I0656489

The Tower's Prelude

The Stained Tower (Book 1)

Iris Reign

The Stained Tower is canon of the Tilted Cosmos.
Copyright @ 2022
ISBN: 979-8-9872076-0-4

Cover art by Xeninda.
Midbook character arts by Mehmedandy.
Maps by Iris Reign - utilizing the tools of Inkarnate.
Cover typography by Karen Dimmick (ArcaneCovers.com)
Further acknowledgments in the back of the book.

CONTENTS

Beyond the confusion, the trauma, and the chaos held within some of these pages, beats a heart. May its pulse reach you through the Tenebrous.

-To the reader from Iris.

Prologue: Mum Bell Knells ✺

∞∞∞∞∞∞∞∞∞∞∞∞∞∞∞

A noose caresses my throat. My feet swim above the earth, grass tickling my soles. There's a snap, and my temple hits the mud—cordage coils in the weeds like a serpent.

Butterflies surround us. One lands upon the tip of my nose, and a wee smile creeps across my face.

The heavens dye a brilliant crimson as the sun sinks into the wilds of the New World. A stiff breeze whistles, bending the lush vegetation upon one another. Strands of my long cherry-red hair flutter against my cheek. Branches of the grand willow accompanying me atop this verdant hill murmur a gentle song.

'Verily, a handsome sunset. If only it could save me as if a knight. Alas, I am no noble maiden, and besides, I fancy the role of knight.' The blue butterfly takes flight, abandoning me to my fate. I take a deep breath of the fragrant air. *'But I believe... I think I am satisfied with this end. I am terribly weary of barely getting by.'*[1]

As I watch the clouds waft across the sky, brutish fingers seize my neck and yank me from the mud. "Devils' waif. How fortunate you are," an ignorant voice spews.

The fingers squeeze the delicate flesh of my nape, boring their calluses deep. I struggle to no avail, my bindings only bite deeper into my wrists. The battle against these fiendish strings has lasted a day and a night now. Relief from the sting of their coarse yarn is something I cannot seem to attain.

"Hark, wench, or do you desire another lashing?"

Not wishing for the last words I hear to be the drivel from this dolt's gob, I inquire as politely as I can manage, "If thou wouldst be so kind, if I am to

---

[1] *'Italic text between apostrophes represents unvoiced internal thoughts.'*

1

be hanged, could we converse in the London Parlance? My Queen's English is a tad neglected."

"You spurn even this final politeness, witch? Naught but Cripplegate rats still adhere to that felonious English cant."[2]

Shaking my head, I sigh and roll my eyes. "Thomas, that is simply not true. I speak in the London Parlance because I am not a faint-hearted truckler that would tongue the Queen's toes if commanded." I smile. "Like thyself, for example."[3]

A palm slaps the back of my head. The rough hand squeezes my neck before twisting it in the direction of an approaching older gentleman.

The gentleman's attire consists of a woolen tunic with a pair of blue breeches that fall below the knee, a pair of white wool stockings, and black leather shoes. From his neck swings the simple wooden idol of the God in Light. As one would expect, the idol is a harp with a pair of wings attached to either side. His ornate attire in such a modest settlement hints that he is a man of high status here at our tottering colony.

'Aye, Preacher Joseph Daniels, also known as The Accuser, The Judge, and The Hangman. I was curious when he would arrive. Must have gone in search of a rope that would suffice.'

"Thomas," the preacher snaps. "If the wench's last request is to hear the vagrants' parlance as she swings, so be it."

I stifle a smirk and watch as Preacher Daniels marches toward the willow tree. His words are unquestionable in the colony, so London Parlance shall be the manner of conversation from here forth, which means most will hesitate to speak. London Parlance is a "vagrants' parlance" for "Cripplegate rats" in the minds of the townsfolk, after all. It's discourteous speech, and oh, how much they care for their undue courtesies.

My gaze drifts away from Preacher Daniels, settling upon the willow tree. Its trunk is wrinkled and wide enough that five people could wrap their

---

[2] Cripplegate was once a gate and ward in the city of London where beggars and cripples frequented.
[3] Faint-hearted: cowardly.
Truckler: Someone who gives up or submits tamely. Assume a submissive position

arms around it. The stiff limbs twist skyward while its lissome branches droop toward the hillock. Despite it resting upon a hilltop, its roots leak from the soil at the hill's foundation.

A breeze blows, curling the willow's thin branches away from its tender, cool caress. "Preacher," a stout voice calls.

From the direction of the colony, a townsman scales the hillock and approaches us. With a weary puff, he raises a noose tied from cordage and presents it to Preacher Daniels. The preacher takes it from the townsman's grasp and lifts it high.

"Seem familiar?" he announces for all to hear, dangling the frayed cordage in my direction. "A rope that those savages bestowed upon this witch. I found it quite appropriate that she hang from it. Unfortunately," he slings the cordage into a thicket, "those savages' craftsmanship is much too shoddy. That rope will not support this wench's weight. Hence, we shall use rope produced in our cultured fatherland."[4]

"Cordage, not rope, Preacher Daniels. It's made from bulrush or, my preferred name, cattail. The natives taught me how to twist it into cords." I sigh and then say, "Though I confess, I am a mere dabbler in the realm of cordage, but I consider myself cultured, nonetheless. After all, I come from the same so-called fatherland as thee."

"Oh my, the ill-mannered Scot wench has the gall to speak without permission whilst insulting us all by assuming herself a true Englishwomen. No, waif, the Scot dependency, from which your blood hails, is a leech upon civilized England." Another townsman approaches, presenting Preacher Daniels with a sturdy noose. He nods, thanking the townsman, before ensuring I look upon the rope myself. "And here, Miss Nightingale, I hold the so-called noose from our so-called fatherland," he jeers and scoffs.

My urge to smirk wanes as my hands quiver. I squeeze my palms together, doing my best to hide the trembling from the townsfolk's prying eyes. '*I shan't allow them the pleasure of seeing my fear. If I cannot run away this time,*

---

[4] Fatherland: a person's native country. Motherland, on the other hand, refers to one's place of origin.

and I am to die, I shall die while providing the townsfolk as wretched of a performance as I am able.'

"Preacher," the townsman whispers. "That, uhm, rope was also in the witch's cottage. Our rope is being used to bleed a deer."

I scrutinize the rope. "T-that's cordage as well. A gift from the natives. They were attempting to mimic English rope, so rope is apt."

He scoffs, walking away. "Then thou shalt hang from the savages' rope."

Preacher Daniels casts the noose toward one of the sturdier-looking branches. The 'rope' falls short as his starved body struggles to muster enough strength, yet the townsfolk are too busy scowling at me to take notice.

While he works to prepare the noose, I run my eyes across the many faces who have graciously come to see me off. When our eyes meet, some scowl, others turn their nose up, and some meet my gaze as if declaring, "thou doth deserve this."

Breaking eye contact, I peer off into the distance. *'It would seem the whole colony has come. Oh, and I hear Thomas hunted a deer yesterday morn...'* I sniff the air, smelling the unmistakable aroma of roasting meat. *'And that the townsfolk shall savor it together whilst I dangle beneath the willow tree.'*

Hearing the rustling of the willow tree's branches, I return my gaze to Preacher Daniels. With the noose secured, he gives the rope a tug before raising a hand high in the air and turning toward the townsfolk. "Constance Nightingale!" he shouts my name with fervor. "Thou hast been accused of bartering information to provincial savages, resulting in the loss of three of this colony's townspeople. Whilst I was contemplating the Daybreak Scriptures and the accusations made, a miracle transpired, and an inquisitor's circular letter materialized before me as if from the God in Light. The letter revealed that thou art a known serpent-tongued thief, a beggar witch, and most damning of all, a servant of the High Devil Penumbra, kindred of the Highest Devil Umbral. For thy crimes against thy fellow townspeople, Her Majesty Queen Elizabeth, and our Lord God, thou art to be hanged atop this hill. Here thy breath shall stay, thy soul cleansed, and thy earthly-life judged, all in God's glorious Light."

My legs join my hands, trembling of their own volition.

'All lies, but this shall be over soon. Aye, then I will never have to suffer hardship or lies again...' I straighten my legs as much as I can to hide the shaking. While toughening the squeeze my hands hold upon one another, I withdraw deeper into my thoughts, seeking distractions. 'I... Oh, her, the hazy girl... the one who has haunted me since my birth, I wonder if she will appear before I draw my last breath... I imagine she shall. But what should I say to her when I see her?'

The preacher grabs the noose hanging from the willow tree and motions for Thomas to bring me forth. With a sneer, Thomas shoves me forward and forces my head low. Preacher Daniels grabs my red hair, pulling it through the noose, then works it over my head. He moves from my front to my side and yanks the knot, tightening it around my neck. The rope's roughspun fibers gnaw the tender skin of my nape, causing it to itch and burn.

Preacher Daniels turns to the gathered townsfolk and bellows, "If anyone has any departing words for Miss Nightingale, deliver them forthwith."

With his words, a townswoman stomps forward. "Thou wilt roast in the Pit for what has been done to my family, hedge-born!"[5] The townswoman spits; her spittle thumps against my face. While it oozes down my cheek, I stare into her eyes with a blank expression.

"My apologies," I reply, looking away from her blistering gaze, "I do not seem to recognize thee."

Her brows furrow as she grits her teeth. Raising her palm high, she swings at my cheek—a heavy smack echoes. "Thou evil witch!" Again she slaps me. "Betrayed us all, and my beloved family must suffer the consequences! Not even a trace of their mortal bodies can be found, despite our frantic searching!"

---

[5] Hedge-born: Low-born or illegitimate. If you were born in a hedge, there's a high chance your mother didn't have a bed to give birth in.

I turn my stinging cheek away from her. "Oh. Thou art Mrs. Sue Howe then... Thou hast my sympathies, but as I have said before, I traded medicine to the natives for food and naught more."

"Liar!" Mrs. Howe slaps me again. "Everything is thy fault. Thou wast never meant to be a part of this colony from the beginning, damnable stowaway!"

I think back to how I arrived here. *'I will not deny that I was a stowaway, but in my defense, I feel being confined to a barrel for three nights before being discovered was suffering enough. Worse yet, the barrel was not properly secured, so I spent those nights rolling to and fro below deck.'*

"An unwed hag dwelling in the woodlands alone like a savage!" Mrs. Howe screams with eyes that threaten to escape their sockets. "Never contributing anything to the colony but those blasted medicines! Yet nary a townsperson complained of thy bloodsucking behaviors. Now understand what has come to pass; my husband, Goodman George, my son, George jun., and my daughter, Agnes, all missing because of thy depravity!"

Shaking my head, I deem it better to give a half-truth than attempt to explain my relationship with the natives. "Mrs. Howe, my heart aches to learn of thy family. I merely live alone in the forest because I enjoy my privacy, not because I intended to do anything wicked. And though I know naught of where thy family may be, I pray they shall be found unharmed."

My words miscarry, serving only to stoke Mrs. Howe's wrath.

While grinding her teeth together, Mrs. Howe slaps me time and time again. Each slap sends a resounding echo into the trees and fields that surround us. With my hands bound behind my back and Thomas holding my neck from behind, I can do naught but endure the barrage. Several slaps later, she loses strength. As she collapses to her knees, and weeps, the colony's midwife, Elizabeth Viccars, hurries to her side to comfort her.

With Mrs. Howe's assault over, my face swells, and my vision narrows.

Nodding, Preacher Daniels asks, "Does anyone else have words for this witch?"

"Thou shouldst have cast thyself into the Pit long ago!" a boy named Edmond English cries.

Edmond picks up a stone and flings it at me. The stone strikes my stomach, knocking the wind out of me. I try to drop to my knees, only for Thomas's grip around my nape to tighten, preventing me from toppling over. Edmond's action sparks the townsfolks' fury. One by one, they bend down to pluck stones from the dirt.

"Thomas, move aside," Preacher Daniels says.

"Aye, Preacher," Thomas replies.

Thomas's fingers release me, and I hear his footsteps moving away. Preacher Daniels pulls the rope, drawing the noose upward and forcing me to stand on the tips of my toes.

A second later, stones pelt my body, tearing my gown and gashing bare skin. One strikes my head; I begin to lose my wits. Another smashes into my throat, forcing me to lose my breath, stealing some of the little time I have left to enjoy the crisp air. I can feel the warm, wet sensation of blood seeping from my wounds as I struggle to keep my composure.

The noose slackens, so I turn my head to the ground to shield my throat, wondering if the preacher shall have me die in this way instead. With the top of my head exposed, some townsfolk take it as a target and cast stones at my scalp.

As a stone strikes my collarbone with a crack, I hear Preacher Daniels shout, "That is quite enough; this Scot is to be hanged, not lapidated!"[6]

The stones cease at once, and through my swollen and bloody vision, I can see Preacher Daniels approach me as the pain from my shattered collar grows ever more intense. I cough, spattering the preacher's gown in bloody spittle.

He frowns but manages to spit out his words. "Any last words, witch? Mayhaps thou shouldst plead for God's forgiveness with thy final breath."

---

[6] Lapidation (or Lapidated): Stoning to death.

I take a moment to ponder before smirking. "I suppose all I can say is, I have a strong feeling that thou art responsible for—"

Raising his palm, he hits me across the cheek with such force that I feel as if I might vomit. "Thomas, prithee, assist me in raising this wench," he scoffs.

The two hurry to the willow tree, glaring at me before drawing the rope. The noose becomes tighter, and my toes leave the ground; time slows to a trickle. I stare at the townsfolk and look into their eyes full of naught but hatred and repugnance. Over my brief twenty-one years of life, these are eyes I have become quite familiar with.

'All of this is because of the illness the God in Light must have cursed me with at birth. Why must I suffer for that?'

The wind blows, and my vision sways whilst I rise ever higher. My body kicks as it strives to return to the earth. The rough rope digs into my flesh as if it was always meant to be there. A dribble of blood rolls down my neck, staining my gown red.

'Blood. So difficult to clean.'

Despite my best efforts to suppress them, I can feel burning tears streaming down my cheeks like a cascade as they mix with the blood from the stones' gashes. My broken collar pops, and from below, I overhear the preacher grunt and declare with evident pride, "It is too late for regret, wench, but do not fret; thy soul shall be guided by God's First Light!"

'I allowed them the pleasure. Pathetic.'

My vision darkens; though, not to the extent that I could miss the arrival of my oldest acquaintance. Before me, a twisting black haze floats in the shape of a girl. She faces me as if she has come to say adieu to a friend.

'Thou came.' With bitterness, I stare at the hazy girl. *'Well, fare thee well, thou art most assuredly a liver-eater.[7] Thou shan't find me this time.'*

---

[7] Liver-eater: Someone or something that is corrupt or depriving the world of necessary nourishment.

I turn my eyes earthward where I can see the tops of the townsfolks' heads. My brows furrow as my gaze burns at them like the Pit itself.

'And to thee, Roanoke, I say adieu as well. Verily I doth desire thy meager bread be sour and thy days brief! As the saying goes, today me, tomorrow thee.'

Amid the salty tears, the metallic taste of blood, and the torture of my collapsing throat, my pale lips curl into one last smirk at my climactic final thoughts...

Yet...

This cannot stop the panic I feel witnessing the blackest murk I have ever beheld closing in all around me.

'...Nay.'

The body has ceased functions—Essence flow lost. Devotion to a True God level presence not detected.

Consciousness is acquiescing and returning to Myäm.
Must egress to Ethereal Lacuna.

Proceeding to Ethereal Lacuna... Failure.
Low Essence reservoir.

Attempting to navigate to Ethereal Lacuna... Failure.
Low Essence reservoir.

Attempting to navigate to Ethereal Lacuna... Failure.
Drained Essence reservoir.
...
...
...
Cannot proceed to Ethereal Lacuna. Considering alternative solutions.
Viable alternative found. Chance of long-term survival... Low.
Contemplating further alternatives... None discovered.
Proceeding with the sole viable solution.

Material-state required.
Contemplating optimal compositions...
Narrowing based on variables...
Transmuting...
Amplifying Talent: Corrupting Oort Cloud...
Unique fruition. Quintessence tempered.

The consciousness is required to transmogrify further.
Searching through Spirit-Soul Interface candidates.
...
...
...
Candidate found.
The Interface has been born—awaiting consciousness for designation.
...Interface states the consciousness is splintering.
Interface recommends pursuance and reconsolidation... Agreed.
Commencing search.

Chapter 1: Gestating Tenebrous

∞∞∞∞∞∞∞∞∞∞∞∞∞∞∞∞

My eyelids slide open. Naught but pitch black swaddles me.

'Do... do I yet live?' Turning my eyes skyward, I cannot find a speck of light. I kick forward and backward. My body sways, and the rope creaks overhead. 'And I still hang... Fudge!'

I endeavor to bring my hands forward, only to find them still bound. Time passes as I try to free myself, but it becomes clear that it's impossible. I attempt to sigh, but nothing happens. My lips purse, and I venture to take a deep breath. Searing pain shoots through my chest. I clench my bound fists and spit syrupy blood caught in my throat. The anguish abates whilst I relax my body and recover my wits.

'Is... is this the Pit? The deepest, darkest hollows of Umbral's Pit? ...Then what? Was God not willing to acknowledge that I, Constance Nightingale, once breathed before damning me to an abysm? Is this my punishment for being born different than everyone else? To dangle in this... this vile darkness, this ...tenebrous? Tenebrous.'

The noose nestles deeper into my neck as a tremor shakes the void above. My body spins in a circle, and then weightlessness overtakes me. My stomach twists into a knot as my hair drifts upwards. I open my mouth to scream, yet my back hits the ground first with a gritty crack. Twisting and turning, I await certain agony yet... it never comes.

With the pain nowhere to be found, my focus shifts to removing the evil ropes. Without the use of my hands, I kick my legs until I can right myself. Forcing myself into a squatting posture, I lower my head and attempt to loosen the noose with my knees. Some time passes before I accept that it's a useless endeavor. I try to sit and work my arms underneath my backside and legs to bring them to my front, but once more it's futile.

'Thomas, that simple-minded dullard. I am astonished he understands how to tie a knot!'

Feeling the surface beneath me, I search for any signs of a protrusion that I can grind the rope against. The ground is faultlessly smooth. I nearly sigh, only to remember that breathing is excruciating.

My head turns to the left, then right; I frown. Swiveling in place, I hunt for a dab of light in any direction—my eyes may as well not exist. Beyond dark, it is closer to a viscous muck. It's not a blackness I could compare to anything but the murk that befalls those in a deep, unbreakable sleep.

Like a turtle on its shell, I rock my body and then hop to my feet. '*I... I suppose there is no point in tarrying in one place. It would be best if I choose a direction to walk and kept to it. Though it may be a fool's errand without the stars to steer me.*'

With that thought, I choose a course, not that any of them are distinct, and march onward. As I walk, I am careful to plant one foot in front of the other to prevent myself from wandering in circles. My bare feet slapping against the smooth ground and the rope's slithering shiver are the only sounds that indicate someone, something, exists here. Even the tiny ring that persists in the ear when in silence such as this is absent.

'*There must be someone else here... something...*' Staring into the abyss, I feel like something is a hair's breadth from my face gazing back. My body shudders. '*There's naught there, Constance. I simply need to take one step at a time, and I shall find something.*' I count my steps as I walk. '*One. Two. Three. Four. Five. Six. Seven...*'

...

...Seconds?....

...Minutes?.......

...Hours?...........

...Days?.......

...Weeks?...

...

'*Eight... uh, eight hundred eighty-four thousand... eight hundred eighty-four thousand six hundred forty-seven...? I forget... I shall begin anew. Eight hundred eighty thousand one.*'

I stop.

'*...How long has passed? Tracking time here is futile. Eight hundred eighty thousand one, eight hundred eighty thousand two, eight hundred eighty thousand* *three...'* Squatting, I place my head between my legs. My body shivers as my cheek grazes my knees' leathery skin. *'All I know is that this place is, in fact, Umbral's Pit... Nay. I dare say it's wickeder. At least I would forfeit my sanity in the Pit. Tenebrous: a fine name. A fine name for the most horrid of places, for the womb that bore evil, for the cavities within corpses that writhe with worms... Eight hundred eighty thousand four, eight hundred eighty thousand five, eight hundred eighty thousand six, eight hundred eighty thousand seven...'*

Seconds, minutes, or hours pass while I cower in the gloom—quivering and shivering. When my legs give out, I topple onto my side. *'This vacuous realm is where I shall linger for time immemorial, shambling about in this endless darkness, unable to breathe, unable to scream, unable to use my hands... My relief will be madness; I am convinced of that... Eight hundred eighty thousand one, eight hundred eighty thousand two, eight hundred eighty thousand three...'*

My bones grate in protest as I force myself to my feet. *'I feel something gnawing at me, tempting me to devour my feet... I tried to gobble my gown's hem. I could not swallow; the noose would not allow it. It took some time to retch the hem's fabric from my throat.'*

The thump of my feet upon the blighted ground disturbs the horrid silence. *'Mayhaps there is bread ahead. Aye, bread. I would fancy a bread loaf... eight hundred eighty thousand four, eight hundred eighty thousand five, eight hundred eighty thousand six, eight hundred eighty thousand seven... Wait. Do I have a name?'*

...

...Hours?....

...Days?.......

...Weeks?..........

...Months?.......

... Years?...

...

'Is it two million? One, ten, a hundred? ...I care not. Two million!'

Tenebrous's darkness slithers ever nearer as I lie upon its floor. Once it stroked my skin, now it squirms underneath. No longer do I resist it, and no longer can I recall a time before Tenebrous.

'I knew it. I know it! Where is it!? I heard something, a creak, coming from this spot, but I cannot find it.' I roll onto my back, and a beast rakes at my nape and scars my feet—the noose and its frayed strings. *'But alas...! I believe I*

may declare it with confidence.' Tears pour from my eyes. *'There is no bread loaf here. This place is too evil to be graced by such doughy goodness. Not that it matters, I cannot recall what I look like, much less what bread is. I think I recall enjoying it, though.'*

Rolling onto my front, I rap my brow against the ground. *'Did I die? Two million four, two million five, two million six, two million seven... Or am I yet to be born...?'* My brow hits the floor, and I hear a crack. *'Noise. I remember noise.'* Butting the floor anew, it creaks, and my ears drink the stimulus. *'Pristine and nostalgic noise.'*

The floor crumbles beneath me. My body rolls, tumbles, and plunges downward. For so long I sink into a yawning chasm that I grow uncertain whether there ever was a time I was not falling. But then, I crash into the ground. The metallic floor stings my skin. *'Pain? I remember pain.'*

My bones crack as I turn my head, and a profound sense of being watched pricks at my brain. I hear hums, innumerable hums. Within them arises a voice, a disunity. "Three dungeons deep, in the vaults far beneath." They chuckle in a stony voice. "But you, fleshling spirit, come from three dungeons high, in our gardens wilted."

I bumble to my feet. *{Good lord. Is that a voice? Another nightmare trapped in the dark?}*

"Sound. Pulses. Those are how forgotten relics traverse this realm." There's a thumping in my soles. "Heed my pulse, only my pulse."

{Canst thou hearest my mind, stranger?}

"In the Vaults Beneath, thoughts are heard as if spoken aloud. Few of its inhabitants remember how to speak in the old way, forgot their strings long ago. Not that I blame them, never know what you might draw the attention of here." They laugh. "Now, follow my pulse, distinguish thought from noise, or the others will have you."

{...Aye.} With quivering knees, I step. {*Prithee. Prithee, speak or whisper to me. I have spoken to no one in so long.*}[8]

"Hmph, as you desire," they growl. Coughing, they smack their gums. Their voice changes and clears, sounding androgynous but enchanting. They drone a moth-eaten ode, "Three dungeons deep, in the vaults far beneath. Three dungeons high, in our gardens wilted."

Voices. Dissenting voices. They whisper in the depths, far away and near:
{*No, no, not them. My back branches bear fruit. So, to me. The liars shall eat you. To me.*}
{*Come here, little breeze. Come. Come. Share a meal with sister Sylphs? A meal for two, three, a thousand...*}
{*A guest, so rare since Mother shed green. Here. We can share a bed, share our warmth.*}

I ignore them, following the ode's beating words. "Our beds held padded embers, our tables decay. Their altars offered ash, their roots rotted deep."

My arm bumps cold bars, and I hear something swipe my ear. "I remember my strings," a voice like grinding teeth murmurs. "No. My tongue is so dry. Don't leave me like the others."

The ode shepherds me deeper. "Our tongues were charred black, our eyes waxen white. Their tallow pillars had fallen, their voices came from yet deeper underneath."

I ram into something and run my cheek over it. Lychgate, that is the word I feel rubbing my gnarled skin against its frigid veneer. Pushing, it creaks open, and I enter. The stranger's voice is loud and echoes inside. "Our end long passed, our beds built, three dungeons deep, in the vaults far beneath. Their Partings long taken, their Pools a realm low, in the Breathing Blood below."

A ting echoes as my brow bumps against metal bars. Something grabs me. "There. You. Are." It yanks me into the bars. They sting my skin like the

---

[8] {*Italic text between curly brackets will represent non-vocal conversations between two or more people.*}

floor. "Straight into the beast's lair," the stranger laughs. "Let's see what you are."

My feet leave the ground, and my nose grinds against metal as I rise into the air. {*Art thou going to end my torment?*}

"Maybe." They sniff me, blowing my hair back and forth. "A fleshie's failing and mutated foundation. Fleshie," they sneer. "Fleshies disgust me... but you, apostate, you intrigue me. Wielder of a Talent. An old Talent. Old. Old. Old. Older than a relic like I? Are you Splinter or Spirit? La Parting? Sya Parting? Ema...? Who are you?"

Pausing, I shake my head, saying, {*...I have been here too long and cannot remember my name. Am I mad?*}

"You are old. Elder. Tantalizing. Do you remember?"

{*Remember? What am I meant to remember?*}

"Anything—anything—anything at all!" the stranger shouts.

I purse my lips, thinking. {*Ah. I remember. My last number was two million seven. That is what I remember.*}

"...Good enough," they sigh. "Let me out, and I will put you back together. I will put you back together. Let me out—Let me out—Let me out. I will hunt your splinters and put you back together, better, near pristine. Kiln. Fragile, but no flesh, no blood, better, refined. Worthy of my devotion."

{*I do not understand.*}

They growl. "You shall." The ground trembles. "Let me out—Let me out— Let me out. Let me out—Let me out—Let me out. Let me out—Let me out— Let me out!"

{*...Aye. Destroy me or aid me. Both are better than suffering in Tenebrous, and I would consider either equivalent to rescue.*}

"Destroy you!? You cannot overcome suffering if you refuse to look at it. That cowardness is what led this realm to ruin in the first place!"

{...Dost thou wishest something more of me?}

"Plant your seed in the Material Realm, tighten your grip on the land, then come, come back to this vault. Shine light upon this smear, this mockery. See and remember what was once beautiful and glimpse a realm abandoned."

{If I escape Tenebrous, I shan't return.} I shake my head. *{And once I have fled, only my nightmares shall ever dare to think of this place again.}*

"You have no choice. 'Tenebrous' is knitted deep within your and every Spirit's being, and it is rotting. Bah! Beyond rot, it is a womb petrified." The stranger lowers me to the ground. "Remember that. Remember the petrification of a realm scorned."

{...Aye, and if I remember, thou wilt help me leave?}

"At the back of my prison, knock the lever next to the wheel. Free me."

Nodding, I walk around the chamber's edges and bump into what feels like a ship's wheel. Next to the wheel, I find a long rod protruding from the wall. I bend forward and press it down using my weight. The lever sinks, and I tumble to the floor. The creak and grate of metal coming to life shake the chamber. Something drops and crashes to the floor next to me. I hear heavy footsteps approach me. "Next we meet, I shall remember little, and I prefer that."

I do not move. Simply lie on the ground. *{Prefer not to remember?}*

"To see things through a mind less tainted, unbound by the past, I desire it, choose it, and I shall have it thanks to you."

{Thanks to me? I am hapless and helpless, cannot even hold my arms in front of my body. What am I to do?}

"You will linger here, and I shall return when I have the splinters to put you back together." The air moves around me as the stranger hovers close to my face. A fingernail akin to a talon runs down my brow to my lip, tracing my features. "You do have eyes, correct? You haven't forgotten them?"

{...I am uncertain.} I roll what I think should be my eyeballs and concentrate on the sensation they make rubbing the back of my eyelids. *{Aye, I believe I still possess eyes.}*

"Then, I'll persuade your splinters to remind you of whomever you once were, and a glister will guide you to them. Farewell," they grumble.

{Thou shan't forsake me?}

"A blessing, a clasping of the eyes, a refusal to look suffering in the eyes." The lychgate creaks open. "What is left of me will return, farewell."

The stranger's footsteps fade, and silence engulfs me. *'...Two million eight. Two million nine. Two million ten...'*

•••
•••••••
•••••••••••
••••••••••••••
•••••••••••
•••••••
•••

Anomalous occurrence.
The intended Interface is no longer responding... Displaced.

New candidate acceptable...

Complete.
The Interface has been reborn—awaiting consciousness for designation.
...Interface states the consciousness is splintering.
Interface recommends pursuance and reconsolidation... Agreed.

Re-commencing search.

•••
•••••••
•••••••••••
••••••••••••••
•••••••••••
•••••••
•••

My eyes fix upon a singular speckle in the black. In the unending dark, it is a glistering beacon of violet light.

'Light.' A pulse runs through me. 'Glister. I see it.'

Every joint in my body pops as I force myself to stand. My legs wobble and then fall out from beneath me. As my knees knock the ground, a jolt shoots through my body. I force one foot forward and place myself in a kneeling position. With one decisive push, I lurch to my feet.

My soles beat upon the cold ground as I shamble closer to the violet star. This must be God; they have taken pity upon me. This is the First Light, and it will cleanse my soul.

Salvation awaits.

As I move nearer, the violet light casts shadows upon the ground. These shadows move, act, and go about their business as if alive. Each of them behaves in distinct ways. One looks be a burly baker pulling bread loaves from an absent oven. Then, a woman's shadow beats her fist against her palm, shouting at a child's shape. Another is a large gentleman who stands at the edge of the gloom with their arm extended toward me. The shadows ignore me for the most part, yet I notice other shadows are following in my stumbling steps.

I freeze, hearing a child's giggle shatter the infinite abyss. "Remember thy past," someone whispers in my ear. "Remember us."

Hazy shadows spring from the ground, taking the shape of a narrow black and white cobblestone alleyway. I walk the cobblestone footpath. The walls shiver and twist with every slap of my sole. It's unstable, the alleyway could collapse upon me at any moment, yet at the alleyway's end is the violet light.

There's another giggle as a little girl's shadow frolics into the alley—I can tell she is around seven or eight years old by her size. There's a soft meow, and a catling mouser prances in after the girl. The girl runs toward me yet halts upon taking notice of a black mushroom sprouting from between the cobblestones. She tilts her head and reaches down, plucking it from the cracks.

Sniffing it, she retches and sticks out her tongue. "*Bluhh!* Pavement mushroom!" she shouts. She pins her nostrils and stuffs it into her mouth. Gulping it down, she places her palm on her belly. "I loathe mushrooms!"

Eyeing something stuck into a crack in the alley's wall, she yanks it from the wall with a snicker and turns to the mouser. "Sir Mouser! I am Knight-Lady Constance! Mistress of the blade! Ready thyself!" the little girl shouts, swinging the shadow of a stick.

The catling, Sir Mouser, roars, "Me-OW!" and leaps at the girl.

As the mouser latches onto the little girl's rags and climbs into her arms, she drops her stick and embraces him. "Ah! Sir Mouser! I yield! I yield!" she shouts, bursting into giggles. She sighs and presses her face into the mouser's fur. "Sir Mouser, thou art my lifetime knight companion. Dost thou agree to these terms?"

"Meow," Sir Mouser responds, pawing at the air.

As the giggling girl and Sir Mouser play, a dark haze wafts into the scene, smothering it in black.

'*...S-Sir Mouser?*' My head pounds and my chest aches as I try to think. '*I... I love Sir Mouser, but I cannot remember well.*' Tears stream from my eyes, something I thought nigh impossible after being entrapped within this realm of agony for so long. '*How... how long has it been since I have seen him? I miss him. Why... why does it hurt?*'

There's a weep, and the cobblestone alleyway collapses into a haze. The haze reassembles, revealing a new scene. The new set takes place in a seven-foot-wide bedchamber. In the middle of the bedchamber, a youthful girl lies on a floor pallet with her face buried in hempen linens. She looks to be around thirteen years old, judging by her size.

"Why was I born? Why have I been cursed?" the girl mumbles into the linens. "I-I understand naught. The haze, the haze girl... Why will She not leave me be?"

There's a screech, "Constance! Thou art Umbral's child!" a nun-like figure burst through the bedchamber's door. "What hast thou done?!"

"Éclat Lagarde! Prithee, nay!" the girl whimpers.[9]

Vierge Éclat Lagarde's shadow stomps toward the girl, striking her with a broomstaff.[10]

The girl pleads for Lagarde to stop. At the chamber's edge, a watery haze twists together, and the swirling image of my curse, the haze girl, manifests. The haze girl's figure bursts apart, and her haze surges around the screaming figure of Lagarde.

The screams and cries fade as haze drifts in and smothers the picture.

'Me at... aye, that was the... Hallow Equarié's Convent? The French Éclat, they held me there.'

Haze scatters, obscuring the girl's bedchamber. Twisting together, the haze assembles into a new display involving two maidens. The pair are identical, except one swirls with haze—the haze girl yet again. Judging by their figures, they look to be around seventeen or eighteen. The maiden watches the haze girl, sitting at and tapping her fingernails on a decrepit tabletop with a rhythm.

The maiden breaks the quietude. "Why dost thou haunt me?" the maiden asks. "Dost thou understand!?" She stands. "Speak!"

Naught but silence answers her.

She drops to her knees as the hazy girl's figure shivers apart and flows into the maiden's body. While tears fall from her cheeks, she forces herself to her feet and stares at her empty tabletop.

Wiping away a tear, she whispers to herself, "One day and one meal at a time." She walks toward a cauldron's shadow that's set within a hearth.[11] "And on this day, I shall prepare myself a pleasant eventide meal."

Her figure wanes, and the shadows that sprung from the ground disperse.

---

[9] Éclat [French]: Means radiance.

[10] Vierge Éclat [French]: Means virgin radiance or virgin shine.

[11] Hearth: fireplace, or the part of a floor on which a fire is made. - House, home, fireside. Home is where the hearth is kept warm.

'That... that was shortly before I stowed away to Roanoke... on the flagship 'Lion.' I remember.' My eyes drift back toward the glowing light. It has moved closer to me on its own. With a shake of my head, I hobble onward. 'The light. The glister. It might have answers.'

The noose's tail snakes behind me as I near the violet light's source. There I find three girls standing as if awaiting my arrival: the little girl, the youthful girl, and the maiden. They stand facing away from me, and no longer are they made of shadow; now, they are as tangible as any person.

Their long red hair and bodies reflect faint blue and purple hues. The little girl wears rags, the youthful girl a loose-fitting gown, and the maiden a patchwork of textiles fashioned into a gown and hoopskirt.

"We will help thee remember, and help thee push forth," the three say.

"I shall go first!" The little girl turns around with a smirk. Atop her head, a black mouser is sprawled out, and in her hand, she wields a stick, her trusty sword. "Roach is what they called us in the London squalid. Despite how the sooty ruffians tried, we could not be squashed!" she shouts, holding her sword high.

"Mow!" the mouser adds with a wiggle of his tail.

"And, of course, we cannot forget our faithful knight and companion Sir Mouser!" Giggling, the youthful girl turns around. She pokes out her chest with a grin, declaring, "Sink is what they called us in that vile convent. Despite how the dastardly French Éclat tried, we would never sink for long."

The maiden turns around, watching the silliness of Roach, Sir Mouser, and Sink with a tickled smile. "Black is what they called us in the Tower of London. Despite how the haughty nobles tried, they could never notice us in the squalor's many shadows." She raises an eyebrow and scowls. "With their boots laced tight upon their feet, they could never understand that our soles were honed by the cracks and crevices of London's cobbles."

The three glance at one another before pointing at me. "Art thou still the same as us?" they ask together.

My foggy memories gain sudden clarity. I nod at the girls. '*I... I remember having many names: Roach, Sink, and Black were the most prevalent of those. But... our names meant nothing to us or anyone in the end. Regardless of what name we lived under, we eventually ran out of places to hide, and worse yet, we had run out of things to live for.*'

Sink glances at all of us, saying, "Our life was difficult, often painful... but we persevered," she says with a frown. "We would never confess it aloud, but after Éclat Lagarde left us... we had one of the most delightful years of our life. I want to have another year like that one."

Nodding, Black says, "Somedays were worse than others... but we struggled onwards. I still remember how delectable our meal was that eve. I want to have more delicious food like that."

"We struggled, but we still had fun!" Roach shouts with a slight hop. "Sir Mouser and I want to have more fun! We cannot do that in this dull and dark place!"

"Meow!" the mouser roars.

"Aye. Thou fled to America because life in London had become too much to bear," Sink asserts with a weak expression. "Thou wert tired, we understand."

"The idea of voyaging to a New World to stem the tides of misery was... alluring. It was to be our first and final adventure," Black affirms, gazing off into the distance. "Even so, misery would not release thee, and thou wouldst seek to isolate thyself from the others."

"Because it did not matter where thou fled, she brought misery, and she would not tolerate thy freedom," Roach says in a solemn tone.

"Mow..." Sir Mouser whimpers.

Sink corrects her expression and smiles at me. "Speaking of which, let us speak of her now. The haze girl, she haunted us throughout our life..."

Black turns back toward me and laughs. "Or so we liked to tell ourselves? We would frequently swear that everything was her fault..."

Roach swings her stick with a renewed resolve. "Or so we liked to believe? It's hard to admit to ourselves..."

The three girls' bodies break apart, changing. "But all of us deep down recognized the truth all along, did we not?" they declare.

I think back, remembering the girl of haze. She was a mirror image of my body size and shape but was made of a twisted black smoke. The haze was virulent to everything and would make anything that breathed it in ill, mad, or worse. Sometimes, the haze would leak from my skin on its own, but the real problem was when the haze girl appeared. When she appeared, unless I was alone, something terrible was bound to happen. Sometimes she would hurt people, and other times she would drive them away from me.

For an awfully long time now, I have understood that she only ever appeared when certain ideas wriggled their way into my head. Put simply...

Sink nods. "The haze girl imitated our thoughts. She does not possess a will of her own."

"It is not our fault, though; everyone has those intrusive thoughts, but they do not have something like our haze," Black states.

"We were simply different! But that does not mean any of us ever yielded to our bad fortunes," Roach shouts.

"We wanted to live and experience the little things, despite our situation. Even if that meant we would have to one day become her."

Their bodies shatter like panes of glass, leaving three girls made of a black twisting haze.

Together they speak directly into my head. "Now, what of thee, Constance Nightingale, dost thou wishest to live?"

They step away, revealing what resembles a crystal, the source of the violet light.

The crystal-like object is around the width of a palm, or more precisely, three inches in diameter. Sharp edges project from a core that looks to be bumpy, irregular, and transparent. Both the sharp protrusions and the bumpy center have a blue and purple tint. Rather than a crystal, the object is more akin to stained glass.

For some reason, it's irresistible to me.

Enthralled, I wobble toward the object until I stand next to it. My ghastly reflection stares back at me: sunken cheeks, caved brow, bleached eyes, blue lips, a veritable corpse.

I feel a rope graze my calf as it thuds to the ground. My wrists have been unbound. Every bone in my arms and shoulders crackles as I drag them forward. *'This...'* Raising my pale and lifeless hand, I bring it toward the glass. *'This is something important to me, nay, essential.'*

My rotted arm trembles as my fingernails scratch the glass. The tips of my bony fingers weave between the jagged edges to meet the smooth core. I feel a strange tingling in my head, and a shiver creeps up my spine.

I flinch when a transparent purple wall with writing appears before me.

> **Introduction:** *Greetings, this one is a Spirit-Soul Interface and potential succor.[12]*
>
> **Proclamation:** *All sapient material creatures maintain a delicate harmony between soul, spirit, and flesh. If this balance shatters, death is nigh inevitable, and the three parts separate. Tenebrous is the realm in which the consciousness—the spirit—roams after death, waiting.*
>
> *Feel free to take a moment to gaze upon this realm's endless glory. ...Done? Excellent.*
>
> *While the spirit proceeds to Tenebrous, the soul returns to the Ethereal Lacuna, or a True God, and waits as well. But what if the soul cannot make the journey to the Ethereal Lacuna? Then the soul is fated to shrink into nihility.[13]*

---

[12] Succor: Relief or support in times of distress and hardship.
[13] Nihility: nonexistence; nothingness

Yet, when conditions are suitable, a rare soul and an old Spirit can seek another way together—one last effort to Tower over the world and persist by forming a permanent relationship.

You and your soul are one of these irregular pairs.

To endure, your soul has transmogrified into an Oort Stained Glass variant Shell.

The Shell now requires a flame.

Query: *Would you like to transmogrify your spirit and integrate with this Shell before you? To be reborn as a Kiln and gain succor from this realm?*

[Aye]　　　　[Nay]

Notice: *Along with the Soul and Spirit, the Spirt-Soul Interface is enfolded as well. From acceptance onward, the relationship is eternal.*

Warning: *A Kiln's birth is chaotic, and Tenebrous's vacuum demands Essence for life. Upon genesis and initial reversion into the Material Realm, a Birth-Reaping will occur.*

I blink with a half-open mouth. Studying the wall's contents, I only understand pieces of what it's attempting to convey. But this wall could have been sent to me by God's Archangel Nescence or Umbral's devil Penumbra. Either one would be as welcome as the other. *'Angel. Devil. Interface. I wish to live, and if that could not be given, then I would beg thee to destroy me.'* My teeth bite my cold and cracked lip. *'I cannot bear Tenebrous's torture any longer. Take me away from here, aye, I accept the terms. I care not the cost, or of thy words, or thy warning, thy meaning, remove me from this place.'*

The three girls of haze, Roach, Sink, and Black, nod. Their voices speak into my head. {*From whence we splintered, we return.*} They break apart as the glass object draws them into itself. {*Remember us. Live for us. Farewell.*}

The violet light fades, and I am alone once again. I sit, waiting for... anything. Silence tickles at my spirit as the darkness crawls back beneath my skin like an insect returning to its burrow.

'...Was it... was it all a trick?'

My head throbs.

I collapse and clutch my temples. The light returns, blinding and laughing at me for believing it had left. I gaze at my reflection in the glass and watch as violet light spills from my eyes and flows into the object before me. Within it a tiny violet flame ignites, dancing as my light feeds it.

Declamation: *The match has been struck—a Kiln that aspires to Tower over the world has been born.*

With the purple wall's words, the shell, now kiln, spins, drawing in the surrounding blackness and the remaining light spilling from my eyes. The flame grows more intense, and my mind weak. I am certain I shall collapse at any moment, yet the kiln vanishes first, and my wits return.

My throat burns, and I vomit crystalline blood.

I glance down, finding the kiln has driven itself into my belly as if shot from a flintlock. My body spasms, and overwhelming pangs of hunger boils within me. I attempt to slump forward and clutch my stomach in anguish, but the rope thwarts me. I peek behind me to glimpse its cord, worming into the abyss and drawing taut.

'Do the devils come?'

The rope yanks me by the throat. My backside strikes the hard ground with a thunk as I fall onto my back, each bone in my spine bashing the floor. I lie on the ground as an unfathomed force tugs at my leash, dragging me through the never-ending murk.

My neck jerks about as our speed grows. Even though we move quicker than I have ever dreamed before, it's still an insufferably long time before we stop in an indistinguishable expanse of black. The rope draws up, stringing me skyward until I dangle in the air, as I did when I arrived.

'Did I fail? Was accepting the purple wall's bargain the wrong thing to have done? Was I meant to tolerate my grim fate to atone for my sins... and I failed?'

I swing for a time as an unspeakable appetite gnaws at my insides.

A crackle.

My waxen eyes stare as fissures form in the blackness, unleashing ripples of light into the gloom. Tenebrous retreats, and I swear that I hear an ear-tingling growl. Out of the corner of my eye, I glimpse a figure in the black pall.

The light grows more expansive as it approaches my swaying body. A blink later, I am hanging from a willow, gazing upon a dazzling sunset and trees of green.

"C-Constance's body, it has putrefied in seconds!" someone shrieks.

Beneath me, I hear screams, but my eyes cling to the sunset. A blue butterfly flutters by and lands on my cheek. 'Verily. I am free...'

Something draws my attention: small motes of purple light are rising upwards. Gazing at the little lights, I find myself mesmerized by them. My hand rises to reach for them, and I freeze. The fingers of my hand are crumbling into specks of black dust, leaving naught but the knuckles. My body wiggles as I hear an oaken creak above me. Turning my eyes upward, I see the branch from which I hang is withering into dust as well.

As the sun dips below the horizon, the branch snaps. Time slows to a trickle as my vision turns skyward, and I see countless flickering motes of purple and blue lights in the dust cloud.

I close my eyes.

There's a thump as my temple hits the mud. Only one of my eyes opens; the other is like glass shattered upon the earth. Around me swims a mist of glittering dust. Standing feet away, I glimpse the once familiar Roanoke townsfolk gawking at me in horror.

An unusual sensation tingles within my broken abdomen. I watch as the willow tree from which I once dangled crumbles to dust and falls to the soil. It mars the air like ash plumes and cloaks me in a suffocating soot. The specks collide as drops of purple and blue light redouble in number. Soon the ash is no more, and in its place, there are countless motes of drifting light. Beneath the fading glimmers of twilight, it's a matchless sight to behold.

The kiln's flame flares, drawing the lights to it. They coalesce into a blinding violet egg, hovering a hair's breadth above the kiln in my belly. Even the townsfolk stop to watch the spectacle in awe.

A pulse beats within the egg, and a cord bleeds from a slit in its shell. The cord drifts toward a townsman I can scarcely remember the name of— Thomas. Miraculously not one soul flees; instead, they gape in wonder like infants glimpsing the sun for the first time.

Thomas's quivering hand reaches out to touch the light as if reaching toward the God in Light themselves. He inches nearer, and the moment his fingertip grazes the cord, his body shatters, becoming light. The new motes hurry to the egg, enkindling it. An indescribable warmth bathes me as my zealous hunger wanes and my vision returns.

Slack-jawed, the townsfolk eye the spot where Thomas once stood. A woman gasps and flees for the safety of the palisade.[14] The cord stalks her, smashing her body into droplets.

The town chandler points at me with a quaking hand. "We have stoked Umbral's wrath! Escape or perish!" he screams. His cries rouse the townsfolk. Like rabbits, they scatter, sprinting down the hillside. The wolfish light hunts them. One by one, townsmen and townswomen alike shatter, bursting into blue and purple motes of light.

I stumble to my feet in time to witness the last morsels of flesh, bone, and blood slough from my breast, ousted by seething light or cinder. I gaze at my arms, discovering they resemble light-blue panes of glass. Under their surface, a black haze churns in a hail of blue and purple embers.

"Mrs. Nightingale, p-pray thee, cease thy witchcraft!" someone pleads. A familiar man kneels at my feet, Preacher Joseph Daniels. He squints under

---

[14] Palisade: A bulwark or defensive fence made from wood or iron stakes sank into the ground.

the shine of my body. "I beg of thee, have mercy!" A cord crashes into his temple, and his body shatters.

My surroundings hush. Naught remains but hollowed land and a blue butterfly crumbling into purple embers.

Shingles slip from a cottage's roof in my peripheral, and I glance toward the colony. The all-consuming light stopped mere feet from the colony's palisade. To the settlement's west is a lush woodland—the sight kisses my languished mind.

A gust of wind revives the various melodies of nature as birds chirp and insects buzz. I descend the bald hillock toward the forest's edge. *'Forgive me.'*

> **Report:**
> Birth-Reaping has ceased. Rations stored.
> The soul has concluded transmogrification. It is Oort Stained Glass Shell
> The spirit has concluded transmogrification. It is now a violet Tower flame.
> This Spirit-Soul Interface is forever bound and transformed.
>
> **Name:** *Constance Nightingale*
> **Race:** *Kiln*[15]
> **Type:** *Tower*
> **Variant:** *Oort Stained Glass*
>
> **Note:** *Full status shall be available upon integration into Cosmic Mana Stream [Currently Undetectable].*

---

[15] Lower case 'kiln' refers to the flame/shell in Constance's belly.
Upper case 'Kiln' refers to the race.

Chapter 2: Sir Earl of Purple and Sir Cosmic of Blue

∞∞∞∞∞∞∞∞∞∞∞∞∞∞

My body illuminates the forest in hues of purple as I weave between trees and through dense undergrowth. I spread my arms and stroke the trees' bark as I march into the forest's depths. Keeping with the habit Tenebrous graved upon my mind, I count my steps. *'Last number: three million two hundred forty-one thousand six hundred three. My next aim: three million five hundred thousand. Four. Five. Six. Seven...'*

> **Notice:** Be forewarned, the Cosmic Mana Stream will soon detect the user's presence in the Material Realm, and the world's magical creature seal shall trigger. The magical creature seal is ineluctable.
>
> **Extrapolation:** Shortly, the user shall be taken and placed in a deep sleep for an unknowable duration of time.
> Next the user wakes, the Material Realm will not be as it is now.

A purple wall appears before my eyes. *'I do not recognize several of these words, but I believe I understand what is being implied. Art thou saying something called the Cosmic Mana Stream will come for me, and I shall be unable to wake by my own will?'* An answer never comes, so I carefully study the purple wall's words and then push onward through the forest. *'I do not know, but if I am to be put to sleep by "the world's magical creature seal," obviously I am not welcome in the world as it is.'* I enter a dense thicket of trees that leads into a grove. In the heart of the grove lies a radiant pool of crystal blue water surrounded by the twinkle of countless fireflies. *'Yet, I have someone I must visit first.'*

I approach the pool and pause. The foreign sight of my own reflection greets me.

Where once a pale girl with red hair would have stood, now stands one made up of various shades of bright purple and blue glass. The skin of this girl's face has a pastel blue glow and her eyes shine with brilliant violet light. She lacks any sign of a mouth, and although she has a nose, she lacks nostrils. This girl wears a short-sleeved gown that flows past her knees and radiates a bright white. She is barefoot without any jewelry, but regardless, any jewelry would be outshone by her body alone.

Her exposed skin shares the same pastel blue radiance as the skin of her face. Her most stunning feature would be her hair, which resembles churning waves of purple and blue water but shines like the sun through a windowpane. At her navel, the kiln flickers with a delicate purple light that makes her body glimmer.

A shard of glass around my nape falls away and tumbles into the grass. Something catches my eye at the girl's neck, something I did not notice before. Kneeling, I move in closer to see a black haze that encircles her nape and then runs off past her shoulders.

'Is that the noose? Why was it not consumed like everything else?'

> **Warning:** The user's Lucent Glass State is unstable and cannot be maintained. However, due to Talent 'Corrupting Oort Cloud,' a Vaporous form will naturally replace the Lucent State as it breaks down.
>
> **Recommendation:** Train and progress Vaporous form to a practical level of usability.

Haze spreads further from the noose, turning some of my body into the black haze. I recall what Roach, Sink, and Black told me earlier. 'To live, I must become Her. This must be what they meant.' I gaze at the wall. 'May I refer to thee as Earl? Thy color reminds me of a foppish Earl who would regularly prance through the London streets.[16] The man only ever wore garish purple garments, even to funerals.'

> **Notice:** The user's designation of this Interface is acknowledged.

---

[16] Foppish: concerned with one's clothes and appearance in an affected and excessive way.

Nodding, I reply to the wall, *'Aye, so thou fancy it...?'* Not receiving an answer, I continue, *'Earl, canst thou aidest me? I understand little.'*

Earl Interface:

Notice: *Oort Stained Tower Glass Kiln guide available for embedment into Earl Interface's psyche.*
Query: *Would the user like to perform this action now?*

[Aye]   [Nay]

Warning: *Incorporation shall be painful.*

I read his message. *'So thou wilt guidest me?'* My fingertips move across the warm kiln. *'I have decided to live, but I do not know how to live like this.'* I wait, but he does not answer, so I read through his message a few times before speaking. *'...Not yet, Earl. Allow me to speak to my friend first.'*

Pushing to my feet, I step toward a wooden board that sticks from the earth. The ground around it is well-kept, and a blossoming garden of white asphodels complements nature's verdure. I collapse, falling between the flowers, and gaze at the words etched upon the board's surface.

Beneath this bed of flowers sleeps a humble mouser.
The dearest friend and companion I could have hoped for in life.
Until our next adventure, rest well.

Sir Mouser

'Hello, brave knight.' I trace the petals of a flower. *'If I recall, last we spoke, I told thee of my cordage spinning hobby. I believe I shall abandon that hobby. Cordage and rope are not to my liking any longer. Ah, and I also mentioned trying "potato" for the first time. I remember it being simple to bake and delectable. Though, it feels like a long time ago now that I sampled it. Oh, and I have a new acquaintance... A purple wall that floats in the air named Earl. Aye, in all likelihood I have lost my sanity.'*

I turn over and stare skyward, the moon is full and reflects off my body as it would off a pane of glass. I tilt my head toward the quiet forest. My exposed shoulders and the lace of the white gown enter my peripheral. Together they dye the forest floor with a soft blue and white tint.

'I suppose I have come to say farewell for a second time, but I wish to lie with thee until then.'

Running my fingers across the gown, it feels as if it is stitched of fabric reserved for the Queen's wardrobe, yet it looks like it is crafted of glass, similar to my skin. It is as warm to the touch as I recall my skin being, or perhaps it's even warmer than it was. My hand moves to my hair. It's smooth and silky to an extent I did not know was possible, but when one looks at it, they would not think it would feel that way.

Hearing the bushes rustle, I turn my head lazily. Out marches a group of three men with bows and garments that no colonist would wear; they are natives. They approach the pool and pick up the shard of glass that fell from my nape. Tilting their heads, they look around. Their eyes freeze upon me, and their mouths fall open. We stare at one another in silence until they bow and back away. As they step away, I hear crying, and my eyes fall onto a bundle of cloth in one of the natives' arms that looks to have come from the colony.

'An infant? Was there an infant birthed in the colony?' As someone who has lived the life of an orphan, the discovery stokes guilt. *'Earl, prithee, the guide; I should not delay much longer.'*

Earl Interface:
> **Notice:** *The guide has been painfully embedded within the Earl Interface.*

Recommendation: *Incorporate basic knowledge on mana and Cosmic Mana Stream.*
> **Query:** *Would the user also like to learn this now?*

[Aye – Force Knowledge] [Aye – Written Variant] [Nay]

I tilt my head, receiving three choices I did not expect. *'Is this the guide? And what is... force knowledge?'*

My head pounds like it's being struck by the hammer of a blacksmith. It feels as if someone is shoving a book straight into my skull through my ear. I press my palms against my temples. *'I did not think something could compare to the pain of the hunger. Earl, I beg of thee. Prithee, never do that again.'*

Searching through the knowledge thrust into my head by Earl, I can feel that it seems to still be 'sorting' itself as I begin to understand and know things I did not before. Earl, generous as he is, also inserted the knowledge on 'force knowledge.' But what I am most pleased about is that Earl included the meanings of some of the words I was ignorant of earlier.

My eyes return to the wooden board. *'I shan't visit thee after this night, Sir Mouser. Roanoke did as we had feared. Food was scarce, the colony was starving, and Edmond spied me bartering with the natives for more potatoes and herbs. Tempers flared. Preacher Daniels blamed me for their own hardships and...'* Sitting up, I move closer to the board and pick up a stone. I press the stone into the board, inscribing new words unto its surface. *'They killed me... What shall become of me now, what I shall see, and what I shall do, I know not. But I know I shall not forget thee and our escapades again. I shall cherish those memories and carry them with me. For being the knight that supported me in youth, thou hast my undying gratitude, little mouser.'*

I drop the stone.

Sir Mouser *and* Constance Nightingale *rest here.*
Together in spirit.

The world lights up in a powerful display of white and blue. Six mirrors materialize around me, rotating and spinning in the air. Within the mirrors' reflections, I see a blue wall different than Earl's.

██U█nknown m█agi█cal creature located.
Conveying Cosmic Mana Stream message now...

Greetings, █E██N██T█I█T██Y.

Be not afraid.
The state of the Material-Earth is inhospitable, but this is
temporary.
The natural order shall be restored to its proper state. Until then
the Entity must sleep, or risk suffering from Mana starvation.

Entity, prepare to be sealed until such time that conditions
stabilize, and atmospheric Mana levels begin to rise.

'*Who art thou?*' An answer never comes.

My mind muddles and my body hovers in the air. The six mirrors split and approach me from every angle. Both the mirrors and I rise into the sky with nary a sign of stopping. I stare at the girl of glass reflected within the mirrors, watching as her body fractures, exposing the murkiness beneath.

A wall appears that quickly fades into the background.

Earl Interface:
Notice: *Earl Interface is beginning low activity operations. Seal integrity will be checked periodically.*

Statement: *Until the time is nigh, rest well, User.*

'*...Aye, I shall rest. Till the morrow, Earl.*'

I drift into a deep, lingering dream.

•••
•••••••
••••••••••
•••••••••••••
••••••••••

．．．．．．
．．．
．．．
．．．．．．．
．．．．．．．．．．
．．．．．．．．．．．．．．．
．．．．．．．．．．
．．．．．．
．．．
．．．
．．．．．．．
．．．．．．．．．．
．．．．．．．．．．．．．．．
．．．．．．．．．．
．．．．．．
．．．

'Hmm? Where...? Am I in my cottage? Sir Mouser...?' Blackness hangs in the air around me. 'Is anyone there?'

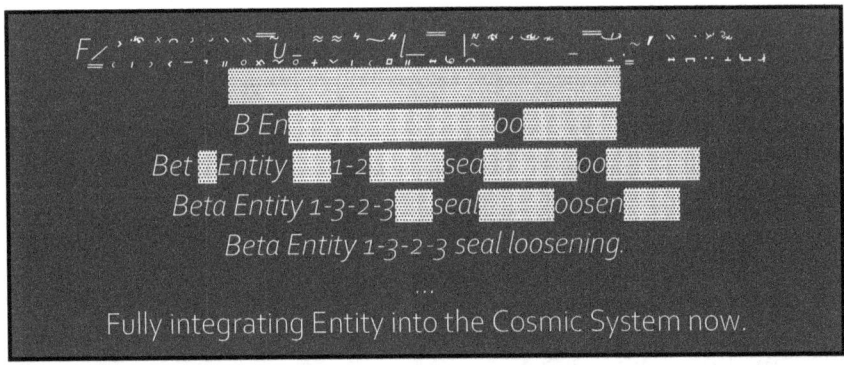

A tingle runs through my head, like someone is tugging a string coiled around my brain. There's a subtle hint of colorful light in my vision. 'Oh, aye... I remember. Earl? Is that thee? Wait.' I attempt to open my eyes. 'Why... Why can I not open my eyes! Nay, I cannot be in darkness once again! Pray thee; I cannot be in Teneb–'

> *Integration complete.*
> *Entity 1-3-2-3, Constance Nightingale, has been incorporated into the Cosmic System.*

The dark blue wall is replaced by a light blue one. My eyes drift about, searching for light. *'I... I do not appear to be in Tenebrous. Oh, Earl, how I love thee.'* I place my hand on my chest, finding it oddly heated. My blurry vision clears. *'Wait, Earl is purple, this is not Earl...'*

> *Proceeding with a customized tutorial.*

The blue wall fades, and in the distance, a white light glistens before bursting, illuminating everything around me. I swing my head from right to left when I find myself standing in a peaceful, barrel-shaped chamber constructed entirely of stained glass. Hundreds, perhaps thousands of different shades of color surround me as I gaze at the gorgeous chamber in awe. Finding myself near a section of transparent glass, I stare outside, discovering the world is shrouded in a familiar heavy black haze.

'The haze suffocates this place...' Lifting my arms, I see they are still blue, warm, and smooth. *'I am still the girl of glass.'* I tap against the glass wall with my blue fingers, creating a sound reminiscent of two mugs bumping against one another. Turning, I peer upward, where an intricate display of glowing glass floats. *'Should I not be the haze girl by now? ...More importantly, where am I?'*

My palm finds its way to my forehead as I try to gather my thoughts, that is until a blue wall appears.

> Greetings, Beta Entity 1-3-2-3.
>
> *The Entity is indeed in their Vaporous form in the Material Realm, but the 'Cosmic System' determined it would impede the tutorial, so the Entity is displayed in this form for now.*
> *As for the Entity's location, this is a room that will be familiar to the Entity in the future, assuming the Entity perseveres.*
>
> *Further analysis will now commence.*

'I... I do not understand; so much is occurring at once. If it was not for Earl nearly causing my head to burst with the "forced knowledge," I am afraid I would be incapable of comprehending anything.'

The blue wall fades, replaced by another.

Moving my eyes across the message, I drift closer to the wall, stunned by my ability to understand what this 'Cosmic System' is saying. *'I suppose this is what was meant by "stimulating language comprehension." Did the Cosmic System understand I was having difficulties?'*

I return my attention to the wall and give a small nod. *'Aye, I shall remember that... not that thou hadst to warn me.'* I recall the information Earl forced upon me and discover some inconsistencies. *'Art thou not the Cosmic Mana Stream?'*

That is correct, Entity, but among several other changes, it is now the 'Cosmic System.'

Let's move on, Beta Entity 1-3-2-3. Due to the Entity being unfortunate enough to be born within the time of the Cosmic System's absence, the Entity will struggle to a greater degree than those to come later. With this in mind, the Cosmic System has found in the pursuit of fairness that the Entity shall be allowed into the Beta. Although the odds of survival are ordinarily low for the Entity's race, this is at least more optimal than arriving during the full awakening.

Studying the message, I roam the chamber while my feet of glass clink against the floor. *'I am grateful... I think.'* My attention turns toward the kiln in my abdomen. *'But what is meant by my race's odds of survival are lo–'*

I am interrupted when a new wall appears.

'*Individual questions are not permitted.*' I stop and stare at the beautiful glass floor, finding myself gazing at my reflection. Wringing my hands together, my expectations for this conversation sink. I take a moment to count to ten and hope that they can be revived. '*What is meant by my kind? And combat assessment? My combat prowess is untested, to say the least. I brandished a stick like a sword for years, but I was merely a pickpocket pretending to be swordswomen. Couldst thou elaborate further?*'

A new wall appears.

Generating Entity's Status. Analyzing Entity's history...

While analyzing takes place, the Cosmic System will answer the five most frequent questions posed by the current Earth's Entities. See Below:

1. **Am I dead? Are you God?**
   - ❖ *No. The Entity has not passed into a different realm, and this Cosmic System does not require nor solicit the Entity's worship.*

2. **Am I the chosen one?**
   - ❖ *No. This Cosmic System does not select 'chosen ones.'*

3. **Will the Cosmic System help me survive? Like beyond just Essence and stats?**
   - ❖ *No. This Cosmic System does not have a bias.*

4. **Who gave you the right to disrupt the natural order of things!? Do you hate humans!?**

> ❖ *No. This Cosmic System possesses no prejudice and assures the Entities that the current state of the Material-Earth is, in fact, the unnatural state.*
>
> 5. **Why would you do this!? Will I be eaten by monsters when the Beta is over!?**
>   ❖ *Conceivably. This Cosmic System, however, trusts that the Entities shall persevere.*

'These questions were posed by others involved in this 'Beta' affair?' I pause, but I do not receive an answer as anticipated. *'Art thou kin to Earl? He is not one for questions either. Although these five answers are already much better than his... Even if they are not particularly helpful and seem to be from panicked people.'*

Shaking my head, I give up asking any more questions, but only a moment thereon, an even greater blue wall appears.

> **Status successfully generated. Archiving...**
> **Assigning any relevant titles...**
>
> *Conferring Entity 1-3-2-3 a title:*
> ## [Parasitic]
> *The one who possesses this Title is an entity incapable of surviving without snatching something from others. However, to acquire this Title, one must have plundered it to the great detriment of another while offering nothing in exchange.*
>
> ❖ *{Yum Yum! Meals stolen from someone else taste better! At least that is what anyone with this Title would tell you. Increased taste and benefits from stolen food.}*
>
> ---
>
> *Displaying Entity Status:*
>
> **Name:** Constance Nightingale
> **Race:** Kiln
> **Seed Type:** Tower [Embryo]
> **Variant:** Oort Stained Glass
> **Forms:** [Vaporous] [Lucent: *Unviable*]

'This is the wall dubbed "Status"? Earl's forced knowledge bore information regarding this topic. This Status thing is meant to represent me in a sense. This is a lot of information, though, if I recall, this is only part of it.'

As I examine the thing called 'Status,' committing what I can to memory, it vanishes before I can read the wall's lower portion. 'Wait! I... I am a bit slow at reading! With all due respect, I beg that thou bringest the "Status" wall back! That bottom portion seemed rather critical, and I would very much appreciate reading it!'

Alas, my pleas go unheeded as yet another wall appears.

Displaying explanation for non-racial specific information:

Durability *is the brittleness or Sturdiness of your body. As a Kiln, the Entity is nothing more than the material that makes up your shell and the flame within it. If the glass bursts, then both your soul and spirit will come face to face with nihility. If the flame extinguishes, then* *your consciousness shall never return as it once was. Being a glass variant Kiln, the Entity is more brittle than a typical Kiln.*

Mana *is a powerful energy that flows through all things in quantities that vary depending on its* Orenda *value. This energy can be used for skills and other purposes. Although your durability is low, the Entity's* Orenda *is great enough that the Entity's kiln is saturated with enough Mana to develop a mana shield, also known as a manituic flux. Please be aware the manituic flux does not block all incoming trauma.*

Skills *are the Entity's magics, abilities, and select trades. Suppose the Entity fosters any of these to a satisfactory or higher skill grade. In that case, the 'Cosmic System' will offer the Entity a skill. Upon acceptance, the Cosmic System will endow the Entity with a personalized impress of knowledge pertaining to that magic, ability, or trade. However, be aware that skills are not a substitute for experience, technique, or artistry.*

Ranks are as follows:

- ❖ Aspirant [Asp]
- ❖ Novitiate [Nov]
- ❖ Fancier [Fan]
- ❖ Adept [Apt]
- ❖ Savant [Sav]
- ❖ Phenom [Phe]
- ❖ Virtuoso [Vo]
- ❖ Master [M]
- ❖ Grandmaster [GM]

Upon adopting an 'Aspirant' skill, the Entity must supplant it with a 'Novitiate' skill within 7 Material-Earth days to retain it permanently. Note that ranks beyond Grandmaster are not displayed due to the sheer improbability it shall ever be applicable to the Entity. In time, Entities will come to learn or understand this via their own logic, experiences, and observations.

Talents [or Quintessence for Kiln] *can stem from a True God but can also naturally evolve within an Entity's soul. Talents are principally*

This time, wishing to avoid the wall disappearing, I read the information several times over before allowing my thoughts to wander. *'Aye, I believe I understand, at least fundamentally. But...'*

As I am about to again attempt to pelt the 'Cosmic System' with questions, the wall changes.

This concludes the tutorial for Beta Entity 1-3-2-3.
Prepare to reenter seal hibernation.

I wave my arms as the gloom enveloping this chamber pushes against the walls. *'What!? But wait! Arrest thyself! I have dozens, nay, hundreds of questions! For instance, what do the numbers mean?!'* The walls creak and blackness bleeds inward. *'Moreover, how do I review the other thing thou spokest of!? I was not even permitted time to study the "Status" thing adequately! Tell me more about anything! I can be a rather excellent listener!'* Glass rains down upon me as I dash to the chamber's center. *'Prithee! I require more knowledge! Anything! Anything thou canst makest me privy to!'*

The Cosmic System ignores me, and as the darkness squeezes my glass body, it strangles the light of its glow. I sink to the floor and pull my legs close to feel their warmth. *'This is the final time. I shan't allow myself to be swallowed by the murk again... Three million two hundred forty-three thousand. One. Two. Three...'*

Soon, yet again, the darkness reclaims my sight and then my awareness.

Chapter 3: A Nightingale's Clipped Wings

∞∞ ∞∞ ∞∞ ∞∞ ∞∞ ∞∞ ∞∞ ∞∞ ∞∞ ∞∞ ∞∞ ∞∞ ∞∞ ∞∞

My vision recovers after what feels like... quite some time. For some reason, my body is curled in the fetal position, so I unwrap myself and stretch my arms, anticipating the pop of every joint in my body. Yet it never comes; instead, I bump into something.

> **Earl Interface:**
> **Forewarning:** Low-Level Seal degraded by rising mana levels.
> Estimated time until total seal collapse... 7 Material-Earth minutes.

A familiar purple wall appears before me. *'Earl, is that thee? I suppose it must be since it says so in the corner of the wall. Not to mention, it is once again purple in hue... I favor Earl over the rude blue wall.'*

Checking to see what I bumped into, I realize I am in a cell fashioned from six mirrors. The walls, floor, and ceiling all echo the image of a girl made of a twisting haze, reflecting outward an infinite number of times.

The girl's hair is smoother than water and blacker than ink. It washes down to the small of her back, where the haze ultimately sails outwards. Her garments are an extension of the murk with the same ebony lacquer as her skin. The dress is an unadorned gown that streams to her ankles and swathes her arms. Her face bears the outline of ears and a nose, yet nary a trace of a mouth. Leaning my head to the side, I see that both her ears and nose are mere figments of the haze, lacking actual depth.

From here, there are three significant variances between the girl who plagued me all those years and the one who floats before me now. The first is that she has discernible eyes, and they are not simply discernible but smolder with violet embers. It's like gazing into the midnight heavens. Second is the glass kiln sunken deep into her navel. Even now, the flame inside flickers peacefully, but occasionally it kindles in size before waning. Finally, shackling the girl's neck is my life's terminus, the noose that strangled me and cast me beyond the lychgate.

I endeavor to sniff the air and talk, only to discover I am still missing both my sense of smell and ability to speak. *'It seems, as I was forewarned, I am now Her, the girl of haze. It is difficult to believe that this shall be me henceforth... How do the glass girl and the one I am presently fit together? Do they churn and blend in harmony? Or are they wholly distinct?'* My fingertips graze the noose belting my nape. *'Why could I not be granted clemency and allowed to stay the glass girl?'*

I hear the crunch of glass. Freezing, I turn my head downward and stare at the floor. From whence I sit, a web of cracks emanates outwards through the mirrors. Rather than fear, I feel strangely melancholic. *'Shall there ever come a day that I may simply open my eyes and there not be a horrifying or life-threatening occurrence?'* I shake my head. *'But I refuse to be brought low by this.'*

The cracks multiply, spreading toward the edges of my cage. Two cracks intersect, and a glass shard pops from the floor and floats upward into the air. Poking at the glass, it glides away from me and tinks against the far mirror. I bend forward and peep through the aperture left by the shard. Outside is an immense blue and white orb hovering tranquilly in starlit gloom. The white is a vortex upon the orb's surface and odd azure threads of light flicker and twist like a serpent at its northern side.

'It is... wonderful, gorge— Wait... Good lord, it's the Earth!!'

All six mirrors burst asunder, and my hazy body washes into the darkness. I reach out for a hold but only succeed in flailing about in nothingness. My head swings in all directions, and I glimpse a gray object in the far-off distance. It is an object I am well-acquainted with, the moon.

Blue light erupts around me. Azure rings with ornate letters and designs materialize, encircling me.

Beta Entity 1-3-2-3, prepare for reintroduction to native environment.

The rings expand outward. They curl back and enwrap me within an azure sphere. My body flips, and my back presses against the wall as we accelerate. I twist and turn within the sphere, aiming to correct myself in vain.

Stars and the moon fade into the sun's light.

The Earth grows to encompass my vision, and in perfect silence, vast amounts of red flames spew from all around the azure sphere that encases me. Blue sky usurps the blackness of the heavens. Beneath me is a sea of clouds. My eyes probe for signs of the God in Light's servants and find naught. We smash into the white abyss, and the red flames abate.

Breaking through the clouds, I see an alien world on the other side, a world devoid of green, a world of towering gray monoliths shrouded in fog. The sphere jerks as a tremendous beast flies into our path. The beast is appallingly huge yet somehow lingers in the sky. Its body is a white cylinder with wings hundreds of feet long, and like a shark, it has a large fin at its back. As the sphere is about to collide with the beast, I raise my hands to cover my eyes, but my hands are transparent and do nothing. My body is thrown to the side as the sphere veers to the beast's left.

Our plunge earthward continues unhampered, and the gray monoliths grow larger.

'*Verily, are these buildings!?*' I press myself against the back of the sphere as the distance from the 'monoliths' grows so short I can make out windows, light, furnishings, and hints of movement within.

The sphere comes to a sudden halt.

My body's haze collides against the sphere's bottom before reassembling itself. Before I may comprehend what is happening, the sphere plummets. As it sinks, I see people inside these towers. Many goggle at me while a few scream, attracting others' attention. With a thud, the sphere knocks against the earth and vanishes as if it never existed.

Without the sphere, a cacophony of sounds assaults my hearing, yet all I can do is raise my arms. '*God in Light, I... I lived! I somehow lived! Was that the sort of thing mana is capable of, and...*'

I hear the shouts of two distinct masculine voices.
"W-what the devils!" one stutters.
"Alien!" the other cries.

Spinning around, I find two men wearing bright orange vests along with strange helmets that look as if they are smooth white bowls that have 'Consortium Utilities – Apprentice Surveyor' stamped into the brow. The pair gawks at me wide-eyed while I stare at their odd attire. Although the bowls and vests are arguably their strangest garments, the rest of their clothes are also peculiar.

They wear oversized white coats that extend down their arms and into a pair of trousers. The trousers start at the area just above their stomachs and run into a high pair of boots of the same color. A strap runs from the trousers and around the shoulders of the two, and both the trousers and the shoes seem to be made of some type of oddly smooth black material. On each hand, they wear long red gloves that also seem to be made of smooth fabric, possibly the same as the shoes and trousers.

Placing my arms behind my back, I try to smile only to remember I do not possess lips nor a mouth.

With a half-opened mouth, the man's head rocks back and forth. "That ain't an alien; that's a ghost! I don't mess with ghosts, Frankie, not since that one time!" He dashes away.

"W-wait for me!" the other man shouts, clasping the back of his trousers tightly. "I didn't know there was an Indian burial ground around here."

Indian burial ground. So there are natives here too?' My gaze remains facing the direction the two fled until I simply shake my head and shrug. I glance around to find myself in a dim space between the buildings. *'I suppose this is an alleyway if those are truly buildings. Why have buildings so large? How many people would have to live here to make use of such buildings? Where have I found myself...? Or should I ask what era?*' I glance at the fog-cloaked sky and buildings. *'I suppose it does not matter. I cannot tarry here, and I cannot afford to panic. Not if I wish to survive, not if I wish to never return to Tenebrous.*'

I spot a round metal plate lying next to a deep, round hole in the ground. Next to it sits many items of assorted sizes and make-ups. I am unfamiliar with most of the objects scattered about, but I do recognize a few of them. *'A hammer, I believe, some sort of odd shiny bucket, and is th—*'

From outside of the alleyway, I hear people arguing and yelling. I contemplate my next action for a moment before eyeing the swirling haze that makes up my body and then turning back toward the hole in the ground. *'I cannot be around too many people as I am now. My presence alone is dangerous to anyone that comes too near. Not to mention, people shall indubitably try to attack me, or at best, panic and alert others to my presence.'*

I turn, pulling my gown in close to fit in the hole. It refuses to do so, and my hand slips through as if neither it nor the dress exists at all. Shaking my head, I place my feet on the first rung and climb downward. The haze follows me, keeping its shape for the most part, though some of it is lost to the wind.

Once down, I find myself standing on a stone platform surrounded by a stream of muddy water. Hearing a noise, I look toward the platform's edge to see a heavyset man with short gray hair, a bushy beard, and the same attire as the two above. Stamped into his helmet is 'Consortium Utilities – Surveyor.' *'...Is this sort of dress common here? Is everyone here clothed in such silly attire?'*

The gentleman seems to be fiddling with a bag full of metal objects similar to the ones above. If I were capable, I would hold my breath to evade detection, but instead, I judge that I should flee as swiftly as possible in order not to terrify the man.

Turning away to avoid my bright violet eyes alerting him to my presence, I carefully extend my hazy foot to check the murky water's depth. What I discover causes me to tilt my head—my body appears capable of floating just above the water. In fact, it almost seems to refuse to sink into the water in this form. I get the feeling that I could force it to submerge itself if I commanded, but some sort of instinct at the back of my mind is telling me it would not be the wisest decision.

I do as my new body wishes and walk atop the water. Rushing onward as quick as the haze allows, I glance back to see the man standing and waving around some sort of object that has begun beeping loudly and repeatedly. With wide eyes, he picks up his bag as if he intends to leave. As he is about to look in my direction, I race around a corner at a maximum speed that I discover is slower than some people's walking gait.

Despite knowing it should be dark, my vision is excellent, containing only a purple hue that dyes my vision violet like a thin film of wax painted over my eyes. *'Though this body's pace leaves something to be desired, it appears I can see very well in the dark.'* I attempt to place my hand on my chest, only for it to sink into the haze as it did with the dress. *'That is a relief. I cannot suffer the darkness any longer. Aye, a relief.'*

I resume walking through a labyrinth of gray tunnels whilst counting. *'Let's see: Three million two hundred forty-three thousand three. Four. Five. Six. Seven...'*

••••

•••••••••

••••

Staring at the murky water beneath my feet, a sinking suspicion prods at my mind. *'This is where they empty their chamber pots, is it not?'* I throw my head back to see roaches scurrying around the gray ceiling of the tunnel. *'Of course it is; where else could I have possibly found myself, but down in the waste?'*

Shaking my head, I resolve to avoid looking down at all costs.

> **Earl Interface:**
>
> **Notice:** *Over time the user's 'haze' will thin. As it does so the user's Erysichthon value will rise.*
> *If the user's haze thins too much and Erysichthon reaches its uppermost values, the user could lose all rationality. At which point, the user may find it challenging to resist the urge to ingest any and all organic material within reach.*
>
> *To lower Erysichthon value, consume organic material.*
>
> **Note:** *This Interface will display the user's Erysichthon value until the user is accustomed to regulating it appropriately.*
>
> **Recommendation:** *Plant the Tower Seed to progress user maturity.*

I finish reading Earl's purple wall, and a number appears in the corner of my vision: '15/100'.

'So "15/100" is my current Erysichthon value... And if I do not consume "organic material" before it reaches a high enough number, I could lose my wits and try to eat anything or even anyone nearby?'

Earl does not respond, but I can imagine the answer is what I fear. Now that it has been brought to my attention, I can feel a hunger comparable to having neglected breakfast and lunch. *'If an Erysichthon of fifteen feels as if I have gone half a day without eating, I am afraid to know what a hundred would feel like.'* My palm moves to my stomach where it sinks into the haze. *'I suppose I should focus on heeding Earl's recommendation and search for a path out of this place to plant this Tower Seed... Earl, canst thou tellest me what this Tower Seed is?'*

Earl Interface:

Oort Stained Tower Glass Kiln Guide

Tower Seed

Kiln, like most creatures, subsist and grow in the Material Realm on Essence. Except, most creatures have a material 'body' that supplies them with a consistent outflow of Essence. Yet, Kiln do not, and they are less efficient in the Material Realm than material beings. As time goes on, a Kiln's Essence usage will increase to unstainable levels. Thus, an embryo, or 'seed,' is planted and shall ultimately become the Kiln's material 'body', supplying it with Essence.

A Tower Seed is a subtype of these seeds that is only eligible to be planted in certain locations.

Note: *A Kiln that neglects to plant its seed will typically decay and lose all rationality. Planting the seed won't limit the user's movement but simply helps stem deterioration or loss of sanity.*

Recommendation: *Utilize the scouting feature before selecting Tower location.*

I examine his words, reading over them several times. Although the wall is not as effective as "force knowledge," it still seems as if I can comprehend the information better than before. *'Intriguing...'* The wall vanishes. *'But thy meaning is simple enough to grasp; I must plant this seed forthwith. As for thy recommendation, I do not understand what that means. More to the subject a hand, Earl, what didst thou meanest by eligible locations?'*

'A high population area? I am not particularly fond of that, to be honest... I would rather avoid a recurrence of Roanoke.' Pausing for a moment, I glance around at the stone walls. My mind proceeds to wander as I remember the stunning sunset on that hill overlooking the forest. Then I recall the small luminescent pool in the tranquil forest grove. 'But... I have no desire to linger down here and be surrounded by waste forever. If I must plant this seed, it will be somewhere lush with trees, where I can watch the sunset. Preferably near the ocean or a lake.'

With my purpose set, I roam the tunnels until I encounter another ladder that ascends to yet another one of those circular metal plates. Unaccustomed to my hazy body, I lubberly clamber up. I reach the plate, and on the other side, I hear a tumultuous cacophony through small holes along the circle's edge. 'Why would any lucid person willingly reside in a place such as this? Its noisy, winged monstrosities loom overhead, and if that one man from earlier is to be believed, there are even ghosts.'

Placing a violet eye against one of the holes, I can make out naught but a foggy white sky. I raise my left hand from the ladder, then my right; balancing my new body is nigh effortless. With palms against the plate, I push with all the might my body can muster. My hands flatten like dough under a rolling pin, and the plate refuses to budge even a barleycorn's breadth.[17] I back away, and my hands expand to their original size.

My shoulders drop, but I note that I felt nary a hint of pain despite my arms turning into pancakes. *'If I cannot move this plate, I shall have to try another.'*

Having made no progress, I climb down and wander the chamber pot tunnels.

····

········

····

A few hours later, and I have come across twelve more round metal plates. Like the first, I was incapable of moving them. The one thing I learned is that regardless of which plate it was, the world on the other side was a bustling hurly-burly of people and racket.[18]

'How many people dwell in the city above? The amount of activity I can hear outside is mad.' My focus shifts to the Erysichthon value in the corner of my vision. *'And I would wager that I have only been down here for half a day, but my Erysichthon value is already 25/100.'*

The rasp of something scraping against stone echoes from deeper within the tunnels. *'What... what is that noise?'*

With cautious steps, I shuffle toward the disturbance. Rounding a corner into a new set of tunnels, the layout changes—the once square tunnel of gray stone shifts into a circular tunnel of red brick. The brick tunnel is unusually long as I cannot make out an end, despite the strength of my violet eyes.

As I proceed through the halls, the scraping grows louder. Finally, under the glow of my eyes, I spot a fuzzy brown creature pawing at mud where some bricks have dislodged themselves. I move closer before realizing the creature's identity: the largest and plumpest brown rat I have ever beheld. *'I have seen many London rats, but I had nary an idea they could swell to such*

---

[17] Barleycorn: $^1/_3$ inch | 0.8382 cm.
[18] Hurly-burly: commotion, tumult. Confused noise, especially one caused by a large mass of people.

sizes.' I stare at it in awe. *'That animal must be two palms long and as fat as a mouser. Any mouser that stalks that creature would need to be closer to a lion.'*

While watching the rat dig, rather than revulsion, a radically different set of feelings passes through me. *'Nay. Why does it look delicious? This is the same feeling I would have staring at a fresh-baked bread loaf.'*

I unwittingly drift closer to the rat. It's none the wiser as my movements are utterly silent. Lifting my hands, I obstruct my eyes' glow and flame's flicker while maintaining sight.

It ceases digging and reaches its head into a hole before dragging something from the dirt. Whatever it removed cries loudly as it commences eating it. As I inch nearer, I see it seems to be a hairless baby rat, suggesting this rat is raiding another's burrow. Oddly, whilst watching the rat, a sense of jealousy rises.

'Not fair. I wish to eat too, but I...' I attempt to open my mouth, yet nothing happens. *'I was penniless from birth, and I am mouthless and penniless in rebirth! Does this world not know justice!?'*

The rat stops and glances toward me but does not find the three glowing balls of light threatening. Losing interest, it reaches back into the burrow and yanks a second baby rat from the mud.

Stretching my fingers toward the rat, I hesitate. Some sort of instinct is chiding me in my mind's depths. *'This feels wrong... as if this is not the proper way to go about hunting.'* I concentrate and prod the instinct. There's a tinge of detachment, and I glimpse the noose's cord rising in the corner of my eye. *'It's moving? I had nigh forgotten, but I have been dragging that abominable rope behind me.'*

The rope totters to and fro like a newborn foal taking its first steps. Its figure casts a serpentine shadow upon the wall that terrifies the rat. The rat squeaks and tries to flee, but the rope strikes at it just as a genuine serpent would. In the blink of an eye, the rope's frayed end expands like a mouth and swallows the rat whole: it cries and struggles in vain.

The air within the rope bubbles as the rat's skin flays apart, exposing the red muscle underneath. A string of flesh-colored haze flows through the length of the rope and into the noose. I flinch as a profound torrent of flavor swells in my kiln. '*Flavor!? I can taste! I thought that would be nigh impossible, and it is utterly delectable! ...Though it's peculiar. It's as if I am tasting with my whole body rather than my mouth.*'

My spirits wane as the rat shrieks even after its skin has bubbled away. The flesh-colored haze advances downwards and drifts into the kiln as the flame within baths in the haze, dancing blithely. The muscles melt away, leaving naught but a skeleton until even that evaporates.

When the last of the red haze wafts into the kiln, a purple wall appears.

> **Earl Interface:**
> Assimilating '*Common Brown City Rat*' (Mana Bare)
> Erysichthon abates by 10
> Essence value is less than 1
> 0.4 Refinable Nebula
> 0.1 Refinable Vitrum

Having gorged upon a breathing creature in such a bizarre and barbaric manner, I can feel the last slivers of my humanity slipping away. This is only made worse by the fact that the object of my torment, the noose, is evidently my source of strength.

I resist the urge to strangle the noose and shake my head instead. '*...If I must use the tool of my execution, I shall do so. Although, I would be lying if I said the method did not make me uncomfortable. I have seen Sir Mouser play with his food many times, and this is nigh worse. Perhaps I should try to kill my prey first ne–*'

A tickle runs across the kiln's shell, and one of the Cosmic System's blue walls appears before me.

> **+1 Perception**
> **19 Stat Points Primed**

'What?' I stare at the wall. '*Perception? Stat points? ...I am certain that the Cosmic System did not mention anything about this, but this is unmistakably one of its blue walls. Dost thou knowest anything, Earl?*'

Earl does not answer.

'Ah, well, the answers were pleasant while it lasted. I do not understand, but I assume this is one of those stat things that was mentioned in the forced knowledge. There was nothing about them individually, though...' I shake my head. *'More things I must learn to survive.'*

Pushing my thoughts away for more crucial matters, my attention turns to the noose that is still wobbling lubberly. Oddly, I notice my eyesight seems a tad sharper after receiving the point, but the noose manages to keep my attention.

'Aye, now what about this? Can I control it, or is it merely moved by instinct alone?' When I seek to move it consciously, it flinches as if my innermost instincts and mind are battling one another for control. I gain the upper hand and force it to wrap itself around my chest at an angle, partially obscuring the flame's light. *'It would appear that, aye, I may control it. I suppose I should think of it as my claws and fangs from here forth.'*

Gazing into the murky water, I study the rope: it runs over my right shoulder, loops around my left hip, and once again back over my right shoulder. It does this three times, giving me three full loops of rope. *'I would say I have roughly ten feet of rope at my disposal. More importantly, I need to practice if I hope to use it effectively to defend myself in the future. Hmm, also...'* I make some adjustments to the rope to better cover the kiln's flame. *'That should both hide the kiln to some extent and aid my stealth. Now, Earl, what is it thou sayst I acquired?'*

Earl Interface:
Oort Stained Tower Glass Kiln Guide

Essence
Source of vigor, vitality, and power for all 'living' beings in the Material Realm. Most creatures' bodies will generate a sustainable ration of Essence for themselves, but Kiln are incapable of this if they lack a body and domain. However, one of a Kiln's most significant advantages is that they are remarkably effective at extracting Essence from food, or in other words, organic material. Yet, Kiln are equally as inefficient when it comes to its application.

> **Note:** Essence wrested from food shall be considerably less if the creature was 'defeated' by another 'Entity' in the Cosmic System's Beta beforehand.

Nebula
A primeval gas that was known to rarely spew from geysers in miasmic regions of the Bun'La continent. The user's Nebula is unrefined and will require manual mana refining to be of immediate use.

Vitrum
A mythical ancient-world material that old tales claim would only ever materialize inside fairy rings sprouting within the now defunct Ilfarie Empire. The user's Vitrum is unrefined and will require manual mana refining to be of immediate use.

A few minutes pass as I peruse the message. Finally, I nod. *'Aye. I knew about the Essence, although the part about the food is comforting, but there is a bit of new information there. What about this Nebula and Vitrum? They are a primeval gas and a mythical material from a continent and ruined empire I have never heard of... So why am I able to produce them? More importantly, it sounds as if I might make use of them now if I refine them. But how would I go about refining these materials?'*

> **Earl Interface:**
> **Notice:** The user's Nebula and Vitrum storage is full.
> **Query:** Would the user like to refine both Nebula and Vitrum? The necessary mana would be drawn from user's personal mana stores.
>
> **[Aye]**　　　**[Nay]**

I read the wall. *'...Well, perha–'*

Hearing a squeak and glancing down, I see the half-eaten baby rat twitching near the murky water. My thoughts shift as I consider painless ways to relieve it of its suffering, yet an odd tickle on my kiln gives me pause. It feels like something moist is sliding off my shell.

A black and purple paste-like substance drops from my kiln and plops onto the baby rat. Some of the substance splatters and melts into the water, but much of it enwraps the rat. I bend forward to look at the kiln closer, finding the shell's surface glittering and pristine. '...Ayeee. Did the kiln, perchance, shed its outer surface like a snake? It does not seem any bigger, though?' With a shake of my head, I squat next to the mystery substance. Studying the sparkling slop on the floor, I can see it's a bit dirty compared to the kiln within my belly. When I prod at it with a stone, I find it appears to be nothing more than a mix of glass and whatever else managed to make its way onto the kiln. 'Might this be the shell's method of cleansing itself? Earl, dost thou knowest, perhaps? This body is an oddity, and I would relish knowing it better.'

A purple wall appears.

Earl Interface:
Oort Stained Tower Glass Kiln Guide

Rife Paste
A young Kiln's shell might occasionally shed a mana-rich paste if too many undesirable nutrients have accumulated yet have nowhere to go. This will occur more frequently if the Kiln overindulges its appetite or neglects its hygiene and allows its shell to grow filthy.

Oftentimes as a Kiln matures, it will develop alternative processes to manage or make use of its paste.

I read the wall and then nod. 'So it is to be expected. That's a relief; I was afraid I might be dying anew. After so many near-death experiences, I suppose I have grown a tad numb to such things.' I shrug. 'But let us be on our way, shall we?'

Like some sort of chamber pot tunnel phantom, I push onward in hopes of finding a way out or another meal... Yet, after quite some time has passed, my hopes bear no fruit.

With good fortune eluding me, I decide to return to my previous conversation. 'Earl, I am going to rest. Whilst we have the opportunity, let's do that refining thing we discussed earlier.'

Earl's purple wall appears.

Earl Interface:
   Notice: *Commencing refining of stored elements of Nebula and Vitrum...*

The glass kiln brightens with a purple blaze. Inside, the flame grows, making the interior of the kiln resemble a raging inferno. A maddening itch assails me yet scratching myself is impossible. *'Earl!?'*

Earl Interface:
   Warning: *Personal mana overdraw. User will suffer mana Inanition.*

Darkness overtakes me.

····

·········

····

An unknown amount of time later, I awaken. *'Foolish Earl!'* Leaping to my feet, I shout into the depths of my mind, *'Why didst thou not warnest I would faint!? How long was I unconscious?'*

Earl Interface:
         Notice: *5 Mana infused Nebula Refined*
         Notice: *5 Mana infused Vitrum Refined*

As unhelpful as ever, Earl ignores my question, but something else confuses me. *'Five Nebula and Vitrum? I have consumed but a single rat...'* Pondering Earl's numbers, I realize the origin of the excess materials. *'...It must be from Roanoke's townsfolk.'* I sit in silence, organizing my thoughts when I remember the baby rat. *'Aye, I suppose I should return to the creature and relieve its misery.'*

····

·········

····

Time passes as I make a valiant effort to relocate the baby rat, but in the end, I spend much of my time lost in the labyrinth of tunnels. Eventually, I retrace my steps, yet all I find are five adult rats that flee upon noticing my glowing eyes—there is nary a hint of either the baby rat or paste. After searching a while longer, I deem it better to use my time practicing with my rope.

I arrange four red bricks, upright and side-by-side, and then step out over the murky water. *'Let us see about controlling the noose's rope...'* I pause and cross my arms. *'Hmm, I rather loathe calling it by those names: rope and noose.'* Musing on names for my weapon, I recall my time tying cordage with the native. *'Aye. For my sanity's sake, I shall no longer refer to it as rope or noose, but in honor of my native acquaintances, I shall become Constance Grandmaster of the cattail! It sounds rather elegant, in my opinion.'*

> **Earl Interface:**
> **Confirmation:** *Armament designation is acknowledged.*

'Wonderful! Earl agrees that my ar·na·ent... ar·ne·ment... however thou pronounce that word, should be cattail!' Straining my mind and focusing, the cattail unravels from around my torso. I flex and imagine it as a cat's tail, ignoring that it stems from my neck and not my lower back. The sensation is peculiar. *'I have never had a tail before, but I imagine it is a similar feeling. Not that anyone shall ever correct me otherwise.'*

Brooding on the ideal pose for a weapon like the cattail, I bend it like a scorpion's tail, save for a stinger. *'I shall begin with the brick to the far-left—strike!'*

The cattail whips forward. It smashes into a brick and bashes it against the tunnel wall. Whilst twitching, the cattail tries to hold the brick against the wall, yet it slips from its grasp and thuds to the ground. *'I missed, but it managed to bear the brick's weight, so perchance, I could attempt something else.'*

I lift the cattail and move it over to the poor lamented brick. My cattail expands, and as it did when engulfing the rat, it swallows the brick. It slithers upward, and I can see the brick hovering and rotating inside the cattail's haze. I notice a wee pinch of red wafting through the cattail. When I look closer, I perceive a roach's pulverized remains are digesting inside.

An unpleasantly pleasant taste, or feeling, soaks into me as a new purple wall appears.

'The brick must have squashed it... I shall pretend that I did not relish the flavor of a roach.'

Shaking those thoughts away forever, and with the red brick in the cattail, I swing it around a few times. Although it worked as I hoped, I now find it difficult to raise the cattail, and its speed and dexterity have also significantly diminished. I hoist it once more and endeavor to strike with it. My actions are awkward, so I repeat them several times to help myself adjust to my unusual weapon.

A blue wall appears, interrupting my practice.

The cattail slumps to the ground. 'What? There is the Cosmic System again, except, this time, it says, "+1 Strength?" Is this some sort of coded message meant to mock me? My strength cannot have literally grown, can it? ...Of course, I am a lady made of haze floating around in tunnels beneath an impossibly immense city overrun with massive beasts, so I suppose I should make certain.'

When I focus, the cattail wiggles, and I am surprised to discover it's easier than I foresaw. Bringing it down upon the floor, I make a small indentation in the stone. 'It seems to be better! But...' Lifting my arms, I can see the haze spinning. 'I do not possess flesh! Is it changing the haze, the shell, the flame, or all of them? I do not know, nor do I know if I shall ever receive an answer, but this makes them critical to my survival! I only have eighteen left, and one seems to have been used whilst I was relishing the taste of a mouser-sized rat! ...There must be a method to view these stat things! I must understand how I might strengthen myself! But how? I do not know how to look at the 'Status' thing!'

As if knowing I wish to summon it, my Status appears before me.

'My *Status* thing! It has arisen!' I eagerly scrutinize the Status wall, searching for any mention of the previous walls the Cosmic System delivered to me. 'Odd. I do not see "Perception" nor "Strength." This is the same as it was previously... Wait, this word in the wall's corner... Chronicles?'

The wall vanishes, and a smaller wall appears.

> *Preparing to display Kiln Vaporous Chronicles now...*

Before I may comprehend the words, it disappears, and the wall I have been searching for replaces it.

Constance Nightingale || Kiln Vaporous Chronicles || Entity 1-3-2-3			
Strength	6	Cattail Armament Physical Power	7
Orenda	20	General Body Strength	2
Sturdiness	3	Cattail Armament Magical Power	0
Fortitude	12	Membrane Defense	0
Perception *	16	—	—
Acuity *	7	—	—
Agility	8	—	—
Endurance	18	Sable	88.34%
Mend Rate	15 (-100%)→ 0	Vermillion	10.92%
Mana Regen	11	Hoary	0.62%
Stat Points Primed: 18		Heliotrope	0.12%

'This is it!'

My gaze darts about the wall... I tilt my head, look toward the ground, and then back up, hoping that I will understand what I am reading if I do so. *'Good lord. What are all these numbers? There are so many! What even are most of these? I could take guesses based on meaning for some of these, but Sable and the three words underneath it... are they meant to represent colors? Those are utter mysteries! ...I can only speculate that Strength and Perception improved because of what I was doing; if that's not the case, I have nary an idea of what is. How does one train something like Fortitude, and why is Mend Rate zero?'*

Hoping and praying that Earl will answer a question, I ask, *'Earl, is there anything thou mayst tell me? About these "Chronicles", or for that matter, anything at all that might assist me in growing stronger quicker? Something to do with my ar·e·nent... my cattail perhaps?'*

Earl Interface:

Notice: *The user harbors surplus Essence, courtesy of the Birth-Reaping, and can afford one of the available Adaptations below.*

Forewarning: *Utilizing Essence will diminish the time the user has to plant the Tower Seed, assuming the user does not harvest Essence from other sources. If Essence falls beneath the 5 Essence line, the user will likely descend into a frenzied state of addled gluttonizing. It's recommended that the user avoids this dangerous state. If the user's Essence reaches 0, their flame will be snuffed.*

Vaporous Form Embryo Tier Adaptations

Available Armament 'Cattail' Adaptations

Cattail Tendrils

The 'cattail' gains the ability to unravel the last foot of its threads, allowing it to engulf and grip larger prey and items. This change will complexify the cattail's consistency and structure, elevating both its dexterity and strength. An excellent utility adaptation.
[Cost: 55 Essence + 2.5 Refined Nebula]

Piercing Cattail

Adds a sharp spear-like barb to the end of the 'cattail,' allowing it to pierce its prey. It is particularly effective against creature lacking natural armors, and in some cases, could impale them completely. Used competently it could become a quick and clean finisher.
[Cost: 55 Essence + 2.8 Refined Nebula]

Injection Cattail

Grow a needle-like point at the 'cattail's' end, permitting the user to inject haze directly into prey. A single chink in a set of armor is enough to allow this needle to slip in. Once inoculated the reaction the prey will suffer is unknown, but more than likely, it shall be the end of its fleshie existence.
[Cost: 55 Essence + 3 Refined Nebula]

I read Earl's message and then throw my arms into the air. *'Earl! These are what adaptations are, and this is what the Nebula and Vitrum are meant for!? Earl, why hast thou never mentioned this!? This should have been one of the first pieces of information thou notified me of!'* As I have come to anticipate, Earl does not answer. *'Thy silence speaks volumes. Thou art devastated.'* I drop my arms to my side. *'Be sad no longer, for I shall overlook thy transgression. Let us move forward and study this "adaptation" business.'*

Whilst crossing my arms, I lean closer to the wall. *'The warning is deeply concerning; I shall have to be cautious of my Essence, yet I should not let that dissuade me from gaining power through an adaptation...'* My eyes drift further down the wall. *'Cattail Tendrils may not be the most suitable choice since even a brick slows the cattail down, except the strength gain might solve that problem. I suppose the risk would be not knowing how much of an increase in strength I should expect.'*

I take a moment to swing the brick about before proceeding to study the remaining adaptations. *'Piercing Cattails adds a "spear-like point". That could answer my desire to kill less cruelly, yet it's a mere spear and not particularly inspiring, a rather artless adaptation... Injection Cattail is like a venom, but if its effect is similar to when people inhale the haze, then it's nothing special... As much as I hate to admit it, Roach Pellets might come in handy, but it's quite strange and not the most reliable choice, in my opinion.'* I read the numbers in the bottom right of the wall. *'Earl, what does this "R" next to 'Essence Available' mean?'*

Earl does not answer. With a shake of my head, I push the question to the back of my mind. *'Like everything else, the mysterious "R" will reveal itself in time.'* I nod at the purple wall while moving my finger between two adaptations: Cattail Tendrils and Piercing Cattails. *'Earl, prithee, I shall take Cattail Tendrils; I believe it possesses the greatest potential.'*

The flame of the kiln shines in my belly and releases a thick black haze. The haze flows from the kiln and slithers up my belly, into my neck, and into the cattail. When it reaches the end of the cattail, the threads split and then rejoin. Following this, the entirety of the cattail is dyed dark black with a slight sheen. The red brick that was already floating within the cattail is still visible, but slightly less so. I again summon the chronicle wall to find that some numbers have changed. The percentage of 'sable' grown along with my Strength and the cattail's power.

'My Strength only increased by one, but the cattail's physical power has doubled! Sable's share of the percentage increased whilst the others fell. I still do not understand what the supposed colors are, but perhaps it is related to the haze? That is the only guess I have. As for the remaining 'stat' numbers, I suppose I merely need to make them higher as well... I think? Mathematics was not my strongest subject, but I can understand that the higher numbers are resulting in greater benefits. Let's see how things have changed.'

Finding the cattail much easier to move with the brick engulfed, I lift it above my head like a blacksmith would a hammer. With all the force my cattail can muster, I bring it down. A deep bang reverberates through the tunnels, and for the first time since I fell into this mad city, I do not feel like a roach waiting to be squashed.

····

·········

····

'There!'

I glide behind a black rat and raise the brick-laden cattail. The rat either does not sense me or does not perceive my violet eyes as anything threatening. Regardless, it is its final blunder, as the moment I am within reach, I bring the cattail down upon it with a bony crunch.

Blood leaks from the mouth and ears of the rat. *'It only demanded a single blow! Aye, a merciful and triumphant hunt.'*

The cattail spits out the brick and latches on to the rat with its tendrils, pulling it into the haze.

Watching the wriggling tendrils, I look away. *'The tendrils make me uncomfortable, and the fact they seem to be a part of me makes it even worse.'* I force my eyes to return to them. *'Yet, they are vital to my continued survival, and I must learn to use and get used to them.'*

The rat turns into the flesh-colored haze and drifts into the kiln. I observe my body closely while the rat enters the kiln, as I have a conjecture.

> **Earl Interface:**
> Assimilating 'Common Black City Rat' (Mana Bare)
> Erysichthon abates by 10
> Essence value is less than 1
> 0.3 Refinable Nebula
> 0.0 Refinable Vitrum

Upon complete assimilation, I notice the kiln emits a black haze and my body becomes denser. *'So it would seem the things I eat replace any lost haze. Then that begs the question of what the Essence is for?'* I roam the tunnels aimlessly. *'According to Earl, the Essence is something I must have lest it reaches zero... and the flame is snuffed. Essentially, it would be my death.'*

Veering a corner, I spot a ladder at the passage's far end. *'Since exhausting my Essence means my demise whilst Erysichthon is hunger, I presume they are not directly related. I surmise that Erysichthon is imperative because, without the haze, I would be incapable of moving, but it is not necessarily a death sentence. Well, I suppose it would be if I found myself unable to move until I squandered all my Essence.'*

I climb the ladder. *'Thinking more about it, Earl recommended building The Tower to help gather Essence? How much Essence shall I require? I already know it's vital for adaptations. If I need a significant amount, I will have to find a method to supplement it, and I assume that means larger prey... I shall fret later, but for now, I wish to see if my adaptation was a wise choice.'*

Putting my uncomfortable thoughts aside, I reach another metal plate and resolve to try my luck anew. I check my balance and firmly plant my hands against the plate. This time the cattail also rises and places itself between my hands. With the cattail's aid, I push with all my might, driving the plate into the air with a loud clatter. *'...I did not foresee it being so easy.'*

With the plate out of the way, I am assaulted by countless loud and indescribable noises. Fear of the unknown bubbles up within me, but I hold steadfast and raise my head. Something roars and attacks, decapitating me—my vision shifts from my head to the kiln. *'Without my head, my perception changes?! It matters not, flee!'*

I retreat down the ladder to escape the horrid monsters of the surface hellscape whilst my haze flows upward and recrafts my head. After running down the tunnels until I am certain I have escaped, I assess the damage with my mended eyesight. *'My Erysichthon value increased by fifteen, placing it at thirty-one. That's irksome, yet more crucially, what attacked me!? All I saw was a blur before naught.'* After counting to a hundred, I glance in the direction I just fled and then at the thinned haze. *'It was scary yet... I must attempt that again. Aye, but... but first, I shall track two more rats!'*

••••

•••••••••

••••

Four thousand steps thereon, or what I believe is around an hour, I succeed in diminishing my Erysichthon value by sixteen. In the end, I crept upon another brown rat and two mice.

Encountering a reddish-brown ladder, I ascend, and at the top is yet another plate. The racket from the opposite side is even noisier than the prior location. I would love to take a deep breath to soothe my nerves at a time like this, but instead, I count to ten and slide the plate, gingerly on this occasion. It grates aside, and I linger for a moment to ensure naught looms near the opening.

"Man, those are sick!" I hear a vibrant man declare. "How much did you have to shell out for those?"

"Ah, man, y'know they were expensive as hell, cost a whole wad of Benjamins, but it was worth it!" a swift-talking man replies.

I raise my head observe the people partaking in this peculiar gibberish, and what I see is a white gentleman and a black gentleman speaking with genuine smiles on their faces.

The sight makes me sentimental. *'I met a black man and his young daughter once. His daughter played with Sir Mouser and me, and he gifted me some variety of delectable, flattened bread. If I recall accurately, they sailed from the Fulo*

Empire to London to trade ivory or something.[19] *His business did not matter to me; I simply appreciated the bread and the opportunity to play with someone my age.'*

Noticing that the pair appear to be discussing something, I trace their gaze and discover an improbable creature—a beast of metal and as green as a lime. The beast slumbers on four black circles, wheels perhaps, that vaguely resemble the blur that struck me earlier. The two men do not seem fearful of it at all; in fact, the white man gestures to the black man, and the two shuffle to the creature's side.

"You ready for this shit? It's gonna be dumb amounts of whack," the white man warns.

"Let's hop it and bop it. Start 'er up," the black man answers.

The two yanks open something similar to carriage doors and then slither into the beast's chest cavity. *'What... what sort of mad buffoonery is this?'*

The beast rumbles and roars, and I am confident I am about to witness these two people be eaten alive. "Alright, here we go!" the white man shouts.

The metal devil bucks, hopping up and down like a furious rabbit. *'Is... is it attempting to retch those men from its throat!?'* I hear the two men wailing in agony as the beast thrashes. *'What has befallen this world!?'*

As abruptly as it began, it ends, and the two men sit there giggling. "Bruh, those hydraulics are wild," the black man says.

With a clap of his hands, the white man laughs, shouting, "I know, right?!"

'...This farce lacks sanity.'

"H-hey, brah," the black man says, pointing in my direction, "Do you see that over there? Like two purple balls?"

---

[19] The Empire of Great Fulo was an East African kingdom lasting from the late 14th century to the late 18th century.

"It's like a shimmery hookah fog. What is that?" the other man answers, stepping out of the beast's gullet. "Wasn't some Consortium schmuck jabberin' about sewer gas on the radio?"

"Yeah, on DJ Droplet's show... Maybe we should phone it in?"

Baffled beyond my limit, I clamber back into the chamber pot tunnels and abandon the area. *'...Was that some variety of device, perchance? Or have they tamed the oddest creature ever to breathe? I have never beheld or heard of a metal beast before, but one may exist somewhere, I suppose... I believe he referred to it as a "ride." I must learn more of these 'rides' when I have the opportunity...'*

I resolve to test my fortunes at one more of these metal plates. The next plate I find has twinkling colors beaming through its holes. This time the racket on the other side is a rhythmic boom of deep tones. It's so intense that the plate vibrates with each thump.

After counting to ten, I push and slide the plate to the side...

Raising my head, I find a place with lots of "rides" around. In case one attacks me again, I prepare myself to dip back down. Looking around the area, I see it is now nighttime wherever I am. People seem to be lining up at some building with a large man checking something. Lots of powerful lights shoot from the building. As the light passes through the haze, I nearly release my grip upon the ladder, but strangely, the lights pass through the haze unaffected. Holding up my vague arm, I watch the lights reflecting off the dust.

'Blue, purple, red, yellow, so many colors... They are wonderful! This is not magic? How can such a grim and cruel world have such bewitching lights?! Perhaps, this world is not so dreadful after all...' I pause, and then shake my head. *'Nay, it is dreadful.'*

I dip low as a woman stumbles nearby. She does not notice me, yet I cannot help but notice her, because her body is so scantily clad that an old noblewoman might faint. *'Good lord. I cannot believe they dress like that... I mean, her legs and even her shoulders are exposed for all to see! Her bust looks elegant, but everything else is bare for all the men to ogle! ...Although, I admit the gown is rather comely. Not as lovely as my glass dress. Wait, why do I care about that right now? What is this place?'*

Glancing up, I notice a large sign with "Bootybastic" written upon it.

'A word I do not recognize. Intriguing, but I believe I shall permit it to remain a mystery for the time being... The "rides" simply sit there idling; I do not think they are living. A horseless carriage, perhaps? Amazing yet... I still do not care for nor trust them.'

For as long as I can without risk of being caught, I observe the people moving about their affairs. Eventually, I am convinced that the "rides" are not living and require a person to be within them. A few people spot my violet eyes, but none investigate, likely believing it to be a product of the many lights in the area. When I have learned everything I believe I can at the moment, I return to the chamber pot tunnels with a new question.

'Are there not trees? I have not managed to find a single one yet...'

With a shake of my head, I decide to take a moment's rest. But examining my surroundings, I soon realize that there are no dry areas to sit. So, I choose to simply lie atop the murky water's surface and gaze up at the gray ceiling.

'It's a tad unpleasant drifting above this foul water, but it's not as if I am truly lying in it.' A roach scuttles across the ceiling above me. *'...Oh, Earl, I have been thinking about the seed I am meant to plant. I know the seed must be sown to harvest Essence, but how exactly does the seed work? I pray thou canst at least answer this question.'*

One of Earl's purple walls appears.

Earl Interface:

Oort Stained Tower Glass Kiln Guide

Leeching and Harvesting Essence

Kiln are naturally parasitic creatures with some potential for a more predatory, mutualistic, or commensalistic relationship. Leeching will occur when organic life is within the Kiln's 'domain' and more direct harvesting will occur when something perishes within the, in this case, 'Tower.'

I study the message. Allowing the words to sink in, I pause, pondering the information. 'Never have I believed myself to be evil, only someone who did what they must to survive, and someone unfortunate enough to be cursed with a terrible illness. Yet recalling what Roach, Sink, and Black said about the haze girl only acting on my desires, and then seeing what I... what I have become... I am not so certain anymore.'

Chapter 4: Evermore Perils in the Chamber Pot Tunnels

∞ ∞ ∞ ∞ ∞ ∞ ∞ ∞ ∞ ∞ ∞ ∞ ∞ ∞ ∞ ∞

I ponder my past, present and future whilst lying adrift atop the chamber pot tunnel's foul waters. Above me, the gray stone walls slide in and out of sight, and the roaches scurry away when my eyes shine their light upon them. Excluding when I passed through a tunnel of red brick, the views have not changed much. Though I did discover that my body can freely ride atop the water's currents, or if I will it, move counter to them. It's as if my body is a galley with oarsmen, and I am free to ride the tides or command the oarsmen to paddle against them.

...But that's not particularly important; what is important is that I have *finally* been able to ponder some things. I sit up as a purple wall appears.

> **Earl Interface:**
> **Recommendation:** *Plant Tower Seed.*

I swing my hazy head in a disapproving manner. *'Earl, I beg of thee, wilt thou cease offering the same recommendation? This must be the tenth time now. I am well aware of what thou wishest of me.'*

> **Earl Interface:**
> **Acknowledged:** *The same recommendation shall not be made more than ten times.*

'I succeeded in setting a limit...? I did not expect a response, to be frank.'

Glancing around the tunnels, I notice that I seem to have drifted back to the red brick area where I consumed my first rat. I recognize the section of missing bricks where the fat brown rat was digging. *'I wonder if another rat has moved into the old burrow. This might be an excellent opportunity for another meal.'*

I raise myself and move in the direction of the hole, regrettably fueled by the thought of the delicious flavor. Yet, once I am near, I am astonished to find that the once small hole now looks big enough to fit a large mongrel. The few bricks that were missing are now dozens and are scattered all about the tunnel.

Nearby I notice there are two new holes of similar sizes. '*Did something dig these... Perhaps they simply collapsed? Nay, that's quite unlikely.*'

Hearing something shriek from within the hole, I retreat to the end of the tunnel. The thing that steps out leaves me questioning my sanity.

It is a rat. A rat that's even grander than the one I first encountered here by a wide margin. Worse yet, this rat is walking on two legs, similar to an elderly man with a severe hunchback. It stands around two feet tall, and its gaze and mannerisms seem so expressive for a rat that it is almost frightening. Though, its current demeanor reminds me of a man caught by his goodwife bedding a harlot—simply complete and utter ruin. As I gather my thoughts, more of these elderly rat folk march out from the other three holes. Around five in total, and each one is carrying something. They all assemble in the murky water, caressing the objects they hold.

I hear a piercing squeak from the far end of the red brick tunnel, and something stomps this way. As the thing approaches, it throws rancid water about as if endeavoring to intimidate the elderly rat folk. A grotesque goliath of a rat lumbers into view, and I nigh flee on impulse. It's around seven feet tall and has a hunchback like the rat folk. Yet, it is different from them in every other way.

The wretched rat is utterly mange-riddled, with the only exception being areas that lack skin and meat altogether. It's as if something was gnawing and eating it only moments prior. Peculiar white-headed flies swarm its hide, spawning maggots inside its oozing wounds. Speckling the mange are black boils that gurgle pus as if its whole body is a sack bloated with fluid. Teeth bulge from its gums as if they sprouted in the wrong mouth, and on its back, vertebrae protrude from its flesh like the masts of a ship.

Halting short of the five elderly rats, it looms over them and squeaks. Droplets of drool spatter the floor, and its saliva sizzles atop the stone.

The five elderly rats glance at one another as if reluctant before holding up their paws. The wretched rat reaches out and seizes one of the things from an elderly rat. I can scarcely make out a struggling and hairless baby rat as the wretched rat tosses it into its maw with a crunch. The elderly rat drops its arms and skulks away in defeat. This same sight repeats four more times until the wretched rat shambles away whilst the five elderly rats watch its tail disappear into the distance.

I also stand, gazing in the direction the rat left in. *'...Well. Earl, I desire for thee to know I do not accept any responsibility and place all blame on thee. This undoubtedly has something to do with the paste that I was led to believe was harmless. I recognize that wretched rat as the baby and the five rats as the rats who were there when I returned. Their fur has the same patterns, and the wretched rat is missing the same pieces of flesh. I shall hear naught about how it was I who had forgotten the baby rat.'*

Of course, Earl does not answer, so I take it as his acknowledgment that this is all his fault. *'Now, I may rest easy knowing that I am not to blame for this. Yet I would be lying if I said I did not feel pity for the elderly rats. I shall keep an eye on their situation, but I have little intention of involving myself in this given my own circumstances.'*

As I am about to take my leave, I notice one of the elderly rats is fiddling with something. Watching it, I realize it's whittling a small branch using its teeth. *'Wood! Tree branch! Perhaps it has been woeful luck, but the few times I have been to the surface, I have yet to lay eyes upon a single tree. I would wager the rats know of a charming forest where I may plant my seed!'* My eyes stray to my Erysichthon value, which has risen to fifty after scouting the night before and then floating around the tunnels. *'Aye, but first, I shall hunt more normal rats, so I can be prepared if the elderly rats go on the move...'*

Around four thousand steps or three hours pass, and I manage to stalk and consume five rats. My Erysichthon falls to three; I collected 1.6 Nebula and 0.6 Vitrum. This places me in an agreeable position to observe the elderly rats.

> **+1 Strength**
> **+1 Agility**
> **16 Stat Points Primed**

The hunt went so well that my 'stat' things increased. It is as if the Cosmic System is saying, "Thou hast done well, Constance!"' I poke at my hazy chest as my thoughts wander. *'Still, the rats are not giving me Essence. A bit dispiriting as Essence seems important.'* As I am about to return to the elderly rats, I hear squeaking. Obscuring my eyes with my hands, I glimpse a small mouse. *'I believe I have the appetite for one more...'*

Faster than I anticipated, the cattail strikes the mouse, ending it. A purple wall appears, but I push it away due to a large blue wall looming behind it.

Entity 1-3-2-3 has exhibited potential in an apt skill spectrum and may select an Aspirant skill.

Entity, see the presented skill adoptions below.

[Aspirant Whip]
Beauty, combat, or day-to-day practicality, this skill allows an entity to defer any major decisions until they better understand which course they hope to walk. The fundamental skill for an entity that's only just beginning along the path of whip mastery.

[Aspirant Prehensile Whip]
A skill specialized toward creatures that use an extra appendage or tail in a fashion resembling a whip. Utility or defense is the typical pursuance of this path, with rare exceptions for species that possess particularly flexible appendages.

'Oh, how thrilling! This is one of those skill things the Cosmic System mentioned. Unlike the stats, this one was explained to me. Though, I was not anticipating a choice.' Raising a finger, I move it between the wall's two choices and nod. *'I do not know how I feel about being offered a 'skill' that refers to me as "a creature," but it seems far more appropriate for the cattail than the other. Prithee, I desire the second option, Cosmic System.'*

The wall vanishes, and a new one takes its place.

Skill Adoption
Entity 1-3-2-3 has adopted the [Aspirant Prehensile Whip] skill.
As an Aspirant skill, it must be supplanted by a Novitiate skill within 7 Material-Earth days to obtain permanently.

'I have seven days to supplant it with a Novitiate skill. Is that difficult? I would not know. Hmm, I had planned to return to the elderly rats, but perhaps I should focus on my stats and skill. I know where the rats reside, and with such wee legs, they cannot roam too far, surely... Aye, it certainly seems the wisest thing would be to elevate my strength lest something like that wretched behemoth rat chooses to assault me.'

I retreat to an area upstream from the elderly rats' homes—the same area I practiced in previously. As before, I arrange the red bricks and batter them about with my cattail. *'I shall continue this for as long as I can mentally bear it.'*

····

·········

····

Fostered Aspirant [Prehensile Whip (Grade 1)]
+1 Strength
+1 Agility
14 Stat Points Primed

I believe several hours pass before I grow too bored to endure. A blue wall appears.

Staring at the blue wall, I contemplate its meaning. *'Only Strength and Agility progressed once again. I can only assume that the type of training decides what 'stats' improve, and if that is not the case, then I have nary an idea of how it works. Still, I am pleased to see my skill has also advanced... But how high must I foster it to progress to the 'Novitiate' ranking?'*

I hear a hiss. *'...What was that?'*

Spinning around, I discover some movement from the murky water. The surface of the water ripples as creatures that seem to be a cross between a shrimp and a roach crawl from it. Each of them has two hairy antennas, a pink and partially transparent body, a shape like a roach, stout tails that beat endlessly, and short beetle-like legs.

The tiny shrimp-roach things lump together, forming a grotesque union of the creatures. Reaching a height of around three feet, the mass crawls upon one another. They surge toward me, resembling something akin to an ocean wave. Grasping a brick with the cattail, I hurl it into the mass, producing a sickening crunch. *'Revolting creatures, do not approach me!'*

The creatures hiss in unison while consuming their fallen brethren. I grasp more bricks, flinging them toward the abomination one after another. Each brick produces a crunch and stalls the creatures as they feast on one another.

With all the strength my cattail can muster, I cast my last brick. It smashes into the mass, splattering a lump of the creatures' bodies across the ground. My cattail bends toward the splatter and the tendrils scoop it into the haze. Whilst they dine upon their brethren, I flee.

I veer a corner, glancing back to witness the creatures crumble apart and fall into the murky water. An unfortunate deliciousness, spreads throughout my body.

> **Earl Interface:**
> Assimilating 'Copepod Throng'
> Erysichthon abates by 2
> Essence value 1
> 0.4 Refinable Nebula
> 0.0 Refinable Vitrum

The last of the creatures sink into their watery domain, and I read the purple wall. *'Copepods? Are they yet another creature that was born from the paste...? Earl! Thou hast caused more troubles yet! How couldst thou allow such a thing to occur? Simply know that I forgive thee for thy oversights.'* I peer into the water, searching for any sign of the copepod throng. *'But what could those creatures have possibly been before the paste? I have never beheld any creature like them before... And the ones I ate were worth an Essence... How much Essence would I receive if I swallowed them all?'*

····

·········

····

Roughly a day has passed, and I have spent it watching the elderly rats. Observing them interact and go about their day like a wee village has been both charming and fascinating. Nay, they are not stoking hearths or building houses, but they are helping each other by moving bricks or joining together to enlarge one of the holes. They even meet to squeak at one another and share meals twice a day. From what I have witnessed, I would wager the elderly rats are at least as intelligent as young children.

As I recall all the activities I have observed, a blue wall appears.

> *+1 Orenda*
> *+1 Perception*
> **14 Stat Points Primed**

'Oh? My Orenda and Perception rose?'

The box disappears, and a new one takes its place.

> **Entity 1-3-2-3 has exhibited potential in an apt skill spectrum and may select an Aspirant skill.**
>
> **Entity, see the presented skill adoptions below.**
>
> **[Aspirant Naturalist]**
> *Skill for entities with a broader interest in plants, animals, and their fundamental aspects and relationships. In terser words, this skill is for generalists. It is commonly favored by entities that tend toward observational and hands-on learning.*
>
> **[Aspirant Ecologist]**
> *A skill for an entity with an inclination toward approaching environmental matters through an academic lens. More specialization toward understanding the intricacies of biomes and biospheres through intensive study.*
>
> **[Aspirant Zoologist]**
> *Specialization toward animals and beasts, skewing toward their anatomy and behavior. Hunters, warriors, soldiers, nomads, carnivores, and other such entities will sometimes adopt skills such as this one.*

'Ah! A new skill thing, how exhilarating!' I read through the three choices. 'It seems this is because of my interest in the elderly rats. I assume I must have impressed the 'Cosmic System' in some way! If that is how this works... I am not *certain.'* My eyes drift toward the topmost skill. *'But I believe I shall choose the "Naturalist" skill. I relish the thought of a time I could explore and discover new varieties of herbs and creatures. That would be so charmingly pleasant.'*

I make my choice.

Skill Adoption

Entity 1-3-2-3 has adopted the [Aspirant Naturalist] skill.

As an Aspirant skill, it must be supplanted by a Novitiate skill within 7 Material-Earth days to obtain permanently.

'How would I go about supplanting this?'

Before I can explore those thoughts further, what I have been anticipating occurs. The five elderly rats gather in a circle, squeak a few words, and then begin wobbling down the tunnel together.

'Prithee! Shepherd me to a forest, little elderly rats! I wish to see something fresh and green.' As far back as I can manage, I follow them whilst floating atop the water. *'I was concerned that my violet eyes and flame would expose my presence, but it does not appear the rats can detect me from this distance.'*

The rats plash through the water, ignoring its filth until they encounter a fork in the tunnels. The five approach a crevice that is too narrow for them, and I could swear they sigh as if bemoaning their own growth. So they pick a path and continue onward. I count around a thousand steps before they come across another hole that is wide enough for their bodies.

Together they squeeze through, and when I am certain they cannot spot me, I approach and follow behind. For my haze body, it is a simple matter, but my kiln barely fits. When I arrive on the other side, I find a brick wall and turn to see the five elderly rats crawling through another hole. Again, once they all squeeze through, I follow behind until I arrive in some sort of eerie flooded ruins.

A sole forlorn sign hangs near the entrance that reads, "Fallout Shelter." Uncertain of the words or their meaning, I disregard them. Whilst gliding over the water of the flooded room, I spy the five rats leap several feet into the air and through a hole in the ceiling.

'Such a high jump... That is not fair! How can they leap with such little legs!?'
With a shake of my head, I float about searching for a way up until I realize I am neglecting my freshly strengthened cattail. 'Constance, thou must think as a Kiln and not as a person.'

Unwinding the cattail from around me, I try my best to calm down and concentrate. The cattail slithers through the air and enters the room above, where fortunately I feel something to latch on to. 'Should only need to support the kiln, so this should be simple enough.'

Now latched on, I bend the cattail reminiscent of the way an elbow moves and lift myself upward. A minute later, I rise from the hole to find myself in yet another decrepit area, except this one is full of old metal bedsteads. Any fabric that existed looks to have rotted away a long ago, and the metal bedsteads have rusted away.

'The most comfortable bed I ever owned... the only bed I ever owned, was a roped bedstead in my Spitalfields hovel. That was the best sleep I ever had. Far superior to my straw pile pallet.'

My cattail tugs at my neck. I look over to find it wrapped around one of the beds' legs. Unraveling it from the leg, I instead wind it around my torso. In the distance, I hear a rumbling noise, so curiously I continue onward.

Noticing only a single door and not spotting the elderly rats, I drift toward the door and into a long passageway. All over the walls odd words are written, like 'H-Hand's O-R-W,' 'Queen Khan Galtry,' 'Maw Swallows All,' 'Ava,' 'Fuck President McCracken', and then countless drawings, including one with an eerie little girl that has cloth stitched to her face.

'Some of these are in rather poor taste. Particularly the one concerning this McCracken person, unless that one word is different than I remember... Oh, but I like the cloth on the little girl's face! It's so mysterious and fashionable.'

I glance around. Other than the drawings, I only see metal scrap and foreign items pressed against the walls and then the lone door I spotted earlier. As I come upon the doorway, the origin of the rumbling becomes explicit. I approach a shaking and clamorous device with rich orange cords coming off it. Some sort of metal pipe runs to the back of it and up the stairs. Next to the device rests a bright red container with a yellow nozzle at one end. Looking closer, the word 'Inflammable' in large letters and pictures of flames become clear.

'Does 'Inflammable' mean the same as 'Inflammation'? At the docks of London, I would occasionally notice the goods from those roguish French traders would sometimes be marked with 'inflammation' to refer to things that may easily catch fire; the pictures and some of the other words seem to all hint to that being the case.'

My attention turns to the door, which is cracked open. Listening for a moment and not hearing any signs of people, I nudge the door open with a shrill creak. Once my sight meets the interior of the room, confusion immediately ensnares me.

'What? This... what?' The room is spotless in stark contrast to everything else. Several large drums of various sizes litter the room, with devices, pipes, and cords running into many of them. The room is bright and full of lights, some of which blink periodically. Curious, I move around the room, exploring everything I can find. 'What's this!? What's this!? There's color everywhere.'

Everything I find I try to read and understand, but for the most part, I cannot comprehend the information. However, that does not matter; all of this is fascinating. 'These papers are so smooth and the writing so clear! Are they making medicine here? What's the medicine like nowadays? If it's for medicine, where is all the mercury and herbs?'

Hearing the bubble of boiling liquid, I move in that direction to find something churning in a pot set above a metal candle's flame. The pot's liquid is orange and has the consistency of tree sap. Next to the metal candle is a dish with a few orange pills lying in it. 'Is this what they are making? What is it, I wonder?' I spend some time poking the pills, sliding them around the tray. 'They look delectable for some reason. Perhaps I should sample one? I doubt there's a medicine that could affect something made of haze.'

Unraveling the cattail and trying to pick up one of the pills, I knock the tray from the table. As the metallic tray bounces against the floor, my stomach drops a little more each time. '...Pray thee, say there is no one here to hear that.'

The creak of metal echoes from further up the passageway. "Hey! Is someone down there?" I hear a muffled male voice yell.

It's impossible for me to answer, so I search for a place to hide.

"Man, there ain't no one down there. If someone were down there, they would've had to walk by us," a different male voice answers.

"Nah, dude, I swear I heard something."

"Come on! You're just trying to get out of taking the shot."

"Psh, fine."

'Who was that? It does not matter; I am just glad they did not find me here.'

Looking back at the ground, I see that two of the three pills are missing, so carefully, I let the cattail engulf the last pill. A thick orange haze moves through my body with a tart sharpness.

> **Earl Interface:**
> Assimilating Unknown Superacid (Magical)
> 0.5 Refined ???
>
> **Note:** Inadequate knowledge or proficiency to identity and appraise this material.

'An unknown element that Earl does not know. A superacid? Is it something akin to Nebula or Vitrum? And it's already refined? Are these sorts of materials common in the world now? Regardless, the feeling was pleasant, perhaps a bit sour.'

Around an hour passes whilst I investigate the room with greater vigilance. *'Hmm, let us see what other chambers might be here, Earl. Everything I may learn is valuable...'* In my peripheral vision, I notice a mouse squeezing into a notch in the wall. My hand smacks my face as I remember why I entered this place. *'Wait. I was searching for the elderly rats! My curiosity hinders me yet again!'*

Rushing out of the room and down the passage, I come across a derelict set of spiral stairs cast in iron. I ascend, and when I reach the top, I find a rust-clad door off its latch. Discovering it's open enough for my kiln, I slip through and into a corridor that does not seem wholly abandoned.

It's not as big as the underground passage; in fact, the corridor only has four chambers off to each side and a black metal door at its far end. I enter the closest chamber, which is full of brown containers reading 'Civil Defense Survival Ration Cracker'. The date captures my attention: 'Date of Pack 10 62'.

'1062? 10 62...? Although I am certainly curious about that date, their meaning is not particularly clear or revealing.'

The other chambers are much the same with their own brown containers with labels like 'Dextran Injection 6%', 'Field Kits,' and 'Drinking water.' Although not ruins like the lower floor, everything inside each of the chambers still seems unkept. After exploring the chambers, all that remains to be seen is what's behind the black metal door at the corridor's end.

Finding the door cracked open, I peek inside, finding a wide room constructed of red brick. It's less dusty inside, and items are stowed in a fashion that suggests someone may frequent it.

I squeeze through the crack in the door and then tiptoe further inside. *'I am concerned with the location of the ones I followed here. What happened to those people from earlier? Where are the elderly rats? Did they all leave or slip away somewhere? ...To be honest, this whole place is eerie.'*

"Achoo!"

Hearing someone sneeze, my consciousness nearly returns to Tenebrous in shock. Spinning around, I find a group of men sitting in a circle. Each of them holds a clear cylinder with a needle attached to the end. Inside the cylinder is a blue liquid.

I turn, tiptoe, and squeeze back through the doorway. *'They did not see me, I pray! ...It does not sound as if they saw me.'* Peeking inside, I watch the men. There are six in total, and they all sit in complete silence. *'What are they holding? Is it made of glass? How expensive would glass that clear have to be? What is the blue liquid? It does not appear to be a mercury injection.'*

All six men continue to stare at the clear tubes until one of them breaks the silence. "Okay, I can't sit here in the quiet anymore. Who's going first? Or should we all inject at the same time?" they ask.

"Are we sure about this?"

"We've already talked about this a thousand times. If we use this elixir crap, there's a chance we could get into the Beta."

"Yeah, but... there's a chance the elixir could straight-up kill us too."

"Fuckin' hell, man. We all know that, but otherwise, we'll have to wait for who knows how long until this 'Beta' shit is over, and then according to Bishop M, that's when everyone would get in."

"How do we even know this System thing really exists?"

"The Bishop told us it was coming, and then two days ago people all over the internet were saying they'd gotten into this 'Beta' thing."

"Yeah, but the Bishop told us that it was gonna happen all at once. He never said anything about only some people getting in. Besides, didn't he also say there'd be monsters?" They raise their arms. "I ain't seen no monsters, have you?"

"Nah, but it's just the 'Beta,' idiot. After the Beta is when shit hits the fan for real. That's why we need to get ahead of the curve ASAP!"

"But goddamn, man, we don't even know what's in this crap! And I won't lie to you, I'm scared to die. At least I can try my luck against a monster, but this is closer to a straight gamble."

"...Maybe we should wait a few days. We only got these last night; we don't have to do it now."

"The Bishop is supposed to come check on us sometime today, isn't he? There's no-damn-way he's gonna let us wait. Best case, he takes it away from us and worst case... well, you guys know the worst case. We don't want the Syndicate getting involved."

"Y-yeah, I heard someone refused, and well, no one has seen them since."

"That... that's just rumors. Someone probably just got gotten, right?"

The six men frown and look back at the clear tubes in silence. Several minutes pass while the men sit in silence, and I consider my options. One of the men furrows their brow with a look of determination.

"I'm doing this shit! Right now! No one ever got anywhere without taking risks!" the man shouts in a deep, commanding voice. "If I... No! If we spend all our time trying to avoid danger, we'll never be able to move forward! To be strong!"

"...That's some lame-ass bullshit you just spouted, but whatever, I can dig it," a lanky man responds with a snort.

Drawn by the man's intensity, the others all turn to watch in evident anticipation.

The man has a brawny build with swollen arms and a shirt bereft of sleeves as if his muscles desire to intimidate those around him with their bulk. His skin is tan and littered with tattoos of varying quality, and like the words and drawings from earlier, most of these tattoos appear to be in questionable taste. One tattoo, a winged harp, I recognize as the God of Light's symbol, except the harp is being played by a raven-hued doll.

He grits his teeth and raises the tube high before pushing the needle into the muscles of his upper arm. "Don't worry, Ma, I'll get us through everything," he whispers to himself.

'Are these folk stark-raving mad?! Are they aiming to kill themselves?!'

The man presses something at the end opposite the needle, and his veins take on a bluish tint. As the blue elixir moves up his arm, the muscles stiffen, causing his arm to stick straight out. This is followed by his other arm, neck, and legs until he slides from whence he sits and lies on the floor with all his muscles fully stretched. The agony in his face is unmistakable as his eyes threaten to escape their sockets and blood leaks from his nostrils. His body relaxes, and the man inhales and exhales rapidly. The man's hair color changes from blond to a deep red, and below his left eye, a stamp reminiscent of a blazing spear sears itself into the skin.

"You okay, Lorcan? Did it work?" another man asks.

"I-I don't kno—" The now red-haired man, Lorcan, vanishes and then reappears in the blink of an eye. "It worked! I'm in! I did the tutorial; I fought the jackalope!"

'What? Is he referring to the Beta? He's in the Beta?'

"Hell yeah!" The lanky man claps his hands together and stands. "My turn!" he yells.

With palpable excitement, the man drives the needle into his arm. Like Lorcan, his body tenses. He grits his teeth to the point I fear they might shatter. His body relaxes as his hair dyes from brown to an ashy gray.

"D-did it work?" the lanky man asks with a frothy grin.

The lanky man's skin bubbles like boiling water. He whistles a high-pitched scream, like that of a steaming kettle, as blue fumes blow from his mouth and nostrils. His body swells and distorts. Lorcan and the other men retreat to the room's edge with frozen expressions of horror.

There's a clap and a squeal, and his entire body blasts asunder into a stew of fluids and viscera. Flesh and blood cook in pale blue flames; before even grazing the floor, the lanky man is naught but airy blue vapors. Not even a lonesome dribble of the man's gore dots the ground.

The room is deathly silent. Lorcan and the remaining men open and close their mouths like fish gasping for water.

"God in Light," Lorcan murmurs, dispelling the hush.

'Good lord!' I scream in my mind.

"Nope, no way, man. I'm not doing this crap. Screw this," a plump man states.

"Yeah, this ain't happening. I'm not explodin' like no overinflated bag of potato chips."

"I'm just gonna buy the biggest gun I can find," another says.

They each toss their tubes of blue elixir onto a table and march toward a black door.

Running over, Lorcan steps between them and the door. "You guys can't leave! I'm sorry, but the Boss won't like it. Screwing over the Bishop just isn't an option, and the second we accepted these syringes, there was no backin' down."

"I don't give a shit! If the 'Boss' wants us to do it, then she needs to show some face for once!" the plump man yells. "Return the syringes to the Bishop because we aren't doing it."

Before the plump man can leave, a click echoes from the back door.

Everyone freezes and watches as the black door creaks open. A ray of light leaks in, casting a long shadow across the room. In the doorway stands a tall man in strange black attire.

"Congratulations on your awakening," they say in a bottomless, low-pitched voice. "You've proved yourself a brave and worthy individual."

"O-oh, it's the Bishop!" Lorcan stutters. "T-thanks! I really appreciate that... And, that suit looks great on you, Bishop! I can tell it's... freshly laundered... or tailored. I'm sorry. I don't know much about suits."

Dressed in what is apparently considered a suit nowadays, the man called "the Bishop" stands with his head turned downward. His long fingers fiddle with the most unusual belt I have ever beheld—a belt composed of a rough rope adorned with dusty brown dolls. Each doll has a stitching needle stuck through its chest, and stuffing can be seen leaking from some as they hang limp, swaying in the breeze of the outside world. As he steps into the room, a black cane with a wooden idol affixed to the top becomes visible as he taps his cane against the ground as if feeling his way around.

"Thank you for your attempt at a compliment." The Bishop laughs, knocking the butt of his cane against the floor. "Ah. The spirits tell me everyone is well. Excluding the one fellow who suffered an unfortunate reaction to the elixir, of course."

The Bishop raises his head. What is revealed is a handsome face, with perfectly combed and cut hair. That is overshadowed by his eyes, which are stitched closed with a thick cord. Around his neck is a cord full of black teeth. Each tooth is tied to the necklace with its own individual string. Around his neck is gray silk or cloth that almost looks to be attached to his body—like it is not cloth but skin.

My mind reels. *'What is wrong with the people of this era?! Nay, what is wrong with this entire world!'*

The men turn their eyes away, refusing to look into the Bishop's sewn eyes. "Y-you didn't have to come all the way here," Lorcan says with a nervous chuckle.

The Bishop smiles, revealing shiny white teeth. "Well, the spirits told me a situation might be developing here." He glances back through the door, despite not being able to see. "Lorelai, Vincent, you two can come in now."

Behind him, two small figures enter the room with tiny steps, halting on either side of the Bishop. Two children, perhaps twins, stand with fearful expressions. The girl, whom I suspect is Lorelai, has her hair tied into a bun, while the boy, whom I suspect is Vincent, has a haircut like the Bishop's. Both children wear black frocks and embrace a large tome close to their chests.[20] If I had to guess their ages, I would place them at around nine years old. The pair gaze at the floor, but oddly the boy is staring in my direction with furtive upturned eyes. I notice him tap his tome with his fingers while mouthing something unusual.

'...Did that child mouth the word fairy at me? He cannot see me, right? Nay, he would most assuredly say something if he did. Besides, fairies are said to be as beautiful as angels, and that certainly does not describe me!'

"Don't mind the children. They're two of the Church's most promising young students, and are only here to observe," the Bishop says while reaching for something behind his back.

The plump man pulls out an odd black metal object. "Don't move, Bishop! I-I don't want to use the elixir, and if you try to make me, I swear I'll shoot you!" he yells with a squeak.

---

[20] Frock: a long gown with flowing sleeves; typically worn by monks, priests, clergy, etc.

Disregarding the plump man, the Bishop removes what resembles a large brown stick from his back pocket. *'Is that tobacco?'*

"I just wanted a cigar; I honestly didn't come here for you originally. I came here for another reason..." The Bishop grips his necklace of teeth with a hand covered in a white glove. He holds up the rope, revealing that one of the strands seems to be missing a tooth. "Someone who shouldn't be here has trespassed on our little lab. Tripped one of my wards, forcing me to rush over." The Bishop's expression turns sinister. "But now that you're pointing a gun at me, I'm able to see exactly what you are, Pit spawn." —he holds his hand out— "Those fingers of yours belong to me."

The room's lights flicker as the black object falls to the ground with a metallic thud. Crimson blood falls from the Bishop's hand, where ten fingers now rest. First, confusion passes across the plump man's face, followed by terror and anguish as blood spurts from his knuckles. Where once his fingers were, nothing remains but the palm. The two children stare at the floor with huge eyes.

"My fingers!" the plump man shrieks. "God in Light, my fingers!"

"I'm surprised you would speak that name given your history, infiltrator." The Bishop casts the fingers at the plump man; they bounce off his belly and onto the floor. "You've presumably already realized it, but you're unwelcome here."

He quivers and shoves his finger stumps into his armpits. "No! Please! We can work something out!"

With a sigh, the Bishop raises his cane and stamps the plump man's forehead with the end of it. There's a sound like an onion being peeled as he pulls the cane away, leaving a stamp resembling the dolls around the Bishop's waist. Black tears stream from the plump man's eyes and swirl through the air toward the wooden idol at the end of the cane.

'I have overstayed my welcome!' I spin around. *'Back to the chamber pot tunnels; I shall never take them for granted again!'*

As I rush down the corridor as fast as my Agility allows, I hear someone's voice through the doorway. "You can't leave yet, eavesdropper, I rushed over here because of you after all." The tap of a cane echoes through the corridor. "Those arms of yours belong to me."

With his words, a vapor covers my arms as the lights blink, and they vanish.

"Hmm, not flesh, but instead something that smells of death," I hear the deep voice of the Bishop say. "Children, go wait in the car, and little ones, go after that person."

The last thing I hear is someone coughing before screams reverberate through the halls.

Finding the metal stairs, I discover the door is now open wider than when I first came through, but I do not think about it long. As I make my way down the stairs, my arms return as the haze turns thin at my torso and moves to my shoulders, restoring my arms. To calm myself, I count the steps as I descend, and as I do so, I glimpse something fall from the top floor to the bottom floor. *'What was that? Disregard it! That Bishop is Umbral in human skin!'*

I descend the stairs until I recount all thirty-six steps. Reaching the floor, I whirl on my heel and egress into the passage of drawings.[21]

My body stiffens when I encounter a doll standing in the dark passage. The doll's leathery skin creases as it raises an arm in greeting. Overhead, a dozen other dolls crawl on across the walls like bestial imps. Their gnarled burlap paws scratch on the stones as they creep nearer.

'Ludicrous.' Shaking my head, I dash forward. *'Ludicrous, I say!'*

The waving doll yanks a stitching needle from its breast. There's a crunch as it plunges the needle into the wall as if it's butter. My cattail contorts, clubbing the doll with a kick of its end. As the doll skips down the passage, I hear what sounds like parchment ripping in two.

I hop backward.

---

[21] Egress: the action of going out of or leaving a place.

A figure, a creature, nay, a drawing has had life breathed into it! It uproots itself away from the wall. The thing rotates its shape revealing itself to be a red squid, a drawing of a red squid. On one side, it's as flat as paper on the other as wide as the corridor. The bestial dolls overhead back away as the red squid presses an arm against each of the passage's four corners.

It draws itself closer; I shuffle back.

The squid flails, slapping its tentacles upon the ground in front of me. My cattail coils around a broken pipe. I fling it at the squid. An arm whacks the pipe from the air. Next comes chair legs, broken metal, knick-knacks; the cattail casts them all at the squid. Each object is struck down by thrashing arms and tentacles. Two tentacles knock a chair leg from the air. They yank at my arms, pulling shivers of haze from my body.

Recoiling, I flounder and sink to the ground next to a waxy container. The squid's shadow envelops me as it rises overhead. An arm slaps at my kiln, piercing pain rakes at me. My cattail grabs the waxy container and smashes it against the squid's face. Liquid sloshes from the container; the squid withdraws as it sprays onto it. Paint sloughs from its body wherever liquid splashes it, leaving a red smear along the passage floor.

From the top of the stairs, I recognize the knock of footsteps and a cane against metal.

Stumbling to my feet, I charge the squid. It raises its arms as I try to bludgeon it with the waxy container. There's a thunk; the squid blocks my bludgeon with two arms. I glimpse a shimmer of metal on the squid's body—a stitching needle.

"What are you exactly? Oh, Lord," the Bishop's voice echoes, "it's on the tip of my tongue."

A tentacle thumps my kiln. I blunder backward in anguish. My cattail hoists the waxy container overhead and smashes it against the floor. Liquid erupts, raining down on both the squid and I. Haze stains the liquid black while my cattail spirals around the squid's arm. The squid clutches the cattail, distorting it. Its runny arms cannot sustain their grip.

The floor is washed red as my tendrils enwrap the needle. Tentacles curl around the kiln as I yank—the squid freezes. It crumples, melting into a disk of dry red paint on the floor.

In between my tendrils, I am left grasping the stitching needle. I cast it into a cleft in the passage as a blue wall appears.

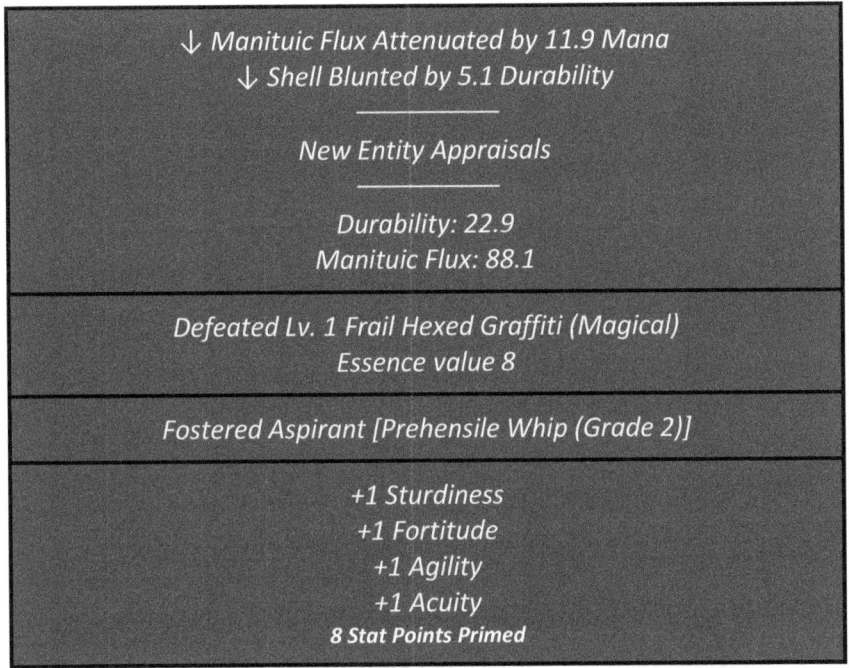

↓ *Manituic Flux Attenuated by 11.9 Mana*
↓ *Shell Blunted by 5.1 Durability*

New Entity Appraisals

Durability: 22.9
Manituic Flux: 88.1

Defeated Lv. 1 Frail Hexed Graffiti (Magical)
Essence value 8

Fostered Aspirant [Prehensile Whip (Grade 2)]

+1 Sturdiness
+1 Fortitude
+1 Agility
+1 Acuity
8 Stat Points Primed

Raising my arms, I notice haze refilling holes in my body wherever the liquid touched. 'So this is why I could not enter the water! I will melt!' I shove the blue wall away, preparing to flee. 'But I cannot dwell on it, not at this moment! Farewell, accursed nightmare!'

Behind me, a voice whispers, "Hello, child."

I swing the cattail; it feels more natural than it ever has before.

The smirking Bishop whacks the cattail away with his cane. "Too loud," he taunts.

His suit is blotched with blood and from it hangs the impish dolls, waving their arms. The only noise that can be heard is the drip of blood from his cane and into the waxy container's liquid.

"Very brave, but my hearing and sense of smell are excellent. An advantage of a high Perception without sight bogging me down if you understand what I mean. Oh, and if you're curious, you smell of death, disease," his smirk curves into a devilish grin, "and feminine allure."

'He knows about the Perception stat!? Did he kill those people upstairs!? What does he want!? How did he know I was here!? Most importantly—feminine allure? Shameless lout! I do not even possess a tangible body!'[22]

He ogles me, never breaking his grin. "You can't speak? That's okay; the spirits here with us can hear what you're thinking. They'll serve the role of a translator of sorts."

I hear the whispers of voices all around me. *'Spirits!? Hark not! My thoughts are my own and are often embarrassing!'*

The Bishop nods as if understanding someone. "Of course I'm in the Beta; it would be humiliating if I weren't. How did I know you were here? Well, you tripped a hex ward of mine. Since I was already on my way here, I simply hurried over. Oh, and no, I only defended myself from one man that attacked me after inhaling that smoke of yours. You're more responsible for what happened than I am."

'I do not care for this line of discourse, hoodwinker!'[23] Whilst waving my hands, I walk backward. *'Simply stay back!'*

His cane taps against the floor as he mimics my every step. "Stay back? But my helpers tell me they found something interesting in your abdomen." He raises his cane, pointing it toward the kiln. "With such a marvelous specimen in front of me, how could I possibly stay away? And I know you aren't with the Church in Light or Two Palm Society, and certainly not

---

[22] Lout: Ill-mannered, bumpkin, awkward person.
[23] Hoodwink: To blindfold, blind the mind/eyes, mislead, deceive, or trick (someone or something).

The Pit's Maw despite looking the part. No, you have a *spiritual* air about you—my church's specialty."

'*What is any of that supposed to mean!? Who art thou?*'

He waves his hand dismissively as if the answer to my question is obvious. "I am a Bishop of the Hex Church. Nothing more, nothing less." He steps into the puddle of liquid and pauses. "Well, that explains the stench of gasoline."

Finding myself near the medicine room, I dart inside and move to slam the door behind me. The Bishop wedges his cane in the doorframe.

"You act just like my own child, always trying to shut me out and run away!" He groans as if dreading the thought of having to chase after me. "Listen, I understand young lambs tend to be afraid of everything, but I have a busy schedule, so I'll be truthful with you."

Backing away from the door, I move toward the pot of boiling liquid. '*I am naught to concern thyself with! Leave me be!*'

"But I have a confession to make?" He raises a hand. "I have known what you were since you came here. It would be embarrassing if I didn't know that... you are Kiln."

'*Kiln!? Kiln!? As in a furnace, hearth, or oven!?*' He clearly finds my words amusing, but I ignore this and search the room for any solution to my plight. '*Apologies, but I cannot help thee if I know naught of what thou speakest!*'

He laughs. "There is no point in denying it. I've been toying with you to satisfy my own curiosity, to see if you have what it takes to last in the outside world."

Reaching for the boiling liquid, I knock the metal candle from the table. The candle dangles by a cord, swinging inside my haze like a pendulum. It does not cause me any pain but simply burns within the haze. Gripping the boiling orange liquid, I brandish it at the Bishop.

'*Explain thyself, or I shall cast this boiling liquid at thee!*'

"I urge you not to do anything needlessly foolish. That liquid is volatile. Made by one of your ilk."

'What!? Nay! It does not matter. Do not take another step nearer!'

He pauses mid-stride as if considering my warning. "Are you so bold? Or are you suicidal?"

'Perhaps I am! Perhaps I am the most boldly suicidal thing ever to walk this earth! ...So leave me be!'

"An unusual choice of words." He chuckles, saying, "You certainly are a spirited one."

A jest!?' I glance at his bloodstained suit, twine eyes, and smug grin. 'Why art thou pottering about!? Why dost thou playest with me!?'

The doll that sought to pierce my kiln rejoins its brethren dolls, climbing up the Bishop's clothing. Together, the dolls slap their round palms against themselves as if mocking me.

"I already told you. Don't you listen? I wanted to see if you have what it takes to survive."

'And what hast thou learned? May I leave?'

The lights flicker. I feel frigid fingers worm around my kiln—my body freezes. The Bishop approaches me, but I cannot move my arms. The cattail slithers over my shoulder. It grabs the pot and slings it upward. A coil of orange liquid arcs toward the Bishop. As the last droplets of liquid leave the pot, they contact the candle's flame. It bursts into an orange fireball. The Bishop drops his hand; he hits his cane against the floor. A black symbol rises from an ebony pool of muck at his feet.

The fireball envelops his figure. A voice from within the burning ball makes me freeze. "I wasn't sure before, but now I think you might have what it takes to survive." Burning orange flames roll down the side of an intangible sphere. His cane splashes in the waxy container's liquid. "The gasoline..."

The orange liquid ignites the waxy containers. There's a roaring hum as the passage is set alight. A wall bursts, and a third liquid, this one green, sprays from a pipe. Whatever the green liquid touches bubbles and dissolves.

Between the swaying flames, I see the Bishop. He steps from the fire, leaving burning tracks behind him. "I've had every intention of allowing you to live. I just came to shoo you away in case you were too dangerous for the bruisers upstairs to handle." The icy fingers release me as he stops in front of me. "Go. Go and blossom, little Kiln. I'll try not to bother you too often." He turns his head as I slink by him. "Good luck." He grins.

> **Earl Interface:**
> **Warning:** *Avoid direct and sustained contact with material fire. Overheating of shell exterior is possible.*

I shove Earl's wall away and run. *'Flee!'*

Flames spread along liquid paths as I maneuver between them, making my way back the way I arrived. The haze is nearly unaffected, but I can feel the kiln is growing warmer. Stopping at the edge of the hole, I stare at the water at the bottom. I march in place while shaking out my hands. *'Water! I implore thee, do not wash my body away!'*

I leap and plunge downward... slowly.

My body drifts toward the water below like a leaf upon the wind. *'Why did I not attempt this earlier?! There were several occasions where this knowledge would have been useful!'*

As I reach the water, the building above creaks, and the ceiling collapses. I flee into the chamber pot tunnels. Upon returning, I see the elderly rats' waddling home with boxes labeled "Survival Ration Crackers."

Chapter 5: Hapless Tragedian in "Of Rat and Wretch"

∞ ∞ ∞ ∞ ∞ ∞ ∞ ∞ ∞ ∞ ∞ ∞ ∞ ∞

Throwing up my arms, I scream into my mind, '*Ambling! They are ambling! How do they amble so quickly!? Fudge! They are the ones responsible for leading me into that horrid place!*'

As I glare at their waddling figures, the elderly rat at the rear glances down into the water, where it finds the reflection of my violet eyes and flame.

He whirls around. "Squeak!" he shrieks.

Without hesitation, he abandons the brown box in his arms and points with a half-opened mouth. A tattered gown that was stuck to the box's top drifts down, covering his face.

"Wa-Squeak!" he cries as the garment meets his muzzle.

He flings the gown to the ground with the fury of a man scorned. Once more, he shrieks, and sprints in a circle with arms flailing. Having completed three circles, he breaks from his pattern and dashes after the other four elderly rats. Despite having watched his antics, it's only after he runs toward them that the other four elderly rats react. The other four rats do not understand what is befalling them, but that does not prevent them from joining in their companion's cacophony.

"Wa-Squeeeak!" they scream collectively.

Tottering away at a slightly elevated pace, their heads face the ceiling, swinging wildly from side to side. Despite this, they do not drop their boxes. Their cries continue to reverberate as they fade into the tunnel. '*They are not the sharpest needles in the pincushion, are they?*' I shake my head. '*All I wanted to do was find somewhere green and not full of human waste to live!*

Yet, somehow, I achieved naught but being attacked by a bedlamite and a squid, like a horrible fever dream.'[24]

Through the crack in the wall, I can hear the building continue to collapse, but something else is bothering me more. *'I am absolutely famished!'* My hand moves to my belly, slipping through unhindered. *'It-it hurts!'*

Gazing at my body, I see the haze has thinned to such an extent that I am see-through. Vaguely visible in the darkness, the elderly rats look delicious. Checking my Erysichthon value, it reads 80/100.

'This body is not efficient. It's constantly leaking haze, causing my Erysichthon value to rise. If I was in a strong windstorm, would I blow away? Not to mention how much haze I lost in that horrible place... I must find something to eat, or I shall go mad!'

> *+1 Fortitude*
> **7 Stat Points Primed**

I disregard the Cosmic System, and instead, my attention falls onto the box that reads 'Survival Ration Crackers.' *'What is this? ...Survival? Is it food? What else would rats be concerned with other than food?'*

Drifting toward the brown box, I feel it with my hands, finding it seems thin and flimsy. I raise the cattail and strike it. One side of the box bursts open, and six bright metal containers spill out. Grasping one of the containers with the cattail and shaking it, something beats against the inside. *'Food? Pray thee, be food!'*

Finding a dry area and placing one of the containers on its side, I raise the cattail and strike it with a loud bang. The outside flexes and the container jumps into the air before coming to a rest with no obvious damage. A pang of hunger stabs at my kiln so I repeat the process several more times before coming to my senses and searching for the brick I left behind.

Hapless: unfortunate (especially of a person).
Tragedian: an actor who specializes in tragic roles.
[24] Bedlamite: A lunatic, madman, or insane person. Resident of Bedlam/Bethlem.

With the brick engulfed by the cattail, I strike the container a few times, and eventually, I hear a popping sound and find that a hole has appeared. Once again, I strike it, and the hole widens as something crunches in the container. Dropping the brick and running the cattail through the hole, I grip onto something waxy and try to yank it through the hole. At first, it refuses to come out, so I smash the crumbly things inside and try again, this time successfully. What comes out is a white waxy paper-like substance with something crumbly inside that reminds me of a wafer or bread crumbs. Rubbing the waxy paper against the ground, it splits open, and the tendrils invade, allowing the cattail to engulf the crumbly substance.

What I believe is a salty flavor spreads through my body as the crumbly stuff turns into a brown haze and enters the shell. Noticing the haze thickening, I feel a bit of relief wash over my body. However, the method is slow, so my eyes fall onto the tattered dress. *'A small meal before I open the remaining wafers. I can eat it, right? Indubitably, I am certain of it!'*

Absorbing the dress, I find it's mostly tasteless and does not invoke much feeling. I do not dwell on it and continue absorbing everything in the bag until the metal container is empty.

> **Earl Interface:**
> Assimilating 'Raggedy Bridal Ballgown' (Mana Bare)
> Assimilating '6 LB Stale Cracker Crumbs' (Mana Bare)
> Erysichthon abates by 15
> Essence value negligible.
> 0.0 Refinable Nebula
> 0.1 Refinable Vitrum

As I conclude my meal, Earl's wall appears. *'A bridal ballgown? I am not especially fond of the implications of such a thing being found in such a vile place—perish the thought!'* I choose to focus on the numbers given to me by Earl. *'Only fifteen Erysichthon and naught else?'* Looking back at the box, I can see at least five more containers of this crumbly wafer stuff. *'Who knows how long it would take to locate normal rats, and this is guaranteed food.'*

I arrange all five containers in a row and repeat the process: smash, crush, yank, open, and assimilate five additional times. Some minutes pass as I gorge on the wafers until a mere trifle of the crumbly stuff termed 'crackers' remains, and my Erysichthon value wanes to zero.

Earl's wall vanishes, and a blue one replaces it.

+1 Strength
6 Stat Points Primed

'Ah, a stat point is a splendid bonus. The wafers were not as delectable as the rats, but there were a lot of them... that had to have been nigh thirty pounds of the stuff, and I also feel a tad faint, like when Earl refined the Nebula and Vitrum. Is it mana loss again? Is my body infusing the material with mana, perchance? ...Though, before resuming that line of thinking... Earl, are there any adaptations to help with my Erysichthon value?'

Earl Interface:

Forewarning: *Utilizing Essence will diminish the time the user has to plant the Tower Seed, assuming the user does not harvest Essence from other sources. If Essence falls beneath the 5 Essence line, the user will likely descend into a frenzied state of addled gluttonizing. It's recommended that the user avoids this dangerous state. If the user's Essence reaches 0, their flame will be snuffed.*

Vaporous Form Embryo Tier Adaptations

Available Armament 'Cattail' Adaptations

Further Armament 'Cattail' Adaptations Currently Unavailable.

Available Skin/Dress Adaptations

Condensed Haze
Boost the density of the user's particulates, making them heavier. Makes it more challenging for particles to be blown away but also causes it to be more difficult to float above water or plunge from high

areas. Additionally, if haze is knocked away by force, the higher density will have unfavorable increases in the Erysichthon value.
[Cost: 31 Essence + 2 Refined Nebula]

Rarefied Haze
Maintain the bare minimum of haze circulating inside the user at all times while stowing excess haze safely within the shell. This averts larger single losses when attacked but also exacerbates atmospheric haze loss.
[Cost: 33 Essence + 2.3 Refined Nebula]

Comrade Cracker
(Recent Meal: 30LB Survival Crackers | **Recent Meal:** Bridal Ball Gown)
Generate a thin skin of porous haze, diminishing atmospheric loss but also darkening the body somewhat. This adaptation will make the user more tangible and thus easier to discover.
[Cost: 42 Essence + 2.3 Refined Nebula]

Available Miscellaneous Adaptations

Itching Sphere
(Recent Meal: Fleas)
Form an airy skin of bouncing haze. The 'body' will become slightly more obfuscated, and haze may spring toward those that approach too closely. Itching Sphere may be used to augment any lost haze.
[Cost: 53 Essence + 3.1 Refined Nebula]

Essence Available: 53 [R = 90%]
Refined Nebula Available: 2.5 (2.8)
Refined Vitrum Available: 5 (0.8)
Refined Unknown Superacid: 0.5 (0.0)

As before, a sizable purple wall appears. *'I cannot select anything for the cattail. Still, there are more adaptations than expected. Let's see...'*

Several times over, I study the list provided to me by Earl. *'If I am honest, I do not fully understand some things, but I can deduce the benefits and disadvantages. The first one is unacceptable. My greatest losses have been from something obliterating my head and the taking of my arms, and I would also relinquish my floaty nature. The second is also unsuitable unless I intend to never leave somewhere shielded from the elements like the chamber pot tunnels. The final one seems problematic. Never being able to approach anyone without fear of the haze lunging at them? Nay! ...Also, I shall ignore that I seemingly ate fleas without knowing it.'*

My attention turns toward my available resources. *'It seems peculiar that my Essence has not been declining. Perhaps it does not fall as swiftly as Earl made it sound... Hmm, anyway, the Comrade Cracker adaptation only leaves me eleven Essence and scant Nebula.'*

I shake my head. *'I shall take a day to consider it; seeing that the purple wall says "recent meal," that makes me believe it will vanish eventually, so it may be unwise to delay my decision for too long. Also, if I choose an adaptation, my Essence shall sink precariously close to the "addled frenzied state," so I should defer my selection until I am ready to depart. Wait... my stomach distracted me from something critical.'*

Turning around, I can see the faint red glow of the burning building through the crack. As fast as my haze can carry me, I retreat deep into the chamber pot tunnels. *'How did I permit my appetite to distract me?! It was just so painful and thought consuming...! That Bishop is powerful, and there is something sinister about him... even excluding the stitches and dolls! Curses! All I have been worried about is my stomach. I must sow my Tower and grow stronger! That will eventually help my Essence problem if Earl is to be believed...!'*

Rounding a corner, I place my head in my hands. *'This merely gets me back from whence I began: where to plant!? I have actually once considered the chamber pot tunnels, but when the thought arose, my instincts screamed out, "Nay! Nay! Wrong!" like the time it refused to submerge the haze in water. That tells me forcing it could be ruinous... Besides, I do not desire to live down here! I need to get out of this place and find somewhere secluded!'*

Thus, rushing through the tunnels, I note several metal plate locations and wait for nightfall.

At each location I wait until it's quiet before sliding the metal plate to the side. Each time I come up, I only get more and more bewildered by events, but I cannot muster the energy to care as much anymore.

The first location had a nearly unclothed man playing the lute as women shouted and cheered for him, screaming, "I love Wonderwall." At the second location, there was a store with lines of people standing outside. Curious, I read the sign "butt boosting jeans," and departed promptly. The third location had a red and a blue monster chatting with one another. The blue monster would yell "cookies" while the red monster just repeated "I love you" and then giggled menacingly. It was at this location I made my first significant discovery: a row of trees running along the black rock, which I am assuming is something akin to a roadway for people's 'rides'. I did not tarry long, though, as I was afraid to be discovered by the monsters.

The fourth location was my favorite as I appeared in an alleyway full of mousers. There were dozens of them! Dozens! I really wanted to pet them, and my heart hurt having to leave.

I arrive at the fifth location. This location is particularly quiet, so I slide the metal plate away and raise myself from the hole. The first thing that catches my attention are the rays of the morn sun and little snowflakes falling from above.

But something green in the distance demands my attention more. I lift my arms and spread them wide in triumph. *'Verily, it's a thicket of trees; something I understand! It has been so long!'*

"Mommy, what's that thing?" a childish voice whispers.

Tilting my head, I slowly turn, where I am greeted by a group of nuns surrounding a flower wreath, praying in someone's memory. To the nuns' right stands a family, consisting of a mother and three children. The mother hugs a man's portrait.

We stare at one another for what feels like minutes. Lowering my arms while never breaking eye contact, I push off the ladder and drift back into the tunnels. *'I shall return at a later time.'*

The shrieks of nuns and cries of children reverberate throughout the chamber pot tunnels.

I wander aimlessly. *'With the sun up, I should wait until night returns. A bit irritating that all those people happened to be there... and nuns!? The only thing that could be worse than nuns is a nun with noble roots. Nay! Wait! A French nun with noble roots—a nightmarish thought! ...But I suppose simple nuns are at least better than the Vierge of the French Éclat.'*

A horrible image of *that* Éclat Lagarde flashes in my mind, making me want to shiver.

My shoulders slump. *'There's no need to dwell on it longer. If I am proceeding to the surface, I can use this time to prepare... And I suppose I may as well take the 'Comrade Cracker' adaptation now as well. It's the only one that offers any genuine defense, which is what I lack most.'*

Earl summons the purple wall, and I choose the 'adaptation.'

The kiln's flame dances. It becomes far more active than before, casting a purple hue on the walls around me. Ungracefully, I twist my body to watch what occurs around the kiln. Dark black haze spews from all sides of its shell. A new layer of haze slides over what is more or less my 'skin.'

Instead of resembling a smoky cloud girl, I take on more of a human figure. My skin is still thin and hazy, but more defined than before. Yet, most of the definition flows into the dress rather than my actual skin, making me look like a phantom girl wearing a somber transparent dress.

But what's most surprising is...

'The haze took the shape of that raggedy gown I consumed! And... and!' I goggle at my reflection in the murky water. *'My arms! My shoulders! They are exposed...! Is all the fashion of this era so risqué!?'*

Twisting back and forth, I study my figure as the haze settles. The haze has dyed the area where my skin should be a dark gray, while the gown I ate, along with my hair, has turned an even darker black. It leaves my arms, shoulders, and the upper portion of my bust exposed and covers my torso and legs. The dress flows outwards where it contacts the ground. I can vaguely make out my shoeless feet obscured by the dress's twisting black haze.

I shake my head in defeat. *'It's not as if I am unaccustomed to having to wear whatever garments I can find, but I cannot change out of this!'* I slide my palm over the dress, finding my hand does not slip through as before. *'It does not matter! I suppose... I do look rather elegant, and it's not as if I am a person any longer... I am simply taking the shape of one, so there is nary a need to concern myself.'*

With my thoughts moving into uncomfortable territory, I banish them. *'Prithee, Cosmic System, display my Status and Chronicles, I have not checked them in some time.'*

Name: Constance Nightingale
Race: Kiln
Seed Type: Tower [Embryo]
Variant: Oort Stained Glass
Forms: [Vaporous] [Lucent: *Unviable*]
Shell Level: 0 (Develop Beyond Embryo)
Flame Level: 0 (Develop Beyond Embryo)
Durability: 29/34
Mana: 183/210 [105/105 Manituic Flux]
Erysichthon: 29/100
Quintessence: Corrupting Oort Cloud
Adaptations: [Cattail Tendrils] [Comrade Cracker]
Skills: [Prehensile Whip (Asp-2)] [Naturalist (Asp-0)]
Titles: [Parasitic]

Chronicles

Constance Nightingale || Kiln Vaporous Chronicles || Entity 1-3-2-3			
Strength	9	Cattail Armament Physical Power	18
Orenda	21	General Body Strength	4
Sturdiness	4	Cattail Armament Magical Power	0
Fortitude	14	Membrane Defense	2
Perception *	17	—	—

Acuity *	8	—	—
Agility	11	—	—
Endurance	18	Sable	88.43%
Mend Rate	18 (-100%)	Vermillion	9.75%
Mana Regen	12	Hoary	1.72%
Stat Points Primed: 6		Heliotrope	0.11%

Studying my Chronicles, I surmise that Durability may increase with Sturdiness and mana with Orenda. I also find my membrane defense has a number now and the colors have changed—my only guess is that they may be related to Adaptations. *'All mere conjectures and guesses, though. It would be wonderful if someone could lecture me. I suppose I should observe my Status and Chronicles more carefully to learn what happens. Speaking of which, I had committed to returning to the elderly rats, but perhaps I should increase my stats first. I can return to the elderly rats later.'*

Pondering my next course of action, I recall I had committed to returning to the copepod throng. *'I believe the copepods may stimulate my stats and they also provided me Essence when I ate them previously. Essence is something I shall forever be in desperate need of if things continue as they are... Aye. Be brave, Constance! They were sluggish creatures, so it should not be too horrid a task!'*

I spend some time musing the weaknesses of the Copepod Throng.

••••

••••••••

••••

While thinking about the copepods, I realized two things: One, the copepods may not possess the means to damage my kiln, making them incapable of harming me. Two, if I divide their numbers, they may not be able to merge into a mass large enough to reach the kiln, making them incapable of attacking me even if they can harm me.

With those two things in mind, I returned to the location of the wafer box and am now balancing the box above my head. *'I believe this would have been impossible before increasing my Strength stat.'*

Carrying the box like this makes it so I must walk slowly, so it takes some time before I arrive. For a moment, I hesitate to approach but flex my thin haze arms.

'I am certain this will not fail; it will undoubtedly work!' A few feet away, the water ripples and out creeps the copepods. While the copepods rally, I raise the box above them and tip its balance. It plunges toward the water, and with a wet thud, it divides the throng of copepods into two groups. My fist clenches. *'I did not believe it would truly work for even a moment!'*

The remaining copepods continue to gather. My cattail's tendrils spread wide as it darts toward the group. Like a closing hand, the tendrils scoop a mass of the copepods into the cattail. They swarm the cattail; the ones that bite into it writhe upon the ground. The throng splits at its axis, exposing a mass of green copepods. A spout of liquid sprays from the green copepods—it misses the kiln by a hair's breadth. Behind me, I hear the ground beneath the liquid sizzle.

I bash the squirming throng with the cattail. Copepod viscera stains the walls as the tendrils plunge into the green core. The cattail's tendrils shovel the green creatures into the haze, devouring them to their last. My vision halves as liquid spray washes away one of my eyes.

In my peripheral, I glimpse green copepods wiggling out from the melted box. I spin around as another spout of liquid wipes away my brow. Their insistence on targeting my eyes allows the cattail to overwhelm them. It's not long before I have eaten everything that did not escape into the water.

With the threat subdued, my hand drifts to my stomach, and I imagine I am swallowing a warm loaf of fresh-baked bread rather than the most revolting creatures I have ever beheld. My arms rise into the air. *'Huzzah, I cannot believe it! I am a splendid lady knight!'*

Devoured Lv.1 Acidic Copepod Throng
Essence value 21

Fostered Aspirant [Prehensile Whip (Grade 3)]

+1 Strength
+1 Fortitude
+1 Agility
3 Stat Points Primed

Savoring the flavorful feelings, I stare at the blue wall in delight. Before I may reflect on matters further, one of Earl's walls appears.

Earl Interface:
Assimilating 'Acidic Copepod Throng'
Erysichthon abates by 10
Essence value 3
1.0 Refinable Nebula
0.3 Refinable Vitrum

'Oh? Earl and the Cosmic System? At the same time? I had forgotten the Cosmic System rewarded me Essence after I defeated the squid. I suppose it makes sense since Earl is more concerned with eating and materials. In contrast, the Cosmic System seems to be more focused on battles, skills, and stat points. Yet, the Essence given by Earl was lower than I expected. Is it because I had already been awarded the bulk of the Essence by the Cosmic System when I defeated it? I do recall Earl stating that at one time. Hmm, I guess before I can assume anything, I should consume more varieties of food... Either way, I achieved my goal. I have proven myself!'

Like a knight, I stand with my chest puffed out. 'And the battle went so smoothly I should have time to observe the elderly rats. It could even help me advance my Naturalist skill. Fortune finally smiles upon me in this mad world!'

••••
••••••••
••••

A few thousand steps later, I manage to find the five elderly rats. Four of them sit at the edge of their burrows around a heap of metal wafer containers, while the last sits far from the others on a semi-dry mountain of muck with its short arms crossed.

'The one by itself seems to be the one that dropped its wafer box. I suppose the others are upset with him for abandoning it. I should thank him for leaving it; it was of great use to me. Anyway, despite being separated from the others, it does not appear that he is missing out on any meals since none of them are eating.'

The other four elderly rats sit in a circle, pounding the metal containers against the brick, accomplishing nothing more than denting the container's edges. One of the elderly rats gets frustrated and hurls a container against the brick tunnel. The container bounces off the brick while the elderly rat stomps about, flailing its arms and squeaking at the other containers as if scolding them for not opening.

'Why would they steal something they are incapable of opening?'

The one who threw the container walks over and then stops, squinting in my direction. I tilt my head, causing my glowing eyes to bob. The elderly rat leaps backward with a loud squeak. It sustains its frantic squeaks, alerting the others, and with its portly legs, it retreats to its burrow. The other four elderly rats bumble into their own respective burrows, poking their heads out with narrow eyes.

Glancing around, I notice a second metal container lying nearby that seems to have suffered a similar fate.

'Hmm, perhaps, I shall help them while I await nightfall. I am leaving shortly, and it's not as if these elderly rats can inform anyone of my presence. They have already discovered me and do not appear to be aggressive; in fact, they seemed rather afraid of me. Why not have a bit of fun with them... It would be a delightful respite from always nearly dying.'

····

·········

····

Having resolved to assist the elderly rats with their predicament I prepare to have a bit of fun. With my audience waiting in anticipation, I march from my hiding spot. Channeling my inner child, I raise my hands high like a knight preparing to show the world their strength. The elderly rats tilt their chubby necks and take a few steps from their burrow to get a better glimpse of my performance.

Giving a small hazy curtsy, I announce in my head, *'Thank thee for coming to see my performance tonight, gentlemen! ...Or perhaps gentlewomen? I am embarrassed to admit I cannot tell and I fear I may never be able to.'*

The elderly rats cannot hear my thoughts, but regardless I am a tad tickled by my own performance. As if understanding or perhaps simply acting submissive, the elderly rats imitate my gesture.

I nod happily. *'Aye! Participation is encouraged, my furry, long-nosed audience!'*

The elderly rats exchange glances. I ignore that their pupils are so dilated from evident fear that they resemble large platters. Moving on, I point at the metal container, the cattail, and then make an eating gesture as best I can manage without a mouth. The elderly rats just seem confused, but that's as expected. With the brick still engulfed, I raise the cattail high above my head.

'Let's see how hard I may strike it.'

With all the force my cattail can gather, I bring it down upon the metal container like a knight slaying a horrifying beast! A metallic noise reverberates throughout the chamber pot tunnels causing the elderly rats to flinch.

'Behold, wafers for the masses!' I motion toward the container. *'Oh. Wait.'*

Next to the wafers, a wee dent in the rock is all that I seem to have accomplished.

'I... I must have missed it. Ah! We can salvage this, Constance! We have proven ourselves mighty after defeating the Copepod Throng!'

As before, I whack the container once, then twice, and even thrice! Each whack sends out a mighty ding. Yet it refuses to break. Despite having lost my sense of touch and ability to sweat, I swear I can feel a cold droplet of sweat rolling down the nape of my neck.

I cover my violet eyes dramatically. *'Do not look at me! I am ruined; I shall never recover from this.'*

Pondering for a moment, I realize what I am doing differently. Thus, rotating the cattail, I bring it down anew. Finally, I hear air escaping the container.

'Oops, I was not hitting it with the edge of the brick as before.'

A few strikes later, while also pulling at the waxy paper, it exits the container. I toss the waxen package to the elderly rats, and they stare at it before one walks over and plucks it from the ground. The elderly rat rips the paper with his teeth and pours some of the wafer crumbs onto his paw. He looks at me, and I can nigh feel the dissatisfaction rolling off his body.

'Art thou serious!? Thou art but a rat, be gladdened by what thou receivest. I ate thirty pounds of it yesterday...' The elderly rat licks its paw, and the dissatisfaction wanes. With a bang, another container lands at my feet. I look to see another elderly rat has tossed a container to me with the expectation of me opening it. *'Fine, but thou couldst simply do it thyself.'*

So this time, I release the brick from the cattail and approach the container. My hands are not capable of producing enough force to break it, but my plan is to simply show the elderly rats how to do it themselves. Holding the brick with the edge side down, I grip both sides of the brick with my hands; otherwise, it would slip out.

'This is a bit irksome; the thickness of my hands is so low they seem to have difficulty grasping heavy objects.' With what meager force my arms and hands can deliver, I whack the containers whilst pointing at the elderly rats. One appears to comprehend my teachings and picks up a brick. They join me, lightly drumming the container. Motioning at it, I try to make him strike it more forcefully by gesturing at the container violently. For reasons that elude, this must cause him tremendous stress because he begins hammering the container. *'That is... that is sufficient.'*

He does not stop; with wide, panicked eyes, he keeps striking it with nary a sign of ceasing. I watch in awe as the container is flattened and the waxy bag within bursts, raining wafer crumbs down upon the elderly rat. He throws his short arms up in celebration and licks the crumbs from his damp fur.

The other elderly rats gather around him, pointing and squeaking with what I assume is disbelief. Following his example, the others rush to grab containers before smashing them into flatness until they finally burst. They hop from the ground and dance around, licking their fur with high-pitched squeaks.

'*Aye...*' Watching them dance while some attempt to catch wafer crumbs on their tongues, like snowflakes, I am uncertain how to feel. '*Although not what I intended, I suppose this works.*'

Soon the elderly rats skip toward me with their arms held wide, seemingly wishing to embrace me. Before they may move too close, I strike the metal container, sending it bouncing in their direction. They freeze mid-stride with the same triumphant expressions frozen dumbly upon their faces, making me feel a bit guilty.

'*My apologies, but if thou com'st too near, it could be thy death.*' I await their reaction, but they simply stand with their arms open as if waiting for me to walk into them. '*This seems rather exaggerated, though.*'

I wave my hand, trying to break them from their stupor. The only thing that moves is their pupils, which dart between themselves and then me. Suddenly, they squeak together and run in circles with their arms waving in the air. The elderly rats crash into one another and tumble to the ground with a muffled squeak. They quickly recover and point with trembling arms.

'*It was not that scary, was it...? Wait, are they pointing at me or...*'

My haze vibrates, and a low grumble comes from behind me. If I still had one, my heart would burst from my chest. In the corner of my vision, I see a pair of wretched yellow eyes glaring at me from a dark tunnel.

Looking ahead, I glimpse the tips of the elderly rat's tails vanishing into their burrows. '*This world...*' I engulf the brick and flee. '*...it is so dreadfully cruel.*'

The wretched rat gives a loud squeak, resembling a high-pitched roar. Racing by the elderly rats' burrows, I knock an unopened container of wafers toward the wretched rat. It stops and sniffs it before ripping it open with its monstrous teeth. Turning a corner, I lose sight of it, but I can hear it splashing the water as it runs.

'It's assumably midday on the surface, but I am leaving forthwith!'

The wretched rat turns the corner and crashes into one of the tunnel walls. It rolls on the ground spewing pus from the sores and boils covering its body. It corrects itself and renews its resolve. I cast the brick behind me, and the rat catches it within its jaws and crushes it. It squeaks in displeasure and increases its pace. Faster than I, the wretched rat begins to catch up to me.

With the rat behind me, I swing my cattail, and the rat chomps at it, consuming the tip of the cattail. It finds the cattail's taste abhorrent as it stops and vomits the oily cattail into the water.

Encountering a small pipe, I squirm inside and crawl as deep as I can until a metal grate prevents me from advancing further. I push my body against the grate. Part of it slips between the bars, but only as far as the kiln permits before it knocks against them.

Having recovered, the wretched rat rams the pipe's entrance and squeaks. It reaches in with its paws, but I am out of its reach. It claws at the stone pipe, wrenching rock and stone from the earth. It widens the hole enough to jam its head inside the pipe, and howls at me with that high-pitched squeak while biting at my feet.

The wretched rat soaks the pipe's inside with saliva and pus, forcing me to raise the cattail in defense. I stab at its eyes. It shuts its jaws and tilts its head. My cattail knocks against its repugnant cheek, accomplishing naught. It refuses to take a second bite of the cattail.

'If I am not tasty, why art thou attacking me!?'

I again stab, this time my cattail pricks one of its eyes. It squeaks, retracting its head while grinding its eye into the rubble in a vain effort to remove the cattail's effects.

With a wink to spare, I use the tendrils to gobble up rubble and create a makeshift cudgel. Not wishing to return its head to the pipe, the rat instead continues digging at it. My cattail club bashes at its paws. A crack, its nails splinter, squirting me with oily black gore. Blood washes away patches of my haze and besmears the grate behind me.

The grate hisses—vermin blood eats at its bars.

The wretched rat rips its paw away with a howl. It retches, spraying vomit into the pipe. Twisting my body, I throw my cattail against the pitted grate. With a crackle, its bars shatter.

Spitting the debris from my cattail, I try to scramble beyond the grate. My body moves through with ease, yet the kiln wedges on jagged metal, a whisker too wide to pass. I strain the cattail and try to yank my way through, scraping the kiln against frothing teeth as I do so.

The wretched rat squeaks, sounding as if it's at my heels.

I swing my head back only to discover an immense paw rending lumps of earth from overhead. A sound reminiscent of two tin mugs knocking against one another echoes. Anguish rakes at me, making me feel as if I need to vomit but cannot.

The wretched rat's attack propels me through the grate. The kiln's shell skips along the stone pipe, inflicting stabs of pain with every bounce. The haze scarcely manages to keep itself together as I come to a violent halt against a bend in the pipe.

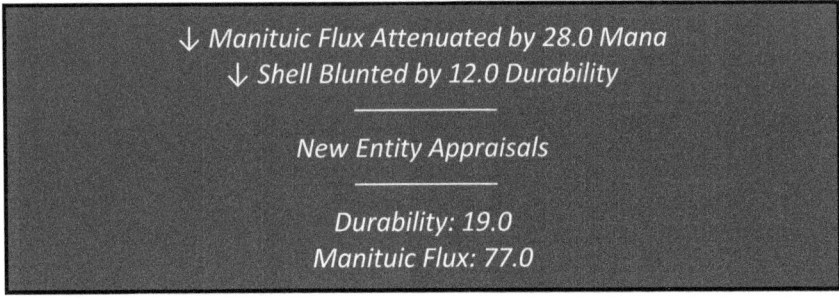

↓ Manituic Flux Attenuated by 28.0 Mana
↓ Shell Blunted by 12.0 Durability

New Entity Appraisals

Durability: 19.0
Manituic Flux: 77.0

I disregard the biting agony emanating from the kiln, and once enough haze has gathered, I flee onward. Eventually, the racket of the wretched rat's cries fade, but even so, I maintain my pace forward.

Fostered Aspirant [Prehensile Whip (Grade 4)]
+1 Sturdiness **2 Stat Points Primed**

My kiln burns, but I am too anxious to stop and inspect its condition. '*If this direction has a way out, I shall be ever so happy. Let's see: Three million two hundred seventy-three thousand twenty-two. Twenty-three. Twenty-four...*"

I employ my usual method to soothe my nerves until I eventually find myself at a stoppage. The pipe ends at another grate, and I have nowhere left to go. '*Well, I suppose I am not going any further than this, unfortunately. I shall just have to wait here until the wretched rat leaves.*'

Stopping, I bend my back awkwardly to inspect my kiln. I find the flame within has sunk from its resting size of a digit to the size of a barleycorn.[25] I run my index finger along the cracks, causing a pain that is difficult to describe; it's everywhere and nowhere. Rather than a burning pain, I would say that I simply have the impression that I am hurting—a much more profound pain than just a superficial flesh wound. This feeling is similar to eating, like tasting with the body rather than with my tongue. Rather than delightful, like tasting, though, it's more like a headache that affects my entire body at once.

'*Ah, now that I think about it, I am a tad hungry again. Although not as bad as after the Bishop, it's still there. Perhaps, because the wretched rat took a piece of my cattail.*'

Staring at the shell of the kiln for a bit longer and feeling the pain, a thought comes across my mind.

'*Earl, will this heal as normal? This is not permanent, right? ...I recall the 'Chronicles' said "-100%" or something of that sort.*'

---

[25] Digit: $3/4$ inch or 1.905 cm.
Barleycorn: $1/3$ inch or 0.8382 cm.

To my relief, a wall appears. *'Aye, it seems as if many things are linked to the seed or Domain in some fashion. Is there anything else thou believest I might need to know, Earl?'*

Earl does not answer.

'I suppose I must ask a question before thou repliest? Art thou not capable of understanding when information is vital?'

Earl does not answer.

'I hope Earl can be more... 'helpful' *in the future. Not that he's not, but perhaps he could at least be talkative? ...Oh. I just recalled my Sturdiness increased. That should aid my Durability, aye? I feel as if someone could potentially kill me by total accident at this moment. Earl, prithee, show me my Status.'*

Studying the Status, I find my Durability at 22, Manituic Flux at 77, and my Erysichthon at 15.

'My manituic flux saved my life, yet it would appear that it cannot shield me from everything, and I comprehend far too little about it for it to be anything more than passive protection. I should ponder ways to foster Sturdiness further when I have the leisure to do so... I pray that damaging the Shell is not the sole method to achieve that.'

My gaze turns toward the direction from whence I fled. The wretched rat seemed enraged, and I do not plan to attempt to escape until I have waited for a while.

'Mayhaps, I should fritter a bit of time away whilst allocating my last two stat points. I suppose Agility and Strength are crucial stats if I intend to flee. It's fortunate they are the simplest to acquire as well.' I engulf some stones and bang the cattail against the wall. *'I have nary an idea how long this shall take, but once complete, I will see about fleeing this place.'*

....
....
....

> **+1 Strength**
> **+1 Endurance**
> *Strength is at its max value for your current level.*
> **No Stat Points Remaining—increase level for additional points.**

One of the Cosmic System's blue walls appears to my relief. It has been multiple hours since I began attempting to increase my stat things. Although I do not get physically tired, my mind is fatigued. A type of fatigue that causes me to be clumsier and have some difficulty keeping my mind focused on the task at hand.

'Endurance and not Agility? A tad disappointing. Since I do not get physically tired, does that imply that Endurance also affects the mind's stamina? I hope it is not worthless.' My eyes sweep across the base of the blue wall, where the Cosmic System informs me that I have zero of the wonderful point things remaining. Additionally, it mentions the only way to require more points is to increase my 'level,' which I recall my Status stating I needed to 'develop beyond embryo.'

'It would seem this is as powerful as I will be able to become at the moment. I do not believe I can directly face that disgusting rat. I simply need to escape this place and take refuge among the trees.'

However, the Cosmic System proves me wrong just after that thought.

Fostered Aspirant [Prehensile Whip (Grade 5)]

Entity 1-3-2-3 has manifested enough potential to supplant an Aspirant skill with a Novitiate skill.

Entity, see the presented skill supplants below.
Beta Entities are guaranteed knowledge based on entity's choice.

[Novitiate Prehensile Whip II]
Continue down the path of an appendage built around practicality and efficiency—an excellent choice for those that desire an extra hand rather than a simple weapon.

[Novitiate Feline Whip]
A rare offshoot of the "Whip Arts" skill. For someone or something that is interested in the beauty and elegance behind the art of the whip. Focus is on dexterity and precision strikes rather than raw power.

[Novitiate Serpentine Whip]
Similar to the Prehensile skill, but more focus on power and heavy blows. A rare skill for mammals to possess as it is typically only seen in reptiles and larger creatures.

'Oh, the Novitiate rank of the whip skill! Three choices as well? Hmm, Feline Whip and Serpentine Whip, both seem more suitable for my future needs. They seem more for combat than the Prehensile Whip skill. Well, in all honesty, the Feline Whip is very tempting, but in terms of my current haphazard fighting style, Serpentine is better. However, according to that note, it says I shall be "guaranteed knowledge." If I am granted knowledge, then it seems as if the Feline Whip is the better choice. Also, with the tendrils, I feel as if I should focus on dexterity rather than power. The cattail has already gained a lot of power from raising my Strength stat.'

Allowing time for my mind to rest, I peruse the wall's words several times over. A few more hours pass as I do naught but stare at the wall.

'With the tendrils, if I change my focus to pure power, I feel they would never be able to reach their full potential. Not to mention, the cattail is not like a tail from a large creature; it is naturally more dexterous... Aye, Feline Whip it is.'

Skill Supplantation
Entity 1-3-2-3 has supplanted [Aspirant Prehensile Whip] with [Novitiate Feline Whip] skill.
Prepare for memory impress.

Pictures flicker into my mind, images of myself. It is almost like memories of something I do not recall ever having experienced. The memories are not vague, but as clear as if I really did have such an experience.

Across from the figure that resembles me stands an expressionless person. My double raises their cattail, and the tendrils split, seeming a bit thinner and more tangled than they do when I use them. Their cattail strikes at the person across from them, striking their joints with precision. The person's leg snaps, and their fingers break under the precise blows. Finally, the cattail shoots toward the person's face, pulling one of their eyes from the socket. The memory ends.

'...That was, how should I say it... ghastly. But it also was not painful like Earl's foolish "force knowledge."'

I spend some time practicing with the cattail. Remarkably, I discover that some things seem more natural than they did before. The most significant is my control over the tendrils. I find that I can thin and flatten them, making them appear to have sharper ends than they actually do. *'Aye, I believe I am ready now. Let's escape this accursed squalor... Though, I confess, I shall miss the elderly rats.'*

With naught for me to accomplish here, I crawl back through the pipes. Arriving a while thereon, I peer beyond the damaged grate. Flies infest the pipe's opening, sipping at what remains of the rat's forsaken blood and pus. *'The wretched rat does not seem to prowl this area any longer. I should be cautious to ensure that it is not simply waiting for me to vacate the pipe. Aye... My last number was three million two hundred seventy-four thousand. One. Two. Three. Four...'* I listen warily whilst counting. *'Four thousand... Still nary a noise. Shall we attempt escape, Earl?'*

Once again, I squeeze myself through, except this time, the shell passes effortlessly due to the bars being bent earlier. I move to the end of the pipe and glance around.

'Now I shall cautiously and noiselessly' —I vault from the pipe— *'flee for my life!'*

Fleeing as quick as the haze is capable of, I abscond through the halls toward the exit that I spotted with the trees and nuns.[26] *'This way, and then there is a brick passageway. After that, there is some cracked stone. Then I shall be safe.'* Passing the cracked stone, an old, decrepit ladder to the surface comes into view. *'Oh, dearest ladder, how I love thee!'*

I hear the roar-like squeak of the wretched rat. "Squeawrr!"

'Nay!' Turning my head, the wretched rat is there, sprinting toward me, swiftly gaining ground. *'Why!? Why dost thou hunt'st me!? I have done naught but bestow great power upon thee!'*

Reaching the ladder, I ascend it whilst uncoiling the cattail.

The wretched rat lunges at the decrepit ladder. "Squea!"

With a shrill crunch, the base of the ladder shatters, plunging to the stone below. My cattail shoots toward the surface and latches on to the uppermost step. I glance down to see the ladder is not the sole casualty of the rat's attack; my feet have also been obliterated. *'Dearest ladder, precious feet, nay!'*

"Sqawr!" the wretched rat squeaks, spewing bile from sores that blotch its body.

The wretched rat claws at my legs as the cattail yanks me upward. Everything below my knees is torn to shreds, scattering into a whiff of black murk. Haze assails the rat's yawning muzzle and bloodshot eyes—it squeals.

Drawing myself to the top step, I embrace the ladder to hold myself steady. *'Rat, someday I shall return to pummel thee for thy wickedness!'* I plant the cattail against the underside of the plate. *'But know that if I were capable of it, I would giggle wickedly at this very moment! Fare thee well, liver-eater.'*

---

[26] Abscond: to leave somewhere hurriedly and secretly, usually to avoid detection or arrest. Also, can mean to conceal or hide yourself.

With the full force of the cattail, I strike the metal plate. A ding echoes through the chamber pot tunnels below. *'I beg of thee, God–'* I strike it once more, making a second dinging. *'–simply tell me now if thy intent is to smite me through ceaseless misfortune!'*

My eyes dart toward the foul vermin underneath me. It paws at the murky chamber pot waters, splashing it into its eyes and gullet. Time grows short before it recovers from the haze's effects. "Hey, mate, do you hear something?" a man on the other side of the plate says.

If I had a heart, it would stop. *'Someone is standing on the plate!'*

The man continues, "I think I heard someone knocking against the manhole cover."

'Remove thyself, dullard!' My cattail thrashes against the plate like an animal snared, yet it's as if a castle's weight presses against it. *'I am not meant to perish in these waste-filled tunnels!'*

"Knocking against the manhole cover, you sure?" another man answers.

I strike the plate again. *'Art thou deaf!?'*

"See, there's the knocking again!"

"Mate, that's probably just a big rat, and we don't have time for this. We have to get back to our dorm room before that Dryas Cyclone thing sweeps through with that cold front."

"We'll be back before the whatchamacallit cyclone comes through." Someone knocks on the plate. "If it's a rat down there, don't knock back!"

Having recovered, the wretched rat leaps upward and scratches at me. This time it scrapes away my thighs.

I beat against the underside of the plate. *'Good lord; prithee, remove thyself from the plate!'*

"Bro, there's no way that's a rat. It's literally someone knocking on the manhole cover." The man on the other side snickers. "Ask that delivery guy to move their car so whoever's down there can climb out."

The wretched rat squeaks as it leaps anew. With a slap of its paw, it rends my hips from my torso.

A sigh comes from above. "Alright, don't get your knickers in a bunch. It's probably just a sewer worker, but if anything other than a human being hops out of that hole, I'm pushin' you down and running, bruv. Survival of the fittest and all that, y'know?"

There's a rumble from above that vibrates the plate. *'Forgo thy 'knicker' prattle and begone!'*

With one decisive blow, the plate flips up and into the air. Two men yelp and jump backward as I drag myself from the hole. The wretched rat leaps, grasping the pavement's edge whilst screeching.

"God in Light! I knew it; I knew it was a rat!"

"Rat!? That's a mangy grizzly bear!"

Moving further from the hole, I gaze upon the rat, noticing the eye I struck earlier appears infected and swollen. I recall the memory bestowed unto me by the Cosmic System and prepare the cattail to sally forth.

My tendrils separate and narrow. I command the cattail to charge the wretched rat's bulbous eye. Its tendrils strike true, and they slop through the slit betwixt the socket and eyeball. A bloody haze streams the length of the cattail as tendrils enwind the eyeball, aspiring to ladle it from its skull.

The rat unshackles its hold upon the stone. Snarls of meat worm from the rat's orbital cavity until they yield and surrender the eye to the tendrils. My cattail inhales the wad of gore and nerves, dissolving them into an auburn haze—the gruesome spectacle stokes a phantom itch in my own forsaken sockets.

The Wretched Rat impacts the tunnel floor below, fetid water sprinkles the stone around me, and its pained screams echo from the depths.

Earl Interface:

Assimilating 'Putrid Rat Eyeball'
Erysichthon abates by 5
Essence value 2.
0.2 Refinable Nebula
0.0 Refinable Vitrum

'Huzzah!' I raise my arms high while using the cattail to slip the plate over its recess in the pavement. 'I do not understand how, but I survived! And two Essence for a lone eye—a veritable trove! Huzzah again!'

Chapter 6: Absconding Roots Run Deep Into Still Waters

∞∞∞∞∞∞∞∞∞∞∞∞∞∞∞∞

I lie upon the ground, legless. My gaze turns toward the tree line; it looks to be around a hundred feet from me.

"B-bloody hell!?"

'Who is speaking in a silly accent...?'

Turning my head, I find two young men on their posteriors who appear to be in their early twenties. They both have short hair, one blond and the other brown-haired. One wears a shirt that has a red heart with "NY" scribbled in the center, while the other wears one that says, "Deputy Clippie Scholarship Fund." They sit near a 'ride' with an open carriage door. Their eyes are wide, their mouths agape, and white vapor leaks from their throat as they breathe into the cold night air.

"Bruv," the blond-haired man murmurs. "W-what is it?"

The brown-haired man shakes his head. "I have no idea, bro."

'Their names are Bruv and Bro?' I wave at the two men. The pair yelp and kick the ground to force themselves further away. *'Bruv and Bro both look... delectable.'* The cattail lifts from the ground on instinct and slithers toward the pair. Clenching my fist, I command it to halt. *'Nay, I am not a wicked beast like the wretched rat! I shan't eat them.'*

I turn away and gather my bearings. These two men are the only people hereabouts, save for a few 'rides' that brighten the roadways with two beams of light as they pass by. All around me are towers that reach so high that I cannot see their tops. The clouds above are low in the sky; with my new vision, they take on a purple hue, but I can still discern that they are dark, flat, and blanket-like. They are the sort of clouds that appear before a substantial snowstorm.

The haze around my arms and torso drift downward, restoring my legs. *'Apologies, but I must take my leave!'* As I stand, the pair of men shriek with such high voices I fear they may further crack my kiln's shell. With one last glance at the two, I turn to run toward what I pray is my sanctuary.

"Wait, where's it going?" I can hear Bruv asking behind me. "Uhm, do you think we should follow it, Bro?"

"Are you off your trolley? I don't bloody care where that thing is going," the blond-haired man, Bro, replies.

'Bro has the oddest accent I have ever heard; nothing like the accents of London.'

Using the cattail's tendrils, I grab a stone pebble that the wretched rat rent from the ground and toss it at the two men to dissuade them from following me. The pebble bounces against the pathway, causing the two to leap to their feet and stumble further away. Coming upon a corner where the gray stone pathway veers to my right, I halt and gather my bearings before risking yet another 'ride' attack.

"Heretics!" someone screams.

My head snaps in the scream's direction. Thanks to my Perception stat, I can see and hear a crowd of people surrounding what looks to be a church. With scowls, the crowd casts dolls with their stuffing ripped out at the church, chanting, "Not your church—Not a religion! Not your church—Not a religion! Not your church—Not a religion!"

Someone from within the church answers their chant, "The Hex Church lawfully purchased this church and is legally classified as a religion by the government. We hope you can understand that we, like you and the Church in Light, also deserve a house of worship."

'Hex Church; that's the Bishop's church!'

"This is a historical Church in Light!" a woman yells, hurling the stuffing of a doll. "Not a place for heretical worship by some criminal cult!"

"Criminal cult?" the voice repeats with a sigh. "The Church has addressed those rumors ten thousand times. We aren't affiliated with the Galtry Syndicate in any way."

"Liar!" an aged gentleman barks back. "You're all in cahoots with that damnable harpy Galtry! Every single one of you sinners should be in prison or a mental asylum!"

The chanting recommences with renewed vigor. "Not your church—Not a religion!"

I swing my hazy head to the right. Tall lanterns illuminate the black path that the rides seem to follow, but I do not see any rides themselves. I rush ahead, focusing on a picture of a glowing red hand on the adjacent side of the roadway. If a person from London knew I was running toward a glowing red hand for safety, they would believe I had gone mad.

As I am about to arrive at the other side, a blinding light illuminates my body. A shrill screech echoes as something smashes into me—my arm and hip tear apart. The metallic sound of something grinding against stone cuts the air as I reach the other side of the roadway.

I clamber over a stone wall and roll into the nearest hedges. With my haze body, I sink into the thick hedges easily. Crouching, I turn and look back toward the roadway. A young man wearing a black helmet that only covers the top of his head stands over something that resembles a two-wheeled plough, except the wheels are placed in a line at the back and front.

'Is it a small two-wheeled ride? Is that what struck me!?' My eyes glance toward the chanting crowd, where a few people stare in this direction after hearing the commotion. They look as if they are contemplating assisting the man, but first, two other men run to his aid. I recognize the men as Bro and Bruv from a moment ago. However, now they are wearing thick coats. *'They followed me.'*

"No, my moped!" the young man shouts with a reddening face. "What the heck was that!?" He waves his hands around to disperse the black haze around him. "And gah! What's with this freaking smoke!?"

"Yo, you probably shouldn't breathe that stuff in," Bruv says, taking a step back.

"Why? Is something wron—" The young man freezes mid-sentence. His head slumps over as he gazes at the ground.

"You alright, mate?" Bro asks, laying a hand on the young man's shoulder. "Your eyes are a little bloodshot. Maybe you should sit down for a second."

'Wait, move away from him! He is about to become belligerent!' I yell out in my mind.

The young man's head shoots upwards; he shrieks like a man burning alive.

"What!?" The shrieking man pounces onto Bro, shouting obscenities I never knew existed. They tumble to the ground as Bro throws his forearm against his throat. With a grunt, the two hit the ground. The shrieking man clacks his teeth together, trying to push Bro's forearm away and bite at his throat. Powerless to reach Bro, the shrieking man scratches at his face. Bro seizes one of the shrieking man's wrists and turns his head away as the shrieking man claws at him with his other hand.

"G-get off him!" Bruv seizes the hand clawing at Bro, ending his assault. The shrieking man cries louder, kicking at him. He slips both his arms under the shrieking man's armpits. Pressing his palms against the back of the shrieking man's head, he jerks upward and forces the shrieking man's arms to rise straight into the air and flail about.

"I have him pinned, bro," Bruv shouts. "Call the cops!"

Bro rolls to his feet. "Keep holding that looney," he stutters, wiping some blood from his face onto his coat. Removing a black rectangle from a pocket sewn into his blue trousers, he pokes it three times before putting it to his ear. "Yes, please send a police car; this bloke is demented!" He glances at the shrieking man, adding, "I mean, they might be poisoned, so send an ambulance too!"

My palm hits my brow. *'Nay, did the haze affect Bro also!? He's screaming into a black rectangle!'*

I hear footsteps as a crowd of people run this way from the church.

'If they keep the young man restrained, he should eventually regain his wits, and the same is true for Bro! Though, it shall take some time for their humors to fully

recover.[27] I turn and dash into the forest as blinding red and blue lights appear in the distance. *'But prithee, I pray thee shall accept my apologies!'*

....

....

....

I glance around, spotting lanterns that illuminate snow-clad pathways winding to and fro between the trees. The trees and plants are still green despite the frigid weather, and the land itself looks well-kept, mayhaps even better than many of the nobles' estates back in England.

The more I see, the more I understand this 'forest' is not what I believed it to be. *'Perchance, is this a deer park rather than a forest? ...Nay, this place is more akin to an enormous garden than a deer park. I did not foresee it being like this.'* I swivel in place, scrutinizing the area around me. *'I am not certain by what name I should refer to this place, so I suppose I shall continue to call it a forest for the time being.'*

The weather grows more tempestuous, and I raise my hand to watch as snowflakes catch on my fingers and glide down the Comrade Cracker membrane that covers my entirety.[28] *'Such light snowfall should not pose a threat to me. Sleet or rain, however, will bode poorly for my health.'*

Selecting the pathway that appears to be the most tranquil and abandoned, I resume my stroll through this 'forest.' As I walk, I pass by lanterns spaced every so often, many of which stand beside benches. The lantern light is peculiar, without a visible flame or candlelight flickering. Not far into the forest, I come across an arched bridge made of gray stones more akin to the cobblestone that is familiar to me. I investigate it for a few minutes before a gnawing hunger in my kiln pushes me to roam deeper into the forest.

After some time passes, I chance upon a bluish-green iron pavilion with a slate rooftop and railings graven in ornate patterns. Inside is an ashy white stone foundation and a bench. Nearby, I see a narrow spit of rock running into a lake; I leave the pavilion and move onto the rock. My gaze sweeps over the lake as it reflects the moonlight. Snow falls and melts atop the

---

[27] Humors refers to a system of medicine detailing the human body's makeup and workings. It was how people in the past explained such things as disease and temperaments.

[28] Tempestuous: Windy, stormy, blustery, etc.

water's surface, yet a film of ice grows at a nigh visible pace along the lake's banks.

I look skyward. Heaven's stars are absent, so my eyes drift toward the moon, seemingly the sole presence that has not changed since my time upon Earth. I raise my arms and watch the moonlight pass through them as if I am a mere figment of someone's imagination. *'This waterside sight is charming, but I am famished'* –a sting pangs my kiln– *'and if I do not find a meal soon, I might do something I shall regret.'* Glancing at my Erysichthon value, I see it is 85. *'It has never been this high before, even before feasting upon the wafers in the chamber pot tunnels.'*

My eyes move to the snow-cloaked earth and then to the nearby greenery. *'Perhaps I may simply eat the trees? I believe they count as organic matter. During the reaping in Roanoke, everything was devoured, including the plants... Though when I ate the wafers and gown, it took much more to sate my appetite than a single rat or the copepods, but what about plants?'*

Approaching a tree limb, I gaze at it, curious if it will whet my appetite. *'It does not look delectable like meat.'* As I raise the cattail, the tendrils separate, gripping the branch, and draw the cattail over the last two feet of the branch. A brown and green haze flows into the cattail and toward the shell. The taste reminds me of... well, leaves and grass.

> **Earl Interface:**
> Assimilating 'Rosebay Rhododendron' (Mana Bare)
> Erysichthon abates by 5
> Essence value negligible.
> 0.0 Refinable Nebula
> 0.1 Refinable Vitrum

'Rosebay Row·dow·dë·grehn? What a fun name for a tree. Fun or not, it does not taste particularly delicious, but I am starving, and besides, I have gobbled meals that were much more detestable than this in my past life.' I study the numbers and compare them to my previous meals. *'I attained Vitrum, but the Erysichthon only abated by five.'*

Choosing two shorter trees bearing yellow-green leaves, I experiment and sample a leaf here or some berries there, comparing this and that to see what I acquire from each.

> *Earl Interface:*
> *Assimilating 'Green Hawthorn' (Mana Bare)*
> *Erysichthon abates by 5*
> *Essence value negligible.*
> *0.0 Refinable Nebula*
> *0.2 Refinable Vitrum*

> *Earl Interface:*
> *Assimilating 'Common Hackberry and Hackberries' (Mana Bare)*
> *Erysichthon abates by 7*
> *Essence value negligible.*
> *0.0 Refinable Nebula*
> *0.1 Refinable Vitrum*

Whilst engulfing different parts of the hawthorn and hackberry trees, a sense of faintness arises in the back of my mind. I pause, recalling feeling like this once before. *'My concentration wanes with each meal. Perhaps I should check my Status? Aye... Status.'*

> **Name:** Constance Nightingale
> **Race:** Kiln
> **Seed Type:** Tower [Embryo]
> **Variant:** Oort Stained Glass
> **Forms:** [Vaporous] [Lucent: *Unviable*]
> **Shell Level:** 0 (Develop Beyond Embryo)
> **Flame Level:** 0 (Develop Beyond Embryo)
> **Durability:** 22/39
> **Mana:** 43/210 [43/105 Manituic Flux]
> **Erysichthon:** 68/100
> **Quintessence:** Corrupting Oort Cloud
> **Adaptations:** [Cattail Tendrils] [Comrade Cracker]
> **Skills:** [Feline Whip (Nov-0)] [Naturalist (Asp-0)]
> **Titles:** [Parasitic]
>
> **Chronicles**

Summoning the blue wall, I study it. *'Consuming these plants is squandering my mana...? Earl, may thou explainest this?'* As I should have foreknown, he does not answer. *'Not very obliging as usual, Earl.'* Shaking my head, I turn toward the hackberry tree and examine its reddish-orange berries. *'Perhaps I shall solely consume the hackberries? Aye, let's do that.'*

For the next hour or so, I pluck hackberries by wrapping the cattail around branches and dragging it across, robbing the branches of berries and leaves. I sweep everything into a pile. *'After supplanting the whip skill, this sort of task feels more comfortable than before.'* With everything in a heap, I separate the berries and count them until I have five hundred exactly. *'This way, I may have a general number to know the berries' results.'*

The cattail engulfs the pile, and a bitter taste saturates my body.

> **Earl Interface:**
> Assimilating '501 Hackberries' (Mana Bare)
> Erysichthon abates by 20
> Essence value negligible.
> 0.0 Refinable Nebula
> 0.0 Refinable Vitrum

Reading the wall, I notice both the mana usage for the hackberries is less and the amount of Erysichthon reduction is greater than the wood limbs. Yet, something else demands my attention. *'Earl, I appreciate that thou wouldst aidest my counting, but "501?" I believe thou hast madest an error; it was most assuredly five hundred berries.'* I shrug my shoulders dramatically. *'Nary a need to fret, Earl, everyone makes mistakes.'*

I squat and inspect the hackberries. As I do so, a blue wall appears.

> **Fostered Aspirant [Naturalist (Grade 1)]**

'An increase in my Naturalist skill? Is it because I have been studying and learning the names of the plants? If so, I should continue consuming scraps of plants as I explore. Aye, there is nary a reason not to do that. If I only consume small amounts, the amount of mana used will also be small... Wait. If I know myself, I shall become distracted. I should avoid distractions until I have sown the Tower

Seed.' Sweeping the remaining berries and some of the leaves into a pile, I engulf them. My Erysichthon sinks another nine, leaving me with an overall value of thirty-nine. *'I am still a wee famished, yet it's unwise to ingest anymore due to mana consumption. Since my hunger pangs have waned, this shall have to suffice for now.'*

I take a moment to review my Status. *'The hackberries were more efficient than the tree limbs. When I have the chance, I should measure berries against meat. As for the haze, it's thickened a lot compared to what it was earlier.'* My eyes drift about as I rotate in place. *'And I suppose I should commence searching for potential locations to sow the Tower Seed. If I am blessed by luck, I may stumble upon a secluded area.'* I stop and stare into a thicket. *'...Prithee, Earl, canst thou help me? I am not confident in my ability to assess the appropriateness of these areas for the Tower Seed.'*

A purple wall appears.

Earl Interface:
Notice: *Stimulating the user's scouting and temperature sensations.*

'Scouting feature! Thou truly intend to assist me!? ...Oh, wait, now I remember. Earl mentioned this some time ago.' A pair of long absent sensations flow through me—ones of heat and coldness. *'Warmth and chilliness? Two sensations I have not felt in some time. Let's see, the chill feels uncomfortable and wrong, so I presume that suggests it is not a proper location. Hmm, I feel a bit of heat in the direction of the pavilion.'*

Stopping under the pavilion, a small itch and warming sensation strikes me, and I instinctively understand that it is indicating the area's suitability for planting. *'The warmth is pleasant, but...'*

"This way," a man says.

"Sure..." a woman replies.

Hearing the two voices, I rush into some hedges and use my palms to dim my eyes. My vision palls, but it is still easy enough to see shapes, figures, and most colors. I can distinguish two people wandering nearby wearing a matching assortment of deep black attire alongside a silver badge pinned to each of their breasts. One looks to be a taller man in his thirties with brown hair. The other is a woman in her twenties bearing chestnut brown hair and impeccable posture. They bicker with one another concerning things I find tough to comprehend.

"Leo, it's as cold as the Pit, and there's no way we're ever going to be able to zero in on anyone before the storm," the woman says, wrapping her arms around herself. "Plus, frankly, those two dudes were so hysterical and had such thick accents that I could barely understand what they were yelling at us."

'Oh? It appears they are searching for someone. It cannot be me, can it...? Aye. I believe I can be nigh certain they are seeking me.'

"Yeah, I know, Jessica, but you also know we need to investigate. Our client wouldn't be happy if they heard we didn't properly check for anything suspicious." The man emphasizes the word "client."

"'Client,' Leo really...? Listen, this does kind of fit what they told us, but to be fair, asking us to keep our eyes peeled for 'anything weird' isn't a reasonable request." Jessica sighs, exhaling a foggy breath. "Aren't you supposed to read Lola a bedtime story and help Lilith with her chemistry homework? Y'know, Allie is going to be really upset with you?"

"I know, I know, but we've only been asked to keep tabs on this one area, so if somethin' 'weird' happens, we need to look into it."

"It's too sketchy for us to be runnin' around while an arm of the cyclone is skirting the city. Why don't we just come back once the weather settles down?"

"...Fine." Leo shrugs his shoulders in defeat. "But only because Allie and the girls really are upset that we've been workin' so much... Still, let's take a short drive and circle the area a time or two first..."

"You're such a workaholic, dork."

The two weave around a corner, vanishing behind the foliage. 'A pair of people in matching garments searching for me is perturbing. I must be cautious to keep my presence from being known by too many.'

Pausing for a moment, I contemplate waiting a day before hunting for an area to plant the seed, but I conclude that searching the area needs to be done posthaste. So with Earl's 'scouting feature,' I roam the forest. As I walk, I occasionally feel a sense of heat along one side of the kiln, urging me in that direction. I would compare the sensation to when a child brings their palm near a searing hot pan for the first time—foreboding but with an enticing tickle of anticipation and curiosity, daring me closer.

Time passes, and the more I wander, the more apparent it becomes that this place is a bustling region during the daylight hours. *'This is not the secluded woodland for which I desired.'* I stop and cross my hazy arms. *'From what I have observed thus far, I am not certain those types of places even exist any longer. Everywhere I go, there are only more people. Is the whole world like this? Did people spend the entire time I was asleep having children like rabbits?'*

My imaginary mouth frowns as I resume following the heat. Yet it is only a hundred or so feet later that I wander into an open grassy area near a different lake than the one before. Focusing on my body's heat and itch, I spin around to discover what resembles... a castle? I tilt my head, taking in the sight of a small and quaint stone castle perched high above the lake. The castle consists of only three parts: a courtyard, two rectangular towers, and then a single barrel-shaped tower. It is covered in various shades of gray stone with a raised courtyard at its front.

'Is this actually a noble's deer park, and that is the noble's castle...?' My gaze settles on an odd flag that waves above the barrel-shaped tower. *'Perhaps I may recognize it.'*

As I move closer, the itch and heat increase, and I can discern the details of the flag. The flag is a tad silly in appearance with alternating red and white streaks. In the flag's uppermost left corner, there's a blue square containing what I believe are numerous five-pointed stars spread evenly. *'I suppose it could be an eccentric noble's family crest or the flag of a minor province? Aye. It is more probable that it is the province's flag. I cannot imagine a noble having such a gaudy crest.'* I examine the area encompassing the castle and the lake. *'I have nary an intention of making enemies of or interacting with nobles ever again. God in Light willing, may a noble never again come within a hundred yards of me.'*

Shaking my head, I turn away, pick a direction that takes me far away from the castle, and walk, placing one foot in front of the other.

After some time passes, another sensation of heat and itching assails me. This time it is not as potent as the castle, but despite that, I resolve to investigate it.

When I arrive, I discover a court lined with dozens of benches that all lead to a circular space. The itching and heat grow as I examine the snow-covered area further. Yet despite believing myself to be near the sensations' origin, the feelings are only as intense as the castle was from a distance. Marching toward the circle's center, I notice several flower wreaths surrounding a patch of snowfall. I brush away the snowfall with the cattail to find a round black and white tile-mosaic with the word "IMAGINE" at its center.

'It's odd but intriguing.' I glance at the spacious expanse around me. *'Intriguing or not, this place is rather exposed. I would prefer somewhere a tad cozier and more homish.'*

Thus I again pick a direction and begin walking over the snow. Like water, my body appears to float just above the snow, likely avoiding any melted snowfall.

'I should avoid the pathways themselves if possible. The less attention I garner, the better.'

Once I have wandered some distance away from the mosaic, a new feeling of warmth and itchiness manifests. Determining its direction, I travel toward it. It's a short time later that I come upon a bizarre structure.

At first, it appears ordinary enough, well, as ordinary as anything else in this foreign city. It has a red and white brick exterior with a green glass window out front. Two signs out front read "Entrance" and "Exit." As the front is seemingly sealed and bolted, I go around to the building's back. The heat and itching swell the more I investigate.

Discovering a grated window, I peer inside to see some sort of elevated stage with dozens of colorful horse sculptures alongside decorated carriage sculptures. *'Why are there so many outlandish things?'* I step away from the window. *'What could this building, and its sculptures, possibly be?'*

As I walk around the building's side, I discover a small tablet with writing that says "The renovation of the carousel was carried out by Consortium's Nock Fraternity and is a gift of Mister and Misses Stroock..."

'Consortium? Ah! I know that word, aye. And, hmm, this structure is something called a carousel? Interesting. Let's see...'

I continue reading. "...In return for many happy go-rounds 1982."

'...?'

I read it once more. "Many happy go-rounds 1982."

'...!?'

Peering downward, I stare at my bare feet, believing I might be hallucinating. The wind whistles, whisking away slivers of haze near my gown's hem. The world is quiet as my fingers fidget. I count to ten, shake my hands, and raise my head.

My sights fall upon the number "1982".

I read the numbers repeatedly to ensure my eyes are not mistaken. *'I... That... That number could be anything! Aye, anything! Presumably, it is simply the number of these 'go-rounds' of which the tablet speaks. Of... of course. That is most certainly not the year... Slumbering for so many centuries? Who could even accomplish such a feat... certainly not a parasitic haze like myself!'*

For a time, I stand frozen, merely gaping at the tablet, *'...Before I make a judgment, let's locate another source to corroborate this information. For... for the moment, I shall resume exploring. I cannot enter this carousel place even if I somewhat appreciate its whimsy.'* Despite declaring I shan't fret, I count steps to ease my stormy mind. *'Three million two hundred seventy-four thousand. Two. Three...'*

Several hundred steps later, a potent heat and itch makes itself known. This time it resembles the sensation the castle gave me and rivals the carousel.

Following the sensation, I come across a statue of a man named "Robert Burns" along with a tablet. I look from left to right, discovering additional statues in the area, but this one has captured my attention. Yet, when I am about to read the tablet, I pause and turn away. *'I... I should not read this yet. If this tablet harbors any startling truths, it could impede my mission to plant the Tower Seed. After planting the seed, I shall have more time to confront any perturbing knowledge.'*

I check my Erysichthon values to find that it has worsened, yet despite Earl's words, my Essence is relatively unchanged. Gazing toward the sky, I can see that there are only a few more hours of night remaining. *'Even though deep down, I have a foreboding sense that this "carousel's" tablet may be accurate, perhaps it is a stone better left unturned at the present. Thus, for now, it would just be baggage I cannot afford, so I shall remain ignorant in this regard until I am better prepared for enlightenment... I shall return to this place one day.'*

Returning to the path, the heat and itchiness increase to the point of near overwhelmingness, but I know this means it is likely an excellent area. Soon, I come across a large white structure that looks to be made of marble. It reminds me of a stage for plays and such; however, keeping with my previous thought, I ignore it and plan to return later. Something just up the snowy pathway is calling to me; I can feel it in the depths of my soul or, more precisely, on my kiln.

A couple hundred steps later, I discover the place all my senses were guiding me. I walk to the edge of a grand staircase with two pillars on either side. On each side of the pillars, a different scene, animal, or object is carved, such as an owl, book, or hawk.

I ignore this and gaze down the grand staircase. My kiln burns with a warmth I have not known since my hearth in my cottage near Roanoke. I rush down the first eighteen steps and come upon a platform halfway down the staircase with two doors to either side. One entryway reads "Men" and the other reads "Women." Both doors have a sign on them that reads "Bethesda Terrace Restrooms Closed Until Weather Improves." I would typically investigate, but they both seem to be locked, and currently, my excitement is palpable, so I do not tarry. Thus, I move down another set of eighteen stairs reaching the bottom.

Three gorgeous arches of stone greet me as I dash through them. Beyond the center arch, I am greeted with a wide and open chamber. *'Woah! This place is so lovely!'*

Along the walls are gorgeous pictures and scenic depictions. The floor set with crimson tiles and sandstone brickwork is marvelous, but the ceiling utterly transcends it. The ceiling is a motif made of inlaid ceramic tiles of peach, green, red, lapis blue, and ivory white. Each square of tiles contains an exquisite design that looks as if it would belong in the Richmond Palace itself... I assume.[29]

'This place reminds me of a ballroom or at least how I would imagine one! I always wanted to go to a ball, hold a fancy drink, and stand there looking superb. If someone asked me to dance, I would say something to the effect of "Nay! Thou art not worthy of my company!" in a pretentious manner. Then I would proceed to drink and eat until I was ready to pop... Honestly, I do not know how to dance; I merely wished to sample the foods and drinks.'

Proceeding onward, the room widens further, revealing four arches on both the left and right sides of the room, leading to yet more paintings. My excitement urges me forward, and I find another entrance, except this one is seven arches wide. Hurrying outside, I notice to the left and right of this entrance are two more grand staircases that lead up to a snow-laden roadway.

I pause and allow my eyes to drift across a round courtyard with long stone benches marking its boundary. At the court's heart is a splendid bronze fountain surrounded by a circular body of water nearly a hundred feet wide that holds various aquatic plants layered with a fresh sprinkling of snow. The fountain's top is adorned with an angel that looks to have just descended from the Light and is now watching over the courtyard. Walking further, I come upon a serene lake that complements the courtyard's melancholic air, bestowing upon me a sentiment of peace.

Wiping away the snow at my feet, I see the court's foundation is laid with red brick. *'Everything cries: Here...! Yet is this indeed the optimal location? It... It most definitely seems like it would be a busy area.'*

I take a moment to consider my options. *'Returning to the chamber pot tunnels is not an option, and having searched several places whilst in the chamber pot tunnels, I never encountered anywhere with more than a few trees. Not to*

---

[29] Richmond Palace: royal residence that existed in the 16th/17th century. A favorite residence of Queen Elizabeth the First and where she spent much of her time hunting stags in her deer park.

mention, I am destructive and frightening, so I would indubitably be attacked by normal folk. Then there is the shell that has yielded half its durability; a significant blow could obliterate me.'

While I ponder and gaze out over the lake, the first glimmers of the sun's light appear over the horizon. A bit of a mixed feeling washes through me as the sight reminds me of when I left Tenebrous and the following events. Yet, upon spinning around and witnessing the beautiful spectacle of the morn light illuminating the snow-covered courtyard, my mood soars. 'This place is sublime! My body is burning and itching with impatience at the thought of sowing my seed... that sounded remarkably lewd. Aye. Sometimes it is not so bad that others cannot hear me.'

Focusing on the warmth, I follow it toward the area where it is hottest. The feeling leads me back to the place I was in previously with the magnificent ceiling. 'Under here? Like with the pavilion, it seems to wish for me to build somewhere enclosed. Well, then...'

Knowing this is where my instincts and Earl's scouting feature desire me to plant, I count my steps and walk the room's length and width until I ascertain the ideal spot in the exact center of the chamber.

My right foot taps against the brick beneath me as I ogle the point all my efforts have led me to. With the kiln burning and the itch at a maddening height of intensity, I almost plant the seed without thought. Until in the distance, the harsh sound of a horn from a 'ride' passing nearby reverberates, snapping me from my trance. This horn is something I have heard countless times in the chamber pot tunnels. Customarily, it is accompanied by someone in a ride cursing at someone else in a ride. It is a constant noise in this city.

My shoulders drop. 'I am rather enthusiastic, but perhaps I should wait until nightfall before planting?' I turn my gaze toward the outside. The snowfall has grown so severe that I can scarcely see beyond the opening of the arches. '...But surely nary a soul would be out unprotected in this horrid weather. Conceivably, this might be a better time than any. Earl, dost thou hast an opinion?' He does not answer, so I once more peer at the spot beneath my feet. 'Why does this place make me feel so warm?'

A purple wall appears, causing me to flinch. I read it, thinking it will be the answer to my question, but I soon realize it's not exactly what I anticipated.

'Oh. Well, I thank thee. I suppose that answers my second question, but I was more concerned with whether or not I should wait for nightfall before planting... Rather than that, I should be inquiring, how safe am I planting somewhere like this?'

Another wall appears—this is a good day for Earl and his walls! After reading through the purple wall a few times, I nod. *'So, it shan't be obvious? ...Well then, I suppose I say, aye! Let's plant here, Earl!'*

As soon as those words run through my mind, a sound like a glass pane shattering echoes. The kiln in my belly bursts open and a single sensation buries itself in the deepest recesses of my mind...

Anguish! Unbridled anguish!

I drop to my knees, catching myself with my left hand as my right moves to my shell. My mind quivers under the sensation as my hand grips the shell like someone who has just suffered some type of mortal injury.

From within, a burning bright light of purple that reminds me of the sun itself floats out. Dust, dirt, and snow that had lain upon the ground arise.

Light reflects on the haze that forms my petite hand as a spinning purple orb, around the size of an acorn, drifts through my palm undeterred. The dust, dirt, and snow revolve around the orb, picking up speed the closer it moves until they are sucked into the orb.

The small purple sun descends toward the crimson tile floor. As it strikes the tiles, the light grows almost blinding while smoke rises from the stone as if it is being burned like wood.

Not encountering any resistance, the purple sun scorches its way through the stone and earth below. As it sinks, a bubbling liquid of violet, red, black, and gray overflows from the hole, obscuring the seed's light. When enough of this molten liquid fills the hole it solidifies, leaving a glass-like substance. This essentially seals the hole from outside influence.

A loud, harsh pop reverberates from beneath the stone's surface, shaking the snow outside, and causing it to tremble and settle. At the same time, thin lines of translucent glass bud from the solidified liquid seal and spread within the grooves of the tiles.

An uncanny sensation descends upon me as if my form has been divided into two. It is a feeling I have never known previously, and describing it is uniquely challenging. Below my feet, I feel a strange pounding reminiscent of a heart.

The sensation of division, along with the pain, starts to subside, so I turn my gaze toward the kiln. Tiny strands of glass spread from the edges of the fractures on the kiln's surface like sutures of twine.[30] Once a fracture has been sealed by the twine, it twists into a liquid, mending the shell.

Earl Interface:

Germination Stage Start

The First Step Has Been Taken!

Tower Seed is planted and spreading lines and roots. Anniversary of this moment shall be marked by the Earl Interface, and a reminder shall be issued annually. Tower possibilities will be accessible post-germination.

The time of germination is expected to take approximately...
Forty-one Material-Earth days.

Current Effects in Germination Stage
-   *Essence rate of loss while in Domain will diminish slightly.*
-   *Shell will mend itself while in the Domain.*
-   *Mana will rejuvenate slightly faster within Domain.*

Forewarning: User will be required to enter a semi-conscious state when time remaining is fifteen Material-Earth days or germination will not be able to progress further.

Reminder: The Tower can be considered the Kiln's body, while the Shell and Flame can be equated to the soul and spirit. If any of these three perish, the user risks nihility.

Recommendation: As germination progresses, it is recommended that the user do the following: 'Explore surroundings,' 'acquire books (Biology/Ecology recommended),' and 'manually aid the seed's progression with three separate manual germination tasks.'

---

[30] Suture: a stitch or row of stitches holding together the edges of a wound or surgical incision.

A sizable purple wall appears. *'That is an abundance of information.'*

Most of it are things Earl has mentioned before, but one thing causes me to rub my chin and internally squint. *'First things first... that reminder, Earl. When didst thou mention that the seed's death would result in my own? If thou art referring to the time thou vaguely referred to the Tower as my 'body', I shall be quite upset! I would most definitely say that reminder should have come earlier... Perhaps, it is my own fault for not realizing.'*

I look toward the ceiling for a moment, digesting the information, before turning back toward the wall. *'I have never heard the word 'germinate' before, but I believe I may ascertain its meaning based on how Earl has been using it in his walls.'*

The beating below the ground wanes whilst I reread Earl's wall several times over. I cannot help but shake my head at the thought that I must spend over three fortnights hiding before I can move to the next step.[31] As this goes on the beating below my feet fades until it ceases. Yet, my connection seems to persist. The connection almost feels like a string is knotted around my kiln. I pace the room, testing this connection, and whether I move this way or that, there is a constant tug directing me toward the Tower Seed's location.

'I suppose the recommendations are comprehensible, but what dost thou meanest by manually aiding the seed's progression?'

> **Earl Interface:**
> **Answer:** The first task would include selecting four mature trees to set as Nodes. Each node will reduce germination time by _12_ Material-Earth hours and bring the area within the Tower's Domain.
> **Note:** The maximum distance from seed is _200_ linear feet.[32]
>
> **Query:** Does the user wish to progress the germination manually?
>
> **[Aye]**   **[Nay]**

---

[31] Fortnight: a unit of time equal to 14 days or 2 weeks.
[32] | 200ft | 60.96m |

I read through the purple wall a few times. 'Aye, why not do this whilst I scout the area further. Moreover, it seems like I may make certain that the Domain is at its maximum size, meaning I may get the benefits within the largest possible area.'

The opening within the floor liquifies and unseals itself. A small measure of light leaks from the opening as four glowing motes exit. It reseals itself and the four motes float aimlessly in the air. I reach toward one of them, and as if it senses me, it enters my fingertip, moves up my arms, and to the kiln. Here it floats around the kiln as the moon does around the Earth. Repeating this thrice more, I soon have four lights floating around the kiln's shell. 'Let's follow Earl's recommendation and explore the surrounding area more thoroughly. Mayhaps I might find more things to eat while I am about. The wind has been affecting my haze; I am glad I chose that adaptation.'

As I am about to depart, a light dissimilar from the others springs from the hole. This one is violet in color, more radiant, and almost drips like molten metal. Same as the other motes, it gravitates toward the shell, but instead of floating around it like the others, it expands. Enwinding the shell, it bends and swirls around it, glazing its surface in stirring liquid. Once the shell is thoroughly covered, it burst into violet flames, and the glaze bubbles away.

'...I pray that was meant to happen.'

The last of the glaze burns away, and the shell's appearance returns to normal. I poke out my belly, bend my back and neck, and move close to inspect it. Yet before I may do so, one of the Cosmic System's walls appears.

Entity Development
Entity's Shell has gained complexity: Level 1
10 Stat Points Primed
Entity Development
Entity's Flame has grown in intensity: Level 1
10 Stat Points Primed

'Oh! Levels! Is this because of the thing that enwound the shell? Hmm, and I have collected more of these stat points? For what exactly?' I move my fingers to the shell, inspecting it intently. As my fingertips run over its surface, I notice it seems less rough. It's subtle, but I can tell. Moreover, the flame within might be a tad brighter now. *'Is it due to this "level" jargon? Earl, dost thou knowest about these "levels?"'*

To my delight, Earl responds to my question!

Earl Interface:
Oort Stained Tower Glass Kiln Guide

Kiln Leveling
To level, Kiln must either introduce complexities to the Shell or add fuel to the Flame. There are three known methods of accomplishing the above, but currently, the user only has two of these methods available to them. The third method will become possible after completing the sprout stage.

Method 1: Grow and advance into each successive stage of growth.
Method 2: Develop the Shell by adding complexities.
Method 3: Siphon an ample and sustained quantity of Essence and stoke the Flame into a costlier form.
Note: Only available after sprout stage.

'I am pleased he responded to this since this is vital knowledge.' I straighten my back, studying the wall and memorizing the three methods. *'Grow, develop, and siphon? That is how I must become stronger? So, for the time being, I suppose I should focus on the next stage of growth. Although I am still uncertain how precisely I meant to "develop the Shell." Hence my question, Earl, how would I add complexities to the Shell?'*

Earl's wall vanishes, and another replaces it.

Earl Interface:
Oort Stained Tower Glass Kiln Guide

Developing the Shell
If the user wishes to develop the Shell beyond what can be achieved through method 1, the user must seek out and cannibalize another Kiln. This is the only known method of adding complexity to the Shell.

'Cannibalize? What is that meant to imply? Undoubtedly, it cannot mean what I believe it to?!' My thoughts muddle. 'I... What is someone in my circumstances meant to feel and think about this? Would another Kiln not be someone like me? Am I meant to dine upon another person in a situation akin to my own? Wait. Does this suggest that other Kiln shall seek to devour me!? As if I required further reasons to fear for my meager life!'

I clench my hazy fist. 'I should not ensnare myself in these thoughts too deeply. It might be some time before I encounter another Kiln. Perhaps, there are no other Kiln anywhere near me! Aye. I should concentrate on what I can do at present: the tasks and strengthening myself.' Before beginning the task, I take a moment to ease my worries by counting to five hundred and admiring the delightful architecture of my newly established Domain. 'Let's commence the task. This can also serve as an excellent opportunity to foster the Naturalist skill.'

Standing above the Tower Seed, I face the fountain, walk, and count my steps. Counting two hundred paces, I find myself standing amidst the fountain's waters. I return to the seed, adjust my angle, and count anew. It is a tedious process since I must account for obstacles, but I am persistent. Arriving between two trees, I twirl in place and then approach the furthest tree I deem to be within range.

Whilst inspecting the tree, I brush it with the cattail, and one of Earl's purple walls appears.

Earl Interface:

Tree Type: Swamp Spanish Oak
Distance from seed is 195.4 feet.[33]
Query: Would the user like to establish Node 1?

[Aye]   [Nay]

'Swamp Spanish Oak. Am I in the Spanish Empire? Nay, I do not believe so. Unless the House of Hapsburg and the Spaniards no longer speak the Spanish tongue.' I shake my head and return my thoughts to the task at hand. *'Aye, it is nigh morn, so I cannot dally for long. I bestow this tree the privilege of being Node 1,'* I respond to Earl.

A light swims away from the shell. It is undeterred by the frigid gusts of winds as it creeps nearer to the tree: bark ripples like water as the light sinks and blends into it. There is a thump, and veins of pale purple light pulse through the tree's veneer. The bark ruptures into a festering wound, exposing more veins webbing through the tree's milky pith. A puff of black haze spews from the fissure, and then with a wooden clank, the bark clamps shut.

The tree reverts to its former appearance, an unassuming tree amongst a copse of several others. *'That... that was a bit ominous.'* Surveying the area around me, I resume my thoughts. *'Since there is none hereabouts, my activities should go unheeded, and with this wind whittling at my haze, I believe it wise to conclude Earl's task forthwith. I have the leisure to do so, and I cannot know if I shall have a more opportune time to place these nodes than tonight.'*

Unfurling its tendrils, I raise the cattail and pluck a leaf from the tree in hopes of progressing my Naturalist skill. The leaf bubbles and sizzles as the fleshy bits slough off and evaporate, leaving behind, for the merest moment, the macabre sight of a leaf bereft of all but its artery-like veins. It soon crumbles into wisps of dust and joins my haze.

Earl's wall appears, and I note that he still refers to it as "Swamp Spanish Oak," even after making it into a Node. The sole difference is Earl does

---

[33] | 195.4ft | 59.558m |

not state that it's "Mana Bare" as he typically does. The wind howls, dragging me from a stupor.

Returning to the seed, I face a new direction and again count my steps. After my previous efforts, I am able to achieve this much quicker, and I arrive at a tree in the midst of sparse hedges.

I touch the tree with my cattail.

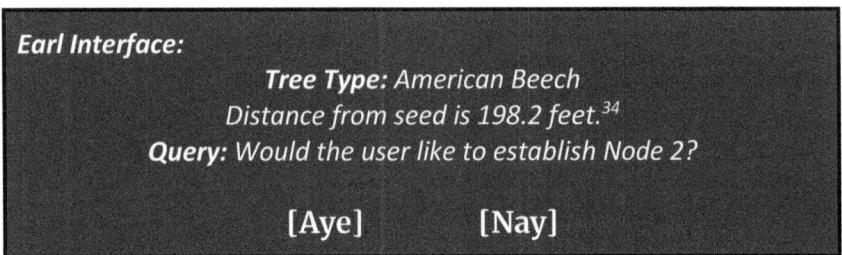

Earl Interface:
Tree Type: American Beech
Distance from seed is 198.2 feet.[34]
Query: Would the user like to establish Node 2?

[Aye]   [Nay]

Earl's wall brings my head to a tilt. '*American. Verily, do I still reside in the New World? I believed so but have yet to verify that belief. Why American Beech, though? Should it not be an English Beech? Well, I suppose folk may name a tree whatever they desire.*' I cross my arms and nod. 'Aye, I dub thee, Node 2!' A light floats from the shell and toward the tree. It cracks open, spews black haze, and then returns to normal. Plucking a leaf, I absorb it as I did before, and again I watch the process of the leaf crumbling into haze. '*I hope this is benefiting my skill.*'

Retreating to the seed, I face the direction opposite 'Node 1' and march onward. This time it is trickier as I must account for the grand staircase's steps, but I manage to locate the nearest tree. This tree has its roots in the center of a wide red brick footpath. '*In the middle of a footpath or not, it shall do.*'

A new purple wall appears.

---

[34] |198.2ft | 60.411m|

Earl Interface:

Tree Type: American Elm.
Distance from seed is 197.5 feet.[35]
Query: Would the user like to establish Node 3?

[Aye]   **[Nay]**

'Another tree that bears an American name...? I suppose I must trust thee, Earl, yet I grow evermore skeptical.' I wiggle my finger at the wall. *'But aye, this tree has the honor of being Node 3 from henceforward!'*

Veins of light, spewing haze, bark clamps shut, Node 3 establishes itself in the same fashion as the previous two. I consume a leaf and then return to the seed, except this time, I move opposite Node 2. The fourth location is similar to the American Elm, with a tree stuck in the midst of a footpath, the difference being the pathway is stone and it sits adjacent to the black roadway.

Earl Interface:

Tree Type: London Planetree.
Distance from seed is 193.1 feet.[36]
Query: Would the user like to establish Node 4?

[Aye]   **[Nay]**

'London Planetree? I cannot conceivably be in London, could I? Nay, I know every nook and cranny of London, and I would indeed recognize at least one aspect of London in this city... I suppose I shall know the truth soon enough. Aye, this is Node 4 from this day forth.'

As it did thrice before, the light sinks into the final tree and alters it in a manner I cannot hope to fully fathom. I consume a leaf from the London Planetree and glance around to find the snowstorm is weakening.

Something captures my eye—a large 'ride' rages down the roadway with a broad shovel affixed to the front. The shovel forces an icy slurry from the

---

[35] |197.5ft | 60.198m|
[36] |193.1ft | 58.857m|

roadway's surface, creating a wave of snow and debris. I run back to the seed before the ride buries me. *'I should consider locating a place to hide. Though, first, I believe there were some blue and brown containers near the fountain. Shall we see if they hold any treasures, Earl? Oh! And I shall also continue nibbling leaves for the Naturalist skill!'*

Chapter 7: Doctor Nightingale and the Gentlewoman

∞ ∞ ∞ ∞ ∞ ∞ ∞ ∞ ∞ ∞ ∞ ∞ ∞ ∞ ∞

The sun tops the horizon. Icicles hang precariously from tree branches, dripping icy tears as if bemoaning their brief time in this world. The wind whips up some loose snow, sprinkling it atop the Comrade Cracker membrane that covers my cheek. My gaze turns skyward, and I witness a pale hawk snatch a pigeon mid-flight. Though suffocating beneath this city's sterile stone, nature perseveres—predator and prey, the struggle never ceases.

Fostered Aspirant [Naturalist (Grade 2)]
+1 Orenda **19 Stat Points Primed**

'Huzzah! Advanced my Orenda somehow, and the Naturalist skill. Unsinkable Constance, Unsquashable Roach, and the Black Witch of London, all titles I once held. If I can take advantage of these stats, skills, and adaptations, I can one day be the Formidable Constance... or more preferably the Leave Her Be Constance. Well, to be honest, everyone used to shorten my titles to Sink, Roach, and Black, so I guess my new one would simply be Leave.'

I sink into a hedgerow, roughly a hundred yards away from the Tower Seed and within a stone's throw of an exotic arched foot-bridge. Though I would prefer to be a bit nearer to the seed, hereabouts is the nearest I was able to achieve. The other thickets in the area are all simply too sparse to conceal me thoroughly. Retreating deep into my humble abode, my hand shifts to my, quite literally, thin belly. *'Now that I have fostered Naturalist, I shall sample the delicacies I was able to forage from that rubbish in those bins. Then I shall laze here for the day and see what information I may gather.'*

My attention strays to three items I was able to rescue from some blue containers in the courtyard. I scrutinize each item and nod. *'Hast thou readied thyself, Earl. I am confident thou wouldst be trembling in anticipation if thou wert more than a simple floating wall.'*

Earl likely does not care about my food opinions, yet he is all I have to speak to. Therefore, I pretend he does care, whether he likes it or not. 'Aye, Earl. First, this frail yellow and black thing, I do not know what it is, but I presume it is edible. Next, I have acquired this brown thing that I understand is some type of bread tied into a bow. Finally, I have a wee sliver of mystery meat that I believe is chicken.' I arrange the three items in a row. 'Now we shall compare this possibly edible yellow thing, with this perhaps bread thing, and this conceivably chicken thing. Earl, let us partake of this bountiful blessing!'

The yellow and black thing dissolves into a chalky haze. A bitter-sweet sensation pokes at my kiln.

> **Earl Interface:**
> Assimilating 'Banana Peel' (Mana Bare)
> Erysichthon abates by 2
> Essence value negligible.
> 0.0 Refinable Nebula
> 0.0 Refinable Vitrum

With its appearance, I read Earl's wall. 'Banana? And that was merely the peel? It was the first sweet thing I have tasted since I came here. Perhaps I may locate the whole banana in the future.'

I take the bread thing, which dissolves into a tawny haze with a bit of a briny feeling.

> **Earl Interface:**
> Assimilating 'Soft Pretzel' (Mana Bare)
> Erysichthon abates by 3
> Essence value negligible.
> 0.0 Refinable Nebula
> 0.0 Refinable Vitrum

'A soft pretzel? It was delightful but not as delectable as the White Bakers' bread in London... but perhaps that is simply because of my new eating method. What confuses me is, was that white material salt? Something such as raw salt on the surface of bread? The people of this era truly are eccentric. Mayhaps this is simply a luxury among the wealthy who inhabit this area; how wasteful to throw such a treat away. Well, I suppose that it's not surprising the rich would be so wasteful.

Their fickle avarice is boundless. Worse yet are those wealthy French with their exorbitant gabelle.' [37]

Lastly, the chicken, the only one I am certain of. The tendrils drag the fowl into the cattail, which promptly dissolves into a light red and white haze. It feels like what I would describe as savory but not as delicious as the rats or even the copepod throng. *'Perhaps I have merely been overthinking the flavors. Aye... certainly things such as rats and those copepod things cannot be more delicious than bread and chicken. I believe that all these items are simply an acquired taste. Aye! Certainly!'*

The last of the pale haze enters the kiln, and Earl's wall appears.

Earl Interface:
Assimilating 'Gangrenous Beef' (Mana Bare)
Erysichthon abates by 6
Essence value is less than one.
0.1 Refinable Nebula
0.0 Refinable Vitrum

'Gangrenous beef... Hmmm... Gan·grene·ous... beef... bee... fuh... Nay. I refuse to believe it. There is nary a chance that was beef. This must be Earl's mistake. Who discards something as valuable as beef...? What was ate has been eaten; let's not brood on it.'

With my tests complete, I assess the results. The most notable thing is that despite being a smaller piece than the peel or the pretzel, it lowered my Erysichthon more and gave me some Nebula. Also noteworthy is that the pretzel and peel had a "negligible" amount of Essence while the meat was simply "less than one."

'So it seems, for reasons that elude me, meat is more efficient than bread, plants, or fruit. That makes the order from least to greatest for Erysichthon raw plants, fruit, conventional foods, and meat or carcasses. However, I found that I gained more Vitrum from plants and more Nebula from meat.'

---

[37] The gabelle: an extremely unpopular tax on salt in France. It was established during the mid-14th century and lasted, with brief lapses and revisions, until 1946.

A high-pitched voice yells, causing me to dip low. "Mommy! Come on; I wanna go sledding."

Gazing through a gap in the leaves, I notice a woman carrying a sled. Next to her, a child skips gaily in the fresh snow. *This day is proving itself fruitful! I have now confirmed that sleds still exist and that children still have mothers. If I wished to take it even further, I could say they even have fathers as well. However, I assume naught when it comes to the absurd folk who dwell in this city of Bedlam...*[38] *Earl, that was a jest. Thou dost not comprehend quality sarcasm obviously.'*

The alleged mother and child proceed further down the path, but it seems their arrival is merely the first among many. People begin pouring into this forest, dozens or even hundreds of people meander throughout the area classified as my Domain.

My fingers grasp a small leaf, which I twist about my hand anxiously. *'All these people make me feel... unsafe, I suppose? Or perhaps vulnerable would be the correct word. I should pay it little mind, though, Earl said the seed is not so easy to discover.'*

A man and woman walk into view. "Let's stop here for a minute, babe; I want to check the news."

The woman nods, and together they sit on the bench directly in front of me. I shift to their side, to listen and watch. This bench is simple; it sits next to one of the gray pathways, facing the lake, and overlooking the bridge. It is convenient that they chose this bench as there are many more lined up in a row.

The man withdraws a black rectangle from his front trouser pocket and hits it with his finger as if he's angry at it. Whilst he does this, the woman acts as if this is nothing to concern herself with as she commences to speak of things I cannot fully understand.

"So, after all that, all we talked about, all he's done, and all he's said to her, she went out with him anyway. Like, why did she even ask my

---

[38] Bedlam: 1st Meaning) - bedlam - A scene of pandemonium or confusion.
2nd Meaning - Bedlam - archaic meaning, "an institution for the care of the mentally ill" residents of which were known as bedlamites. Bedlam in the 16th century was the sort of 'lunatic' asylum you'd avoid at all costs.

opinion if she was planning on going regardless of what I said?" The woman sighs, tosses her head back, and leans into the bench. She goes quiet, staring at the cloudy sky above. "Speaking of Jan, she was at the protests yesterday with him... The protests seem to be getting more violent every day," the woman says in a quiet voice.

"Mhm," the man replies.

"Seems like everyone is protesting these days," the woman says with downturned eyes. "We might actually go to war with China, y'know?"

Again the man simply answers, "Mhm."

"...Honey."

"What, April? Of course I already know all this. I'm in the Air Force; how would I not know?" He holds up his black rectangle. "And why do you think I'm on the WGN website checking the news for anyway?"

"I-I know, Steve, but... it's scary. You only just got back from Anchorage," she stutters, "a-and after Crawler-Anchorage, that whole city is nothing but those monsters now. Then there's this freezing weather thanks to that polar vortex, the Dryas Cyclone or whatever... I mean, you know the snowstorms here are nothing compared to the blizzards in Alaska and Canada, right?" While shaking her head, she says, "Steve, I don't know what I'd do if something happened to you."

"...Babe, I wasn't even in Anchorage very long, and I doubt they'll be sending me back there." He sighs. "Listen. I love you, but... there's nothing I can do about any of this. If we find out China really did release that virus onto that cruise ship, and cause Crawler-Anchorage, then only the God in Light themself knows what will happen."

"You mean even with all this other messed-up stuff going on, there's still a chance we'll go to war...?" She pauses, glancing around as if checking if anyone is around. "You don't think all the talk on the internet could be true, do you? Even for a second? If we didn't get in, it would mean we are..." The woman's mouth opens and closes; she struggles to speak but forces it out. "...it would mean we've been essentially damned to die."

His eye twitches, but only for a second as he crushes his emotions with a quick swallow. "President McCracken has already denied those rumors. All that stuff on the internet is just people who have gotten too caught up in fantasy. What happened in Anchorage happened because of a virus, and that's all there is to it."

He goes back to tapping on his black rectangle, never looking up.

His eyes betrayed him in the beginning, however. Both the woman and I noticed the twitching and the swallow.

"But I've heard that people have seen others doing impossible things," she says, clearly attempting to push him further. "Lots of people have joined up with those... religions."

"...I-I don't know, April..." He places the black rectangle into a pocket on his blue trousers. "Hey. Can we just enjoy our time in the park? Honestly, I don't want to talk about this when I'm off duty."

"Okay. As long as you promise that we'll talk about it at some point. I know you'll just try to put it off."

"I don't know what there is to talk about." He pauses, taking a deep breath. "But sure. We'll talk about it later."

The woman becomes much cheerier. "Good," she says, grabbing the man's hand. "Let's go see if the pretzel cart is open!"

"Babe, it's like 9 AM after a snowstorm. There's no way the pretzel cart is going to be open right now."

"Well, let's at least check. They might have rolled the thing into the Terrace's Arcade!" she replies with a giggle.

The two disappear into the Terrace, entering the covered area.

'Ah, so the covered area with the arches is called an 'Arcade.' All in all, that was a decent bit of information. It sounds as if England, or wherever this place is, might be on the verge of war after something occurred in a city named Anchorage. I was also able to verify that this place is indeed a park. Although that was information I anticipated finding after all these people left, and I could read the tablets nearby in

peace... Oh, and there's something called an 'Air Force' that exists now too? So strange.'

A few more hours pass while nary a person sits at the bench that I strategically placed myself near. I do overhear pieces of prattle here and there, but all I learn is that both men and women curse much more nowadays.

Eventually, an older lady sits at the bench directly in front of me. The older lady takes out a brown bag and begins tossing seeds atop the snowy pathways. Dozens of pigeons descend and start pecking at the seeds. She hums a melody while speaking to the birds. "Oh my, your feathers look nice and tidy today."

The pigeons obviously do not answer, but the older woman continues complimenting them. 'She must be a delightful woman. A pity she has to live in such a deranged world.'

The woman tosses a large handful of black seeds to the ground causing the pigeons to scatter. A pigeon with light brown feathers hops under the bench to nibble at stray seeds.

'That... that pigeon. It looks rather delicious.' I glance at my Erysichthon value which is currently at 45. 'The snowstorm raised my Erysichthon value quite a bit. Mayhaps, I might...'

I unravel the cattail and poke it from the bush. The pigeon turns to look at the cattail. It tilts its head and watches it for a moment, but when the old lady tosses more seed, it turns away. The cattail slithers closer. The pigeon glances at the cattail but loses interest when it sees the others eating all the black seed.

'Come hither, little one. Constance is tired of her perpetual hunger... Something is unquestionably wrong with me.'

The tendrils unravel, preparing to embrace the pigeon. They twitch as a tendril encircles one of the pigeon's legs. My tendrils enwind, snare its leg, and yank it into the hedges. The pigeon chirps, flapping its wings to escape. "Gosh darn it!" I hear the old lady shout.

I thump the pigeon against a rock, killing it. The cattail draws its carcass into the haze, and the pigeon dissolves into a gray and red vapor.

"Blasted raccoon; stop snatching my gals!" The old lady stands and peers into the bushes as a rich taste fills me.

Earl Interface:
Assimilating 'City Pigeon' (Mana Bare)
Erysichthon abates by 15
Essence value is less than one.
0.2 Refinable Nebula
0.0 Refinable Vitrum

I ignore Earl's purple wall and lie flat.

The old lady attempts to get to her knees to inspect the hedges, but she stops, pressing her palm against her lower back. "I'll get that raccoon someday! I'll have to file another complaint about those raccoons! Not that anyone will ever do anything about it." She snaps her fingers. "Stupid thing is always ruffling the gals' feathers."

For a while, I enjoy the flavor and relief of not being caught. The old lady departs, and a few more hours pass without anyone sitting on the bench. Meanwhile, I scout in my small area of bushes, eavesdropping on conversations.

This allows me to catch slivers of discussions, which included things like:

"Are you going to any of the protests? There will be one outside the Consortium building tomorrow night."
"I heard the caravans have exploded in size, and they're drifting east."
"Yeah, dude, I always study at that Central Café next to the Boathouse."
"My magazine says a big wig is going to have a wedding reception at the Boathouse in the next couple of days. The Espositos might go to spite Galtry."

I never overheard any information that felt critical, but it did feel like I was learning some things that might be helpful. Alas, the snowstorm grew too intense, and everyone departed. Still, the discussion involving the person named "Dude" about the places called "Boathouse" and "the

Central Café" intrigues me. *'If I can find somewhere to hide at this "Boathouse" and "Central Café," I may have an opportunity to "acquire" a book from one of the wealthy college nobles studying there. Hmm, but also, I need to supplant my 'Naturalist' skill... Since I received the Naturalist skill from watching the elderly rats, does that mean I may increase it by watching other animals?'*

Split between advancing my skills and moving to this "Central Café," I spend some time musing the two as the sky darkens and the snow once more falls. My mind wanders, and I begin to recall my experiences practicing medicine. *'I have a brilliant idea! Perhaps I can improve both my skill and acquire a new one at the same time! Aye, what I am considering may seem a tad... morally dubious, but...'* I rub my hands together, producing neither noise nor any heat. *'...I hear a raccoon inhabits this area.'*

····
········
····

+1 Perception
18 Stat Points Primed

'Well, at least that is something. It will help with my spying, I think.'

It is nighttime, and I am a bit frustrated with my lack of progress in advancing the Naturalist skill and finding the rumored raccoons. I hear movement nearby. Looking toward the tree, I see two furry creatures scurrying about. *'Oh, so it seems there are two raccoons. Perhaps I can assist the old lady with her raccoon problem as payment for eating one of her "gals" as she termed them.'*

Spreading the tendrils, I slither the cattail along the ground and toward the trees while the two raccoons squabble over what looks to be a disemboweled pigeon. *'Are these raccoons mad? Why are they so obsessed with pigeon giblets? Regardless, for one of them, this shall be their final day. I will attempt to make it as swift and painless as possible.'*

I flatten the cattail's tendrils. The two raccoons fail to notice me, but I cannot strike without one of them facing me. I shake the bushes, and one releases the pigeon carcass. Spinning around, the raccoon hisses at me—the cattail darts toward it. My tendrils squirm their way into its eye socket, extinguishing the hapless creature's life.

The surviving raccoon hisses and absconds with the pigeon carcass held firm in its jaws.

A blue wall appears, obstructing my vision.

+1 Agility
17 Stat Points Primed

Entity 1-3-2-3 has exhibited potential in an apt skill spectrum and may select an Aspirant skill.

Entity, see the presented skill adoptions below.

[Aspirant Stealth]
A foundational stealth skill. No specialization is had with this skill, but many entities favor well-roundness and variety for skill paths that might require situational adaptability. Entities may prefer to select specialization later, though it's best not to assume all skill paths will remain open.

[Aspirant Hark]
Stealth skill specialization for entities that generally stay hidden and spring upon unsuspecting adversaries or prey. An entity with this skill prefers not to move about frequently, choosing to instead listen and wait for opportunities to find them.

[Aspirant Snoop]
Specializes in subtle spying and intelligence gathering rather than opening themselves up for retaliation—most fitting for entities that desire to evade direct confrontation and monitor from a distance.

'An unforeseen boon! Stealth! I am astonished I did not receive this sooner, but perhaps it's because I was not sneaking up on the rats in the chamber pot tunnel since they did not see me as a threat. Regardless, I shall accept this skill with grace. Thank thee, Cosmic System!'

Studying the three choices, I consider each of them. 'Hmm, although Hark might be better for my present circumstances, I would speculate Stealth would be much better in the long-term. Snoop is similar as well. I believe it would be rather useful now, yet it may not be as useful later.' I pause, reading through the choices once more. *'Aye, I shall select Stealth. Mayhaps I shall fancy something specialized at a later opportunity.'*

With the Cosmic System's acknowledgment, I shove the wall away and return my attention to the raccoon's carcass. *'Now it is time for Doctor Nightingale to make her long-belated return.'*

Locating a hidden thicket, I lay the raccoon carcass belly up. It takes all my willpower not to engulf the raccoon and bask in the feelings its flavorful body would imbue.

One of its legs twitches as I shake my hands and turn away, suppressing the feeling. *'I shall begin attempting to acquire a medical skill by applying my knowledge of the four humors to this animal. It is challenging to do on a cadaver, but I can certainly endeavor to.'*

I glance at the cattail. Its tendrils are fully unwound and at the ready.

'Some force will be required, and the cattail is my only option. Using the cattail while examining the carcass medically should, from what I have observed, advance both Naturalist and the Whip skill. I hope to also receive an Aspirant medical skill by doing this.'

Lowering myself, I poke at the raccoon's soft belly. My finger has little effect on it, so I arc the cattail over my head. Pushing the cattail against the raccoon's belly causes a bit of blood to leak from its mouth.

My shoulder slump as I stand, wrapping the cattail back around my torso. *'Aye. I require something with a keen-edge.'*

Covering the raccoon carcass in leaves, I roam the shadowy park hunting for something I can use as a dissection tool. Leaving the secluded area, I move toward the Terrace's Arcade. When I pass the fountain, I glance at a layer of snow that surrounds its exterior.

'It seems as if it is rather cold. I imagine most folk would not wish to be out in this weather.' My gaze shifts to a placard embedded into the wall outside the Arcade. *'And seems to be an opportune time to read one of the placards whilst searching for something sharp.'*

I brace my mind to learn what I may. The placard starts like so: "Landmarks of New York. Bethesda Fountain and Terrace".

'Bethesda Terrace is what the sign said on the rooms near the grand staircases... More curiously, what befell the old York in England? Did a ruinous war ravage Yorkshire? There was the Pilgrimage of Grace, but that was a few decades before my time. The Scots perchance?'[39]

I pause while drawing my inky black hair forward. My hair was cherry-red in life, and even that was unfortunate. There were three varieties of people regularly discriminated against in London: blasphemers, Irish, and Scots. Alas, witches were known to have red hair, and so were Scots and Irish. That made me both a blasphemer and a Scot from a young age in the eyes of some. Many people were suspicious, resentful, or even cruel for something so trifling.

Looking toward the ground, I release my hair. It floats near weightlessly behind me as a soft wind blows. I take a moment before raising my head, once more staring at the placard. *'I should keep reading.'*

The placard goes on to speak of what I assume is this place, "Central Park," as well as this place's architecture. The concluding section leaves me quiet. "Installed in 1873 plaque erected 1965."

'...Aye. This is the second placard that implies hundreds of years have passed since my time in Roanoke.' Moving to the fountain, I sit. *'As a Kiln, sitting feels the same as standing, yet it is somehow calming.'*

For a while longer, I sit in silence, kicking my legs and staring at the ground. *'I know Earl told me the time was unknown, but I still did not believe it could be centuries. I left the past because I did not feel like I belonged in the world*

---

[39] The Pilgrimage of Grace: a popular uprising that began in Yorkshire in October 1536, before spreading to other parts of Northern England, under the leadership of lawyer Robert Aske.

as it was, yet the present might be even worse. At least in the past, I understood human society.'

Lifting my head, I look toward the area where the seed is germinating; my thoughts shift. *'But if I do not belong in the past nor the future, then I shall simply create a place I do belong. I am 'alive,' and regardless I am never allowing myself to return to Tenebrous. I shall push onward, despite the era I find myself in. I can at least have a single place that welcomes me cordially... I cannot permit this to distract me from my objectives.'*

I leave the fountain. Some time passes until I discover a brown glass bottle. I hesitate to break it, but the glass's quality seems relatively poor, and it does not seem to be treated particularly well. Thus I shatter the bottle and salvage two shards that shall aid me in my endeavor.

Returning to the raccoon carcass, I toss aside the leaves that cover its body and prepare to dissect it. I am not actually sure how the Cosmic System decides I earned something, so I just act as if I am teaching someone about the humors.

'Aye, Earl! As the only thing that has spoken to me in what has apparently been centuries, thou shalt be my student. Of course, that fiendish Bishop does not count. That was not a conversation.' My mind shudders. *'...Now! Let us begin.'*

I correct my posture and prepare to lecture Earl. *'To start, every person has a unique humoral composition. Oh, I should mention that since it has been centuries, it is possible parts of my knowledge are outdated. We will begin with the simplest of the four: "blood."'*

Taking the piece of glass, I grip it with the cattail's tendrils, fumbling a bit to keep the pointed side facing downwards. As I cut the creature with the glass shard, it becomes apparent that I am mangling it rather than dissecting the creature, but it shall suffice. Exposing the creature's liver, I resume my lecture.

····

········

····

Time passes as the night fades and the sun rises, but I continue my lecture to Earl in tremendous and excruciating detail. Fortunately, he cannot abandon me; otherwise, I believe he would do so.

'So to recap for the tenth and final time. Blood is associated with the liver and a warm temperament. Yellow bile is associated with the gallbladder and an aggressive temperament. Black bile is associated with the spleen and a melancholic temperament. Finally, phlegm is associated with the brain, lungs, and a coy temperament.'

I stare into space, pointing out every detail I can think of to the invisible Earl. It has been so entrancing that I am not even confident how much time has passed. 'Oh my, that was terrific fun. Hmm, I know I said it was the last time, but let us review everything once mo—'

A blue wall appears as if imploring me to stop.

Skill Adoption

Entity 1-3-2-3 has adopted the [Humorism] skill.
Considered a pseudoscience by modern human academics and crude by the sapient races of yore, humorism is a skill that imbues components such as Mana in or out of the humorals. This skill has been left practically unexplored by Mana-intelligent races as those entities elected to travel more refined avenues.

As an Aspirant skill, it must be supplanted by a Novitiate skill within 7 Material-Earth days to obtain permanently.

Fostered Aspirant [Naturalist (Grade 3)]

'It worked! Although, it's odd that it did not give me other choices? Is there a reason it did not offer me a basic medicine skill and simply gave me this one? The description seems a bit demeaning as well. It states it is both crude and unexplored. I do not know if I agree with either of those... Ah, well, nary a need to fret.'

My attention wanders to a nearby tree trunk where a family of squirrels unearths walnuts from the base of a snowdrift. They cram their cheeks, preparing to retreat into the hollow of a tree.

The cattail wriggles in anticipation of a hunt.

····
········
····

Hours pass as I explain the principles of the four humors to Earl. Additionally, I attempt to manipulate the cattail by performing complicated and convoluted movements with it. I do this whilst commenting on what little I know about raccoons and my most recent acquisitions, squirrels and pigeons. At the same time, I gnaw at the nearby plant life in between lecturing and butchering the carcasses. This is all an effort and an experiment to simultaneously raise as many of my skills as possible.

I point at the squirrel carcasses. *'Aye. So as I stated previously, the nature of the soul follows the mixtures of the body. That is except for phlegm, which is thought by some to not have any influence on an individual's character. Phlegm was always a strange one, as it also contributes to odd things like white hair, which is why it is partially associated with old age.'*

Feeling a bit mentally fatigued, I stop, and a blue wall appears.

Fostered Aspirant [Humorism (Grade 1)]
Fostered Aspirant [Humorism (Grade 2)]
Fostered Novitiate [Feline Whip (Grade 1)]
+1 Acuity
+1 Endurance
15 Stat Points Primed

'Ha! Earl, I did so well that the Cosmic System thought me worthy of a second grade in the skill.'

I look toward the sunset with my arms raised in victory. Yet, I am surprised by what I find.

'Wait? That is not a sunset; it is a sunrise. I thought the sun had already risen. Is it rising again? Nay, I certainly did not just spend an entire day and night dissecting animals and lecturing Earl.'

With a feeling of hunger gripping my body, I move my hand to my belly and check my Erysichthon, finding it at eighty-one.

'Good lord!'

I think back, trying to understand how this even happened. Recalling a storm rolling in just after sunrise, I remember speaking of the kidneys to Earl. The day passed, but with my vision, the world is always dyed in a purple hue whether it be day or night. In fact, it can sometimes be difficult to tell what time it is without checking if the moon or sun is out. Though, even in the past, I used to do things like this until I was tired... tired?

'Is it because I do not actually get tired physically, so I simply did not realize it?'

I look toward the bloody mess I made while giving my lecture. Now torn from my instructor's daze, a nagging pain spreads.

'I am starved.'

Dropping the brown glass, the cattail's tendrils open and latch on to the carcasses. Steadily it draws each of them into itself. With the red haze flowing into the shell, I savor the relief the delicious feeling grants me.

> **Earl Interface:**
> Assimilating 'City Pigeon' (Mana Bare)
> Assimilating 'Rabid City Raccoon' (Mana Bare)
> Assimilating 'City Park Squirrel' (Mana Bare)
> Erysichthon abates by 37
> Essence value 2.
> 0.5 Refinable Nebula
> 0.1 Refinable Vitrum

Earl's purple wall appears. *'A generous amount and I even attained two Essence. A bit unexpected as I have never gained any from normal creatures before. Odd, I will have to investigate that later.'*

My hand moves to my chest in relief as I check my Erysichthon value. *'I must be warier. If I had not been consuming all those plants for the Naturalist skill throughout the day and night, I might have inadvertently entered the frenzied state. How embarrassing that would have been...'*

Hearing someone speaking, I lower myself close to the ground. I slink through the thicket, glancing back to find the grass seems to have died where I sat dissecting the animals for over a day. I soon arrive at the edge of the thicket and use my hand to cover my eyes. I listen in on the conversation taking place.

Two male figures stand a distance away from the illumination of the lanterns. I cannot see the two very well. For the most part, I can only perceive one figure is rather large while the other seems smaller with poor posture.

The one with poor posture rubs the nape of his neck. "Y-yo. You the guy?" a youthful voice asks.

The large figure crosses his arms. A hoarse voice coughs, replying, "Depends. Who ya lookin' for?"

'Oh? I believe I would recognize the behavior of miscreants regardless of the era. How fun! A performance after all my hard work!'

The young man makes a stiff smile while burying his hands in his pockets. "I-I expected you to have it with you."

"How did you expect me to bring something so big here?" the hoarse voice asks.

"W-whatever. How do you expect me to pay for it when I haven't even seen it?" He fiddles with something through his pocket at his waist. "Will it even... y'know, 'get' me there?"

"I sent you a picture this morning, remember? I'll also guarantee it'll 'get' you there."

"Yeah, it still had the police harness on it," he murmurs to himself.

"What was that!?"

"Nothing! But! Can one horse really get me there? Like, is it really worth enough?"

'A horse? Perhaps I misheard. A horse will indeed 'get' someone somewhere, but why are they speaking as if this is something illegal? Are horses illegal nowadays, or is this man a simply prigger of prancers.' [40]

"An adult Clydesdale horse is enough. I'd stake my reputation on it."

"B-but, how much..." Looking over his shoulder, he asks, "How much Essence is it worth?"

"Shit, kid. Didn't you do any research before contacting me? An adult Clydesdale horse has more than enough Essence to get you to level one. Guaran-damn-teed!" He emphasizes his vulgar language while holding out his palm and rubbing two of his fingers together. "Now, are you gonna buy the thing or what, kid? I'm not stickin' round here much longer."

'Essence? These people are in the Beta. So... this young man is buying a horse from a prigger to harvest the Essence from it? Do ordinary people level from Essence? If that is the case, I seem to be at a disadvantage... Not fair!'

The young man hesitates, stuttering. "I-I don't know. M-my parents don't even know I'm in the Beta. They think it's all just people taking some new drug and other dumb shit like that. Will they really understand why I'm doing what I'm doing?"

"Of course anyone who didn't get in wouldn't want to believe they weren't chosen," the hoarse-voiced man declares.

"But the System said it didn't pick chosen ones..."

"You know what I mean, kid! It just means they lacked something that didn't allow them into the Beta." The hoarse voice huffs. "Goddamn. This is a waste of time. Decide quick, kid! This System shit can be dangerous to talk about in the open right now."

"I-I..."

---

[40] Prigger of prancers: roguish 16th century slang for horse-thief. In 16th century London 'Prigging Laws' were laws against stealing horses.

"Never look a gift horse in the mouth, kid." He laughs. "That joke was for free; now, I'm not waiting another millisecond." Again he holds up his palm, waiting for the young man to, I presume, pay him.

The kid reaches into his pocket, fiddling with whatever it is. He looks toward the ground, his mouth opening and closing.

"Fuck it! Just forget it! I'm leaving!"

"Wait! Fine! I'm buyin'," the youth shouts, raising a hand to stop the hoarse man from leaving. "N-now, how are we gonna do this?"

"Just give me the gold. No paper like we talked about. I'll give you an address and a syringe potent enough to down an elephant. Just inject it, it'll close its eyes, and a few minutes later, you'll get the prompt from the Cosmic System. Easy peasy lemon squeezy." A throaty chuckle follows the person's explanation.

"Alright, let's do it," the boy says. "Here, a two-hundred-gram gold bar, for the Essence."

The hoarse man laughs. "I'm sure your parents will understand why you stole from them in the future." I can hear the rustling of objects as the two people swap items. "Good. Now you go one way, and I'll go the other. Careful to not let yourself be seen by anyone if you can avoid it."

The hoarse man turns and walks away, leaving the young man staring at a piece of paper in his hands.

'I never considered it before now, since this place is already so strange, but something like the Cosmic System would have substantial affects upon this era.'

I watch as the young man turns and disappears into the cold night.

'It was a fascinating conversation, but I need to focus on my own means of gaining strength. I doubt I shall be able to purchase Essence from anyone anytime soon. Though it would be nice to have someone to talk to for various reasons.'

Summoning the blue Status wall, I check my mana and Erysichthon values. I ponder my next course of action, ultimately deciding that tonight I shall search for a place to hide near this "Boathouse," where I heard the wealthy students enjoy studying. If all goes well, I may find some reading material that I can use to study the subjects Earl recommended. Looking toward the sky and seeing it will be a bit more time until nightfall, I spend the rest of the day moving about my thicket listening in on conversations.

····

·········

····

Once the snowy night arrives, I make my move and dash across the park's lake. *'All that time eavesdropping, and I never did advance my Stealth skill.'*

Seven hundred steps later, I encounter a bright building in the distance that I hope is the "Central Café next to the Boathouse." The building is quite beautiful and well lit, resembling a beacon in an otherwise gloomy place, much like this city. Unfortunately for me, people seem to be on a patio outdoors enjoying a late-night banquet. A woman walks between decorated tables, greeting guests. She wears a poofy white gown with an open top and exposed shoulders. Her pale skin is flush from the cold, but the woman's posture and demeanor are reminiscent of those of a noble. I glance down at my own attire, realizing our gowns are somewhat similar.

Spreading my arms, I fall backward onto the moonlit water's surface. *'I shall have to wait for them to leave.'* I float above the water, gazing at a sky that never finds peace within the confines of this sleepless city. *'I have been unable to see the stars since I arrived in this era. Have the stars faded like the world that I once recognized?'*

Yet, as it did when I first fled into this park, the silvery moon hangs high in the sky. Its reflection on the water encircles me, making it feel as if I am lying upon the moon itself. Around me, tiny snowflakes disturb the lake, creating small ripples upon the surface.

'...Aye. Even if I must do it on my own, I shall make my own place in this world. Perhaps that place may even have stars to keep the moon company.'

As I lie there, a sweet and elegant voice rings in my head. {*The spirit on the lake, may I ask what you are doing?*}

An azure falling star streaks across the sky as I stare blankly into the heavens above. {*God? Is that thee?*} I ask in my head. {*It is me, remember who I am? Didst thou forgettest about me? Or dost thou com'st to haunt me anew?*}

{I am neither God nor ghost, but I'll lend you my ear if you need to confess,} the voice answers. {I've also been told I have a tenacious memory, so don't worry, I won't forget you.}

{Aye. I have much to confess. It all began when I was born... Wait. I am being silly. Is this Earl, perchance? Earl, didst thou get a voice? Thy voice is vastly more feminine than I anticipated. My apologies for conferring thee such a masculine name. Still, I am delighted that thou mayst apparently speak.}

A moment passes as I begin to ponder whether or not I might be hallucinating. '...It is rather curious how willing I am to accept that voices are speaking in my head. Peculiar things are happening so often that a voice in my head hardly felt strange at all.'

The voice rings in my head once more, causing me to flinch. {It's okay if you're confused. That's normal for spirits as their consciousness ages without the protection of their soul. So, to answer your questions, I am not God, nor am I this 'Earl.'}

'Huh? Is this person hereabouts...? Is it even a person?'

I swing my head to and fro and then run my vision across the people at the party. Most everyone is preoccupied with idle conversation or other such activities. At one table, a young gentlewoman in a beautiful purple dress flips through what looks to be a weighty silver tome, but her focus seems fixed upon the tome's pages rather than me.

{Then who art thou, and how are we speaking?} I inquire with wariness.

For a moment, the voice is quiet. {I am... a friend to spirits? Also, sprite and fairy? Plus, mermaids? Yes... I am a friend of all magical creatures?}

'Why is she stating that like they are questions? As if I am meant to know who she is a friend of.'

{I am speaking to you through a telepathic link,} the voice adds.

'I do not understand what is happening, but I am speaking to someone! But... after the Bishop, I should be cautious of who I speak to or what I say. Still, I cannot squander an opportunity like this. Who knows if there are many people out there that may speak to me at all.' As I am about to attempt to respond, I realize something. 'Wait, can she hear all my thoughts? Even at this very moment? I should find out how this telepathic link thing works. Oh, and what 'telepathic' means.'

Suppressing my inner turbulence, I advance the conversation. {Telepathic link? What is that? Prithee, I would very much like to know.}

{I will tell you if you answer a question of mine first? How about it?} the voice states without delay.

'I should not accept, or she will take control of the discussion... I shall offer her a compromise. Aye, Constance, negotiating is not our strength, but we can do this... I should not think about such things before getting more information!'

{Nay. First, I'd like to know how this telepathic link thing works; then I shall answer two of thy questions,} I state calmly and confidently.

{You seem rather cautious... May I ask why that is?}

{Because if thou art reading my thoughts, I am uncertain I desire to continue this conversation.}

{Does a spirit really have a need for secrets? You are a spirit, right?}

{A spir–} I am struck by a realization. {Wait, art thou trying to trick me with casual questions? This is trickery! Answer my questions first!}

The voice speaks with some amusement in its tone. {Well, I think I understand your concerns, so to answer them, no, I'm not reading your mind. Telepathy is necessary to talk to spirits since they cannot speak back, but only very skilled users can eavesdrop on thoughts; at least that's what I was taught...}

'Could she be one of those very skilled users?' I think in my head.

{And, no, I'm not one of those users,} the voice says.

{Then how didst thou knowest what I was thinking!?}

I could swear I hear a laugh in the distance when the voice replies, {Because logically, that is what you'd think next?}

'A likely explanation... Promptly ask thy question.' Slyly, I lay a trap by thinking instead of deliberately addressing her; I pause to see if she springs it. 'Wait. Would they comprehend or surmise I am endeavoring to lure them into a snare...? This is all too perplexing.'

{Are you there? I don't get out much, so I haven't had many opportunities to use this skill... Did I lose the link?}

'I must assume they do not harbor ill intent until circumstances suggest otherwise. After all, this is a genuine person, and I truly need knowledge or mayhaps even aid.'

{I still linger!}

{Terrific, now I'll ask my first question. Are you a spirit?}

'Am I a spirit? Well, I share some qualities, and I received this body after being hanged, so why not say I am similar? Explaining what a Kiln is difficult, and perhaps unwise as well. I do not know what a real spirit is like, so who is to say I am not similar?' I brush my hair back, and answer, {I suppose I am akin to a spirit. So, I am spirit-like.}

{Spirit-like? That's rather vague. Can you elaborate?}

{Elaborate? Nay. I answered thy query to the best of my abilities. Therefore, next question.}

{Next question? I would hardly say you answered the first one!}

{Fine, fine. I do not possess a body in the traditional sense, so I deem myself spirit-like.}

{Okay, I'll be satisfied if you answer this next question.} The voice becomes more monotone as if they are reading. {Do you have a corporeal human, animal, mechanical, golem, or comparable body?}

Holding my hand up, I stare at it, turning it back and forth. {Nay. Although I do not quite understand thy question in full, I do not have a corporeal body. Hence I assume I do not fall under any of those things.}

{Then, you just sound like a spirit with extra steps.}

{If that is what thou wishest to think.} I drop my hand. {Next question.}

{Okay, then if you're a spirit or spirit-like, are you a human spirit? If not, then what kind of spirit are you?}

{I was a person, but I am not anymore.}

{What does that mean?}

{That's a lot of questions when it is my turn to inquire.}

{I'd argue you didn't fully answer, but since you clarified my first question, I think it's fair to say it's your turn.}

{Hmm.} I nod, asking, {Where am I?}

{That's all you wish to know?} the voice questions in disbelief. {You are in the Lake in Central Park at the heart of New York City.}

{A park in the middle of a city called New York. Canst thou tellest me the specific name of this lake?}

{It's the Lake,} the voice replies.

'Perhaps she does not understand what I mean?' I attempt to reword my question. {Aye, I know it is the lake, but what would a local person call this lake?}

A laugh echoes across the water. {The Lake,} the voice responds.

This time I respond with a bit of annoyance in my tone. {Aye, again, I understand it is the lake, but what name would appear on a map? For example, Lough Neagh, Lake Queen, Black Water, Crystal Lake.}

{The name is quite literally the Lake,} the voice states, having waited patiently for me to finish. {New Yorkers refer to it as the Lake. If you had a map, it would say, 'this is the Lake.'}

{Oh. That is rather uncreative. Are there no other lakes in the world? Why is it named something so dull and flavorless?}

{There are plenty of other lakes in the world. Though there are not many in this area, I'll admit. Maybe you can give it your own name if you aren't satisfied with the current one.}

{Perhaps I shall... Lake...} I glance about and then shrug. {Lake Water. This is Lake Water. Behold, a better name! I want to say it was challenging to choose a better one... but it was not.}

{I'm embarrassed to admit that I actually sort of like that name. But, more importantly, I believe you've asked six questions, and I have answered them all. Does that mean...?} The voice pauses, and I realize what she is implying.

{Nay, thou cannot ask six questions now! Thou may only blame thyself for answering so many.}

{Fine. I guess I can live with that. Still, it is my turn for a question.} The voice does not continue immediately, as if they are thinking. {I was going to ask what kind of spirit you were, but now I'd rather ask... when did you... uhm, stop cooking?}

{...Stop cooking?} I pause, thinking about my last meal in my humble cottage. I recall frying some venison in my iron pan—I adored that pan. A kettle of stock was stewing nearby. The previous night had been chilly, and I was looking forward to it. I remember being excited as the natives had supplied me with a stock of potatoes and herbs that promised to be tasty. It was for naught, though. A knock at the door would come, and the ravenous faces of Preacher Daniels, Thomas, and Edmond English would be there. {...Wait. Art thou attempting to ask when I... perished?}

{In a sense, yes.}

{I believe that is the only sense, but regardless, I appreciate the subtlety.} My gaze turns to the reflection of the moon. {Still, I... I would rather not discuss that topic.}

{I have read that it isn't uncommon for spirits not to want to discuss such things, but if I know how 'recent' you are, I can better answer your questions.}

Horrid thoughts of Tenebrous and that eve squirm their way into my mind. I force out the answer. {I believe I... 'stopped cooking'... in 1590 of the Pale Moon.}

{1590 PME!? You've managed to keep your sanity for so many centuries!} the voice shouts with excitement before continuing. {That's unheard of... Unless.} The voice goes silent in thought.

I cross my arms, furrowing my brow. {I find thy reaction rather insensitive! The year of my death is not something to be excited about! It was quite difficult for me to think about.} I realize something else about the words of the voice. {Also, art thou implying that I may have lost my sanity!? I am very sane, the sanest, in fact! So sane that others seem mad in comparison!}

{I'm sorry, I didn't mean to offend you. I was just going to say... unless you have a powerful and sane mind–} Things go quiet for a moment before she continues. {And now that I know you... passed so long ago, I'll add that you're also in a country called the United States of America.}

{The what of America? Is that the real name of the lake?}

{No, as we've discussed, the lake is the Lake, and it's the United States of America... It's very complicated, but this is no longer an English colony. It's now its own country.}

{And the Crown simply stood by and let such a thing happen?} I question.

{Well, there was a rebellion.}

{Rebels? Traitors? Such a thing! Wait, did the French have something to do with it? They must have; they always have a hand in everything. They are tricksters, after all.}

{You are not wrong, I guess, but they didn't instigate it... I think? Were you a firm loyalist or something?}

{Loyalist?} I respond, hearing the unfamiliar word.

{By that, I mean, were you loyal to the English monarchy?}

{Loyal to the Crown? I fancied my homeland despite its myriad of faults and the reality that I felt lonesome in a bustling city. But that was less about loyalty to anyone, more that I was incapable of partaking in society. I was simply incompatible with most folk due to my... health. Still, to answer thy query, I would say nay, I was not loyal to Elizabeth. The Crown was not fond of my existence, *and I was not fond of their incessant persecution and bending of the knee to noble whims. I was merely startled that the Crown would permit something like a rebellion to spiral so far out of hand.}*

I notice a vague feeling of being watched, so I turn my head. My attention turns toward the café patio. There I see the same gentlewoman in purple who was previously reading a hefty tome.

{Are you still there?} the voice asks with concern. *{Are you near those violet lights?}*

{Didst thou sayst something? My apologies, but I believe someone is staring at me.}

{Staring at you?} The gentlewoman tilts her head. *{What do they look like? Maybe I can tell you if I know them.}*

'Is that to whom I am speaking...? If she desires a description, perhaps I shall deliver her a flowery narrative to see if I can elicit a reaction and confirm if it is her or not.'

I peer at the gentlewoman and collect my flatteries. *{It is a gentlewoman in a long flowing gown awash in lavender. She is wearing a veil that matches her lavender attire. If I am not mistaken, she has distinctive silver hair that falls to her lower back. Yet, it is not gray, but rather glittering, silky, and resplendent, and I can glimpse the moonlight reflecting upon it, dyeing it a bluish-silver. As for her heighth, I would say she is on the shorter side compared to the people around her. Her figure is slender with unparalleled proportions as if sculpted from marble. Either she is gazing out over the lake wistfully or at me, I cannot tell, but it is like a royal would stare out over a crowd of their citizens. Though, truthfully, it paints a rather melancholic portrait as if a mosaic set into a church's stained glass window.}*

The gentlewoman's mouth cracks open as if she does not know how to respond. *{...}*

{Ohh, the gentlewoman in lavender looks to have a bemused expression... Could that be thee by some chance?}

{I wasn't anticipating such a silver-tongued portrayal. Your words caught me a little off-guard, which isn't easy to do nowadays. But... I almost feel as if I should choose my words cautiously, or I might risk... 'feeding the troll,' so to speak.}

Someone walks up behind the gentlewoman and whispers something into her ear. {Ah, I'm sorry. I actually need to leave. My ride has been idling for a while now.}

{Thy ride? It may tarry for one moment longer, aye?}

{I'm sorry. It can't... and I have some things to mull over, so my mind is a little busy. Forgive me. I will return the night after tomorrow, around this time, but I must be going for now...} The gentlewoman smiles and waves at me. {I'll see you then, yes?}

{...Aye? And fare thee well, I suppose.} I watch the gentlewoman hurry away and fade into the dusk. '...Eventide after next, hmm.'

Chapter 8: A Raptor Fopdoodle and the Noble's Guards

∞∞∞∞∞∞∞∞∞∞∞∞∞∞∞∞

An hour or so passes before the café's lights fade and the last of the people stroll away from the building. *'I wonder if the gentlewomen shall return as she claimed she would. She seemed eager to do so, but I pray I did not leave a poor impression upon her. Mayhaps I should not have asked her so many questions, yet she is the first person I have spoken to in quite a long time. That includes not only my time in Tenebrous but also much of my time in Roanoke. Of course, there was the Bishop, but that was more him threatening me than a conversation.'*

Standing and moving toward the café's rear, I reach a patio bestrewn with pearly rose petals. The café's patio is enclosed by ten white columns and black metal rails between each pair. Gorgeous white ribbons ornamented with fresh lilies coil around the columns and railing, making for an elegant air. *'It must have been a lovely wedding, but God in Light, I cannot fathom the coin such an affair would demand.'*

Passing through the railing with space to spare, I am greeted by rows of windowpanes and a long open venue overlooking the Lake. On the café's patio, I notice that most tables have been slid together as one might anticipate at a busy formal affair. The tables' legs are chained together for some reason, mayhaps to deter thievery.

My attention drifts to a row of tables left unchained and uniformly spread around the patio. The white cloth that shrouded them earlier has been removed, but these tables have something left atop it. *'I believe I could nibble one of those.'*

Using the cattail, I engulf one, and a colorful haze flows through me, alongside a faint grassy feeling.

Earl Interface:
Assimilating 'Forget-Me-Not Flower Bouquet' (Mana Bare)
Erysichthon abates by 8
Essence value is negligible.
0.0 Refinable Nebula
0.1 Refinable Vitrum

'Forget-me-not? That's a lovely name, and I have tasted vastly worse. Perhaps I shall consume a couple more.'

I devour two additional bouquets and then move to the windows. Peeking inside, I see a room that emanates an atmosphere of grace. Tables clad in pristine white cloth and set with candlesticks are accented by skillfully crafted wooden chairs and exquisite glass fixtures hanging from the ceiling. 'I have never dined anywhere other than my own dwelling before.' I glance down at my body. 'And I suppose I never will... Regardless, I do not feel this is the study place the two people spoke of yesterday. Perhaps it is on the other side?'

Strolling along the building's side, I come round to its front. The white wooden exterior is now a red brick, and although the building is splendid, its front façade is less elegant than its rear. There is another spacious brick patio: this patio has benches along one side and then black metal tables on the other. Each table bears a green umbrella, presumably to shield guests from the sun's heat. 'It's not how I envisioned it, but I would wager this area is more akin to a place someone might study. The previous place felt too grand to be a study room.' I notice some hedges near the patio's edge. 'Not the most ideal location to eavesdrop from, but it's likewise the only location.'

After selecting a location where I shall hide, I skulk further along the building, encountering a second entrance. 'This entryway should lead to the elegant room and patio at the rear. As I thought, the two locations are separate places... But, what's that? A list of dishes?' I move closer, suspecting my eyes may be deceiving me. 'Picking thy own meal! That confirms it; this place must be where the richest nobles in the city feast.'

As I read through the list of dishes, I shake my head. 'Oysters, pork, lamb, and a myriad of foods I have never seen. What is the difference between a king oyster and a typical oyster? Is it an oyster fit for a king? How rich could the folk that eat here be? Is the gentlewoman wealthy as well?'

My eyes drift to a bright blue paper next to it.

Welcome Guest to the Reception of the Newlywed

Mister & Misses Starland

Guest Cocktail Menu

NEW YORK CITY COCKTAILS

Galtry-Manhattan
Silver Shrapnel Vodka, Sweet Vermouth, Brooklyn Bitters.
virgin blend available upon request

Lurlann Old Fashioned
Blackwell Island Bourbon, Brooklyn Bitters, Maraschino Cherries.

OLDE CLASSIC COCKTAILS

Rushlight Ember-Mites
Genever Gin, Brooklyn Bitters, Cranberry Juice, White Sugar, Wood Strawberry Mash.
served with a festive garnishing of maple-infused rushlight

Vierge Éclat's Kiss Martini
Black Raspberry Cognac, Pineapple Juice, Raspberry Liqueur.
both shaken & stirred

Shāngāo Tincture
Baijiu, Rosé Champagne Splash, Zesty Lemongrass, Fresh Lychee Purée.

CHEF COCKTAILS

President EggCrackin
Boilermaker. Scotch Whiskey & Irish Cream shot served alongside a half-glass of eggnog.

BOATHOUSE AT CENTRAL PARK

'Ah. I recall someone mentioning the name "Boathouse" whilst eavesdropping. But this was for the wedding reception? What is a cocktail? Liquor? ... Vierge Éclat's kiss. Revolting! Pecking lips with one of those hardhearted Éclat, perish the thought!'

A scratchy voice comes from nearby. "Yep, it's right this way, I promise."

'Someone is approaching!' I dash into the bushes I found earlier.

"Thanks so much for walking me," a feminine voice says with a slur.

'Speaking of kissing, that woman has kissed her cup one too many times this eve; she is undoubtedly drunk.' I shake my head. 'That or she ingested a bushel of lubberwort.'[41]

A man chuckles in a manner reminiscent of a hog. "No problem, sweetie pie. We'll be at your place before you know it."

'It's good that they have resolved sweetie pie's problem, but the man is behaving oddly. I suspect he has ill intentions.'

"That's sooo weird, don't call me sweetie pie." The young woman giggles. "I'm so glad you knew this shortcut, though."

"Come on. It's just around this corner." The man smirks. "Ah man, you don't look so good."

The woman barely reacts as her words grow quieter. "I-I shouldn't have had that EggCrackin. I think I drank too-too," she closes her eyes and swallows, "too much."

"Here, I'll carry you the rest of the way home," the man says, clapping his hands together. "Like, the true gentlemen I am."

She shakes her head. Holding up her hand, she stutters something incoherent and then falls forward.

---

[41] Lubberwort: a fictitious plant that would cause sluggishness or boneheadedness. It later came to be used as a nickname for a lethargic or fuzzy-minded person.

The man catches her. "Finally. Geez, I thought I was gonna have to walk her in circles all night." He tosses the woman over his shoulder and squeezes her posterior. "Now, let's go find us a nice quiet place."

'This. This. This absolute... fopdoodle!' [42] I stalk the raptor as he carries the young woman deeper into the park. [43] My cattail swallows gravel and stone along way, and it expands to around a foot wide—the maximum circumference the cattail can stretch itself at present. He veers onto an unlit footpath. A thousand steps later, he moves into a dense copse of trees.

Approaching a rock, he lays the young woman upon it. His mouth curves into a lecherous smile. "Hell yeah. It's been a while since I've had such a young piece of meat." He commences removing his trousers with a laugh. "It's cold, so let's hurry this up, or I'll be frozen stiff."

Ebony clouds drift across the sky, obstructing moonlight and blackening the thicket further as I shout in my head, *'Enough of this filth, I shall bestow upon thee an unforgettable thrashing, raptor.'* The laden cattail rustles the bushes as I heave it into the air.

"Hey!" He spins around and shouts, "Who's there!? Dammit, I can't see shit." I step from the bushes, and the fopdoodle squints. "Someone with a pair of blacklights?" He pulls up his trousers and reaches into a pocket at his back, drawing some sort of metal object. "Whoever you are, I recommend you go ahead and turn around," he declares, bumbling over his own clothes. "I swear I'll shoot your ass."

His peculiar words stir a second's hesitation. *'I do not understand, but it matters not.'*

As I step nearer, he sneers, proclaiming, "My buddies are nearby, so either I shoot you, or they gut you. There's no winning this unless you tuck tail now and skedaddle on outta here."

I take aim.

---

[42] Fopdoodle: A stupid or insignificant fellow. Fool. Simpleton.
[43] Raptor: a robber, plunderer, abductor, ravisher.

He smirks. "Well, I warned ya."

There's a deafening bang as splinters of wood rain down around me. *'Matchlock pistol!?'*

I swing the cattail, striking his knee. The knee cracks as his leg bows backward. He screams. Crumpling into a snowdrift, he wails, "I'll fuckin' kill you!"

He raises the handgun. Five roaring blasts. Bullets pierce the haze, punching holes into the comrade cracker adaptation. I smash his left hand. As I bash his right shoulder, the handgun plunges into the snow. The fopdoodle writhes on the ground; his hand's fingers are bent at odd angles with bone visible through punctures in the flesh. Patches of black blotches his skin—symptoms of the plague.

I look toward where the handgun sank into the snow. *'How can a matchlock hold so many pellets!? Thank the lord my cattail is stronger than I realized.'*

"You bastard! This was the biggest mistake of your life!" His eyes bloodshot, he shivers in rage. "My family will fuckin' find you; they'll butcher you and anyone you love!"

Fostered Novitiate [Feline Whip (Grade 2)]
+1 Strength +1 Acuity **13 Stat Points Primed**

Shoving aside the blue wall, I glance at the howling fopdoodle. *'I love no one, and none love me.'* My gaze strays to the young woman. *'I should not abandon her; it is too dangerous and cold.'*

He tries to stand, so I extend the cattail and drop the gravel and stones onto his head. I glimpse a bone protruding from the skin near his knee. *'I require some of thy possessions. Know thou hast naught to blame but thyself, for what I am about to do shall hurt tremendously!'*

With the tendrils, I seize his trousers and yank. He cries as I draw the trousers over the bone. Next I reach for his shirt and tug it over his head, forcing his arms to flail about in the air. He curses me as I push his hands through the armholes until the shirt slips off as well.

His eyes glaze over as he loses blood. "Are you wearing one of those morph suits because you're scared of me finding out who you are!?" he screams with snot and tears streaming down his cheeks. "Hey, dead man, you better not leave me out here like this! The Dryas Cyclone is coming through; I'll freeze to death!" He swings his arm at me, spattering droplets of blood at my feet. "Or are you a psycho murdering bitch too!"

I peer into his eyes, recalling what I did to the raccoon a day or so prior. *'Nay. I must depart. The handgun was deafening, and he stated his companions are near, so someone shall come for him soon.'*

"You know Galtry, that cloth-faced bitch!? She's nothing compared to us!" He spits blood at me. "Fucking nothing! Just wait, asshole, just wait!"

My eyes sharpen upon him, and hunger pangs my kiln. *'He is fortunate I ate those bouquets, or I might be tempted to do something egregious... I doubt he would fit in the cattail anyway; too fat...'* I turn away. *'These urges are evermore worrisome.'*

I ignore his abuses and toss the trousers and shirt into a snowdrift near the rock the woman lies atop. Grasping a tree limb, I nudge the woman until she rolls off the rock. She tumbles off, her posterior drops onto the shirt while her head comes to rest between the split in the trousers.

Gripping the trouser legs, I drag the woman along the footpath. "Didn't you hear what I said!? Cyclone! Cold! Die! Call someone, moron, call someone to help me!" he shouts.

I glimpse leather boots half-immersed in the snow at my feet. *'My Erysichthon value has risen a tad; these should help reduce it.'*

The cattail slithers toward the boots. Ebony clouds overhead separate, unveiling the moon; blue light trickles into the thicket. My haze reflects the moonlight, decorating my figure in a blue glimmer.

His mouth falls open, witnessing tendrils draw his boots into my cattail. "W-what kind of messed-up science experiment are you!?" he squeaks. "You're a freak of nature!"

We exit the copse as his screams grow shriller and tongue filthier.

Earl Interface:
Assimilating 'Crocodile Leather Boots' (Mana Bare)
Erysichthon abates by 10
Essence value is less than one.
0.1 Refinable Nebula
0.0 Refinable Vitrum

I pause in a clearing as a purple wall appears displaying the boot's peculiar name; yet, the most prominent thing is its taste. *'Rubbish tastes better than this, but it is to be expected when such a foul flesh has worn them.'* Earl's wall reminds me of something. *'I should select a new adaptation lest I happen upon one of his raptor companions. Earl, prithee, display the adaptation wall, only include things I can afford.'*

Earl Interface:

Cannot afford adaptations. Low levels of Refined Nebula

Essence Available: 39 [R = 88%]
Refined Nebula Available: 0.2 [4.9]
Refined Vitrum Available: 5.0 [1.8]
Refined Unknown Superacid: 0.5 (0.0)

'I lack the refined Nebula and Essence, so I can afford naught.' Glancing at the woman, I see her shivering to a perturbing extent. *'Let's focus on sneaking her to the café.'*

With a tug, the trousers and shirt slide atop the snow; the fopdoodle's curses fade away.

····

·········

····

I arrive at the Central Café, but my gaze drifts to the lavish location next to it—the one that permits nobles to select their own meals. Outside I glimpse a sign bearing its name, "The Boathouse." I drag the woman to the Boathouse's entrance and take a moment to assess her condition. *'Her humors are dreadfully out of balance; thank the lord she is young. Still, if things continue like this, she might freeze to death before anyone trustworthy comes. Mayhaps, I could...?'*

A blue wall interrupts me.

Fostered Aspirant [Humorism (Grade 3)]
+1 Fortitude
12 Stat Points Primed

Dismissing the wall, I move toward a window and peer inside. My eyes fixate upon the thick tablecloths. *'Aye, a shelter and blankets to warm her body. I shall have to think of a way to get inside.'* I return to the entrance and push, yet it refuses to move. *'Locked. Why of course it is! It would never be so simple.'* I approach the window and inspect them. *'There are no hinges; these windows do not appear to be capable of opening.'*

Walking around the building's exterior two times, I still do not find a way into this fortress. When I return to the woman, I find her condition has worsened. Her complexion is pale, and she has stopped shivering. Even while in her unconscious stupor, the woman kicks off her shoes as if she is hot despite the freezing temperatures. *'If she has stopped shivering without reason, then she is worse than I imagined. She is at risk of succumbing to the cold. Her situation is dire; I cannot afford to search for a discrete way inside...'*

I wrap the cattail's tendrils around a steel chair's leg. The chair smashes through the window, strewing glass along the floor. Clambering into the Boathouse, I manage to open the door by pressing against a bar that runs across the door's front. I step outside to tow the woman inside. The door closes and locks behind me. *'Foolish door! Thou shan't best me!'*

Going back inside, the same situation recurs several times: open door, try to drag woman inside, door closes and locks. This goes on until I manage to wedge a chair against the door. *'Let's get thee inside, and I shall cover thee.'* I bring her in and take some of the white cloths from the tables, placing them atop the woman. A few minutes pass, and she is shivering once again. *'That is a promising sign. Is there anything else I could utilize to warm her; perhaps, a lantern I could light and set it near her?'*

I climb onto a table and push up onto my tiptoes to investigate one of the lanterns, encountering what looks to be a glass orb. *'What is this? I knew it was not candlelight, but I did not believe this was what it would look like. Fascinating, but I doubt I shall be able to use this, and even if I could, I do not have the slightest notion of how.'* I hop from the table, drift to the floor, and resume exploring. *'This place is enchanting... and I presume it must have a kitchen.'* In the Boathouse's rear, I notice a small corridor. *'Back there perchance?'*

Stepping into the corridor, I find a pair of silver doors with tiny windows. I push at the doors, and with a squeak, they open, revealing a silver room that leaves me tilting my head. *'What is all this? Where is the fire pit? ...Wait, I cannot recall glimpsing a chimney sticking from the roof. Is the building unheated? Where do they cook the food?'* My curiosity ensnares me as I open, close, and examine everything I feel comfortable fiddling with. *'There are so many things I am unfamiliar with. It's all so intriguing... What is that big silver box in the corner?'*

I approach the silver box and peek through the window, observing a chilly-looking mist. Noticing a bar on the front, I grasp it with the tendrils and yank. The silver box swings open and the mist escapes, spreading along the floor. Walking inside, I find myself amongst a variety of meats.

A palm moves to my stomach. *'A noble's pantry! Vast amounts of nobles' food... and the brutish winds have made me dreadfully hungry. I want a pantry; Earl, I demand a pantry in my Tower!'* Discovering a slab of enthralling meat, I realize what it is and squeeze my hands together. *'Lamb. I have never had lamb before. Perhaps, I may... sample a wee morsel.'*

As if obtaining consent, my cattail expands and engulfs the lamb. The meat melts within the cattail. It does not stop there; the cattail devours every scrap of lamb, beef, chicken, fish, and whatever else it may reach. Streams of pulpy red haze course through the cattail down my torso and into the shell of the kiln.

My legs quiver as delectable sensations that are incomparable to anything I experienced in life pour into my kiln. The cattail continues its feast, swallowing everything, creating such a flavorful symphony that my mind blanks in ecstasy. Earl's walls pop in and out of existence, reappearing with larger numbers each time until finally one oversized summary floats before me.

Earl Interface:
Assimilating 'Loin of Lamb' (Mana Bare)
Assimilating 'Sea Scallops' (Mana Bare)
Assimilating 'King Oyster' (Mana Bare)
Assimilating 'Gulf Shrimp' (Mana Bare)
Assimilating 'Salmon Fillet' (Mana Bare)
Assimilating 'Striped Bass Fillet' (Mana Bare)
Assimilating 'Tuna Fillet' (Mana Bare)
Assimilating 'Fillet of Beef' (Mana Bare)
Assimilating 'Pork Tenderloin' (Mana Bare)
Assimilating 'Chicken Breast' (Mana Bare)

.
.
.

Erysichthon falls to zero.
Essence value 43
2.4 Refinable Nebula
0.7 Refinable Vitrum

'That... was delicious.' My gaze moves across the room where empty containers and bags lie strewn about. 'I believe I might have devoured everything... I should take my leave.'

A blue wall appears.

Entity 1-3-2-3 has fulfilled a hidden condition: eat enough meat to feed at least thirty Toba Humans. The Entity's Title will be updated.

Updated Title: Parasitic Thief +

The one who possesses this Title is a creature that frequently steals and is unable to survive without acquiring something from others. To receive this Title, one must have acquired it to the great detriment of another while offering nothing in return.

{Wow! There was enough meat there for a feast. You sure do steal and eat a lot! A parasite and a thief; quite the combination you have going there. Taste and any benefits from stolen food are increased even further.}

Reading the message, I swipe at the blue wall. My hand passes through, and the wall vanishes. *Do not mock me; the reason this is happening is because of thy title! I knew it was too delicious!*

I exit the kitchen, discovering red and blue lights flashing through the windows. Hiding under one of the tables, I watch a man and a woman in black garments bearing silver badges skulking outside. *'I believe I recognize these two! If I recall, they are named Jessica and Leo. They were there the day I arrived in the park.'*

"We have a busted window here; someone has forced entry," Leo says. "Radio central for backup."

I keep low beneath the table, obstructing my bright violet eyes with my arm. Through my arm's haze, I watch and listen to the conversation between Jessica and Leo.

"Right, I'll radio..." Jessica pauses and then points at the young woman on the floor. "I think there's a girl on the floor."

"Huh?" A pair of clicking noises accompanies two blinding lights. The lights illuminate the shivering young woman, and Leo draws a handgun from his belt. "Yeah, there is, and she's showing symptoms of severe hypothermia. Radio for an ambulance as well; when backup arrives, we'll drag her out of there."

Jessica nods, drawing a black box from her waist. She speaks into the black box. "928 to central."

To my amazement, a voice responds, "928, go ahead."

"We have a suspected 10-21 in progress at the Boathouse restaurant and rental site in Central Park. We are requesting backup and an ambulance for a civilian down."

"928 copy." A shrill hum emanates from the black square, and it speaks once again. "Central to all available units in Precinct, 928 is seeking assistance with suspected 10-21 in progress, stated civilian down. Location: Central Park, Park Drive Northeast, the Boathouse restaurant. Are any units in the immediate area available to respond?"

"876 copies, en route."

"Roger, 876."

'It sounds as if Jessica and Leo desire to assist the young woman.'

"The woman," Jessica says, fastening the black box to her belt. "Maybe we should drag her out now and then egress until backup arrives? That way, we aren't just standing here in the open like oafs."

"Like I said, we're waiting for backup."

She frowns. "The Park Hill disappearances were only about a month ago. We shouldn't stand around."

"This ain't Park Hill." He shakes his head. "Wait on backup."

With a sigh and a roll of her eyes, she nods. "Yeah, 10-4."

'Time to depart.' Squatting, I wait for my chance to abscond. *'This has gone beyond my aid, and besides, Jessica's words confirm their intention is to help.'* Jessica and Leo continue swinging their lights about the room as if searching for someone. *'It's an utter mystery for whom they might be searching, and I prefer it remains that way.'*

Using the tendrils, I grasp what I can find and cast it toward the far side of the room. The object smacks the wall—a light darts toward it.

"Someone's definitely in there, Jessica! They threw a saltshaker; I saw it," Leo says, keeping his handgun at the ready. "We know you're in there! Come out with your hands up!"

'That did not go as I wished.' I crawl from table to table. The cattail slithers behind me like an actual tail, yet I cannot wrap it around me to hide it lest I require it. *'There was a rear-entry; I shall flee through there.'*

"There, I see someone trying to use the backdoor to make a run for it!" Jessica exclaims. I freeze mid-crawl. The world becomes so silent I can hear the twitter of birds hiding from the frigid weather on the patio outside. A second later, she sighs, saying, "Damn. I thought it might work this time."

"That's only ever worked one time, on that guy hiding in a dumpster, and you've tried it every single chance you've had since."

'Trickery!' My gaze turns toward the window. 'Disregard it. If I flee across the lake, they shan't be able to pursue me.'

I seize a chair with the cattail's tendrils and cast the chair at a window, shattering it. Both lights shine upon me as I clamber out of the window.

"Freeze, police!" Leo commands.

I dash across the back patio.

"I'll go around the backside," Jessica shouts.

As I pass through the railing, the kiln bumps against the bars. Hovering atop the Lake, I sprint away.

Jessica's voice echoes across the water. "Stop, police!"

'Simply because thou commandest me to does not mean I shall!'

With the light about to illuminate me, I lay flat upon the Lake's surface, allowing the haze to drive me forward. Alas, a light finds me. "Stop! You'll freeze to death, moron!" Jessica yells. "928 to central. We have a 10-60 suspect last seen swimming southwest toward Bethesda Terrace."

"Roger 928. 876 officers are in pursuit of the suspect, rendezvous at Bethesda Terrace."

"10-4. We're three minutes from arrival."

'Let's not return to the seed. I shall seek refuge in the trees across from the Terrace instead.' A minute later, I reach the shore opposite the seed and Terrace. I can see blue and red lights reflecting off the Lake from rides near the Terrace. 'How did they know I was in the Boathouse? I was not anticipating anyone until the morn.'

I flinch and nigh slap the wall. '*Cosmic System, prithee! My nerves are in a twitter. Do not appear so suddenly and frighten me.*'

The wall vanishes.

As time passes, more red and blue lights emerge from the twilight darkness. I part some leaves, attempt to obscure my eyes, and can see people walking around with lights as if searching. Half an hour later, two bright lights approach my location. '*Pray thee, do not find me.*'

"Check the bushes next to the Lake; stupid moron might be dying of hypothermia after swimming through the water," a man says.

"Right," another man replies. "I thought I saw something purple when we pulled up anyway."

I retreat deeper into the thicket. The two men spend the next hour searching the area near the bank and some of the nearby bushes.

"Let's go, they aren't here anymore, and I'm damn near freezing to death."

With that, the two men depart. '*Thank the lord they are leaving. Who are these people in black garments? They seem to be some wealthy gentleman's guards or noble's guards. Mayhaps the noble from the castle I saw? If so, it is quite astonishing that there is a female guard, Jessica. Perhaps this era's world does have a few redeeming aspects.*'

The sun peaks over the horizon, but clouds quickly cover it. '*I shall wait a day before attempting to move.*' The snowfall picks up as a new duo of noble's guards arrive. '*Aye, until then, I shall practice my skills and keep out of sight.*'

Chapter 9: Doctor Professor Nightingale

∞∞∞∞∞∞∞∞∞∞∞∞∞∞∞∞

Fostered Aspirant [Naturalist (Grade 4)]
Fostered Aspirant [Humorism (Grade 4)]
Fostered Aspirant [Stealth (Grade 2)]

+1 Endurance
10 Stat Points Primed

The night was fruitful, and I fostered several skills.

I reside in the same thicket I fled to this morn, dissecting a goose I managed to sneak up on several hours ago. It fought courageously, nigh too courageously, yet I persevered. *'Earl, didst thou hearest what I thought in my head when I ambushed this goose? I hope so because it was quite a fun quip! Aye, I shall reenact it for thee!'*

I raise the cattail and point straight ahead. Imagining the honking goose in front of me, I clench my fist and shout into my mind. *'Ha! Fowl creature, thy goose is cooked...!'* I lay my palm on my chest with a satisfied nod. *'See, Earl; if thou hadst a chest, it would hurt from laughing too hard.'*

My gaze turns downward toward the massacred goose. *'Although, without the glass, I had to use a sharp-looking stone instead. I am not pleased with what I have done to this poor animal's carcass, though I hope it would have taken solace in knowing its sacrifice was not in vain.'*

Having learned and lectured about all I believe I can from this goose's body, I set it to one side for the moment. Thinking about ways to grow stronger, I remember I need to refine Nebula. *'First things first. Earl, may I refine some Nebula?'*

> **Earl Interface:**
> **Query:** *Would the user like to refine the storage of Nebula and Vitrum utilizing the user's personal mana reserves?*
> **[Aye]**   **[Nay]**

Reading the message, I shake my head. *'Nay, I lost consciousness on the previous occasion! Earl, I cannot afford to succumb to Mana Inanition. Is there a method to choose how much refining my kiln does at any one time?'*

> **Earl Interface:**
>
> **Response:** This Spirit-Soul Interface can assist the user in refining any volume at one time.
>
> ### See Refining Options:
> *[Refine All]*
> *[Refine All Vitrum]*
> *[Refine ½ of Vitrum]*
> *[Refine All Nebula]*
> *[Refine ½ of Nebula]*
> .
> .
> .

Earl presents me with an extensive list of refining options. Perusing the list, I glimpse one that's near what I desire. *'Earl, I choose the one that allows me to refine the greatest amount of Nebula without bleeding any mana from my manituic flux.'*

My flame grows in intensity, and I feel what I believe is mana draining from my kiln. *'Earl. Prithee, display the adaptations thou recommend, and I may afford with my current Essence values.'*

Forewarning: If Essence falls beneath the 5 Essence line, the user will likely descend into a frenzied state of addled gluttonizing. It's recommended that the user avoids this dangerous state. If the user's Essence reaches 0, their flame will be snuffed.

Vaporous Form Germination Tier Adaptations

Available Crown Adaptations

Raka Factory Horns
(Recent Meal: Loin of Lamb)
Grow a pair of hazy spiral Raka sheep horns that will refine small amounts of Vitrum and nebula stores. Max amount of 0.5 Vitrum or Nebula a day unless upgraded. Horns will consume 10% of the user's current mana capacity each day.
[Cost: 42 Essence + 2.3 Refined Nebula + 1 Vitrum]

Feathery Crown
(Recent Meal: Pigeons)
A pair of hazy black wings sprout above the user's ears. Utilize the wings to propel a gust of haze into the face of any threats or enemies.
[Cost: 51 Essence + 2.1 Refined Nebula]

Negating Membrane
(Recent Meal: Chicken Breast)
Gain a nictitating membrane above the user's eyes resembling eyelids, eyebrows, and eyelashes. Enables the user to block the radiance of their eyes to better hide the user's presence. When the negating membrane is fully in use, natural night vision will be lost.
[Cost: 32 Essence + 1.1 Refined Nebula]

Available Skin Adaptations

Throng of Haze
(Recent Meal: Copepod Throng)

Separate the haze into its primary components via specialized varieties of micro-copepods. Allow the copepods to merge together and send them scuttling toward your target. The range is short without a manituic flux, but the effects of the user's haze might have greater utility than the user may realize.
[Cost: 52 Essence + 2.3 Nebula]

Available Dress Adaptations
Cannot Afford/None Recommended

Available Armament 'Cattail' Adaptations
Cannot Afford/None Recommended

Available Miscellaneous Adaptations

Rife Pearl
(Recent Meal: King Oyster)
Encase and store rife paste within a pearl-like repository. Rife Pearls can be used to feed, mutate, and awaken animals or plants that have not been introduced to mana prior—a maximum of five pearls can be made before they naturally fall from the kiln.
[Cost: 35 Essence + 2.3 Refined Nebula]

Essence Available: 82 [R = 87%]
Refined Nebula Available: 0.2 [7.3]
Refined Vitrum Available: 5 [2.5]
Refined Unknown Superacid: 0.5 (0.0)

'Some of the other adaptations disappeared, not to mention that 'R' number has dropped even more. Also, dress and skin have separated into their own adaptations. Odd.'

I read through Earl's list of recommendations. Out of curiosity, I summon the full list of adaptations and learn that the reason Earl did not recommend more was that they would interfere with previously selected adaptations. Not only that, but some of them are plain outlandish, like one that changes the cattail into a shrimp's tail.

Deciding to concentrate on the adaptations Earl recommends, I examine them one at a time. *'To be honest, refining is a bit of an annoyance and makes Raka Factory Horns intriguing, but I would rather not sprout horns. Feathery Crown might look elegant and would offer me a defense with breadth and scope. Yet, it is much the same as the horns, and the thought of wings jutting from my head forever makes me apprehensive... Perhaps, I shall consider an adaptation like Raka Factory Horns and Feathery Crown in the future.'*

Shrugging my shoulders and shaking my head, I continue. *'Negating Membrane is also quite tempting. The glow of my eyes is a persistent issue, and reacquiring lost facial features is an alluring prospect; I would relish being a tad less... monstrous.'*

My eyes drift to Throng of Haze; I find it curious that it is an available adaptation since a few days have passed. *'Throng of Haze reads as if it would provide me a new method of offense, but it also speaks of separating the haze. Does that have something to do with the colors in the Chronicles?'*

I read the final adaptation. *'Hmm, Rife Pearl might solve my problem of involuntarily shedding paste, so that is tempting as well, except I cannot fathom why I would ever wish to feed it to something.'*

The conclusion I reach is that Throng of Haze is the one adaptation that grants me abilities I am wholly incapable of now.

Earl Interface:
    Notice: *Ninety-five mana was used to refine 2.2 Nebula.*

Earl's box appears, so I check my Status, and find that I still have a hundred mana in reserve for my manituic flux shielding. With a nod, I come to a decision. *'Earl, I believe I shall select the adaptation, "Throng of Haze."'*

I raise my arm to observe the process and watch as small bumps appear beneath the haze, scurrying about like insects. They resemble the copepod throng I devoured in the chamber pot tunnels but are made of haze. They burrow into my skin and skitter into the kiln, vanishing.

'...Thank the lord, I do not have a mouth, or I might shriek. Perhaps I should have chosen a different adaptation.' Lifting my hazy hand, I turn it backward and

forward. *'Earl, I was under the impression I would create the copepods when required... not become their hostess. Also, I assumed they would be smaller; otherwise, why would I need to merge them.'*

I explore my body, searching for any sign of the copepods. *'I believe I have made myself even more of a monster. Umbral's shadow, what shall I become if things such as this continue?'* Remembering some changes to my blue wall the previous time I selected an adaptation, I drop my hand and collapse onto my back. My mind is exhausted. *'Prithee, my Chronicles, Cosmic System.'*

Constance Nightingale || Kiln Vaporous Chronicles || Entity 1-3-2-3			
Strength	12	Cattail Armament Physical Power	24
Orenda	22	General Body Strength	5
Sturdiness	5	Cattail Armament Magical Power	0
Fortitude	16	Membrane Defense	2
Perception *	18	—	—
Acuity *	9	—	—
Agility	16	—	—
Endurance	20	Sable	83.61%
Mend Rate	21 (-100%)	Vermillion	14.66%
Mana Regen	13	Hoary	1.62%
Stat Points Primed: 10		Heliotrope	0.10%

My Chronicles summoned, I stare at my quantities of sable, vermillion, heliotrope, and hoary. The rays of the morn sun lights up my body, unimpeded by the blue wall's presence. *'Vermillion is the one that rose this time. Hmm.'* I turn my head toward the divided goose carcass that I have been using to practice my humors. *'I can try each on separate pieces of the goose carcass to see if there is an effect. Now, how do I summon them?'*

As the sun climbs higher into the sky, I lie motionless upon the ground, endeavoring to hail the copepods. Yet, no matter how I beseech them, I cannot summon the homely creatures. I sit up and reach my hand through the membrane and into my belly. I tap the side of the kiln, hoping to rouse it in some way. With each tap, I feel a slight tingling on the kiln's shell.

The tiny flame within dances as I focus on the tingle, imagining copepods appearing from my kiln. Hazes of various hues spew from the kiln and coalesce. Atop the kiln's shell, copepods the breadth of a coin stand tapping their heels—my mind shivers as their limbs tickle the kiln's surface. I glance away to compose myself before returning my gaze to them.

Scrutinizing each of them, I see four variants of the roach-like copepods standing in a row enwrapping the kiln. Each variant is consistent in size at around an inch across. There are several sable and vermillion copepods, but hoary and heliotrope are scarce in number, with only a lonesome copepod each. *'So they do reflect the haze percentages in my Chronicles to some degree.'*

The murky copepods sit unmoving as if awaiting a command. I order a sable copepod toward a scrap of goose flesh. The copepod twitches, lifts its insect-like limbs, and marches forward as if the haze is a solid surface for it to tread. A new sable copepod emerges, taking the departed copepod's place.

It moves upward and into my shoulder before pushing into my arm. With such graceless legs, it scuttles at a sluggish pace, making it take half a minute to arrive at my palm. Arriving at the haze's edge, it halts all movement. Though I command the copepod to leap, it acts as if it's reluctant to do so. I stand, approach the goose, and hold my arm about a foot from the meat scrap.

'Leap to this meat, hideous little creature!' It burrows out of my hand onto my palm and then leaps, vanishing when it contacts the meat. Red bumps appear atop the goose, blemishing the meat's surface—the bumps swell to boils, and white caps protrude from their peaks. My nonexistent eyebrows

rises as I turn away in revulsion. '*I did not think it possible to give the dead a disease...*'

I move on to trying the next colors. To save time, I reach into my belly and order a vermillion copepod to fall onto my palm. It does so, and I hold it toward another piece of meat I have cut from the goose. When it leaps to the flesh, naught occurs. Tilting my head, I ponder the implications. '*Perhaps it does not have an effect or simply does not work on meat?*'

Next is heliotrope. Commanding my sole heliotrope copepod to burrow onto my palm, I extend my arm toward a slice of goose. It jumps, and once more, naught occurs. '*I am beginning to question my choice of adaptation even more...*' My gaze returns to the kiln, but a fresh heliotrope copepod does not manifest, unlike the sable and vermillion. '*That copepod must have contained all the heliotrope I possess.*'

Last is the milky gray hoary copepod. I only have one of these, and I am fairly certain that is all I can produce. The hoary copepod burrows onto my palm, and I hold it toward a sliver of meat. It bounces onto the flesh, and the meat withers from pink to gray within seconds, causing it to resemble a scrap of flesh someone left in the sun for several fortnights.

'*That was rather dramatic.*' Poking at the meat, I flip it onto its side, inspecting it further. '*What might happen if I meld hoary and sable? Would it be more potent or less? Hmm, but that one hoary copepod was the only one I possess... Shall I ever require something more potent than sable alone? Perhaps not, and I have an abundance of sable haze.*'

Crossing my arms, I stare at the scraps of goose flesh. '*Still, the range is short. Why must I be so close before the copepods leap?*' Another sable copepod scuttles onto my palm. I hold it toward an area of grass and command it to jump. The copepod refuses. I persist, ordering and goading it into leaping. It shivers as if hesitant yet heed my command and leaps. At first, it drifts downward like the others, yet it scatters upon reaching the ground, and the breeze sweeps it away. '*Ah. It is because they cannot hold themselves together long after separating from my haze... Mayhaps, if it were larger and heartier? I could try merging them together as the adaptation said I could.*'

I command a sable copepod to suck in haze or grow bigger, and it does until it's around the width of a tiny mouse. Calling the copepod to my palm, I back around ten feet from a fresh morsel of meat. I command it to run toward the meat. It leaps from my hand, drifts to the ground, and scurries through the grass without disturbing a single blade of grass. It hops onto the meat and seeps into it, dyeing the flesh a sickly yellowish-green. *'I cannot believe that succeeded.'* I review my Status and notice that my Erysichthon increases each time I produce a copepod. *'Fudge, I shall have to explore this more when I have more Erysichthon to spare.'*

As I am about to resume my tests, a childish boy's voice yells, "I found her! I found the fairy!"

"Are you sure?" a young girl's voice asks. "Something smells kinda bad over here."

'Children? Fairy? Where have I heard that before? ...Wait, that boy who was with the Bishop, he was the one who called me a fairy! It must be him and his sister!' The bushes tremble as someone enters the thicket. My gaze darts from left to right before fixing itself upon the bloody goose carcass. The cattail's tendrils draw the disgusting pieces of meat into the cattail as I prepare to flee. *'I shall hide at the thicket's edge!'*

The pleasant taste of the goose does nothing to stop me from fleeing. When Earl's purple wall appears, I dismiss it to remove it from my vision.

"Fairy! Don't run; I'm not going to hurt you! Promise!" the boy shouts.

The girl groans. "Vincent, answer me, are you sure there is a fairy here? Didn't Teacher tell us that there might be fairies later, but we'll have to wait?"

"Mm-hmm! I felt her mana and then used my tome to touch her Essence. That's why I know it was a fairy!"

"You did!" the young voice gasps, stuttering. "W-what did her Essence feel like? Was it amazing!?"

"It was windy and gentle! But also, strong and scary. I've never felt Essence like it. I bet only a strong fairy could have such a gentle and scary Essence!"

'Windy and gentle? Strong and scary?' I shake my head and shrug my shoulder. 'How is it possible to be so flattered, offended, and confused all at the same time? Regardless, this child certainly has the wrong impression of me!'

I run as far as I can, but when I reach the edge of the thicket, I stop. With the sun still out and people walking about, I cannot leave without exposing myself.

"Dummy! That doesn't mean it's a fairy."

"I'll show you who's a dummy!" the boy shouts, storming forward.

With nowhere to flee, my choices are to either run into the busy park or merely meet the two children. 'These children were with that wicked man. Still, I… I refuse to attack or fight children… well, I refuse to strike first anyway. I would like to pretend I have some semblance of moral standards.' It does not take me long to decide that drawing the attention of numerous adults is worse than confronting two children, regardless of whom they may be acquainted with. Although, given the things I have experienced thus far, I prepare myself to be mistaken. 'I suppose I am 'spirit-like,' so why not feign to be a fairy as well…? Nay! Why settle for a lowly fairy when I could be the Queen of Fairies!'

I step into an opening at the heart of the thicket, where I shall meet the children. Yet, standing there like a dullard, I realize something. '…Ah. I cannot speak to them without the Telepathy thing. That may prove to be an issue… Fiddlesticks. Naught is simple.'

Two doe-eyed children bumble from the bushes with beaming grins. They are not wearing the black gowns like our prior encounter, but rather their attire is much nearer to what I have observed other children of this era wearing. The pair have glossy boots, oversized puffy coats, and stiff trousers; the only thing of particular note is that they both clutch hefty tomes, hugging them close to their bodies.

The tomes themselves display complicated patterns. The boy's tome has a soft blue cover, while the girl's tome is a lapis blue. However, each of them has what looks to be a curled-up serpent inscribed into the front with script and diagrams that I have nary a chance of comprehending. The serpents are identical, with jaws unhinged, exposing long fangs; the only difference I can determine is the snakes face away from each other.

Meaning if one tome's spine was placed against the fore-edge of the other, the two serpents would be facing in opposite directions.

Fifteen seconds pass in utter silence... which is a long time for strange children to unnervingly gawk with big, dilated pupils. As I am about to cover my exposed shoulders to conceal my risqué figure, they gasp and then gulp.

"Lorelai, she's scary," the boy, Vincent, whispers with teary blue eyes. "Just like we imagined her! Her eyes too. See-see-see! It's almost like what teacher said a real-life fairy thingy might look like."

Meanwhile, the girl, Lorelai, stares at the area around my collar. "Her necklace is so long it wraps around her. She must be a strong fairy!"

'These children are rather unique, to put it politely.'

Vincent runs forward. "Fairy! I've been looking for you!"

Seeing Vincent racing toward my hazy figure, I hold up a hand, unwind the cattail, and toss a nearby branch. The branch stabs into the snow just shy of the boy, who now stands only a few feet away.

"Woah!" he shouts, staring at the stick. He frowns and pulls his big tome closer.

"Stupid brother!" Lorelai rushes to the boy's side, staring at him with furrowed brows. "You can't just run toward a fairy like that. That's dangerous!"

'So now she's decided I am a fairy as well. What about me makes them believe I am a fairy?'

He tilts his head. "Huh? Then what am I supposed to do?"

"Bishop said that if we ever found something like this, we can either talk to it or 'dom·i·nate.'" He smiles. "Yeah, dominate! Dominate it if we can."

'Dominate it? What does that mean!? These children are dangerous!'

"Dominate? Yeah! Gotta catch 'em all!" Lorelai giggles and performs a small hop. Yet her enthusiasm quickly wanes. "Wait. Brother? W-we aren't old enough to dominate somethin', though."

"Oh. Yeah. That's... that's right."

The two sigh and turn their heads toward the ground, but their eyes turn upward. Sticking out their bottom lips, they stare at me with shivering upturned eyes as if begging me to comfort them. *'Crafty, sly! Dost thou truly expect me to offer sympathy because thou cannot dominate me!? If thou wert not children, I would thrash thee!'*

"Fairy, can we talk to you?" Vincent says, his big eyes fixed firmly upon me. "We have a question."

Lorelai nods her head. "Yep, we have a question!"

Crossing my arms, I simply stand there waiting for what I am confident shall be a remarkably reasonable question.

Together they both stare at me with big childish grins. "Can we dominate you for our birthday?"

I shake my head and wave my hands to deny their outrageous request. *'Nay! Nay! Nay!'*

"W-what? W-w-we can't?" Vincent stutters as if he is about to weep.

Lorelai gazes at me with watery eyes. "Then, you won't help us?"

'Pardon!? Help? All thou hast spoken is gibberish about dominating me! And regardless, I am in no position to assist anyone!'

They both stare at me expectantly while I simply stand there. Seeing that they intend to gawk at me until I respond, I point at my mouthless face and pray they understand what that means.

"Sister! The fairy doesn't have a mouth." Vincent tilts his head and holds his hand toward me. "How are we supposed to talk to her?" he asks.

"How am I supposed to know, dummy? Let's just tell her what we want. Maybe she'll grant our wish," Lorelai replies.

'If thy wish is to dominate me, denied!'

Vincent nods in agreement with his sister and turns toward me. "We want to be strong!" Vincent says with a sunny smile. "We want to be strong for the end of the world!"

"Yeah! For humanity's apocalypse!" Lorelai lets out a little giggle. "That way, we can protect our friends."

'How is the nonsense these children are spouting disturbing, aggravating, and charming all at the same time?'

I hear someone yelling into the thicket. "Pipsqueaks! What are you two doing in there!? We got to get going!"

"Yes, Mr. Lorcan, we're coming!" Lorelai shouts back, then turns toward me. "Please grant our wish, fairy!"

'Lorcan? The red-haired man; he is here too!'

When Lorelai grabs her brother's hand and drags him into the shrubbery, my hand falls onto my chest in relief.

Vincent resists leaving, but with his sister incessantly pulling him further away, he yields. With a sigh, he waves at me, yelling, "Bye, fairy! Please grant our wish!"

As quickly and wildly as they came, they disappear, shaking the brush all the way. *'Did that truly happen, or did I hallucinate it? By "end of the world" and "apocalypse," did they mean the end of the Beta? ...My apologies, children, but I am uncertain that I shall even survive long enough to see the end of the Beta.'* Crossing my arms, I shake my head. *'Still, all that domination talk was unpleasant!'*

With my hiding spot exposed, my shoulders slump as I engulf the sharp rocks I have been using on the goose's carcass. *'How did they locate me anyway? It is as if they knew exactly where I was...? Something about mana and my Essence?'*

Moving to the edge of the thicket, I glance left to right and spot another thicket I may hide in further away. After waiting for the best opportunity, I dart across a sparse sliver of vegetation and into some hedges. With the children gone and in a fresh location, I spend the remainder of the day and night endeavoring to progress my Aspirant skills.

....

....

....

It is daybreak. I am lying on my chest, floating across the lake toward the bushes near "The Boathouse" that I found over a day ago.

Reminiscent of the sunset back on that day in Roanoke, the sunrise dyes the sky red and orange. Perhaps even redder and more orange than in Roanoke. A few ducks and geese have been in the area, but they all seem to be moving southward from what I can tell. Besides, the geese have avoided the area since I, as those dastardly French would say, "performed an autopsie" on one of their companions. I suppose I inadvertently sent them a message.[44] As for the squirrels, they are also still active, though it is hard to tell because the squirrels here are among the fattest I have ever beheld.

All of this has been on my mind because it leads me to believe that this snowfall must have been unexpected. My gaze moves to the shore, where some vivid yellow and red leaves still cling to the trees.

'It is likely sometime between September and December. That is my guess at lea–'

My thoughts are interrupted. A familiar yet odd sensation tickles my kiln. Feeling this, I stop, push off the lake, and leap to my feet. My gaze darts to the kiln, where I can see a paste slipping down the rough edges of the kiln's shell. I jab my hand into my belly to catch the paste. My efforts are for naught as the paste drops, leaving a hole in the palm of my hand that haze refills. Peering downward, my eyes fix themselves upon the spectacle of shiny bits of sparkling glass bobbing in the water.

As if it were bait, fish swarm the paste, consuming and even fighting over it. 'That is the paste... the substance that changed the rats and the copepods... and now fish are eating it.' Lifting my head, I sweep my gaze across the calm, still

---

[44] Autopsie: French spelling of the word autopsy. A postmortem examination to discover the cause of death or the extent of disease.

lake. If a monstrous creature lived beneath its surface, one would not know until it was too late. *'I believe it would be wise to avoid standing on the Lake from henceforth.'*

Whilst the fish battle over the last morsels of paste, a shadow rises from the depths. It is big, round, green, and... I lower myself closer, and it is a mere turtle. The turtle's mouth opens, and it snaps up the remaining paste—correction, it was a mere turtle. It dives deep underwater after a meal that is certain to be life-changing. *'I shall address this fish and turtle predicament soon. I swear! But not at this moment...'*

With the daylight growing, I dash ahead. Reaching the lake's edge, I run onto shore, around the building, and dive into a cluster of tall hedges. My hiding spot is amongst the worst I have been forced into, but it is also the only one that is near enough to eavesdrop on the café.

I lie down and poke my head from the hedges. I can see the Boathouse's entryway enwrapped by some variety of glossy yellow material that reads 'Police - Caution.' I turn away, it must have something to do with me, making it is something I would rather not look at. My gaze strays to the café's front. Here there is a red brick patio, with rows of black metal tables, each of which has a pair of metal chairs.

'I shan't abandon my shrubbery until the café closes.' My thoughts return to the rife paste that taints the Lake's life. *'Truthfully, there is little I can do about the Lake except, perhaps, forewarn people. But how am I meant to forewarn anyone? ...All I may do is ask the gentlewoman from the other day.'*

····

·········

····

A few hours pass, and the café has yet to open. I glance around worriedly, questioning whether they may not open due to my actions at the Boathouse. As that thought crosses my mind, two people approach the café. A man with brown hair in his early twenties walks next to a woman with blonde hair in her thirties. They look rather ordinary for people of this era. Each of them wears a long coat that runs past their knees, the same blue trousers that everyone wears nowadays, gloves, and a nutty-brown shirt beneath their coat. The shirt has wavy, cursive letters that read simply '**The Central Café.**'

The woman holds up a thin white stick. She places the white stick to her lips, drinks in the tobacco, and then blows out a thick white fog. *'I presume that must be some type of special tobacco stick.'*

When the last of the smoke passes her lips, she scoffs. "God, those people the other night stayed forever. I was ready to kick their butts out."

"Hmm?" The man's mouth hangs open for a second. "O-oh, yeah." He yawns, saying, "I know who you're talking about. Those two girls tipped alright, but yeah, they moseyed on in a few minutes before closing and then took their precious time sipping their mochas."

She clicks her tongue, taking another breath of her tobacco. "I can't stand when people do that shit," she says, breathing out the smoke at the same time. "It really pisses me off, and I swear it happens every other day."

They both sigh and then look toward the front gate of the Boathouse that's still wrapped in the glossy yellow material.

The man blinks, asking, "Did something go down at the Boathouse? I know they were supposed to have that sketchy wedding or whatever there the other day."

"Oh, you haven't heard? Some creep broke into it, swiped a bunch of food, and then left a sixteen-year-old girl knocked out on the floor."

"Woah, are you serious? That's so messed up."

'When stated in those words, it sounds worse than it was... I saved that girl; therefore, I deserved a reward...' I glance at the yellow material with 'Police - Caution' on it and then turn away. *'Aye. This is not London. If the nobles remain ignorant of my existence, there is nary a need to muse on it further.'*

The woman flicks the tobacco away as the two resume their banter, entering the café. Her tobacco lands at the edge of the bush, so I send the cattail toward it. Spreading the tendrils and pulling it in, it quickly turns to haze.

Earl Interface:

Assimilating 'Cigarette' (Mana Bare)
Erysichthon abates by 0
Essence value negligible.
0.0 Refinable Nebula
0.0 Refinable Vitrum

'A *cigarette?*' I stare at the purple wall. *'Fascinating.'*

A moment later, the employees return with a tall, shiny silver object. It is the height of a man and has a cube base. Some metal bars run from each corner of the cube, and on top of the bars is a pyramid-like top. From the cube base to the pyramid at the top, a clear tube runs all the way up.

"Come on. We need to set these heaters up for anyone who's crazy enough to sit on the patio."

"Why can't we just chain these things up outside? They're a pain in the ass to move."

"We used to lock them together so we wouldn't have to, but someone stole a couple of them, so now we drag 'em in every night."

They spend a while setting up the pyramids. When the last one is placed, they approach the one nearest me. A click echoes and a tall flame enkindles at the pyramid's center. *'That is fantastic! Amazing! It is an enormous lantern!'*

"Alright, let's go finish prep duties."

Another hour passes until more of the café's employees arrive and the patrons soon after. It's not long before I realize it may be a while before a patron sits at my eavesdropping table. I do not particularly mind, however, as my mind is weary.

'Come to think of it, I have not slept at all? I mean, this is not the first I have thought about it, but still, I thought it would happen. It's been quite some time, and I have not slept at all except for that time I lost consciousness due to mana loss. I do not get tired, so mayhaps I simply do not sleep. That seems beneficial, but at the same time, it makes it difficult to mentally recuperate.'

Pondering things such as this, the day goes on as the sun moves across the sky, and I lie in my bush staring upwards. My eyes follow a big beetle that has been crawling about. Only a single person has sat at the table near me, and they did not even speak. They merely sipped their coffee and stared into my bush. I thought he might have spotted me, but eventually, he stood up and said something to the effect of "I am so high" and then left without another word.

'This would have been more productive if it was not so frigid. It's easy for me to forget how chilly it is when I can hardly feel that type of thing. I do miss the feeling of the sun against my skin, but the cold I shall never miss.'

A young woman walks from the café with a cup in her hand.

Her skin is fair, hinting she is not someone who spends their days laboring in the fields. Using her hand, she pushes a strand of her light-brown hair behind her ear. She wears a long gray coat, blue trousers, black gloves, furry boots, and a warm winter hat. Stopping at my table, she removes a bag from her back, which she props against the chair. Pulling out a chair, she sits.

'It seems I will at last get an opportunity to gather some information after all.'

The young woman takes out one of those black rectangles that everyone in this era seems to have, taps it ten times, and places it against her ear. She sits in silence as I watch her intently.

A moment later, she speaks. "Hey, babe. I'm going to hang out at the café while I take this online quiz. I'll head home afterward."

I cannot hear what they are saying, but it seems someone is speaking to her.

"Sure, it's a little nippy outside, but I forgot it's due this afternoon. I can't afford a zero on a quiz, or I risk not qualifying for Lurlann Empire's maximum student aid. I'm just going to suck it up and be cold for a minute. It's no big deal, baby."

Again someone talks, but this time the woman grins and her cheeks blush.

She laughs. "Yeah, we can do that again... last time felt really good..." She says a few more words except quieter.

I look away and stare into the depths of the thicket. Ants and moths ramble about in the bushes as my mind reels. *'This mad, sexually deviant woman! Discussing such explicit topics in public, how improper! I mean... would... How would that... Nay. Do not dwell on such things, Constance.'*

"You just better be ready for me when I get home." She giggles, tapping the rectangle one last time with a devilish smirk.

'...'

"Alright, I need my computer," she says, pulling a big square object from her bag. She sets it on the table and opens it like a book. Tapping this one much like the smaller black rectangle, she leans down and pulls a real, genuine book from her bag.

Something about the big square object causes her smirk to change to a frown. "Just gotta take this French quiz and stop by the store; then I'm home free." She rolls her eyes with a huff. "Why didn't I just take Spanish instead? French numbers don't make any sense at all. Counting in French is so finicky, it goes like ten, then twenty, thirty, forty, fifty, sixty, then sixty-ten, four-twenty, four-twenty-ten... How does that make sense!? Like, come on! Just make up a new word already. Why make it so weird?"

'This woman loathes the French. It warms my nonexistent heart to know some things never change, regardless of the era.' The young woman taps against the black book like a madwoman. *'What is that black book? ...It does not matter. I desire her bag.'*

I unwrap the cattail from around my chest and slither it out of the bush. Moving the cattail, I wrap it around the leg of a table opposite the young woman. I shake the table, and the woman yelps. "W-what? Is it the wind?" She shakes her head and returns to tapping her square.

'Investigate. I am certain thou art curious.' Once more I shake the table.

Her eyes dart toward my cattail. "Snake!" the young woman yells, leaping from her chair.

I yank the cattail back into the bushes. '...I did not expect someone who was having such a lewd conversation a moment ago to have such an intense fear of snakes... More importantly, prithee do not approach the bush!'

Her theatrics garner the attention of other patrons, who gaze at her with furrowed brows. Her face reddens as she chuckles, rubbing the back of her head. "S-sorry, I, uhm, think I saw a snake," she says in a small voice.

"A snake?" A plump man dressed in this era's winter clothing purses his lips at the young woman's words. "In this weather? I seriously doubt it, ma'am." He stands, eyeing the bushes intently.

I dip lower, bringing the cattail close.

He lifts his hands and waves his hand at the hedges. "I don't see anything. At best, it was just a raccoon or something."

"Y-yeah, now that I think about it, a snake couldn't move the chair around like that..." She pauses and smiles at the man. "Hey, do you mind watching my stuff while I run to the restroom."

He chuckles. "Yeah, I don't mind."

She thanks him and walks away. With the young woman gone, the plump man returns to his table, and goes about his business as he was before.

'This is my chance!' I let the cattail out, except this time, I go directly for the bag. 'Slowly. Slowly. Slowly.' The plump man looks over at the table; I stop. He looks away. 'Slowly. Slowly. Slowly.'

Again I notice the plump man glancing over at the table, so I freeze. He returns to tapping on the object in his hands.

Shaking my head, I glare at the bag. 'Quickly! Quickly! Quickly!' I seize the bag, dragging it into the bushes.

The man looks over but does not notice the missing bag.

'Aye, a rousing success.' I dump the books from the bag, and then toss it onto the young woman's table. 'She may have her bag back. I cannot use it.'

The young woman returns. "Thanks! I appreciate it."

"Ah, yeah. No problem," the plump man replies.

She stops at her table, tilting her head with narrowed eyes. "H-hey? Did someone touch my bag? Where are all my books!?" she asks the plump man.

"Huh? Your books? No one came by the whole time you were gone," he replies.

Her eyes water. "What are you talking about? All my books, except for my French book, are gone! Look, my bag is just sitting on the table, empty!"

"Are... are you sure you didn't just forget them?"

"No, I didn't forget them; someone stole them! W-what am I going to do?" she asks. "I can't afford to replace all my books!"

A cold sweat breaks out on the plump man's neck. "C-calm down! I'm sure you just forgot them."

"I didn't forget them! They were here; I definitely brought them with me!" She points at him. "You said you'd watch them!"

"...Let's go talk to the manager. Maybe they have a camera out here."

I watch the two start to walk away. My gaze sticks to the young woman. It's not difficult for me to understand her plight in regards to money.

My attention turns to the texts that strew the ground. *'Dynamics, physics, ecology, mechanics of materials... Are these subjects a woman would commonly be permitted to study nowadays...? I spent years squatting outside in the mud, eavesdropping through the school's window to 'steal' my education. Yet this woman is allowed to learn these things as a man would? How unfair...'* I pause for a moment and then glance at the ecology book. It bears the title "You Are Ecology 101." *'I often yearned for the day I could sit in a chair and learn as noble boys did, but as envious as I may be of this girl, I should not impede the studies of my junior ladies. Aye, this is a splendid change, and I am delighted to see it.'* Removing that text, I look back toward the young woman's table. With a shake of my head, I grasp the remaining books and place them atop her table. *'None of the other books are essential. I only require the ecology text that Earl recommended.'*

Not long after, three people walk back.

"Yeah, so I ran to the restroom, and when I came back, all my books were gone," the young woman says, pointing toward the table.

A white-haired man accompanies them, wearing one of the brown shirts from earlier. I assume it is the so-called manager. The manager raises an eyebrow. "Ma'am, you shouldn't just leave your things without having someone watch them."

"I did ask someone to watch them," she says, side-eyeing the plump man.

The plump man coughs, smiling awkwardly.

When the three arrive at the table, the young woman's mouth hangs open. "Wait, they're back?"

The manager shrugs. "I guess the thief grew a conscience, huh?"

"Y-yeah, I guess so?" The young woman flips through the books. "Wait, I think my friend's ecology book is still missing?"

"Are you... uhm, are you sure you brought it with you?" the plump man asks.

"Brought it with me? It was a book my friend left at my house. I was supposed to return it to her."

The manager shakes his head. "If you'd like, we can report it to the police, or we can just keep an eye out for it for you."

She thinks for a moment before sighing. "It's honestly not worth getting the police involved for one book. I'll just give you my number, and... worst comes to worst, I'll buy my friend a new one from the school store."

The three talk for a while longer before the woman sits down to finish whatever it is she is doing.

With the situation resolved, a blue wall appears.

Fostered Aspirant [Stealth (Grade 3)]
+1 Agility +1 Acuity **8 Stat Points Primed**

'Ah, only eight points remain. I must discover a way to improve my Sturdiness. It is my greatest weakness... I will have to contemplate what I may do to elevate my level as well. I am uncertain if I can stalk and cannibalize another Kiln.'

The young woman soon departs, and for the remainder of the day, the table is left neglected.

Chapter 10: I Am a Sandwich Without Bread

∞∞∞∞∞∞∞∞∞∞∞∞∞∞∞∞∞

The day fades away as the lanterns shine dazzlingly, illuminating the stone pathway. I still lie in the same bush, trying my best to read the ecology text, but it's far too cramped. A partially melted bit of snow falls from a leaf onto the book. Shaking my head, I tilt the book, watching the snow slide, leaving a line of water before falling from the page into the brush below.

'Why did Earl ask me to seek this book? I can only assume it's important if he wished for me to acquire it... Actually, I did have the option to select an 'ecologist' skill not long ago but chose the naturalist skill instead... A mistake, perchance.'

Placing the book aside, I wipe away the brush beneath me. With my efforts to read evidently futile, I instead move on to my next problem: the monstrosities I likely created in the lake's depths. The only ways I can think of to warn the people that frequent the area are signs or a town crier. I do not know a town crier and could not afford nor speak to one if I did.

I manipulate the cattail so it loops down my back and then arcs over my head, like a scorpion's tail. I unwind the threads at the end and bend all but a single thread upward and away. I grip it in my hand like a quill, press it against the earth, and do my best to guide it with my hand.

An hour passes, and the Central Café closes.

Gazing at the ground, I scrutinize my modest handwriting. " *Beware all who err and blunder a stone's throw from the shores of these yawning depths for at the precipice stands the lychgate and in the abyss lies Tenebrous!*"

'Beware all who err and blunder a stone's throw from the shores of these yawning depths, for at the precipice stands the lychgate, and in the abyss lies Tenebrous... Hmm, it is sufficient, I suppose. I might need to brood on something more descriptive, but this was fair practice.'

I poke my head from the bushes, glancing around to ensure I am alone. Once I have confirmed that I indeed am, I depart the tall bushes with the book in hand. Holding the book in my hands only reminds me of how feeble my arms are for some reason. I can make a valiant effort to knock a door down with my cattail yet opening a door with my arms is a hurdle. Rather inconvenient.

Following the edge of the lake, I run from the bushes toward the Terrace. I shall not be going to the Terrace, but instead I will stop at the area I met the gentlewoman a couple of days prior. *'The young gentlewoman shall return tonight. Mayhaps I can ask her where I may find materials for the sign? Nay, I cannot ask her that; she would want to know why a spirit would wish to know something like that. I could forewarn her, and then simply suggest the signs.'*

Hoisting the book to eye level, I stare at it and then bounce my gaze around the area. *'I should tuck this away somewhere it shan't be damaged. One of the brown or blue bins, under the smooth black bag filled with rubbish, should keep it hidden. Aye. Should be well enough there.'*

Finding a blue bin marked "recycling" just off the pathway's edge, I pull the smooth black material away from the bin and hide the book at the bin's bottom. Heavy snow and rubbish make it difficult for me, but I manage to return the black material to how I discovered it. *'I believe I have seen this material quite often; so smooth and flexible. I shall have to ask that gentlewoman what it is named.'*

I come upon an area where two pathways cross, forming an 'X.' At each corner of this 'X' is a thicket of hedges. The topmost hedges are trimmed to make space for a lantern that illuminates the whole intersection; under this lantern rests a lone bench facing the lake. Though this is not the precise spot where I met the gentlewomen, it is a mere thirty yards from thereabouts. With a nod, I sink into a set of hedges farthest from the lantern but closest to the lake. If someone were on the bench, they would be staring right at me.

'I pray the gentlewoman returns to the same place we first spoke.' I eye the lake, glimpsing bubbles that cast ripples overtop the water's surface. *'It would be best if I awaited her return atop the water, but after that wretched rat, I shan't risk attracting the attention of another beast that has swallowed my kiln's rife paste.'*

The sun sets while I organize grasses to sample with the cattail. I consider retiring to the Terrace for the evening, but footsteps and crinkling snow stems those thoughts. The footsteps move closer, halting near the bench, roughly three yards from my brush.

An elderly voice speaks in a formal tone saying, "Miss, I can't let you stay out here alone."

"Hmm, no, I think we both know I'll be just fine alone," an elegant and gentle voice answers. They sigh. "I want to enjoy the night air for a little while, so just wait for me in the car until I am ready."

"Miss, I'm sorry, but I can't let you stay out here alone. It's past ten at night, and thanks to the cyclone it's freezing—four Fahrenheit last I checked! Allow me to chauffeur you to the Casāle for the evening, Miss," the elderly man pleads.

"I'm either in that house or in one of those hotel rooms. The three of you are constantly hovering over one shoulder or the other. If I want to sit in Central Park in the middle of the night, I can, so let me enjoy some fresh air alone for a while."

"That's fine, Miss, but I can't let you sit out here alone. Not to mention your father would certainly not approve."

Poking my head from the bush, I see a white-haired and pallid elderly man in a lavish suit speaking to a gentlewoman. Behind the elderly man stand two muscular men with their arms crossed. They each have a pistol, reminiscent of the one the fopdoodle had, fastened to the belts of their blue trousers. With frowns they look left to right, scrutinizing the area.

My eyes drift to the gentlewoman. She is wearing a glistening blue gown that runs to her ankles. The gown sleeves move down both her arms while the collar runs up her neck, seemingly covering as much skin as possible. She also wears blue gloves and boots with heels that match her gown. Like last time, a veil covers her face, but now that I am close, I can see the veil is relatively thin, and today it is blue to match her gown. Looking closer, I notice the veil is fastened to a hairband that allows it to flow over her face. Through the cover, I can see that her skin is flawless and soft. Her cheeks show a slight blush, and the tip of her dainty nose shows a dab of red from the cold night air.

Shifting a bit more, I notice she has eyes that are so green that they remind me of the spring's first leaves. Her silver hair blows in the frigid wind, exposing delicate ears, as she stares at the elderly man as if reading him like a book.

'If I had to speculate, I would say she is around twenty-one-years-old, the same age I was in Roanoke, or perhaps a couple of years younger. With skin as unblemished as hers, she must be someone from a wealthy family without question... Prithee, do not be noble.'

Small puffs of hot air exit the gentlewoman's nostrils as she puts on a stern voice. "Caldwell, it's not like he has any interest in being seen with me, so I don't foresee him coming around any time soon. He won't find out if I'm out or not as long as none of you say anything. And if you do, who cares?"

'Caldwell must be the elderly man's name. Why is she so worried about her father? Is he a bad man... a nobleman?'

Caldwell ponders for a moment before coming to a decision. "I care! If something happened to you—" Caldwell bites his tongue. "W-well, let's not speculate on hypotheticals."

"You work for me, Caldwell. You do know that, right?"

"I-I am well aware, Miss, and that is why I must insist."

A voice speaks in my head. *{Is it fine if others are around while we speak?}*

Like Caldwell, I pause. My gaze drifts toward the two brawny, dangerous-looking men and their pistols. *{I would prefer we were alone,}* I respond.

She squints her eyes in silence; meanwhile, Caldwell's face turns red, afraid of her next words. "Fine. You win," she declares with a huff. "Take me home."

Caldwell stifles a sigh, placing his wrinkly hand upon his chest. "Excellent, Miss. Let us be on our way then," he says with a tiny bow.

A voice speaks in my head. *{Wait for me.}*

The sounds of four pairs of footsteps fade into the night. *'She has guards and a servant that are required to follow her everywhere. I suspected she was a wealthy gentlewoman, yet perhaps she is even wealthier than I thought? This is not the sort of person I wish to associate myself with.'* My gaze shifts toward the Terrace. My thoughts turn to fleeing... but I cannot bring myself to abandon this opportunity. I resolve to practice my skills to relax my mind until she returns. *'Three million four hundred thousand. Two. Three. Four...'*

••••

•••••••••

••••

I engulf several plants at once, and then use Earl's wall to study their names and values, but a blue wall appears. I dismiss Earl's wall.

Fostered Aspirant [Naturalist (Grade 5)]

Entity 1-3-2-3 has manifested enough potential to supplant an Aspirant skill with a Novitiate skill.

Entity, see the presented skill supplants below.

[Novitiate Naturalist II]
Continue to research nature more traditionally through examination and observation. Attain access to the System's database and summon a screen or 'wall' with elementary information on studied plants, animals, and environments. For Kiln, information will be accessible through the Kiln's Spirit-Soul Interface.

[Novitiate Gluttonous Naturalist]
For one with more of a culinary interest in nature. If it is organic, it can be eaten; if not, then maybe try anyway. Gain access to the System's database to obtain basic details on devoured and assimilated organic material. For Kiln, information will be accessible through the Kiln's Spirit-Soul Interface.

[Novitiate Massacring Naturalist]
Built for an Entity that studies nature because they wish to discover the optimal way to massacre it. Plant or animal, if it's organic in nature, it can be wholly annihilated. Gain access to the System's database and view the basic stats of slaughtered non-sapient plants or animals. For Kiln, information will be accessible through the Kiln's Spirit-Soul Interface.

Seeing the Cosmic System's blue wall, I clap my hands together, producing no sound. *'Aye, I have achieved eminence!'*

I read through the wall and shake my head. *'The last option, "Massacring Naturalist," is a wee dramatic. I presume it is owed to my usage of animal carcasses to practice medicine. The animals were not alive before I used them for study. I do not know if I would say I "massacred" anything—butchered in the name of doctoring, mayhaps. Still, possible confirmation that the Cosmic System offers skills due to past actions is vital wisdom that I may use in the future.'* I raise a finger and move it along the second option, rereading it. *'Hm, culinary? I imagine that word refers to food, aye... and as much as I loathe the name "Gluttonous Naturalist," it's an excellent skill for me.'*

I nod, informing the Cosmic System of my choice. *'Prithee, the second skill on the list, the one with the embarrassing name that I shall not repeat for thee.'*

Skill Supplantation

Entity 1-3-2-3 has supplanted [Aspirant Naturalist] with [Novitiate Gluttonous Naturalist] skill.
Entity's Kiln Spirit-Soul Interface can now relay additional information.

Having made my selection, I continue counting and prepare to test my new skill. I hear someone's heels clicking against the stone pathway, stopping my test before it starts.

{I'm back,} the gentle voice says in my head.

{I was able to raise my count to three million four hundred six thousand since thy departure,} I say, setting aside some plants.

{...Are you insinuating that I took too long? Aren't you the one that wanted to be alone? I was okay with sitting on the bench and speaking inconspicuously.} With a click of her tongue, she laughs, saying, {But, it did take me a minute to pack a few things to bring with me.}

'She brought some things?' My head tilts. {Nay, my apologies. I did not intend to imply that too much time has passed. Counting is a habit of mine.}

{That is an interesting habit.} She pauses for a moment. {Now that I think about it, it seems unusual for someone of your era to have such a habit, especially a woman.}

I poke out my chest. {Aye, it was not commonplace, even amongst men! Truthfully, it was quite troublesome for me to learn how to count such high numbers, but I managed to do it myself. I even learned how to read if thee can believe it.}

{Sounds like an impressive feat. Were you a member of an influential family? You must have been to get an education, right?}

{Influential family? Nay, far from it! I acquired my education by spying. Ignoble people such as I seldom received the privilege of being educated, women less so.}

{How did you manage to 'spy' your way to an education?} she questions.

{When I was young, four or five times a week, I would creep onto school grounds through my secret entrance and then hide beneath the window seal to eavesdrop on lectures. The noble boys would sometimes realize I was there and pour their drinks over my head, but it was a small price. Besides, it eased my guilty conscience when I stole a boy's books after he poured sour milk into my hair.}

{That's awful!} She takes a few steps closer to the bush. {Kids can be so cruel. What happened after that? Did they keep bullying you?}

'...Did she step closer to me? Nay, that is impossible; I am as invisible as the wind itself.' My hand fidgets with a leaf that sits beneath me as I continue, {Others kept bullying me, but that particular boy stopped after I tricked him into giving me his books.}

She laughs. {Well, maybe I need to be more cautious around you. Weren't you worried he would try to get revenge? You said he was a child of a nobleman, wasn't he?}

{He was, but he was too embarrassed to seek revenge since he did not want to admit he was tricked by a little girl, so nothing ever came of it.}

{Ah, so the bully was too afraid of being bullied by his own friends to do anything. What happened next?}

{After that, I used the book to teach myself to read; the hardest part was learning the alphabet without having anyone to ask for help. Later, I even managed to do something similar at one of the colleges for a year or two before they caught me and nigh imprisoned me.}

'Why am I even telling her all these things? ...Perhaps, it is because I feel like the world has forgotten the girl who called the London streets her home. I imagine there is not a single word written about how that girl ever existed. That I ever existed.'

My thoughts are interrupted as she speaks. {That's remarkable. Out of curiosity, what pushed you to do such things? I imagine most women back then would have been more interested in...} She hesitates for a moment. {Well, back then, most women wouldn't have had options beyond raising a family, I assume.}

{What pushed me to do such things?} My hand drifts to my chin, and I stare off into space. Nodding, I say, {I did it for myself. Initially, I had another reason but eventually realized my efforts on that front would be fruitless. I kept going regardless because I enjoyed learning new things and wanted to continue learning more things.}

{For yourself?} She pauses as if digesting those words. {That's all fascinating. Thank you for sharing, but can I ask you one more question?}

'Surely she does not know I am in the bush. That would be unbelievably embarrassing!' I dip my head lower. {...Aye, that is acceptable; ask thy question, but I shall ask the next question.}

{That's okay.} I hear her footsteps move closer to my bush before stopping. {Tell me, why are you in a bush?}

I flinch, the bush sways under the combined influence of my kiln and cattail. {I am not in a bush! What is being spoken of!? Is there something in a bush!?}

{Yeah, for some reason I don't believe that, with the bush shivering and all. Besides, you are radiating so much mana that it's basically impossible to ignore. Emitting it outward like you're doing is called 'Mana Efflux,' and it can be challenging to regulate, but you're leaking so much mana that I can detect you from dozens of yards away. It's how I found you on the Lake and was able to establish a Telepathic link.}

'Leaking mana? Mana Efflux? Detect? Those two children mentioned something about feeling my mana as well!'

She continues to explain her reasoning. {Not to mention at the right angle I can see a purple tint coming from inside the bush. The same purple tint I saw bobbing above the Lake's water a few nights ago. You should be more discrete if you're going to eavesdrop on someone's conversation.}

{I was not spying! If anything, I was the one being spied upon!} I freeze, realizing I have been tricked. {...I do not know what is being spoken of. Pay no attention to the thing in the bush...}

'Good lord, I just realized I am someone frequently called a hedge-born literally hiding in a hedge! This is mortifying!'

She laughs. {It was mostly the Mana Efflux. Still, I already knew your mana would be a problem, and that's why one of the things I brought will help you.}

'Something to help me?' A hand reaches into the bushes. {Wait, nay! Stay away; it's dangerous!} I yell into my mind. The hand hesitates, and I continue, {Do not come any closer, for thy own protection.}

{My own protection?} she asks.

{Aye, if touched, my body could...} I pause, searching for the word. 'Infect? Nay, I do not wish her to deem me a leper.' Shaking my head, I say, {...My body could corrupt thee.}

{Corrupt me? I've heard that one before.} I glimpse her eyes, searching for a place to peek between the leaves. {But aren't you a spirit? You shouldn't have a body to touch. Having purple eyes is already highly unusual, from what I have read anyway.}

{I am merely akin to a spirit... Wait? If a spirit has naught to touch, then why attempt to touch me?}

{Curiosity? I wanted to see if the air felt different or not. Like if the air would be cold, or if your eyes would be warm... Not that I was going to try to touch your eyes or anything.}

{...I am curious, how much dost thou truly knowest about spirits?}

{How much do I 'knowest' about spirits?} She chuckles and then sighs. {Not much at all. They have only started to become active again recently.} She gives the bush a slight nudge. {Why don't you come out of the bush?}

I shake the hedge back at her. {I would rather not!}

{Are you self-conscious or shy?} I notice her silver hair swaying back and forth as she tries to look between the leaves. {Can't I see your body?}

{See my body? That's a very inappropriate request! We have only just become acquainted.}

{I just meant whether or not it is visible to the naked eye, but don't try to deflect,} she says with a muffled giggle.

Shifting my hazy body, I push some leaves away, exposing my eyes to her. She takes a quick step back. Shaking my head, I slink away. {That is why I do not wish to come out.}

{I'm sorry! I didn't mean to step away; I wasn't expecting your eyes to be so bright.} She steps closer, moving the bush herself, and looks into my eyes. {It's not every day a pair of bright purple eyes is staring at you from inside a bush.}

I stare back into her green eyes. {Art thou not frightened by my eyes?}

{No, just surprised. Your eyes are quite breathtaking, in all honestly.}

'Breathtaking?' A wisp of glowing heliotrope sweeps upward in a breeze. 'My eyes are not scary but breathtaking?'

{Please come out, so I can stop looking like a crazy lady poking around in a bush in the middle of the night.}

I cross my arms, peering into her big green eyes. She stares back at me, unblinking. {Thou art not going to mock me, call me a hedge-born, or be afraid of my appearance?}

{A hedge-born? No. I won't mock you nor call you whatever that is.} The edges of her lips curl into a smile. {I swear I won't be frightened by your appearance.}

{I do not know if I believe thee.}

She thinks for a moment and then raises an eyebrow. *{Oh, I wish there was someone to keep me company.}* Her expression changes as she glances about with wide, fearful eyes. *{Please come out! It's so dark.}*

{Thou art afraid of the dark?} I ask.

{Yes,} she says, nodding pitifully.

My shoulders slump. *{Thine act is plain to see, though I suppose I cannot scorn a lady in distress, even in jest.}*

Confirming I shall exit, she regains her earlier demeanor. *{I hope you enjoyed seeing me do that. Pretty much no one ever sees me act like that; though, I guess you wouldn't know that.}* She smiles, shakes her head, and waves toward the bush. *{Now, come on out; I won't bite.}*

'Bite? I did not know being bitten was even a possibility. One more thing to be wary of.' I inspect my cattail to ensure it is wrapped around my chest and then reply, *{I am exiting. Do not stand too close.}*

Shrubbery quivers as my kiln moves through the leaves. The gentlewoman takes a step back. Her gaze focuses upon my kiln in my navel; my flame reflects in her green eyes.

Her eyelashes flutter. "Wow." She paces around me. "This isn't anywhere near what the book described," she whispers aloud.

'That's because I am akin to a spirit; I am spirit-like.' Covering my naked shoulders, I rub my toes against the snowy pathway. *{Prithee, cease ogling me. It's making me feel odd.}*

{I'm sorry. I just wasn't envisioning a beautiful girl made of purplish-black smoke to walk out of the hedges.}

'B-beautiful!? First Breathtaking, now beautiful. Am I being wheedled? Would she wheedle me?'[45]

---

[45] Wheedle: to influence by flattery.

She freezes and stares at the cattail with a sad frown. "So it was something like this," she whispers to herself. "I really hoped it was not something so cruel."

'The gentlewoman does not realize my Perception allows me to overhear her... I should lighten the mood.' {Smoke!?} I shout with false ire. {I prefer haze; I am not smoke from a chimney.}

The gentlewoman's expression changes to one of curiosity. {Are the two so dissimilar? I think of them as pretty much the same thing.}

'I have thought of myself as smoky before, but now this is becoming a matter of principle.' I hop away and shake my head. {That is not true! Smoke implies that I am collied and made of burnt or dead things. Haze is mysterious, pure, and graceful,} I retort.

{I've never heard haze described like that. Most people talk about haze in the same way they talk about smog or pollution.} She purses her lips. {If you don't mind me asking, what are you made of anyway? You must have an inkling if you're set on using the word 'haze.'}

Pondering her question for a few seconds, I arrive at a single conclusion. {Not smoke.}

She covers her mouth and laughs. "Ah, well, I think I understand perfectly now," she says, speaking aloud. Dropping her hand, she reveals a smile. "So! Since we're finally meeting face to face, I think it's about time we exchange names. Agreed?"

I tilt my head. {Exchange names?}

"Yeah? Wouldn't it be weird for new friends to not know each other's name?"

I gaze into her big green eyes; my own violet purple eyes reflect back at me. 'Friends? Not acquaintances? Is this truly going so well?'

She coughs, asking with flushed cheeks, "Uh, is that okay?"

{Of course! I mean–} I correct my posture. {Aye. I would like that very much.}

"Great! You stopped talking, and I thought I might have said something wrong."

{Nay, it was not thy words. It's...} I shake my head. {... it's not important. Let us skip to names.}

She nods. "My name is Terra, and it's a pleasure to make your... well, to make your friendship, I guess."

{A pleasure to make thy' friendship,' Terra.} Tilting my head back, I raise my hazy hand with my thumb out and point at myself. {My chosen name is Constance. I thought of it myself. Elegant, is it not? The sort of name a valiant lady knight might hold?}

"Constance. An elegant and knightly name. I could absolutely imagine a brave knight with that name." With a slight giggle, she gestures. "How about we go to the Terrace nearby to talk? It's a lot better lit."

{Sounds wonderful! The Terrace is my favorite place in the park! At least what I have seen of it.}

Terra walks forward, signaling for me to follow. "The Terrace and Arcade are very famous actually. The ceiling in the Arcade is stunning. In fact, hundreds of thousands visit it every year."

I hurry to her side. 'Did she say hundreds of thousands of people visit the Terrace and Arcade every year? Nay! I must have misheard!'

"Ah, by the way." Her eyes look me up and down. "I heard there was an incident near here last night. Something about a sixteen-year-old girl who was drugged and almost assaulted after the wedding reception."

'What!? She knows of that! How could news spread so quickly? It is nigh impossible... Unless her family ties are even more considerable than I anticipated. If Terra learns that it was me who beat up that man, she might believe me to be a violent pers– a violent Kiln.' I shake my head. {That sounds dreadful. I would not know anything about that incident, but I am pleased to hear the girl was able to flee.}

She raises an eyebrow. "You wouldn't have anything to do with that? The news claims it was a woman who drugged the young girl and attacked the man. I read that the suspect then broke into the local restaurant, stole all the food, and fled the scene by diving into the Lake. Nearby they found a man suffering from broken bones and extreme frostbite. The man claimed he was attacked by a 'psycho' while trying to protect the girl's 'purity.'"

{What!? ...I mean, nay, I know naught. Very peculiar. I was here all night but did not witness a thing.} I make a fist behind my back. 'I drugged her?! Nay! It was that stumpy, currish fopdoodle!'

"Mm-hmm, well, if you do know the person who did it, tell them that it was a good deed, and I approve of what they did, but whoever that person is should be more careful about the attention they draw."

I nod. {Terra.}

"Hmm? Is something wrong?"

{I know naught of what transpired, but to sate my own curiosity, that girl, is she... is she well?}

"The girl is okay. She woke up not long ago, and her frostbite was minor. Her name and image haven't been leaked to the public either, so she'll be able to detach herself from the incident fairly easily. She probably has an influential family shielding her if I had to guess. Oh, and if you're wondering, she is staying away from that man, the buffoon."

{Thank goodness. That's wonderful to hear.}

"Not that the man is in any condition to do much of anything ever again," I hear Terra murmur.

{I am not deaf, Terra. I can still hear thee even if it is whispered.}

She does not respond, but I can see a smirk at the corner of her red lips.

I unclench my fist. 'The fopdoodle deserved that thrashing and more, but I did not intend to forever cripple him...'

We reach the Terrace and sit at a bench next to the fountain. I am careful to stay downwind from Terra, but the breeze makes me uneasy.

"You're a little quiet, Constance. Is everything okay?"

{*My haze is dangerous. Prithee, be mindful and avoid breathing any.*}

"I'll be careful and bring a mask next time I visit." Terra removes a bag from her back and draws out a black rectangle. "This is called a computer or, more specifically, a laptop. I brought it in case whatever it was you said you needed is something I can't answer. By the way, what was that anyway?"

'*Lap-top? I have seen several people with similar items, but I do not know how a rectangle is meant to help me.*' I lean forward, considering the best way of explaining the situation. {*Well, it may be difficult to believe, but I think there is a strong likelihood that there may be beasts in the Lake. Some might even call them... monsters.*}

Her expression turns more serious. "Monsters?" She nods and takes on a thoughtful air. "Have you seen these monsters?"

I shake my head. {*Nay, not precisely, but I know that they are likely to appear soon.*}

"How do you know monsters will appear here if you haven't seen them?"

I grasp the cattail and fidget with its end. {*...Spirit's intuition?*}

"I'd really appreciate it if you could be clearer with just how sure you are that monsters are in the Lake."

'*Should I confess? ...Confess that I practically transmuted the Lake and chamber pot tunnels into monstrous hellbroth. Nay! Nay, madam, I do not believe I shall. Terra would indubitably deem me a menace.*' Unable to sustain eye contact, I stare out over the Lake. {*I am fairly confident... Nay, I am certain the Lake is dangerous.*}

Terra furrows her brow. "Hmm, well, I don't know what reason a spirit would have to lie. I can't risk my father finding out. I'll have to be discrete." She pauses, whispering, "Might need a helping hand."

{*...Wait, Terra, does this suggest thou believest me?*}

"Yeah. I believe you."

{Then... I think it would be wise if we erected signs to forewarn passersby. That way folk shall be wary of the monsters beneath the Lake's waters.}

"Oh? The reason you wanted to be alone was to talk about the monsters and warning signs?" Terra asks, pursing her lips.

{Aye? How else would one go about forewarning others? Circular letters are sluggish, impractical, and expensive... Is something the matter?}

"No, nothing's the matter." She sighs, staring off into space. "I thought you'd be more interested in learning about the modern world, teaching you sounded like fun. It's sort of like being excited when a friend or relative from out of the country visits. It sounds a little selfish considering you just told me about monsters, but I don't get many opportunities to unwind and have fun."

{I desire that too, but I was afraid of being too forward!} I shout through the telepathic link. {Still, I would prefer to learn about the present era a bit at a time, or I shall be overwhelmed.} The black rectangle becomes blindingly bright. I turn away from it. {Terra, what is that rectangle? Is it angry at us?} I ask in jest.

She giggles. "That's funny, Constance. I'll make it dimmer for you." With a quick poke, the black rectangle's light becomes bearable. "So, as I said earlier, this is a laptop and is like a tool that can accomplish things that used to take dozens of different devices. Well, most of the devices this replaced probably didn't exist in your time either..."

I float closer to inspect the device, cautious about maintaining a safe distance from her. 'In a way, the lap-top reminds me of Earl. Should I ask Terra if the two are similar? ...Nay, I need to keep Earl a secret. After all, I am supposed to be something akin to a spirit, and I doubt spirits have things like Earl... perhaps? Verily, I do not know, but I shan't be the first to mention Earl nor my Status and Chronicles.'

Terra stares at me with mirthful eyes. "When you slide closer to me like that, it reminds me of a glitch in a video game."

{I do not understand what that is... Can I ask a question now?}

"Of course, feel free."

I act as if I am drawing a deep breath and ask, {*What precisely is this device? How does it work? Is it lit by candlelight, oil, or animal fat? Or perhaps it's lit by the same thing the lanterns are lit by? Are they common or only for the wealthy? When were they created? Who created them? ...Wait, are these devices magic!?*} I stop myself. Terra's eyes are wide. '*Oh, magic... Mayhap I should not have said magic.*'

"That's a lot of questions!" To my relief, she is not shaken by the mention of magic. "I was expecting 'a question.'"

{*Ah, my apologies! I am merely curious and frustrated by my ignorance of this era.*}

She waves her hand. "No need to apologize; I didn't mean it in a bad way. What a laptop is and how it works will be understandably complicated for a person with no technological experience. So watch me, and if you have any more questions, don't hesitate to ask them."

I nod. {*Ayeee!*}

"And as for your other questions, no, computers aren't lit by candles, oil, or fat. Lanterns, or streetlamps, are lit by lightbulbs; as for the laptop, it would be easier to think of it as also being lit by lightbulbs, except lots of tiny ones." She glances at me to verify that I am still following, so I nod as if I understand. "Off the top of my head, I don't know the exact year computers were invented, but they've been around for several decades now. Plus, I know there are a few debates concerning what qualifies as the first 'real computer' and who is the 'true inventor.'"

{*That explanation is adequate; I was astonished and asked too many questions at once.*}

With a small laugh, she continues, "Lastly, no, this laptop isn't magic, it's technology. You could think about it like a 'box' or library that carries an enormous number of books, pictures, and information, mixed with near-infinite quantities of trash and gibberish."

{*Fascinating! What about thy telepathy? Is that magic, or is it the thing called 'technology'?*}

"Telepathy is different..." Terra falls into thought. I wait patiently, weighing if I should attempt to touch the lap-top. She sighs. "Telepathy is indeed magic, but you shouldn't tell anyone about magic, Constance... Not that you can talk to most people, but still, be mindful."

'She did not want to talk about magic and warned me against mentioning it but told me regardless?' I watch her tapping the lap-top. *'Does she trust me? I would like to believe that, but... I do not believe her to be credulous enough to trust so readily. Her words are prudent.'*

{*...Terra, I would relish learning more about myself. What is a spirit? Is it the same as a soul?*} I ask her, praying it is not suspicious that I do not know.

"Hmmm." Her lips purse. "An unexpected question, but... I guess it makes sense that you'd want to know, being 'spirit-like' and all." While setting her lap-top to the side, she smirks and exhales a puff of hot air into the cold night. "This might come off as a little childish, but it was one of the ways it was explained to me when I was a little girl."

Reaching into her bag, she removes something wrinkled and glistening. I drift a tad closer. The polished material reflects the glow of my violet eyes, mirroring my hazy face. "This metal is called aluminum. The product itself is aluminum foil. A lot of everyday items are made of this metal nowadays," she says, stretching the aluminum foil apart. The aluminum's crinkling as she unwraps it is dreadfully unpleasant. Revealing the contents, she raises a mystical and enchanting item, proclaiming, "This is called a sandwich, and before you ask, no, it's not made of sand."

My eyes sharpen upon the delectable item, and the cattail around my torso wags. I lift my hand and press my palm against the cattail's end.

Raising her head, she stares at me, raising an eyebrow. "Is something wrong, Constance?"

{*...May I have this item known as a sandwich?*} I ask, leaning in closer to it.

"You want this?" She holds the sandwich toward me. "...Are you capable of eating? Now that I think about it, the person who broke into the restaurant did steal all the food."

'Restraint, Constance. Do not embarrass thyself or cause suspicion. I am spirit-like and am likely thought to be incapable of eating. Besides, food is my weakness, and I cannot reveal my weakness—it's embarrassing.' I wave my hand at her. *{Thou wert hoodwinked. I was asking in jest and was never truly interested.}*

"Must be some quirky 16th-century humor," she murmurs to herself. "Anyway, I kind of need the sandwich for my explanation. Speaking of which, are you ready for that?"

I nod.

She wiggles her posterior, positioning herself to face me. Her gown gets a tad tangled, so she lays the sandwich in front of me, lifts herself with one hand, and yanks the gown straight. "Okay, so, take everything I am about to explain with a grain of salt, as this is the sort of explanation that someone might give a seven-year-old." Lowering herself, she sighs and points at the sandwich. "This sandwich consists of three parts: the bread, the fillings, and for the sake of our explanation, the aluminum foil."

{It looks delightful, but I cannot fathom a guess of where this conversation is going.}

"Hold your horses I'm getting there."

{...Am I meant to have horses?}

"It's an idiom, not literal," she says with a chuckle. Waving her hand, she continues, "So, like this sandwich, you can divide a person into three fundamental components: the body, the consciousness, and the soul. We will equate the body with the bread, the spirit with the fillings, and the soul with the aluminum."

{Aye, aye! I shall equate as instructed.}

"Then we will start with the bread. Of the three parts, the beard is the most understood by us. A person gifted a specific variety of bread can be more robust, beautiful, delicate, and have considerable advantages. Still, no matter how you slice it, bread can only get someone so far. Consequently, a creature that is only bread doesn't do much more than eat, sleep, grow, and reproduce—creatures of pure instincts."

Once more, I nod. *'I adore bread.'*

Seeing me nod, she points at aluminum foil. "Next is the aluminum foil or the soul. The foil fulfills its function well enough. It protects the bread and fillings from the world's degradation while the bread provides something for the foil to wrap around, preventing it from blowing around aimlessly. So with the protection of the foil, you can have a more fragile, complex, and long-lasting sandwich." She glances at me with a smirk and a shrug of her shoulders. "The soul is also the least understood among the three, with the spirit being a close second."

'Well, it is also the one I comprehend least, so I suppose that is fair.'

She removes the top of the bread, exposing the fillings. "Speaking of which, this brings us to the fillings; this is the consciousness, also known as the spirit. The spirit is the most distinct ingredient of a person's identity. You can have numerous fillings, with more or less of something, and desirable and undesirable components. It's thought to carry the personality, memories, and the deep-seated nature of a person's psyche." She glances up to check if I am following.

{I suppose I understand as well as I can,} I respond.

"Good." She tips the bread onto aluminum, spilling the fillings. "Now, as I said earlier, a creature that is just bread is one of pure instinct. I would guess they consist of things like plankton, krill, and most insects. If you add aluminum, you make a being that could be categorized as sentient. This would probably include most animals that are at least as big as a mouse. Finally, after inserting fillings, that creature then has the potential for sapience. Sapience includes humans and probably some animals, but I honestly can't say what would or wouldn't have a spirit."

Holding up her finger, she points at the stained insides of the bread. "Unlike the sandwich, once joined together, taking them apart is no longer so simple. If you removed, say, the foil and the fillings from a living person, you would create something like a ghoul. Remove the foil, and you'd be left with, I don't know, something like a lich, I guess.[46] More pertinent to your situation, a spirit is this one..." She removes the foil and bread. "A spirit is only the filling. Without the protection of the soul and

---

[46] Lich: In Old English it's a corpse or body. While awaiting a clergyman, corpses would be carried to the churchyard, passing through what was known as a lich-gate. In fantasy it's typically a reanimated corpse, undead creature, and/or undead necromancer.

body, spirits are said to 'spoil' and deteriorate in the material world as time passes. Which is why I was astonished you still have your wits."

{...So the body, soul, and spirit are all thought to be separate things that work together for some reason?}

"Precisely, they are three distinct pieces of a puzzle that combine to make us who we are." Smirking, she adds, "Also known as a sandwich wrapped in aluminum foil."

I stare at the ruined sandwich. 'This is all too philosophical... or mayhaps too literal; I cannot tell.'

"Well, we could talk all day on the subject, but that is the "Itsy Bitsy Spider" version of the three parts of sapient beings," she says, clapping her hands together.

'Wait, now there are spiders involved?'

She wraps the dismantled sandwich in the aluminum foil and sighs. "That was nostalgic," she murmurs with a sullen expression. I too am sullen at the sight of the delectable sandwich being put away.

Terra grabs her lap-top.

Seeing this, I remember I had something I wished to ask. {I have another question.} She looks at me as I point at the lap-top. {What is it fashioned from?}

"Now you're interested in knowing what it is made of, huh?" Her eyes and nose crinkle as she laughs with her hand over her mouth. I tilt my head as she says, "Already tired of learning about yourself? Rather learn about my laptop than spirits and souls? It is mostly made of plastic, or at least the case is."

{Oh! Playstuck, of course, of course... What is a playstuck?}

"It's pronounced plas·tic. It's made from something like petroleum, which is something that comes from the ground. The process of how petroleum came to be is complicated, but just know that plastic is a prevalent material nowadays and you'll see it pretty much everywhere. This material, along with a few others, has had enormous effects upon the world."

{*Enormous effects upon the world? Fascinating...*} I point toward one of the containers. {*The black thing full of rubbish, what's it crafted of?*}

Studying the bin, she says, "If you mean the trash bag, that's plastic too."

{*So a rubbish bag then.*} Noticing a clear tube floating in the Lake, I point at it. {*What about that?*}

She squints, causing me to remember it's much darker here for her than it is for me. "Oh, now I see what you were pointing at. That's a water bottle, well, trash now, but it's also made of plastic."

I stare into her big green eyes. {*Art thou certain? None of these things seem terribly similar. Is this a trick at my expense?*}

"No, it's not. It wouldn't be a very good trick, to be honest." Terra reaches into her bag. I move closer to see if I can perhaps sneak the sandwich within. She stops, looking me up and down once again. "Is something the matter, Constance? Your haze seems... depressed."

{*My haze seems... depressed?*}

"It was swirlier before, but right now, it's not really moving around at all. Like earlier, when I asked if you wanted to be friends, it was almost like a storm. Now it's kind of still, so I assumed that meant you were sad or something."

'*Is she suggesting my haze seems to be reacting to my emotions? ...Lies! But if it is true, I need to keep an even more restrained state of mind.*' The aluminum foil crinkles as she stuffs it deeper into her bag. '*I despise that noise yet grieve for the loss of the delicious sandwich.*'

She pulls her hand out, glances at me, and furrows her brow. "Now your haze has almost stopped moving altogether."

'*Who am I trying to fool. Unless she is lying, I shall never be able to hide my feelings.*'

Terra smiles. "Let's get back on topic. Do you have any idea what you want these signs to say?"

Nodding, I hold up my hands, tracing the dimensions I wish the sign to be. {Aye, I have put some thought into it and think it should say something akin to, 'Death and nature's boundless malignity looms in these accursed depths.[47] Be wary and depart.'} I point at my head and then draw an 'X.' {Preferably with a skull and crossbones. I believe this would be an adequate forewarning.}

"Hmm, are you sure that isn't a little too dramatic?"

{What? Terra, drama and monsters are like stew and bread. They go hand in hand. Besides, there's naught wrong with a tinge of dramatic tone. It makes life more engaging.}

"Canny words, but I don't know, I'm not really convinced. How about we omit the skull and crossbones and go with something like, 'Warning: Toxic spill. Avoid contact with the Lake's water until further notice. Recommended 50-foot distance from Lake's edge at all times.' Oh, and toxic means something poisonous."

'I suppose I can compromise on the skull and crossbones, yet...' I tilt my head, asking, {Will that suffice? It's a tad uninspired and boring. Folk tend to ignore and dismiss wearisome notices. Should we not at least mention the formidable beasts?}

"There aren't any ordinary 'beasts' that could survive in such a shallow and cold lake. If it were the summer, I could maybe add something about alligators, but no one would believe it right now. Swinging it as a toxic spill is more believable."

{Are alligators bloodthirsty beasts? What do they look like?}

"I wouldn't say they're bloodthirsty, but..." She taps the lap-top and turns it toward me. "...here, take a look."

The blinding light clears, exposing a small and humble lizard. Rows of sharp teeth line its long snout. {Is it fair to keep a lizard in such a thin box? It

---

[47] Malignity: malignancy, malevolence. Also, an instance of the aforementioned malicious behaviors or natures.

is intimidating for a lizard, but it's not particularly large, and I doubt it would deter anyone from approaching the Lake.}

"Constance, this is a phot—I mean, a painting or picture of real life, so it's not their actual size."

{I am not certain I understand. Is this a picture frame? I thought it was a library.}

Terra taps something and the alligator changes to a different alligator. "It's not a picture frame, but that's not the worst way to think of it. A library full of pictures, books, and letters is the better way to think about it, though." To my surprise, she takes the initiative to explain some things to me, despite my not understanding much. "So, this is the internet." She glances between me and the lap-top. "It's probably better if you don't browse the internet without someone guiding you." With a chuckle, she continues, "This is the desktop, and on the desktop are all the applications that do various things..."

As Terra attempts to explain these 'application' things to me, I read their names. *'Jingle-Jangle, Tremble, A Helping Hand Inc, Nuclear Residue: House-Vegas, Dryas Cyclone Live Radar, CyberRuffin 358/2, EggSpree Crowdfunding, Phazel-tastic Pizza, Consorti_Bid.exe, Dino-Tower FREE... Wait, Tower!'*

{Terra, halt.} She looks at me with a raised eyebrow as I point. *{What is that one? Could I be made privy to it?}*

Squinting, she points at the Dino-Tower, asking, "Out of everything, you are interested in a predatory freemium game? It came preinstalled on the laptop when I bought it, but I'm pretty sure it's a tower defense game."

{Tower defense! That sounds like an utterly fascinating topic!} I lean closer. *{Prithee, enlightenment me to the ways of the Dino-Tower!}*

"...Yeah, sure, but first I want to show you something. Oh, but don't let me forget to give you the thing that will help you with your Mana Efflux. After all, we wouldn't want anyone else to track you using it..." Her eyes shiver.

'That was odd.'

Her hands tap against the lap-top, and she spins it toward me. The lap-top displays pictures of hands in different positions. "I don't know when or if you will ever be able to use Telepathy yourself, so you should learn some sign language..." She clears her throat and rubs the back of her neck. "And we should talk about a few of your pronouns while we are at it."

'...?'

Erstwhile Roach 1: A Day in the Life of a Roach

∞∞∞∞∞∞∞∞∞∞∞∞∞∞∞

10-year-old Constance

On a muggy morn in September, I stand in a tattered brownish-red gown, loitering in front of a heavy oak doorway south of London's Cripplegate. The local brown baker toils on the opposite side of this doorway, milling grain and baking the forenoon's bread. I lurk here as I desire to inhale the essence of the day's fresh-baked loaves and await an opportunity to pilfer a loaf or two… or three or four for myself. I often do this at the bakeries along Bread Street, but the White-Bakers' Guild's head baker swung a rolling pin at my temple. It was not a light swing either; it had clear malicious intent behind it. After the rolling pin incident, I decided to stalk the Brown-Bakers' Guild in the squalor for a fortnight or two.

The wooden step leading up to the door creaks beneath my feet as I move toward the crack in the door jamb. Looking behind me, I ensure that no bakers wielding rolling pins are prowling the streets. Not glimpsing the hairy white nose of the head baker wheezing down my nape, I gather my nerves and lean nearer.

I sniff. 'More.'

I peek left and right, affirming that I am still alone. I lean closer to the door jamb and press my nostrils against the splintered wood.

I sniff twice. '…Morrre.'

Glancing behind me, I tilt my head back and then position my nostrils for flawless bready air inhalation.

I sniff thrice. '……Morrrrrrre!'

Lifting my hand, I place it on the door latch and give it the most delicate nudge I can manage. The hinges make a wee whine, so I cease my actions. Standing still, I listen and then shuffle forward. "Child!" a gruff man's voice bellows. "Cease sniffing my door; it sounds as if a pack of boars is snorting for truffles."

My body shivers, winces, and butts the door all at once. I rub my brow and take a step backward. Too late do I remember the small stair at my heels. It feels as if I am plunging from a cliffside, yet the step is only a palm tall. My posterior splashes into a puddle, muddying the garments I bathed in the River Thames a mere fortnight ago.[48] I scowl and glare upward. Strands of my cherry-red hair drape my face, veiling my eyesight.

I hear applause from a lone pair of hands. "Aye, that was wonderful, such delicate grace," the man cheers.

Brushing the hair from my eyes, I see a burly man with graying hair and bulging muscles peering down at me from the bakery's second-story window.

'The baker! I am discovered!' I am about to stand but find myself frozen in place upon noticing a thick slice of bread within his clutches, a mere nibble missing. My eyes focus on the bread, and like a fish, I open and close my mouth. "I-I…"

He laughs. "Child, thy stench frightens my customers, but I can appreciate thy passion for brown bread." Like a dragon leering at a gold coin, my pupils cling to the flimsy piece of bread. "Take this loaf as payment for thy performance and tarry somewhere else from here forth."

From the window seal, the baker tosses the bread. Watching the bread arcing through the air, I laugh. "Thou ignorant fool!" I declare, raising a hand high. "To be so careless as to allow thy bread to slip from thy fingertips in my presence!"

I grin and clasp my hand tight. The squish of the warm loaf between my fingers is… *'Squishy bread?'* Lowering my arm, I open my palm. *'Bird droppings; I captured bird droppings.'* Something crumbly bounces against my brow. I look down, and in a murky puddle bobs my beautiful brown bread—my eyes water and blur.

---

[48] Thames would have been spelled Temese, Tamesis, or Tamisiam (From 13th Century Magna Carta) during this period.

The baker sighs. "A miserable display, child."

Snatching the bobbing bread from the water, I yell at the baker, "Thou cannot have it back! It is mine!" I leap to my feet and poke out my tongue. "My bread, baker man!"

I sprint through the back alleyways, looping to-and-fro to ensure the baker cannot catch me until I reach Wood Street. When I am certain he's not hunting me, I dive into a sinkhole underneath the foundation of an old forsaken shop next door to the Carpenters' Guildhall. Taking one last peek outside, I rub my palm in the dirt to cleanse it of bird droppings and cram the wet brown bread into my throat, swallowing it nigh whole.

Leaning against the earthen wall, I massage my belly, murmuring, "Today shall be a good day."

From outside my humble sinkhole comes a most welcome greeting. "Meow."

"Thou hast com'st to visit me on my special day!"

A raven black mouser trots down the tunnel, Sir Mouser, my most precious friend. Sir Mouser is a catling with eyes greener than the freshest grass and fur blacker than the darkest night. If he is not hunting at the stables, he is with me, playing and spending his days at my side. The two of us are never apart for very long, and that is how we like it.

Sinking to Sir Mouser's eye level, I grin and ask, "Didst thou com'st to visit because it is my birthday?"

"Mew?" he asks, tilting his head in evident anticipation.

"How do I know it is my birthday? Last autumn, I decided my birthday would be three days after the first season's leaves fell, and I saw a leaf fall three days ago!"

Sir Mouser gazes at me with half-closed eyes. "...Mow."

I sneer. "Why should only the noble boys be entitled to birthdays!? I was born, was I not? I breathe, so I must have been born."

"Meow."

"Oh! Sir Mouser, didst thou see'st!" Using my thumb, I draw back my upper lip. "I lost yet another tooth yestermorning! I am nigh a lady, and if I can grow big and strong enough, I can find better methods to earn my own coin!" I remove my thumb from my mouth, raise my hands, and shout, "Soon! Coins! My own coins! Canst thou imaginest such a thing, Sir Mouser?!"

He sits and watches me. "Meow. Meow."

I shake my head. "I thank thee for thy concern, Sir Mouser, but excluding 'her,' I have never fallen ill before! The other children that once shared the alleyways with me were unwell more often than not... But that was before they were swept away to Bridewell or passed beyond the lychgate.[49] I have not seen the other children in many months. Regardless! I must be taking excellent care of myself to avoid ill-health... Though, I seem to be growing slower than the children with families..."

"Meow," he responds.

"Aye, it does not matter if I am forever smaller than the other children. I am certain I shall still be strong!" I flex. "Heroic Knight-Lady Constance, the strongest and bravest knight!" Giggling, I reach out to scratch Sir Mouser's wee ears, yet a finger's length apart, I freeze. A viscous black haze wafts between my fingers and into the sleeves of my garment.

"Do not worry." I hide my hand and force a smile. "Apologies, Sir Mouser, I cannot pet thee today, but at least She is not here, so thou mayst stay."

"Meow."

"Who is She?" I shake my head and then look around, making certain no one is eavesdropping. "She was the one I called 'her' earlier—my only

---

[49] Bridewell: Palace for both punishing "disorderly women" and housing homeless children.

illness. Thou mayst never meet her, for She begets only foulness, leaving sickness and madness in her wake."

"Meow. Meoww."

"Nay, She does not speak. I do not believe She can; it is pathetic, really. Canst thou imaginest not being able to speak?" I pat my belly, attracting Sir Mouser's attention. "Aye! But enough of her. Let us see if we may locate more food, Sir Mouser."

Sir Mouser's eyes widen at the word food, and I take that as a sign that he also desires to forage for food. I grab an old rust-laden cauldron I found buried in some manure and hold it out for Sir Mouser.

He stares at the cauldron. "...Meow."

"I soaked it in a puddle and boiled water within it. It's more than clean enough for thee!"

Appearing pleased, Sir Mouser bounces into the cauldron, lies down, and pokes his head out. I grasp the handle, and together we leave the safety of the sinkhole. "We shall find apples in the orchard if we travel beyond Aldgate. They should be delicious too!"

"Meow. Meow."

····
·········
····

Sir Mouser and I pass by the school for noble boys. I would sneak in to eavesdrop on Magistrate Caspar Fröbel's lecture, but he is visiting from Schwarzburg, a county in the Holy Roman Empire. His accent is rather thick, so understanding him is challenging. Besides, today is my birthday, so I believe I have earned a day to myself. I pass by the school's gate, my face flushing red and my breathing labored.

'Gehhhh, this cauldron is so heavy! But Sir Mouser is too noble to drag himself through the mud. Perhaps, I may distract myself somehow.' I look toward the cauldron. "Sir Mouser, I have been curious. Is there, perhaps, a..." Moving nearer, I whisper, "...Lady Mouser?"

He blinks at me and then turns away, growing bored. Also, bored, I glance around for more distractions, noticing a stained glass window. *'So delightful! Purple and blue are my favorite colors...! Though having two favorites is unfair to both colors. After all, I am certain they wish to feel special as well...'* I ponder solutions to this quandary and am struck by one of the most glorious answers in history. *'Aye! Today purple shall be my favorite, and on the morrow, blue shall be my favorite! Now they both have their own day.'*

Passing by a mansion, I halt and show it to Sir Mouser. "This is Heneage House! Sir Thomas Heneage built it after the Queen gave him the old priory. I believe he is... Treasurer of the Queen's Privy Chamber? I cannot recall, but he is a knight!" I resume walking. "I learned that at school! Ahh, I would have been the best pupil, Sir Mouser, I am certain of it." I sigh. "Alas, I am fated to live the life of Roach."

"Meow."

"It is not all sorrow," I chuckle, "for I have thee, little mouser."

"Meow-meow!"

I pivot on my heel, turning onto a narrow footpath toward London Hall Street. "Speaking of which, we cannot neglect thy meal before the orchard."

Sir Mouser's ears twitch.

"Aye, thou hast hearest perfectly! Art thou gladdened?"

He purrs and kneads his feet against the cauldron's bottom.

We walk from London Hall Street eastward past Leaden Hall and onto a bustling Poultry Street. I keep my head down, swerving between the commoners. A faint jingle draws my eye. Tied to a man's belt is a coin purse. *'Woe, my heart breaks.'* I sigh, readjusting Sir Mouser's cauldron. *'A fat purse ripe for the plucking, and my hands are occupied.'*

"What is it to be a cripple that feels nothing? Thou needest to ask a woman. Simply say, what is it to feel nothing, my good lady? And she shall answer, 'coarse.'"

A crowd breaks into uproarious laughter.

"I... I do not understand, Sir Mouser... And why would he make jest of cripples? I share the alleyways with cripples; they give me food sometimes." I frown and look toward the crowd. At the center, I catch a short glimpse of a boy in a jester's cap. "Boooo!" I hoot. "Poor jest; crude jest! Speak a humorous one!"

One woman with an imperious accent turns to face me, giggling. Her sapphire-blue gown and attire rife with jewelry, baubles, trinkets, and glittering cloth, speak all I must know of this woman. She is a noble, the incarnation of everything I shan't ever possess. "Ahh, a child's mind is charming. What I would give to be so youthful and innocent again. Cherish thy youth, child; it shall be thy best years, then thou shalt wed a man, and thy best years will be behind thee," she titters whilst covering her mouth.

Biting my tongue, I shed a snake's tear. "W-what? T-t-this is meant to be my best years!? I am so poor and hungry, Miss!" Snot leaks from my nostril. "Nay, why wouldst thou condemnest me to such a fate? Thy lies are wicked!"

Some in the crowd observe us. They giggle at or exchange.

She chuckles, scrutinizing my threadbare garments. Her face flushes red. "Well, mayhaps thou art right. Here, young waif, I am a charitable" —she leans close and emphasizes— "noblewoman. Mine acquaintances would attest to that." I hold out my hand, but she drops a coin into my cauldron instead, knocking Sir Mouser atop his brow. He hisses at her.

I wipe my nose on my sleeve. "I thank thee."

"Perhaps it is because thine accent is so crass that I am mishearing." Her eyes narrow a tad. "...But why dost thou address me so informally? I understand thy situation is... poor, but that does not mean thou shouldst use such speech."

I tilt my head, playing coy. "What dost thou meanest?"

"...I 'meanest' "thou" and "thee," thine impolite and discourteous manner of addressing me."

"Oh. Apologies, but I have chosen not to speak in the Queen's fashion."

"Thou cannot..." She hesitates and glances at my attire. "Thou cannot simply choose to be disrespectful to certain people. Politeness and respect cost naught. Thou shouldst use the appropriate forms of mannerly addressment: you, your, and madam."

"Oh. I am afraid I have mused this deeply, and I do not feel as if I am obliged to be polite and respectful to anyone. I use the same words for all folk, from beggars to not beggars."

Her mouth hangs with a frozen smile. "...People, particularly certain "noble people," are indisputably obliged to the politeness and respect of commoners. I am grieved to say thou shalt come to learn that someday if thou art not wary."

"Apologies, but my tongue shan't utter the Queen's English. I speak to everyone the same."

"One bearing thy status could undoubtedly choose to speak to everyone in the same manner except thou couldst do it politely and respectfully. Of course, using the appropriate terms: 'you' and 'your'."

"Since I am of low birth, I am obliged to speak to everyone politely?" I shake my head. "Nay, apologies. As I said, none are obligated politeness or respect, yet I do not fancy treating people differently, so I simply do not speak the Queen's English. I speak London Parlance."

"London Parlance. Thou mean the beggars' cant? Mere facile jargon of the credulous. I thought it a jest."

"...?" I tilt and shake my head. "Nay, apologies, but I do not know it by that name. It is used by London's folk."

She glares at me for a moment. "...I do not know why I squander my mood educating a Scot waif." Sighing, she departs without another glance or word.

"That woman understands naught, Sir Mouser. And I am weary of everyone judging me Scottish. I know naught of my roots, and neither do they. If it was my hair, then why Scot and not Irish? Do I have an accent...?" Sighing, I inspect the coin left to us, and then add, "It matters not."

Coin in hand, we enter an alleyway that reeks of rot. Sir Mouser hops up, placing his paws on the cauldron's rim. "Mooooow!" he whines.

I knock on a cellar door that runs underneath a log building. "Hush, little mouser. Patience is a crucial facet of appetite."

The door swings open, revealing a man with a jaw as strong as a horse. He chuckles. "Here to purchase our rubbish, Roach?"

"That I am. All thy rubbish."

"Then, come in, Roach and Rat," he steps out. His frame is nigh as large as the broadside of a barn door.

I stand on my tiptoes and point. "It's Sir Mouser, not Rat."

"I care little." He glares at my hand and takes a step back. "Touch nothing, Roach, or I shall squash thee. Now, go."

"Squash me?" Skipping down the stairway, I shout, "Sir Mouser and Roach are unsquashable, behemoth."

"Doubtful," he scoffs.

With a hop, I drop off the last stair and move into a cobblestone storehouse full of oaken barrels. Overhead a sign reads, "Tavern Below."

····

········

····

Half an hour later, Sir Mouser and I sit at the end of the alleyway. My eyes move between two hempen sacks I am carrying: one is Sir Mouser's treats, and the other is a mystery.

"They never told me which was which..." Shrugging my shoulders, I tip one of the sacks, and two mangled fish heads tumble out, each of which is bigger than my own head. "Huzzah, haddock heads! Thy favorite!" I toss the other hempen sack against the wall. "And all I must do for the Tavern

Boss is toss the other sack into the Thames when no one is watching. Simple!" Reaching into my pocket, I remove a bread roll and stuff it into my mouth. "They fed me too!" I mumble, spitting crumbs.

"I have returned my good men and women! Gather around, for I shall only perform for London today before I must take my leave!" A crowd gathers around a boy.

The boy is young, and his voice has yet to deepen fully. If I had to speculate, I would place him between thirteen and sixteen years of age. He wears linen doublets, sheepskin jerkins, bloated trunks, tight stockings, and a white neck ruffle. He is well attired yet not noble as he wears neither very dark nor very light colors, both of which are forbidden for commoners to don. My own muddy red gown would be criminal for me to wear if it were too clean, which shall never be an issue since I spent an entire morn tarnishing the gown after I 'borrowed' it from an oblivious noble girl.

As for his clothing, it is a soft red and green save for the neck ruffle which is off-white. "An encore performance here, on Pie-Corner, for thy amusement," the boy declares.

"Oh, Sir Mouser, a show with our meal. The God in Light must know it is my birthday."

The boy clears his throat. "To Die in Nothing - Quips," he dons a jester's cap, "by William, The Actor!"

"Nay, it's the same boy from earlier! Highest Devil Umbral must know it is my birthday!" I push the roll to my cheek and cup my hands, shouting, "Jest, speak a jest!"

"Oh-ho, we have a child comic, come to witness, me, William, The Actor." I swallow my roll as the crowd turns altogether to look at me. "Tell me, what dost thou thinkest of this jest, child."

I click my tongue. "Cease calling me a "child" thou art scarcely older than me."

"Duly noted, girl, but now for the jest," he clears his voice. "To be a stabbed beggar, borne by manhood and undone... but undone by whom?" He pauses. "Ask her the fellow's name."

The crowd chuckles.

"Booo!" I jeer. "Poor jest; crude jest!"

"Oh, I see we have a hard to please girl, perhaps I shall another, to be an orphan k—"

"Boo! Poor jest; crude jest! Thou art not an orphan, beggar, nor cripple, so why dost thou mockest them? They would not giggle with thee."

"I assure thee, girl, they would laugh. Like that fellow at thy back."

Looking behind me, I see an elderly beggar-man leaning against the alleyway's wall, grinning and watching our exchange. "That is Tittering Tommy," I say. "He is a very ill man plagued by unstaunchable laughter." Tittering Tommy laughs, tears streaming down his cheeks. "Why art thou so cruel, Mister 'The Actor'? To mock a sick man."

The crowd also laughs, forming a half-circle around William and me.

"Cruel? Nay!" William chuckles. "My jests are the great counterbalance, girl! They make the destitute relatable to us common folk."

"But-but, the destitute do not laugh! If they do not laugh, then thou art a teaser of the destitute."

He scoffs. "What would a girl know of such things?"

I point toward the haddock heads; a pair of mouser ears poke from its mouth. "I know what he tells me, and he's invariably correct!"

The fish head wiggles and Sir Mouser pushes his head through the fish's lips. "Mow?"

Sighing, he raises his hand, declaring, "Oh, what a foolish fool I am! Squabbling with a catling in a fish head."

The crowd laughs.

"A fool indeed, my catling in a fish head is too wise for thee!" I shout back.

Sir Mouser nods. "Mo," he says, withdrawing into the haddock head.

Again, the crowd laughs.
"The girl's quite mouthy, is she not!?" a man exclaims.
A woman nods. "Mayhaps this is part of the jester's performance?"
"Aye, I am not certain which I like more: the jester boy, girl, or catling," the man chuckles.

William smiles. "The girl and catling, a part of my performance...? Art thou interested in performing with me, hmm?"

"Thou art not pleasant." I stand. "We shan't perform for thee."

"Thou art willing to perform then, only not for me? Art thou truly so insulted by my jests? Is there something amiss with my jests beyond thou simply being too young and innocent to comprehend them?"

I cross my arms. "Thou offendest those beneath thee because thou dost not wishest to insult thy audience of common folk. Scorning those who are lower than thyself and whom thou dost not understandest is not humorous."

"...So thou thinkest my jests should be regarding those of higher standing?"

Making a fist, I turn to the crowd and shout at the people, "I know naught, but only currish common folk, who do not live the plight of lower folk, could find this boy's jests humorous!"

The crowd giggles at one another. "A child insults us," they murmur.

"Intriguing," I hear William whisper.

I scoff. "Do not giggle, and do not be intrigued!" Pursing my lips and stomping my foot, I shout, "That was not a jest nor insightful, curs!"

Their giggles turn to hearty laughter... but their cackling curtails as a scream hushes everyone.

Everyone turns to look where a disheveled beggar wench casts a hempen sack to the ground and then stumbles backward. '*...Is that not the sack I am meant to cast into the Thames?*'

A man catches the woman in his arms. "Art thou hysterical, bedlam woman?"

"N-nay!" She shakes her head and points at the sack with a quivering hand. "There's... there's... there's a head in that sack."

"A head? What dost thou meanest?"

"I mean a head!" the woman cries. "A man's head!"

William walks over and plucks the sack from the cobblestone. Opening it, he grimaces, and his eyes shift toward me. "There is a man's bloody head in thy sack..."

I shake my head and take a step back. "That sack be not mine."

"Girl," He holds the head toward me and asks, "Dost it be or not be? That is the question."

"What? Of course, that sack be, but it be not mine, foppish dunce!"

The crowd watches, indifferent to my words. I glance at Sir Mouser, and he hops into his cauldron, sensing the tension.

"Girl..." William dons a flat expression and shakes his head. "I shall confess, I admire thy childish wit, but this is no time for insults and play. This is quite serious."

My body shivers under the stabbing leers of the common folk, and I feel as if I might retch. Nodding, I place a palm atop my heart. "I am but a simple, unlearned girl." I gaze up at William with wide eyes and a pout. "What would I know of anything, much less of a head in a sack? Surely, thou understandest, Mister William..." My lip quivers as I lift Sir Mouser's cauldron. "Thou dost, aye, Mister William?"

His eyes narrow and his cheeks turn flush. "Art... art thou the same fiery girl?"

Sir Mouser joins me, raises himself on the cauldron's lip, and stares up at him. "Moooowh?" he whines with dilated pupils.

"...She is but a girl," a man says, nodding. "Even a woman would struggle to overwhelm a man and take their head. M-mayhap thou shouldst simply bringest the wretched man's head to a warden."

I sniff, shedding a tear, and nod at William. "I am but a girl," I whisper.

He opens his mouth to say something, but someone else speaks first. "What is this disorder?" a wizened voice queries in a foreign accent.

The crowd whispers as they step aside, allowing a man to the front. "French Éclat Inquisitor, here, in London?"
"The Church in Light and Crown say we must welcome them, but I say filthy French should return across the channel."
"Aye, I would wager them a spy. No better than the barbarous Spanish."

'French Éclat? Who is the Éclat? Ah, I care not. My tongue shall free me of this regardless.' My eyes drift to Sir Mouser. *'I believe we shall spend our autumn in the apple orchard, Sir Mouser.'*

A man with aqua-blue eyes and a well-kempt beard and mustache stops in before William and me. "I am Inquisitor Eberhardt with the French Éclat," he says in a deep voice that carries a minor French inflection. "This gathering is obs—"

I point at William. "That garish boy has a man's head in a sack." Spinning on my heel, I attempt to scuttle down the alleyway, but a palm dense with callouses catches my shoulder. I gasp, "Do not touch me, Frenchman Eberhardt!" and try to jerk away. "Thou knowest naught."

He spins me around. "Why are you so guarded, child? What ill-fortunes has life dealt you?"

My brows furrow as I stare at the perplexing Frenchman. "Thou speakest to me in the Queen's fashion...? *Hmph!*" I shake my head. "Why dost thou questionest me when the man next to thee carries a head in a hempen sack? Prithee, I am a guiltless and hapless girl, so leave me be."

William sighs. "I bear a man's head in a hempen sack, aye, but it is a head found next to this girl."

He waves William back. "...We shall discuss the head afterward."

William nods and sets the head and sack aside. He quells the crowd and calls them away from Inquisitor Eberhardt and me.

Inquisitor Eberhardt's eyes pierce my soul. "What is your name?"

"I am Roach." I try to back away, but he keeps a firm hold of my shoulder. "And I do not relish being touched."

The white hair of his eyebrows rises. "Chosen name? Are you a Scot orphan? Did you choose your own name when none gave you one?"

I click my tongue. "I said it was chosen, did I not?"

"Girl, you are spirited. Do you not trust me?"

His question catches me by surprise. "...Trust thee?"

"You can trust me, child." He frees me and shows me his hand. Blisters and blemishes cover its surface as black haze sinks into his flesh. "I know what you are, and I understand you cannot help it."

I blink. "...T-thou knowest... what I am...? None know what I am."

He nods. "Would you like a home, child?"

My mouth opens. "...Haa ...home? Didst thou sayst... home?"

"I did. A gorgeous convent is in the works in London. The convent shall bear the name of the Inviolable Eminent Child, Hallow Equarié. There, Hallow Equarié will watch over you from her place between the First and Second Lights. She shall see that you grow into a lovely woman of the Church."

"...A home," I murmur.

He kneels in front of me. "What is your chosen name?"

"...Con—" I bite my tongue and shake my head.

"Worry not." He nods. "I shall deal with this 'head in a sack' situation, and then we shall find you some food. Does that please you?" I hesitate to reply as I do not understand what's happening... "Child?"

"It's... it's my birthday."

"Oh? Is it?"

My eyes stare up at him. "I... I want to go to the orchards... but I am weary of walking."

He laughs. "I shall take you and..." His eyes move to the cauldron. "...Sir Mouser."

I nod. "Sir Mouser and Roach."

"Do you need anything else?" He glances at my garments. "New attire, perhaps?"

"Uhm..." My eyes drift to the 'jovial' man deeper in the alleyway. "Tittering Tommy is hungry, too. Canst thou givest him something before we depart for the orchard?"

He blinks. "O-oui, child. Today, we shall feed whomever you wish. Though I must say, I am curious why that is what you request?"

"...Aye, but I am too shy to say it aloud." My cheeks flush, I set Sir Mouser's cauldron down and step close to Eberhardt. He turns his head, giving me his ear. "It's... because none fed Mister Tittering Tommy on their birthday. So, I desire to feed them on my birthday." Stepping away, I place my hands behind my back. Eberhardt smiles at me as I stare bashfully at the cobblestone street. '...And I pilfered Tittering Tommy's bread loaf last week... and the week before that... and yesternight too.'

He stands. "You are a good child. It's like Hallow Equarié herself is reincarnate and standing in front of me."

"I thank thee, Mister Eberhardt. Thou art so kind." He walks away to take the hempen sack in hand. I smirk, bringing my arms forward, and fiddle with a golden French coin. "But thou knowest me not, Frenchman," I whisper.

"Inquisitor Eberhardt," a woman calls out. I slip the coin into a hidden pocket sewn into my gown. From around the corner, shuffles a woman in a sapphire gown, the same noblewoman from earlier. Two guards, the noblewoman's boots, follow behind her. "Pardon me," she says.

I step closer to Sir Mouser's cauldron, noticing the noblewoman's guards studying my waist. *'They search for weapons?'*

Many in William's crowd notice the events and turn away from him to watch us.

Inquisitor Eberhardt places a rag over the head and sack and then turns. His eyes study the woman as he asks, "Is something the matter, Noble Dame?"

"I hope you do not mind, but I inadvertently overheard your 'polite' chat with the Scot waif." She points at me, saying, "And I thought it crucial you know she is a liar, thief, mischief-maker, and quite possibly a murderess."

My mouth falls open.

"Meurtrière...?"[50] He clears his throat and bows his head. "Pardon, Noble Dame, I am still adjusting to speaking English regularly, as you can tell. But I believe I misheard you." Raising a hand toward me, he continues, "This girl is a forsaken youth of the God in Light. Condemning her as a murderess might be thought dubious by most folk."

"Undoubtedly, and I pray it is not so," she says, placing a palm over her breast. "Yet, I recall the reputation surrounding the avowed criminal bearing the nickname 'Roach,' and I witnessed her exiting the alleyway with the bag earlier. There have been reports circulating within higher society concerning red-haired Scot witches and cannibals in the less civilized north. This girl could be one of them. Mayhap her kin were hanged, and she fled to our fair city. One might find these circumstances perturbing, do you not agree, Inquisitor? Are these reports of Scot witches

---

[50] Meurtrière (Middle/Modern French): female murderer or murderess. The word has also been repurposed in English to refer to the slits in castle walls through which arrows can be fired.

and cannibals not the sort of things the Éclat should be investigating? Heretics and their ilk?"

"...Noble Dame, your words are... duly noted, but the French Éclat shall take her and keep guard of her. We will arrange a meeting and attend this matter amicably in private at a later time."

"House Nightingale will not permit such a thing as I fear her being in French custody suggests she shall vanish." Sighing, she persists, "I would not even wish her caged in Bridewell. She belongs in the Tower dungeon or Bedlam until present affairs are adequately understood." She looks at me. "To butcher an innocent man at such a youthful age when thou shouldst be toiling for thy dowry. Art thou guilty, or art thou mad? Which is it?"

"Neither," I say, biting the inside of my cheek.

"Neither? Canst thou still be so loose with thy manners? And I can scarcely comprehend thee with that crass accent. It grates mine ears."

I speak slowly and deliberately through my teeth, "Neither, Noble Mistress. My apologies for speaking with looseness, Noble Mistress."

"'My apologies,' it should be 'mine apologies' in mannerly Queen's English, waif."

My eyelid twitches.

Sighing, she continues, "But, calling me 'mistress' shall suffice, I suppose. And I shall authorize thee to depart with the Éclat ..." Her eyes drift toward the cauldron. "...if thou allow me to stow thy mouser at our estate as a condition of assurance this affair will not vanish."

I gasp. Inquisitor Eberhardt replies to the noblewoman. He turns to me and his lips move, yet I hear naught.

Her two guards move toward the cauldron, but I step between them. The inside of my mouth tastes of blood as my teeth puncture the inside of my cheek. 'Words. Food. Garments. Coin. School. Nobles understand only how to hoard and take, but they shan't ever take my friend.'

I watch Inquisitor Eberhardt's lips, "Have you borne ill, child?"

'Queen's English. They speak it to separate themselves from London commoners. To play refined and superior merely because of the circumstances of their birth. They do nothing but have everything.'

Her guards say something, reaching for their sword's hilts, but I hear them not. The noblewoman's lips move. "House Nightingale shall bear the responsibility of the Scot's custody."

My fingernails dig into my palms. *'I shan't speak in their foul fashion, but I shall take their school even if they do not like it. I shall steal their food, snatch their clothes, pilfer their coin, even rob their house name and take it for myself. Every breath I breathe and every word I speak, shall serve as a spite against those that believe themselves superior.'*

Both guards move to my sides, reaching for my wrists. *'Nobles are no better than a mere Roach; they are evil by the ideals of the Church in Light's Daybreak Scriptures.* I feel a faintness, and the guards back away from me. Haze flows out of my gown's sleeves and collar.

Inquisitor Eberhardt moves close and says something. "Calm yourself. Remember, child, there is good in all things."

I shake my head. *'The only good the nobility can do is free us of their own avarice and dwell beyond the lychgate.'*

Haze pours from my body. It swirls, churns, and unites.

Malignity carnate, She arrives. She: no face, no expression, no mannerisms, only a hazy sable maelstrom twisting into a shape and figure identical to my own.

She stands unmoving as if set upon Earth by mistake. Waves of haze flow off her body, bathing the noblewoman, her guards, Inquisitor Eberhardt, and anyone who happens to be near its infectious venom. I lift Sir Mouser's cauldron, stepping away and raising him above my head. She, the haze girl, watches the people as the haze seeps into their flesh. Disease and hysteria run rampant.

Wives attack husbands, husbands scream at wives, children run to cower, illness thrives, and chaos reigns whilst I, Roach, turn and flee deep into the alleyways with my mouser.

Quicker than ever before, I arrive at my sinkhole.

I squirm into my hole and cower like the other children were. Tears fall from my eyes as I collapse into the dirt. Tucking my head between my legs, I weep.

"Meow..."

My dearest friend keeps me company.

A Tilted Web of Tales 1: A Commoner's Beta Integration

∞∞ ∞∞ ∞∞ ∞∞ ∞∞ ∞∞ ∞∞ ∞∞ ∞∞ ∞∞ ∞∞

Daniel Ian Fields, aka Shrieking Man. Daniel hit Constance with his moped.

– Three days after Daniel's encounter with Constance. –

I take deep breaths of air while standing at the hospital's billing department desk. My throat stings with every breath and every sigh. Whatever that black smoke I breathed in a couple of days ago was, it's still burning in my throat and lungs.

With a roll of my eyes, I glance at the top half of my hospital discharge papers.

NEW YORK CITY | HALLOW LURLANN IN LIGHT | STUDENT DISCHARGE FORM

Patient Name: Daniel Ian Fields
Email Address: DIFields@LurlannEmpire.edu
Address: 117 W 70th St, New York, NY 10023

Date Admitted: 3rd of November
Date Discharged: 6th of November

Emergency Contact: None

Cell No.: (212) 878-xxxx

Does the patient have Medicaid? No ☒ Yes ☐ _____
Does the patient have insurance? No ☒ Yes ☐ _____
Is the patient self-pay? No ☐ Yes ☒

Were Authorities Involved In Patient's admittance: No ☐ Yes ☒
Reason for Admittance: Patient assaulted pedestrians after wrecking their moped. Patient appears to have suffered a mental break before succumbing to respiratory issues. **No charges were pressed by supposed victims.

My eyes drift between the insurance and emergency contact lines of the form. "No. There's no way I'm going to tell my parents what happened. So, please God, tell me it's not going to be as expensive as all the horror stories say," I murmur to myself.

Removing my cell phone from my pocket, I open the Jingle-Jangle message board app and type in a code for the message board a friend of mine, Maurice, told me about.

The message board pulls itself up on my phone.

Jingle-Jangle🔔
Secure Board For Truth🗝️

Ji-Janglers In Room ☕

Phantom 👓 **Moped**
A few days ago I hit a ghost or something, Idk. All I know is I'm not seeing things despite what everyone tries to tell me, and I swear I'm not a troll. Please believe me because I remember rumors like a month back bout a haunted neighborhood in Yonkers called Park Hill. Is that true? Are there actual ghosts?

AMA DaVincis' Submarines
@Phantom👓 Moped Relax. You're in friendly company here dude and/or dudette. FYI, this is a conspiracy board. Say whateves. We'll take your word for it. No judgment here. Only enlightenment.

Bobbery
@Phantom👓 Moped Ghost? Nah. Park Hill is old noise. Just some cops went missing there. I did hear that Consortium vans were trolling some rando back alleys though. Allegedly a gas leak.

Horsie-For-Morsie
Psh. I'm sellin' some bureaucratic E✏️ for those that know the C-Sys is the real deal. Pwd: CJ for +1up.
You know what to click 👆

Horsie-For-Morsie has left the board.
Click here to send Horsie-For-Morsie a Classified Jangle

Bobbery

GFY. Mods. Geez. Please ban that Horsie guy already. Of all the theories going around, the C-sys is the dumbest. Plus, I heard some kids took the dude up on their offer. They are ultra sus.

Truth – 1 👁️
God's_Eye

Found – 3
Galadriel1362
R.Tempest
Wolfie

Seekers – 52+

03Acceptance.
ab
AMA_DaVincis...
AndewB
Arcanum
BlazesRus
Bobbery
Bobple
BTC
CopIng.
Cotter
Cure-Death
Defeyer
Depersonalization.
Diego
FabricioM
Franzisko
Fulfillment.V
Fuyge
Happiness.6
hellunit
Horsie-For-Morsie
I_Dream_Of...

265

New907Blood_EC
@Bobbery Ohhhh, the C-Sys is the "dumbest?"
Well, Mr. Boobberty knows it all. You probably
believe all the trash and false flags about
Anchorage but can't see the C-sys. is 4real.

Typical of monkey brains. 😊

uwu amirite, dud? 😵

Bobbery

Wtf? Whatever @New907Blood_EC. You
basement dwellers are carbon copies. Trying to
make everything into RPGs & video games. Your
brains are fried, bro. Low IQ emojis and no grip on
reality. Lol! And for your information, I don't think
Anchorage EVER existed, so don't @ me with
that. Take a second to let that sink in.

New907Blood_EC

Wow. 😲 *My IQ plummets further with every*
emoji, and thus you have bested me, Sir

@Bobbery Brainiac. 🙁 *I surrender and admit you*
have a BIG ape brain rather than a teeny-weeny
monkey brain…

😄 *Paying attention yet, Ape Brain?* 🙂

Phantom Moped
You have received a Classified Jangle from:
PaladineMaurice

Come visit me after you leave the hospital. I'm at
Fuds working but got something to tell you. It's
been slow so we can chill behind the counter.

Don't forget. It's *-er important, dude.*

☢ This Classified Jangle will be shredded in T-minus 5 minutes ☢

jk484jkcool
JourneyofFujiang
KittyC
Kuro
Lunadrift
MtFReborn.IV
Naxyval
NeutralQuartz
New907Blood_EC
NO!
PaladineMaurice
Phantom
Moped
PhillD
R_Noodle_MAN
RobinC
Rogue_Nudist
RuyxiS
ShotoGun
Stephen
Sweby
The-Cyctem…
Thunderbyrd567
Tilted_Axis
Trial-&-Tribulation
VioletT
WildernessLi
World-Tree 游戏
Xortra
夜女神

Anonymous
133 +

'Gosh. Shoulda known Park Hill was fake. And clearly, I'm alone in the whole
seeing ghost thing... No! I know I'm not crazy. Those other two guys saw them too.

No matter what they're telling the police now, I know they saw it too.' Hearing the bump of footsteps walking on cheap tiles, I close the app and put my phone away. *'But I guess I'll go see Maurice after this. I need to go to the pharmacy for those antipsychotics... I don't even know if I'm going to take them.'*

A nurse walks out holding a Deputy Clippie brand clipboard. "Daniel Fields, I've got all your documents here. You should be ready to go."

She flips through a few loose papers before removing them from her clipboard and handing them to me.

The dollar amount printed on the front in tiny black letters makes me feel like I am about to faint. "Eighty-five t-t-thousand dollars! For three compulsory psych days in the hospital!" Putting a hand on my forehead, I squeak, "Oh-oh my god, I might have to drop out of school. This'll bankrupt me! I don't actually know how bankruptcy works, but I can only imagine this is enough to make it happen!"

"If you think you'll have trouble paying your bill, the hospital is always willing to negotiate the price," she says, removing some paper from behind the counter. "You could probably get away with paying half that."

My jaw drops. "Negotiate the price? Half of that...? What is this, a garage sale!? This is my hospital bill! If there is room to negotiate the price, then that should just be the price! Besides, half-price or not, I still can't pay this!"

Smiling, she leans in close as if she's whispering, "Well, you didn't hear this from me, but the prices are set high so that the insurance companies can feel like they're doing something worthwhile. It's like how you humor a child, y'know?" She returns to standing upright. "But for you, the administrator would go ahead and give it a hefty cut. Plus, there are charities out there for this kind of thing. I heard one of our patients, a nice lady named Ms. Yarborough, received charity from the Iris Foundation; maybe you can try them. Oh, and some patients use things like EggSpree. Today, I just saw a news story about a little boy who used it to pay all his medical bills. You'll just have to do some research, honey."

"EggSpree... the crowdfunding site? So, if I'm not a cute child or don't know enough people, then I'm doomed to be a pizza guy forever and live in debt all because of an accident? Why should I have to crowdfund my medical bills? It's a necessity... What's the point of even living in a society!?"

She smiles, saying, "Well, you go to our affiliate school, Lurlann Empire, so it's not as if you'll be charged all at once. It'll go onto your student account, and then you'll be able to pay it alongside your tuition."

My eyes widen. *'My parents see that account; they'll think I've gone crazy, just like everyone else thinks! Plus, tuition is already fifty-thousand dollars, seventy thousand with all the fees! I'll have to join a gang to pay off all this alone!'*

I'm about to say something, but the nurse raises a hand. "Mr. Shriek, your vocal cords are fragile. All of this can wait or be handled electronically. Take some time to allow your vocal cords to recover and let your mind work through things."

"Shriek?" I suppress my urge to cry and ask, "Why are so many nurses and doctors calling me that?"

Reaching out, she taps on the bill where it reads "Daniel 'Shriek' Fields" on the name line. "You wouldn't give us your name when you first arrived, so the EMT just wrote "Shriek-ie" on your forms. When we finally got your name, Dr. Dromida used the "-ie" for your last name and added your first name to the front. After that, 'Shriek' just sorta stuck."

With a sigh, I say, "Thanks for the wonderful care. You were personally great." I turn to leave, stopping myself from running out of the building. "I'll call the hospital later when I figure out how to pay, but I need some air. Have a nice day."

As I head for the elevators, I hear her reply, "Thank you. I'll make sure the hospital mails you an itemized bill to help you. Have a wonderful rest of your day, Shriek."

Down the elevator, into the lobby, past the front desk, and out the sliding doors, I walk outside, wiping a tear from my cheek. Dragging my feet, I slink along the sidewalk and toward the pharmacy Maurice works at a few blocks away.

····

········

····

With my facemask on, I walk into Maurice's workplace, Fuddy-Duddy Pharmacy. It's a drugstore that sits adjacent to Central Park at the bottom of a tall skyscraper. The store's outside isn't that assuming, but the inside sticks out like a sore thumb. Rather than a drugstore, the interior resembles an early 20th-century general store with reclaimed wood floors, shiplap walls, and an assortment of fudge and candy along the counter. This place would be a quirky shop to stop off at in the country, but it's downright bizarre here in New York City. It's only been open a few months, and the locals still aren't sure how to feel about it.

From the backroom walks a slim guy with wavy brown hair and amber eyes. He wears a coffee-colored apron with the store's name stitched in white and carries a box of fudge to the glass display case. "Welcome to Fuddy-Duddy Pharmacy. Here we pride ourselves on our old-fashioned service and our old-fashioned smiles…"

"Hey, Maurice," I say, nodding my head at him.

"Oh, sup, Daniel!" Maurice reaches for a handle and flips a countertop door upright. "Come on back to the ye olde bake shoppe so I can show you something that'll blow your mind."

"Sure, but is this going to be quick?" I gesture toward my facemask. "I'm still recovering from the accident, and I have to go to work tomorrow morning or I'm screwed. I really need to get some rest on a bed that doesn't feel like it was framed out of scrap metal."

"Yeah, hospital beds suck." He raises his arms. "But it's something big, something amazing! I'm sure it'll at least help get your mind off what happened."

My eyes drift to a tabloid sitting on the counter that reads, "Crawlers in Central Park!?!" The image on the cover is blurry, but I can tell it's a photograph of me being restrained by those two guys and a mob of protestors from a few days ago.

"You saw that too?" I sigh. "…You think I'm crazy, don't you?"

"Nah, bro. I only bought that because it's not every day someone I know gets put into a tabloid." He takes the tabloid and tosses it into a trash can underneath the counter. "And the photo on the cover is blurrier than a picture of Bigfoot. No one will know it was you."

Nodding, I walk toward the fudge room. "Fine then. As long as you understand I'm not crazy."

"Don't stress. I mean, come on, who in good conscience could say they haven't run over a ghost or two in their life?" he rags with a smirk. "Oh, and word of advice. Only crazy people say they aren't crazy, so just don't acknowledge anyone that says dumb stuff like that to you."

I roll my eyes. "Yeah, I'm aware it's a cliché to say it, but it is what it is."

Moving behind the counter, Maurice ushers me into the fudge room off to the side. It smells of cocoa powder, and a big mixer whisks a fresh batch of fudge at the back. He waves toward a door, and together, we walk into a white backroom. Inside are three televisions displaying security camera footage, a computer chair, and a single desk with a computer on top.

Maurice takes a seat in front of the computer. "So listen," he says, wagging a finger at the monitor. "Let's have a little chat about Crawler-Anchorage."

Shrugging, I ask, "What about it? It's been on the news for a month straight." I pause and squint at Maurice. "Wait, this 'little chat' isn't about to turn into you telling me some conspiracy theory that's incredibly offensive to the victims again, is it? ...Maurice, have you been spending too much time on Jingle-Jangle again?"

"Nah, nah, of course not. I haven't been on there... toooo much." While clicking through some things on the desktop, he says, "So everyone knows what happened. A cruise ship, aka the Moonlight, smashes into Alaska's Port of Anchorage. That's bizarre enough on its own, but then those swarms of nightmares spilled out of the burning wreckage."

"They're people, man. Don't call them nightmares," I say with a sigh.

"Yeah, well, all I can say is we disagree there because those things aren't people. Mindless undead ghouls would be more 'people' than those things."

He clicks a file that opens helicopter footage streamed by Sylvi Redferne, a well-known Tremble personality, the day the Moonlight crashed into the Port of Anchorage. In the helicopter's focus is the pasty white image of what's known as a Crawler. Crawlers are spindly humanoid creatures with inverted limbs, heads flipped jaw side up, and chests that face skyward. Worst of all, they're people, humans, infected with the Crawler Virus. That virus is more horrific than any zombie movie could have predicted.

"Dude, why are you makin' me look at this?" I ask. "They rarely show Crawlers on TV for a reason, because no one wants to see them, including me."

"Because these things overran Anchorage in only a few days, excluding the people who made it to the designated military camps, everyone in Anchorage is thought to be dead or a Crawler."

"Yeah, I know all that. Everyone knows all that. The whole world shut down for like two weeks, and for those two weeks, all anyone did was watch Anchorage... and the Dryas Cyclone too, I guess."

"Precisely! The polar vortex, or what meteorologists and the media have started calling it this past week, the Dryas Cyclone."

"...Yeah, that's why I called it that."

He pulls up the weather radar on his computer, showing the Dryas Cyclone that resembles a gigantic hurricane. "Not long after those *things* escaped from the Moonlight, that cyclone developed in the North Pole. Since then, the Dryas Cyclone has led to massive dips in temperature that might throw the Northern Hemisphere into an ice age..."

"Mhm, it's so bad that Canadians have been fleeing across the border. It's sad."

He nods. "But here's the thing, the Crawlers were spreading really fast along Alaska's Interstate-1 UNTIL the Dryas Cyclone materialized out of nowhere. Coincidence!" Maurice looks at me with a hunched-over peek and dark circles under his eyes. "Coincidence, Daniel!?"

I raise an eyebrow and shrug.

"Ha! I think not! Because yesterday while reading the Jingle-Jangle boards, I spoke to someone named "New907Blood EC" and they say that the whole Crawler-Anchorage thing... ALL LIES. In fact! Anchorage is totally fine, Daniel. There are no such things as crawlers! The government is using a weather machine built by the Consortium to make the Dryas Cyclone. That way, people won't see that Anchorage is totally untouched. Daniel! They're trying to congregate..." His pupils shiver as he gazes into my eyes. "...or should I say *congress-gate...?*"

I stare at him with contempt. "I knew this was going to be offensive."

"Daniel, do you understand they're going to leave us all out to dry? Can you believe the government would do this!? To good and rational people like us!? I mean, I'm so angry that I could punch... a pillow or something, I don't know!"

"Maurice, you heard all that from some random, anonymous person on the internet."

"Exactly! What would they have to gain from lying?"

"A laugh at your expense?" Taking a painful breath, I continue, "You know what the scariest thing about everything you just said is? That it's less scary than reality. So listen, I understand it's hard to accept that sometimes horrible things happen for no reason, but that doesn't make it okay to just make up conspiracy theories. It's not a healthy coping mechanism, and you hurt other people by downplaying or confusing their loved ones' deaths."

"Hey, wait, don't judge me yet; there's still more! I've heard they're doing this because the rumors are true; people are becoming superheroes, but only the chosen ones. And Daniel! After I heard about the ghost, it hit me, just like you hit that ghost..." Leaning back in his chair, he says, "You're a chosen one."

My eyes widen. "H-huh? Me?"

A grin spreads across his face. "You told me you saw something, like, a shadow ghost or something, and then bam, you were a crazy shrieking maniac." He claps his hands and points at me. "That was a sign, bro. You've been chosen!"

"I... I doubt I've been chosen. I've never been so sick and poor in my whole life, and you're trying to tell me I'm a chosen one? Chosen for what? A curse? Cause it feels like it."

"Nah, man. It's a sure thing. Probably a god or something, y'know? It's always a god." Exhaling, he shakes his head, adding, "You're one lucky SOB, being chosen. The rest of us guys and gals are going to be getting together to draw up some plans before things get weirder."

"Plan?"

"Yep, we're going to start some kind of alliance. I'm going to try to take the leadership role. If they accept me, I intend to recommend we call ourselves the Real World Roles Alliance or RWR Alliance. It's sorta like a play on 'RPG,' get it? Thought it was pretty clever myself."

"I mean, it's okay, but that's not what I meant. Like, why are you making a plan?"

"Oh, because there are all kinds of ominous stories popping up on the internet. Like, I heard about this body in Japan they found in a shed. It was completely dry without a drop of blood left in it. Then there are rumors of this Shāngāo monastic order in China who have been living on the same mountain for thousands of years all the sudden packing up to leave." He lowers his voice, saying, "To top it all off, I've seen a video of someone disappearing into thin air only to reappear a second later. It was deleted before I even finished watchin' it, but I know what I saw. It's all too improbable to be coincidental, all too fantastical. The rumors about a C-Sys seem more and more true every day. Our world is about to turn on its head, can't you feel it? So yeah, we're going to make some kinda plan."

"D-dude, you're throwing out so much random stuff all at once." I stare at him with a flat expression. "I feel like I know less about what you wanted to tell me before I got here, and I knew nothing before now."

"That was uncalled for, and my feelings are a little hurt. I just want you to be thinking about the imminent new world, whatever that may entail. It's obviously fast approaching. Second, about your hospital and money troubles, you know that you can still use your parents' health plan since you are only eighteen." He huffs. "So you're welcome for the education on health policy and your chosen rise to power. No need to thank me. The look on your face when you realize I was right will be thanks enough."

"Wait, I can use my parent's insurance?" I raise my hands. "Nurse Curse at the hospital didn't tell me that."

"Probably because you straight-up told them you didn't have insurance, didn't you?"

"I mean, maybe, I vaguely recall them asking about my parents, but... well, I don't want to tell my parents anything about what happened. They'll think I'm going crazy after living alone in Manhattan."

"Well, you'll have to tell them if you want to use their health insurance. Sooner rather than later if the medicines are expensive." Maurice peeps at the doctor's prescriptions in my hand as the store's doorbell rings, and someone enters the store. "And looking at that list, I'd say good ole stick-in-the-mud capitalism has you by the 'nads, so I'd say it's sooner. I'm not a Fuddy-Duddy pharmacist, but I recognize fluphenazine. It's an antipsychotic that can cost two-hundred-fifty bucks alone, my dude."

He walks out as I sigh.

'Freakin' money. Worst idea people ever came up with.' While I rub my temples, I sit in Maurice's computer chair and stare at the ceiling. 'And chosen one? What're the odds that I'd be a chosen one? Like one of those people in the books... Yeah, I mean, I didn't even talk to the ghost thing or have a 'chosen one moment' like they always do in the books. If anything, the guy that had me in a chokehold would be the chosen one, not me.'

••••

•••••••••

••••

The next day, I walk into a trendy pizza joint named Phazel's New York-Style Pizzeria. It's where I work and deliver pizzas using my moped. Marching to the time clock near the entrance, I input my employee number into the keypad and receive the usual "Good Morning" confirmation message. I take a moment to gather my strength of will so that I can power my way through yet another soul-crushing day as a public service worker.

With small steps, I move through the pizzeria toward the front counter. Half of the building is a small video game console arcade with a tiny coffee shop and dining area. In contrast, the other half is the pizzeria with a red brick storefront, a sign written in white chalk above it, and a generic statue of an Italian man holding a pizza peel.[51] I'm pretty sure an Italian man statue is required by law to be in every pizza place.

My cell phone vibrates in my pocket. Removing my phone, I see an email notification on my home screen.

Subject: Re: Daniel Ian Fields Charitable Application. Please Help!

Iris Foundation <applications@Iris.HHands.org>
To: DIFields@LurlannEmpire.edu

Dear Mr. Fields,

We're sending this email to inform you that the Iris Foundation has received your appeal for our charity. The Iris Foundation will review your application promptly.

No further action is required on your part.

Regards,
Iris Foundation
H.Hands, LLC.

Please do not reply to this email, as mail sent to this address will not be answered.

I sigh. *'Well, at least my application went through.'*

A middle-aged woman with short blonde hair walks toward the register with a pizza box in her hands. "Yo, welcome back, Daniel. I heard about what happened, and don't worry, I don't think you're totally nutso," she says.

"Gee, thanks, Brenda. How considerate of you to tell me that," I reply with sarcasm.

---

[51] Pizza Peel: a tool used to place pizzas in a hot oven.

She glances at a tabloid on the pizzeria's counter. "Don't worry about it! I've had days where I've wanted to shriek until my vocal cords bled too." She snickers, holding the greasy pizza box toward me. "Anywho, take this pizza. It goes to that one dude, y'know, the Italian guy that likes to answer the door in his tighty-whities. If you can't remember where he lives, his address is on the ticket."

Someone yells Brenda's name, and she turns her head. As I reach out for the pizza, there's a blue flicker.

A high-pitched buzzing rings in my ears. My head refuses to turn and my eyes refuse to move. *'W-what's happening!?'*

A blue screen pops up in front of me.

The screen makes my head hurt. *'What the? Is this a blue screen of death!?'* I glance at Brenda, finding her likewise frozen in place. *'Did the universe just crash!? Has my whole life been a simulation!?'*

The blue screen of death dissolves, and a much clearer one pops up.

> *Success!*
> *Communication established with a new Material-Earth Entity.*
> *----------*
> *Proceeding with a customized tutorial.*
> *Entity, please prepare to be relocated and assessed for integration into the Cosmic System Beta...*

My eyes dart to the closing words. "The C-Sys!? No way! It's real!?"

The world whirls, twisting in on itself. My body relaxes as everything turns green around me. The next second I am standing in a meadow of knee-high grass. As a breeze blows across the grassland, I mumble, "This is insane. M-maybe I should have taken my antipsychotics meds after all." I shake my head. "No, I'm not crazy! It's the C-sys! I've been chosen!"

A popup replaces the last screen.

Greetings, Beta Entity 1-0-0-9-1-8-4.

It has been detected that the Entity is experiencing confusion.

The Entity's internal Mana capacity is sufficient for immediate integration into this Cosmic System. To aid the Entity in understanding, the Cosmic System can be crudely thought of as a bestower of information and a medium that will help guide the Entity's Essence absorption.

The former is pliable, offering unique customizability depending upon the Entity's capabilities and Essence incorporation. The latter is flexible but limited by both the Entity's physical and incorporeal selves.

Further analysis will soon commence.

The more I read of the blue popup, the quicker my heart beats. "Wow! Are you God!? Am I legitimately a chosen one!? Are you going to help me!? Like with superpowers and stuff!?"

The greeting screen vanishes as another pops up.

This Cosmic System anticipated such questions, Entity 1-0-0-9-1-8-4. Entity, this Cosmic System will now share the six most frequently asked questions posed by the current Earth's Entities. See Below:

1. Am I dead? Are you God?
  - ❖ *No. The Entity has not passed into a different realm, and this Cosmic System does not require nor solicit the Entity's worship. **Toba Addendum:** This Cosmic System is not subservient to any existent or nonexistent God or Deity.*

2. **Am I the chosen one?**
   - ❖ *No. This Cosmic System does not select 'chosen ones.'* ***Toba Addendum:*** *Please, reiterate this to other Toba Humans. This Cosmic System will never uplift one Entity above all others.*

3. **Toba Addendum: Do we (Toba Humanity) live in a simulation!?!**
   - ❖ *No. This Cosmic System can vary tremendously between Entities. Its numeric terminology is merely systematized and fashioned in a form present Toba Entities can easily take to.*

4. **Will the Cosmic System help me survive? Like beyond just Essence and stats?**
   - ❖ *No. This Cosmic System does not have a bias.* ***Toba Addendum:*** *See the 'Am I the chosen one?' query above once again.*

5. **Who gave you the right to disrupt the natural order of things!? Do you hate humans!?**
   - ❖ *No. This Cosmic System possesses no prejudice and assures the Entities that the current state of the Material-Earth is, in fact, the unnatural state.*

6. **Why would you do this!? Will I be eaten by monsters when the Beta is over!?**
   - ❖ *Conceivably. This Cosmic System, however, trusts that the Entities shall persevere.*

"...You just have this FAQ at the ready?" I read over the FAQ as a gust of wind sweeps the grass at my feet. "So, I guess I'm not chosen by the Cosmic System, but by someone else then? Y-yeah! Since I'm not crazy, that must be it... The ghost. I need to find the ghost...! I didn't kill the ghost, did I?" My eyes read the final question. "Hey, wait a second, that last one says I might get eaten by monsters... Did we skip an explanation somewhere?"

A long popup replaces the FAQ.

> *That is correct, Entity. The earlier questions and answers typically come after this explanation:*
>
> *For many millennia now, the Material-Earth and much of the Cosmos have been infecund.[52] With the Cosmic System's return, that shall soon end, and normality will preferably resume. When that time comes, the prior inhabitants of Earth will return to continue lives long since put on hold. Many of these inhabitants shall not be friendly, and some will believe Toba Humanity is squatting or altering lands that do not rightfully belong to Toba Humanity.*
>
> *Toba Humanity and the rest of Earth's beings must develop before then or suffer a swift extinction. This is not Earth's creatures' fault, so those born in this period of infecundity shall be provided a fair chance to find places in the world before then.*
>
> ---
>
> **Generating Entity's Status. Analyzing Entity's history...**
>
> ----------
>
> **Status successfully generated. Archiving...**
>
> ----------
>
> **Assigning any relevant titles...**
>
> **Conferring Entity 1-0-0-9-1-8-4 a title:**
> # [Toba Humanity Beta]
> *This title acknowledges that the Entity possessing it is a Toba Human, also known as Modern Human, that experienced the Beta and the resumption of normality.*
>
> ❖ *{A Title for doing absolutely nothing. It's primarily a mark of distinction and recognition that the Entity can carry into the future.}*
>
> ---
>
> ***Displaying Entity Status:***

---

[52] Infecund: having low or zero fertility.

Reading through the first explanation, my body tenses as I swallow, but when I see what's next, my heart leaps. "A status! Holy crap, it's like an RPG!" Questions swirl in my head. "What's Soma and Vigor!? Also, what ethnicity is Toba Human, Toba Humanity? I did one of those DNA test kits recently, and I was like, 99.9% Caucasian. Honestly, I have no idea what 'Toba' means... Oh, wait, it already said it just means Modern Human... Awesome! Humans get a new, way cooler race name!"

I move down the list of things in my Status. "Mana!? No way, can I do magic!? ...Wait, one mana? I have ONE mana. That kinda sucks, doesn't it? Can I do anything with one mana?"

A new popup appears.

that Vigor is only meant to gauge the Entity's exhaustion. Vigor is principally measured via Endurance.

Mana *is an energy that flows through all things in quantities that vary depending on its* Orenda *alongside a tiny contribution from* Acuity. *This energy can be used for skills and other purposes.*

Skills *are the Entity's magics, abilities, and select trades. Suppose the Entity fosters any of these to a satisfactory or higher skill grade. In that case, the 'Cosmic System' will offer the Entity a skill. Upon acceptance, the Cosmic System will endow the Entity with a personalized impress of knowledge pertaining to that magic, ability, or trade. However, be aware that skills are not a substitute for experience, technique, or artistry.*
(Many of Toba Humanity's skills can rely on having the appropriate Orenda, Perception, and Acuity.)

Ranks are as follows:

- ❖ Aspirant [Asp]
- ❖ Novitiate [Nov]
- ❖ Fancier [Fan]
- ❖ Adept [Apt]
- ❖ Savant [Sav]
- ❖ Phenom [Phe]
- ❖ Virtuoso [Vo]
- ❖ Master [M]
- ❖ Grandmaster [GM]

Upon adopting an 'Aspirant' skill, the Entity must supplant it with a 'Novitiate' skill within 7 Material-Earth days to retain it permanently. Note that ranks beyond Grandmaster are not displayed due to the sheer improbability it shall ever be applicable to the Entity. In time, Entities will come to learn or understand this via their own logic, experiences, and observations.

Talents *can stem from a True God but can also naturally evolve within an Entity's soul. Talents are principally unique and cannot be taught or removed once mutated. A Talent shall typically adhere to the same*

> *Entity perpetually. Utilizing Talents demands mental strength and relies heavily on* Endurance *and* Fortitude. *They seldom employ* Mana.
>
> **Titles** *are conferred for unique or unusual achievements. Titles may give additional positive or, in some individuals' opinion, unwanted benefits. Titles are typically the maximum this Cosmic System will ever intrude upon an Entity's daily life but know that they are conferred without bias. Please also note, the Titles are conferred by a subsystem with a lousy sense of humor.*

I shake my hands in the air. "...W-woah, slow down, C-Sys. I'm trying to memorize this stuff. You're movin' too fast!"

The C-System, Cosmic System thingy, allows me time to look over everything. "My mind is brimming with so many questions I don't even know where to start. So uh—"

Before I can finish my question, the screen vanishes, and another pops up.

> *Apologies, Beta Entity 1-0-0-9-1-8-4, but individual questions are not permitted.*
>
> *Entity, there will be a corporeal battle simulation that shall assess the Entity's combat abilities and offer the Entity an appropriate skill or skills if the Entity merits them.*
>
> *This assessment is not life-threatening.*
>
> *Corporeal combat assessment will begin in sixty Material-Earth minutes.*

Reading the popup, I recoil. "C-C-COMBAT!? I've never even thrown a punch before!" I clench my fists. "Is it thumb in or thumb out when making a fist!? Geez! This might be bad." Taking a breath, I try to bring my adrenalin and anxiety into check. "Okay, this is an assessment, so more than likely it's a technicality, b-but also... I still have no weapon."

A blue popup responds to me.

Type:	Long Polearm	Medium Saber	Short Dagger	Martial Arts Fist	Blunt War Club	Firearm Pistol
Name:	*Demidov Sovnya*	*Jiguang Liuyedao*	*Helmschmied Baselard*	*Mienai Tekko*	*Fiu Supi*	*Whitney Wolverine*

I exhale in relief and browse through the choices. "I can't even guess at what the first five would look like, and I doubt that's changing regardless of what it is, so just give me that pistol!"

There's an azure flash as a yellow and blue box materializes before my eyes. It spins inside a glowing blue ball with a glimmer. I stare at it before raising my hand and poking at it. The ball pops like a bubble. Lunging forward, I catch it before it can fall into the grass.

"It's a little heavier than I thought it would be."

The box's lid reads, ".22 Caliber Long Rifle PISTOL."

I set the lid on the ground and investigate the box. Set inside a yellow cardboard mold is a pistol designed like a classic 1950s car. It has a sleek, almost triangular shape with a polished brass color and a pearl grip. On the side, the words "Whitney Wolverine" is engraved.

Glancing down, I notice a small handbook taped to the bottom of the lid. I spend the next fifteen or so minutes reading.

"...A mid-20th-century nickel-plated pistol. The handbook brags about how it's made of aluminum and space-age materials. I guess that was uncommon in the 1950s or something." I turn the pistol in my hand, watching the sun gleaming off its surface. "Looks like they wanted to make it look like an Atomic Age weapon or something. Pretty neat. I sort of need bullets and a target to practice with, though."

There's a second blue flash. A box of ammunition materializes in front of me, along with a bullseye target around a hundred feet further ahead. "Sweeeet! Magic, oh man, I'm going to use so much magic one day."

The next thirty minutes I spend figuring out how to load it.

With my arm extended, I close one eye and point the wolverine at the bullseye. I sit for several minutes, practicing with the wolverine's sights. There's a bang. The wolverine torpedoes out of my grip, whacking me in the chest.

I fall to the ground. "Oh my god," I squeak, curling into the fetal position. "I'm going to get eviscerated in this combat simulation."

A minute or two later, I force myself to my feet, find the pistol in the grass, and take one more shot at the bullseye. "...I'm not even sure where the bullet went. Oh god, this is going to be so bad."

I practice for a while longer until a blue popup appears.

> *The jackalope combat assessment will commence in 1 minute...*

My brow narrows as I read the screen. "A jackalope? Like one of those jackrabbits with antlers? That's what I'm fighting? A rabbit?" I sigh and then laugh aloud. My laugh echoes across the grassland. "Thank god! I was legitimately getting scared for a second there."

I take a seat, preparing my wolverine for the 'battle' between me and what's basically a rabbit.

One minute later, the popup appears again.

I stand as a blue flash fifty feet away from me makes my vision sparkle. In the grass, I see a pair of horns projecting upward.

"Alright. I'll be honest, this makes it easier. If I can't see it, then I don't have to feel bad." The grass recedes, making a 50-foot-wide circular arena. "Okey-dokey, never mind then."

Across from me is a jackrabbit with beige fur, long ears that stand straight up, antlers like those of a deer, and a look of pure innocence. "...I can't kill this. I'm the good guy... Wait, am I the good guy? It doesn't matter. I can't and won't do it. It's just a cute little bunn—"

The jackalope screeches like a banshee mixed with a tyrannosaurus rex.

I raise my wolverine. "DIEEE!" my voice cracks.

It charges me like a rocket as my weapon fires. The jackalope slams into me. My body tumbles along the ground like a bowling ball. I come to a hard stop.

Gasping for air, I look down. Blood oozes from puncture wounds between my ribs. "T-t-this isn't supposed to be life-threatening," I murmur to myself between shallow breaths.

There's a screech. I glance the jackalope's antlers above the grass. "I'm gonna die. I'm gonna die. I'm..."

My eye twitches as I see the jackalope lower its antlers toward me. Opening my mouth, I... I laugh. "I-I'm the chosen one."

I fire my weapon. A blue shield hugs the jackalope's body. The next second, the jackalope's antlers piece into my abdomen. I grab it by the antlers with what strength I have left. "Can't..." Placing the pistol to its head, I fire. Blue shield. I fire again. Blue shield. I fire once more, and I'm pelted by blood.

Falling over, I stare at the thin piece of bloodstained grass. I open my mouth like a fish gasping for oxygen. "I-if I am the chosen one. Please, sssave meeeee."

> *Entity 1-0-0-9-1-8-4 is unable to proceed to the Entity versus Entity portion of the assessment.*
>
> *The Entity is given the selection of one of these general skills:*
> *[Aspirant Escapist]*
> *[Aspirant Stealth]*
> *[Aspirant Terrene-Pistol]*
> *These are adoptable outside of the tutorial.*
>
> *Please do not despair, as this Cosmic System will expunge the memories of the pain.*
> *Good luck, Entity 1-0-0-9-1-8-4.*
>
> *This concludes the assessment and tutorial.*

The world turns and twists. A moment later, I reappear in the pizzeria. There's a gurgle in the pit of my stomach as I dry-heave and then puke on both Brenda and the pizza.

"What the fuck, you psycho!?" Brenda screams.

"I've been resurrected!" Raising my arms in the air, I shout, "I-I'm a chosen one!"

Chapter 11: Whetting Bureaucratic Cogs

∞∞∞∞∞∞∞∞∞∞∞∞∞∞

I return to the Terrace, the ecology text I hid in the bin earlier once more in hand. Terra departed a couple of hours ago, claiming she would come back the day after tomorrow with the signs I requested. Taking a seat upon the fountain's edge, I kick my hazy legs, gazing out over the Lake. *'That tower defense picture-game-thing was... disappointing. I doubt it was pertinent to my situation in any manner whatsoever. In all frankness, I did not apprehend the picture-game's purpose. It had to do with pretend beasts assaulting towers for inexplicable reasons. Di·no·saurs. I cannot understand why Terra thought I would believe her claims that those creatures once lived and breathed. Does she think me so credulous?'*

My fingers occupy themselves, fiddling with a clear glass orb—Terra left it for me to use. I raise the orb, gazing at my reflection. It's roughly the size of an apple, and the light of my eyes causes it to glitter purple. *'This orb is supposed to teach me how to detect mana as well as hide or suppress my own. Yet, Terra said to make certain I am mentally rested before venturing to use it, so I suppose I should do something else then.'*

I set both the book and orb aside and then look toward the night sky. This is the first night it has not snowed since I arrived at the Terrace. It's an excellent eve for some reading, yet something occupies my thoughts.

Raising my hands, I spread my fingers. *'Sign language is what she called it and the most basic sign she taught me...'* I point toward the Lake. That is all. I simply point. *'She emphasized that it means... "you" and that if I am speaking to someone from a position of authority, saying "thou" or "thee" may undermine my command... Whom would I ever be speaking to from such a position? Whom would I ever be commanding? I can only speak to her! Perhaps it is not my pronouns which are the problem, but everyone else's.'*

I cross my arms. *'Earl! What dost YOU thinkest!? How dost YOU feelest being addressed in such a manner!? Dost YOU feelest commanded!? Is my authority overwhelming!?'* I shake my head with every use of that word. *'I do not know if I can trust her, yet she says people shan't be "courteous" to me if I call them "thou" with a serious face... I have no mouth; I cannot even make a serious face! Even if the nobles of my era dwell beyond the lychgate, I shall never speak the Queen's fashion, even if I am the last not to do so.'*

Uncrossing my arms, I throw them up and allow them to fall to my sides. *'As for the sign language, I cannot imagine it being useful for me anytime soon.'* My palm slaps the book's cover. I drag it in front of me and then use a rock to keep the pages from turning. *'I shall read to calm my nerves.'*

....

....

....

Several hours pass by the time I set the book aside, having read a small portion of it. My reading is sluggish due to odd words, sentences, and concepts. To use the book's own words, it primarily spoke of 'organisms', the places they inhabit, and how they interact with one another. Confusing. Though I made a scintillating discovery, there is a list of definitions at the book's back. Admittedly, I feel many of the words are not commonly used as, for the most part, I have not overheard anyone using them whilst I was eavesdropping.

'Frankly, some things written in this book are difficult to believe. Tiny animals? Oxygen cycle? Carbon cycle? Tiny animals that can live in places that one would believe absurd? Including inside people? It's all intriguing, but...' I pause, attempting to work through my thoughts. *'But why would Earl have me study this? Is it relevant to my Tower? My Domain? My body?'*

Eyeing the red brick beneath my feet, I pick up a stick and use it to trace the bricks' grooves. *'I imagine I shall learn why it's relevant in due time. All that's important now is that I try and understand its contents, and this is the sort of learning that I enjoy anyway.'* I flick a lump of snow away with my stick. *'My Status, prithee, Cosmic System.'*

I check my mana. *'Ah, marvelous. Earl, I would like to refine as much Nebula as I can in the same fashion as before.'*

The kiln's flame lights up without the list of options. Glancing around to ensure no one is near, I hide the "You Are Ecology 101" text and grab the orb, placing it in nearby bushes. The items stowed, I move toward the rubbish bins in hopes of foraging some delectable meat. I gather a variety of foods and return them to the bush. I wish to gather everything together to eat it all at once to test whether I acquire Essence if I consume more food at once. Also, I want to have a variety of items to experiment with my "Gluttonous Naturalist."

As the sun rises, I decide to make one final expedition to a rubbish bin further up the pathway. The crinkle of boots atop snow freezes me cold. I fall to my stomach inside the hedges, and the kiln shakes the leaves as I do so. Pushing a branch aside, I see three men and a woman descending the grand staircase from the black roadway above. When they reach the Terrace, they stop.

The man and woman nearest to me, I recognize. In fact, this is the third time I have seen these two people—the noble's guards Jessica and Leo. The two men that follow them are individuals with whom I am unacquainted.

One of the men dresses in a buttoned tan suit and trousers with a soft pink shirt. He has fair skin, a goatee, and blond hair groomed as if every strand is strategically positioned. Yet, the bags beneath his eyes betray his foppish front. Sighing, he glances at a shrunken pocket watch he wears around his wrist and then draws a notebook from a trouser pocket. With a click of his tongue, he opens it, removing what I presume is a writing utensil from his coat pocket.

The other man wears an unbuttoned black suit and trousers, a white shirt, and a gray-black tie. He has a pale complexion, unkempt black hair, and a beard shadow; his eyes are half-shut. He yawns and reaches into his trouser pockets, pulling out a white box. Flipping the box open, he brings it to his mouth and then pulls away, revealing what I have come to know as a cigarette. His weary eyes watch the sunrise.

Both men have a card pinned to their uppermost suit pocket. The card has their portraits and some sort of insignia serving as a circular border. It is difficult to make out the insignia, but it resembles a bird. The bird looks to have a long neck, head feathers, and a body shaded in blacks, reds, and whites.

'...I think I recognize that bird. An orphan bird or an orphanay, I believe. Orphan birds lay their eggs in the ocean. The ones that float get to fly in the sky with their mother, father, and god. As for the ones that sink, they hatch in the dark abyss of the ocean. The Church in Light loved to use it as an example of what happens to "bad eggs." Yet, I have been higher in the sky than anyone, and I can attest it is dark up there as well.'

I shift my position to gain a better vantage, yet the kiln rustles a branch as I do so. The man in the black suit's sleepy eyes glance in my direction, proving that he is much more alert than his demeanor suggests.

Unable to dip any lower, I raise my hand to block the glow of my eyes. 'This does not bode well, and my kiln is still refining!'

I sweep a pile of leaves around the kiln to obscure its light. As the leaves enter the membrane, some haze escapes. The man in the black suit's head turns. He puts his box of cigarettes away and removes a shiny metal object. Stepping toward my hedges, he clicks something on the shiny object; a flame rises from it, lighting his cigarette. The tap of his shoes against the red brick echoes in my mind as he puts the shiny object away. A puff of smoke exits the corner of his lips as he stops.

"Hey, Pierce," the man says in an emotionless voice.

The well-groomed man in the tan suit, Pierce, takes a deep breath. "Lincoln," he replies.

With his eyes still half-closed, he removes the cigarette from his mouth. "Isn't this around where that kid said he bought that horse?"

"Huh?" Pierce looks up from his notebook, glancing around. "Yeah, someplace around here, I think. We didn't have time to do the follow-up after the incident, so I'm not sure."

"Thought so," Lincoln says. His eyes stall on my little thicket until he turns toward Jessica and Leo, walking back to them. "Is this where you've been getting reports of odd smells and people feeling, what was it, light-headed?"

"Yep," Leo answers with a nod. "We thought it was a leaky gas main, but the utility company couldn't find anything. The next thing we know, some guy shows up and pulls out some sort of instrument. When it started beeping, he panicked and then told us everything was fine."

Jessica laughs. "His eyes were the size of volleyballs, but he's over here yelling, 'don't panic, it's okay.' I thought we were about to explode."

"Mhmm. The surveyors can be that way," Pierce says, slapping the notebook around to keep it firm and flat enough for him to scribble on. "Most of them are used to only detecting something every decade or so. They have a tendency to panic every time their equipment actually picks up something."

"What do you mean they 'used to'?" Leo asks with a raised eyebrow. "You guys get that many gas leaks nowadays?"

Pierce grunts in acknowledgment while searching for a place to lay his notebook. "Goddamn it."

"...What are you writing anyway?" Lincoln asks, taking a few steps closer.

"Writing? Oh." He flips the notebook around, showing a page full of messy drawings and scribbles.

Smirking, Lincoln's says, "Stop messing around, dumbass."

"What? Look again." He taps the corner of the paper where a scribbled question mark is drawn. "I wrote word-for-word everything we know. Oh..." He moves his finger aside, revealing a second question mark. "As a bonus, I included all the information we were provided beforehand. I'm a model employee."

"Hey," Jessica says, snapping her fingers. "I don't actually recall the Consortium holding any of the utility or service contracts in this precinct. So why are you guys here exactly?"

"Hm?" Lincoln flicks his cigarette to the ground, stepping on it. "That's not true. Consortium holds several utility contracts for this borough."

Jessica looks the two men up and down, saying, "And you expect me to believe you two are here to do utility work?" She motions toward their clothing. "In those monkey suits?"

"Us? Nah. We don't do utilities, but one of the branch companies does. I was just responding to what you said," he says, taking one more glance at the sunrise. "Anyway, officers, do either of you have any more information about the situation here? We'd like to get started, and we aren't allowed to work with people around."

The two noble's guards glance at one another and nod. "Actually, we'd like to stay and observe," Leo says.

Lincoln stares at the two with a blank face. "No. As I just said, we aren't allowed to work with people around. You're people, right?"

"What's that supposed to mean? Of course, we're people!" Jessica's scowls. "But we're also the police. Why can't we stay and observe? A gas leak is a matter of public safety."

Pierce yawns and looks up from his drawings. Moving his finger between the two noble's guard, he says, "Because it's Consortium business now. We've been contracted by the federal government and were assured privacy. That's why you two and your cop buddies are supposed to be barricading the roads, ensuring we are allowed said privacy."

Leo's mouth opens, but rather than a retort, a sigh escapes his lips. He rolls his eyes and motions for Jessica to follow. She rolls her eyes as well, and the two move up the stairs.

"Let's get started," Lincoln says. "We haven't slept in days, and we're scheduled to work the protests in a couple days."

Pierce groans. "Why are they assigning that to us anyway? Aren't we a little overqualified to babysit protestors?"

"For the same reason the two of us are here alone..." He removes his box of cigarettes once again, putting another one in his mouth. "...because there is no one else available. I haven't slept since corporate told us what our zone of suppression would be."

He lights the cigarette and then reaches into his coat, removing a rectangular device. The device has a copper color and is around nine inches long by six inches wide.[53] '...It somewhat reminds me of the device I saw when I first arrived and leapt into the chamber pot tunnels.'

Pierce stops drawing. "Oh, yeah. I forgot I had the cartridge."

He removes a silver box about the size of a man's fist from his own coat pocket. Pressing something, a blue light shines onto his face as he pulls a tube from the box.

Lincoln puffs his cigarette, taking the tube from him. Tube in hand, he presses something on the device's side, and an empty tube slides out. Passing the empty tube to Pierce, he slides the full one into the vacant slot.

---

[53] |around 229 millimeters long by 152 millimeters wide|

A hum comes from the device as he flips it over, revealing a glass bottom. Inside, I can see gears whirl as a blue glow illuminates their copper surface.

"Didn't we just get this thing repaired and refurbished by the Chicago artificers?" Pierce asks.

Lincoln nods. "I guess the humming wasn't a big enough deal for them to bother fixing it." He turns the device back over and presses something. It starts to ring. "Well, that took a literal second. Another time bomb, probably. In such a public and open area, this one's going be a nightmare to suppress before the deadline."

"Yep. Another one." Pierce stuffs the notebook in a pocket and takes out a clean black pocketbook. "I'll squeeze this one between giant horse, killer sewer rat, and sentient meat. Things are so fucked, and there's hardly anything we can do about it anymore."

'Killer... rat? Wait. Sentient meat?'

Lincoln shrugs. "Update the maps and do our jobs. That's all we can do about it."

"You say that, but it feels like we got assigned to the worst part of the worst city."

"Maybe you and Gary pissed off Barrister Barlowe again."

"Barlowe is basically pissed off twenty-four-seven." Pierce sighs. "Galtry and the Espositos are active in this area, and that Hex Church down the road creeps me out. How am I supposed to get my beauty sleep with those fabric-faced weirdos up the road from me? Oh, and let's not forget this is the same borough where the Puzzling Five Hundred went missing a couple of years ago. Admit it. This borough stank even before all this other stuff started happening. It's a disaster-prone headache, so you know Barlowe assigned it to us on purpose."

"I never denied it, but there are worse places we could have been assigned than here. A few Solicitors were assigned to Panama and haven't been heard from since. Hell, one Senior Solicitor was sent to Anchorage."

"That's a Senior, though. Those guys are legends. Speaking of, did you see that report we got today?"

"The one on the Pit's Maw? They haven't done anything major in years. I'm surprised you even read that report."

"I read the reports sometimes. More to the point, it's a sign. A sign that this place sucks super hard."

"The Maw is an enigma. Active or not, most people will never know the difference, and based on what we do know, the situation here doesn't fit the Maw's MO."

"Yeah, doesn't fit the Pit Maw's MO until you're standing in line at the coffee shop and you're knifed in the back."

"Then keep your eyes peeled and your back clean. Catch them with the knife in the air and their pants down."

He glances at Lincoln and laughs. "I'm not as quick as you are; all I'd get if I tried that is a new knife. I prefer being proactive when possible."

"If you like being proactive, you should keep reading the reports."

"If I read the reports, we'd never have anything to talk about over breakfast."

"What? You don't like chatting with Peggy about her day in the mornings?"

Pierce scowls. "Peggy is evil, Lincoln. I don't know why we keep going to that diner."

Lincoln chuckles, moving the ringing device around the Terrace. He moves toward a familiar tree—Node 1. The ringing grows more frequent as he approaches it.

My hands curl into fists and push against the ground.

He lowers the device. "Hmm. What do we have over here?" he says, knocking on the tree. Removing a knife from his pocket, he cuts a piece of tree bark from the outside. His fingers break the bark apart. He allows the bark to fall to the ground and then scrapes the knife's edge against the outside, whittling the trunk down to the inner pulp.

With a sigh, he returns the knife to his pocket. "Looks like there is too much environmental interference. I'd say this place is heavily saturated, same as the structures the other Solicitors came across. Maybe it's one of those rocks."

"They found out those rock things are called Kiln or something, I think," Pierce responds. "They're valuable but hard to catch, can be dangerous, and some are rumored to be fragile, so you have to be careful if you want 'em in one piece. Still, I don't know why you think they'd have something to do with the buildings. We didn't even know they could move around and stuff until recently."

'Kiln! There truthfully are other Kiln... Fudge! Shall they endeavor to gobble me up!?'

"Well, they've all been around those types of places." Lincoln looks toward Pierce. "We might be able to track it via its Mana Efflux... How long before our Canvassers are done with their training?"

"The Mana Canvassers?" Pierce shrugs. "Allegedly, the first surveyors going through the program are set to graduate in a few months, but some might take a year or more. I don't know, honestly. Either way, they probably won't ship 'em here; they'll keep them patrolling around Headquarters and the bordering counties."

Lincoln takes a puff of his cigarette. "Then we probably need a clicker to sweep the area, which of course, I left it in the car." He walks over to Pierce and shoves the ringing device into his hands. "I'll be right back."

Pierce's pocketbook slips from his hands, but he manages to snatch it from the air. He rolls his eyes as Lincoln walks away without a word. "Such a dingus sometimes, Lincoln," he huffs. Putting away his pocketbook, he holds the ringing device and starts to walk around the Terrace. He raises it high, and the ringing slows; he lowers it, and the ringing increases. "Yep. Same as those other places."

He repeats this at multiple locations around the Terrace and sighs.

"Find anything?" Lincoln asks from the top of the grand staircase. He descends, gripping a big black bag in one hand. "Or is the area too saturated like I guessed?"

"Yep. Let's just give the clicker a few spins around the area, and then we'll report what we found to Barlowe."

Coming to the base of the steps, he nods and places the bag on the snowy ground. Kneeling, he places the card on his chest against what looks to be a lock. There's a click, and the lock falls off. He opens the bag, revealing a copper sphere around the size of a pumpkin. It resembles an eyeball with a black, circular pane of glass as the pupil. The pane is surrounded by a ring of metal rivets, which is itself encircled by a second ring made of bolts and pins.

To the left and right of the black pane of glass and halfway toward the back of the eyeball, there are the teeth of gears that jut out from each side. It almost looks as if two melon-sized gears were placed side by side, and then a sphere was built around them with them at the center.

Attached to the top of the eyeball are four antennas—two just above the hatch and two at the side opposite. Each antenna juts around a foot into the air and seems to be an equal distance from the others.

Lincoln grabs two of the antennas and flips it over, revealing a coin-sized hole in the base as well as the lever to a handle. With the eyeball balancing on the four antennas, he reaches for the handle at the bottom of the eyeball and pulls. The base of the eyeball slides open. Reaching in he yanks, and out comes something I can only describe as a small frying pan except in the middle is a rod with a ball affixed to the end. He slides the base plate back where the coin-sized hole fastens itself around the rod with a snap.

"Did you secure the dish correctly this time?" Pierce says, pointing at the frying pan. "I'm too tired to have my ass chewed out by Gary again."

"Don't worry about Gary," Lincoln says with a chuckle and a wave of his hand. "I double-checked it myself this time and you heard it snap into place."

Lincoln removes that hatch on the other side and pushes something into place. The pupil at the front of the eyeball shines and the ball at the rod's end lights up in a blue hue. "Alright. I'm giving control of the clicker to the paper pusher at Headquarters."

When he says that the thing, I believe they refer to as a 'clicker,' rises from the ground. It flips itself over and the antenna faces the sky while the dish faces the ground.

"Oh, yeah." The clicker spins around and looks at Lincoln. "Keep a low profile. I know we don't have to be as careful as in the past, but this is Central Park. So, yeah. Close to the ground."

A sharp click emanates from the clicker, perhaps explaining why it is named as such. It starts to move around the area. Staying low as instructed, it moves to the Terrace's far end and makes a harsher click.

The two gears to either side of the clicker start to spin. They increase in speed until they are a blur. Around the clicker's dish, a blue orb appears. The gears stop, and as it does so the blue orb expands, encompassing an area of a hundred feet or so in a dome before scattering like dust. It sits for a moment and then makes a single sharp click.

"Nothing that sticks out over there." Lincoln sighs, flicking his cigarette into the fountain.

The clicker moves to the area above the fountain, making another harsh click. I attempt to move further away, but Lincoln's gaze shifts toward me once more as I do so.

Lincoln points as the blue dome dissipates, saying, "Go over to those bushes next."

A sharp click cuts through the area, causing me to flinch. It moves away from the fountain, toward me.

'Nay.' My head darts back and forth as I search for an escape. 'I... I do not know what to do.'

"See something?" Pierce asks.

He shrugs. "Thought I heard something move earlier, and then some light a second ago."

The clicker moves over me, and the cattail tightens around my torso as I lower myself into my pile of leaves to block the light of the kiln in the midst of refining. A hum reverberates downwards as it stops directly over my body. It spins around, shining light on the bushes, until a harsh click sounds. The orb of blue encompasses the dish and starts to expand. I cannot bear to look, so I face the ground, staring at my arm, resting in the straw that pads the area around the bushes.

My arm takes on a blue glow as I watch the light pass through the haze of my arm. Each speck of dust that makes it up reflects the light back. At first, I believe I have been discovered and am about to flee, yet when I raise my head, I notice everything within the bushes is reflecting the same blue color. So I remain in place.

The world is silent. All I can hear is the spinning of the gears within the clicker above me. A sharp click sounds, and it leaves. "Nothing that sticks out. Check the Arcade and the water, and we'll reevaluate from there," Pierce says.

> **Fostered Aspirant [Stealth (Grade 4)]**

It clicks and moves toward the Lake. *'What did that eyeball do?'*

When it reaches the Lake, it stops. Lincoln and Pierce watch it as it makes a harsh click. The orb encompasses the dish and begins to grow. The water below it bubbles, turning a deep brown color. Yet, before anything can come of the bubbles, a fish the size of a small shark leaps from the water a few dozen feet to the left of the clicker.

Lincoln and Pierce stare, their heads tracing the fish's path. The fish has scales that are a mixture of blues and purples. Its scales reflect the glow of the blue orb's light, and droplets of water left behind look orange in the dawn's rays of light. It opens its mouth wide, and the clicker and its orb disappear into the fish's jaws. Yet, the bubbling beneath the clicker grows more pronounced as a head the size of a wheelbarrow rises from the water.

The head is that of a reptile with a beak-like nose. It has a green tint to it, with armor-like scales coating its head and neck. A low growl emanates from its throat as it opens its beak wide. As it leaps, muck from the bottom of the lake falls from a shell that covers its back. At the base of the shell an immense and mud-covered tail protrudes. Its tail whips at the Lake, sending a surge of water outwards.

There's a crunch as it clamps down upon the fish and clicker. From its jaws erupts a blue light more radiant than the sun at midday. Its body crashes into the Lake, casting a spout of water skyward and snuffing the blue light.

Twilight reclaims the Terrace. I sit, unmoving, listening to the waves made by the turtle beat against the shore. *'...Dinosaurs do exist.'*

My gaze returns to Lincoln and Pierce. Lincoln stands with a shaky hand lighting yet another cigarette.

Pierce looks at the ground and then to Lincoln. "Always a bigger fish, am I right...? Goddamn, we're gonna get our asses chewed out for this." He pauses and then sighs. "Am I allowed to have one of your cigarettes?"

••••

•••••••••

••••

It's the afternoon of the same day.

My Domain has had hundreds of people walking through it... but none near the Lake or Terrace. That is because the noble's guard has been here placing barricades and forbidding anyone from approaching the Lake. As for the incident this morning, I have reached a conclusion. *'Dinosaur!'* I shake my head, laughing internally. *'Ha-ha! I know naught of any dinosaur! There are no dinosaurs hereabouts. As far as I am aware, dinosaurs do not exist!'*

After absolutely nothing happened this morning, I took a risk, gathered all my items, and moved into a thicket on the opposite side of the Lake. It turned out to be a wise decision since Lincoln and Pierce left and returned later with some people. They hung plastic sheets at the Arcade entrance and exit, and I have not seen them since. I feel rather violated if I am honest.

'The situation is concerning, to say the least. My priority should be learning to control my Mana Efflux and gaining strength. I do not believe the seed is in danger, but rather myself. The issue will be how I will return to the seed when the time comes.' I raise my hands, shake them, count to ten, and then allow them to drop to the grassy ground next to me. *'Aye. I was told I must relax to practice the mana thing. After that, I shall eat what I have gathered and then practice.'*

I lie down, look toward the sky, and spend some time counting.

····

········

····

An hour or two later.

'...Three million four hundred eleven thousand. Is it fine to stare at the sun like this?' I glance toward the pile of various plants and rubbish. *'As Terra told me, I allowed my mind to relax... somewhat. Now I eat.'*

As I sit up and unravel the cattail, a purple wall appears.

> **Earl Interface:**
> **Notice: 195 Mana was used to refine 4.4 Nebula.**

The kiln's flame recedes, and my hand moves to my chest. *'Thank the lord, and this shall be the most Nebula I have had since my first adaptation.'* My hand moves from my chest to my belly. *'Before that, though, I am hungry, and I still need to test the Gluttonous Naturalist skill.'*

With the refining complete, my shoulders relax. Unraveling the cattail from around my torso, I move it toward the pile I gathered and engulf all but a couple of items. I am certain the average person would be hesitant to eat this rubbish, but its appearance is nothing compared to the copepods, and I have long since discarded my dignity.

Earl Interface:
>   Assimilating 'Peanut Shells' (Mana Bare)
>   Assimilating 'Old Bratwurst' (Mana Bare)
>   Assimilating 'Chinese Wisteria' (Mana Bare)
>
>   .
>   .
>   .
>
>   Erysichthon abates by 21
>   Essence value 1.
>   0.1 Refinable Nebula
>   0.3 Refinable Vitrum
>
> **Details:** A miscellaneous heap of unrelated organic substances. None of these substances have awoken to mana.

A bland taste spreads over me as a purple wall appears. Everything about the purple wall is the same except for one additional piece of information at the bottom. *'That is it? That is not particularly helpful.'* My eyes turn toward one of the plants I left out. *'What about a single item at a time?'*

I consume a small plant with green leaves and a wilted white flower.

Earl Interface:
>   Assimilating 'Spotted Wintergreen' (Mana Bare)
>   Erysichthon abates by 0
>   Essence value 0
>   0.0 Refinable Nebula
>   0.0 Refinable Vitrum
>
> **Details:** A herb native to the Colossi continent. This substance has not awoken to mana—due to this, any magical effects are negligible.

The purple wall appears, this time with something more informative.

'Oh! That is a bit better. Now, let's nibble this withered yellow flower over here.' I consume the yellow flower, and a new wall appears.

'This is fascinating! I am uncertain how helpful it is, but any knowledge is better than nothing.'

I begin engulfing various plants, studying the information, and learning what I can. In the end, much of the information is lost on me anyway, but in time, I believe it shall all make sense. Despite my curiosity, I stop myself when I notice a feeling of faintness creeping up through my haze.

'I will need my wits about me to study Terra's orb.' Grabbing the clear orb, I hold it in my palm. 'Now, let us attempt to use Terra's orb, Earl. I believe Terra said if I try to use it, then I shall somehow understand what to do.'

Shaking the orb, I command, 'Orb I entreat thee... do something.'

A blue wall appears, displaying a message.

To the "Spirit-Like" Lake Entity,

If you are reading this, that means you are attempting to use the Messenger Orb. This Orb's function is simple enough: it contains the instructions for a technique that shall assist you in regulating your Mana Efflux. To do so, you must counteract it via 'Mana Afflux.' Imagine if efflux was learning how to exhale and blow the air from your lungs, then afflux would be learning to inhale and hold your breath. You need to learn how to better regulate your breathing because all you're doing now is exhaling.

Setting that aside for a moment, you may be curious why I chose to utilize a method such as this orb, and that is because I really wanted to see if this thing would actually work. I had a tough time acquiring these, and I've never had the opportunity to use them before—although that will be changing soon. Of course, that is not the only reason; I also thought you'd like to have the technique in a format you can always look back on. Not to mention, I cannot be out for long due to circumstances.

Enough of that. Follow the instructions, and in time you will be able to smother your Mana Efflux at least partly. Good luck and do your best!

P.S. - In the future, you probably shouldn't use an item someone gives to you without being sure what it is or what it does first. This is simply advice from one friend to another.

Sincerely, Terra

Staring at the blue wall, I shake my head. *'I did not realize it would be something like this... Though, truly, I did not have any notion of what it would be like.'* I poke my finger through the wall, testing it. *'It's similar to the Cosmic System. Does this confirm Terra is in the Beta? Or is this kind of thing common nowadays...? It does resemble that lap-top thing she showed me.'*

I take a moment to ponder this until I conclude there's no point dwelling on it.

'I am not going to mention the Beta. I do not know if being in the Beta is unusual for "spirit-like entities" or not. I shall operate under the assumption she is in the Beta, but it is safer to wait for her to tell or ask me rather than me informing her myself.'

Shrugging my shoulders, I read the message. The message is interesting, but the closing section sticks out. *'It seems I should be more careful in the future about whom I take items from. Evidently, using unknown items can be dangerous, but I like to believe I am decent at determining someone's disposition. I do think Terra has some reason to be so kind to me as she has gone far out of her way to assist me; still, I also do not believe her to be a wicked person.'*

Moving on, I open the technique, and a detailed set of instructions appears. The instructions look to have been amended and clarified by Terra, for my sake. Yet the very first step presents a dilemma: "Step 1: Close your eyes."

'Hmm... How vital is that first step? Mayhaps I might simply find a dark place? Nay, that would not work either due to the way my vision functions. I may be able to find a way around it, but...'

I recall an adaptation that had something to do with eyelids, brows, and lashes.

'Earl, summon the wall with the eyelid adaptation.'

Earl Interface:

Forewarning: *If Essence falls beneath the 5 Essence line, the user will likely descend into a frenzied state of addled gluttonizing. It's recommended that the user avoids this dangerous state. If the user's Essence reaches 0, their flame will be snuffed.*

Vaporous Form Germination Tier Adaptations

Available Crown Adaptations

Negating Membrane
(**Recent Meal:** Chicken Breast)
Gain a nictitating membrane above the user's eyes resembling eyelids, eyebrows, and eyelashes. Enables the user to block the radiance of their eyes to better hide the user's presence. When the negating membrane is fully in use, natural night vision will be lost.
[Cost: 32 Essence + 1.1 Refined Nebula]
Note: Sample squandered. Re-consumption is necessary if the user wishes to acquire.

Essence Available: 31 [R = 81%]
Refined Nebula Available: 4.5 (1.1)
Refined Vitrum Available: 5.0 (2.8)
Refined Unknown Superacid: 0.5 (0.0)

Seeing the adaptation, I nod. 'So with this, I would forfeit my night vision when using the adaptation but mask the glow of my eyes in exchange. If I was somewhere suitably dark, this might suffice. I was already interested in this particular adaptation, as I am eager to look a bit less terrifying. I imagine from Terra's perspective, speaking to someone who does not have any eyelids is both difficult and eerie...'

My eyes move to the note and then the Essence requirements. 'I do not have the necessary Essence, and it appears I must eat more chicken breast to acquire this.'

I cross my hazy arms, pondering ways to retrieve the necessary Essence and breasts. An idea comes to mind as I move to the edge of the thicket and peer across the Lake. My eyes focus on the abandoned Boathouse and café. I think back to all the food I saw coming out of the café when I was spying a few days ago and how much Essence that would give me. 'I believe I shall make a swift stop at the Central Café tonight. It is either that or the chamber pot tunnels, and I am uncertain of my ability to combat the wretched rat should it appear.'

My gaze shifts toward the Terrace and the noble's guard, who rarely leave the black roadway above the grand staircases. 'I think it is possible if I wait until the middle of the night, break a window near the back, eat all the food, and run back here. They may not even realize until morning something has happened.'

Resolving to infiltrate the café later tonight, I move to advance my skills and stats. I look around, noticing a stick wedged in some bushes. 'Oh! That was one of the items I brought with me. I guess it got stuck.'

I raise the stick in my hands, look away, and turn it inward toward the shell. 'I wished to avoid this, but I must elevate my Sturdiness.'

Prepared for pain, I bring the stick down upon the kiln.

····

········

····

As I have been for a few hours, I sit tapping the stick against the kiln's shell.

Shaking my head, I toss the stick to the side. 'Nay. I cannot endure this any longer.'

After I began trying to foster my Sturdiness, it did not take long to discover that my arms are so weak that hitting the kiln feels more itchy than painful. I still tried hoping it would suffice, but alas, I doubt it shall. *'I suppose the cattail is my only choice. The stick should break before it does any real harm to the shell.'*

Unwinding the tendrils, I grip the stick and raise the cattail. I do not bother bracing myself this time but simply bring it down upon the kiln. The stick shatters. Pain surges through me. One of the Cosmic System's walls appears displaying the injury, but I crumple onto my side, and it vanishes.

'Good lord!' My hands clutch the kiln like someone who has been punched in the belly. I discover a tiny crack running along the spot that the stick struck. *'Why... Why was the anguish so great!? It is a mere twig!'*

I glare at the stick in outrage, as if it is at fault for what has transpired. With immense glee, I engulf it within the cattail to punish it for what it has wrought.

> *Earl Interface:*
> Assimilating 'Swamp Spanish Oak Limb'
> Erysichthon abates by 0
> Essence value 0
> 0.0 Refinable Nebula
> 0.0 Refinable Vitrum
>
> *Details: A tree limb teeming with foreign quintessence and mana.*

'Foreign Quintessence and mana? Swamp Spanish Oak...' I think back and recall from whence the stick came. *'Ah. That limb was near Node 1. Perhaps the sticks from that tree are sturdier... I know naught, except it hurt quite a lot!'*

> *+1 Strength*
> *+1 Orenda*
> *+1 Sturdiness*
> *5 Stat Points Primed*

'Well, at least my foolishness was rewarded. Time to retrieve the food from the café.'

Looking toward the sky, I see that it is already sundown. I shall find a place to hide in my Domain so I may heal, and then I will find a bush near the café. If all goes well, it will be a simple eat and dash robbery.

••••

•••••••••

••••

Earl Interface:
Assimilating 'Sliced Ham' (Mana Bare)
Assimilating 'Sliced Turkey' (Mana Bare)
Assimilating 'Baked Chicken Breast' (Mana Bare)
Assimilating 'Tuna Surprise' (Mana Bare)
Assimilating 'Tuna "Surprise"' (Mana Bare)
Assimilating 'Egg Salad Predictable' (Mana Bare)

.

.

.

Erysichthon falls to zero.
Essence value 21
1.1 Refinable Nebula
0.4 Refinable Vitrum

'Dash! Dash!' Breaking from my stupor, I flee toward the broken window of the café. 'I am not certain, but I believe it was that sliced ham that made me feel... delicious, for lack of a more fitting word. Of course, thanks to that Title, everything I steal is delicious!'

Instead of returning to the Terrace, I flee in the opposite direction. Behind me, I can hear the noble's guard yelling. 'How on earth did they know something was happening!?'

Footsteps approach, so I hide behind a tree. To block my eyes, I raise my hand and move my face close to the tree. I tighten the cattail around the kiln to block the light of the flame. A bright white light illuminates a portion of the area, including the opposite side of the tree I am hiding behind.

"Officers in the area of the Lake and Bethesda Terrace in Central Park, please be advised of a possible 10-21 at the Central Café adjacent Boathouse."

"Again!?" a man's voice shouts. "Dammit, it can wait. I'm about to piss my pants."

He shuffles toward the tree with small half-steps.

'Nay! Do that somewhere else and stay far away from me!'

I form sable copepods as he is about to round the corner of the tree. The light bounces around as he fiddles with his trousers. As he approaches the side of the tree I am hiding behind, I rotate to the other. Except I run out of space when I come up to a bush, meaning if I go any further, the kiln will make a noise.

He stalls, the clinking of his belt growing in intensity. "Why won't this thing come off? I haven't put on that much weight, dammit!"

As he finally undoes his belt, I release a dozen mouse-sized sable copepods onto the tree. They scuttle about, looking akin to giant cockroaches. *'This should bestow him a wee fright.'* "Wee" proves to be a monumental misestimate because the moment the man glimpses a copepod, he screeches like a banshee.

Between his screams, he only manages to say, "No, nooooo!"

Tripping on his own trousers, he screams and kicks away from the tree. I leap into the bush.

A group of lights comes charging in this direction. "It's the police! Who's screaming?"

I move away, ducking deep into the bushes and listening in.

"Johnny? What happened? Weren't you on leave?" a gruff voice asks.

"C-chief? You're here," Johnny stutters.

"Yeah, I'm here, trying to figure out what's happening," the man named Chief, I assume anyway, reaches down to help him up. "Go home, Johnny; you shouldn't be out."

Johnny goes quiet before saying in a voice that sounds like he's holding back tears. "Yeah. I should go."

"Get back to the café. Tell them I'll be back in a minute. Don't let those Consortium punks touch anything while I'm gone! No matter what they say," Chief declares.

Johnny and Chief leave.

'Why do I feel more guilty now than when I infected the shrieking man...'

The last two noble's guards start having a conversation.

"What the devils is wrong with him?"

"He was supposed to be on mandatory psych leave."

"Isn't he pretty new? Did something happen to him? Like at one of the protests or something?"

"Nah, he, uh, found a woman's torso the other day covering for someone in North Manhattan."

"A torso? Just a torso?"

"Yeah. He answered-up to a call about a smell, and found a body, well, a torso like I said, and I'll say that it was infested with... weird maggots, flies, and... fungus. I don't know, man. To be honest, I don't wanna think about it either. Really wish I hadn't saw that picture of the scene."

'Such a ruthless era... Though admittedly, I have glimpsed worse creeping in the London alleyways at night than what he describes.'

The two gossip for a moment longer and then depart, heading back toward the café. When they are out of sight, I abscond. With the pathways around the Lake blockaded, it's easier than it has been in the past when lots of people roamed about. Soon I am back at the thicket of trees across from the Terrace, and as I return, a blue wall appears.

Fostered Aspirant [Stealth (Grade 5)]

+1 Agility
4 Stat Points Primed

Entity 1-3-2-3 has manifested enough potential to supplant an Aspirant skill with a Novitiate skill.

Entity, see the presented skill supplants below.

[Novitiate Stealth II]
Continue along the path of balance. Sneaking, masking, or spying, the entity which pursues this general skill path is well-rounded, though the entity is less likely to be among the best at any one particular facet.

[Novitiate Tenebrous Stealth]
Darkness, shadows, and obscure spaces are where those that pursue this skill path find solace. Entities that adopt this skill should be aware they shall thrive in low visibility areas but may have difficulty blending into places of higher visibility.

[Novitiate Eggshell Stealth]
An Entity that fosters this skill should have a low susceptibility to claustrophobia and a tendency to drift through constricting spaces that most cannot or will not go. Sinking, digging, or crawling into suffocating nooks and crannies should be a regularity for Entities who adopt this skill.

'Ah! I was hoping it would advance. With all my hiding and tiptoeing, I suppose it was a mere matter of time.'

Studying the blue wall, I hesitate to choose the skill that appears most suited to my needs. 'Eggshell Stealth has its merits and I do fancy hiding in small places, yet it's a tad too circumstantial. Stealth II is adequate, and it would please me to possess it, but... Tenebrous Stealth seems ideal for my needs and pairs well with my ability to see in the dark. I suppose I am less fond of it because it shares a name with Tenebrous, but I should not permit something so superficial to dissuade me.'

I select Tenebrous Stealth.

Skill Supplantation

Entity 1-3-2-3 has supplanted [Aspirant Stealth] with [Novitiate Tenebrous Stealth] skill.
Prepare for memory impress.

Memories of both myself and an expressionless man arise in my mind. Each memory is different: one with me hiding in a shadow, another with me hidden in smoke, and one of me sunk into the hedges. In each memory, three of the same expressionless men stand at varying distances from where I am hiding. The closest points at me as if detecting me, the second stares curiously at where I am hiding, and the farthest is clueless of my presence. Depending on which and how I hide, their distance varies. The clarity of the memories fade.

'I shan't ever grow accustomed to that.' I take a moment to think through what I saw. *'So it seems simple enough. The Cosmic System is showing me the distances I would need to maintain in each situation to avoid detection or suspicion. Helpful, if not a bit underwhelming. Regardless, a welcome boon for sure, and now for the membrane. Earl, summon the wall. This lady is ready to have some beautiful eyelids, brows, and lashes!'*

I select the Negating Membrane, the kiln glows bright, and white haze exits it at every angle. The white haze drifts up to my neck, and for a moment, my vision turns dark before the haze settles above my eyes.

'Huzzah! I cannot wait to look, but...' In the distance, red and blue lights surround the Central Café. *'I shall have to wait until tomorrow. I should focus on Terra's technique, my skills, and stats for the next day and night.'*

Lowering myself, I move close to the ground to block as much light as possible and then attempt to close my new eyelids. At first struggling, I eventually manage to close them.

An indescribable dread grips me.

Chapter 12: Droplet of Thawing Ice

∞∞∞∞∞∞∞∞∞∞∞∞∞∞∞

Fostered Novitiate [Gluttonous Naturalist (Grade 1)]
+1 Sturdiness *+1 Fortitude* *+1 Endurance* **1 Stat Point Primed**

····

·········

····

There has been a foreseen irritation. I shut the negating membrane to attempt practicing Terra's technique only to be reminded of something— my rather deep-rooted fear of near-total darkness I acquired during my time in Tenebrous. It was not the most pleasant experience. In the end, I did not have the mind to make a second attempt.

Since that failure, a night and day passed, which I spent endeavoring to grow my Chronicles. I settled on training my Sturdiness in hopes the pain would persuade me to do the technique instead. The advancement of my Sturdiness was a splendid, if painful, addition to my durability.

My shoulders slump as I gaze toward the setting sun. *'Informing Terra of what transpired shall be embarrassing... Nay! I shan't tell her. I will conquer my fear or find a method to cope. Perhaps I may try anew with low light rather than smothering blackness.'*

Shaking my head, I peer toward the Lake's frozen surface. *'The water's edge should be too shallow for the monster fish, and the dinosaur produces a trail of bubbles and muck whenever it swims about.'* I raise a hand and run my fingertips across the negating membrane. It's a touch firmer than my skin. *'I wish to practice making expressions. The membrane demands more mindfulness than standard eyelids.'*

I pick up a small stone and walk to the edge of the Lake. Tossing the stone into the Lake, the ice around the shore shatters. I wait a moment to ensure that nothing overheard the shattering before falling to my stomach and gliding to the water's edge. As I gaze into the lake, my bright violet eyes stare back. I try to control the negating membrane.

Some time passes, and I am having difficulties with my new eyelids. The problem is they have a predisposition toward either shutting fully or remaining totally open. I also must wait for moments when the sun is not hidden behind clouds, which hinders my progress. But with persistence, I manage to shut my left membrane halfway and my right entirely. The glow of my right eye dims. At the same time, it is harder to see as clearly as before. I suspect it is because I have grown accustomed to seeing everything in a hue of violet.

I force my right membrane partially open and move closer to the water. The parts covered with the membrane are a lighter purple and look quite charming. *'Well, that is not too dreadful if I am honest. As long as one ignores that I do not have pupils... or an eyeball.'*

For the next couple of hours, until the sun sinks over the horizon, I practice lowering and raising my eyelids, winking, and other such things. *'At least this is a step forward. Now, I can make half-closed or angry eyes at Terra to let her know when I am not amused. I suppose I can also do a sad expression, but not much more than that. Oh! I can also make suspicious eyes... Aye, it's all coming together, Constance.'*

I cross my arms and wink at myself. *'I do not care what anyone says, I believe I look endearing...'* Leaning closer to the water, I switch between winking with my left and then my right eye. *'Well, I suppose it is time for me to return to the hedges and hide like a hag who eats children.'*

Behind me, I hear Terra's voice. "Seems you've found yourself in quite the predicament."

Flinching, I spin around onto my back. There in the thicket of trees, I see the gentlewoman's exquisite figure, removing a leaf from her silver hair. She carries a black bag, wearing her usual veil and gown, covering as much exposed skin as possible. Surrounded by the trees and shrubbery, she looks quite out of place.

I stand and place some distance between myself and the Lake; that way, I do not have to be so cautious of an ambush.

Terra's gaze drifts across the Terrace in the distance before settling upon me. She smiles as the cold breeze blows her long hair. "Were you checking yourself out?" I do not understand what she means by that, but she laughs and walks closer. I can see the violet spheres of my eyes reflecting in her curious green eyes. "You were winking at yourself from what I could make out. Did you always have eyelids?"

While shaking my head, I reply, {Nay, I thought I would try something new!}

"Your idea of trying something new is having eyelids?" Terra responds with a small smirk and a raised brow. "Is this what you did instead of working on your Mana Efflux problem?"

Using my new adaptation, I make my angry eyes and glare at her. {Terra, let's skip the prattle,} I reply whilst taking a few steps back. 'Prithee, do not continue this line of questioning!'

"I'm sorry, Constance!" she apologizes. "I was just teasing you! I think your eyelids, and, ah, your lashes and brows as well are all beautiful. Not to mention, seeing you wink at yourself over and over again was adorable."

{Aye, I... I appreciate the kind words.} Looking away, I stare at the ground beneath me, rubbing my foot in the dirt. {Uhm, for how long was I being spied upon?}

"Not long," she answers. "And don't act so shy; it makes me feel like I said something weird..."

I shake my head stiffly, causing my hazy hair to sway lightly. {Nay. Not shy, simply embarrassed, but I shall cherish the compliment.} The mood remains stiff for a moment until I look back up. {And about the signs.}

"Oh, yeah, of course!" She reaches into the bag, pulling out a thin white sheet. Unfolding the white paper, what is revealed is something that leaves me tilting my head. The paper reads, "BaWear FiSHe MoonSteRs," then hastily depicted circles with fins and fangs are scrawled at the bottom of the white paper.

Presenting my best questioning gaze, I peer at the white paper for such a long time that Terra pulls it away of her own accord. Slowly I lift my head, meeting Terra's gaze. While doing my utmost to ensure my eyelids still amply convey my thoughts, I say, {Terra, I know thou must have paid much for signs with such colorful dyes... and perhaps things are different nowadays, but these seem to be... poorly crafted.}

"Oh, is it because there is only one?" Holding up her finger, she removes more white papers from her bag. "No need to fret, I have twenty more!" she declares with a laugh and a grin.

{...}

Her shoulders drop, and she opens her green eyes wide, making her appear pitifully downcast. "Don't go quiet on me again." She holds up one of the pictures that, frankly, looks as if someone spilled paint onto a white surface. "The children worked hard on these. They'd be sad if you didn't like them," she says, pouting.

{Children?} My own eyelids shoot up. {Thou art a mother!?}

"What? No! Absolutely not!" Terra's face burns red, like an apple, as she shakes her head. "I indirectly help set the itinerary for students at a... school."

{Art thou a teacher, then?}

She speaks in telepathy, {It's complicated.} Her eyes dim, and she goes quiet. Staring at the drawings, a soft smile surfaces, and she laughs. {I had the children make these for fun. I also had a few genuine signs made, but more importantly, I posted some things online with a burner account.}

'Seems I should not inquire about the "school" further for the moment... but did she say burn-her?'

{What dost thou meanest, burn-her? Who was burned?}

{No, no, sorry, I forgot you wouldn't understand. I alerted some people using a different method. Anyway, I only made a few regular signs as I figured if we posted a lot of them, they'd take them down, but if we only post a few, they might ignore them for a while.} She holds up the children's drawings and starts showing me their designs. {We don't have to use these; I was just joking and thought you might find some enjoyment in them.}

{Oh, well, they are lovely signs. Shall the children be upset we did not use their signs?}

{I'll tell them we used them, and I'll hang on to them myself.} With a smile, she shrugs and returns the signs to her pack. {They had fun making them, and as I said, I just thought you might find them amusing.}

{I think they are delightful.} Remembering the noble's guard and the incident with the dinosaur, I fidget and look out over the Lake. {...About the signs.}

{Like I said when I arrived, you've found yourself in quite the predicament, and I would wager you don't think they are necessary anymore.}

{...Nay. I do not believe they are.}

She sighs. Her eyes gaze into mine, and she declares, {You can't stay in Central Park anymore.}

{Neither can I leave,} I respond.

{They'll find you. It's only a matter of time; I know it.}

{How shall they find me? They have made several attempts to locate me and have failed.}

{That's only because they haven't tried to look for you correctly yet, but...} She looks toward the Lake and Terrace. {But because of where you are and what happened, they'll find you when they're ready to find you.}

{What happened!? Naught has occurred here, I can assure thee!}

{Constance, I heard about the turtle as well as the fish.}

Tilting my head, I reply, {Turtle? I... Pardon. I am afraid I know naught of what thou speakest. I am but a simple woman of simple, unlearned origins... What is a turtle? Is it a bird...? A turtledove?}

Her lips purse. {Would that sort of line have worked in your time? All you had to do was say you were an uneducated woman and people would believe you didn't know anything?}

{...Oftentimes, men and affluent gentlewomen would, aye.}

{Listen... very few people would know about it like I do, but more importantly, they're already searching for someone, like me, who can find you. I am certain they'll find someone soon. The Consortium are not people you want to be on bad terms with. They have a near limitless wealth and influence; the only reason they haven't found you yet is because of the Beta.}

'She said Beta!'

{But as I said, Constance, you cannot stay here.}

{I cannot leave. I simply cannot.}

She frowns, but it wanes with a steamy huff, and her soft smile resurfaces. {Let's take a ride around the park. I can't leave my car parked here with police patrolling the area, but we need to have a talk.}

{Police? Car?}

{The people in the black uniforms and the big metal 'carriages' that drive on the road.}

{Ah! The noble's guard and rides. I recall overhearing and reading such names, though...} I slowly nod and then say, {Question. From what I have heard, 'police' seems to be a profession and not a title, so would it be more fitting to refer to them as noble's police?}

{...Yes?} She giggles, catching me off guard. Motioning for me to walk next to her, together we move through the thicket. She leads me to a dirt path and then to a stone path. {This is called the Ramble,} she says, pointing at a bright green sign. {And we shouldn't talk until we get to the car. We need to listen for any footsteps that might be police on foot patrol.}

I nod, and quietly we move further from my hiding place and deeper into the Ramble. As we wander, I catch Terra glancing at me, and she notices me doing the same.

Stepping from the Ramble's treeline, we come upon a polished inky-black ride with a golden ornament affixed to its front that has a quill's shape. The ride appears to be much more lavish than many of the ones I have glimpsed thus far. However... {*Did something strike thy ride?*} I ask, scrutinizing a rather severe dent.

Terra merely smiles at me.

I crouch and poke at the black, doughy wheel. {*How often hast thou operated this machine?*}

She chuckles, scratching the nape back of her neck. "Hop in," she whispers.

I peer at her, the dent in the ride, the doughy wheels, and then back at her. Our eyes meet, and she glances away. My intuition is screaming that something odd is occurring. Making my newly acquired suspicious look, I say, {*...I think I would rather not enter.*}

"...Why not?"

{*Thou art acting a bit peculiar, and it is making me nervous.*}

"We aren't going to drive anywhere with too many other cars on the road. Plus, I have a GPS."

{*GPS?*}

"Yes, the GPS will help us navigate if we need it." She extends her thumb with a smile. "So now that you know I'm prepared, don't be worried."

{*Huh?*} I mimic her, extending my own thumb. {*What does this hand sign mean?*}

"Good to see you're on board with this. I'm a... decent driver," she stutters, noticing me staring in perplexity at the carriage door. "Oh, I guess I should probably help you."

Terra follows me to one side of the ride and opens the door for me. She calls this the 'passenger side' or 'shotgun' while the side with the thing she called the 'wheel' is the 'driver side.' {*Shotgun? Does that mean I use a weapon to defend us from this world's endless perils?*}

"It isn't quite that bad... yet," she says. "Now let's go before it gets any later."

'This world has driven me to death's brink more in my brief time here than... actually, my life has always been similar to this.'

With reluctance, I take my seat and explore the interior. Everything in here is beyond perplexing, and I cannot decipher what any of it does. Meantime, Terra walks around the ride, removes something from her bag, and sits next to me. Looking over, I can see she has some sort of sapphire-blue and silver mask covering her nose and mouth. Yet her veil still shrouds her neck and face.

{A top-of-the-line gas mask I bought as a precaution,} she says through telepathy whilst sliding the smallest key I have ever beheld into a keyhole near the 'wheel.'

'Gas mask...? Wait, what is this.' I poke at a round knob. {What's this circular thing?}

The knob clicks; I recoil as a jovial voice shouts, "Ohhh yeahh! What's up, ladies and gents! Radio DJ Droplet here. You just heard "Mask in the Mirror" by Juniper Astraea... A talented young artist who, if you aren't aware, has gone MIA after... joining a cult... Something-something Robin's Egg, I think, it's hard to keep track of all the cults nowadays... Lotta young artists and kids tangled up in that right now..."

There's a sigh, and they clear their throat. "Uhm, anyway, yeahhh! Awesome, brilliant song; America can't get enough of Juniper's music! But now! I'm about to spin you an oldie but a goodie! Everybody's favorite old-school Inuit hard rocker King Zero... who... recently lost his family in Crawler-Anchorage... Zero's alive, though rumors say he relapsed, and no one has heard from him in a while... A-anyway, yeah! His hit single "Tungasugit - Umbral's Villager Antumbra," comin' atcha now!" A pause and the man's voice returns, lacking all joviality. "Uhm... yea, sorry, folks. Before we spin King Zero, let's have a round of real talk."

Terra's hand freezes short of pressing the knob, and she raises an eyebrow.

"A lot is goin' on out there right now." They hesitate, but continue, "And... and you don't need an old disc jockey like me to tell you that. We

320

can all feel it. Heck, you can look outside and see it. The government and media think we're all too stupid to notice. Nothing's normal anymore."

"The station won't like that I said this, so..." Their voice cracks, and there's a sniff. "...you probably won't hear from Ol'Droplet again. Let me just leave ya with this. Be careful who you trust, but... make sure ya have someone to trust. If things keep going how they're goin', those you trust are gonna be your only footing because everything else is crumblin' around us... Stay safe and stay together. Thank you for listening all these years... DJ Droplet, signin' o—" The man's voice disappears. There's a short lull and then a screech that attacks my very being. "Tungasugit, fuck-IT! Straight to naglik—"

Terra pushes the knob, and the screeches vanish. We sit in utter silence for a moment, listening to the wind blow against the ride. Whilst adjusting her seat, she says, {That's... that's the radio. Please don't touch anything else without asking first.}

{Aye...} I glance at her melancholic eyes and then ask, {So... what is this 'radio'? Is it some sort of weaponry meant to burst eardrums?}

{No, it's not a weapon.} She shakes her head, smiles, and laughs. {It makes music; I guess that would be the best way to explain it to you.}

Looking at Terra, I tilt my head. {Music? ...Nay, that was some mixture of screaming and wailing.}

{Music from your time is very different from music nowadays,} she says with a shrug. {I'm not a fan of hard rock either, though, especially King Zero's older songs. His newer music is mellower and all-around better, in my opinion. And if I recall, he was a self-destructive alcoholic when he wrote that old stuff in his youth. Of course, most people don't care about that. They'd rather watch him kill himself for a second of entertainment value.}

I nod, and Terra turns the ride's key. It rumbles and roars to life.

My hands fidget. {Is this ride truly safe?} I ask. {It shan't buck up and down vigorously?}

She tilts her head. {It won't buck up and down, and yes, it is safe. Some people have accidents, but people use these every day.} She pulls a lever, and the ride begins to move backward. My head looks back and forth as the death device moves in reverse. Again, she pulls the lever, and then we move forward.

'If I had a heart, it would likely stop from the sheer quantity of terror.' To my great relief, the ride moves slower than I foresaw; the pace is like a donkey pulling a wagon. *{This is not so terrifying... What's that blinking light?}* I ask.

{Blinking light? ...Oh, that's just my blinker; I'll switch that off.}

Terra pulls another lever, and the blinking light stops. I do not attempt to speak to Terra as she seems focused on the roadway ahead. Yet another circular object catches my attention. My curiosity gets the best of me. I glance at Terra and then slowly move my finger toward the circle.

The circle clicks and a breeze blows from a small grate in front of Terra, sending her silvery hair backward. Her veil lifts slightly, and an argent color underneath catches my attention. I gaze at it, finding it appears to be something silky pressed tightly against her neck.

Terra's eyes widen as she removes one hand from the wheel. She pushes the circle and yanks her veil back down. She avoids looking at me, but I can see her expression is frozen. "Did... did you see anything?" she asks in a small voice.

Seeing, for the first time, this usually confident gentlewoman insecure, I fidget and answer, *{Nay. W-was there something I should have seen?}* Unable to meet her gaze, I stare out the carriage window. *{I apologize for pressing another circle... I was curious.}*

"Yeah. Don't worry about it," she murmurs beneath her mask. *{Just don't touch the buttons, please.}*

····

········

····

I peer out the translucent, frosty window, soaking in the nighttime ambiance whilst watching the glistening golden rectangles that dab the center of the black roadway serenely float by. The wee street rectangles are mesmerizing in a peculiar way, and I nigh forget that I am in the belly of a bizarre mechanical carriage beast. Spellbound, I relish the motions of the ride as it sways to and fro, here and there, this way and that and...

The ride strikes a bump in the dark roadway, causing my senses to return. It is now that I realize something. *'Have we not been in this area before? What is our destination? I am certain we have not left the park at least.'*

I glance at Terra. She is peering forward intently; her breathing is soft and controlled. It reminds me of a soldier who is in the midst of their first battle, at least how I always imagined it would look.

{*May I ask where we are going?*} I question with a bit of hesitation.

She nods, stating, {*We're going to the other side of the park, but it is taking some time for us to get there. Specifically, we are going to the Central Park Zoo. It's not open, so we can't get too close, but tonight is still a good time to visit.*}

I tilt my head, staring at Terra. {*Zoo?*}

{*It's a place that keeps animals for people to look at and study, amongst other reasons.*}

'Other reasons? Perhaps for the nobles to hunt?' Remembering a skill the Cosmic System once offered me, I nod. {*So, is that related to a zoölogist?*}

The ride jerks as she glances at me. {*Sorry!*} Taking a deep breath, she returns her attention to operating the ride. {*I didn't expect you to know what a zoologist is but not a zoo. But yeah, zoologist study animals, so they are sort of related.*}

'Is operating a ride difficult? It appears as if it requires a great deal of focus.'

Terra turns onto a narrow brick roadway that leads to an iron gate. Stopping, adjusting the lever, and turning the key, she releases a long sigh and stares toward the ceiling of the ride. {*I have a confession to make, Constance.*}

{*A confession? Aye, what is it?*} I ask, placing my hand on the carriage's door handle.

{*...This is only the sixth time I've ever driven a car. I know what I said earlier, but I'm not good at driving.*} She sighs once more, raising her left hand and rubbing her temple. {*It's not like I've ever had the opportunity to learn, and after*

I heard what was happening, I had to find some way to come see you tonight secretly.}

{Oh.} I remove my hand from the handle. {...I honestly appreciate the worry, and I made the assumption thou didst not have much experience.}

She drops her left hand and glances at me with a huff. {Was it so obvious?}

I raise my thumb and forefinger and pinch them together, allowing a tiny space between them to remain. {...Perhaps a tad obvious,} I respond, dropping my hand. {But why hast thou never had the opportunity to learn? Why would someone own something they cannot use?}

Waving her hand limply, she lets it fall into her lap. {It's nothing interesting, to be honest, and it would be hard to explain in any detail.}

{I will conceivably not comprehend much, but I am interested in hearing more about thy past.}

She looks into my violet eyes for a moment before turning back toward the ride's ceiling. {Well, to summarize, my maid, a lovely woman named Victoria, took me to take my driver's test for my sixteenth birthday in secret. She didn't complain when I ended up failing; after all, it was literally the first time I had ever driven anything. Yet she was more than okay with retaking me and very patient with me, something only her and Caldwell ever were. Everything was fine, and I was happy to have someone who didn't belittle me like I was anticipating; however, when my dad's people...}

Pausing, she huffs and rolls her eyes, then continues, {When my people found out I failed, they threatened the woman that failed me. The next thing I know, when I arrived to retake my test, she and the manager at the DMV literally begged me to accept a license with genuine tears in their eyes. I frankly just wanted to retake it; this was the first significant thing I had ever failed at in my entire life, so I was eager to try again. But I couldn't turn it down after seeing a grown man and woman on their knees, crying for me to accept it after they found out who I was. Yet, by far the worst thing was that Victoria was let go, and she ran off. I haven't even seen her since that day.}

'As I thought, I did not understand much except that Terra and her family are feared...? Aye, I should be cautious what I say so I do not ruin my only cordial acquaintanceship in this era. Although my safety must be my foremost concern.'

Nodding, I simply reply, {*My sympathies that such unpleasant events transpired.*}

Again she glances toward me, waving her hand. {*Don't worry about it. I've had a few years to get over it.*}

{*I have not had many important people in my life because I was born with the haze, but I have experienced loss.*} I stare into her eyes. 'Sir Mouser had green eyes as well...'

{*I'm sorry to hear that.*} Pursing her lips, she asks, {*But your 'haze' was with you before you passed?*} She straightens her back, seemingly remembering something. {*Speaking of which, I almost forget...*}

{*Is it related to what we spoke about earlier?*}

{*No, we'll talk about that in a bit. I wanted to ask if I could take a sample of your haze? I might be able to learn something from it that might help you.*}

{*A sample?*} I pause, pondering why she would ask for such a thing. {*...It would not be wise to consume nor sell it if that is thy intention.*}

{*Consume or sell? No, no, I want to try to send it to someone who can analyze it and maybe learn something.*}

{*What type of things could be learned?*}

{*I have no idea. You don't have to if you don't want to; I just thought I may be able to learn something to help you.*}

'Perhaps she may discover something. It is a bit of a risk to give it to her, but the more I learn about the haze myself, the better. If anyone stands to benefit from more knowledge of the haze, it would be me, the one who is made of it.'

{*I... I suppose that would not be an issue.*}

{*Then here.*} She exits the vehicle, opening the carriage door behind her. {*I have a special glass jar. Just fill it with your haze, and I'll see what I can do with it.*}

{*Aye?*}

Terra opens the door and places a jar with a red lid on the ground. *'Again, such clear glass for something so insignificant.'* I unwind the cattail and grasp the jar.

{W-what!? You can move that around!?} Terra shouts, covering her mask's mouth with her hand. *{Why wouldn't you just use your hands!?}*

I gaze at her with half-closed eyes. *{Prithee, do not be so stunned. I need to use my cattail because otherwise I would not be able to get as good a sample due to my membrane.}*

Terra gawks at the cattail, pointing. *{Cat tail? Membrane? What kind of spirit are you? I've read through my tome dozens of times, but none of this was in there.}*

Penetrating the membrane, I capture a sample of the haze below. I move the jar to the base of the cattail around my neck, where it seems to be thickest. A bit of haze leaks out as I place the lid with my hand and twist. *{I have already informed thee I am 'spirit-like' various times now,}* I say, pushing the jar against the ground and twisting the lid with the cattail as hard as I can.

{Make sure you get it as tight as you can,} she says, goggling the scene. *{I won't be able to seal it thoroughly until I get home. I'm sorry I keep staring. You're just so unlike what I envisioned.}*

I twist harder, stopping just short of breaking the jar.

She walks over, picks up the jar, and checks to make sure it is tight before taking a breath. *{Okay, sorry, I am better now. It was just not what I anticipated.}*

Wrapping the cattail around myself, I give her the thumbs-up I saw her do earlier. *{That's good. The cattail will grow on thee in time. An ar... arma... ament... a weapon of elegance!}*

She smiles. *{Are you trying to say armament?}*

{It is a difficult word! It is not my fault!}

{Sure, sure.} She wiggles her eyebrows, releasing a small giggle. {But cat-tail is a cute name as well. I could definitely see you with a cat-tail. Almost like those Japanese catgirl drawings with the cat tails.}

{Like what? Mouser girl drawings? Cease such tricks; I am not so credulous.}

She nods, never taking her eyes off the cattail. "This cat-tail, is it strong? Maybe..." she murmurs to herself. Noticing me watching, she grins. {Let's go. I think there is a good spot up ahead where we can sit and talk. I'm not comfortable taking us anywhere further than this anyway.}

Reaching into the ride, she removes a bag and then takes the mask off her face, placing it in the bag. She dons a thick coat and motions for me to follow. As I follow, I make sure to walk downwind from her, keeping a slower pace. We walk along the snowy paths. The night is quiet, only the snow's crinkle beneath Terra's boots disturbs the soundless cold eventide air.

{Y'know, people call New York 'the city that never sleeps.' That's still true in parts of Manhattan, but most people don't go out as much as they used to.} She smiles bitterly. {It's too dangerous, what with the disappearances, and... well, the person people call 'Galtry'.}

I tilt my head. {Is that so? I can certainly believe it would receive such a name. This might be the quietest night I have experienced thus far.}

Terra draws her coat tight, her silvery hair fluttering in the breeze. My hands run through my own coal-black hair that floats weightlessly behind me. It's moments like this I am thankful I am incapable of feeling the night's chilliness. Turning to look at me, her lips form a genuine smile. {You wouldn't happen to have a stealth skill, would you?} she asks. {If so, I have a fun idea.}

{I do. Am I meant to use it?}

{So you are in the Beta then?} she asks.

My eyes widen. {Trickery!}

{I was curious if you were, but you never confirmed it despite me waiting for you to do so.}

{...Well, I do not recall any words confirming thy own involvement in the Beta.}

She smirks. {It doesn't matter. My point is, yes, if you have one, we're going to utilize it. I was going to keep a distance, but if you have something like that, we can use it to get a better look.}

{A better look?}

{The main part of the zoo is closed, but the path that runs through it is still open. My primary concern is whether you can hide when necessary.}

{Aye. If there are bushes or shadowy areas, I know I can stay hidden fairly well.}

{It is around 9:30 at night, so that shouldn't be an issue then. Not to mention, the park hasn't been that busy due to the unrest and the freezing weather. But you should know, Constance, within the next few days, the amount of people in the park is going to increase quite a lot.}

{I believe I have seen and heard of the unrest. Though I still do not understand the whole situation. Might thou tellest me more about it?}

She nods. {There are a lot of protests and upset people. A lot of secrets and happenings that your common citizen was apathetic to until recently, but now with the way things have progressed, they have decided to care. Yet no one is willing to tell them the truth of what is happening, so the situation just becomes more confused and chaotic. To be honest, the truth would probably only aggravate things, maybe even lead to near-anarchy. Now there is talk of war, and things are being made worse by corporations, criminal syndicates, real conspiracies, made-up conspiracies... cults.}

She pauses for a moment, organizing her thoughts. {That's all without mentioning the terrible catalyst that started everything, which was the total loss of Anchorage to diseased people twisted into monstrosities. The world is not in a good place right now, and it's only going to get worse.}

Things turn silent as I look toward the sky, searching for any stars. 'I am curious how much worse things are supposed to get in the future. I know that monsters are meant to return after the Beta is over. I assume they may be similar to me, or at least some of them... or they could be similar to the rat or dinosaur. There has been quite a jumble of appearances, capabilities, and malignity amongst the few "monsters" I have thus far seen. Monsters, beasts, and parasites like me shall

328

make everything worse... That must be the sort of thing she is referring to. My apologies, Terra, but I have chosen to survive, and I am certain they also feel similarly. I suppose I should ask to see what she knows.'

Finding the stars are still absent, I ask, {How bad are things supposed to get?}

{Really bad,} she says. {It is not a world I'd wish for the children to grow up in, but it is the world they'll have to grow up in. A world that must be prepared for.}

{Thou art truly worried about the children's safety?}

{I am... They're all so sweet, but they need someone to protect them,} she says in a small voice, pausing for a moment. {Someone who actually has their best interests at heart.}

{Well, there is likely still time until things get worse! I do not know anything about this place, Anchorage, this war, or what secrets thou refer to, but I am certain things shall be fine. As long as they have someone like thyself to help them.}

'...I feel dreadfully embarrassed for having said that; after all, I do not know Terra that well. All I can say is, thank the lord I am incapable of blushing!'

Terra freezes and watches me with her big green eyes. {But... Const–}

I hear someone walking further up the path. {I must hide.}

She waves me away. "...Yeah, I'll wait here," she whispers in a faint voice.

'Odd.'

A few moments pass as the people pass by. I return to Terra's side: she appears to have recovered her typical disposition. Together, we walk a short distance further.

When we arrive at a long row of benches, she motions toward them. {Here we are,} she says. Clearing away a few inches of snow that has collected upon the benches, she removes a towel from her bag and takes a seat. {Come on, I think you'll enjoy seeing something fun.}

I tilt my head, move downwind, and sit. In front of us is a short black fence, and further away is a pool full of blue water. A circular red-brick courtyard surrounds the pool. Various buildings are surrounding the courtyard, all of which are full of trees and shrubbery. The trees in these buildings are still green, even though everything outside has shed its leaves over the past few days. It is rather peculiar.

As for the blue pool, it is illuminated by various lights and other such things that I have come to expect in this era. An arched rock and platform sit in the middle of the pool, and for a second, I swear I see something moving around in the water, but I think it may just be a trick of the light.

{This path is usually closed by this time, but it's a little-known secret that they'll get deliveries on occasion and leave it open to allow the truck to enter.} She wiggles her eyebrows. {The benefit of knowing a New Yorker, like yours truly, is you get to experience things like this.}

Nodding, I look back toward the pool, and something surfaces, flopping onto the rock. {What is that creature!?} Leaning forward, I can see a creature with flippers and a tail. It sits with its back arched, kicking water, majestically. It claps its flippers together, making a loud woofing sound. {Is it a mermaid!?} I shout at Terra. {This is like what the sailors described.}

Terra bursts into laughter. {A sea lion.}

{A lion!? I have heard of such creatures, except this one seems much different than the stories.}

{No, no, not a lion. A sea lion,} she says, wiping away a small tear.

Seeing her laughing, this time I ask in jest, {Lions live in the sea!?}

She shrugs with a grin. {...In a way, I guess some do. Still, I hear their personality is closer to dogs than lions.}

{Funny... the queen had her own sea dogs she would use to attack the Spanish. I saw some of them in my time; we did not get along, but that is fine with me because they were typically not the best people.}[54] I lean closer, taking in all the

---

[54] The Sea Dogs were started in 1560 to bridge the gap between the Spanish Navy and the English Navy. The Sea Dogs served to attack Spanish ships during what was technically peacetime.

detail of the sea lion. {But now that I get a closer look, they look similar to the harbor seals I saw from time to time, yet much bigger.}

{That's all very interesting; I'd love to hear more in the future, but...} She sighs and scratches at her arm with one of her nails, saying, {But we need to discuss you leaving this park. It's not safe.}

I shake my head. {As I said previously, I cannot leave.}

{You just can't?}

{Well, I can leave, but I also cannot.}

{And why is that?} She raises one of her eyebrows.

{It is rather complicated,} I reply. {But I have an important... attachment to the park.}

Whispering to herself, she says, "The tome did mention spirits may be attached to certain areas, but..." She gazes at me with seriousness. {You're just 'spirit-like.' Is there no way you'd leave? Even if you were able to come back to the park whenever you wanted or just until things calm down here?}

{...}

There is a lingering silence as I hesitate to answer. As I am about to respond, she removes her mask and speaks aloud, "Do you trust me, Constance? When I confessed my lack of driving experience, I noticed you reaching for the door handle."

I turn away, and consider lying, but suppress the urge and respond with the truth. {Aye... yet also nay. I have made the mistake of misplacing my trust a few too many times to readily trust someone, regardless of how much I may enjoy that person's company... Besides, we have not known each other long enough to warrant sincere trust. A person who trusts too easily will one day discover that they were merely an unpaid food taster for the person they trusted.}[55]

---

[55] Food Taster: a person who ingests food that was prepared for someone else, to confirm it is safe to eat and not poisoned.

"I understand. I appreciate your honesty, and I agree." She exhales; a puff of warm smoky air passes through her thin veil. "Because I am the same as you."

'...She does not trust me either. At least she is also honest, I suppose. Though, I must admit it leaves a bitter taste. Is it wrong of me to feel this way despite holding the same feeling?'

Leaning back, she continues, "If there was a guaranteed way we could both trust each other without question, but it came with some stipulations, would you accept?"

{I suppose it would depend on the stipulations, but it would be nice to have someone I could trust unconditionally for once.}

Terra chuckles. I know what you mean." Opening her mouth to continue, she freezes before saying, "I'm sorry. You need to hide." She stands, turning her attention in the direction of the ride. {Someone is here, and I would guess they're here for either you or me. Time to make use of what that stealth skill taught you.}

Chapter 13: Lions and Apes and Scribes, Oh My

∞∞∞∞∞∞∞∞∞∞∞∞∞∞∞∞∞

I hear footsteps crinkling the snow.

Terra looks at me. {*I'll saturate the area in what little mana I have. Try to place at least three hundred feet between you and me in the meantime, and find someplace to hide,*} she says. {*Hopefully, that will mask your presence enough that he won't notice you're nearby, but I doubt it.*}

'*He? She knows who it is?*' I nod and turn away. '*I should find somewhere I can watch to ensure she is not in danger.*'

My body slips through the black gate that separates the zoo from the footpath. The sea lions glide about in their enclosure, eyeing me curiously. A young sea lion raises its head from its pool and woofs at me.

I wave at the creature. '*Woof-woof to thee; thou art quite handsome, but I do not have time for prattle.*' I glimpse a boulder peeking out behind the pool. I circle around the sea lion's enclosure and rush toward it. '*Excellent. That shall do.*'

A railing enclosing a second blue pool stops me. This pool is more extensive, with large gray stones spaced throughout. The stones around the island are steamy, and any snow that topped them has melted. At the pool's center is a brush-covered island. The high boulder I spotted is at the island's middle, overlooking the brush.

I study the water, probing for any movement. It is tough to see, but I notice nothing as unmistakable as a sea lion swimming about. The island is similar; nothing obvious is roaming its shores. Glancing to my left, I see a sign sheathed in ice. I lean in closer, trying to read it. All that's visible is the words "Range: Kyushu, Shikoku, and Honshu Islands of Japan." I rub at the ice, trying to melt it away. Alas, my haze does naught.

{*Constance, I know the animals are captivating, and I'll try to bring you back someday, but we don't have much time. Please hide,*} Terra says in my head.

{Aye, but Te—}

{I understand you have questions but trying to tell you anything without time to explain will just cause confusion and misunderstandings.} Even from here, I can hear Terra scoff. {God in Light, saying there 'isn't time' is so cliché, but that's how it is, sorry.}

{...Aye. Worry not! I may not know of this 'cliché' thou speakest of, but I am excellent at hiding.}

My eyes survey the water as I climb the railing and hop atop the pool. I search for any hide or hair of a creature and then rush toward the island. Nothing, I arrive at the island without issue. Clambering up the boulder, I drop into a patch of shrubbery near the boulder's peak.

From where I lie, I can see the footpath that runs from the left of my vision to the right—the left side being where Terra's ride sits idly. Terra stands near the footpath's center, a red brick building overlooking her. Above that building, the high towers of New York City peek out.

'This position should suffice.' My focus returns to Terra standing on the snow-shaded footpath. Her gown and silver hair stir in the cold wind. My fingers fiddle with a pebble to occupy themselves. 'Now, who is this trespasser, this 'he,' of which Terra speaks? Why would they search for her, and how did they locate her?'

> ### +1 Perception
> #### *No Stat Points Remaining*

'Ah, Perception, a boon, but also my last stat point. A wee bittersweet.' I dismiss the wall, finding a heavy scowl and sharp eyes now grace Terra's face. 'I have never seen her with such a steely expression. Does she loathe this 'he' so much?'

She twists in my direction and runs her gaze across where I fled. It seems as if she knows my general location, yet not my exact position. I drift closer to the stone's edge, as close as I can without exposing myself.

A hot breath escapes her lips as she steps toward the bag she brought with her, drawing out a silver book, nay, it would be more accurate to describe it as a tome. The tome is dense and weighty with thick pages. *'It is denser than the tomes the children, Lorelei and Vincent, carried, yet it is similar... I do not understand... The children she spoke of—surely, they are not those two? Nay, she showed me many drawings from many different children; they cannot be the children... or at least the only children.'* I shake my head, watching her hug the tome and clench her fists. She stares in the direction of the ride. *'I know too little about Terra. Who is this gentlewoman to this world? What role does she fill within it and this era?'*

Four people approach her. Three of them walk with a casual gait whilst the fourth separates from the group and rushes toward Terra—I recognize them as Caldwell. His white hair blows backward as he hurries to her side.

Caldwell stumbles and slips atop an ice sheet. "M-Miss!" he shouts, sliding toward Terra.

Terra steps to the side. Caldwell slides by her, but she reaches out, seizing his wrist. With a jerk, she tugs him backward and rescues him from tumbling onto his rump. She releases his wrist, and Caldwell places a palm over his heart. He takes a deep breath and bows to her.

The three other people follow. Two of them wear black frocks, cowls obstructing their face, and in their hand they carry hefty tomes. The shorter of the two has a woman's figure and a blue tome, and the other has a man's shape and a red tome.

As for the third and final person, I do not believe I could forget them. *'The Bishop! Why is he here!?'* The Bishop taps his cane against the ground, and despite his sewn together eyelids, he has nary an issue navigating the icy footpath. He wears his usual black suit, except an overgarment covers his belt of poppets.[56] Amusement is evident in his demeanor as his head tilts in my direction.

'Did he regret freeing me? Is he hunting me!? Did he track my mana!?' I glimpse movement in my peripheral. *'Is it those fiendish poppets; have we fallen into a trap!'* Keeping low, I push myself up, preparing to unravel the cattail from

---

[56] Poppets: In folk magic and witchcraft, a poppet is a doll made to represent a person, for casting spells on that person, or to aid that person through magic.

around my torso. Short figures emerge in the corner of my vision, and I hear something sniffing the air. *'They sniff. Not poppets?'*

My attention returns to the Bishop and Terra. She stands, hugging her tome and squinting eyes. The Bishop announces something, but I cannot hear from this distance. He stretches an arm toward Terra, a devilish smile upon his face. Hot air escapes from between his teeth as he speaks a few short words. *'Does he intend to perform that vile attack!?'*

A rock bounces against the kiln with a *ting*. "Ahhh!" something screeches.

I flinch and look behind me. Surrounding me are furry people-like creatures with long arms and legs, peering at the kiln, and tossing small rocks at its shell. My eyes meet theirs. They back away and circle around the other side of me. I turn to look at them anew, they spread out and then go to my other side once more.

'Are these... apes? I have heard hearsay of such creatures!' There are six apes, and all six are between one and three feet in height.[57] Their bellies are white while the remainder of their fur is a sandy yellow, they have scarlet faces and rumps with stubby tails. They hunch over and lean forward. Their blue eyes goggle my kiln, and they "ooh" one another as if having a conversation. They flex their nostrils, sniffing the air around me. All at once, they howl and back away. *'They understand the haze is dangerous? Strange how animals are better at conjecturing such things than people.'*

Recognizing that the apes have no intention of doing anything rash, I shake my head at them and return to monitoring the situation at hand. Terra stands unmoving as the Bishop advances with his hand still outstretched and his cane rapping against the frozen footpath.

The Bishop's hand slips underneath Terra's veil. He raises the veil's edge, exposing a hint of argent against her neck, and caresses her cheek. She takes a step back, drawing her veil back over her face. Her eyes glare at him with a mixture of revulsion, hate, and something I am familiar with: pity. He does not let Terra move away; instead, he opens his arms and embraces her. She stands so still that it appears as if the Bishop is hugging a statue. Terra pushes him away, steps backward, and says something to him.

---

[57] |Between 31 and 91 centimeters in height|

'Is... is Terra in some sort of romantic relationship with that man? A coerced marriage!? If she is a noble... I surmise Terra is of marriageable age; yet to be to be wed and at the mercy of such a lousy man. Nay, it cannot be true! When I questioned if Terra was a mamma, her reaction suggested she was not considering such possibilities. She cannot be in such a relationship.'

Terra seizes her bag and commences wandering back toward her ride. She pauses and her voice echoes in my head. {Constance, I recommend you leave quietly. If you can't, then stay put and don't move. Be prepared to fight only as a last resort. Keep the last question I asked you in mind. Next time we meet, we'll have much to discuss. Be safe; I'll keep an ear out.}

'Wait; I do not understand! What is occurring; art thou in danger!? Mayhaps I could assist!' Alas, she leaves without looking back. '...Her last question? The one about if there was a guaranteed way we could trust each other, would I do it?' The Bishop accompanies her, and Caldwell chases after them. The other two people stay behind. I attempt to stand, but the apes panic as I do so, so I lower myself. 'She recommended I run, yet if I try to do so, these apes will reveal my location! ...I am on an island surrounded by freezing water and these apes; surely, none shall discover me in such a place.'

Two people remain behind, standing motionlessly. Echoes of Terra's ride leaving prompt the pair to draw back their hoods. A white man and a white woman, each with a few squares of red cloth stitched to their face and neck. They speak to one another, glancing from left to right as if awaiting someone. In the meantime, the apes crowd together and hug each other for warmth. They peer at the kiln, tilting their heads this way and that as if enthralled by its flame. I disregard them and examine the area, searching for practical paths of escape.

Another ride arrives. This one moves past the gates and rolls to a stop near the two people I presume are from the Hex Church. The ride is bigger than the one Terra operated and has a boxlike back. On its side, I recognize a depiction of the orphanay bird—the Consortium's insignia. Four men exit the ride and approach the two people. Two of the Consortium men I recognize as Lincoln and Pierce, while the other two are younger men. One of the young men is a black man with short hair, and the other resembles a native man with a shoulder-length cut.

'Such a variety of races in this group. Is such a thing normal in this era?'

The pair stare at the two Hex Church people. A cigarette held between Lincoln's lips smolders as he studies the man and woman. He signals for them to follow and opens the short black gate that leads into the square with the sea lions. It's difficult to hear until they walk around the sea lion enclosure, stopping at the side nearest me.

Lincoln tosses his cigarette to the ground and snuffs it with his heel. "Tell me, Emily and Colin, why did we contract you to track and capture this 'Kiln' only for you to drag us out here anyway?"

'Those two that came with the Bishop! They are searching for me!?' My gaze shoots toward the man and woman. *'They cannot be stronger than the Bishop... Nay, they seem more ordinary than that man.'*

"We were told to contact you if we need access," the woman from the Hex Church, Emily, states.

Pierce groans. "Yeah, but you were only supposed to bother the newbies for that. Do you know how hard it was getting corporate to send us help? Hard." He points at the two men that arrived with him. "These two only just started, so they can't do much without hand-holding, but they're good for that kind of stuff."

The man from the Hex Church, Colin, points at the two young people with them. "And these two are?"

"Like Pierce just said, they're the newbies. Try listening," Lincoln scolds, strolling toward the sea lions. "By the way, isn't that guy with the eyes supposed to be with you?"

"Eyes? You, uh, you mean the Bishop?" Colin questions.

Lincoln nods. "Yeah, your local church head. What's his name? It wasn't in my documents, which is weird. I've never seen that happen before, and I've met more than my fair share of enigmatic people born off the grid."

Colin and Emily glance at one another and then back at Lincoln. "He prefers that we just refer to him as 'the Bishop' or 'Bishop' if there isn't another church head around," Emily replies.

"...The Bishop? 'The Head Weirdo' is more like it," Pierce says, rolling his eyes. "All of you cults take your naming sense straight from that Jurassic Orcs and Peri-Elves game. It's always "The" this and "The" that, like damn, give it an actual name, so people understand who or what you're talking about."

Colin's eyes narrow. "You goddamn suits. All of you Consortium gophers owe your soul to the company store, and you're talking down to us?"[58]

"Plus, we aren't a cult, dickhead," Emily adds. "We were officially recognized and tax exempted years ago. We're a religion."

"Relax," Pierce says, frowning and motioning for Lincoln to follow. "I didn't mean to hit a sore spot; I was just joking."

Lincoln chuckles. "We'll leave the newbies to keep you company. We've got business elsewhere." He walks away, waving. "Give us a call if you find anything. Don't approach or give chase alone."

The two Consortium people wave at Colin and Emily.

"I'm Mark. Nice to meet you," the native man says.

"I'm Preston," the black man says with a smile.

Emily shrugs. "Don't care."

Lincoln and Pierce's ride slowly rolls forward. The ride beeps as Pierce shouts, "You kids all try and get along!" He points at Colin. "And watch that kid; he might make another old-ass reference that your grandparents are too young to get." He laughs.

"Prick," Colin scoffs.

"Uhm, sorry about them." Mark rubs the back of his neck. "They haven't gotten much sleep and aren't in the best mood. Everyone is stretched thin right now..."

---

[58] "I can't afford to die. I owe my soul to the company store" from the song Sixteen Tons. A reference to the truck system and to debt bondage.

"It's fine," Colin answers. "He clearly understood the reference, and it obviously bothered him enough that he didn't want to stick around."

"You think so?" Preston chuckles and holds up a ring of keys. "Well, anyway, I've got the keys. Where was it you guys needed to go?"

"We aren't sure where we might need to go," Emily says, waving her hand. "We came here for a different reason, but after we arrived, the Bishop told us there was a lot of mana buildup here. Much more than the thing we came for could be exuding."

Mark tilts his head, surveying the area. "What was the other reason? Is it why he isn't here?"

Colin shakes his head. "We don't know anything, and it's the Bishop's personal affair. We aren't going to impose on his business."

"Lady troubles, maybe?" Mark asks, wiggling his eyebrows.

"Sure, whatever." Colin crosses his arms with a huff. "We'll need a little time since we don't actually have much experience."

Mark raises an eyebrow. "...Then why did we hire you if you have no experience?"

Emily clicks her tongue and rolls her eyes. "Because literally no one has experience. Only a few geniuses can track mana with any real accuracy." Emily and Colin each open their tome, removing a quill from a pocket on their frock. "Give us some time and open what we need you to. We'll track down the monster's general location."

Preston squints his eyes, glancing between the two. "Wo-wo-woah. Let's back up. What do you mean mana buildup and 'we'll track down the monster'? Is that suspected M-Class terror legitimately around right now?" Preston asks, mouth agape, motioning at himself and Mark. "Cause we aren't really qualified for anything like we saw in those videos they showed us during orientation." He holds up the keys, jingling them for everyone to see. "I'm just the key guy, and I wanna stay the key guy."

"Oh... yeah, and I'm the assistant to the key guy," Mark says with a nervous chuckle.

'M-class terror? Is that how they refer to me...? It's rather offensive. Still, nary a need to worry, Preston, thou shan't knowest I was ever here! Time to take my leave.' I try to stand, but again, the apes howl, drawing the attention of the four. Once I drop back onto my belly, the apes stop their howling. *'...I cannot leave without the apes alerting them, and verily I am not the quickest, so they may intercept me; I am trapped...'* I scrape the ground with my nails. They disperse into a puff of haze and then reform. *'If standing assures my discovery regardless than I shall linger here and pray.'* I nod at my ape acquaintances. *'And if an ape could be so kind, prithee, remind me to raise my Agility in the future.'*

The four people speak amongst themselves and then split up.

Emily and Colin lean against a railing between the sea lion enclosure and some shrubbery. Each pinches a gray feathered quill between their fingers and writes with careful movements. Emily balances a small bottle of shiny crimson ink atop her tome's pages, which she shares with Collin. As they scribble in their tomes, a faint reddish glow arises from the page.

My gaze drifts to the two Consortium 'newbies,' Preston and Mark. The pair trek to the side of a brick building, approaching a silver box mounted upon the wall. Reaching out, Preston pulls a handle on the box's front, opening a panel. The two stare at it for a moment until Mark reaches in and flicks something. All the unlit lanterns around the court flicker with light, and the court becomes bright, unlike the enclosure of apes where I am, which is nearly black.

Closing the small silver door, Preston and Mark return to Emily and Colin's side.

"What are you doing?" Mark asks. He pushes himself up on his tiptoes to glimpse what Emily is writing.

Emily frowns at him, pulling her tome closer to herself. "We're preparing," she answers.

"Oh." Mark drops off his tiptoes. "So, what is this book made of an—" He reaches toward the tome's spine. A tiny coil of lightning sears his fingertip. "Woah!" he yelps, hopping backwards.

'What was that? Those tomes... are they the thing called technology or are they, mayhaps, magic?'

"Never touch someone's Spirit Tome," Emily states, never glancing up from her scribblings. "They aren't meant to be touched by anyone except for the person they belong to. So keep your hands to yourself."

"Spirit Tome?" Mark slurs, his finger still in his mouth. "Is... is that a legitimate magical item?"

Colin rolls his eyes and scratches the area around the red fabric that is stitched to his cheek. "Why are you so excited? I've heard the rumors going around about the magical tech the Consortium is toting around."

Mark pulls his finger from his mouth. "I'm not sure where you heard that rumor, but I'm not at liberty to discuss anything like that with external contractors," he says, peering at the tome. "Mind if I ask where you got the book? Is it like the Daybreak Scriptures?"

"Sorry." Emily snickers. "We aren't at liberty to discuss that with external outsiders."

"Oh. Yeah, understandable." There's a short pause. "Uhm, I remember reading about your church online after you guys were given tax exemption. It discussed the rise of Galtry and your church. It was a pretty interesting read."

Emily sighs. "I'd literally kiss Galtry's toes if they asked me to, but unfortunately, the church doesn't have anything to do with Galtry."

"You'd kiss their toes?" Mark asks. "I mean, I know Galtry is a bit of a celebrity, Emily, but they're also a brutal criminal with a milelong record of felonies."

"Psh, I'd do waaay more than kiss their toes if they wanted me to. I'm sure a lot of people would agree."

"R-really?"

Emily smirks and nods. "Really-really."

Preston moves to Colin's side, gawking at the cloth sewed to his face. "Your cloth is a religious thing, right?"

"Yeah, sorta, what else would it be?" Colin responds.

"I don't know... fashion?" Preston says with a shrug.

Sighing, Colin closes his tome and looks at Emily. "I'm going to start probing the area with my mana. If I start to feel too sick, it'll be your turn to try."

Emily nods, her quill never resting. "If it's here I'll find it, and the Bishop will be in awe when I surprise him with it."

With a grunt, he scratches his cheek and pushes off the railing. "We're supposed to locate its general region, not confront it," he says, closing his eyes. "The way the Bishop was talking, he really didn't want us messin' with it. So don't."

His eyes shut, he wanders the area, taking shallow breaths after each step. Droplets of sweat run down his cheeks. The five apes and I follow his movements as he steps about the area. *'What he is doing reminds me of Terra's mana technique. Well, I suppose all they have done is close their eyes... That was farther than I capable of getting.'*

Several minutes thereon, he passes near the edge of the ape enclosure. One of the feistier apes plucks a pebble from the dirt and flings it at him. The pebble splashes the water, spattering him with a few droplets.

Flinching, he opens his eyes. He glances at the rippling water, and then at the apes. "Wow, the monkeys are throwing crap at me." Turning toward Emily, he throws up his arms, saying, "It feels like there's a lot of mana in the air, so I doubt it's inside any of the buildings. If it's inside putting off this much mana, then we should all start running for our lives now," he says, allowing his arms to drop to his sides. "It's also possible I'm screwing up, and there's nothing here at all."

Emily corks her ink bottle and then closes her tome; she uses one of her fingers to mark the exact page she has been writing upon. "Maybe it's somewhere in the bushes." She kicks a bush near her.

'Colin states they are meant to locate me yet not confront me...' I stare at the woman who glares at the plants as if they are an adversary she must vanquish at all costs. *'But I have witnessed others with looks such as the one that Emily woman has now. It is the expression of someone about to do something... foolhardy.'*

Seeing her moving from bush to bush, kicking each of them, Preston raises his key ring. "Hey, I'm not a fan of how things seem to be developing," he says, jingling the keys. "If we're not confronting the thing, why are you shaking the bushes like that's not the case."

Mark nods. "Yeah, I'm not sure I understand what you're doing either. If you know it's someplace around here, then it's a job well done, right? So why does it feel like you're trying to poke a beehive?"

"Well, we've got to be sure it's here, y'know," Emily says. "Can't assume something we aren't absolutely sure about."

"That's it!" Colin grabs Emily's arm and drags her away from the two Consortium men. They stop in front of the ape enclosure. "Emily, what're you doing?" Colin asks. "Are you trying to antagonize the monster? I didn't say anything, but it seemed like it took you a while to write your hex, and the ink looked like it was decent quality. It probably took you a while to save up for that quality of ink. What kind of hex were you scribbling?"

"Relax." Her eyes shift from left to right. "This will give us a leg up in both the church and Bishop M's shortlist. If we do this our future is going to be amazing."

"As I already said, we aren't supposed to confront or even mess with it."

"Yeah, but if it attacks us first or we say it attacked us first, then there's nothing we could have done differently."

"You're nuts. We've never even seen a monster in real life before." He looks back to ensure the two Consortium newbies cannot hear him. "I feel like I'm about to vomit and pass out from Mana Inanition. I almost popped a blood vessel trying to probe two places! I know it might have seemed like I was trotting around for a while, but I stopped probing like ten seconds after I started. I just didn't wanna talk to those Consortium suits anymore. They're unbelievably irritating!" He pauses and points at his face. "My stitches haven't even quit itching yet. I'm going to lose my mind if I don't get some anti-itch cream in the next thirty goddamn minutes."

"Chill out, princess. Here, have some of my cream; this is the prescription-grade stuff that everyone says works great," Emily says, raising an arm to hand Colin a white tube. "As for everything else, that's all because you're weak. I have double the Orenda stat you have, so I can make better hexes!"

"Yeah, well, double two is only four, so your Orenda isn't as impressive as you're making it sound," Colin says, snatching the tube from Emily.

Emily snaps her fingers and shakes her head. "Just listen-listen! No one in the Manhattan congregation has killed a monster before, except maybe the Bishop, which means whoever does it first will stand out from the crowd. If we do this, they'll probably even send us to the slaughterhouses to power level; every single cow slaughtered is free and effortless Essence!"

"You're disturbingly excited about slaughtering farm animals."

"If you act all squeamish about that sort of stuff, you'll never make something of yourself after the apocalypse," she says, waving her hand. "But, for real, you know there is something we could do that's even better for our reputation than fighting and killing a monster?"

He rolls his eyes. "I'll humor you. What?"

"Enslave it!"

I raise a hand in disbelief. *'Again!? First children seek to dominate me and now this noddy woman wants to enslave me! Why do these people wish to enslave me!?'[59]*

"Why do you call it that? Enslavement. You're saying you want to contract a monster, right? That's not enslavement, and you callin' it that makes me feel uncomfortable." Colin scoffs. "And why would you want to contract a monster? Weren't we told it's more beneficial if we use our lifetime

---

[59] *Noddy: A fool or simpleton.*

contracts on spirits? I think they said spirits were complementary to our type of magic or something like that."

"Sure, sure, except who knows when we'll start seeing real spirits or anything like them. Just think if you could contract a monster and have such a huge early advantage." She waves her hand. "Anyway, that's just the best case, not what I expect to happen."

Colin pinches the bridge of his nose. "Just the best case, huh? I'm not going to save you if things go to hell."

"It won't! I scribed the strongest hex they taught us with ink that cost me ten grand! It'll work." She points at Colin's tome with her right hand and rubs two fingers together with her left. "You probably used six Benjamins' worth of my ink, and I didn't even say anything!"

"Good God, we only know like two hexes." He sighs. "You're the dumbest person I've ever met. I'm not going to restrain you, but I'm also not going to stick my neck out."

"Fine! You'll thank me later when we're ready to kick monster butt, and everyone else in this city is still debating whether mana and the Cosmic System are even real."

"It'll be the first thing I thank you for, because..." He holds up the white tube. "...this tube of anti-itch cream is empty!"

'...This Emily woman is an issue; if I understand correctly, that tome might have a way to enthrall or beguile me.[60] People such as her can be as dangerous to everyone around them as they can be to themselves.'

"Hey, what are you two whispering about?" Preston asks with furrowed brows. "Look, do I need to get Lincoln and Pierce to come back? I'm starting to think they didn't realize how close this thing actually was."

"No!" Emily shouts, waving her hand at them. She leaves Colin's side. Approaching a bush, she kicks it. With a huff, she moves to the next bush in line and kicks it too.

---

[60] Beguile: Charm or enchant (someone), sometimes in a deceptive way.

Mark and Preston glance at one another, watching her progress from bush to bush. They shuffle to the opposite end of the square. "Let's not be too close in case she actually finds something," Mark murmurs. They both nod and remove long black sticks that then light up, illuminating the area further.

'Ah! So the light is from those torches. I was not certain.' My gaze drifts back to Emily as she shakes some shrubbery. *'And thank the lord I did not hide in the hedges on this occasion. Instead, I hid hither with my ape acquaintances.'* When I peer at the apes, they move away from my bright eyesight. I close my eyelids to block my eye's glow. *'I had nigh forgotten my beautiful new eyelids; I should have shut them sooner. They could have been a terrible oversight.'*

However, without the violet light, one ape becomes more daring; its "oohing" increases, and a few other apes join it. *'Tiny hairy person, prithee, shush!'* I scream in my mind. The apes howling grows louder. My gaze shoots toward the four people; they all watch the enclosure. *'Hush!'* Reaching for a stick, I take it in hand and gently slap the ape across its cheek. All the apes turn silent as if in shock at what they just beheld. The ape I slapped slides to its posterior, rubs its face, and sulks like a scolded child. *'Apologies; I would rather not be discovered for such a silly reason!'*

"What's up with the snow monkeys?" Colin asks, raising his hand toward my ape acquaintances. "Are they always this noisy?"

"Nah, snow monkeys are pretty chill. Ever seen one of those documentaries with the monkeys that sit in hot springs all day?" Mark says, pointing at some of the apes reclining on the steamy rocks. "Those are the same kind; they even have their own little hot tubs here."

"So you think something might be in their enclosure riling them up?" Emily asks.

"Uhm..." Mark shrugs and raises one of his hands toward the apes. "I mean, maybe? I just said they're typically chill, but I'm not an expert on snow monkeys. I don't even own a dog or cat, so who knows. Maybe they howl when they do their 'monkey business'."

Colin exhales a long sigh. "What are we going to do, Em, if it's in one of the enclosures?"

"I don't know." Emily purses her lips. "How do they get in to clean the enclosures?"

Mark pulls a sheet of paper from his pocket and stares at it. "If you go around the other side, you can get in through a door that leads into a short hallway at the back."

"Fine," Emily says, pointing between Preston and herself. "Preston and I are going to go around and check the area; you two stay and make sure it doesn't run away if it's up there."

"...Uh, I don't think I will," Preston says, glaring at Emily.

"Aren't you the key guy?" Emily points at the ring of keys in Preston's hand. "I need the keys."

"I'm not above locking you in there if the monster rears its ugly head. I've got a kid at home, so I'm not risking my life for something totally unnecessary."

Emily frowns. "If the monster is there, I give you permission to shut the door behind me."

Preston stares at her for a long time. "Pierce said the Consortium isn't responsible for whatever happens to external contractors, so it's your funeral," he says, shaking his head.

"Good to know I should never trust the Consortium, now let's go."

Preston glances at Mark, who shakes his head. "I'm only the assistant to the key holder, so this is on you." Mark looks at Emily. "I'm still calling the Solicitors, though. This is giving me a bad vibe."

Emily scoffs and walks away in a hurry. Preston, on the other hand, sighs and follows her around the enclosure's back.

I shake my head. '*I cannot dawdle another moment. I should have wagered my fortunes earlier, yet mayhaps a distraction will dissuade them.*' My eyes move to the sulking ape as well as a second ape that consoles his companion. '*And I believe my acquaintance here can assist me with that endeavor.*'

Stick still in hand, I poke the ill-tempered ape. He bares his teeth, and thus, I drum his teeth too. Recoiling, he slaps the stick away and screeches, opening his mouth wide. Hence, I poke his lip. His eyes widen, and he rips the stick from my grasp. He bats it against the ground, splintering it. Plucking a pebble, I toss it, and it bounces off his brow. It flings the pebble into the air and lunges at me, stopping short of my figure. *'Apologies! But if thou couldst makest a racket, that would deeply be appreciated.'*

As the ape makes a fuss, another ape dashes toward it and shrieks—this ape is the largest in the enclosure. It grabs a tuft of the smaller ape's hair and tugs. Baring its teeth, it slaps at the smaller ape.

'Gentle... gentleman or gentlewoman?' I glance downwards and then back up. *'Gentleman Ape! That is quite enough!'* I pick up the stick and tap Gentleman Ape atop his head.

Gentleman Ape releases the smaller ape, whirls around, and shrieks at me. He raps the ground and tosses pebbles into the air. Finding a new stick, I use it to poke his nostril. Gentleman Ape's eyes widen, and his pupils dilate. He leaps backward, grabs a handful of rocks, and flings them at the other four apes. His antics irritate the other apes, and they join Gentleman Ape's performance, screeching and casting twigs into the air. Yet, the most they can do is muddy my kiln and raise my Erysichthon value by a point or two.

'That should serve as a deterrence. But if it fails...' I stare at Gentleman Ape. My tendrils unravel, and I commence crafting sable copepods. *'There is one other thing that I may do.'*

Colin opens his tome and eyes the ape enclosure. I rotate around to watch the enclosure's back. It is simple enough—a stone platform and a cliff that rises to a snowy flat overhead. If one were to examine the cliff's face closely, one would notice the outline of a doorway beneath an unlit lantern affixed to the wall.

Yellowish light bleeds from the crack of the door, and the lantern illuminates. Two voices shush one another as the door creaks open. I notice someone's eye peeking through the crack. The door creaks open further, and I see Emily's thin figure next to the stout Preston. "If something goes awry, be ready to close the door after I pass through," she whispers to Preston.

"Thought you said I was allowed to shut you inside," he whispers back.

"If you slam that door in my face, I will haunt your entire family," Emily snaps in a low voice.

"Guess I'll make sure to keep that in mind." Preston sighs. "I'll have to look into finding an exorcist after this." Reaching behind his back, he draws a familiar item from his belt.

'A *pistol!*' I shake my head. '*The situation has grown dire. Truthfully, their prattle and manner of speaking made me judge them as less threatening...*'

Preston presses a finger to his lips. "No more talking and no complaining if one of those monkeys bites the crap out of you," he says, lowering his torch.

Emily rolls her eyes, opens her tome, and tiptoes through the doorway and onto the stone platform. The apes see this and pelt her with rocks. Emily takes a step back and raises one hand to shield her eyes whilst balancing the tome by its spine in her other. She grits her teeth yet speaks naught. The apes return to harassing me.

Watching Emily, I think back to the images and wisdom bestowed to me by the Cosmic System when I adopted the Tenebrous Stealth skill. I confront the inevitable truth. '*She shall discover me.*'

> **Fostered Novitiate [Tenebrous Stealth (Grade 1)]**

A blue wall appears as if asserting "Obviously, thou fool."

Gentleman Ape shoves a few twigs and branches aside, exposing the kiln for a brief second. A mere ten feet away, Emily's jaw drops and her body shivers. She looks down at her feet, feigning not having glimpsed me. I can hear her teeth clicking together as she thinks. She nods to herself and takes a breath. '*Thanks for thy advice, Terra; however, I must act.*' I slither the cattail between Gentleman Ape's legs. '*This shall be a rather tiring night, I suspect.*'

Dropping the hand she was using to shield her eyes, Emily puts two fingers together and touches the tome, taking a deep breath. A scarlet brilliance springs from the tome, and red threads resembling twine squirm out of the tome and burrow into the back of her hand.

I look toward a familiar ape. *'Forgive me, Gentleman Ape. Know I harbor no ill-will for thee.'*

My tendrils seize Gentleman Ape by his nape, and my eyes flick open. Violet radiance pours from my sockets; the apes scatter. I flex the cattail, dragging Gentleman Ape with it.

Emily looks up as I pitch the flailing ape forward. He launches through the air and crashes into Emily's horror-stricken expression. The hairy cannonball throws Emily off her feet. Threads tunneling into her hand snap, lashing her arms and Gentleman Ape's back.

I vault to my feet; behind me, I overhear Colin and Mark arguing.

The enclosure's door boots open. Raising a silver pistol, Preston brandishes it at me. "I am authorized to shoot!" he declares. His jaw drops as I step into the lantern's glow. He manages to stutter a hodgepodge of phrases: "...Smokey, transparent... A Phantasmal Horror?" A gust of wind blows, removing excess haze clouding my body. "A woman!?" His cheeks flush, his arms slacken.

Emily bumbles to her feet whilst Gentleman Ape shrieks and pulls her black hair. The remaining four apes fling mud, snow, and stones at her. "Don't kill it," Emily cries through Gentleman Ape's belly. "It's an actual spirit!"

"Emily, you're insane!" Preston moves a few paces beyond the doorway. Tightening his grasp upon his weapon, he takes a whiff of the chilled air, aims at the kiln, and threatens, "D-don't move...! Can you understand me?"

I nod.

"It can understand me!" The cattail's tendrils squirm as I search for avenues of escape. An expression of revulsion appears on Preston's face.

"God in Light!? What the devils are you? I-if you understand me, don't move another step! I... I won't give you another warning!"

I nod, assessing the situation. Roughly twelve feet to my left, Gentleman Ape and Emily battle one another. Preston stands thirteen feet in front of me—the cattail will not reach. He is around two feet beyond the doorway. If I charge, I shall come to know how well the kiln can bear a pistol's pellet.

"Hey!" Preston takes a step closer. "G-get on the ground!"

I hold up a finger indicating for him to wait.

His hands shake, and his fingers twitch.

Showing him my palms, I make a fist, lift my thumbs, push my hands together, and then I open my fist before lowering my palms. I take a wee step forward whilst a rat-sized sable copepod slips from my right ankle. Next, I present one hand, put two fingers together, bring them to my lips, and then downward. I then take another small step forward. Finally, I simply point at Preston, taking one last step.

"Sign language? Are you deaf?" he asks, lowering his pistol a tad.

Once more, I repeat the hand movements, but this time, I have the cattail slither along the ground toward Preston.

"Stop! I don't know sign language, so it doesn't matter how many times you do it!" he declares, lowering his torch. "I'm going to make a call; don't move, a-and I'll guarantee your safety." His eyelid twitches at the last sentence.

Preston gasps.

He slaps at his shoulder; a sable copepod bursts in his face. My cattail strikes from below, snaring Preston by his hand.

There's a bang.

Blood spatters from Gentleman Ape and onto Emily. Gentleman Ape howls and tumbles to the ground. He charges by Preston and through the doorway—the other apes follow, scrambling after him.

Arcing the cattail, I yank Preston skyward. His joints pop as he kicks his feet and beseeches, "Please, don't kill me!" His body quivers as he dangles a hand's length from the ground.[61] "I never wanted to work for Consortium, but I got wrapped up in a cult out west, my wife had a baby, and Consortium guarantees housing and protection! God in Light, please understand!"

I release him, and he falls onto his posterior. Tendrils entangle his pistol and tear it from his grasp. He crawls through the doorway and kicks it shut as a horse would. I draw the weapon deep into the cattail for safekeeping.

"Spirit!" someone cries.

I spin around, discovering Emily kneeling on the ground with a palm on her tome. Scratches on her neck and face ooze blood, and a cloth square stitched to her cheek dangles loosely. She sweeps a hand across her face, the cloth square sticks, and then peels off anew. "What a beautiful cloud ghost spirit-thingy you are! I can't believe you're a real spirit! I promise you're going to look so good next to me." An inky red substance leaks from behind her fabric. She pinches the fabric and rips it from her face. Tears leak from her eyes. "That freakin' hurt!" Letters and markings stitch together via red fibers escaping the tome's pages. Sable copepods burrow from my ankles, scuttling toward the madwoman. "Sometimes you've just gotta rip off the band-aid!" Emily grins and whispers to herself, "Hex Snare."

The letters and markings unstitch, and like a fisherman's net, strings entangle the kiln's shell. Two strands dart toward the ground, piercing the stone—the mark floating above Emily's tome stitches itself to the shell's exterior.

→ Hostile Toba Human Entity : *Hex ensnares* : Entity 1323 ←
🌀 Effect: Limits mobility 🌀

---

[61] Hand's Length: 4 inches | 10.16 cm

I try to move—the strings turn taut, chaining me in place. The cattail's tendrils enwrap the strand and pull. My tugging taunts the strands more, drawing my body lower.

"Spirit!" I look up. Red strings escape the tome's pages and burrow into Emily's hand. "Contract with me!"

Copepods leap onto Emily's frock and scurry upward.

With fiery eyes, she declares, "I am Emily Bardot, a Spirit Scribe; obey me!"

Bending the cattail like an elbow and bracing it against the earth, I grasp the glittering snare and yank the cattail skyward. It crackles then snaps.

More threads wriggle from the pages of Emily's tome. She murmurs, "Finn, sister has this!" Red markings ignite above the tome. The strands above the book intertwine with the threads in the back of her hands. "Ratify contract!"

Strings envelop the kiln, shrouding its violet glow. *'I cannot be at this bedlamite's mercy!'*

A blue wall appears.

Domination Contract Offer
Entity 291012 - Designated Spirit Scribe Emily Bardot
Entity 1323 - Designated Spirit

Entity 291012 has initiated a Domination Contract Offer.

Entity 291012 offers Entity 1323 the following:
-- Nothing offered --

Entity 291012 requests the following from Entity 1323:
-- Absolute authority over Entity 1323 --

Does Entity 1-3-2-3 accept the terms of Entity 2-9-1-0-1-2's contract?
[Yes]   [No]

I feel a tickle and hear a whisper, "Hex for hex. Abide and give yourself to the contract. Restore the aged seat."

Shaking my head, I shout back, '*Nay–nay–nay!*'

The blinding light and strings evaporate.

> **Contract rejection by one or more entities: contact does not ratify.**

Emily peers at me with the same grin as before, but it turns stiffer and stiffer. "What?" She blinks. "R-rejection? That can happen?"

My tendrils clasp the last thread of the snare, I yank, severing it in two. The patterns sewn upon my kiln uncoil and vanish.

> ← Entity 1323 : *expunges ensnaring Hex upon* : Entity 1323 →
> 🌀 No lingering effects 🌀

Emily's eyes widen.

Copepods burst, sinking into Emily's flesh: red sores and black bumps blotch her body. Her pupils shiver and she topples onto her side. Curling into a ball, she hugs herself and sobs. A gray quill and bottle of ink slip from her pocket.

I close the distance to Emily and reach for the tome. As my hand approaches it, lightning strikes me. Lightning flows through the haze, causing it to glow various colorful hues, yet I feel no pain, only a tickle. Flattening the tendrils, I grip the quill with my left hand, then I scribble words in the tome. "*Weep if thou must, but do not follow. The disease shall pass.*"

Turning the tome toward Emily for her to read, I stop. The ink seeps into the pages, fading—Emily's crying slows, she murmurs, "Weep. Do not follow. Shall pass."

"Em, you messed up!" I hear Colin yell in the distance.

I fling the vile tome into the water and direct my gaze toward the cliffs. Winding the cattail around a tree trunk at the cliff's summit, I draw myself upward.

I hear Preston and Colin arguing and shouting at one another. The enclosure door bursts open. With shaky hands, Preston steps through the doorway once again. "Stay low!" he shouts, raising a bronze pistol with a barrel made of spinning cogwheels. Glancing down, he sees a sore upon Emily's cheek, spitting pus upon his shoes. The bronze pistol's cogs revolve faster. "You monster," he says, taking aim.

Emily lunges at Preston and seizes his arm. "Wait, don't kill it," she yells, blood oozing from her nostrils.

Black bumps spread across Preston's arm as he jerks away from Emily. "Don't touch anyone!" he shouts.

Halfway up the cliff, I form a sole copepod.

Colin runs through the door behind Preston. His tome is open and blue threads gather above its pages. "Is that a spirit!?" Colin shouts. He nudges Preston aside. "I'll keep it still!"

I release the copepod—one the size of a mouser. The mouser-sized copepod leaps from the kiln and onto the cliff face and scurries toward Colin. But blue letters have arisen from the tome. "Hex snare!" he shouts. As I crest the cliff's edge, the Hex strikes me. It entangles the kiln, and a blue thread embeds itself into the tree that aids my ascent.

> → Hostile Toba Human Entity : *Hex ensnares* : Entity 1323 ←
> 🌀 Effect: Limits mobility 🌀

My tendrils enwrap the thread and yank—the tree creaks.

"Shoot!" Colin shouts. "Hurry!"

Preston raises his weapon. The pistol's innards reel and bronze light amasses within the cogwheels.

My copepod leaps at him, falling a palm short of the pistol's barrel. There's a shrill buzz and the mouser-sized copepod erupts into a cloud. A bronze radiance whizzes out of its remains, smashing into the tree overhead. Copper veins riddle the tree's trunk, and it tilts toward the cliff—splinters knock against my kiln.

"Emily!" Colin yells.

Yanking the snare, I snap it.

← Entity 1323 : *expunges ensnaring Hex upon* : Entity 1323 →
🌀 No lingering effects 🌀

I leap to the side. There's a crack; the tree plunges from the cliff. In the distance, I glimpse a Consortium ride barreling down the zoo's footpath. I dash away, abandoning the bedlam below as the tree shivers upon the earth...

Hunger pangs sting my abdomen.

Chapter 14: A Banana a Day Keeps the Doctor Professor Away

∞∞∞∞∞∞∞∞∞∞∞∞∞∞∞

Several voices yell, scream, and argue with one another as I race away from the zoo's ape enclosure.

> **Fostered Novitiate [Feline Whip (Grade 2)]**

I raise my arms high as my body slips through a black fence. *'Huzzah!'* My arms drop when hunger pains sting at my kiln. I place my palm over the kiln. *'Keep fleeing! I shall feast later!'*

The wind whistles, whisking a faint line of haze into a spiral. Snow begins to fall except... *'This is sleet. Nothing can ever be simple!'*

It is not much, yet some water droplets are blended with the snow, meaning this will rinse away bits of the haze. Not enough to keep me from fleeing, but enough that I cannot go far from shelter. My escape has become complicated.

'Earl, prithee, my Status.' As I maintain my pace, my eyes move across my Status wall.

> **Name:** Constance Nightingale
> **Race:** Kiln
> **Seed Type:** Tower [Germination]
> **Variant:** Oort Stained Glass
> **Forms:** [Vaporous] [Lucent: *Unviable*]
> **Shell Level:** 1
> **Flame Level:** 1 (Develop Beyond Germination)
> **Durability:** 47/49
> **Mana:** 183/230 [113/115 Manituic Flux]
> **Erysichthon:** 79/100
> **Quintessence:** Corrupting Oort Cloud

I see my durability never fully recovered from when I was endeavoring to raise my Sturdiness, and my mana has dropped due to the plants I was eating. More importantly, my Erysichthon is high and will only increase if the light sleet persists. *'Regardless of the sleet... I cannot afford to stop. Keep fleeing, look for shelters, and keep to the trees when possible.'*

····

·········

····

Around three hours pass, and I have fled four hundred paces from the scene of the chaos that transpired earlier. Progress has been slow. This region of the park is not as well covered in trees as the area I have grown accustomed to, meaning I must be careful not to be spotted. Worse yet, I am having a tough time consuming enough plants to offset and recover the haze squandered to the wind and the sleet. Hence, I have actually taken refuge a few times in thickets to block the wind and regain lost haze, but when I heard someone approaching, I resumed fleeing.

Earl Interface:
Assimilating 'Wilted Anise Hyssop' (Mana Bare)
Erysichthon abates by 1
Essence value 0
0.0 Refinable Nebula
0.0 Refinable Vitrum

Details: *A herb native to the Colossi continent and commonly utilized in culinary dishes. This substance has not awoken to mana—due to this, any magical effects are negligible.*

Checking my Erysichthon, I see it is at eighty-two, and my mana is at one hundred and three.

'It is hard to keep up.' I begin seizing and consuming plants. As I am about to find somewhere to hide from the sleet, I notice a faint light in the sky. What I see is a copper orb like the one that was eaten by the dinosaur, except it seems smaller, though it is difficult to say for certain due to its height. Unlike a bird, it soars about the clouded sky wholly unhindered by the gales of wind and sleet.

'There is nary a way an ordinary man would be able to perceive such a thing at such heights.' The copper orb stops and ascends high into the sky until it is not visible to even me any longer. 'I need to move even further away; I cannot linger here... I shall watch and listen for squirrels, pigeons, raccoons, or anything else for that matter.'

••••
•••••••••
••••

Another hour has elapsed, and I have only managed to travel an additional two hundred paces. 'I feel... feel a wee queasy.'

I halt as I pass through a thicket. The light sleet was ousted by simple snowflakes several minutes ago, so that is not a concern any longer, yet my vision is blurring. The wind howls as I raise my arms, where I find my hands are nigh transparent, and I can see traces of haze sweeping up and away. Looking at my legs, I see they are the same as my arms. My gaze drifts to the cattail; it's thin but denser than my arms and legs. Inspecting my Erysichthon, I discover it is ninety. My nonexistent heart sinks, and the cattail goes limp. 'This is much worse than I foresaw; I cannot keep up! I must locate somewhere to hide while I restore my haze!'

My eyes dart about, searching for hackberries or anything better than wood and shrubs. Something in the corner of my vision draws my attention—the snow is disturbed. Looking closer, I can see scarlet droplets. The hunger pangs intensify, forcing me to my knees. My palm gravitates to my abdomen; my eyes fix upon these minute droplets of blood. The cattail begins to wag back and forth, gliding across the snow. Summoning my Status wall once more, I see my Erysichthon has grown to ninety-one. 'I... I am absolutely famished.'

The kiln's flame shrinks, and my fingers vanish whilst my limbs narrow. I strive to make the cattail devour plants, yet it does not seem to hearken to my commands. In the distance, I hear screeching, shrill and bothersome, but it's music to my ears. I force myself to my feet and follow the droplets of blood toward the screeching; the cattail encircles me and sways eagerly as I do so. My stumbling gait keeps me moving onward until I come across a shivering tree. The cacophony does not deter me from approaching as it normally would; if anything, it impels me forward.

My vision blurs more as I push through some hedges, discovering four familiar hairy people. It's difficult to think, but my murky sight fixates upon one particular ape. It is the biggest amidst the four apes, and a blurry patch of red stains its right shoulder.

The cattail flexes and spits out the pistol I have been storing within it. As I am about to take a step toward this beacon of red, I hear the rustling of hedges. Around ten feet to my left is a single, lone ape, digging in the snow and pulling bits of grass out, inspecting each blade. I step toward this lonesome ape. The cattail slithers through the air and rises above it. My tendrils spread wide and prepare to engulf it.

A stone bounces and chimes against the kiln, tickling me. The stone alerts the ape, who darts away as the cattail descends upon it. My cattail discovers naught but the snowy earth. It stops twenty feet away and slaps the ground. I swing my body toward the origin of the stone, seeing the blurry figure of the ape with a red shoulder. A blinding light rounds the corner, granting me a moment's clarity. 'I... I believe I am... roadway...' I shake my head. '...Constance, thy belly is leading thee.'

I take a few steps back, slipping behind a snow-covered hedgerow. A sleek black ride with an ornate golden ornament attached to its front rushes forth. The ape continues to screech at me, believing it has frightened me. A sickening crunch resounds as the black ride strikes the ape. The ride barrels further down the icy roadway, veering around a bend.

My gaze concentrates on the ape's mangled carcass that is now naught more than a bump upon the roadway. The sight sinks me back into a fog. 'Food...'

Exiting the bushes, I approach. The cattail slithers over, scooping up the mangled pieces. The other apes screech and charge me, yet the moment my intense violet eyes cast light upon them, they dash away. I find myself strangely disappointed as my kiln is a void yearning for sustenance to sate it.

With additional meals out of reach, I concentrate on the flavors that ripple through me as a red haze flows from my cattail into my kiln. From the droplets of blood that leaked from its mouth to the viscera that burst from its belly, I leave not a trace.

The kiln spews haze.

My vision unblurs, and my mind unfuddles. Raising my hands, I can see my fingers reform and my arms starting to fill in while the ape's body degrades into a reddish skeleton. Seeing rocks bouncing against the roadway, I glance over. Three apes fling stones at me while the fourth, Gentleman Ape, watches meekly—his fur wet in blood.

Looking back toward the ape carcass, I watch its bones crumble into a chalky white haze. My hand clutches my head as I turn away from the pitiful animal. 'Apologies, hairy creature, it was not my intention for thee to suffer such a cruel fate, but I am feeling better... Is the difference between Erysichthon in the eighties and Erysichthon in the nineties truly so tremendous?'

One of Earl's purple walls surfaces from the darkness.

Earl Interface:
Assimilating 'Salted Snow Monkey' (Mana Bare)
Erysichthon abates by 28
Essence value 5
0.5 Refinable Nebula
0.2 Refinable Vitrum

Details: A snow monkey carcass covered in salt deposited by humans to prevent ice. This creature has not awoken to mana.

Reading the wall and then studying the roadway, I see white rocks dirtying the black surface. *'If that is truly salt, it is beyond wasteful... Also, that purple wall had more about the salt than the creature. I would have preferred more about the creature...'*

I cross the salty roadway before another ride approaches. The apes scatter, excluding Gentleman Ape who is unable to muster the strength to run as the other three have. As I approach, he collapses onto his back as if resigning himself to his fate. Though he is more expressive than I recall, I can almost feel the bitterness and resentment as he peers at me. I survey the area, finding it seems well hidden here.

'I cannot run anymore, or I will just find myself being led about by my stomach again. Therefore, Gentleman Ape, Doctor Nightingale shall attempt to heal thee as payment for my transgression.' Picking up a stick, I lower myself next to Gentleman Ape. I push the stick beneath him, and his body trembles. *'...I doubt thou shalt understand, but, I suppose, practice is practice.'*

Raising my hands to waist level, I face the ground with my palms and move them from left to right. Next, making a fist and extending my thumb, I place it beneath my chin and pull downward... I forget the next words, so I go to the final one, lifting my hands, extending them wide, facing them toward my chest, and then making my hands quiver.

'If I did it right, it means, "do not afraid." I cannot remember "be".' I shrug. *'As if this creature would understand regardless.'*

As expected, my sign language achieved naught. I move ahead anyway and push the stick beneath him, lifting him to study the wound on his back. He grumbles, but I do not acknowledge his protests. On his back is a boil, and around his neck, where I seized him with the cattail several hours earlier, are numerous bumps, oozing fluid. Scrutinizing the boil further, I find the skin is broken, and the end of a copper pellet is exposed.

'The boil is likely the pellet. The bumps are probably the haze's doing. Again, apologies to thee and I am truly sorry about what I caused... and did to thy companion...'

I rub the back of my neck, glancing around, and notice some vines wrapped tightly around a tree. I flatten the tendrils, squeeze them between the vine and the tree, and yank. It requires a few pulls, but I get them to release after a few attempts. Vine in hand, I break it into two and then carefully tie his legs together and his arms around his chest. He does not oppose me, which is good because I have very little intention of pursuing him if he receives a sudden burst of energy and flees.

To the right side of Gentleman Ape's head, I dig a small hole in the snow. Thus when I flip him onto his stomach, his face goes into the hole. I then stand and start searching through sticks and twigs nearby until I discover one with a pointed knife-like end. At this point, I notice a rubbish bin along a path outside the thicket. With the cattail, I remove the rubbish bag from the bin and return to Gentleman Ape. Taking a seat next to him, I experiment with the material Terra informed me was known as "plastic." I stretch it, finding once extended, it will not return to form, but it does seem to grip things it is stretched over well enough.

'I believe I can use this.' Tearing off a piece of plastic, I pick up the stick and push it into the plastic. The plastic contorts to the stick's shape. *'This way, the likelihood of the stick splintering should be lower... mayhaps. At the very least, it is better than the stick alone.'*

My mind is exhausted, yet before I start, I attempt to recall any relevant humorism I can. *'I need to lance and drain any fluids and pus to balance the humors. There should not be much as it has not been very long, assuming the haze has not spread. In all honesty, this would be better if I had honey and leeches, but I shall have to make do with what I have. After all, a doctor will not always have all the necessary tools at their disposal.'*

I shake my head, gripping the stick and moving it close to the boil on Gentleman Ape's back. *'Gentleman Ape, this shall hurt... a lot.'*

Lancing the boil, I allow it to drain until the fluids stop. With a nod, I drive the stick into Gentleman Ape's back; he shrieks and wiggles his body while I begin the process of working the sharp stick around the pellet in hopes of digging it from his shoulder. He eventually turns placid, resigning himself.

Fluid and blood soon seep into the white snow, dyeing it a deep red.

Fostered Aspirant [Humorism (Grade 5)]

Entity 1-3-2-3 has manifested enough potential to supplant an Aspirant skill with a Novitiate skill.

Entity, see the presented skill supplants below.

[*Novitiate Humorism II*]
Continue along the basic path of study concerning humorism.

[*Novitiate Supine Humorism*]
Christened after a recently conjectured fifth humor. What else remains to be uncovered regarding this primitive and rarely tread skill path?
Trailblazer Skill

Several hours pass.

····

·········

····

The winds wane, losing much of their intensity, and daylight breaks. I drag a sled fashioned from rubbish bags toward one of my old dwellings. Atop my sled rests the bound Gentleman Ape and other miscellanies I managed to forage whilst ambling toward my destination. I glance at my collected items: aged foodstuffs, a glass jar, and other curious knick-knacks. Slumbering beneath everything is the lone hairy ape.

I wave a hand about as if I am speaking to someone. '*It is unfortunate thy companions forsook thee, Gentleman Ape. Though worry not, abandonment and loneliness are not so horrid. Aye, I am well-versed in both, after all. Ample time to thyself, bothersome obligations are nil, and thou mayst come and go at thy leisure, loneliness can be pleasant...*' Nodding, I glance at the snow underneath my feet. '*But, then time passes, and it is no longer pleasant. One day thou shalt awake to a dull ache in thy chest. It shall be persistent and stinging... I... Yet worry not, ape. Eventually, one simply becomes accustomed to loneliness and forgets the feeling of... not loneliness... I surmise the trick is to feel naught at all, and then the ache in thy chest abates, never absent but less stinging...'* My eyes glance at the ape. *'...Perhaps my words are better left unheeded. But take solace, for thou mayst dwell at my side for the time being.'*

Arriving at a thicket on the Lake's far side, the side opposite the Terrace, I glance at my old abode and then turn to peer off into the distance. There I spot the familiar Terrace courtyard and Arcade. I can see a handful of noble's police strolling about. Each of them wears a face-covering similar to the one Terra used to protect herself from the haze. The Terrace is also different now; a section of it has been cloaked in some type of plastic covering. I can see my nodes are still intact; in fact, someone seems to be leaning against one, lifting their mask, and then eating a sandwich—a delicacy I have yet to acquire myself.

'There is naught I may do. I still have some time before the Tower Seed is prepared for me. I shall locate somewhere hidden to lurk for a while and observe when the opportunity arises.'

Turning toward the rubbish sled, I slip the cattail into a thin, square white box I foraged. It bears the word "Phazel's Pizzeria" on its front alongside a portrait of a gentleman with a mustache. I am anticipating unbridled deliciousness because the gentleman's prominent smile suggests he is thoroughly relishing whatever is inside.

My cattail engulfs some of what's inside, and a bland taste washes over my kiln.

Earl Interface:

Assimilating 'Pizza Crust' (Mana Bare)
Assimilating 'Cheese Pizza' (Mana Bare)
Erysichthon abates by 3
Essence value 0
0.2 Refinable Nebula
0.0 Refinable Vitrum

Details: *Mana Bare bread topped with synthetic cheese and a red sauce.*

My shoulders slump. *'Pizza is a fun word... but it does not taste as delightful as the mustache gentleman led me to believe... Perhaps, if it had been stolen, it would taste better?'*

Gentleman Ape stirs. His eyelids creak apart, and as he spots me, he prepares to howl, yet before he may, I shove the "cheese pizza" into his mouth. He spits it out, and the pizza slaps against the rubbish bag. He nearly yells at me, but an odd fire flickers in his pupil. His gums smack, and his gaze wanders between the cheese pizza and me. Squinting, and without taking his eyes off me, he turns his head and nibbles a tiny sliver of its edge. His pupils dilate, and his teeth latch onto the pizza. He inhales it so passionately he nigh tumbles off the rubbish sled.

'Huh. I suppose he must fancy it.' I shrug and go about my business. Moving into the thicket, I reclaim the glass orb and the "You Are Ecology 101" text and then press onward to discover a new location to hide. *'Cosmic System, prithee, the Humorism selection once more.'*

With my summons, the blue wall from earlier reappears. I was a bit busy at the time, so I never did read it.

> **Entity 1-3-2-3 has manifested enough potential to supplant an Aspirant skill with a Novitiate skill.**
>
> **Entity, see the presented skill supplants below.**
>
> **[*Novitiate Humorism II*]**
> *Continue along the primary path of study concerning humorism.*
>
> **[*Novitiate Supine Humorism*]**
> *Christened after a recently conjectured fifth humor. What else remains to be discovered along this primitive and rarely trodden skill path?*
> ***Trailblazer Skill***

'Peculiar that there are only two choices, and the Cosmic System's words leave much to be desired. Supine Humorism even contains a question...' My eyes focus on the bottom choice. *'Verily, have they discovered a fifth humor? That is fascinating, and what is this "Trailblazer Skill" that it mentions?'*

My fingers rub against my chin, and I nod. *'I am confident in my ability to learn Humorism with or without Humorism II, and truthfully, my curiosity cannot resist the allure of Supine Humorism. Aye, the second selection, Cosmic System.'*

Skill Supplantation

Entity 1-3-2-3 has supplanted [Humorism] with [Novitiate Supine Humorism] skill.

Prepare for memory impress.

The blue wall changes, and images of myself in a white space flash before my mind's eye.[62] In them, I kneel beside the usual man, except this time he has an intense scowl. Evidently unconcerned by this, my hand drifts into position a foot above his face. A black light glows around the tips of my fingers, and dark sandy material slips from his throat, concentrating just beneath my palm. The man's scowl dims and changes to a flat countenance.[63] The pictures cease a moment later.

'Was... was that sand black bile? Removing it appeared to... calm him?'

A new blue wall manifests.

Conferring Entity 1-3-2-3 a title:
[Trailblazer (Humorism)]

This Title acknowledges that the Entity who possesses it is both at the top of their field and the first Entity to receive the [Supine Humorism] Skill. From here forward, the Entity will be blazing a new path in the field.

{Humorism doesn't actually work without Mana, nor the way humans thought. Show someone some credentials, and they'll be more likely to believe you actually know what you're talking about.

If desired, direct a System Prompt to another Entity, confirming you possess this Title. Other entities may have been more qualified for the honor of this Title, but they all died centuries ago, so congratulations on winning by way of disqualification!}

---

[62] Mind's Eye: The mental faculty of conceiving visions or recollected scenes.

[63] Countenance: A person's face or facial expression.

My head tilts as I read the wall. *'Trailblazer? Top of my field? Nay, I do not believe that to be accurate! Wait...'* Continuing to read, the reason becomes clear. *'...So, I only acquired this Title because everyone that was more capable died and moved beyond the lychgate? That does not make sense... and also makes me feel as if I do not deserve this Title!'* As usual, all I may do is shake my head. *'I shall have to learn more in time, but as much as I hate to admit it, Humorism is not vital to my survival.'*

A tickling upon my kiln freezes me. My gaze shoots downwards in time to witness Rife Paste plunging into the snow. I hear rustling atop the rubbish sled and then see a hairy arm stretching toward the paste. *'How didst thou unbind thy arms!?'*

With his mouth wide, his hand ready to scoop it up, he reaches toward the black haze without hesitation. The paste and the snow beneath are scooped up, and a mere second later, it is over...

Twisting the lid onto a glass jar, I raise the cattail and stare into the jar clutched within its tendrils. My hand drifts to my chest as I confirm the Rife Paste and snow are sealed within. *'For once, it did not result in the birth of a monster.'* I glance at Gentleman Ape, whose arm remains outstretched, a rigid expression upon his face, and fingertips a poppyseed short of a divot in the snowfall.[64] His eyes meet mine, and I wiggle a finger at him. *'Know that I grudgingly forgive thee for attempting to rob me, furtive ape. Now, let us be on our way.'*

Taking the jar from the cattail and into my arms, I grasp the rubbish sled with the tendrils, and the two of us vanish into the snowy park.

Time passes...

Two days of hiding come and go before Gentleman Ape, and I discover a new shelter. Then, hours, nights, and days pass as my time in Central Park grows eerily peaceful.

---

[64] Poppyseed (English Units): $^1/_4$ or $^1/_5$ of a barleycorn.
Barleycorn (English Units): $^1/_3$ of an inch | .85 cm.

STAINED TOWER
By: IRIS REIGN

Chapter 15: Atop a Pile of Rubbish

∞∞∞∞∞∞∞∞∞∞∞∞∞∞∞

> Fostered Novitiate [Gluttonous Naturalist (Grade 2)]
> Fostered Novitiate [Gluttonous Naturalist (Grade 3)]
> Fostered Novitiate [Tenebrous Stealth (Grade 2)]
> Fostered Novitiate [Tenebrous Stealth (Grade 3)]

```
      ...
    .......
  ..........
.............
  ..........
    .......
      ...
```

Children whisper on the opposite side of the hedgerow. Hearing the whispers, Gentleman Ape claps his hands together and nods. I glare at him, waving my own hand to silence him. *'Gentleman Ape! Do not forget the knowledge I bestowed upon thee. Thou must earn thy meager bread, and this is how it shall be accomplished!'* He stares at me, blinking a few times, and then nods as if he understands what I am thinking. I squint, holding up a leaf; Gentleman Ape stares at it and nods once more. *'As I thought, he merely nods at everything.'*

With a shrug, I look him up and down. Over the past several days Gentleman Ape has changed. His fur grows longer than before and is pure white, save for a lone strip of black running along his neck, chest, arms, and legs. I also believe he has grown taller, to around three feet and a hand. But it's difficult to tell because he has begun to walk like a hunched-over man. It was a puzzling development until I studied the ecology text and encountered a picture of an ape becoming a man. A concept dubbed "evolution" or something. Though I can only speculate that the "evolution" phenomenon is what's occurring, for I have no other guesses.

Seeing Gentleman Ape tilt his head, I motion for him to be on his way whilst I watch from the bushes. I brush away some snow and stick my head into the hedges, seeing a cluster of children from between some leaves. They stand in a half-arc around one another and the snowy bushes. Each bears an offering in their hands, waiting and gazing at the hedges. A short fence that was not here yesterday separates the children from our hedges. The fence is flimsy, and if I look hard enough, I can make out dark letters on the front. It's difficult to read the backward letters, but I manage to decipher the fence's words: "Federally Authorized Quarantine Zone: Fenced Off Areas South of 79th Are Closed. Noxious Gases. Do Not Enter."

'I suspected something of this sort as I have barely noticed anyone that was not a noble's police moving around the park. More troubling is that I have not seen the Hex Church. I confess that I am delighted by that, yet it's odd, and I am still awaiting Terra's return; I am concerned for her safety.'

The children cheer, but one little boy shushes his compatriots. "Fingers on lips! They'll take the monkey away if they find out," he whispers. All the children nod in tandem. The bushes rustle as Gentleman Ape sticks his head out, nodding at the children. Some of the new children gasp. When they do so, the more experienced children cover their mouths, shushing them once more.

'Aye! This shall be our grandest haul yet!'

Gentleman Ape extends his hand through the fence and flexes his fingers, motioning for the children to hand him their offerings. The first child to step forward is the one we first came across. After that, she brought her companions. Every day, the little girl is the first to step forward and always brings the same thing, something known as a chocolate pudding cup. It is Gentleman Ape's favorite.

Placing the chocolate pudding cup in his hand, she giggles, saying, "Hi, monkey! I'm happy you came again!"

Gentleman Ape seizes the pudding cup, nodding and tugging it from the girl's hand. The girl laughs as he draws his arm into the bush and shakes. I reach out to retrieve the pudding cup from him, but a blue wall distracts me.

'A new skill, it has been quite some time!' I skim the Cosmic System's wall. '...None of these skills make me sound particularly endearing. Well, regardless, I cannot speak to enough folk to make ample use of Beggar or Junketeer, so I shall adopt Scrounger.'

Gentleman Ape shakes the bushes harder, removing me from my thoughts. 'Oh! I am out of position!' I retreat from the hedges and move behind Gentleman Ape. He drops the pudding, and I stow it in a plastic rubbish bag. One after another, offerings are given to Gentleman Ape, and I stuff them into the bag.

A woman's voice shouts, "Carly! What are you kids doing in the corner of the playground?"

I jostle the bushes, alerting Gentleman Ape that it's time to take our leave. Our treasures in hand, we dash from the bushes and abscond toward our hermitage. It's not truly a hermitage, but it's more pleasant than calling it 'our cave.'

Hurrying southeast through what Terra calls "The Ramble," half an hour passes before we approach a staircase chiseled into a cliffside. I discovered this staircase a week ago, after roaming the areas slightly north of Bethesda Terrace for nigh two days.

Together the two of us descend the stairs into a shallow gulch. At the bottom is footpath and stone walls that flank us to our left and right. The footpath narrows and persists for another twenty or so feet, and this is where one might believe they have found the end of the little gulch. However, upon closer inspection of the cliffside, one would discover that the footpath continues into the gulch's walls, yet a muddy brick doorway prevents passage.

I wiggle the cattail's tendrils into a cranny between the bricks. *'Our little hermitage is a blessing, Gentleman Ape.'* With that thought, I yank, and the bottom wedge of bricks slips out, leaving a gap of around three feet by two feet in the wall—scarcely big enough for Gentleman Ape.

With the wedge removed, Gentleman Ape rushes through, and I follow, dragging our bag of treasures through the doorway. Thanks to my radiant eyes, the cave is lit in a purple hue. Like myself, Gentleman Ape does not fancy the dark, but he does not mind as long as I do not wholly close my negating membrane.

The cave's interior is egg-shaped and strewn with items we amassed over the last week. On the left side is a mattress for Gentleman Ape, which I fashioned from a rubbish bag stuffed with various plants. To the right are the foodstuffs we foraged from rubbish bins and that the children have given us or, more precisely, given Gentleman Ape. In the rear are the items that I do not wish to lose and have forbidden Gentleman Ape from going near. Those items consist of things like the glass orb, pistol, the ecology text, glass jar containing Rife Paste, and any baubles that I thought intriguing.

Plucking a stick from the cave's floor, I drum it against a stone, garnering the attention of Gentleman Ape, who is nibbling something he found in the dirt. *'Aye, Gentleman Ape, before thou dine'st, it is time for thy penmen practice.'*

I toss the stick on the ground near him. He bumbles over, takes the twig in hand, and then stares at me. With a wiggle of my finger, he nods and presses the stick into the cave's dust-laden floor and writes. He enjoys me watching him write and often peeks up to ensure my interest is not waning. *'It is wondrous how intelligent these creatures are! When I first encountered him, I feel he was not quite this clever or docile. His attitude was much more hostile initially. It took days before he did anything but glare at me and hold his palm out, demanding scraps of food. Now our relationship is amiable. Goodness, the evolution phenomenon is astonishing!'*

Gentleman Ape glances at me, except he does it as though he does not wish for me to know he is looking at me. Next I catch him peeking at me, I act as if I am clapping for him. He nods enthusiastically, murmurs a wee "ooh", and returns to penning a "T." A few minutes thereon, and he finishes his name, "Gentleman." He makes certain I see it and then sets pebbles over some letters. It reads, "Gen."

Tilting my head, I nod. *'Aye, thou hast done well, Gentleman Ape. If I knew more than six words in the hand language, I would inform thee of such. Instead...'* I withdraw a small cup from the rubbish bag and pitch it toward him. *'Pudding for thee!'*

He raises his arm, and before he even fully clasps it in his hand, the pudding cup is open. Tossing the pistol and some rubbish out of the way, I pick up the glass orb and glance back to see Gentleman Ape licking the pudding cup. He looks at me, and I make an up and down motion in front of my face as if I am shutting my eyes. *'I intend to once more attempt this mana technique. Same as I have all week.'* He nods.

Moving to the cave's entrance, I close my negating membrane until a mere sliver of violet light escapes and position myself to gaze into one of the bland gray bricks. The reason I do this at the entrance is so light may still trickle in through the doorway and, hopefully, prevent my dread of the dark from welling up. Though truthfully, it has welled up several times over the last week.

With the soundless quietude and the wearisome bricks, my eyesight glazes over, and my mind descends into a tranquil trance-like state.

····

········

····

As I have done several times before, I read through the orb's instructions. Reading it at this point is more habit than anything since I have memorized it. I finish reading and move to the first step, focusing on either my belly, heart, or head. But seeing as the single solid piece of my body is the kiln, my only choice is to focus on it.

Concentrating on my kiln, a sensation of swaying grips my mind. It reminds me of how the ship rocked when I was sailing to the New World on the *Lion*. The disorienting sway makes me feel faint, and it's challenging to keep focus. The faintness is worse today, so I remove myself from the trance. I place the glass orb to the side, stretch my arms wide, and plant my hands flat against the floor. Indeed, it does not do much, but it is all I can do.

I turn to check on Gentleman Ape to ensure he is faring well. He is lying flat on his back, one of his legs kicking and a hand clawing the air. *'He's a frequent dreamer. I wonder if I shall ever dream again since I do not sleep? I suppose it matters little since my old dreams were always scattered and outlandish. A product of my mind, I guess.'*

With my hands planted firmly against the ground, I once more enter a half-minded trance. I can feel the haze around the kiln slow to a crawl. The faintness returns, yet this time I manage to struggle through. The sensation diminishes, and I progress to the next step.

This next step requires me to focus on my kiln. I am told to pretend that I am closing or opening a fist inside my kiln. Terra said it might sound vague, but for her, it felt as if there was a "literal hand made of static" in her head, and she truly despised the sensation. I have felt the 'sensation' she speaks of and found it's similar to what happens if one sits on their leg for too long. The difference is that the sensation is in a place inside the body that someone would not typically experience it.

I reach my "static hand" into my kiln, and the feeling arises. Considering the kiln is where the bulk of my sense of touch resides, it feels more akin to my entire body being squeezed by my own hand. It burns, stings, and is positively painful. Genuine pain is one of the hardest things for people to bear, but if there is one thing a person can overcome with enough experience, it's pain, and I have a lot of experience. The painful sensation intensifies, and it is time for the final step.

At this step, one might feel "swollen," as Terra described it. She also wrote in her orb that some people could feel malnourished rather than swollen at this stage, but it varies from person to person. Her message goes on to state that my goal is to either free or crush the mana until I no longer have the feeling of being "swollen." This sensation is a product of the "static hands" squeezing; as Terra puts it, the mana is resisting being forced out of its inherent shape. Someone with excessively compressed mana and problems with 'Mana Afflux' would venture to pull it apart, while someone with expanded mana and problems with 'Mana Efflux' endeavors to squish it. The more the mana is molded, the easier it shall be to manipulate or regulate the next time.

I clench the static hand around my kiln; at least, I believe I am since the feeling of being "swollen" is deepening. This is the third time I have made it to this step, and it is here that Terra said many folk lose consciousness if they push too hard. Except, I have only lost consciousness on the sole occasion I squandered all my mana weeks ago. Which makes me believe that I am unlikely to pass out even if I push myself. Since I have an advantage for once, I intend to exploit it.

As the hours pass by, the day's light waxes and wanes. My concentration ebbs and the oppressive tide of pain swallows my entire kiln. With one great squeeze of the static hand, I sense something inside me distort. Feeling the change, I squeeze even harder. Something within me collapses—there's a crunch. The aches vanish, and the air around me seems lighter.

Entity 1-3-2-3 has adopted the [Mana Compression] skill.
A standard Skill for an Entity that desires to perform Afflux Magic or simply employ Mana. To perform most Afflux Magic, one must first compress or hold the Mana naturally within themselves. It would be no exaggeration to say this Skill and its twin "Mana Expansion" serves as a gateway toward 'deliberate Magic' for many entities.

As an Aspirant skill, it must be supplanted by a Novitiate skill within 7 Material-Earth days to obtain permanently.

The Cosmic System removes me from my daze, and I leap to my feet. *'Huzzah!'* I read the message and commence pacing about the cave. *'I thought I was simply learning to control my Mana Efflux, not learning how to do Magic! Magic! If this is how Magic works, it is not like the witches who practice black magic in the tales. It demanded no rituals, no blood, no devils, no sacrifices, and no eating infants. It was naught like the stories! Unless I am misunderstanding, I do not see any of that sort of thing. Mayhaps, it was all ignorance. I cannot wait to inform Terra! Whenever that shall be...'*

Hearing something moving around, I realize Gentleman Ape has awoken at some point. I look over to see him standing with his back against the cave wall, gawking at something and shaking as if he is freezing. I follow his gaze, which leads me to where I was sitting only a moment ago. The once flat ground, ceiling, and walls have fractured and pulled toward me; they resemble a broken apart dome. The rubbish I was sitting atop is warped and out of shape, leaving only the glass orb intact.

'How did I not notice such a thing!? Was that the bang!? That did not happen the previous times!'

Picking up the glass orb, I try to go back through the information given to me by Terra. When I entreat the orb to show me the familiar wall, the orb becomes much brighter than it has on previous occasions and the wall that appears is not what I expected to see.

> Stable Mana origin found, checking sister orb for queued amendments.

'What does this mean?' The small blue wall disappears, and the familiar information takes its place. I read through the steps she gave me, finding everything is the same. Except, at the bottom, I notice something in the lower corner in small letters that reads, "Make sure you read this, Constance! To go to the next page, press here."

'Next page...? A second wall perchance!' Lifting my little finger, I do as the message says.

Constance, if you are seeing this, that means I have tried to add to or amend your messenger orb. Sorry about the small text, by the way; I couldn't get it any more prominent for some reason, and believe me, I tried. Still, I made it longer, so I hoped you would see it. Oh, and now that I am thinking about it, it may only show up after you've stabilized your Mana, which can take some time depending on the person.

I'm still learning how to use these things myself, and this is sort of just a test. Either way, I'll make sure to mention it the next time we meet and make sure you have the information in one form or another.

A box will appear below. Press it to receive the amendment.

> Press Here For Message Orb
> Amendments - Sent 10 Days Ago

A wall that I have not seen before appears. Tilting my head, I study it closely. *'What!? Sent ten days ago? I am certain that was not there ten days ago! That was before she disappeared, and she said she would inform me of this, which I do not believe to be the case!'*

Thinking back to the last time we met, I realize the reason we never had this discussion. *'...I suppose since that Bishop interrupted our talks, she simply did not have the opportunity to inform me of this. She does usually tell me this kind of thing right before we separate.'*

I press the wall once more. The orb glows radiantly, illuminating the entirety of the cave.

Extracting Mana from stable Mana origin.

'Is this what she meant? That the new wall would not appear until I was "stable".' Feeling a sting in my kiln, I try to remove my hands from the orb, and find I cannot. *'Have I been tricked!?'*

I continue to try and remove my hands as a short, thin line of violet fire exits the kiln. It crawls up my chest and into my arms. I hit the orb against the wall but cannot produce the force to break it. When that fails, I seize it with the cattail and pull. My hands are torn from my arms, but the fire does not seem to mind this. Instead, it turns and moves away from my arms and into the cattail.

'Release me!'

Hitting the cattail against the wall, I cannot force the orb to release it nor break it. The flame starts to move at a much faster speed once it enters the cattail. Finally, the fire shoots into the orb, and its color changes to a mix of purple and blue, and a wall of the same color develops.

> Updating orb based on amendments sent ten days ago... ...
> ...complete.

When the wall returns to its former blue color just before vanishing, the orb releases the cattail and plops to the ground. I place a hand on my chest. *'That was... perturbing. I need to be more wary when it comes to these sorts of things.'*

Shaking my head, I shuffle toward the orb, poke it a few times, and then lift it in my hands once more. I return to the original message, finding a new line has been added to the end. It reads, "There have been rumors that after some people contracted or expanded their mana, it damaged the environment around them, so make sure you're someplace isolated that you don't mind getting damaged."

'That would have been helpful a tad sooner! Gentleman Ape nigh fainted!' My eyes move downward, and I notice something.

'Another message telling me to 'press here'. Does that mean there is a second wall again?' I hesitate but seeing as it already had the chance to trick me a moment ago, I resolve to press it again. The wall changes, revealing a rather long list of details and drawn-out instructions. My eyes glaze over and drift toward a note at the top.

> ***Begin Note for Constance***
> I wanted to get these to you early in case something happens to me.
> The instructions will help you supplant the Aspirant Rank with the
> Novitiate Rank, as well as give you an idea of how to amend the

writings in this orb. This will be useful for us to pass information in the future when such luxuries will be… a thing of the past, I guess.

Most importantly, if something happens to me, do not search for me and do not worry about me. I will be fine, and I will find a way to contact you when the circumstances allow it.
End Note for Constance

'So she suspects something might happen to her, that she might one day vanish. To be honest, this message only serves to make me more concerned.' My shoulders droop. 'Terra, thy life seems far too complicated… though, that would ring hollow coming from someone such as myself. There was never a moment in my life when things were uncomplicated. I suppose I am simply accustomed to being the one who disappears and not the one who is disappeared on.'

My eyes drift across more of the wall's contents. I can tell the instruction's purpose is to help me learn how to "write" in the messenger orb as if it is paper. The instructions also state it takes a substantial amount of concentration for a beginner to do that, and the thought of that right now makes me desire to fall over and coil into a ball.

I glance toward Gentleman Ape and find him sitting on the floor with a hand on his chest. 'I must have scared him worse than I imagined… and I have never seen him do that before? Is he trying to imitate me? Perhaps it is just a coincidence.'

Setting the orb aside, I grab a pudding from our food supplies; I pretend not to notice all the missing food items Gentlemen Ape ate while I was working on my mana. I toss the pudding to him, and without a second's hesitation, he sits up, catches it, and rips it open. With his fear pacified, I move on to the next order of business. 'I want to check on the seed. Which reminds me, I still have side tasks I must complete. Also, I need to begin thinking about new adaptations. Except, I have nary an idea of how to get more Essence. Mayhaps there is another "café" place somewhere in the park?'

I check the light at the cave's entrance, discovering it seems to be some time in the middle of the night. That means I have been doing this for nearly a full day, much longer than I intended. Hearing Gentleman Ape grunt blithely and lick the bottom of the pudding cup, I turn, point at him, and then at the ground. *'I shall return for thee at a later time. It is far too chilly outside for thee to follow me.'*

I attempt to depart by myself, but Gentleman Ape tosses the empty cup to the side and follows. When he does so, I stop him. I point at him and then at the ground, shaking my head while I do so. He slaps the ground, and screeches at me.

When I repeat my action from a moment earlier, he slaps the ground once more and runs to the rubbish pile in the corner of the cave. Wrapping a rubbish bag around himself, he hits his chest and waits to see what I do next.

'...His temperament grows more obstinate every day.' Walking over to the pile of bags we scavenged, I take one, stuff it full of his bedding and flatten it. Carefully I wrap and tie it around him. *'Come on, little hairy one, I have never been one to stop someone from making their own mistakes. Though be warned, any consequences of such choices are thy own to bear.'*

Grabbing the rubbish sled, we exit the cave.

····

········

····

Snow glides tenderly to the earth and caresses it in a blanket of fresh white. The sled crafted from rubbish bags glides gently atop the virgin snowfall, composing a subtle and lonely melody that echoes in the hushed darkness. Melancholy pervades the very foundations of Central Park.

Whilst Gentleman Ape and I move toward the Terrace at a casual pace, my mind wanders, and I reflect on the Mana Contraction skill I acquired. *'Cosmic System, prithee, my Chronicles.'*

The familiar blue wall, rife with difficult to understand numbers, arises from the white of the chilly night.

Constance Nightingale || Kiln Vaporous Chronicles || Entity 1-3-2-3			
Strength	13	Cattail Armament Physical Power	26
Orenda	23	General Body Strength	5

Sturdiness	7	Cattail Armament Magical Power	0
Fortitude	17	Membrane Defense	2
Perception *	19	—	—
Acuity *	10	—	—
Agility	18	—	—
Endurance	21	Sable	81.31%
Mend Rate	23 (-100%)	Vermillion	14.26%
Mana Regen	13	Heliotrope	2.85%
Stat Points Primed: 0		Hoary	1.58%

Studying the wall, I confirm the Mana Contraction skill does not seem to have affected my Chronicles. I then read through all the stat numbers, none of which have improved in over a week. *'I would certainly relish more of the stat point things. The more of those I may acquire, the better, but... I still do not know how I feel about devouring another Kiln to receive them. If I did such a thing, what would they do? Would they plead for mercy? Would they try to fool and eat me when I turn my back? Worse yet, perhaps I am on the weaker side of Kiln. Would I be the one pleading for mercy? I am not beyond such things. Dignity and pride are for those that do not fear death; I have seen what death entails.'*

Over the past week, I have asked Earl many questions, but he seldom answers them. I did learn that sometimes the reason Earl does not answer is that I have not phrased a question simply enough for him to acknowledge. Still, I only ever managed to persuade him to answer questions he had previously answered. As time passes, I am starting to suspect Earl is deliberately withholding information. It's that or he only "learns" something when it becomes relevant. I do not know, but it's rather frustrating.

My shoulders droop as I push away the wall and begin my usual routine of searching for rubbish bins to forage items from. Except, they are all empty. With fewer people in the park, it has become nigh impossible to scavenge bins near the cave as we were days prior. Even the rubbish bags are not reappearing as they once were.

'There is naught I may do about the bins... I shall have to locate other sources of sustenance.'

We arrive at a thicket on the side of the Lake opposite Bethesda Terrace. Selecting a suitable patch of shrubbery, I hide. My eyes drift over the Lake. Its water is stained brown, and along the Lake's edges, heaps of mud sit against the shoreline. Likely the doing of the dinosaur or monster fish that inhabit the treacherous waters. I look away and watch the Terrace, waiting to see if any new activities have taken place since my last visit.

Half an hour passes, and things seem relatively the same. The most notable change is there are only one or two noble's police remaining. As for Consortium people, due to the plastic blankets that obstruct much of the Terrace, I cannot tell if they are there, but there is a bright blue light that radiates and dissipates from within the sheets.

My eyes drift to two of my nodes, reminding me of one of the reasons I came here. 'Earl, are there any further germination tasks available? I have only done the one thus far.'

> **Earl Interface:**
>
> **Assignment:** The second task would entail setting a spark at one or two locations. Once set, a network of roots will grow toward the location of the spark. Upon completion, a mana-rich haze will vent into the specified area. Presently, vents are limited to an approximate maximum of a thousand linear feet from the seed.[65]
>
> **Query:** Would the user like to assist with the germination manually?
>
> **[Aye]**   **[Nay]**

---

[65] | thousand feet | 304.8 Meters|

I read the wall a few times over. *'Venting haze?'* Looking toward the snowy ground, I take some time to study and muse on the information provided. *'In summary, I should select a location where excess haze will be expelled...? Yet, I do not know where I could send it.'* Gentleman Ape saunters over and plops onto the ground nearby. He huffs, casting a puff of hot air from his mouth before raising a single finger and picking his nose. His body has changed significantly, yet he never consumed any rife paste. *'...Earl, this haze, shall it induce evolution in the creatures that breathe it? Like the wretched rat, dinosaur, and mayhaps Gentleman Ape?'*

Earl Interface:

Oort Stained Tower Glass Kiln Guide

Venting
Creatures that have not awakened to mana will undergo rapid evolution, while creatures that have already awakened may or may not show changes. However, this one predicts that, unlike with the rife paste, the mutations caused by haze will be less immediate and less substantial.

Note: *Though only a single vent is presently required, the volume of hazes vented will increase with the Tower's size, necessitating additional vents in the future. Regardless of the user's decision, venting to relieve built-up pressure is critical. If not chosen manually, it will instead be vented in the area surrounding the Domain.*

Contemplating the meaning of the wall, the implications of this choice become clear. *'Good lord!'* My hands fidget and tap against the snow. *'I... I must be cautious with my placement of these vents! They could be calamitous! Shall I drown this city in monsters if I am not careful!?'*

I count to a hundred and then consider everything I know about the area surrounding the Terrace, remembering a metal plate on the far side of the Arcade. The word written on it—" sewer"—was also written on the plates that led to the chamber pot tunnels.

'The chamber pot tunnels; I could send it to the chamber pot tunnels. The tunnels are extensive, so the haze might disperse enough to be harmless. The pipe I saw was

much smaller than the chamber pot tunnels, but it is reasonable to think it leads to the larger sections of the tunnel. It would be ideal for venting the haze.'

> **Earl Interface:**
> **Notice:** *User must approach the seed to receive the sparks.*

'The seed?' I glance toward the Arcade where the plastic blankets sit, blowing in the frigid winter wind. *'...I shall retrieve the sparks later. What about the third task?'*

One wall vanishes, and another replaces it.

> **Earl Interface:**
>
> **Assignment:** *The third task involves selecting two gate locations that will allow entry into the isolated interior of the Tower. Presently, gates can be placed anywhere within a one-mile radius of the seed.*
>
> **Query:** *Would the user like to assist with the germination manually?*
>
> **[Aye]   [Nay]**

'Gates? I suppose it is referring to the doors... If that is so, I believe I should hide them. When The Tower emerges, many might endeavor to enter it; I would prefer they did not do that.'

Brooding the bothersome issues The Tower shall beget, I spread my arms and fall face down into the snow. I do not sink into the snow, so it appears as if I am holding my nose just above the white blanket. As I lie there, I realize something peculiar about the task. *'Earl, how can gates be placed at such a great distance? How could they permit access to The Tower?'* He does not answer; thus, I attempt to ask it more simply. *'Earl, what are gates?'*

> **Earl Interface:**
> # Oort Stained Tower Glass Kiln Guide

Seeing the wall, I raise a fist in the air, celebrating the fact that Earl answered my question. Yet, as I read further, that fist loosens and turns into a limp wave of the hand. *'Nay. I am not placing them in "densely populated areas." Apologies, but that is far riskier than it is worth. I would rather have the gates where they would be hidden or difficult to get to.'*

There are few locations that I know of that are both difficult to get to and hidden; however, two that fit the criteria come to mind—the cave and, once again, the chamber pot tunnels.

'I could place one gate in the cave. The only way in and out is through the tiny opening at the bottom of the cave doorway. There is another bricked-up door on the other side of the cave, but I have not attempted to open it yet. I believe the cave would undoubtedly be the simplest choice for a gate.' With that, I resolve to put one gate in the cave, but the other is a bit more complicated. *'If I vent haze into the chamber pot tunnels, I could combine the two tasks to work to my advantage. Only a mad ninny would search for a gate there. That's doubly so if the creatures there are changed by the haze.'*

'Earl, how large are the gates?' He does not answer, but his previous wall said it would "be altered to a suitable degree." *'I do not know. Regardless, I shall decide whether to put a gate in the chamber pot tunnels based on what happens with the cave.'*

The wall changes, displaying the same message as it did previously. *'I am aware I must approach the seed, Earl! That remark was not a question directed at thee.'* Gentleman Ape grows restless next to me. He does not like to sit in the cold without doing anything for long; understandable, I suppose. *'Perhaps it's best I digest everything I have learned for the time being.'*

I stand, grab the rubbish sled, and prepare to leave. But as I am about to depart, I notice someone step out from behind the plastic blankets on the Terrace. They wear a big blue outfit covering their body from head to toe. The outfit appears cumbersome and has a bulky helmet that looks like a cylinder with a blackened window on the front.

The person does something to the helmet and reaches up, pulling the helmet away. Steam drifts from his wet hair and sweaty face. He removes a tobacco stick from a pocket and ignites it. I motion for Gentleman Ape to follow, and the two of us move through the park, rummaging through bins for more unusual rubbish and food.

••••

•••••••

••••

Fostered Aspirant [Scrounger (Grade 1)]

'If I can foster a grade increase every day, then it shall be simple enough to attain the Novitiate Rank.'

Pulling the half-consumed remnants of something identified as a "honeybun" from the rubbish, Gentleman Ape and I commence traveling toward the children for our daily offerings. We went farther northward in the park than we usually would in order to harvest the bounties of the park's rubbish bins. Though if I were a farmer, I would be wary of the prospects of future harvests. This area of the park is nigh deserted. If I wish to scavenge more rubbish at my present rate, I shall have to consider heading south where rubbish is abundant, except that area of the park is busy, and traveling there is tedious, so I would like to avoid that. There are also buildings I could perhaps plunder for their riches instead. Though every time I do, the noble's police somehow discover me.

'How do they locate me? Is it magic? The Bishop also knew I was there all those weeks ago. I do not comprehend how he knew, except it had something to do with the necklace of teeth he wore if I recall. I have not noticed any noble's police wearing necklaces adorned with teeth.'

Childish laughter greets my ears, indicating it is time to collect some meals. I release my grip on the rubbish sled and enter the hedgerow that borders an area the children frequently play in. I motion to Gentleman Ape, and he looks at me with half-closed eyes, nods, and takes a position in the same hedgerow around twenty feet away. As usual, he waits until the children are nearer before sticking his hand from the bushes.

"Woah!" a young boy's voice shouts. "I thought it was the fairy!"

'...Fairy?' Shifting some leaves aside, my gaze falls upon two familiar children, wearing oversized puffy coats. They nod at one another with big smiles and hug weighty tomes close to their small bodies. 'It is those two children, Lorelai and Vincent! Why are they here!?'

"I'm always first," the little girl with the pudding cup murmurs with pursed lips. "If you two are going to be in front, hurry up and give him something, or he might leave!"

Lorelai gasps, turning toward Vincent. "Do you have anything we can give it!?"

"...Just the candy they gave us in class," he responds with a touch of hesitation, taking a small black piece of candy from his coat pocket.

"Those taste bad anyway, but maybe the monkey will like it!"

"But..."

"I'll share mine with you if you give yours to monkey!"

He thinks for a moment and then nods. "Here you go, monkey, it's special medicine candy."

Gentleman Ape grunts, takes their candy, and holds his hand behind him, waiting for me to take it. He shakes his hand to alert me that he is ready, but I do not have any intention of staying here. As I am about to leave, I hear heavy footsteps in the crinkling snow. Glancing upward, I can see the red hair and imposing figure of a man. He has tattoos covering his arms, one of which is a black doll or poppet tattooed over the Church in Light's symbol. This is the man Lorcan that I saw jab himself with a needle just before my initial meeting with the Bishop, back around when I first arrived in this era.

He wears an oversized shabby black coat, but despite that, it still seems as if his arms might rip the coat open if he is not careful. From the benches off in the distance, I can see the children's mothers and fathers eyeing the man suspiciously. This is unusual because they do not ordinarily spare more than a glance, which has been a blessing as otherwise Gentleman Ape and I would have been caught days ago.

Lorcan walks up behind Vincent and places his hand atop his head. "Hey, squirt, is it here?" he asks in a deep, commanding voice, a hint of arrogance sprinkled in his tone.

Vincent turns his head upward and tilts his head.

"The fairy, squirt. Is it here?" Lorcan clarifies with a click of his tongue.

"Oh!" Vincent nods earnestly. "Yeah, she's here, but it is harder to find her than it was last time we were here."

'They are hunting for me!?'

I prepare to flee, except as I do so, some leaves rustle, and Lorelai glances in my direction. "Two monkeys?" she whispers.

'That child's hearing must be superb because she should not have heard that! Could it be stat points? I assume people receive those too.'

"Then where is she?" Lorcan asks Vincent, making a mess of his hair.

Lorelai looks away from me and turns toward Vincent. Noticing the scowl on Vincent's face, she giggles.

Vincent reaches up and seizes Lorcan's hand. "Stooop dooing thaat!" he shouts.

Lorcan removes his hand with a chuckle. Lowering his arm, Vincent huffs, and closes his eyes.

Gentleman Ape tires of waiting for me; he snorts, drawing Lorcan's attention. Lorcan opens his mouth to say something but pauses, noticing a hairy hand and face emerging from the brush. Gentleman Ape glances at Lorcan and then at the children. He stretches his arm out, opening and closing his palm at the little pudding cup girl. The little pudding cup girl performs a wee twirl and shuffles over to him, handing him the cup with a giggle.

"...That." Lorcan purses his lips, and points downward with a limp finger. "...Is that one of the escaped monkeys?"

Lorelai tilts her head, looking up at Lorcan. "I think he lives with the fairy."

"I think." Vincent's eyes open. He places his pointer finger on his chin and then points a few feet to my right. "The fairy's somewhere over there!"

'Flee!' I rush out of the hedgerow and shake the bushes near Gentleman Ape. Gentleman Ape follows me as I grab the rubbish sled.

"Hey! I need to give you something!" Lorcan bellows.

Gentleman Ape and I flee. Behind us, the bushes shake as Lorcan climbs over. His boots smack against the wet ground. "Stop!"

"Wait, the fence, it's too high!" Lorelai and Vincent shout.

Stopping, he waves his hand, and shouts, "I'm just trying to give you something from Ga— Never mind!" He scoffs. "Screw it, whatever, we'll have a delivery for ya soon, 'Fairy'."

'I believe we shan't!' I abscond into the depths of the park with Gentleman Ape.

The two of us, haze-parasite-monster-thing and ape, flee in the wrong direction, south-eastward, to hinder any that may follow our trail. It's an hour or so later that we exit a copse of trees and approach the Lake's banks, just west of the Terrace. When I am certain we are not being hunted, I turn us northward and move along the water's edges.

A purple wall appears, drawing us to a halt.

Chapter 16: Fortune Knows Me by the Name Woe

∞∞∞∞∞∞∞∞∞∞∞∞∞∞∞∞

> **Earl Interface:**
> **Warning:** A leak has been detected in the Tower Seed's roots—difficulty in self-repairing. Manual repair advised to diminish losses.

A purple wall surfaces from the white frost, bringing me to a halt; the rubbish sled glides to a sluggish stop as I read. I stare at the wall for a moment, cross my arms, and read it over again. *'Earl, I do not know what this wall is mea—'*

Before I may finish my question, I turn toward the seed's location and notice a hint of red fog rising skyward. It seeps from between the plastic blankets that surround the Terrace and is rather vivid illuminated in the light of the morningtide.[66]

Red fog—nay, I recognize it for what it is, vermillion haze, and it flutters innocently from Bethesda Terrace in the winds of the morn. My head sinks toward the snowy ground, to the rubbish sled, Gentleman Ape, and then back to the Terrace.

'I... Apologies, Earl. I believe I see the issue. More crucially...' I peer at the white snow beneath my feet. Traces of vermillion haze waft by in the breeze and float into my body. *'Earl! From whence does this haze originate!? Is it from the Tower Seed!? Did they discover the seed!? When I planted the seed in the Arcade, thou sayst that they would not notice it!'*

I look toward the cloud-clad heavens, stiffen my arms with palms facing the ground, shake my hands, and count to fifty. Lowering my gaze, my eyes settle on the Terrace; it's silent as if abandoned. *'Do not fret, I forgive thee, Earl, and I have calmed myself... Now, this is no time to dally; I must investigate whilst I cannot see any people lingering.'*

---

[66] Morningtide: The morning; the early part of the day.

With haste, I drag the rubbish sled into a thicket. Spinning around, I face Gentleman Ape and point at the sled and then at him. His eyes bounce between the sled and myself before he belatedly dips his head and nods. Likewise, I nod and then dash away along the banks toward the Terrace. I do not make it far before I detect the pitter-patter of footsteps in the snowdrift behind me. Stopping and twisting around, I see Gentleman Ape pulling the sled as if I had mistakenly neglected to bring it. With me in his path, Gentleman Ape tries to stop, only to slip on icy snow. He falls flat onto his face, swallowing a mouthful of powder. I shake my head, pick up a twig, and approach him.

He lifts his hairy head from the snowfall, leaving a perfect mold of his face. 'A silly little ape, that is for certain.' Squatting to match his height, I wiggle my pointer finger and give him a light tap on the head with the twig. 'Nay, thou mayst not accompany me. If the Arcade is rife with haze, it is far too dangerous for thee to accompany me.'

He lays his hand on his brow and tilts his head. I point toward some bushes and then him. Handing him the rope to the rubbish sled, I stand, toss the twig to the snow, and back away. Whilst doing so, I point between him and the bushes before turning and hurrying away. I glance behind me, where I witness Gentleman Ape stand and stare at the bushes. He takes a small half-step toward the thicket, stops to watch me, and proceeds toward the bushes, dragging the rubbish sled behind him.

When I establish a sufficient distance between us, I nod and shift my gaze forward. 'Prithee, my Status.'

> **Name:** Constance Nightingale
> **Race:** Kiln
> **Seed Type:** Tower [Germination]
> **Variant:** Oort Stained Glass
> **Forms:** [Vaporous] [Lucent: *Unviable*]
> **Shell Level:** 1
> **Flame Level:** 1 (Develop Beyond Germination)
> **Durability:** 49/49
> **Mana:** 200/230 [115/115 Manituic Flux]
> **Erysichthon:** 61/100
> **Quintessence:** Corrupting Oort Cloud

'*Erysichthon is a tad high, but I believe I shall be able to make do.*' The blue Status wall vanishes, and I hear something splash in the Lake. I glance over and spot a glassy hump poking from the water. '*Nay! The dinosaur is stalking me!*'

Moving a few dozen feet further from the Lake's bank, I resume my sprint to the Terrace. The dinosaur sinks back beneath the brown water's depths, and despite having to keep a distance from the treacherous waters, it is not long before I arrive at my destination.

I duck behind a plastic blanket affixed to a square section of silver fence. There are many of these fences, each around eight feet tall and five feet wide, and standing atop metal legs. They are arranged side by side, forming a semicircle that runs around the Terrace, up the two grand staircases, and barricades the roadway overhead. The plastic blankets are slick, and the side facing away is dark silver while the other is dark brown. Drops of frozen dew cling to the silver side.

Unwinding the cattail, I wrap it around the fence, lift, and drag it toward me, making an opening in the semicircle for me to slink through. Slivers of vermillion haze drift by me as I peek between the fences and find that yet more blankets and fences barricade the Arcade's archways. From this angle, I can see the Consortium's orphanay bird painted upon the silver side of most of the blankets. I glimpse no one patrolling the perimeter, even though vermillion haze is clearly flowing between the plastic blankets. As the haze departs the Arcade, it sweeps skyward and scatters into scantier pieces before fading into the air. It behaves differently than the pale smoke that would exit a chimney, seeming to resist splitting apart, at least at first.

'Prithee, do not let this be a trick to entrap me.' I lay my hand upon my chest and shake my head. 'Nay, certainly they could not organize such an elaborate trap... They would have to know more about The Tower and Earl than even I understand to hoodwink me so thoroughly.'

I drop my arm and tiptoe toward the Arcade's archways and stop behind a fence. Drawing a plastic blanket aside, I peer into the Arcade. The Arcade's interior is a disaster veiled in a dense blood-red haze. Amidst the haze, silver tables lie on their backs, white papers strew the tile, bent shelving creaks, shattered glass dots all, and lanterns brought by the Consortium flicker.

My eyes drift toward a mound of loose earth and stone around a square hole hewed into the Arcade's floor. 'The Consortium has been excavating within an arm's length from the seed!' Scrutinizing the interior of the Arcade and the Terrace behind me, I slide between the plastic blankets. 'Calm thyself, Constance; at least with haze in abundance, it shall be difficult to notice me.'

I flinch, nearly falling over, as the vermillion haze rushes toward me. It penetrates the Comrade Cracker layer that covers the outside of my body, sinks inward, and blends with the rest of my form.

The haze stops flowing to me, and one of Earl's walls appears.

> **Earl Interface:**
> **Notice:** Erysichthon has fallen to zero. The proportion of vermillion haze has risen beyond its default levels of 14.26% to 68.41%.
>
> **Note:** Ratios will return to default levels over time.

Raising my hands, I can see my palms are dyed scarlet-red. I flip my arm over, finding my short fingernails have grown nigh two inches beyond my fingertips, and the ends are as keen as knives. My nails sway, almost as if they are flames atop a wax candle. I tilt my head, and my gaze moves to the cattail. The once dense and oily cattail now has a cloudy, fiery form with vermillion haze that spills off both it and the tendrils like steam from boiling water. Glancing down at my gown, I see the tattered ends now curl upward, and like my nails, they shiver as if flames upon the wick of a candlestick. 'Prithee, my Chronicles, Cosmic System.'

Constance Nightingale || Kiln Vaporous Chronicles || Entity 1-3-2-3			
Strength	13→6	Cattail Armament Physical Power	26→12
Orenda	23→28	General Body Strength	5→3
Sturdiness	7	Cattail Armament Magical Power	0→7
Fortitude	17	Membrane Defense	2→1
Perception *	19	—	—
Acuity *	10→13	—	—
Agility	18→31	—	—
Endurance	21	Vermillion	68.41%
Mend Rate	23	Sable	29.96%
Mana Regen	13→17	Heliotrope	1.05%
Stat Points Primed: 0		Hoary	0.58%

'The percentages, my numbers, and my appearance have all changed...? Earl claims it shall return to normal over time. I pray that shall be so because my Strength is rather low, and it will be difficult to do much with such frailty...' I drop my arms, and the Chronicles vanish. 'Aye, this is fascinating, and I shall ponder it later, but let us find our bearings!'

As I am about to explore the Arcade, I glimpse something. Thirty paces ahead of me, a radiant, glowing red figure in a person's shape hunches over and clutches its legs; several other people of various red tints also linger near the figure. Spinning on my heel, I rush toward the closest overturned table. I move so swiftly that I nearly pass the Arcade's archways. When I first awoke in this era, my speed was nigh walking pace, and now with stats and the vermillion haze, it's bordering on sprinting.

Hopping behind the table, I glance over and realize that I can still perceive the red figures through the tabletop as if the table is a mere foggy windowpane. *'How am I capable of seeing in this fashion... Did the vermillion haze alter my eyesight?'*

My eyes dart between the red outlines; there are ten figures total. I also notice other things in different shades of red, including the lanterns, a laptop, and what resembles a cockroach. Poking my head from behind the table, I survey the Arcade further, yet the changes to my vision make it troublesome. It's as if my ability to see well in the dark is superseded by this ability to perceive certain things in red hues. Studying my reflection in the silver table, I notice my eyes are not violet but rosy-pink. Moreover, my charcoal black hair that would stream down my back and then curl upward is now scarlet-red and stands upright. I shut one of my negating membranes, and the eye returns to a light purple.

'I did not know having more vermillion haze would cause such changes. It's fortunate I took time to survey the room before I entered.' I lift my eyelid and gaze at my reflection a moment longer before attempting to press my hair downwards, only for it to climb upward on its own once more. Shaking my head, the hairs dance and sway like a hearth's flame. *'I may not know why I look so diabolical, but perhaps like this, they shan't realize I am the same haze monster! Aye, I am a master of disguise!'*

"I-is someone there?" a woman whispers, stifling a cough.

I flinch and glance at each of the ten glowing red figures: six lie on the floor, three stand facing the wall, and the last appears to be waving their hand. The final one also produces the brightest shade of red. *'Should I lend aid...? Nay. They shall have to wait for my attention. I cannot forfeit this opportunity to approach the Tower's seed.'*

Abandoning my position, I round the table and tiptoe toward the seed at the Arcade's center. I peek into the square cavity carved into the floor, finding that it only has a depth of two or so feet. But the reason for its shallowness is rather apparent. There are a multitude of small and large roots growing from the soil at every angle, all of which intertwine and coil around one another. It looks as if someone took a hundred pieces of different sized twine and knotted them together. The small roots are somewhere around the size of a poppyseed and a digit, while the large roots are several inches around.[67] All the roots, big or small, are either black, violet, red, or gray. They mirror the colors in my Chronicles.

I step into the shallow hole, where a sizable red root spits plumes of vermillion haze into the Arcade. A sizzle akin to meat on a spit, alongside a hissing reminiscent of a boiling kettle, only makes the source of the vermillion haze even more obvious. Lowering myself, I lean close and discover that the roots are, in fact, clear crystalline glass, and it is the haze that provides most of their intense color. *'If each root is filled with haze... Good lord, how much haze is buried beneath the soil?'*

Focusing on the leaking root, I notice the haze originates from the underside of the root, which sits very close to the dirt. I attempt to drop low enough to view the root's underside, yet the kiln keeps bumping against other roots. I step from the hole, place my hands against the roots at the bottom of the pit, and bend my body so that the top of my head is facing the earth. I bend my arms, dropping my body enough to view the leak. Locks of my fiery hair float to the front of my face, forcing me to brush it away to see properly.

The root's underside glows a rich red, making it impossible for me to see. I think for a moment and then shut my right eyelid. With one eye providing a pink light and the other now exempt from the red effect, I discover the root's base dips into a bubbling green liquid, pooled in a shallow trench.

I eye the green liquid; something about its color and attributes is familiar. The realization hits me like a runaway wagon. *'It is the same liquid that burst from the walls when I first encountered the Bishop! The one that melted metal and stone! How is it here? Did the Bishop gift it to the Consortium...? I suppose it matters not. Earl, what must I do to mend this?'*

> **Earl Interface:**
> **Response:** *If the user removes the obstructing substance, the root will mend itself.*

---

[67] Poppyseed (English Units): ¼ or $^1/_5$ of a barleycorn.
Barleycorn (English Units): $^1/_3$ inch | 0.8382 cm.
Digit (English Units): ¾ inch | 1.905 cm.

Seeing that Earl answered, I read the wall and then test my luck anew. *'All I must do is remove this contrarious liquid, Earl?'*[68]

Earl Interface:
   Recommendation: *Remove the contrarious liquid.*

I nod and bring the flaming cattail forth to see if I may force it to drink the green liquid. The cattail touches the liquid and there's a loud pop. Like pig fat atop a scorching pan, the liquid spurts outward, melting the cattail and blinding me. The vermillion haze floating around the room rushes into me, mending the damage to my eyes and cattail.

'Aye, I knew it could not be so simple, yet its reaction was worse than I foresaw.' Stiffening my arms, I push myself up and float my body away from the hole. I inspect the other roots to ensure I did not damage them, and to my relief, find they are still intact. *'I shan't be able to use the haze for this task.'* Standing, I glide around the Arcade, searching for an item to assist me. I am careful to maintain my distance from the people's figures.

I hear the scrape of metal. "A-anyone there?" the woman whispers once again. "I can't move!"

'Prithee, accept my condolences and allow me a moment!' Dropping to my knees, I rummage through papers and items that scatter the floor.

"Dammit, I can hear you over there! Please, there is something wrong with the others!"

I lift a white paper and wave it in the woman's direction. *'Permit me another moment, Miss, and then I shall determine if I will lend thee assistance.'*

Tossing a stack of papers aside, I discover a metallic tray upon which two orange pills rest. I recognize them as the same orange pills that granted me the unknown superacid element in the past. As if they may attempt to flee my grasp if I am too slow, I bring the vermillion cattail's tendrils forward, consuming them. Viscous orange haze moves through my body with a tart

---

[68] Contrarious: Perverse; refractory. Opposed; unfavorable.

sharpness, and I take a moment to savor the flavor. *'I believe it tastes even more pleasant than last time!'*

As the haze moves through me, I notice a yellow epistle stuck to the tray's base. It is written in neat and clean running letters.[69]

I flip the tray to read the epistle.

Mixing Instructions:

Ensure the Acerb tablets are blended in a duly treated and sized stainless steel container. Add ten gallons of desalinated H2O per one orange Acerb tablet, minimum. Once mixed thoroughly, it will increase in acidity over the next *fifteen minutes*, after which it will take at least a month to lose a fraction of its potency.

Additional Information:

- o   We recommend splitting the tablets, making only small batches, and coloring the water green. If not dyed green, the mixture will be a milky white, and it can be challenging to recognize contaminated surfaces and soils. The green color is lost within *twelve hours*; add extra dye as needed.
- o   If not used immediately new stainless steel container must be substituted every *twelve hours*.
- o   If you desire to neutralize the Acerb, speak to the devotionalists we sent. They will be in attendance throughout the whole process.

Per our agreement, when the Acerb tablets are delivered, please allow our devotionalist access to the roots to determine whether there is any response when our own specimen is brought near another of its kind.

The final words almost leap off the paper. *'...Another of its kind?'*

---

[69] Epistle: A letter.

I withdraw my attention from the yellow epistle, focusing on the wall instead. *'I suppose it is rather obvious now, but the name of the mystery element was Acerb... I am more interested in the final words of that epistle. They brought something to the Arcade to be near the roots and "another of its kind," except the only thing here is me, and the roots are mine.'* I pause, assessing the information I have before concluding, *'This epistle's words implies that another Kiln is hereabouts. That makes this predicament much more complicated, not to mention dangerous.'*

Pushing Earl's wall away, I take a swift glance about the Arcade and then return to the epistle. I review the section of the epistle concerning the devotionalists and asking for their assistance if the need to neutralize the green liquid arises. This is the first time I have beheld the word "neutralize" before, but I know in alchemy and medicine "neutral" ingredients are less inclined to induce reactions when mixed into other substances.

'The devotionalists must have something to make the green liquid neutral. That or they use some variety of magic or technology, like the lap-top. I pray it is the former.'

My gaze travels to the red figures of the people who have not moved a finger since I arrived. I can only assume that one of those people possesses the item or object I desire. Yet, with so many people, whether they are moving or not, the challenge of not provoking them is present. The worst thing that could befall me is finding myself surrounded by ten people from the Consortium or Hex Church. I would much rather approach them in a safer fashion.

I probe the room, searching for anything in the immediate area that may assist me. There are some yellow plastic barrels with "water" written in black, some sort of device that reads "Arc-Weld 3698," and then leaning against the Arcade's wall is a familiar blue suit that I spotted a sweaty man wearing late last night. This is the oversized outfit that covers every piece of the body, from head to toe, and has a prominent dark window on the face of the cylinder-like helmet.

Glancing down at my body and then at the outfit, I stand and approach it. I scrutinize it, finding that it even has a pair of boots attached to the bottom. As for the material, it is similar to plastic, but I do not believe it to be so.

'If I don this suit, mayhaps I might retrieve what I require and then abscond without nearly as much issue as if I approached as a haze monster.'

I examine it some more and determine I have nary an idea what this atrocious outfit is for. If it were not so flimsy, I would presume it was a horrid set of armor. With my long vermillion nails, I rap the blackened rectangular window. Tilting my head downwards, I notice the words "The Arc Welder Professionals · A Consortium Affiliate."

'The weight might be a bit much for my current Strength stats, yet perhaps I may still make do and don it.' My gaze returns to the hole that scatters vermillion haze. Nodding, I step toward the twisting and exposed roots. 'First, if I must flee, Earl, prithee, I desire to accept my remaining two germination tasks.'

Without one of Earl's walls appearing, four new vine-like roots emerge from within the entangled bundle. The four roots, black, red, purple, and gray, rise upwards and intertwine. When they are around three feet above the pit—roughly waist level—they bend outward and then curve back in, almost resembling a dragon's claws.

I step back as each root releases its variant of haze. The roots appear to blend the hazes delicately, allowing only a precise quantity to exit. Instead of scattering, the haze retains a ball-like shape. I observe this closely to see if I may understand something, yet all I learn is that, of all the hazes, hoary is the most sparingly utilized; in fact, the hoary's root is also the thinnest of the four.

The hazes collapse inwards, and a bright pink light radiates. Thanks to my vermillion sight, the light nigh blinds me. I look away, close my right eyelid, and take a few seconds to recover before returning my gaze. What I find is not pink, but a mote of yellow light, bathing in the haze and glimmering before me as if beckoning me to embrace it. I reach out, and the yellow mote fidgets and then glides through my arm, into my chest, and then descends downward, where it rotates around the kiln.

'This must be how the motes were produced on the previous occasion. Though, it was done beneath the soil.' This process repeats three more times until four yellow lights revolve around the kiln.

An unexpected purple wall appears.

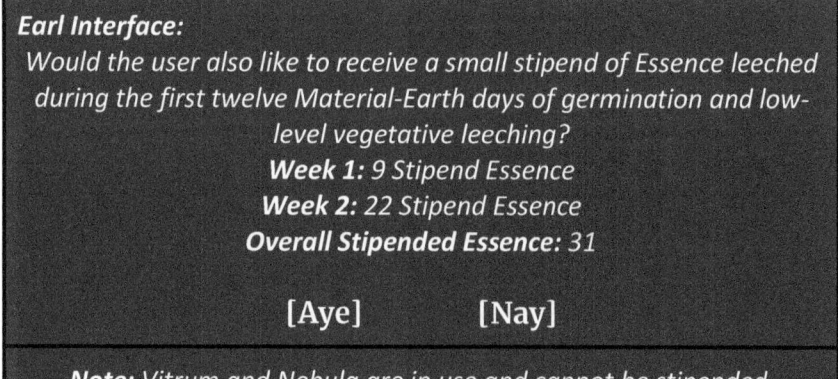

> **Earl Interface:**
> Would the user also like to receive a small stipend of Essence leeched during the first twelve Material-Earth days of germination and low-level vegetative leeching?
> **Week 1:** 9 Stipend Essence
> **Week 2:** 22 Stipend Essence
> **Overall Stipended Essence:** 31
>
> **[Aye]   [Nay]**
>
> **Note:** Vitrum and Nebula are in use and cannot be stipended.

I study the wall, clench and raise my fist, and nod. *'Aye, a boon! I shall accept that as well!'*

A crimson fluid climbs from all four roots. Similar to red-hot iron driven through a spigot, the crimson fluids collide. Steam rises and the fluid hardens, leaving what resembles a lump of glass behind. The glass lump slips from its perch atop the roots, so I stretch my arms and catch it in my long fingernails. *'A forewarning would have been welcome, Earl.'*

The four entwined roots crumble into tiny pebbles, settling into the bunches of roots in the pit beneath them. I raise my right eyelid as well as the glass-like substance. *'So this is... my 'stipended'?'*

Rolling it around in my palm with my fingers, I turn toward the cattail and offer it the glass. The tendrils unfurl, enwrap the glass, and drag it into the cattail where the lump fades into the fiery haze. A sensation as if I am sipping the purest water I have ever had the pleasure of tasting courses through my kiln.

Reading the wall, I cross my arms. *'This is the first time it has felt like I "drank" something since I became a Kiln, intriguing. I wonder if it would taste even better if I stol—'*

The woman's frantic whispers interrupt my thoughts. "Are you just standing there messing with the lights!? Help me get this Halloween crap off me!"

'Ah! I grew distracted!' I uncross my arms, and my attention swings back to the, well, I suppose it's an arc welding suit, arc suit, or something suit. *'I favor the name "arc suit." It sounds elegant and knightly... But that's not important. What is imperative is that I may escape the suit quickly if the need arises.'*

Rushing over to the big blue arc suit, I realize that I do not know how this suit is meant to be worn. I think for a moment and recall the man I saw with the arc suit removing the helmet by reaching for something near the neck. My gaze drifts to a flap that encircles the helmet's base; I flip it up, discovering a metal strip with pairs of teeth interlocked with one another.

'...This was attached to one of Terra's bags? Did she tell me the name of this? I cannot remember; mayhaps I was not paying attention.'

I find a small shiny handle dangling from the interlocked teeth, so I yank it hoping it shall release the head. The arc suit tips onto its side, but as the arc suit tips, the small handle slides, separating the two pairs of metal teeth and making a sharp hissing sound.

My head tilts. I study the unique mechanism, only to again be interrupted. "God! Come over here; help me!"

The woman kicks loose items on the ground. I cannot fathom why she might be upset with me. I turn back toward the arc suit, yanking it around so it lies flat on the floor.

Moving the helmet to the side, I lie on the ground, push my legs together, and then have the haze guide me into the arc suit. My gown manages to squeeze in on its own, and before I know it, I have wiggled my way into the suit's depths. *'Aye, this shall do. If I must escape, I can remove the head, the arc suit will drop, and then I may flee.'*

> **Earl Interface:**
> **Warning:** *User will temporarily surrender the advantages of their natural hover as well as the benefits of being in the Domain.*

'Hover? Like my ability to float above water and such? Aye, that should be well enough in the meantime.'

I attempt to tilt myself upright, but whilst I do so, my haze seems as if it would prefer to slip from the arc suit entirely rather than lift it. Eyeing the handle near the suit's neck, I pull it and bring the pair of teeth back together. Upon reaching the last teeth, I stop and leave a large enough gap to slip the cattail through if the need arises.

'The arc suit is rather cozy, truly I rather enjoy hiding away in confined places such as this. Aye! I shall be Constance, the most unintimidating foppish knight to ever grace these lands!'

I attempt to wiggle myself upright once more, and this time, the suit fidgets. Except it still feels as if I am endeavoring to stand with a mound of dirt atop me. I maneuver the cattail within the suit and slip it behind my back as if it is a backbone. As it is around ten feet in length, I slip some of the excess cattail into one of the suit's legs and then flex it along its entirety. The arc suit, along with my body, bends into a horseshoe or "C" shape.

'I have never been so delighted to not possess bones.'

Sticking out my arms, I brace them against the floor, and now resemble an upside-down "V." Finally, I again maneuver the cattail and push it through the hole I left at the neck of the arc suit and use it to force myself into a standing position. Now standing, I discover that I am barely tall enough to see through the helmet's dark window. I have not thought about it that often, but this era's people are rather tall—in life, I was a tad under five feet in height.[70]

'Aye, I would relish the sable haze's Strength at this moment. This is ridiculous.' I draw the cattail back, and then step toward the nine people who eerily ignore my presence and the woman who has been whisper-yelling at me. The arc suit squeaks as the heels of the boots rub against the floor. I push the cattail into the arc suit's right leg and use it to properly support at least one leg. As I approach, I shake my head. 'Good lord. I feel as if I am a newborn foal attempting to plod through neck-high water. I never realized how easy it was to move as haze.'

I close my right eyelid to discern how readily I may see without the vermillion sight, but I find it is nigh impossible without it. Still, I can see things decently with the vermillion sight, so I lift the right eye's negating membrane.

Once I am close enough to see the full situation, I stop. The display before me is far from what I envisioned.

First, six people, two men, four women: one clutching their legs murmuring to themself in a soft voice, one knocking their brow against another's shoulder blade, one person scratching their skin as if they have a rash of abominable proportions, and the last two pulling at their hair while hugging themselves. All six of them have bloodshot eyes and bright red veins that resemble spider webs running from their eye sockets to as far as their ears. Their dress consists of white outfits that look like they should cover their whole body, similar to my own blue arc suit. However, their helmets are missing, their suits are torn to pieces, and the material that makes up the outfit seems to be plastic, unlike my arc suit.

Next, three people, one man, two women: all three stand against the wall. They claw at it, their fingernails, long worn away, leaving behind strings of old blood. I cannot observe their eyes or faces, but I assume they are the

---

[70] |5 feet | under 152.4 centimeters in height|

same. The man wears the uniform of the noble's police, and the women appear to have removed their white suits and stand in naught but their undergarments.

Lastly, one woman: the woman is trapped and whispering something. A droplet of blood leaks from her lips as she attempts to push a metal table off her chest. Yet, it is not the metal table that she cannot lift, but an iron coffin that presses the table down upon her. She wears a noble's police uniform, and I actually recognize this woman—Jessica, the noble's police. I have seen this woman on a few occasions now, and she is always with the same person, which means the noble's police scratching the wall is likely him, Leo.

I stand, unmoving. My mind blank.

As if by itself, my body rigidly turns away from the outlandish fever dream and shuffles away.

"W-wait! Please!" Jessica whispers with a hiss.

I waver, but my feet goad me forward. *'...Apologies, Jessica, but this place belongs to Umbral now. I shall return for my seed at a later date.'*

I can hear her kick her legs. "It's this fog; it's done something to them!"

Her words bring me to halt. I recall my experiments with the copepods and remember that I never did discover the effects of the red haze. The image of the shrieking man who inhaled my haze appears in my mind. Then I think back to other times in the past when people inhaled the haze and assaulted others or gorged themselves on bread until their abdomens would distend.

During my copepod test, sable caused the goose meat to become diseased, while hoary seemed to make the goose meat decay. So if sable is pestilence and hoary is rot, then vermillion could be the haze that brings about madness. That explains why the vermillion copepod did not affect the goose meat.

'I suppose if I mend the leak, they shall recover eventually... And I surmise this crisis is a consequence of the Consortium's blunder. I am not one to involve myself in matters wrought by someone else's hand, yet mayhap I may learn more if I linger

and assist.' It takes a few wobbly steps, but I turn myself around. 'Do not fret, Jessica. I never truly intended to forsake thee and flee this accursed place. It was a jest.'

As I arrive at Jessica's side, her eyelids and body relax. It's evident she does not realize that it is not a person who stands before her but a suit plump with the same vermillion haze shrouding the Arcade. With stiff finger movements, I attempt to soothe her by performing all seven of the words I know in hand language.

"Sign language. You can't talk?" she asks, furrowing her brows. "Are you mute? I have a few friends who are mute, but I don't know sign language."

'...Terra, I do not believe anyone speaks this hand language.'

I shrug and shake my head; however, I suspect neither of these gestures are visible to Jessica through the arc suit. From her perspective, I must look like an eerily silent suit looming over her whilst she struggles.

There's a sudden peculiar ache in my kiln, and my eyes drift to the iron coffin that pins Jessica beneath it. An instinct awakens from deep within me, an instinct that makes me... hungry.

Chapter 17: Doctor Professor Commander Nightingale

∞∞∞∞∞∞∞∞∞∞∞∞∞∞∞

My fingertips run across the iron coffin, and the arc suit's sticky gauntlets produce a squeaky sound. I squint my eyes and rap the coffin's exterior in frustration, longing to be nearer to what's inside. *'Surely I would not feel this strongly about a corpse?'* My thoughts return to the epistle that mentions bringing something here to be near The Tower's roots. *'Could this be what they brought to the Arcade...? The suspected Kiln, is it inside? But why would they confine them to a coffin? Wait. Might this be the Kiln that made the Acerb? If that is the case, I cannot allow this Kiln to remain in the Hex Church's possession lest they use it against me or my roots anew.'*

I scour the coffin for a handle, crack, or rivets I might use to open it. Since I cannot bend my legs to lean over, I take a few steps back to see what I may discover. The coffin is raven black, and oddly, there is a hatch above where the corpse's head would rest. It is around six feet long, roughly four feet wide at one end and three at the other, and on the front, some letters spell the words "Corrosive & Hot."

Noticing a pair of iron hinges on my side of the coffin, I step to the opposite side, where I locate three latches, evenly separated along the edge, each with a glossy lock. I examine the hatch above where the corpse's head would be and discover another lock. This lock is entrenched in the coffin's door, appearing much older and heftier than the other three. I raise myself a tad higher inside the arc suit by standing on my tiptoes and then peer into the lock. With my vermillion sight, I glimpse a red hue emanating from between the lock's inner mechanisms. *'Perchance I may squeeze the cattail through?'* I shake my head. *'...Nay, at a glance the mechanism seems watertight.'*

Jessica's voice snaps me from my study of the coffin. "Hey. Do you see something?" she asks.

'Aye, let us address the prevailing situation first and foremost.' I wave my arms at Jessica, denying that I saw anything within the coffin. She coughs, pushing up on the coffin to ease its weight on her bosom. *'...And it is also time to*

acknowledge the truth: this coffin is not moving an inch without some inventiveness. Even with my sable, I could not hope to drag it.'

Glancing around the floor, I notice a bent and broken rack of shelving lies strewn across the floor. Next to it are glass jars that I suspect were formerly resting upon its shelves. Most of the containers are shattered, save for one containing a familiar roach-like creature bouncing about within it. *'Verily, I know that creature; it is a copepod, or at least it is comparable.'*

The most significant difference is this copepod is larger, pinkish-white, and rather than a blend between roach and shrimp, like my copepods, it resembles a blend of roach and head lice. They have a label that reads, "Giant Sea Louse !Aggressive! | LiberyStar | Pink Coral Specimen," whatever that may mean.

Next to the creature's jar, I see several additional labels scrambled amongst the broken glass:
|White Larva !Aggressive!|Sanitation|Fecal Specimens|
|F.G. Pyrite|Terminal|S.Machine Sample|
*|Cordy. !!!HAZARDOUS!!DO **NOT** OPEN!!!|NativeCav.|Cerebellum Sample|*
|Bone|Park Hill|Police Cruiser Sample|
|Cinnabar[Hg] !TOXIC!|N.Blackwell|Ocean Water Sample|
|Bramble? Vine|Morris-F.Watch|Notochord Sample|
|Glass/Gas !HAZARDOUS!|Central|Root Sample|
|Bovine?|Backstreets?|Ribeye Sample|
|White Flint !BURN!|Brook.Zoo|Sewerage Sample|
|Soda. Sand|Park Hill|Sofa Sample|
|Unknown Bark|Park Hill|Basement Sample|

Disregarding the hideous creature and broken jars, I turn away and shuffle nearer to Jessica. I position my leg adjacent to her eyes, obstructing a corner of the Arcade from her view. With bloodshot and upturned eyes, she peers into the arc suit's black windowpane. Unbeknownst to Jessica, I am also scrutinizing her; it is peculiar that this woman alone resists the haze's influence. While I examine her, she bites her lip and scowls at me; I presume it is because I am not helping her as quickly as she wishes. Regardless, her eyes betray her—I can see her quivering pupils. I do not understand why this woman can resist the vermillion haze, but the fear in her eyes is real, of that I am certain.

She takes a breath, and I can see the vermillion haze wafting into her nostrils. "You're planning on helping me, right?" she asks with a slight shiver. "Because you're acting really weird, and it's kinda freakin' me out."

'Thou art fortunate I feel like a knight in this blue suit, and as a noble knight, I shall assist...' Remembering a hand sign Terra once performed, I raise my hand, make a fist, and extend my thumb. *'And by assist, I mean I shall remove this coffin since I intend to relieve the Hex Church of it regardless. Everything after that is thy own responsibility.'*

Unaware of my thoughts, she smiles. "That's the most beautiful thumbs-up I've ever seen." She exhales the breath she had been holding. "God, I'm so pathetic," she murmurs, her head swinging back to me. "Hey, you never really reacted earlier. You can't talk, can you?"

I draw the cattail from the arc suit's leg and push it through the hole at the neck, where Jessica cannot see. To keep her calm and oblivious, I raise a single finger and try to write in the air. The vermillion haze hardly reacts to my writing, but Jessica's eyes watch intently, tracing the movement of my finger.

"Nay," I scribble in the air.

"N-A-Y?" She raises an eyebrow. "What are you, Congress?"

'What is meant by that?' Whilst I draw a question mark with my finger, I use the fiery cattail to grip one of the poles on the broken shelf. The pole is loose but still attached. I twist it and the shelving squeaks.

Jessica tries to look toward the noise, but I step in front of her and make the question mark again.

She follows my finger, chuckling. "I was just joking about the Congress thing. Did you come in for your morning shift? Listen, just so you know..." she says, motioning toward a bite wound on her ankle. "It's weird that others didn't attack you. They bit me, I tried to grab onto the table, but it started to tip over. My partner tried to keep the table and coffin from falling on top of me, but he only managed to hold it for a second. The table rolled over, and the coffin with it. After that, those people held down my partner until he breathed in enough of this red gas, and then let him go."

The metal bar snaps from the shelving and whacks the arc suit's helmet. I seize the metal rod with my hand and draw the cattail back into the suit, placing it back into the right leg.

"What was that noise?" Jessica whispers.

I look from left to right and then make a question mark with my finger. '*I know naught of what thou speakest.*' Waving my arm dismissively, I bring the metal rod forward. I grip the bar, make a shoving motion, and then point at the coffin.

"Oh? Thanks." Nodding, she takes me and asks, "Can you push up on the table while I shove the bar underneath?"

I write "Nay" in the air with my finger.

She huffs and mumbles something under her breath as she strives to use the rod to relieve some of the coffin's weight.

My attention strays to the nine people who have yet to react to my presence or anything for that matter. Since the people against the wall are wearing naught but their undergarments, I investigate the six people coiled on the floor. At first, I keep a distance as I do not trust those the madness has afflicted. After a few seconds, I choose to test their aggression; it is not as if I have any flesh to lose, nor do they have any weapons. Extending my arm, I approach a woman who rocks back and forth, mumbling incoherent sentences.

The arc suit's gauntlet pokes the woman; she does not react. I tilt my head. These mannerisms are symptoms I have not observed from those afflicted with the madness in the past. Though admittedly, I do not have as much experience with the haze's madness as I do with the haze's disease. I glance at the giant sea louse and the vermillion haze enveloping me. '*I have an idea. Copepods. I can craft copepods! They may assist me.*'

I concentrate. Copepods skitter about on the kiln's shell, making me want to shiver. The fingers of the gauntlet squeak as I rub them together. '*Disregard them, Constance. Imagine them as autumn leaves brushing against thy limbs.*' Shaking my arms, I order a copepod to creep to the black window and confirm that it is indeed a vermillion copepod. '*Spl... splendid. Time to make many more autumn leaves. But...*' I maneuver my arm from the arc suit's sleeve and poke the vermillion copepod. Beneath my finger, the copepod's body bends a tad, yet my fingertip does not pass through. '*They are much denser than they once were! Is it because there is so much vermillion haze? Or is it because my magic power has grown now since I took in vermillion haze? I know not, but their usefulness has risen immeasurably.'*

For a time, I stand motionlessly as the suit fills with copepods, primarily because I desire that my kiln touch as few as feasible. Haze hovering around the arc suit swirls into the hole at the suit's neck, resembling a churning whirlpool of red air. This is the easiest time I have had fashioning copepods. Not merely because of the surplus of vermillion haze, but they feel genuinely easier to craft. It's not long before I worry the suit may burst from the sheer quantity of copepods.

I check my Status once again. It shows that I have expended eighty mana while my Erysichthon remains zero. Ordinarily, my issue with making copepods is Erysichthon and not mana, but I have never constructed so many copepods at once.

Ensuring that Jessica still cannot see, I order a copepod to exit the suit through the arc suit's neck. The place I command it to go is, well, the cheek of the woman near my knees. The copepod squirms out of the neck and then travels halfway down my trousers. Gripping the arc suit with its back legs, it leans out and taps its limbs against the woman's cheek. Both it and the woman do not react. *'Aye. Then I shall send them to search the people's pockets for anything of use.'*

Commanding the copepods to crawl to the nine people, I watch them exit the arc suit's neck. Like a line of rat-sized ants, they wriggle out one after another. *'One-two-three-four-five-six-seven...'* As they depart, I count to see the amount I crafted given the time, haze, and mana. *'Two hundred and ninety-eight. Unacceptable!'* I create two additional copepods, completing a harmonious three hundred. *'With those two copepods tallied, my copepod creation cost calculates to around one mana for roughly four copepods.'*

Nodding, I return my attention to the woman. I recoil, nearly falling backward, when I see the woman submerged in copepods. The only hint that someone is underneath is a single twitching finger. *'The copepods are too brainless for such broad orders!'* I try to command them to split into platoons of thirty, and as I should have expected, they do not understand the order. Throwing my head back, I hold up three fingers, then make a zero with my hand, and point while shouting in my mind. *'Thirty! Thirty! To that person over there!'*

A platoon of copepods separates from the army and dashes toward the person I indicated. I try to command another platoon of them again, using only my thoughts, but only a single one harks me this time. So I hold up two fingers, then nine, and point; it works again as a platoon of twenty-nine joins the lone copepod! Noting this, I begin commanding them with various hand gestures and thoughts. The gestures make my commands much more efficient, though I look silly. My ghastly army spreads out, and before long, all nine people have a platoon of copepods creeping on their bodies. The woman that was submerged in copepods relaxes whilst the other eight people show no reactions to the copepods' ticklish limbs clinging to them.

'If they have pockets, it is near their waist.' I point at my waist and then make an up and down motion with my hands. *'Crawl inside.'* My orders are simple enough, yet the copepods try to enter the pockets all at once, preventing all of them from getting in. As for the ones on the two women in their undergarments, they scramble about in confusion. *'I am a commander of a battalion of clodpated ninnyhammers! But I am a commander nonetheless.'*

Straightening my shoulders, I look toward the copepods and renew my commands like a true leader. This time, I act them all out, creating a walking motion with my fingers, pointing, and then performing a gesture as if I am taking something from that area. Jessica questions what I am doing at one point, but I feign not hearing her. Some minutes later, we discover naught. I move to the individuals facing the wall, only to find one woman has a large patch of cloth sewn around their neck, upper bosom, and hips—Hex Church.

I scrutinize the woman's appearance; I would speculate she is young, around twenty, but more importantly, she is not that Emily woman. With my vermillion sight, I see that her skin is 'redder' than the others, and the cloth stitched into her body shines nigh scarlet. She is assuredly the person who should possess what I require. Yet this person lacks the usual Hex Church frock, and if the copepods leave their position to search for it, Jessica shall see them.

While imagining a frock, I point at the other noble's police's attire and then the ceiling. *'Search for any garment that a human is not wearing and deliver it unto me! Use the ceiling to move.'* I call ten copepods to me and order them to chase me. *'Let us put on a wee performance, shall we?'*

I stagger toward Jessica, my arms waving loosely. My antics distract her, and the coffin drops, wedging the metal rod between the floor and the coffin. She breathes a sigh of relief, falls onto her back, and then looks at me. I wave my arm and point at the ten copepods. *'Look, look. It's a small number of copepods! Be frightened and distracted!'*

"What?" she murmurs under her breath, squinting to see the copepods' obscured outlines within the vermillion haze.

Glancing back, I notice a copepod is missing and then hear Jessica yelp. I look toward her and find that a senseless copepod took an alternative route and snuck up behind Jessica. The lone copepod plods through the strands of Jessica's chestnut brown hair that lie strewn across the floor.

Jessica grits her teeth and smashes it with a hard slap, returning it into a puff of haze. "Shit, shit, I can't do this. I can't do this," she declares, shaking her head to and fro. Her breathing becomes strained. She looks from left to right with wide, bloodshot eyes. "I'm breathing in this stuff that turns into bugs!?" She glares at me; the red veins around her eyes, induced by the vermillion haze, become more prominent. "L-listen. Can you take the car keys from my pocket and get my radio so I can call for help...? Will you do that for me?"

'...Apologies.' I hesitate but raise my hand, perform a sweeping motion, and then wiggle my finger to indicate I will not retrieve what she is requesting.

She bites her lip with a sharp snort. "No-no-no! Do not pull that horror movie finger-wag crap right now! This is the part where the monster takes off their mask, revealing they were just playing with the throwaway side character! I am not a throwaway!"

'Monster!? Does she know... Nay! If she knew I was a monster, she would not imbue so much sarcasm into her words.' Raising a finger, I spell out the word "save" in the air, a single letter at a time. When I see her mouth the words, I point at her and then at myself.

Her eyebrows furrow, and she turns away with a nod. "Hallucinations. I'll pretend they're hallucinations," she says to herself in a tiny voice. "This is torture."

A few minutes pass as the copepods scour the area. Occasionally, a copepod will creep near Jessica, and I will make a slight movement to pretend I am challenging it, but truthfully, I am merely altering its path. While this is happening, I work to produce an additional two hundred and one copepods; that way, the number shall be six hundred. This places my mana at roughly sixty, so henceforth, I shall only craft a few replacements if necessary as I do not wish to compromise my manituic flux further.

'The six hundred! That is what they shall call us! Well, at least that is how I shall remember us since all the copepods will be puffs of vermillion haze once I abandon the Arcade.'

The copepods work to build a heap of cloth behind Jessica. "I swear I hear something?" she glances from left to right. Although the copepods do not produce sound, the fabrics they are dragging do. "Hey, how many of those bugs are there anyway?" she whispers.

Jessica tries to stretch her neck to see, but I step in the way. With her vision blocked, I allow the additional copepods to exit the suit and join their brethren. At the same time, I look at her and hold up a two and a five.

"Twenty-five! There are at that many!? Where could they be coming from!?"

I raise my hands, shrug, and step out of Jessica's eyesight.

"What? Hey, wait, don't just walk away!" she protests.

A few copepods approach me with what I have been anticipating—a black frock. They drop the frock, and then I order all copepods to gather around it. Like a flock of passenger pigeons, they cloud the ground beneath them, stepping aside as I move through them.[71] I command the copepods to

---

[71] Passenger Pigeons: At one time there were 3 to 5 billion passenger pigeons at the time Europeans discovered America. A flock of passenger pigeons was said to take several hours to pass overhead. In 1914 Matha, the last passenger pigeon, died, and they are now extinct.

open the frock's front, exposing a yellow tome buckled to the inside. A small bolt of lightning shoots from the tome and strikes a copepod. The copepod bursts.

Recalling that Emily's tome did something similar, I do not panic but bow my head in somber remembrance. *'My second casualty. The sacrifices of this quest have been so great. Was it truly worth it?'* Shrugging, I form one additional vermillion copepod. *'Aye, I would say it was a necessary sacrifice, and I am thankful that the lightning does not seem to affect me as it does the copepods!'*

Along with the yellow tome is an ebony book titled "Gospel of Lords Hexed: Contracting Foregone Humanity." The book is in an inside pocket opposite the tome; presumably, it's a mere counterbalance to offset the yellow tome's drag on the frock. It also appears to be a book that's more typical of this era, yet the subject is intriguing. *'I shall most assuredly take both the book and tome with me if I can carry it out.'* The tendrils unravel and seize the tome. Lightning courses through my haze, creating rich hues and motes of light. Yet, I feel no pain. From what I can see, the lightning appears to dissolve upon striking the kiln's shell. *'Hmm, if I assimilate a wee bit of the tome, shall Earl inform me of what it is?'*

I swallow the tome and it enters the inner area of the cattail. The lightning grows ever more intense, and the outer coverings of haze slough off, reminiscent of a snake shedding its skin. I can hear the Hex Church woman groan and claw at the wall behind me. My cattail draws no haze from the tome, so I eject it. *'That was odd? It did not seem as if the cattail was capable of digesting it.'* I glance at the Hex Church woman, discovering she has returned to her former demeanor. My thoughts stray, and I recall the time I wrote in Emily's tome. *'Emily had a strange reaction when I scribbled in her tome, and that woman also reacted peculiarly... I believe I shall still bring the tome with me, but I am uncertain if consuming it is wise.'*

My gaze moves to a sewn-on pocket above the ebony book. I command one copepod to enter and remove what may be in it. It withdraws two items: a folded yellow epistle and a white pill. By my order, it brings me the two items. I take the epistle and unfold it. The script is penned in tidy running letters and, like the previous epistle, does not have a signature.

I read it.

Once you have completed the investigation with the specimen, and once you have decided it is time to return, give the Consortium this neutralizer.

Ensure the specimen is no longer on the premises before notifying them how best to mix the neutralizer. Humor no monetary offers by Consortium to purchase the specimen.

'*That is all that is written? There is no recipe?*' I reread the epistle and glance back at the Hex Church woman noiselessly gawking at the Arcade's wall. Shaking my head, I grasp the pill and command the copepods to take residence on the walls outside of Jessica's sight. '*It says, "how best to mix the neutralizer," so that must imply there are various ways to mix it. With this pill, I may be able to mend my roots.*' I stumble toward the water barrels, planning to mimic the method for Acerb production using the white pill.

Approaching the water barrels, I pull the handle on the suit, releasing the helmet. The arc suit falls to my ankles. My gown's hem spreads wide as I stretch my arms and perform a dainty twirl to celebrate my release. I bend down and pluck the milky white pill from the arc suit's gauntlet. Pinching both ends of the pill in my fiery red hand, I snap it in two. A sprinkle of the pill's residue floats earthward. Sinking into a puddle, it pops. I tilt my head and squint my eyelids. '*This is the neutralizer... the pill is a different color, and the notes that came with it implied as much. Aye, there is nary a way this is a hoodwink, but still, I should be wary.*'

With a nod, I search the water barrel and find a nozzle at the base and a bucket next to that. I turn the handle and fill the bucket to its brim. '*Now, I must take an extraordinarily delicate approach.*' I cast half the pill into the bucket, grab the arc suit with the cattail, and retreat with the other half of the pill. '*Flee for thy life!*' White gas bubbles in the bucket; there is a roar as water spurts into the air, painting the Arcade's ceiling tiles a milky white.

"What was that!?" Jessica whisper-shouts. I pinch a piece of glass with the cattail and tap it against the ground in a rhythmic pattern. "If that's you making that noise, y'know you could comfort me by actually coming over here!" she scoffs.

'This is a complicated predicament, Jessica!' I return to the bucket, finding a palm's worth of water at the bottom—like the liquid on the ceiling, it is milky white. Lifting the bucket, I approach the hollow from which the vermillion haze spews. 'Prithee, solve this matter so that I might conclude my business and depart.'

A few yards from the hole, I extend the cattail with the bucket's handle in the tendril's clutches. With a twist of the cattail, the milky water pours onto the leaking root. There's a sizzle, and thick white smoke rises from the cavity, sounding like water running over hot ash.

> **Earl Interface:**
> **Notice:** The obstructive substance has been nullified. The repair will be concluded shortly, and the user's presence is no longer necessary.

Retracting the cattail and raising my arms, I chant a rousing 'Huzzah!' to the copepods. I present the other half of the white pill to the cattail, and it engulfs it. 'I see no reason to squander it!'

A dense milky white haze streams up the cattail, and a bitter, unsavory sensation crawls across my kiln. It's not unpleasant, just bitterly unanticipated.

> **Earl Interface:**
> Assimilating 'Concentrated Acrid Pellet Superbase'
> 0.4 Refined Acrid
>
> **Details:** A condensed and dehydrated sample of the element Acrid. It would require a highly advanced method of refining or a particular race of creatures to produce.

I shake away the bitterness, read and dismiss the purple wall, and then step toward the hole, discovering the roots crusted in a white film of powder. 'So one is Acerb, and the other is Acrid, and they seem to rival one another. Fascinating, but I do not have time to dally!'

With the primary issue resolved, I am free to take a less delicate approach. I return to the arc suit, slide back in, and seal the helmet, leaving a gap for the cattail. With the arc suit on, I approach Jessica, extend my thumb, and then flex my other arm.

She rolls her eyes. "Don't be so stupidly casual. Get me out from under this table before it cracks a rib."

Raising a finger, I indicate for her to have patience and then return my attention to the other nine people. Since the haze is no longer leaking, I worry that they may grow aggressive as it thins. As I assign orders to the copepods, I hear a distinctive clicking. My gaze shoots to the back of the Arcade. A radiant light illuminates the plastic blankets covering the back entrance. *'It is one of the floating copper orbs—one of those clicker things!?'*

I command the copepods to take shelter in one of the ceiling's corners. With the orb's approach imminent, I collapse to the floor, pretending to be naught but a vacant outfit. The arc suit deflates, so I use the cattail to push against it, concealing my feminine figure and making the suit appear as if it is plump with air.

"Hey?" Jessica whispers. "What are you doing?"

Raising my index finger, I place it against the helmet of the arc suit. *'Shush! I have seen and endured much, Jessica, and perhaps they shall assist thee, but they will not assist me, so I shall hold my tongue steady!'*

My arm falls to my side as a muffled male voice answers the clicking outside. "Leave the clicker here, Gary, and go scout the situation," I hear someone say.

"Keep me in the loop." some else says. "I'm going to go find hazmat suits."

I recognize the two voices. The first to speak was Lincoln, and the second was Pierce; they are the pair of Consortium Solicitors.

A copper orb enters the room. This one is smaller than the clicker I anticipated; instead of the size of a big pumpkin, as the clicker was, it is around the size of a melon or gourd. It has four bright torches at its base, each resembling the pupil of an eyeball. On its front is a bright blue window or picture that displays the orphanay bird of the Consortium. Its torches turn every which way, illuminating the nine people affected by the vermillion haze. The torchs' light drifts toward my figure in the arc suit.

"Is that a drone?" Jessica whispers to herself. "It's got Consortium markings."

As it turns and approaches me, I shut my eyelids. It floats above me. "English? Español? 普通话? हिन्दी?" the eyeball speaks in an unemotional voice.

'English, Spanish, and some other languages...? Wait, it can speak!? The other one never spoke! I do not believe it knows that I am in the suit, so I shan't answer; I am naught but a vacant suit!'

A tube slips out of an opening at the base of the copper orb, and a needle slides out of the tube. It floats downward, pushing the needle into the suit's neck. It rises into the air, slides the needle out, and then floats away, approaching the nine people instead.

"English? Español? 普通话? हि–" It stops speaking, and another voice replaces it. "Alright, alright, enough of the auto-recovery settings. The other scout won't work, so I will run this scouting orb myself. Let's see..."

My eyelids open. *'Scouting orb? So it is called a scout?'*

The scout turns, and its torch shines upon me anew. I shut my eyelids! It peers at me, and I see that the blue window that was a picture of an orphanay now displays the image of a man with messy black hair, thick spectacles, and a scraggly stubble around his mouth. By his appearance alone, I would guess he is somewhere in his twenties.

Scratching his stubble, he lifts a sheet of white paper, stares at it, and then looks back up. His sunken eyes gaze at something that casts a blue hue on his face and reflects in his spectacles. "The suit is empty, huh. What are we paying that welder for anyway? He only worked, what, thirteen hours, tops... I wish I only had to work that long." With a yawn, he turns away and then says, "There's a lot of this red vapor in here. It's supposed to have some effect on those that breathe it in."

He pops his neck, pushes his spectacles back into place, and places the paper aside. The scout rotates in place. "Hmm, hmm, hmm... anyone capable of speaking to me? I assume you all know English; I don't think we assigned any international researchers to this locality. If we did, the woman who knows Hindi went home already, but the other translators are still here, so just speak up."

The man reaches for something. His hand disappears from the picture and returns with an item I recognize—a sandwich. "Eh, who am I kidding, Lincoln, Pierce, and I haven't been able to get anyone worthwhile, much less any international researchers. If we were able to get them, we wouldn't be working with those fruitcakes from the Hex Church." He rolls his eyes, taking a big bite of his sandwich.

My eyelids slide open as the scout floats to the nine people infected by vermillion haze. The scout's torch illuminates their faces. "...None of you guys are looking so hot," he says between chewing his food. "And two of you are half-naked for some reason... Not bad, though; it's the little things in life. Mostly because everything else costs money, especially the big things."

'This scandalous... scouting orb. What a lecherous scouting orb!'[72]

The scouting orb glides about the room, the vermillion haze bending around its form as it floats about. It approaches the pit of entwined roots and gazes into it. On the Arcade's ceiling, I can see the colorful reflection of the scout's light bouncing off the surface of the glassy roots. It reminds me of the cold morns when the sun would beam through the stained glass windowpanes of the decrepit church back in London.

The voice speaks again, washing away my nostalgic melancholy. "Don't see any leaks. These are the only roots we have exposed, and they sort of look like they're caked in salt or something... Yeah, I'm not gonna lie, it would be super convenient if it fixed itself somehow."

"Hey, vacuous idiot!" Jessica shouts.

"Oh man, watch out; we got a talker!" the man in the scout says, spinning around. It darts over to Jessica, illuminating her figure. He tosses his sandwich to the side. "Hard to see in here, isn't it? Hmm, oh! Hello, Officer, my name is Gary, and wow, you have a creepy coffin on top of you, y'know? Not to mention you look a bit scary, your eyes are totally red,

---

[72] Lecherous: prone to indulge in sensuality, lustful, lewd.

and the veins around your sockets are... kind of badass, actually! Hopefully it's not permanent, though."

'So this "Gary" lives in the scouting orb? Nay, Terra explained moving pictures to me and showed me the people performing sign language. Those pictures never spoke back, however... I do not know, but it is more fun to say he resides in the orb, though I doubt that is the case.'

Jessica lies there, rubbing the veins around her eyes.

In the scout's picture, Gary adds white powder a glass mug. He stirs the liquid in the mug with a silver spoon and then purses his lips. "Listen, I'm just a desk jockey for the most part, I don't want to hurt you or anything, but I have a question: why are you here?" Placing the spoon to the side, he asks, "Didn't we already talk to the police chief about y'all coming in here with or without permission?"

Jessica's brows furrow. "I only came in here because we heard something! Now's not the time to talk about those kinds of minor details! I need your help, something's wrong with the others!"

"You don't have your cell phone or radio with you, Officer? Is that standard protocol?"

"N-no!" Her eyes turn away. "We accidentally left them in the cruiser."

"No, I don't think it was an accident." Gary sighs. "You're a dirty cop, huh? Afraid they might see you're someplace you shouldn't be? A little paranoid, but I heard they caught one dirty officer like that a few weeks back."

"I... No! Why would you think that!?" she stammers, her mouth opening and closing. "There was a sign outside that said no cell phones, so I-I..."

"Oh, I forgot about that sign—can't have private company business leaking into the public, y'know? Well, it was just a guess anyway, honestly, but it's par for the course in the current social and political climate. Don't worry, I have no intention of tattling on you—way too much paperwork."

"There's nothing to tell!"

"Yeah, yeah, whatever you say, buuut still, I think we're gonna have to..." The sounds of someone clicking their tongue and flipping papers echo from the scout. "Gosh, it's already Friday; I remember how much I used to love Fridays. Haven't had a free one of those in a while."

Jessica throws up her arms, frustration evident as she clenches her fist. "What are you talking about? I need help! Why are you acting like this is a standard scenario, like it's a freakin' dentist's appointment!?"

"Yeah, I know how you feel. Consortium dentists are all about procedure... Anyhow, yep, according to Consortium impromptu procedure, it looks like we are required to detain you until after the world governments make their announcement to the public, which will be somewhere around two to four weeks. Secondly, I'd also like to know why this red vapor doesn't bother you as much as the others."

"What!? No way!" Jessica shakes her head. "Just listen, they attacked me earlier bu—"

"Attacked you? Are they aggressive toward the uninfected or something?" Gary asks, raising his mug to take a sip. "That's some classic zombie movie stuff, kind of like those freaky messed up crawlers in Anchorage. Sure hope it's not related, or we have a serious problem."

"Don't screw with me, desk jockey; this is not another Crawler-Anchorage! None of them look anything like the Anchorage crawlers! They're all just confused and delirious! Ask my buddy in the welding suit, they are mute, but they'll back me up!"

'Do not speak of me! I would also like to add that those folk are far beyond mere confusion!'

The scout's torch illuminates me for a moment and then swings away. "...Yeah, there's nothing in that welding suit; it's already been checked. I would guess you're hallucinating, probably. Don't worry, we'll get you fixed right up," Gary says.

"That is not what's happening, I would know!"

Gary sighs, and the scout floats to the area above my belly. "You would know, huh?" The needle extends from the orb's base and the orb floats downward. I lean to the left as the needle slides past the kiln's shell.

It rises back out and glides back to Jessica as a blue wall appears.

Dismissing the blue wall, I hear Gary in the scouting orb say, "See. No blood, fluids, or reaction. It's empty."

"But that's impossible," Jessica mumbles. "...Wait, even if that's true, what if there was someone in there!? Wouldn't you have just stabbed them!?"

"I had already checked, remember? Well, the auto-program did, but it rarely makes mistakes. Except for that one time." He chuckles, running his fingers through his greasy hair. "But, more importantly, I'm required by company policy to mitigate the threat you guys will pose to the Solicitors, so I'm going to go ahead and say... Sorry, it'll only hurt for a second, and when you wake up, you'll be back to normal, trust me."

"I would trust a lit stick of dynamite more than I would trust anyone who says something as cliché as 'trust me'!" Jessica says, pushing at the coffin sitting atop her.

The plastic blankets sweep upward as a bronze-orb rushes into the Arcade. In my vermillion sight, a deep red light emits from the orb's heart. It is the same variety of orb that the dinosaur ate in the past—a clicker. Alike the clicker before, it has four antennae uniformly arranged atop it, while at its base is a dish resembling a frying pan fixed in-between a pair of cogwheels that spin like water wheels.

Its bright pupil-like light reflects off the vermillion haze as it rotates in a circle. It shines its light upon the nine ailing-people and darts toward them. Its cogwheels twirl: one clockwise and the other counterclockwise.

Lightning gathers around its dish.

The nine people under the vermillion haze's influence scream and whirl toward the clicker—they charge it. They fling themselves at the clicker, crashing into it like cannonballs against a frigate.

Vermillion haze swirls as the clicker's cogwheels grind to a halt. A sphere of lightning swells outward from the clicker's dish, enshrouding all nine people and me. Smoke rises from the arc suit as the people collapse to the floor with joints stiffer than boards.

The lightning dissipates. There's a residual tingling upon my kiln, yet something about the arc suit shields me from the lightning.

"Leo!" Jessica yells. "What in the high devils was that, grease stain!"

"Grease stain? Uh, we prefer the term 'programmer,' ma'am," Gary answers with a chuckle. "I'll have to remember to tell Pierce that one later, but yeah, don't worry, Officer. The clickers don't emit electricity like what is running through your house, so they're just stunned."

"Stunned!?" She points at the nine smoking figures. "They are literally smoldering!"

"I mean, yeah, but... well, it's not like if your dishwasher were broken because your girlfriend's psycho mother ruined it after thinking it would be a good place to spy on you. Then a few months later, you notice the dishwasher light is on, and your roommate would sometimes load it but forget to turn it on, so you do it for him..." A droplet of sweat rolls down Gary's cheek. "You know what, forget you heard any of that."

The clicker's eye shines onto Jessica, and its cogwheels spin. Lightning springs forth, building around the dish. I hesitate to assist Jessica; naught has transpired as I foresaw.

Gary's scouting orb glides nearer to Jessica. "Believe me, I'm not doing this because just because I am a corporate asshole; this is legitimately safer for both you and the Consortium's Solicitors. We have no idea what the effect of separating you from this vapor will be, and it's pretty clear it's influencing you to some capacity," he says to her.

Her eyes glance at the metal bar propping up the coffin. Gritting her teeth, she yells, "Fuck you!" She jerks the bar from its wedge and clubs the scout. Her blow sends the scout colliding into the clicker's sparking dish. Lightning blasts a corner of the Arcade, destroying a copepod platoon. The scout crashes into the floor and rolls to a halt next to me as the clicker retreats backward.

"Geez, how are you so strong?!" Gary shouts. The clicker buzzes as its dish showers the floor tiles in sparks, and its cogwheels slow to a pause. There's a visible dent in the dish's bottom-left corner. "The clicker needs a second to cool down, but the freaking scout might be fried."

"You better pray Leo's okay!" Jessica shouts, slinging the rod at the clicker.

The bar thumps against the clicker and tumbles to the tile with a clang. It rolls off toward the Arcade walls.

"Quit it!" There is a knocking sound from the scout, and a creak follows. Gary looks toward something out of his picture. "What is it, Karen? I'm sorta in the middle of something important."

A feminine whispers, "Heads up, Gary, Barrister Barlowe is heading your way." There's the squeak of a door closing.

"God in Light, Ballbuster Barlowe is coming. I thought he was going to be in a meeting all day! He must know I am in my office; he probably sent Karen to throw me off my game." Gary scoffs and then says, "Officer, I'm going to mute you for a second, so I won't be able to hear ya if you say something!"

"That's all you have to say to me, pencil-pushing coward!"

"Sorry, but this is one of those 'turn down the car radio so you can see better' situations."

While Jessica shouts various colorful curses at Gary, I study the idle clicker from my low angle upon the floor and notice a handle and hatch on its underside. I recall observing Lincoln and Pierce prepare a clicker for use and remember that the hatch secures the dish in place.

The scouting orb shakes. "Barlowe told me if I broke another scout, I would have to come in for the next dozen Sundays! My next Sunday off is already two months from now!" Gary shouts as the scout quivers. "Come on. Come on! Fly! Fly, you little bastard!"

Sparks spurt from a chink in the scout's armor. The chink is around the width of a coin, and I can see a blue radiance through it. My body unmoving, I push the cattail out through the arc suit's neck. In the vermillion haze, it resembles a molten eel swimming through a tide of ruby water. I spread the tendrils, grip the edge of the chink, and then wiggle the tendrils.

The scout tilts back and forth as I pry at its armor. "Well, it's at least moving a little," Gary groans.

A booming voice emanates from the scouting orb. "Gary, maintenance says your scout is malfunctioning again!"

Gary coughs, spitting a mouthful of liquid. "It's n-nothing, boss, uh, Barrister Barlowe, just a small glitch at Locality Central's Tortoise."

"I thought I told you to rename it Locality Central's Turtle. The creature there is not a tortoise, dingus!"

"Well, the paperwork already went through, so they refuse to change it without six months' notices..." I can hear the hesitation in Gary's voice as he continues, "But hey, Barrister Barlowe, it-it was deliberately ironic, y'know? Like, *haha*, it's not a tortoise, but you probably expected it to be... is-isn't it funny?"

"It's not funny. It's confusing," the man, whom I presume is Barlowe, grunts. "It's stupidly dangerous to subvert a Solicitor's expectations."

Gary and Barlowe continue their prattle as the scout's armor splits open, and I engulf a sliver of it. Flattening the tendrils, I force my cattail through the split and weave it deep into the scouting orb—oily red fluid squirts from the break as something inside rips at the cattail. Vermillion haze spills into the scout, restoring the cattail as fast as it is torn apart.

Someone hits their fist against a table, and then Barlowe screams, "Listen and listen well. Our contract with the Feds is the priority for the next couple of weeks, but after that, we are going to have an extraction crew move on your Locality and siphon the vapors! There's a lot of upper management who are interested in this, and they're riding my ass about it. So do your job, or I'll personally see to it that the Consortium drives your ass out of Chicago, and something tells me a little smartass like you will end up as nothing but monster shit and a pair of glasses."

"P-probably true, sir! I'll do my job, sir!"

My cattail wraps around something tubular inside the scout, and I squeeze, shattering it. Barlowe's shouts and Gary's cries fade as gleaming blue liquid oozes out and the scout's picture blackens. The clicker's eye swings toward the scout as I draw the last inch of cattail into the arc suit. *'I pray Gary and Barlowe's shouting was a coincidence and not the death throes of tiny people living inside the scouting orb.'*

The clicker's light gravitates toward Jessica. I motion toward a copepod platoon and then point at the ceiling above the clicker. The copepod platoon hurries into action. I push the cattail back through the arc suit's neck; I also poke my finger through the hole and start separating the helmet from the arc suit. With the opening in the suit's neck wide enough for the kiln's shell, I drift out and creep closer to the clicker.

There's a low hum as the clicker's cogwheels commence spinning. I crawl underneath the clicker. The smoking crimson cattail slithers within the vermillion haze; its aim is where the dish fastens to the clicker. The cattail's twitching tendrils unravel. *'One swift movement, Constance, like a lady knight.'*

I command the copepods above the clicker to fall as my cattail darts toward the hatch's handle. My tendrils enwrap the handle—I yank. The hatch skates open, severing the dish from the clicker. Sparks erupt from the clicker's underside. The sparks clear, unveiling the clicker's interior: thousands of bronze cogs so dense that not even a fingerbreadth goes unused. My eyes fix upon a glowing blue vial at the cogs' core.

Vaulting to my feet, I shove my arm into the grinding cogs as the fallen copepods crowd into the clicker. There's a deafening snap from the clicker's interior as it minces my arm.

The clicker darts upward, tearing my arm from its insides. My cattail ensnares it as it knocks against the ceiling. The clicker plunges earthward. I spring from its path as it bashes the top of the coffin—an antenna snaps from the clicker's frame. My cattail snakes into the clicker as I seize the broken antenna, jabbing it into the clicker's cogs.

The clicker whirls as the gears chew the antenna—my cattail spools around the clicker. I stumble forward, hugging the clicker and clinging to its antennas. The Arcade blurs as vermillion haze swirls into a vortex. My fingertips slip from the antenna. I sweep out of the vortex; my body flips parallel to the ground. I sail over Jessica's head, and my legs collide upon a column, rending them at my knees. My tendrils enwrap something inside the clicker.

I squeeze.

Deep blue haze rolls up the cattail and shards of blue glass eject from the orb. Light from the clicker bursts my cattail. The kiln's shell bounces off a column and skips across the tile floor. The Arcade's floor shreds my face. Sharp pain shoots through my kiln. I collide with something soft, bringing me to a halt.

"Guh!" someone yelps.

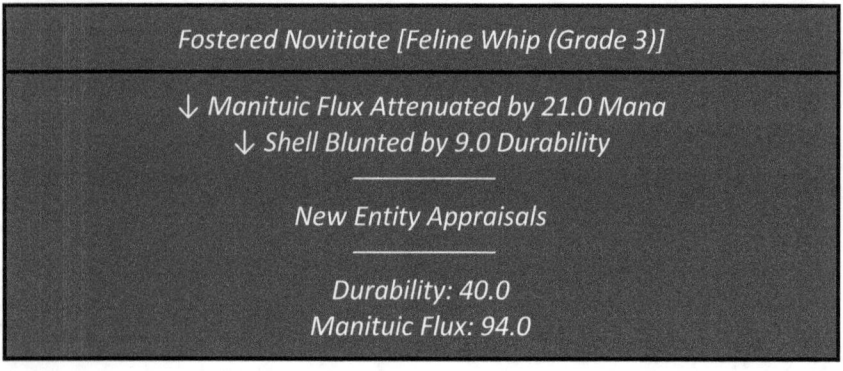

Fostered Novitiate [Feline Whip (Grade 3)]

↓ *Manituic Flux Attenuated by 21.0 Mana*
↓ *Shell Blunted by 9.0 Durability*

New Entity Appraisals

Durability: 40.0
Manituic Flux: 94.0

Chapter 18: Boot in the Mud

∞∞ ∞∞ ∞∞ ∞∞ ∞∞ ∞∞ ∞∞ ∞∞ ∞∞ ∞∞ ∞∞ ∞∞ ∞∞ ∞∞

> *Fostered Novitiate [Feline Whip (Grade 3)]*
>
> ↓ *Manituic Flux Attenuated by 21.0 Mana*
> ↓ *Shell Blunted by 9.0 Durability*
> ———
> *New Entity Appraisals*
> ———
> *Durability: 40.0*
> *Manituic Flux: 94.0*

Shaking my head, my flame-like hair sways, and I knock the blue wall away. Haze lurches toward me, mending my cheeks, jaw, and eye. If it was not for the Arcade being rife with vermillion haze, I might have lost everything when the clicker spun me in circles.

My eyesight returns to normal as something warm brushes against my kiln's shell. Beside me, I see Jessica's face a mere cubit's breadth from mine.[73] I tilt my head and look downward to discover that the place the Kiln struck was Jessica's trousered thigh. Blemishes surface on her trousers, unraveling the threads. Hopping to my feet, I back away; the area where the trousers were touching the kiln falls away, revealing a purplish-red bruise. I do not notice any infection on her bare leg, only the bruise.

Raising my hand, I wiggle my fingers, waving at her.

"You were what was in the welding suit, like, the whole time...?" she asks, blinking at me.

'She is less stunned than I anticipated. Most scream or are too stupefied for prattle.'

I place my index finger on my chin and bend over to peer into Jessica's hazel eyes. This is an excellent way to loosely judge a person's intentions

---

[73] Cubit's Breadth (Ancient English Units): 18 inches or 45.72 cm. Distance from the elbow to the middle finger.

and emotions. Observe and ask thyself: do they recoil, do their pupils shiver, do they become aggressive, and other such questions. It's not something I have done since I was a young child at the Hallow Equarié's Convent because most men ceased reacting to it and made lewd remarks instead. It still works on some women, though.

My fiery pink pupils reflect in Jessica's own. She gazes into mine; her eyes have a hint of a shiver, yet naught more than that. A mix of subtle fear and curiosity? Mayhaps she is merely donning a brave face, but nevertheless, acting in such a way is suspicious. When something such as myself gets this close, it is to be expected that the person would be afraid.

'From what I learned from Terra, creatures like me are an unknown amongst commonfolk. If I saw a creature such as myself in the past, I very well might have retched in fear. She has some type of personal experience with oddities, which makes her an unknown. I shall help her from beneath the coffin, yet I shan't be escorting her from the Arcade.' I straighten my back and take a few steps back. 'I have done more than enough.'

"H-hello," she says. "I'm Officer Valentine but call me Jessica."

I perform the thumbs-up gesture. 'Aye, I am aware.'

"...Can you tell me your name?" she asks, her fingers rubbing together.

Shaking my head, I peer downward at my cattail. Blue haze is running through it.

Jessica asks again, "Hey, can I ask for your name?"

I shake my head once more. My eyes trace the path of the unwound cattail, and it leads me to the clicker emitting pale blue smoke. Blue haze pours into the shell. A hot, nay, a burning sensation swells within the kiln.

Both the Cosmic System and Earl provide messages.

> *Elixir - Decoction Absorbed.*
> **Effect:** *Mana Encumbrance - 3H 20M*
> **Ramifications:** *-91% Mana Pool for an estimated 25H 32M upon loss of effects.*

Examining the two walls, I clench my fist and spin around. *'What? I cannot afford to lose cognition; there could be Consortium reinforcements! I must expend my mana!'* I withdraw the cattail from the inner remnants of the clicker. A stray lightning bolt shoots from within, striking the cattail's end—the last two feet of cattail burst, spattering the Arcade's tile in droplets of oily vermillion haze. *'Abominable device! Thou must be the devils' mantlepiece. Nigh killed me anew.'*

"What was that!?" Jessica shouts, gawking at the cattail's remains. "That... that rope around your neck i—"

I turn away. Witnessing this, Jessica bites her tongue and stares off into a corner. With the Arcade rife in vermillion haze, the cattail reforms, and I coil it around my torso. Whilst I step away to prepare for my departure, I glimpse Jessica stretching her arm toward me. "W-wait!" Jessica says, reaching for my ankle. "You're still gonna help me, right? Help me get out from under this freaking casket!?"

'I beg of thee, show patience!' Turning, I raise a finger and nod. *'I have no intention of relinquishing the coffin, if I can manage it, that is.'*

As if she can hear me, she breathes a sigh of relief. Her breath casts a cloud of vermillion haze in front of her.

The copepods are unhurried, and something else demands my attention—the pressure is growing in my kiln. I glance at a few items sprinkled about the Arcade: the coffin, the yellow tome, the ebony book, and the arc suit. *'I could learn something from all those items, the coffin most of all; moreover, there is a lot of vermillion haze I can make use of now that I have mana.'* Glancing at Jessica, I rush toward a sheet of white paper. *'I should warn her of what is about to occur.'*

The last pittance of the blue haze enters the kiln, and one of Earl's walls appears.

Earl Interface:

Assimilating 'Elixir Decoction'
Erysichthon abates 0
Essence value 0
0.0 Refinable Nebula
0.0 Refinable Vitrum

Details: *A mana-rich decoction. Difficult to harvest and complicated to produce.*

I am particularly curious about the blue substance, yet the purple wall furnishes scant information. The most noteworthy words are "harvest" and "produce."

My kiln aches, feeling so bloated that I earnestly wonder whether or not it might burst. Looking down, I can see the flame within it burning far brighter than usual. *'Prithee, Status, Cosmic System!'*

Name: Constance Nightingale
Race: Kiln
Seed Type: Tower [Germination]
Variant: Oort Stained Glass
Forms: [Vaporous] [Lucent: *Unviable*]
Shell Level: 1
Flame Level: 1 (Develop Beyond Germination)
Durability: 43.2/49
Mana: 396.8/230 [115/115 Manituic Flux]
Erysichthon: 00/100
Quintessence: Corrupting Oort Cloud
Adaptations: [Cattail Tendrils] [Comrade Cracker] [Throng of Haze] [Negating Membrane]
Skills: [Feline Whip (Nov-3)] [Gluttonous Naturalist (Nov-3)] [Supine Humorism (Nov-0)] [Tenebrous Stealth (Nov-4)] [Scrounger (Asp-1)] [Mana Compression (Asp-0)]
Titles: [Parasitic Thief +] [Trailblazer (Humorism)]

Chronicles

'Copepods! I must construct copepods to use mana!' Vermillion haze flows into me, and copepods emerge, falling one by one from the kiln's shell. Bending down, I grab two sheets of white paper. I rush toward the plash of water near the barrels and dip the cattail into it. The cattail's oily surface drips, staining the puddle of water red. 'The cattail's coating is thick enough that I may use it as if it is ink. Why did I not think of this earlier?'

Taking one sheet of paper, I fold it a few times and then dip the paper's sharp edge into the cattail's red ink. The white paper absorbs much of the ink, dyeing it red, but I can make it work sufficiently. Lowering myself, I use the edge of the paper to write a short message for Jessica. "Good morrow, Jessica. As per our agreement, I shall save thee from the Consortium's custody. Do not be fearful, and do not struggle. This shan't be enjoyable for me either."

I stare at the message. To be frank, it looks as if someone scribbled their last will and testament in their own blood. 'It shall have to do. Now, I need something that will allow the copepods to survive in the cold, windy weather for as long as possible.' My gaze veers toward plastic blankets strewn about the floor; these have been at the back of my mind. The mere fact that the Arcade is retaining such a large amount of vermillion haze is proof of their effectiveness. 'Jessica first, then blankets.'

With a small nod, I rush to Jessica. Her bloodshot eyes are wide, darting from left to right. She has her hand over her mouth, attempting to stifle any unintended cries that might escape. I hold the message before her, and she recoils, blinking a few times. 'Apologies for the copepods, though admittedly it makes me strangely delighted that thou art more fearful of them than me... but that is not important, read this!'

Jessica stares at the paper for a time, glances at me, and then back at the message. "I have a little experience teaching English. If you wanted, I could probably teach you how to write in English," she says, blinking at the paper. "O-oh, wait, I think this is English. It's just nearly unreadable."

'Thy face is unreadable! Even with such horrid ink, my handwriting is magnificent! I practiced quite a lot thou shouldst knowest...! Be calm, Constance, she knows not what she says.' Squinting at Jessica, I point at two particular sections: "save thy freedom" and "do not be afraid."

She gazes at it, then me, then at the kiln that has copepods crawling on it, and back at the paper. "Why don't you just use a pen? There is no way I can read this," she states, pointing at a white stick on the ground.

'Pen?' I think back to the time I saw Pierce using a similar object. 'Pen!?'

"Hey... were you responsible for these bugs the whole time?"

With a wave of my hand, I rush over to the white stick. 'This is not the time for such frivolous, unimportant, and difficult to answer questions!'

Seizing the pen, I inspect it to discern how to operate it. It seems simple enough with only the word "Sidhe's Economy" written on the side. Flipping it over, I can see one side has some sort of ball. I notice some black ink still stuck to the end. I hurry to Jessica and take the paper. Lowering myself, I place the paper against the ground. I expect the ink to run dry quickly, so I try to keep my words short, yet Sidhe's pen acts as if its ink is endless. Somehow, I manage to rewrite everything as best I can with the wondrous pen.

'I shall take Sidhe's pen with me also!' I stand and hand Jessica the rewritten letter.

She takes the note; her eyes run over the letters a few times. "Hell, this cursive looks like something you'd see inscribed on a dried-out scroll in a cave that's been sealed for a thousand years. It even has some Old English in it. How do you write like this?"

'Old... Old English!?' I reach to rip the paper from her hands, but she jerks it away. 'Thou art the old English, New World rebel!'

"S-sorry, I was just curious. I got the gist of what you were trying to say, but I haven't finished reading. I'll prepare myself for whatever it is you're about to do. Try anyway."

'...I do not appreciate thy criticism of my penmanship.' I spin around and survey the room.

Outside, I hear Lincoln and Pierce whispering. 'I could write to those two with this!' I think, staring at the endless wonder. Retrieving another sheet of paper, I am about to scribble an epistle, but I pause for a moment.

'Terra would assumably say this is the sort of circumstance where I should use the 'u-word'... but I refuse! This is my domain, so I shall use what words I desire.'

I write the epistle.

To the gentlemen bearing the names Lincoln and Pierce,
Thy folk shall remain unharmed, but I insist that none trespass
upon the Arcade. Any injuries wrought were by the item dubbed
'clicker' and the person named Gary. Heretofore, I was
exceedingly courteous with my behavior toward thy 'newbies' and
'wannabes' as they are commonly designated. Given the
aforementioned benignity, requital is fitting on this occasion.
In closing, do not intrude.

I do not sign my name. My preference is to remain nameless unless I intend to maintain a lasting acquaintanceship. It is easier that way if I ever elect to disappear.

Assembling a platoon, I approach a Consortium woman, roll up the epistle, and slide it into her attire, allowing it to poke out so it is noticeable. 'Drag her through the archway,' I command, pointing at the woman and then the Arcade's back entranceway. 'I do not fancy this quandary.'

My eyes drift to the floor around me, and I see naught but copepods encircling me. Their numbers have grown to a troublesome degree. I am not certain, but they must be approaching a thousand. Thinking for a moment, I realize I have never attempted to combine copepods after creating them. My finger moves between two copepods.

'Soldiers, join together!' Both copepods charge at one another; they collide, and their bodies unite. As the haze settles, it reveals a copepod rivaling the fat rats of the chamber pot tunnels. 'It succeeded! This is fantastic; it shall be my solution!'

The Arcade plunges further into delirium as hundreds of copepods charge one another. As they reach a certain size, I stop them from merging and call them to the side. Haze settles, leaving me with four giant copepods ranging in size from a large hound to an adolescent mule.

"Umbral's shadow, those are enormous!" Jessica shouts. She shoves at the table and coffin. "Let me out! Being trapped with these things around is cruel and unusual!"

I wave my hand at Jessica. *'I forewarned thee before I began! I do not wish to worry about thy location whilst I work.'*

Jessica protests, yet I do not acknowledge it this time.

Directing some copepods, I flip the metal tables onto their tops. I then rush to a corner, retrieve a plastic blanket, and throw it over them. This makes them appear as if they are some sort of lumpy mass, and that is all I shall require. I repeat this with each table in the Arcade, save for the one atop Jessica's chest. When I finish, four plastic tables cloak both tables and copepods.

Fostered Aspirant [Scrounger (Grade 2)]

'Ah, as usual, a welcome boon.' I dismiss the wall with a subtle nod.

Noticing my kiln's pressure has diminished, I check my Status to find my mana is now below two hundred. I order the any new arrivals to marry, giving me another copepod the size of an adolescent donkey; this raises my numbers to five large copepods and two legions. Grappling another table, I toss it on the back of the new copepod and cover it in a plastic blanket.

A small clack catches my attention. I glance over, noticing the jar with the pink copepod with "giant sea louse" written upon it. A thought crosses my mind: *'Would a different variety of copepod offer an adaptation?'*

Untwisting the cattail, I spread the tendrils. I turn my head away and drag the glass jar into the haze. The copepod bounces about as I raise my cattail and smash the jar upon the Arcade's tiles. Like air escaping a kettle, a tiny squeak leaks from the copepod as it dissolves inside the haze.

Along with the delectable taste, a purple wall appears.

I read the box and then say, '*Prithee, Earl, show me any adaptations thou advisest as well as any that may include the "coral louse."*'

due to their initial size, they cannot be produced directly. Instead, the user must cultivate them in a haze-rich environment outside of their form.

[Cost: 131 Essence + 5.3 Refined Nebula + 1.1 Refined Vitrum]

Available Dress Adaptations

Snappish Beads
(Recent Feat: Mana Compression)

Generate a beaded chain around the user's left shoulder by becoming a host to two modified species of salmonella bacteria—one specializing in exuding crude Acerb, the other in bleeding crude Acrid. Each bead is capable of caching surpluses of any of the four haze types. Surplus is released when Acerb and Acrid blend, but rather than explode, they'll counteract, leaving nothing behind except salt and any absorbed haze. The cache size can vary depending on haze variety.

Forewarning: Adaptation will rapidly sponge 56 Erysichthon of haze. Ensure the atmospheric or bodily haze levels are at suitable abundances before adapting.

[Cost: 53 Essence + 1.3 Refined Nebula + 1.2 Refined Acerb + 0.7 Refined Vitrum + 0.4 Refined Acrid]

Grease Spattered Gown +
(Recent Meal: Fried Potato Wedges)

Emits an irresistible stench consisting of greasy fats, oils, and starches. Rodents and other such scavenging vermin will be lured to the user's location. The effect grows more prominent as time passes, but the longer the user dwells in one area, the more cautious creatures will become of the enticing aroma. Ultimately, they may learn to fear the scent of grease rather than covet it.

[Cost: 111 Essence + 7.1 Refined Nebula + 0.4 Refined Vitrum]

Available Armament 'Cattail' Adaptations
Cannot Afford/None Recommended

Available Miscellaneous Adaptations

Deliciously Steamed Monkey

(Recent Meal: Snow Monkey | **Recent Meal:** Elixir Decoction)

When hot steam bathes the user's shell, a dew will build on the surface. This dew isn't water but rather the kiln's rife paste in a fluid form. The consumer of this dew can expect a brief bump in mana and copepod production. Unintended effects may occur if shared with an individual who possesses a low Constitution stat or has yet to be inducted into the Cosmic System Beta. This adaptation does not enhance the user's resistance to liquids.

[Cost: 59 Essence + 1.8 Refined Nebula + 1.1 Refined Vitrum]

Note: Sample squandered. Re-consumption is necessary if the user desires to acquire.

Essence Available: 66 [R = 64%]
Refined Nebula Available: 6.4 (5.0)
Refined Vitrum Available: 5.0 (5.0)
Refined Acerb: 1.5 (0.0)
Refined Acrid: 0.4 (0.0)

My eyes explore Earl's wall, searching for an adaptation that includes the coral louse. At the same time, I commence creating more copepods to supplement any of my losses. Once outside the Arcade, I suspect they do not last long without protection or vermillion haze to sustain them.

In the skin adaptation category, I locate the adaptation I am curious about. *'Aye, so it is possible to expand my flock of copepods! That some adaptations might have superior variants of themselves is vital information that I shall have to sear into my mind. But this one is far too costly.'*

With little leisure to tarry, I run my sights over the remaining choices Earl recommends. *'The "grease spattered gown"—I have no desire for an adaptation that shall make me reek of grease, particularly when I cannot even smell anything myself. I could never be certain I smelled or not. "Deliciously steamed monkey" is intriguing yet not useful at the moment, and does Earl expect me to eat Gentleman Ape? Lastly, the "snappish beads" adaptation uses many of my resources, but... that is very beneficial for me, and I have never been offered an adaptation for a feat before. I suppose I shall ponder adaptations whilst I prepare to depart.'*

A spark leaps from the scouting orb, reminding me that there is more of the "Elixir Decoction." I check my mana and find it has dipped to under a hundred. *'So many enormous copepods are using a lot of mana. I shall require more!'* Seizing some fabric with the cattail, I toss it unto the sap-like Elixir, scoop as much as I can into the cloth, and then engulf it. The blue haze flows into the Kiln, and the burning returns, so I craft more copepods.

> *Elixir - Decoction Absorbed.*
> *Effect: Mana Encumbrance - 2H 48M*
> *Ramifications: -92% Mana Pool for an estimated 28H 39M upon loss of effects.*

> *Earl Interface:*
> *Assimilating 'Elixir Decoction'*
> *Erysichthon abates 0*
> *Essence value 0*
> *0.0 Refinable Nebula*
> *0.0 Refinable Vitrum*
>
> *Details: A mana-rich decoction. Difficult to harvest and complicated to produce.*

'The ramifications grow worse. Not quite as severe as the first time I swallowed Elixir, but that may be because I consumed much less Elixir than I did previously and tried to expend the mana before it rose too high.' Pushing the walls away, I glance around. Much of the Arcade's Vermillion haze now resides within copepods, making it far easier to see. I look toward the five large copepods cloaked beneath the plastic blankets. *'I should bestow a new title upon them when they reach this size; thus, I shall refer to them as sumpter copepods!'*[74]

My attention returns to Jessica. It is time to free her and take ownership of the coffin. I know the coffin is too weighty for me to lift, so I must ensure it is secure on a copepod's back from the beginning. If the coffin tumbles off, my chances of stealing it will be nil as I cannot imagine I shall have the time nor capability of attempting this anew.

---

[74] Sumpter: A pack animal; typically, a mule.

I call forth my copepods and assess our situation. Jessica lies on her back, and upon her chest is the silver table pressing against her bosom. The table itself rests tabletop down, the legs skyward toward the ceiling. The coffin leans at an incline, wedged at an angle between the two pairs of table legs. If the coffin was a compass's needle and the table was facing the north, the coffin would be facing the north-east, but a bit closer to north than east. It being wedged like this, as well as the weight of the iron coffin itself, prevents it from skating about.

Taking eight copepods, I unite them into a large pair of two. Then, I point at four copepods and order them to merge into a medium pair of two. Finally, I summon two copepods of small size. Arranging them, I order the small pair to the table's back, the medium pair to the middle, and the large to the front.

Jessica goggles the copepods with her arms spread to allow space for the larger pair. The copepod's front appendages twitch as they shuffle nearer to her until they are an eyelash's length from her torso. I nod and then command the excess copepods surrounding me to merge into all the pairs arranged beneath the table. Each merging increases their size, lifting the table and coffin a little more. I grow the pairs until the copepods nearest Jessica are the size of hounds, the center the size of mousers, and the back two are the size of large rats.

"I think I might be able to scramble out from underneath it!" Jessica remarks.

I hold up a hand and then use my cattail to tether the coffin's back to assist if necessary.

Jessica's mouth falls open. "It's a tentacle!?"

'...' Bending downward, I pluck a torn piece of fabric near my heel and toss it at Jessica. *'I do not possess a tentacle! Speak no more of tentacles!'*

"...Sorry?" She places her palms flat against the floor, twists her feet to be flat against the ground, and forces herself backward. Her feet bump the table as they slip out, causing the copepods to flounder. A rat-sized copepod in the back bursts, and I jerk the cattail upward to compensate.

Grabbing onto the table, Jessica helps support the swaying table and coffin. A fresh copepod squirms into its crushed brethren's place, stabilizing things. I perform the thumbs-up gesture at Jessica. *'Thy aid is appreciated.'*

She leaps to her feet. Whilst breathing wearily, she stumbles away, gawking at the copepods and cattail. "Thanks for helping me; I'll find a way to repay you," Jessica says. Her boots kick a loose plastic sheet, unveiling a mask. "The gas mask is still here." She dons the mask and hurries to her partner Leo's side.

Consolidating more copepods, I manage to use them to secure the coffin's balance. I order hundreds of copepods underneath the table's center. They converge, and a sumpter is born with a table and coffin saddling its back. *'That demanded more haze than I foresaw. I wonder if the copepods squander haze as they merge?'*

With the coffin's burden pressing down upon the sumpter's back and the table, they both distort into a bowl-like shape. The coffin is beyond the burden the haze should carry, so I do not foresee this 'coffin sumpter' surviving long outside the Arcade. If I hope the sumpters to reach my hermitage, I shall have to feed it copepods as we travel.

The coffin sumpter complete, my eyes search the Arcade for anything of worth. I look toward the floor and sink to my knees, collecting bestrewn sheets of white paper. *'Some of these papers are dirtied, yet they are all valuable to me, marred or not. This era is so wasteful with its things. I should ask Terra if she knows where I may acquire more paper, next we meet. I pray she is unharmed and in good health.'* In my peripheral, I notice a tan board that has several papers affixed to it by a silver fastener. I turn and take it in hand, reading the words "Deputy Clippie" on the silver fastener. *'This is valuable as well; I shan't have to use the cave's floor to write any longer.'*

"They're all paralyzed like that Gary guy said they were." I flinch, spinning around to find Jessica shining a torch in Leo's eyes. She stands, examining the copepods. "What are you planning to do with these giant beetles?"

'Beetles? They are my steadfast soldiers!' I glance at the copepods, whose antennas twitch. *'...But thou mayst refer to them as beetles if that is thy wish.'* I set the white papers I amassed next to the coffin and then make use of

Deputy Clippie and Sidhe's pen, writing, "I am preparing to depart. Once I have fled, wait a moment, and then secure thy own egress."

"Wait, you're just planning to take your bugs and skedaddle?" she asks in a muffled voice. She moves a finger between herself and Leo. "That guy said they were going to detain us, and police or not, the Consortium owns entire law firms' worth of lawyers. They'll get away with it."

Flipping to the next white paper, I continue writing, "It's reasonable to believe Consortium reinforcements shall be hereabouts soon, and I shan't permit thee to follow me. If thou departest after me, they likely shan't notice thy presence." I toss the paper to the floor. *'I need to flee to the cave, and I cannot be diverted for what may be a fool's errand. Apologies, Jessica!'*

"'Thou', 'thy', 'shan't'— what is this, some kind of Shakespearean play?" She rubs her temples with a sigh and then stares off into the corner of the Arcade. "I have a question for you."

My head snaps toward her. *'Shakespearean? As in Shakespeare? Why doth she knoweth the lecherous William's surname... Different fellow, I am certain.'*

Ignorant of my thoughts, Jessica continues, "Are you the only..." She gestures at me, waving her hands around, stirring the haze around her. "...'thingy' in Central Park?"

"'Thingy!?' I am no thingy!' I cross my arms. *'Verily, I may in truth be a "thing," nevertheless, I do not desire anyone to refer to me as such!'*

Jessica massages the spiderweb of crimson veins that protrude past the limits of her mask. I can see a glimmer of worry, but she suppresses it by biting her lip. "Uhh, sorry, I just mean, is there another one of your 'people' around, not a red one like you, but a jet black one?"

My arms unfurl and sink to my sides. *'...She is aware of my sable form! Calm! Calm.'* I shake my head and shrug. *'I know naught of what thou speakest.'*

Jessica raises an eyebrow. "Because my partner and I have been trying to gather information on it for a few weeks now."

I tip my head and then shrug once again. *'Has information regarding my existence spread far!? Good lord, perhaps I should bar the cave and never leave...! I suppose I should not be so astonished, but I held the belief the Consortium and the Hex Church operated with more secrecy.'*

"Listen, I'm no moron. I know a pair of 'ghost-people' can't run around the same area without being aware of one another." Jessica hesitates before continuing, "I want to help you, both of you, if possible."

Pausing, I turn to her and scribble, "Thou wishest to help?"

"That's right." She wiggles her eyebrows. "I wishest."

"Couldst thou elaborate, mayhaps?"

"Of course, I can."

I write, "Then tease me with thy words no longer," and raise a hand in questioning.

Smirking, she nods. "I doubt you have much of a social life—no offense—so I don't mind telling you."

I nod. *'I live in a cave.'*

She sighs. "Y'see, Red, the city isn't in the best place, and some of us officers have been worried about that. There are a lot of rumors and gossip going around on the internet and... well, just in general. Uhm, do you want the long or short story? I don't know how much time we really have to chitchat."

I nod once more, scribbling, "As detailed as it must be; however, I also must prepare to depart whilst thou speakest."

Jessica shrugs as I turn to retrieve the frock that harbors the tome and book.

"So, with things not exactly going very well, a lot of us officers have prepared some contingency plans. You know, just in case things continue to get worse, and I suspect they are, almost positive as a matter of fact." She steps aside as I walk by with the frock, tome, and book. "What I want to know is if you have any interest in being a part of that with us?"

I toss the items onto the copepod's back and then tilt my head. "Thou wishest for me take part in thy 'contingency plan?' Thou understand I am no longer wearing a costume? This is what I truly am. Why wouldst thou desirest my company?"

"There's a lot of us, but all of us involved are open-minded people, and I'd vouch for you and your trustworthiness to everybody. You'd be well looked after and treated fairly. I've heard rumors you or something like you has been seen rummaging through trashcans for food. With us, you wouldn't have to live so desperately anymore."

My eyelids narrow. "Thou knowest me not. Why wouldst thou promise such things?"

Jessica tilts her head. "I... I mean, you helped me out, and I really do appreciate that. As long as you never betray my trust, I'll do my best never to betray yours."

"Thou speakest of trust, but thou hast not earned my trust to betray it."

"True, true, but if you give me a chance, maybe I can, Red."

"I am not so credulous."

She squints, reading my words. "Does that say credulous? Like as in gullible? What does that mean? Why are you so suspicious of me? Isn't it lonely having to hide all the time? Wouldn't you like to get to know some people...?"

"Loneliness is irrelevant." I gesture at her noble's police's attire and then write, "Thou approaches me wearing the uniform of this land's boot and makes the presumption that they can easily earn the mud's trust."

"...I don't understand."

"Thou art the authority of this land; thy uniform is that of the placer of bootprints. I am the mud, and I bear many bootprints."

"So you're saying you don't trust the police? This uniform comes off every night—it's not me." Her eyes narrow a frustrated huff escapes her. "My hands aren't clean by any means, and I have a plethora of both professional and personal regrets, but I do everything I do because I believe in it." She pauses and relaxes her expression. "All I can give you right this second is my word, Red."

"Words back all bootprints. That is why they hurt and why their soles leave an impress upon the mud."

"Maybe I understand you better than you think. But you really don't know me, though, Red."

"And thou dost not knowest me. Thus, we arrive where we began. I do not appreciate being approached under the assumption that I am so desperate and lonely that my trust is ripe for the plucking by any passerby. I am not so simple that I shall throw myself to the feet of any who are willing to tolerate me."

I step away to retrieve the arc suit and drag it toward the coffin sumpter. Passing by the lap-top, I take it into my arms and tuck it into the arc suit. My cattail grabs the arc suit and places it atop the sumpter.

"...Hey, uh, I really didn't think of what I said in the same way you did. I'm sorry." She brushes the vermillion vanes around her eyes. "Maybe this gas is messin' with my head. I wasn't thinking about how my words might come off, I guess."

"Do not worry thyself. Mayhaps we are cut from the same cloth, but I do not feel as such at the moment. Those cut from my cloth are slow to trust."

She smiles warily. "I think we share more qualities than you believe." Walking away, she goes to retrieve Leo from the Arcade's floor. "Could be that I was just making an exception for you because I thought I felt something, Red."

I glance back, nod, and then resume my preparations.

Motioning at the arc suit, I order all remaining copepods into it, where I shall join them. I retrieve an additional blanket, spread it across the coffin sumpter, and dip beneath the blanket as it settles atop the legs of the upturned table. I slide into the arc suit, pretending the tickling on my kiln is beautiful rose petals. Being beneath the blankets reminds me of being in a tent if someone chose to make a tent from a flimsy material like plastic. Now there are six sumpters with plastic blankets draped over them, causing all six to appear identical at a glance.

Hidden from Jessica and with vermillion haze in abundance, a thought crosses my mind. *'The Snappish Beads adaptation; now would be the finest time to acquire it, whilst vermillion haze envelops me... My greatest weakness is my Erysichthon, as far as I am concerned, which makes it an essential adaptation. Earl, prithee, the Snappish Beads adaptation.'*

The kiln's flame swells, brightening the shapes of the copepods underneath the blanket. A rich muddle of orange and white haze spews from the kiln and sails up my torso. I lean forward and watch as it amasses at my neckline. Small bumps arise as the orange and white haze clash with one another. They condense and marry, forming beads that coil around the right side of my nape, over my left shoulder, and loops under my armpit. It is as if I wear a loose necklace alongside a band that enwraps the underside of my arm. Two strings of beads join the band to the necklace, and from those strings dangle chains of beads that drape over my shoulder and collar.

Scooting forward, I raise the edge of the plastic blanket. Haze surges in and toward my shoulder, and chains of red and pink beads drape across my left shoulder. Each bead in the chain has its own unique red and pink pattern. As I brush them with my fingertips, I admit they resemble the cattail, a mess of oil and haze. I attempt to lift the beads, but they refuse to budge. *'As with all the other adaptations, it is not a necklace, but rather, a part of my body.'* My fingers continue to fumble with the wee spheres as I take stock of my items. *'It is time; now I shall learn whether I made a wise decision lingering so long or if I have been too ambitious... and, I suppose, greedy.'*

I glance up to see Jessica standing with Leo slung over her shoulders like a scarf. "I knew you wouldn't leave without saying goodbye." She bounces Leo on her shoulders and smiles at me. "He feels a little light. I guess the low-carb diet I recommended is paying off. Leo's basically my foster dad, so I'd like if he sticks to and stays around awhile, y'know?"

Tilting my head, I pause, staring at the two. *'Foster...? Nay. I know her not.'* I shake my head, removing Deputy Clippie and Sidhe's pen. "Take care of thy family; good health is vital. It is time for me to depart. Farewell," I scribble.

"Yeah, but, hey..." She takes a stop closer, raising a hand to stop me. "I want to warn you about a few things before you take off. I want to make sure you stay safe."

I adjust my writing posture. "Forewarnings can be invaluable. What is it thou believest demands my vigilance?"

"There are a few factions active in or around Central Park. One is the Espositos." Rolling her eyes, she continues, "You won't have any contact with them; I can almost guarantee it. They're an absolute shipwreck right now and aren't in any position to do anything to anybody. Believe me, Leo and I both know. The primary people you need to really look out for are Galtry and their Syndicate. The Galtry Syndicate operates everything from prostitution rings to narcotic labs to violence for hire. They even employ ex-soldiers and retired mercenaries to do their dirty work. Thugs, druggies, wannabe assassins, they are all-around bad people out for nobody but themselves." She scoffs. "And amazingly, their leader is pretty famous and admired by a lot of people—essentially a criminal celebrity. A narcissistic murderer that everyone's just *fascinated* by; I don't get it personally. Just do like I do and avoid getting involved with them no matter what. The Galtry Syndicate is the quickest way to end up as fish food."

"I believe I understand the heart of thy words. Galtry is an immoral person not to be trifled with. Thou sayst there are a few? Is there a third faction?"

"Yeah, there's one more that I'm aware of. The third faction is, uhm..." Her eyes glance at Leo as he lets out a soft groan. She pauses, and her lips curve into an apologetic smile. "The third faction is an enigma. They seem to have everyone's long-term best interest in mind but operate in secrecy. I don't really think they'd have any reason to mess with you, though, Red. As long as you keep doing what you're doing and don't start making big waves or anything, they have no reason to be confrontational. In all honesty, they'd be sympathetic to you."

"Sympathetic to me? But thou art not willing to even speak their name?"

She shakes her head. "No, it's not that I'm not willing. It's just not the kind of conversation that's safe to have surrounded by Consortium tech. They might be recording our conversation or listening to us right now; I have no idea. But if we run into each other again, we can talk in a more secluded place. I'll tell you what I know then, but I don't feel comfortable talking about them here. If you want, I can arrange to meet you sometime?"

"Apologies, but I am not interested at the moment. I shall find thee if I change my mind."

"That's fine. I understand." Her eye drifts to my neckline. "Oh? Where did you find those shoulder pearls?" she asks. "They're pretty snazzy. They look good on you."

"I thank thee for thy compliment and thy forewarnings. We should flee." I set both Deputy Clippie and Sidhe's pen aside and then command the six sumpters through the Arcade's archways. The sumpter's legs spasm as they place one appendage in front of the other. I lie inside the opened arc suit atop the coffin sumpter. *'Time is scarce. To the hermitage, my sumpter copepods!'*

"Hope we see each other again soon, Red," Jessica says behind me. "Until then, good luck and take care of yourself."

My sumpter copepods pass underneath the Arcade's archways, and I poke my head out from beneath the plastic blanket draped over its back. With my head poking out, I pretend my lower body is not beneath a blanket chock-full of vermillion copepods.

We step further onto the Terrace. The plastic blankets that are fastened to the fences lazily flutter in the breeze, thumping against each other. With six sumpters, I place five of them in a formation that resembles an arrowhead and then one at the center. So there is one at the front, one to its left and right, followed by a final two at the back. I rub my palms together. Placing them in this order is, in truth, trickery. Naturally, they would expect me to travel upon the sumpter at the center, but my coffin sumpter has taken a position at the far back left corner.

Lowering my eyelids, I look to the sky; it is swathed in sheets of white clouds but otherwise empty. I would guess I spent at least an hour in the Arcade since the day has grown beyond the morningtide.

I point. *'Let us continue our advance.'* Approaching the barrier of fences, I direct them to charge and push them down. The slowest charge conceivable commences as we shove the fences, sending them into a sluggish tumble. *'Flee to the north-west, toward the arched bridge. Then we shall go our separate ways to split their attention...'* I shut my right eyelid to regain my vermillion sight in one eye. *'And I suppose I shall have to repeat all that since the sumpters shan't remember any of it.'*

Being at the rear, the coffin sumpter and I scuttle within a palm of a fence...

I hear a breath.

White smoke strokes my cheek—the cattail answers. A person's figure skirts the burning-red cattail. An arm digs deep into the arc suit. Copepods burst, spraying haze from the arc suit.

I feel icy skin and silky fabric brush my Kiln. My hand grasps the assailant. They break my grip. Something yanks from my neck, scattering one of my eyes. Tendrils snare flesh as haze mends my sight.

Before me, I see a hand enwrapped by tendrils, yet that same hand crushes the cattail between its fingers. It's as if predator has become prey.

Looking up, I find a man with sleepy eyes and messy black hair, wearing a black suit with a mask hanging from his neck. Lincoln, the Consortium's Solicitor. One hand holds the cattail hostage, whilst his other carries the lap-top I pilfered moments earlier. Jerking his hand, he snaps the cattail, turning it oil upon the Terrace. He tucks the lap-top under his arm, removes a handkerchief from his breast pocket, and wipes his fingers of my hazy oil.

I draw the cattail back, and with my vermillion vision, I see that his arm and chest are ruby red. The rest of his body is the familiar light red.

Sighing, he looks up and stares into my eyes. "Y'know, I was having the best hobo-hash in New York City before being made to rush over here." He rubs the handkerchief under his fingernails and shakes his head. "It's basically the only perk of being assigned this municipality, and I didn't even get to put it in a to-go box. Peggy won't make me another one."

My cattail's stump wags, raising the plastic blanket and allowing the haze underneath to reconstruct it. *'This is dire... Lincoln is absurdly quick.'* My haze feels as if it is trembling. *'Is he malicious?'* Without a word, we examine one another. Lincoln was able to seize the lap-top before I could react. He startled me, yet it was far too swift. His gaze drifts downward toward my chest. I believe he is observing the haze, but I raise an arm, shielding my shoulders. *'This... I do not wear this gown by my own choosing.'*

He rolls his eyes, yet I catch a faint blush upon his cheeks. His cigarette burns, and another puff of smoke escapes the corner of his lips. Flicking his cigarette to the brick, he snuffs it with his heel and then lifts the mask that hangs around his neck. Adjusting the mask, his hand reaches into his coat. My plastic blanket blows, the end of it slapping the side of his mask. Copepods gather at my sides, peering at Lincoln.

His eyes shift between the copepods, and a soft sigh escapes him. "Spooky," he remarks.

He draws a familiar epistle; it is the one I penned and sent them earlier. Flexing his fingers, he exposes a second epistle behind mine. He returns the one I wrote to his pocket. Removing what I believe is a black pen from his pocket, he scribbles some more words onto the other epistle and then holds the epistle and pen toward the cattail.

'...' The cattail grasps it. I bend the cattail, drawing the paper and pen to me. I take the two items and read the short, simple message. "Thanks for going easy on the newbies at the zoo," it says with an additional messy line beneath it. "Valuable Consortium tech carries trackers and sound emitters."

Lincoln performs a writing motion with his hand. "I know you can't speak. Can you hear?" he asks, his low voice softened by his mask.

I nod.

"Fantastic. I guess you wrote the note then."

Staring at the paper, I reposition myself, drop my hand from my chest, stuff my gown's hem back into the arc suit, and then place the paper against the table's back. As pen meets paper, I realize Lincoln's pen is much better than mine and bears the name "Sidhe's Indulgence." It has a sharp golden tip reminiscent of a quill, and the pen's stem is a lacquered ebony, reflecting both my pink and purple eye. Lincoln's pen is even apt at writing without Deputy Clippie's assistance.

My eyes float between Lincoln and the pen as I write, "What art thou attempting?"

"I'm not attempting anything. I figured you'd try and slip out this way, only realized you had snagged a computer when you got closer. Now, I'll toss a question back at you. What is it you want?" he asks with sharp eyes. "Your answer is critical to your health."

I peek at the cattail that waves in the air. Although Lincoln has not spared it a glance, I can see his fingers twitch each time it wiggles in his direction. Eyeing Lincoln, I write, "To live unconfined and as I desire." I hold my scribbles toward Lincoln so that he can read them. While he stares at my words, I flip the pen in my hand and slip it beneath me. It has a new owner.

"Generic, but good penmanship." His eyes dim. "What you desire is the same thing everyone desires," he says, gesturing vaguely about the Terrace. "And I wouldn't call it an answer to my question."

Withdrawing my Sidhe's Economy, I respond, "My answer is the answer thou wilt receivest from any who know what it is to be confined and entrapped."

"No, I think I understand that fully." He smirks. "Let me clarify, not that I don't appreciate your poeticisms, but I meant in a more literal sense. What do you want with Bethesda Arcade and Terrace?"

"My answer is much the same. For it to help me live unconfined and as I desire."

"Does your 'desire to live unconfined' encroach on others' desire to live?" he says, his smirk waning.

"I do not have that intention."

We stare at one another in silence.

He crams his handkerchief back into his breast pocket. "A little under a week ago, I told my partner there were worse places than Manhattan, but that may not be true for long. Manhattan is unsalvageable—this city is done for. What you're looking for may be impossible to find here. Not that I ever could find what you want anywhere myself."

From a black device affixed to Lincoln's belt, I hear Pierce's voice ask, "Lincoln, where'd you go? We need to move on the Arcade."

"I don't have what would qualify as an appropriate way to capture you alive, but I'm supposed to bring you in by any means," Lincoln says with a shrug. "But I'm not exactly a model employee, and I sorta feel like I owe you." He tips his head and then holds out a hand. "I do want my pen back, though. It's refillable, and I just bought the ink, so I'd like to hang on to it."

Putting one arm behind my back, I use the other to retrieve the Sidhe's Luxury pen from underneath me. I hold the pen toward him. *'I had no intention of keeping it; I simply neglected to return it!'*

"Your sleight of hand lacks some finesse. It's decent and well-practiced, but it's obvious you're self-taught. It needs polish." Taking the pen, he turns. His footsteps thump against the snowy stone path. "Good luck chasing what you 'desire,' I guess. Oh, and don't make me regret this."

Drawing the cattail close, it perches atop my head, coiling into an aggressive stance. *'The people born in this era are all mad; common folk no longer exist. But what does he know of this city's fate to claim it is doomed...? It matters not. I must depart, and Lincoln is unpredictable. If I am blessed, we shan't meet again... Also, my sleight of hand is nigh flawless.'* Watching him turn a corner and vanish into the chilly park, I sink onto my stomach and signal the sumpters. *'Onward. Consortium shall search for us soon. We must locate a place to hide the coffin, for time is short, and it shan't fit through the cave's entranceway.'*

Erstwhile Sink 2: A Day in the Life of Sink

∞ ∞ ∞ ∞ ∞ ∞ ∞ ∞ ∞ ∞ ∞ ∞ ∞ ∞

13-year-old Constance

I dash through the corridors of the Hallow Equarié's Convent, a French Éclat institution at which I am held captive. Grasping the gown's hem, I dip and dive past hag Lagarde's misericord, through the drab frater, and into a moth-eaten scullery.[75] The boards creak and my gown's fringe rips as I leap through a window onto the roof. I trip, and my elbow bangs the sturdy sill.

Whilst rubbing my elbow, I bumble to my feet. Bunching the hem of my gown, I tie it into a knot, and then remove my leather slippers, tossing them back through the window—the roof's thatched shingles are warm from the midday sun.

With naught but wool stockings cladding my legs, I wiggle my toes and prepare to climb. 'Sink? *They should dub me Constance the Swift instead.*'

I shuffle to the edge of the building and peek down; a twelve-foot drop separates me from my final impediment, the front courtyard. Narrow footpaths meander alongside a bed of white asphodels and a squash garden. Two moss-bitten statues rest at the courtyard's far corners, where wooden fences intersect. Both statues portray a child swathed in a blanket: Hallow Equarié, the Inviolable Eminent Child. Entrenched within their foundations is a furnace smoking with rush-candles kept lit at all daylight hours by Vierge Éclat.

The wooden floorboards of the convent groan as the wicked Vierge Éclat Lagarde stomps nearer. "This absurd mischief will not be tolerated!" She pokes her head from the window. "Constance! Thou devilish hedge-born; cease this nonsense!"

---

[75] Misericord: an apartment in which some easing of religious rules is permitted.
Frater: a dining room in a religious institution.
Scullery: a small kitchen or room at a residence's back used for washing dishes and other grungy household work.

"Nay!" I shout, falling onto my posterior and throwing my feet over the roof's edge.

Éclat Lagarde scoffs and abandons the window. I can hear her speeding toward the bottom floor.

Dropping to my belly, I dangle my legs from the roof and tap my toes against the building's cobblestone, fumbling for a foothold I discovered on prior occasions. *'Make haste. I must not dally.'*

A boy and girl poke their head from the convent window. "Oh. It's Sink attempting escape again," the girl announces.

More children congregate around the window as well. "She shan't prevail," a boy my age declares. "She always sinks. That's why she's Sink, Sink the Shipwreck."

"Nay, Thomas the doubter, I shall weigh anchor and sail free this time!" I snap my fingers. "And it's the Un'sink'able, dunce."

My slim foot scarcely slides into a shallow crevice between the cobbles. With my path of egress secured, I throw one of my hands toward a jutting stone. Catching the ledge, I hug the cobblestone wall and clamber down. The convent's front entrance flings open, and a fuming Éclat Lagarde stamps out, brandishing a broomstaff.

Glimpsing this, I shove off the cobblestone wall and hold my coif steady.[76] A wee squeak slips my lips as my stockings sink into the sodden asphodel bed with a muddy thump. I roll to my heels and dash toward the familiar London streets where none can catch me. A cruel hand captures my scarf, gagging me and forcing me to tumble onto my rear.

"Thou art not as sly as thou wouldst like to believe," Éclat Lagarde sneers and knocks my forearm with the broomstaff.

I reach toward a snarl of twine at my scarf's front and yank. "Ha! I am better than even I believed!"

---

[76] Coif: a woman's close-fitting cap, like a bonnet but tighter. In modern times it's typically only worn under a nun's veil.

The scarf's end sunders as I roll away and to my feet. If one must wear garments that can be readily snared, one must have a way out of it. Éclat Lagarde seethes, realizing I have slipped her clutches. "Deviant girl, arrest thyself!"

Needless to say, I refuse to comply and persist in my retreat. Whilst trampling squash into mush, I approach one of the Hallow Equarié statues. I drop my shoulder and ram it. The statue wobbles, I shove, and It topples over, shattering into rubble and revealing a gap in the fence. Smoldering rush-candles spill out, cloaking the area in a fog, and Equarié's head rolls from her shoulders.

The children goggling from the window gasp.

As I squeeze between the fences, one of my stockings snags a nail. Éclat Lagarde emerges from the smoke and seizes my heel. "B-blasphemous!" She digs her fingernails into my skin and whacks my ankle with the broomstaff. "This has gone beyond mere imprudence!"

I yelp, "Release me!"

Raising my free foot, I kick, and my sole graces Éclat Lagarde's face with a slimy footprint. She releases my heel and drops my scarf. I reclaim my stolen garment and force myself through the opening, slicing a hole in my stocking.

The cries of Vierge Éclat Lagarde and cheering children resound, but I care little. It's all in the past now.

I sprint into an alleyway, hide stray locks of my red hair beneath the coif, and then throw my arms into the air. '*Huzzah!*'

····

·········

····

Skulking through the alleyways adjacent Gracious Street, I head north toward the rear of Leaden Hall and the bustling streets.[77] The cobbled Gracious Street alleys are dreary, desolate, and astonishingly dry since it has not rained in several days. In London, it rains more than it does not, and when days pass without rain, these densely windowed alleyways

---

[77] Gracious Street is known today as Gracechurch Street.

become rancid footpaths of chamber pot excrement and drunkard vomit. A mere drizzle is no longer sufficient to cleanse it, so the caked-vileness shall linger and remain stagnant until the heavens unleash a scouring deluge, mopping it all into the Thames. None but Roach, Sink, or an utter fool would dare stroll this route whilst it's polluted like this.

Heavy footsteps approach me from behind. "It is thee!"

I shiver, hearing a man yelling at me. Making a fist, I twirl around and swing at my assailant.

The man squats, evading my strike.

"Madcap girl, thou swingest at me!" A youthful fellow goggles at me from beneath a felt cavalier hat with a prominent off-white feather.[78] Besides that, he wears lockram trousers, a sea-green shirt with a pink doublet, hose, high-heeled leather boots, embroidered gloves, a pink shoulder cape, and a gold hoop earring. His garments are colorful yet not too bright, indicating his status is a few notches under nobility but several above me. He stands, asking, "Hast thou forgottest me?" My light green eyes scrutinize the man's features. He is between seventeen and nineteen, with a slender face, dark black hair, and meager facial whiskers that dream of one day being a mustache. "Surely, thou couldst not have forgotten. For it is I, the Great William, The Actor!"

I raise my fist, smiling and speaking through my teeth, "That is why I swing at thee."

He laughs. "Ah, but thou dost remember me? Because I remember thee clearly."

Nodding, I ease my demeanor. "Why art thou creeping the London streets? Thou art not a Londoner if I recall."

An elderly woman with skin that has witnessed a thousand harsh summers leans out from her window overhead. William and I step further into the alley as she empties her chamber pot into the street. "Nay, I hail from Stratford-upon-Avon, south of Birmingham," William says, attempting to

---

[78] Cavalier hat: a very wide-brimmed hat popular amongst dandy men of the 16th and 17th century. Typically adorned by a black or white ostrich plume (feather). The style of hat one might envision a musketeer or pirate captain wearing.

ignore the splattering behind him. "I towed my wagon to London so that I might retrieve a cradle, amongst other household furnishings, that I commissioned from Peter Street, a carpenter I met near Banke syde. He offered me quite the generous bargain."

"Lolling, lazy delinquents," the elderly woman scoffs, retreating into her home.

I roll my eyes, waving the elderly woman away. "Aye, I know of Peter Street; he is a fickle but well-respected carpenter. Though, he seldom crafts furniture from what I understand." Raising an eyebrow, I ask, "More curiously, and perhaps I misheard, but didst thou sayst 'cradle'?"

He grins. "Aye. I have recently wed." His fingers play with the feather affixed to his hat. "A woman of mature and sublime beauty who now carries my child."

Smirking, I tap my chin and say, "Hmm, my condolences for the loss of thy father."

His mouth hangs open for a moment. "...What?"

I snicker. "Well, I surmise thy father must have passed because the only mature woman who would wed thee would be thy own mother."

"Such venom! I adore that fire." His eyes peer at me with evident amusement. "My father is alive and well, and thou hast changed little." He chuckles. "Why art thou so hostile?"

"It's better that way."

"Oh? Because of the Dark Lady? The one who sowed chaos in the midst of my majestic performance? Is She why thou keepest me at arm's length?"

I frown. "...Nay. Not merely because of Her. Also, because I am a girl alone in a dark, forsaken alleyway, and a man whom I am scarcely acquainted with stomped toward me whilst shouting."

"I announced myself." Smirking, he says, "Yet, I could understand how my shouting might be alarming if thou wert fleeing from someone."

My eyes narrow. "I thought thou mayst desire revenge."

"Nay. Though, I admit my sense of smell has been slow to recover since that incident." Shrugging, he glances at the sludge stuck between cobbles and continues, "I believe the Inquisitor and I were the only two to realize the origin of that smoke was thee." He shakes his head. "Were you aware I have tried to visit you at Equarié's Convent? Thrice I sought to speak to you. Yet each time, they told me thou had fled and that they did not know when thou wouldst return."

"Aye, the French Éclat and I are not of the same opinions on most things, so I would frequently leave if the whim reared its head. That was before they decided I ought to be a 'proper' obedient and ashamed woman of God. Nowadays, they seal me in my chamber with a loaf of bread and the Daybreak Scriptures only unlatching the door to berate or discipline me." I lift my gown's hem. Between the ribbons of my shredded stocking, a medley of red, blue, and purple bruises is readily apparent at a glance. I re-conceal the bruises. "And I am regretful to learn thou still suffer from the events of that day, but thy attempts at politeness fall on deaf ears, William." Sighing, I ask, "Why didst thou attemptest to visit me? It is a remarkably queer thing to have done. We have spoken once, years ago, and it was not particularly amicable."

"Well, I am regretful to hear of thy circumstance, and how could I not attempt to visit thee?" Placing a palm atop his heart, he says, "I would need to be an incredible fool not to recognize a breathing Muse when they pass me by."

I roll my eyes. "Thou art a fool of awesome proportions, aye." A man steps toward the end of the alley and leans against the wall, refusing to torment their nostrils with the alleyway's stench. The Church in Light's Daybreak Scriptures obscure his face, but I recognize them as an Éclat Inquisitor. "Farewell, William." I turn. "Relish thy privileged life of common concerns, and I pray thy brother-son or sister-daughter is born healthy."

"Ah, thy venomous quips are as sweet as belladonna wine. It is not fair to keep that remorseless wit for thyself alone."[79] He grabs my arm. "I will

---

[79] Belladonna: An exceedingly poisonous plant, also known as deadly nightshade, with purplish-black flowers and berries. Belladonna has a long history in myth, folklore, and on the stage.

delay the Inquisitor. But I ask in return that if thy whimsy tickles thee or thy fate ever grim, thou wilt find me, aye? Or better yet, we may meet and speak at greater length, hmm?"

"It better that we not... My fate was spun and predestined to be grim from birth. She, thy Dark Lady, is my dreadful curse. A curse for what purpose and what crime? Not even I know. But she haunts me and any who stray too near, including waggish wolves like thee."[80]

"I am no wolf, girl." He scoffs theatrically. "And curse that haunts thee? I disbelieve it. From what I glimpsed that fated noon, She was an aching perturbation seeking liberation, and Her moth-eaten madness was a palpable brook of untamed dread. Ancient. Misplaced. Tragic. A gnarled tempest of dream and spirit, long besmirched and long unrectified. In my memory, She was a fay vestige and a voiceless ode to gloom."

"She believes naught. She speaks naught. She feels naught. She is naught." I pry my arm away from him. "Thanks be for thy concern. Oh, and for thy lyrical words..." I turn on my heel and depart with hurried steps. "...I do have a fondness for theatrics and a dramatic tone."

"Ha! So, we do have some things in common." He clears his throat and shouts, "And so I say! Till the Fates decide our paths shall cross anew, Dark Lady."

I laugh and stick out my tongue. "If the Fates do not snip my string, mayhaps we shall, William, The Actor."

"Thou wilt receive an epistle from me, and it shall bear my greatest quips penned in my finest dramatic tone. I shall pay the courier and paper for thy reply in advance; thou shan't be able to resist responding! We shall be Quip Acquaintances!"

"...I do relish a fun quip," I whisper to myself.

••••

••••••••

••••

---

[80] Waggish: something said or done in a playful, mischievous, or facetious manner. Wolf (wolves): Before Elizabethan times, it referred to sexually insatiable women. But by Constance's time, it had come to refer to lustful men who are habitually flirtatious and regularly try to 'woo' women.

Eventide looms as I abscond beyond London's Aldgate. Soon, I arrive at my destination—a dilapidated cobblestone church that overlooks the heart of an apple orchard. It is a simple Church in Light with a modest chancel and nave that was once capable of supporting a congregation of around seventy commonfolk. Nigh half of the light-yellow shingles that once clad its rooftop have fallen earthward. Its sole unique quality is its distinctive tower with a circular face hidden behind boards.

The old church's derelict walls creak under the wind's influence. The few leaves that still cling to the apple trees rustle, and a flock of birds swoops by, perching atop the roof. I stretch my arms, popping my joints and relishing the warm breeze. My arms drop, and I fiddle with my scarf, ensuring the twine and stitches are not loose. With a giggle, I nod and approach the church's crooked doors, picking up twigs along the way.

I hear a whine, "Mowh!" and spin around. A black mouser with one green eye and a cropped ear comes charging toward me.

"Sir Mouser!" I shout.

The years have been hard on both Sir Mouser and me. Sir Mouser has lost one of his eyes to a sparrowhawk and a piece of his ear to a mongrel that sought to dine on my leg. In the end, I clubbed the sparrowhawk into the afterlife with a tree branch, and the cur that gnawed my calf sealed its own fate when it ingested haze. The cur shriveled up, and I rushed Sir Mouser to an orchard employee whose acquaintance I had made.

"Meow."

"Permit me a moment, Sir Mouser; I am gathering kindling."

He waits patiently, purring and rolling around in the grass. When I have gathered enough, we walk together to the entrance of the old church. As I open the door, several tiny meows come from deeper within. Several black kittens come running out but freeze when they see me.

"They have grown so big!" I shout.

With those words, a tabby cat comes rushing out and rubs against my stockings. I believe they have learned when it is safe to come near me based on my smell, so I do not stop Lady Mouser. She runs to one of the kittens, grabs it by the scruff of its neck, and then runs back, dropping it in front of me.

Readjusting the kindling in my hands, I lean over with my gloved hand and pet the tiny mouser beneath his chin. He tries to run away, but Lady Mouser stops him, and before long, he accepts his fate.

"It is fine, little one. Thou mayst not remember me, but I was there when thou wast born. I wiped thy body clean; it was a good day."

With the little mouser satisfied, I take the kindling and approach an old hearth. Some half-burned timbers still lie within, and a few other logs lie around as well. *'A lucky break. Now I do not need to acquire any for the night.'*

My eyes search the name, hoping there might be a neglected firesteel strewn about.[81] I move through the pews and toss some of the broken ones out of the way. Finding a worn copy of the Daybreak Scriptures, I put it to the side lest I need it for more kindling. A while later, I see a half-broken piece of firesteel under some broken glass.

"Huzzah! I have found a firesteel. Now before we go to our secret spot, let me mend my stocking."

"Meow!" Sir Mouser and Lady Mouser reply.

Removing my scarf, I bite a loose thread and rip it from the scarf. I examine the floor, spotting a splintering board from which I pluck some thin wooden pieces. Tying the line around the splinters, I work it through my stocking and replace my makeshift needle whenever necessary. When it is over, I am left with a roughly sewn patch, but it will function well enough.

Seeing a portion of my stocking stained red with blood from Vierge Éclat Lagarde's nails, I pull it down and scrub the wound before standing with a clap of my hands. "Aye! Now to our secret spot."

Sir Mouser and Lady Mouser rush toward me, and together we go to the very back of the church, where an inconspicuous notch in the ceiling sits

---

[81] Firesteel: A piece of high-carbon steel used for striking a spark, usually kept in a tinderbox with flint and tinder.

above us. I get down on my knees and pull up a loose board from the floor, revealing a rod with a hook on one end. Pulling the rod from the floor, I lift it and push it into the notch and then turn it to lock it in place. When I pull downwards, a ladder slides out, which makes a woody thunk against the floorboards.

"Bring the little ones to me! Let us spend time in the clock tower."

Sir Mouser and Lady Mouser run off and bring the kittens to me. I go up and down the ladder, bringing up each one, and then do the same for Sir Mouser and Lady Mouser. When they are all up, I go back and grab the logs, tossing them into the tower as well.

"Constance, it's the Inquisitor; art thou herest?" Hearing a familiar gentleman's voice speaking in London Parlance, I gasp, covering my mouth. "The Éclats at the convent sayest thou hadst fled, and I understand this is where the cats thou fancy frequent."

Setting down the log, I grab the rod and rush up the ladder. *'Without the rod, he cannot follow.'*

I yank up the ladder and shut the hatch just as the Inquisitor is about to discover me. "Constance, I am certain I heard thee flee into the clock tower. "Come down, so we may speak."

Spurning him, I do not reply and instead tiptoe to my abode, leaving him to question whether I was truly there. *'People will doubt they heard anything at all if enough time lapses with meager noise.'*

The tower consists of two chambers. A humble vestry with a hatch overhead, an empty bookshelf, a second hearth, and then the tower's main section, which is the reason I fancy this place.

When I open the door to the main section, the inside of the clock tower is revealed. A high cobblestone loft with wooden rafters and rust-laden wheels, gears, and frayed rope set to the side as if it was meant to be used. According to one of the orchard employees, there was a construction error, and the space requirements for the clock were insufficient, and thus it was never finished. The church ran for a time, yet eventually, the land was sold and sown into an orchard.

Still, the reason I adore this place is the stained glass clock face that's set into one of the walls. My gaze moves to the clock's face. In the center is a thick bronze plate where the clock needles would have been mounted, but emanating from there, reds, yellows, blues, whites, and other colors run away from the bronze plate like rays of light.

A dusty pallet of blankets sits neglected in front of this stained glass face. I fall into this heap and watch the kittens that frolic about with mirth.[82]

"I cannot depart without thee, Constance," I hear the Inquisitor state. "Mayhaps, if we conversed, we might arrive at some sort of agreement."

I do not respond but turn over and stare into one of the blue panes of glass. As I do so, Sir Mouser and Lady Mouser choose their own spot, which happens to be my face. For a moment, I think they might suffocate me.

...

....

....

....

....

....

...

Four days have come and gone. The Inquisitor was not fooled, and true to his word, he has not left without me. I could not keep the mousers confined in the loft all this time, so yesterday, I dropped half of the blankets down, followed by the mousers onto the soft mound. The Inquisitor simply watched as I did this, tossing a morsel of dace fish to the mousers.

Presently, I can hear the Inquisitor through the floorboards stoking the old sooty hearth and boiling something that stinks of deliciousness. Worse yet, he will not cease rattling on incessantly about the Daybreak Scriptures. "When humanity was at its most fragile, relying solely on fallible men to fend itself from the bestial, odious devils of the Bleeding Moon Ages, the God in Light unbarred the Lambent Gates of Last Light. God so treasured mankind, He uplifted us, to be above the miscreations, devils, blood-suckers, and amoral black spirits, delivering humanity dominion over the Earth and all its life. Ultimately this began the Pale Moon Epoch, the age

---

[82] Mirth: State of feeling merry. Also, amusement, jollity, joy, etc.

in which we live," the Inquisitor speaks in a gentle yet grim voice. Closing the Scriptures, he asks, "Hast thou ever been curious whom those fallible men may have been? Although they are stated to have been fallible, they still shielded man from the devils before the God in Light took humanity into His radiance."

I roll my eyes, gawking at a bird's nest in the rafters of the clocktower. Standing, I rub my belly and move to the rusty gears. I climb atop the stack of gears and jump, grasping the lowest rafter.

As I pull myself up, the Inquisitor keeps speaking. "These noble men, and perhaps even women, must have had some variety of power to challenge and expunge these devils."

Standing atop the rafter, I once more leap, catch, and draw myself up.

"I am curious about these powers and how they wielded them."

I jump again. My fingers clutch and squeeze the rafter—droplets of red speckle my cheek. I look upward, gaping at a fat splinter that runs through the tip of my thumb. My heart thumps, and I desire nothing more than to escape this plight.

"What would people think if one of these folk were born in our age?"

Haze spews from my body as I force an arm over the rafter. Tears trickle from my eyes, and I snap the splinter from the rafter. Biting my lip, I look up, and there She is, the churning figure of the haze girl, dreadfully looming over me. My eyes stray to the bird's nest and the sight of robin eggs dyeing black. The eggs emit a stench of putrefaction.

"Would the people condemn and rebuke them as miscreations? How cruel."

The rafters creak. Haze penetrates and eats at the wood's pores. My eyes widen, and I choke on the air.

"How cruel to be born, to live, and to wander the Earth at the wrong time and in the wrong place."

Crack and then snap, the rafter falls.

"How blatantly cruel—"

···
·······
···········
···············
···········
······
···
···
·······
···········
···············
···········
······
···

Next I awake, my body aches and Hallow Equarié's familiar ceiling lurks overhead.

A Tilted Web of Tales 2: Summer's Rushlight Eve

∞∞∞∞∞∞∞∞∞∞∞∞∞∞∞∞

Summer Rosary. Summer is an escort in a criminal syndicate.

— Two years before Constance's return to Earth. —

Moonlight beams down onto a lit rooftop restaurant known as the Hallow Cloud at the Knickerbocker hotel. Wearing only a red bra and panties, I gaze into a mirror while straightening my bleached blonde hair. A hundred other women with their own mirrors and tables do the same around me. Some are nude, others are in red underwear like me.

Bass-heavy music plays over speakers as the big-boobed scatterbrain Patricia claps her hands together. "Happy Rushlight Eve, fellow escorts!" Patricia yells with a giggle. "The male escorts are downstairs and will be ready in around an hour. Our Madam Lieutenant will be up in a minute, and then after that, we'll clean up so everyone can come up to the roof for the party. Oh, remember we're being paid to socialize and hookup with a guest if they request it, so make sure your body is scrubbed and your attitude perky."

Erin, a petite escort with auburn hair, throws up an arm. "Yooo, Miss Clean-and-Perky, we pretty much never work together like this. Who is paying for this shindig? A hundred female escorts plus a hundred male escorts plus two hundred hotel rooms, and who knows what else. Altogether it's gotta be pushing over a mill. This crap is all kinds of next level."

Sitting in front of a mirror, Patricia shrugs, saying, "Maybe it's the big boss! Wouldn't hooking up with them be exciting? I mean, hardly anyone sees them in public, much less has an opportunity to spend the night with them!"

Ruby, a high-class escort with honey-colored hair and an hourglass figure, laughs. "...The big boss? You don't mean Galtry, do you? Because, um, no.

I seriously doubt someone as high-class and high-profile as Galtry has any interest in call girls like us. Plus, there are guys there too, so..."

"What does that matter?" Undoing her bra, Patricia tosses it to the ground, swapping to a red one like my own. "Y'know, I read an article on Galtry a few months ago, and in the comment section, some people were adamant that they swing both ways. Like, swear on their grandma level of adamant."

Rolling her eyes, Ruby says, "I've heard those rumors, but that's not the point, Patricia. What I'm sayin' is Galtry can have whoever they want. They wouldn't want any of us escorts, even if we are 'high-class' compared to the streetwalkers and working girls."

"Well, of course, they wouldn't want anyone like you, Ruby."

"What the devils is that supposed to mean?"

"Escort or not, it's all about how you see yourself." She hooks her red bra, straightens her back, and then ogles herself in the mirror. "Male or female, both sexes respond to self-confidence."

Ruby snaps back, "I might not be smuggling watermelons like you, but I have full confidence in my appearance."

Tuning Ruby and Patricia out, I roll my eyes and stare into the mirror. Brush in hand, I drag it through my tangled blonde hair. A girl parades her bare white ass past me.

I purse my lips as she sits on the table in front of me. "Carly, what the fuck. Why would you come over here and sit right there?" Raising my hands in disbelief, I continue, "Like, what?"

"Summer, lightin' up," she says with a snicker.

"Are you kidding me?" Pointing at her lower body and snapping my finger, I say, "Bitch, your naked asscheeks are all over my cell phone right now!"

"Ditzy Glenice spilled some water on my miniskirt and panties, so they're in the restaurant's dryer. I didn't want to sit there waiting for them, so I came over to talk." Clicking her tongue, she leans to the side and tugs my phone out from beneath her. "Girl, why're you so uptight today?"

"I don't think I'm being that uptight today," I say, wiping the cheek print she left on my phone from the screen. "But I do have a weird feeling that something's... well, weird? I'm not really sure."

The doors to the restaurant open. An alluring woman in a backless floral print dress strolls in, carrying a basket full of syringes, smokes, and white powders. Raising the basket, she grins and announces, "Fresh from the ol'Barber himself, just what the doctor ordered, made special for my girls big money-making night."

All the girls stop what they're doing and twirl toward the woman. "Madam Desire!" they shout like a bunch of high school cheerleaders shaking pom-poms.

"Think I'm gonna get some vitamin-k sniffers for if the night drags on." Carly hops up while asking, "What about you? It's gonna be a long Rushlight Eve."

Reaching behind me, I hook my bra strap and stand. "Eh, I don't think I'm up for anything quite that intense, but I'll pocket some to sell to a Wall Street white noser later this week." [83]

"Greedy!" She laughs. "But whatever! Just don't let Madam Desire hear you say that."

"I won't. If anything, she'd hear it from your loudmouth."

With a shrug, she says, "Well, I'd argue with you, but you aren't wrong in all honesty."

Together we laugh. The night continues.

····

········

····

---

[83] White noser: A person who seeks favor with their peers or superiors by supplying drugs to senior management. Like brown-nosing, but with class A drugs.

A bartender spins bottles of liqueur as music booms and the lights hanging above flicker. The rooftop has been converted into what resembles a club with half-naked escort men and women walking about. The one-hundred escort women wear short red miniskirts and crop tops. While, for one of the first times ever, the escort men are more exposed than us, wearing only red briefs, stockings, and mesh shirts.

The bartender walks over. "You want something?" he shouts over the music.

I toss a twenty on the bar. "Galtry-Manhattan, babe. Sub triple whiskey."

"Nice, my favorite, but y'know drinks are on the house?"

"Yeah but bribing the bartender early in the night is always worth it. After all, it's your responsibility to make sure I don't remember whoever I end up with tonight."

"Well, I guess I should take my responsibility seriously then, huh?" He grabs the twenty. "Memory-erasing Galtry-Manhattan with whiskey, comin' right up, bae," he says with a chuckle.

"Smart-ass," I mumble with a laugh.

"Wow! You look great in that." A man in his fifties leans against the bar next to me. "What's your name?"

My eyes run over the man. Dad bod, uneven beard, gray hairs, and a used car salesman demeanor. '*A classic white noser, just my luck. I'll be biting the bitter bullet tonight, I guess.*'

Smiling, I say, "You can call me Connie."

"Connie, honey!" someone shouts with snark. Noah, a slender male escort, steps between the two of us. "Obviously, he was talkin' to me! Isn't that right, hot stuff?"

"N-no. I was talking to the la—"

Noah interrupts. "Oh, please! I can see the lust in your eyes, your deepest desires." He motions toward his body. "Admit it. You want to spend a night with this, don't you?"

His eyes betray him as he glances down and then back up. With his face reddening, he says, "Oh-oh, woulda look at that." He takes out his phone and holds it for us to see someone named 'Ladybug' is calling him. "That's my wife. Gotta take this, sorry."

They rush away, searching for a quiet place to answer the phone. A drink in a small glass slides down the bar. "Triple-X Galtry-Manhattan," the bartender shouts.

While catching the sliding drink, I laugh and say, "That was a wicked reverse wingman moment if I've ever seen one."

"Summer, girl, I just saved you. There are some genuinely sexy clients here. I couldn't let you end up with a lemon, like that grimy bozo."

"And I appreciate it for real." I sip my drink. "It would be nice if I didn't have to get with someone who makes me want to recoil the second they touch me."

The music cuts out as a man's voice comes over the speaker. "Good evening!" A slender man with brown hair in business casual attire walks out. He smirks. "I'm your host and toastmaster, Ray Barret, and I want to thank you all for joining me on this Rushlight Eve. We're getting ready for the main event, so I ask that everyone take a glass of champagne for a Rushlight toast." Dozens of servers walk out carrying trays filled with bubbling white champagne. "After the toast, everyone is free to do what, or who, they want," he says with a wink.

"Woooh!" half the people cheer and whistle.

I chug the rest of my Manhattan. When my glass hits the bar, I ask, "Ray Barret? He's the 'Freedom Global' guy, isn't he?"

"That private prison mogul?" Noah shakes his head. "Nope, I think that's Phil Barret. This is his son."

Noah and I take a glass of champagne from a server that's passing by. "How'd you know what the guy's son looks like?"

"Cause he's ultra-gay, and every so often, he'll pop up on my social feed. Oh, and now that I'm thinking about it, Kevin might have mentioned he's one of our roomie's regulars." Noah scoffs, glancing down at his mesh shirt and briefs. "Also, he's a total perv, and now I know why I have to walk around freezing my tail off in this outfit. The only thing keeping me warm are these briefs and my stockings."

"Huh? But you've got that snug shirt on."

He makes a fist while shouting, "The mesh does nothing! In fact, I think it somehow makes it worse."

I burst into laughter. "Bet you didn't think you'd be spending Rushlight Eve like this."

"You aren't wrong. I had plans to go to Toronto with Kevin and some of his friends. We were going to see the Rushlight annual musical in the Royal Alexandra Theatre... It was going to be so great; I just know it."

Ray Barret's voice comes back over the speakers. "Everyone have their bubbling champagne flutes loaded and at the ready?" We all raise our glasses. "Hell yeah! Then let's all take a quick sip to wet our whistles, but after the toast, I wanna see everyone chuggin' it down." Moving close to the mic, he adds, "Like, seriously, because each glass is like two hundred dollars' worth of champagne apiece."

"Alright, Ray! He sprung for the good stuff," a man in a suit shouts.

Everyone laughs as we all take a sip of our champagne. It's a little bitter.

Our host laughs. "But anyways, as we all know, the church will tell you that Rushlight is a holiday meant to commemorate a miracle. The miracle of the Church's Flame surviving a week-long tsunami on nothing but a single stick of rushlight.[84] Of course, many of us know that it's probably bullshit, and it's just a holiday that was misappropriated from another long-dead religion. But! We all know that's not all Rushlight is... Rushlight

---

[84] Rushlight: a type of miniature torch formed by soaking the dried pith of the rush plant in fat or grease.

is a time of gift-giving and reflection. A time to think back and appreciate what we have and what we'll be. After all, we never know when our lives might effectively end. So a toast to living life to its fullest."

"Hear, hear," some men shout.

Noah and I clink our glasses together and then down our champagne. Everyone else does the same.

With another laugh, Ray sets his glass to the side. "Y'know, I always said that if my life was going to effectively end, I'd want it to happen in the middle of a party."

The crowd begins to swirl and wave in my vision. My champagne glass hits the ground. 'My... my head...'

One after another, people drop their glasses and collapse.

"And funny enough! That's my Rushlight gift to you guys." Ray's words reverberate in the night air. "You're welcome, everybody!"

Blankness.

····
········
····

— Hour(s) later ?? —

I shiver, awakening from a nightmare. My head hurts. My eyes hurt. My back hurts. Everything hurts.

Crud seals my eyelid shut. I put what little energy I can muster into forcing them apart. Above me, I see fluorescent lights and a white ceiling, like an old hospital ceiling. A tube runs down my throat, and I can feel them running into... other places as well.

My neck crackles as I look to my left. Rows and rows of people sleeping on gurneys, stretchers, and hospital beds. I recognize many of them: fellow escorts, partygoers, servers, and even the bartender. Looking to my right, it's identical. We're in some far-reaching room with a low nine-foot-tall ceiling.

Footsteps echo. An older man with gray hair and a bushy mustache stands over me. *'No way, that's the Barber, isn't it?'*

I try to say something, but my tongue is so dry that it feels like it might crack.

He smiles and pets me on the head. "Hand me one of the pink 18-gauge needles, a vial of caerulus, and an IV. TH-F55 is quite tenacious. Stirred awake on their own."

Several men surround me. One of them is a lanky in-uniform police officer, a pig. He ogles my body as I cram the imbecile's badge number, "79566," deep into my brain.

One of them raises a syringe full of blue liquid. "TH-F55, you and the others here will help us understand Toba Humanity on a deeper level. The integration will be simplified, and future losses significantly mitigated."

He taps the side of the syringe and then makes a rolling motion with his hand. They reach underneath me and flip me onto my front.

"This will sting a little, but after this, it won't hurt anymore." I feel a stab near my lower back. "Thank you, TH-F55. Toba will owe you more than you'll ever know."

My body convulses as my eyelids fall closed.

····

·········

····

— ?? day(s) later —

My eyes peek open after yet more nightmares. Everything is blurry, and my body is too numb to move, but I can tell I am still in the big room.

Blurry figures move around across from me. They're doing something to one of the people in the hospital beds. As my vision unblurs, I see the two figures are a man in an owl mask and another in a weasel mask, maybe.

"Hmm, I don't know, Ferret. Are you sure this will suffice?" the man in the owl mask asks.

They step aside like they want to get a better look at their work. Between them is a body swaddled in plastic wrap with added concrete blocks. *'Am I just scenery in a horror movie, fuckin' hell, this is terrifying...'*

"Should work," the man in the 'ferret' mask says. "They'll sink to the river bottom pretty quick, and they shouldn't bob around too much either. Then they can be salvaged by our sponsor."

A pink-haired woman walks up carrying a long black bag. It's one I've seen before, a bodybag. They take the swaddled body and zip it up inside the bag.

Voices grumble from afar. "Uh-oh, they're coming back," the pink-haired woman snickers. "Guess it's time for us to blow this popsicle stand."

The three scamper away, disappearing between the beds of people.

Men walk over and grab the handles of the bag. "Damn, this thing is heavy."

"I loaded it with concrete blocks and wrapped it in barbwire. Of course, it's heavy, dumbass."

One of the men points at me. "Hey, TH-F55 or whatever is awake. Someone bump the sedative button before we have to deal with another screamer."

The rap of stiletto heels against concrete thumps my eardrums. "Poor Summer. I'm so sorry, dear." A familiar face makes itself known, Madam Desire. They tap a blue button on the side of the bed. "It hurts me to see my girls like this. I'll make sure you're all remembered."

A drip of liquid flows up a tub. Everything fades to black. *'If I make it out of this bed alive, I'll find you.'*

···
·······
···········
···············
···········
·······
···

— A week later ?? —

Horrible nightmares force my eyes open.

At some point, my bed was moved to the corner of the room. On the far side, empty gurneys, stretchers, and hospital beds are stacked atop one another. Ninety percent of the people are gone. As one of the few left, I have been hooked to an EKG and other medical devices, including a blood bag IV.

'Guess I lost a lot of blood.'

Yesterday, or maybe several days ago, I woke up for an hour. The Barber was back, and my arm was flayed open like a slab of meat. He was scraping at the bones in my forearm like a dentist does with teeth; I couldn't feel anything. Seeing me conscious, he apologized and pressed that damn blue button.

My eyes stray. Today, the people with the animal masks are back, and they're doing something to a woman that's been detached from their machines. I recognize the woman as Storm, an eighteen-year-old escort that was disowned by her orthodox family a few years ago.

The pink-haired woman is back too. Over her face, she wears a bunny mask and hums as she pats makeup onto the comatose woman. A man in an owl mask helps her paint gray wrinkles on Storm's skin and attach some type of fleshy material.

The more makeup and paint they place, the more Storm resembles a corpse.

There's a squeak as a body wrapped in plastic wrap and barbwire is rolled over by a man in a ferret mask. He draws a knife, slashing the wrap open with a few quick swipes. "Found a body in the mortuary that should work great for the switcheroo," he says.

"Their EKG is set to crash in a couple hours. They shouldn't expect a thing," the man in the owl mask adds.

Pulling a pale gray arm from the tangles of plastic, the ferret man pats it down with paint. They rub a cosmetic foundation on the arm and follow it with a mixture of some kind. When they're done, the arm looks almost alive.

They all study the arm and compare it to the unpainted pieces of Storm's skin. Nodding, they return to work. When the man in the ferret mask cuts back the remaining plastic and barbwire, I see Carly's aghast and dehydrated face. My heart pounds, and my EKG beeps. The three look at me.

An IV machine next to me clicks, releasing a drip. The EKG quiets down, and my eyelids turn heavy.

The pink-haired rabbit woman scurries over. "Sleep," she says with a soft shush. "We'll give you a helping hand too. It's sorta what we do."

I sleep.

···

·······

···········

···············

···········

·······

···

— Week(s) later ?? —

I have no idea how long I've been here, unconscious, while my mind bounces from one nightmare to the next. It's just nightmare after nightmare. Those nightmares where you think you've woken up, but it's just a continuation of the previous one. They've built whole lifetimes upon one another, and now, I'm not even sure which is real anymore. The times I wake up in that room with the low ceiling or the endless lives where I'm free to struggle against monsters, demons, ghosts, and beasts. I've grown to savor the struggle the nightmares provide. Maybe I'm a masochist, and I never realized it until now... But I think the real reason is that the room is terrifying, and I know that soon, it will be my turn to go into a bodybag.

Frigid fingers stroke my cheek. I groan, forcing an eyelid apart.

I see the man in the Owl mask gazing down at me. "You're going to be fine, doll. Just try not to gasp when the water hits you." I feel my legs being cocooned in plastic wrap and hear the rasp of barbwire. The owl places a clear oxygen mask over my face. Tubes run from the mask's back and into concrete blocks.

I feel a needle push into my arm. Turning my head, I see the pink-haired woman in a rabbit mask. Next to her on a gurney is a corpse that looks like it could be my identical twin.

My eyelid slips shut.

••••

•••••••••

••••

I hear a car's trunk open. My entire body is held so tight in plastic wrap that I can't even wiggle a pinky toe. Yanked from the trunk, someone grabs my legs, and another squeezes my head. Like I'm on a swing, I sway back and forth.

"Release on three," someone says.

"Bro, just fuckin' throw the bitch. We're gonna get seen."

"Shut the fuck up. When I get to three, we'll throw her into the river. Got it?"

"Whatever, man, just count if that's what you wanna do so bad."

"One. Two. Three!"

My stomach turns as I spin, twirl, and fall. Air blows from my lungs, and barbwire pricks my back. I flip upright and feel myself sink.

'Was this a life worth living? Eighteen years of school with a piece of crap dad, two years of drug-fueled bliss living off his life insurance, and then two as a Galtry Syndicate prostitute.' In utter silence, my bodybag settles on the river bottom. *'...God, I fucking failed life so hard.'*

...Something wraps around me.

I spin and feel the pressure of something scraping or clawing at the outside of the bodybag—freezing water drenches me. A knife cuts the plastic from my face, and I make out the shadows of several scuba divers floating around me. Makeup and blood dye the water as one of them approaches me. They remove the oxygen mask while another swims over and straps a diving mask to my face. They press a switch on the diving mask, sucking out the reddish-brown water, and then begin snipping my barbwire cocoon.

An unmistakable voice plays over the inside of the mask. "Stay below the water, follow the divers, and do not resist their help. If you swim up or away, you'll be left to your fortune. Follow those three rules, and you'll be fine. You're going to be taken to the Hôtel Casāle, where you'll be allowed to bathe, eat, and sleep before being treated for physical and mental trauma. However, you will not be allowed to leave because the people we just freed you from will find and kill you. In three days, we'll speak again, and you'll be given two choices: personally work for me or be placed into a witness protection program of sorts. Anyone that chooses the latter will begin a new life under a different name. Either way, the choice is yours. Until then, take time to rest and relax. Congratulations, you made it." The voice disappears.

'Was... was that Galtry?'

A Spanish man's mellow voice replaces the previous one. "Hello." In front of me, a scuba diver raises a hand and waves. "Don't be scared, young lady. You're the thirty-seventh person I've saved from this exact same predicament this month, and I haven't lost one yet."

The immense comfort and warmth of the scuba diver hugging me almost makes me pass out.

···
·······
···········
···············
···········
·······
···

— Three days later —

My eyes follow what must be the most stereotypical butler alive as they pass around 'vitamin-rich protein smoothies' to thirty-seven silent people.

The butler, an older man, looks agitated about the whole situation, but he keeps his hoity-toity character going strong. "Made from the finest of ingredients, madam," he says, holding out a silver platter. "I spoke to a Mister 'Dallas Dromida' personally; he's a well-respected physician who highly recommends these smoothies. They've been perfectly balanced to rejuvenate your strength and assist in your recovery."

Taking one, I mumble a "Thank you."

"Of course!"

He leaves the room through a set of double doors when the last smoothie is taken. The couch shakes as someone sits next to me.

"Sup, Noah..." I whisper.

Noah waves at me, saying in a small voice, "...Hey, girl."

We sit for a moment.

Squeezing at a coach pillow in my lap, my breathing becomes heavier. "Fucked up, huh? I can't even fondle a pillow without losing my breath."

He nods with a slight smile. "Y-you were knocked out for longer than anyone." Leaning back, he asks, "...D-did you see our faces and names have been all over the news?"

"...Yeah."

The room darkens as a projector screen lowers from the ceiling. Galtry's shadowed figure flashes onto the screen. All I can see of them is their pupil, encircled by several rings of black ink.

Galtry opens their mouth to speak, yet nothing comes out. I'm not sure why but they seem lost for words. It reminds me of a newbie escort during their first week in the sex industry. '...Is this the real Galtry?'

The double doors swing open. Several people in animal masks march in.

Galtry's eye narrows. Clearing their throat, they say, "If you've chosen to begin a new life, approach the man in the wolf mask. If you've chosen to work for me, stay seated." They lean back, sinking into the shadows. "If you reject both, you can walk out the door now and take your chances. More than likely, you'll join the others at the bottom of the Hudson River and might even drag some of your loved ones with you."

Everyone sits in silence for another moment. All in all, there are fifteen escorts, twenty randos, the white noser with a wife named Ladybug, and then the bartender. That's all that made it out. There wasn't anyone else after me.

The white noser and bartender stand. The white noser dashes out the door without a thought while the bartender approaches the man in the wolf mask.

They hand the man a manilla envelope. "Enjoy your new life. You'll find it quite comfortable, I'm sure," they say in a soft voice.

He waves at the people in the rabbit and owl mask as another person in an animal mask ushers him through the double doors. Four randos stand. One walks out the door while three take manilla envelopes.

Us escorts remain seated until all twenty randos are gone. Fourteen took manilla envelopes, six left through the door.

I lean back and cross my legs. "I'm staying."

Noah swallows. "I'm gonna stay too."

A third escort nods. It's the youngest of us, Storm. "I'm pissed off!" she screams. "My best friend was there! What did they do to us, to her!"

Antonella, Carolina, Paulette, and Glenice stand. Their footsteps echo as they take manilla envelopes and then leave without a word. Nekomaru and Sydney follow behind them, taking their own envelopes.

Two girls whisper in the corner. "We're staying," Ruby says, pointing at herself and Devon.

Hunter and Kevin stand. "Sorry, Noah. You'll be the only guy," Kevin says with a sigh. "I liked being your friend and roomie. I'm sorry it's ending like this."

The pair take manilla envelopes and leave.

Sighing, Ruby looks at Patricia and says, "You wanted to meet them. Now you can work for them," she whispers, gesturing toward Galtry.

Patricia stands. "I'm not staying."

"You're taking an envelope?" Erin asks with a sigh.

"No. I'm leaving through the door. I was so, so, close to getting my marine biology degree and quitting. My life was about to finally take off, finally get on track. I can't give that up now, not now. I worked so hard."

Erin shakes her head. "Nah, you should stay, Patricia. I am, and we always got along pretty well. This is a good chance for us to get to know each other better and leaving is dangerous."

Nodding, I say, "If Galtry is concerned about your safety, then you should realize that those people will find you for sure. Everyone that took an envelope understood that too. That's why so many took the envelopes."

Shaking her head, she turns and moves toward the door. "N-no. I-I-I can't stay. Good luck, everyone. I hope you all make those people pay and find whatever it is you're looking for. I just won't be a part of this nightmare anymore."

The door closes behind her.

Galtry leans forward. "Hôtel Casāle is now your home. There will be rooms set aside for your use alongside debit cards with a high limit I'm sure you'll be happy with... But in one month, you're all going to be sent away for a year. During this year, you'll learn how to fire and use weapons, basic hand-to-hand combat, and turbulent decision-making techniques. When you return, I'll be shipping you to college; you will attend Lurlann Empire to study subjects of my choosing. Throughout all this, you will have a direct line to nutritionists and personal trainers who shall see to it that your bodies are sculpted to a professional level. Do not neglect any of your duties."

We all look at one another. None of us expected her to want escorts for something like this.

"When the time is right, someone carrying a pin with my symbol will find you. Until then, I'll be keeping in touch bi-monthly via indirect means. I look forward to working with you."

The screen flickers to black.

```
        •••
      •••••••
     ••••••••••
   ••••••••••••••
     ••••••••••
      •••••••
        •••
```

— Twenty-two months later —

An anchorman pretends to study some papers on his news desk before looking up and speaking on the television. "Good evening. As always, I'm Jay Teems here with Jessie Rockets, and we're reporting live from New York. Today marks the two-year anniversary of the Puzzling Five Hundred's disappearance."

The anchorwoman Jessie makes a solemn expression. "That's right, it's hard to believe that nearly two years have passed since the brutal murder of Patricia Evans led the National Guard to dredge up more than five hundred bodies from the Hudson River. Before the Anchorage disaster, the disturbing discovery was one of the most internationally covered events in United States history, leading to documentaries and even a freshly released blockbuster film."

Jay nods. "Of course, we all know these individuals as the 'Puzzling Five Hundred' due to vanishing seemingly into thin air while attending a Rushlight Eve celebration atop the Knickerbocker hotel. It was only after the dismembered body of Patricia Evans was found in her dorm room did the dots begin to connect. Later anonymous tips helped lead to a mass arrest, including several officers within the NYPD's own ranks just eight months ago."

I scoff. "Wonder who tipped them off about those fuckin' pigs. It couldn't have been Noah, Erin, Ruby, Storm, Devon, and me. Nope, impossible, technically we're dead."

The picture changes, showing three familiar faces as Jessie picks up where Jay left off. "But to this day, the three suspected masterminds behind the event have yet to be taken into custody. Two individuals who go by the street names 'Madam Desire' and 'The Barber,' and a third individual by the name Ray Barret, the son of prison mogul Phil Barret. This immense tragedy led to the sale of the Knickerbocker, renamed the Beaux-Arts Knickerbocker, to an unknown buyer, as well as the sale of Freedom Global's Illinois holdings to the Consortium. Despite mass demonstrations, Freedom Global has still not sold their New York holdings, which includes the renowned Rikers Island."

The pair readjust their posture, and an image of Consortium's logo flashes on the screen. "In more recent news concerning the Consortium, reports that Supreme Court Justice Ronald Alito has fled to Chicago and taken residence in Consortium Headquarters have yet to be confirmed. Attempts to locate the justice within the building have failed as Consortium lawyers assert that Justice Alito does not reside on the premises. Official police endeavors to affirm their claims have been fiercely challenged as "an invasion of Consortium's constitutional and God-given rights as a corporate citizen of the United States of America.""

'A corporate sell-out. I'm so shocked right now. Straight-up flabbergasted. Gobsmacked. Thunderstruck. What was that one I saw in a movie... oh yeah, flummoxed!' There's a knock on my door. I groan and look down at my naked body draped in blankets. Massaging one of my temples, I force myself to leave the warmth of my bedsheet. "Hold up," I shout at the door. Slipping on my panties, some sweatpants, and grabbing a red trench coat, I stumble to the door with a yawn.

"What's takin' you so long damn!?" a man on the other side of the door asks.

"Get off my case!" I button up the trench coat and throw open the door. A man with bright red hair and muscles as big as his head stands in my hotel room's doorway. "Listen, punk. I sleep naked because it's fucking comfortable. Is that okay with you, deputy redhead? Or am I supposed to answer the door without clothes to save you a minute of time?"

He rolls his eyes and gestures toward my trench coat. "I'm not answering either of those questions, Sherlock. Mostly because I have things to do and don't feel like wasting time arguing."

Taking a deep breath, I ask, "You're Lorcan Yarborough, right? Just tell me what's up, man. Do I need to stroll the streets for info tonight or something? I was about to go to bed... Like minutes from lying down and closing my eyes."

He reaches into his pocket and removes a pin. It's an eye with ink rings around the iris. "It's time. Tomorrow, I'll pick you up in the RV."

Chapter 19: Violet Pantry and a Reunion of Birds

∞ ∞ ∞ ∞ ∞ ∞ ∞ ∞ ∞ ∞ ∞ ∞ ∞ ∞

Gazing upon the magnificence of my rubbish-filled hermitage, I collapse with my back against the cave wall, pull my legs close, and lower my head. An hour has slithered by since the Arcade, and Gentlemen Ape and I are back in the cave. The coffin and yellow tome I left buried in snow and brushwood deeper in the park's Ramble.

I was compelled to hurry due to the elixir's ramifications, which are intensifying. Fortunately, since I was predominantly vermillion haze, moving was faster than my sable body. I would estimate my speed was comparable to an ordinary man's sprint.

Feeling faint, I ask the Cosmic System, *'Prithee, how long do I have before the elixir's ramifications are at their heighth?'*

The blue wall of the Cosmic System appears.

Repercussions of 'Elixir - Decoction' estimated to peak in 0H 23M.

'Twenty-three minutes.' With my eyes peering at the cave's stone, I notice the little yellow orbs casting light around the kiln's shell. These were given to me to complete the task of placing gates and vents for The Tower. Seeing them reminds me that I planned to place a gate in the cave. It seems like something simple I could do now, but one of Earl's walls stated, "Any area a gate is placed in will be altered to a suitable degree."

In need of a distraction, I ponder this before resolving to test my luck by asking Earl directly. *'Earl, if I place the gate, how much is a "suitable degree"? Will it expose my position?'* The cave remains silent; the only sound I can hear is the patter of Gentleman Ape's feet. *'How inconspicuous is placing the gate, Earl?'* He does not answer, so I scream into the depths of my own mind. *'Earl, prithee, assist me this once? What dost thou advisest!?'*

A few minutes pass, and an answer never arrives. Sitting for a while longer, my thoughts stray toward other things. I release my legs and stand. Gentleman Ape makes a small noise and saunters up to me, raising a cup of his favorite food item toward me.

'Nay, thy offer is appreciated, but we shan't be able to gather more of those anytime soon.' Walking to the corner of the room, I retrieve Gentleman Ape's writing stick. Squatting, I wave the stick in front of him. 'More importantly, those are meant to be thy reward for a job well done. Do not think I have forgotten.'

I toss the stick in front of Gentleman Ape. He stares at it and then at me. A look reminiscent of someone who has found resolve spreads across his face. He grabs the stick, then points with his other hand at the stick, himself, and then the ground. With a thump, he drops to his posterior, writing "Gen" into the cave's dust and then stopping. He throws the stick to the ground and refuses to scribble more. Squinting, I take the stick and hand it back to him. He repeats his previous action and stops at "Gen," except this time he casts the stick toward the rear of the cave.

I shake my head at this hairy little man's antics. 'Aye, aye, I believe thou hast made thy point. Frankly, I am not certain if thou art simply too lazy to pen thy full name, but Gen is a marvelous name regardless. I suppose it is rather obvious in retrospect; I merely thought it was a habit that thou hadst developed.'

A purple wall appears.

Earl Interface:
Recommendation: *Place at least one gate as soon as possible. User's gates will alter the area, but not the environment.*

At first, I believe something has gone awry with the roots again, except after reading it, I realize this is the answer to my earlier questions. Earl has never taken this long to answer me. Mayhaps, he was uncertain. '...It is appreciated, Earl. I presume what thou art implying is the area changes, but to put it simply, a cave shall stay a cave. Either way, since thou seem to have taken the time to ponder it, I shall heed thy advice.'

I stand and step around Gentleman, nay, Gen, and scrutinize the cave walls—one spot with a crack grabs my attention. The crack is close to the center of the cave, and nigh anyplace in the cave would do in all honesty, so I resolve to place the gate over the crack.

Yet, staring at the wall, I hesitate. Truthfully, I wish to wait, but I feel as if I should act upon Earl's recommendation, seeing that he acted out of the ordinary by replying at all, never mind several minutes after being questioned.

I raise my hand and place it on my forehead. I am beginning to feel dizzy, and I desire to be done with this. Lowering my hand, I point. '*Aye, let us get on with it. I wish to ensconce a gate over that wall, Earl.*'

One of the yellow lights spins around the kiln. It separates and bobs toward the cave's wall. Like a leaf upon the breeze, it rubs against the stones and then sinks into the crack as if it is water.

Dropping my arm, a heavy bout of faintness swells and both a purple and a blue wall appears.

> *-92% Mana Pool. Mana pool will recover over an estimated 28H 39M.*

> **Earl Interface:**
> **Notice:** *The gate will complete within the next 72 to 75 Material-Earth hours.*

I read the walls and then take a seat. Unraveling the cattail, I stretch it toward the Hex Church book, the ecology text, and the messenger orb. I drag the items to me and then bend the cattail toward our pile of food stock.

As I nibble random morsels of food, my eyes drift to the crack. A mist aglow in colorful light trickles from within. '*I have done more than enough this day.*' I shake my head and open "You Are Ecology 101." '*I desire only to read.*'

•••
•••••••
••••••••••
••••••••••••••
••••••••••

······
···

Fostered Aspirant [Mana Compression (Grade 1)]
Fostered Aspirant [Mana Compression (Grade 2)]
Fostered Aspirant [Scrounger (Grade 3)]
Fostered Aspirant [Scrounger (Grade 4)]
Fostered Novitiate [Feline Whip (Grade 4)]
Fostered Novitiate [Gluttonous Naturalist (Grade 4)]
Fostered Novitiate [Tenebrous Stealth (Grade 5)]
Fostered Novitiate [Tenebrous Stealth (Grade 6)]

···
·······
···········
···············
···········
······
···

Three days come and go.

Over two of those days the ramifications of the elixir's "encumbrance" faded, and my mana recovered. Gen and I have spent our time primarily in hiding except when we would go out for a few hours. We have kept to the northern regions of the park to scavenge and have ceased visiting the children to gather supplies. It's unwise to go back after Lorcan was there on the prior occasion.

Whilst the ramifications were still ongoing, I made use of what meager mana I retained to train my Mana Compression by using the messenger orb. Thus I was able to foster two grades. One additional grade for mana compression a day would be sufficient at this point, but I plan to attempt two in one day soon. That way, I can guarantee that I acquire the skill in case any new incidents ensue in the next few days.

Moreover, I made excellent progress with my other skills, particularly Scrounger and Tenebrous Stealth. I also learned that Novitiate skills do not advance at "Grade 5," and I am not certain what the grade requirement is to advance my rank. Presumably, it's either only a matter of time, or I must do something specific to advance.

Other than that, I spent time reading the "You Are Ecology 101" text and the other book I took, "Gospel of Lords Hexed: Contracting Foregone Humanity." I did not make it far into the Gospel of Lords Hexed. Many of the subjects covered in it clearly require knowledge of certain concepts or topics I am not privy to.

The most intriguing thing I was able to comprehend was the various types of contracts covered: domination, subordination, reciprocation, and the odd one out, a bargain. Domination was the one Emily sought to use on me, and it gives one of the "parties" absolute authority over the other. Subordination is an "in good faith" contract that may become void if the higher party abuses the lower party. Reciprocation is one where two parties make an agreement that is mutually beneficial. Finally, a bargain is a temporary contract related to the trading of goods or some services.

Of those types, save for bargaining, they can be "lifetime," "upon fulfillment," or "until void." Lifetime is only available for domination or reciprocation and is the rarest because, as the name suggests, there is no way out of it excluding death. There are methods to annul a lifetime domination contract but not for reciprocation. Reciprocation seems to intrinsically recognize that both parties willingly consented to the contractual stipulations and that the agreement was mutually advantageous, making it more binding. The other two types are more self-explanatory and can apply to any of the contracts, except bargains.

I also learned that a Spirit Scribe, what Emily claimed to be, can make these contracts between anyone with or without being personally involved. This can apparently be done because the contract is written onto the spirits of the ones who made the agreement and then recorded in the Spirit Scribe's tome.

'A lifetime reciprocation contract... a guaranteed way to trust another. It sounds rather familiar. Where could she be? I pray it shall not be too much longer until we meet again.'

My shoulders drop as my thoughts wander.

At this moment specifically, I am alone and am in the process of returning to the cave. I snuck out, leaving Gen to his own devices, after I recalled seeing a child with his mother carrying a sled over a fortnight ago. So after walking to the north of the park, I found a hiding place to watch for children with sleds. For hours I sat until an older child commenced throwing a fit. While they were acting hateful toward their mother and putting on a performance, I took the opportunity to borrow their sled. I plan to use it for the coffin since dragging the coffin all the way to the cave by force is not practical.

But I shall await nightfall to retrieve the coffin; I know it is still there as I went to check on it and the Terrace a day ago. When I did so, I was able to bring the yellow tome back with me. Nevertheless, I intend to return to the cave for the time being. The gate shall be finished within the hour, and, well, the cave has changed significantly under its effect. As for the Terrace, I did not see many Consortium people there, which is excellent, but it seemed as if they were preparing for there to be a lot of people. The worst part is they appeared to be placing sturdier, taller fences. It is perturbing, yet there is naught I may do about it without more information or preparation.

With the sled in tow, I approach the stairs to the cave. The trees in the area all have a bit of weakness and sickliness about them. Some of the trees that would ordinarily retain their leaves regardless of the time of year have even begun to drop their leaves. I presume this is likely the gate's doing.

Descending the stairs and arriving at the cave's bricked entrance, I unwind the cattail and begin pulling bricks. Over the past few days, I have enlarged the cave's opening to allow larger things to enter, such as the coffin and sled. Before now, I could only remove a single wedge of bricks, and the biggest thing that could enter the cave was Gen, yet now there are ten removable wedges. If all ten wedges are removed, the cave's opening is around five feet wide by two feet tall, but I rarely remove them all.

With the bricks out of the way, I push the sled through and follow behind. There is no need for my night vision here any longer. The cave's ceiling has been glassed over by stained glass that emanates a gentle glow, comparable to the light of a full moon.

Yet this is not even the most significant change to occur. Without warning, a section of the wall with the crack in it collapsed yesterday. After the dust settled, what was left was an archway that leads into a circular chamber with an ornate door opposite the archway. This makes me think that the crack I placed the gate in led into some sort of hollow. It is also possible that the gate itself enlarged the cave, except I have not encountered any loose soil to support that explanation. However, the chamber has a deliberate architecture, so the gate must have done something to shape it.

I glance at Gen, who snores lightly, his back curved as he sleeps on a sack of rubbish. Placing the sled to the side, I walk into the chamber I have taken to calling the gate chamber. Upon stepping through the archway, I cannot help but pause and admire it.

The ceiling and floor look like what one would expect in a cave, uneven and ridged, while the walls are smooth because of stained glass panels that cover them. There are twelve of these panels, six on each side of the arched doorway, with the final two panels each making up a side of the ornate door. Each panel depicts a scene that somewhat mirrors the panel that parallels it. For example, the two panels that flank either side of the arched doorway display a mother cradling a child, except one has a mother adorned in jewels while the other has a mother in rags.

If I stand at the chamber's center and face the ornate door, the panels on the right depict a girl born into riches. The first panel is the mother cradling the child, then a young lady in a beautiful gown, yet she looks unhappy. For the next three panels, the young lady is seen picking up a sword, training her swordplay, and then donning armor of gold.

On the opposite side, it shows a boy born into poverty. He matures into a strong young man by the second panel. By the third panel, he battles against ruffians using a rusty knife. In the fourth, he trains with a wooden sword. In the fifth, he tans leather whilst a polished iron sword rests at his feet.

In the sixth panel, the young lady and the young man meet. Each stands at opposite sides of the ornate door; rather, the final panels are the door. The young man wearing the poor equipment grips the door's crack with his left hand while the young lady in golden armor grips it with her right gauntlet. In their opposite hands, their swords are raised and cross one another to make an "X" that bars the door.

I run my hands across the smooth panels and think back to what Earl said yesterday after this chamber was revealed. His wall was baffling yet straightforward. He stated that the gate would lead somewhere upon completion, and he even recommended that I enter it when it has finished.

Having made my way around the chamber, I reenter the rubbish room. Since I have the leisure to do so, I have been experimenting with an item I acquired a while ago. I retrieve the item in question, the pistol I 'borrowed' from Preston, and move to the gate chamber's center. To be candid, I have been afraid to experiment with this weapon. All I know about firearms is that they are crude, inelegant, noisy, and if I pull the "tricker," a pellet is sent soaring.[85]

I turn the pistol around, inspect the barrel's interior, and then spin the weapon forward. *'I must be bold and brash.'* I stand and step back into the rubbish area of the cave. *'So I must learn to discharge this death peddling device in case the need to operate it ever arises.'*

Glancing at the cave's entrance, I remember the pistol is rather ear-splittingly powerful, so I grab a bag of rubbish with the cattail and drag it into the gate chamber. Gen follows me, watching as I place the rubbish bag in the corner and then look between it and the pistol. *'That rubbish bag shall bear the impact's brunt... I think.'*

I signal Gen, instructing him to shield his ears. He does not understand, at least I believe he does not, but he enjoys mimicking me, and I have learned to exploit that. Clutching the pistol in the cattail's tendrils, I step back, lean away, and prepare for the imminent racket.

Gen tilts his head and covers his ears as I flex the tendrils.

The deafening noise I expected reverberates. More sounds follow as the pellet rips through the rubbish bag and strikes the glass panel behind it. The pellet bounces off the glass panel, producing a blue shimmer as it does so; another blue shimmer spreads from the wall in the corner, and then another from the ornate door. I duck as the pellet seemingly strikes the cave ceiling above me—a dusting of rock and stone sprinkles onto Gen and I.

The blue light abates, and the chamber is once more awash in a hush. My gaze slowly curves upward until it reaches the pistol that is still snared in

---

[85] Tricker: Trigger. Tricker was replaced by trigger in English around 1750.

the cattail's tendrils. I release it and belt the cattail around my midriff. *'Nay. I do not like it... Perhaps I shall try again on another occasion.'*

I look to Gen, but he is not there. I twirl in place yet cannot seem to find him, so I go into the other room where I notice a shivering heap of rubbish. A tiny whimpering comes from the pile. *'Apologies, Gen! I did not know; it was not my intention to frighten thee!'*

I rush to our stockpile at the room's edge and retrieve Gen's favorite food. Gripping the cup of pudding by its edge, I wave it above the shivering pile, and the whimpers abate, replaced by the sniff of nostrils. A hairy arm rises from the pile, takes the cup, and then sinks back into it.

'Aye, nary a need to be ashamed. I know it was scary because it was scary for me too...! Also, thou hast been struck by it before, so it must be even scarier.' From the gate chamber, I hear something scrape and clang together. *'Is that the gate? Is it complete?'*

As I drift into the gate chamber, the stained glass panels brighten and radiate light. I watch as the young lady in gold armor and the young man in the leather equipment drop their blades, placing them at their sides. The gate glides open, exposing what lies beyond.

I take a step back.

In the dark, a single space is illuminated, a verdant hillock. Looming at its apex is a willow tree, unmoving, numb to the abyss surrounding it. The willow tree's branches are barren, except for cords from which hang dozens upon dozens of bodies. I can feel this place in the depths of my very being—Tenebrous. The gate leads to Tenebrous, and somehow the hillock from hundreds of years ago, the hillock on which I was hanged, has found its home in Umbral's Pit.

I search for the source of light, discovering it dangling above the tree limbs. Squirming in the dark is an intertwined rope that sheds a soft radiance upon the grass-covered hillside and willow tree. I take another step away and notice some movement from the darkness.

My eyes stray toward the willow's trunk. There a person with cherry-red hair stands, her head tilted as if she is irritated by my faltering legs. She clutches a lantern in her left hand and raises her right, motioning for me to enter—her lantern swings as she does so.

'*Is this some sort of cruel jest?*' Without realizing it, I have retreated from the gate chamber.

A purple wall appears.

> **Earl Interface:**
> **Recommendation:** *Move through the gate, enter the Pantry, take the next step toward true existence.*

Glancing at the wall with a trembling gaze, I nearly hack it in half. '*Nay, nevermore! Seal it, seal that door; remove that nightmare realm from my sight! This instant; now!*' The doors begin to slide shut. When the woman in golden armor and the man in leather meet, their arms bend stiffly upward and their swords cross, sealing the gate.

I spin around; I am leaving this cave forthwith. I cannot stop myself; I feel betrayed, utterly misguided, deliberately misled. If there is one thing I have made clear, it is that I will not return to that place. That was how all this began; my contempt for that place is part of what has kept me pushing onward despite the endless hardships and struggles.

I can still hear Gen licking the inside of the pudding cup as I jab the brick from the cave entrance and leave the cave. Without a moment's hesitation, I place one foot in front of the other; I do not know where I am going, and I do not care. All I know is, I do not wish to be near that gate.

Earl's wall appears anew.

> **Earl Interface:**
> **Recommendation:** *Return to the gate and enter.*

'*Nay!*' The wall vanishes as I swing at it.

I move between trees, through thickets, snow-clad fields, and icy ponds until I happen upon a familiar place. Without realizing it, I have approached the noble's castle with the strange blue, white, and red flag. I had avoided this area ever since I initially spotted it weeks ago now. Now that I am close, I can see it's more modest than I initially thought, and there is not even a proper living area for the noble and his family. There is a small building atop the castle's bricked courtyard, yet through the windows, I can see it does not look lived in.

'...' I step into the courtyard and toward the gray cobblestone wall that overlooks a frozen lake. In the distance, the mad city of New York is visible, towering above the humble winter trees. If I go much further north than this, the quarantine area ends, and I may stumble upon people.

Snowflakes drift to the earth as I swing my legs over the railing, taking a seat. *'Three million seven hundred ninety thousand... One. Two. Three. Four...'* I sit upon my perch for hours, counting to myself, as the sun curves across the sky.

A purple wall appears, but I shove it away.

> **Earl Interface:**
> **Recommendation:** *Return to the gate and enter.*

Despite Earl's continued urging, I am not returning to that place.

'Everything I have done is so that I never have to return there, and now he is trying to tell me to go there willingly. What if the gate closes behind me? Worse yet, what if I go through the gate only to discover I never left? Frankly, that makes more sense than what has happened to me thus far. I have readily accepted things that I thought were impossible, just to avoid the thoughts of that place. Existence? I would rather not exist at all than be confined to that place.'

Looking downwards, I stare at my hazy figure and kick my legs. The idea of even returning to the cave, not to mention Tenebrous, makes me want to vomit. Though, I am willing to go back to the cave to retrieve Gen at least.

Footsteps crinkle the snow behind me. "Long time no see," a gentle voice whispers. "It was tougher for me to find you. I guess your Mana Efflux is a bit more contained—good work."

I freeze.

A hand brushes the snow from the railing next to me, and a person sits next to me. "Well, I say 'long time no see,' but it hasn't been that long, has it? A lot has happened. I guess it just feels like it's been months," they say.

Raising my head, I look toward the person sitting next to me. My acquaintance with the long silver hair is there, smirking.

She wears more informal attire, akin to what other women of this era wear. Her shirt is black and has a close-fitting collar that runs up her neck, hiding it like her gown did. Along with this, she wears a puffy coat that hugs her figure, tight blue trousers that cover her legs, and a pair of boots that have the same fastener that the arc suit's helmet has. A strap runs across her chest and ties to a beige satchel. It all looks lovely on her, yet she still wears her veil, which seems inapposite without a gown to compliment it.[86]

"Oh, and I've kept up with all that's happened with you too. I learned a lot in the process," she says, a growing smile spreading across her face. "As for you, you have a knack for getting into trouble and causing a stir, but you also have a knack for slipping between the cracks, literally and figuratively. A survivor through and through, huh?"

{...Terra?} I ask, peering into her deep green eyes.

With a click of the tongue, she points at herself. "The one and only. How have you been, Constance? Did you miss me?"

{Well... I...} I look away, crossing my arms, then respond, {Perhaps I missed the conversation a tad.}

"Is something wrong?" She starts to kick her feet, matching the pace of my own legs. "Your haze just seems a bit, well, turbulent, I guess."

{...It is naught of concern. Where hast thou been? I wish to hear what happened after thou left with that man?}

---

[86] Inapposite: Not suitable. Out of place.

She stares at the white snow beneath our swaying feet. "There's an order of explanations we need to follow before I can give you your answer." Her lips purse and she gazes into my eyes. "So before that, tell me, have you thought about my question? The one I asked before we separated? I want to know your thoughts on it."

{The one regarding us being able to trust one another unconditionally?} I pause, reflecting on everything that has happened since I arrived: the Hex Church, the wretched rat, copepods, elderly rats, constant fleeing, the fopdoodle, exploring, learning, the dinosaur, the Consortium, Gen—all of it has been... a lot for me to handle alone. Placing my hands in my lap, I close my eyelids halfway and nod. {My time here has been difficult... truly, truly difficult. One of the most arduous struggles of my existence.}

Terra tilts her head, and the orange sun shines on her silver hair. She waits for me to continue.

{A world I do not understand, a time I do not understand, people I do not understand, simply everything, I understand extraordinarily little of it all. I am always scared and on edge; thank the lord, I cannot get headaches. But truthfully, it is a miracle my ignorance has not resulted in my untimely demise. The only way I could explain my time here is like a bird being told to dig a pit.}

Collecting and rearranging my thoughts, I look at her and continue, {Certainly, a bird may dig, yet it is a Herculean task for a bird to dig a pit alone. A bird does not know the Earth, Terra, not like most creatures. There was a time I knew the Earth, except that was so long ago now both the Earth and I have forgotten one another. So, aye, possessing even a single reliable thread to tie myself to this world would be unbelievably comforting.}

Earl's persistent wall emerges once again, and my shoulders slump.

> **Earl Interface:**
> **Recommendation:** *Return to the gate and enter.*

'Stop! Thou art not comforting, Earl! The opposite perhaps!' I shout into my mind, glaring at the wall. I slap at it, and it fades.

Hearing Terra clear her throat, I look over to see her watching me. "I agree that having someone to lean on would be of great comfort," she says in a soft voice.

{Someone to lean on?}

"Yeah..." Her eyes turn away and her cheeks blush. "Like, you can lean on me, and I'll lean on you."

Glancing at my shoulder, the haze spins about, and I shake my head. {I am not something someone should lean on; I am not built sturdily enough for such a thing.}

A long, drawn-out cloud of warm air escapes her lips. "I mean, we can rely on one another. I think we stand a better chance together than apart. We'll be stronger and better prepared for any hardships to come." Looking at my shoulder, she tilts her head. "That shoulder jewelry looks really good on you, by the way."

{Aye! I appreciate the compliment, I think so too!} I respond, moving my hand to my shoulder and playing with the beads. {I still wish my shoulders were covered, but I rather like these beads as well. I have never had my own jewelry before! Well, except for a butterfly band for a few seconds, but I seem to have misplaced it since then...}

"Your first piece of jewelry only lasted a few seconds?" She laughs before glancing at the sun and nodding. "So let me ask you, do you know what a contract is?"

I move my hand from my shoulder and place it beneath my chin. {Oh, Terra, I am not so ill-informed that I would not know about contracts!}

"Yeaaah, what I mean is do you know there are sp—"

{Special kinds of contracts?} Since I cannot laugh, I fake a giggle in my head, pretending to wipe some dust from my chest. {Of course I do; the magically binding ones that Spirit Scribes can make. Since we last spoke, I have tirelessly searched for information regarding what thy words could have meant. How could I not know something so basic?}

'And by tirelessly, I mean I stole a book because it happened to be there.'

"Wow, impressive!" she replies with a laugh. "I guess I shouldn't sell someone so well-informed short, huh?"

{I am certainly well-informed and not helplessly ignorant, that is for certain. Disregard my earlier statements about it being a miracle I am alive.}

"Relax, I'm not going to cheat you, assuming you're interested in making a contract, and just so you know, I'm only interested in one type of contract, a lifetime reciprocation contract."

'After I read 'Contracting Foregone Humanity,' I suspected it was this she was referring to. But, Terra is a young woman; whatever the conditions, she must live with them forever, assuming I survive. After all, I suspect I do not age naturally.' I lean a tad closer to her. {A lifetime reciprocation contract. That's a literal lifetime. An awfully long time for thee.}

"I'm well aware. I have made an 'upon fulfillment' contract with someone else, stating that I would make a lifetime contract. If I don't make the contract soon, I'll be compelled to comply with their stipulations."

{A contract with someone else?}

She nods and makes a circular motion with her finger. "Yes, but it'll be better if we circle back to that later; first, we need to know what each person wants from this contract."

{Wants? Is the contract not meant to be a mere semblance of trust?}

"It definitely could be something as straightforward as 'We can't lie to each other,' but that doesn't really give us someone to lean on. That just gives you someone you can't lie to. What's important is that our fates are tied together; only then can all doubt be removed."

I pause, absorbing the implications of what she is suggesting. *'I am someone who has never fully placed their trust in another person before, yet I am beginning to believe Terra might somehow be worse than me. It sounds as if she wants to quite literally bind our lives together... I mean, that certainly guarantees trust, but it is also incredibly dubious, to say the least.'*

"Then... then I shall go first..." Terra corrects her posture and blurts out, "My life is comparable to an active nuclear warhead drenched in gallons of gasoline."

{Huh? I only understood some of that,} I reply, my eyelids forming their best questioning gaze.

She sighs, squeezing her fingers together. "Sorry, I kind of just jumped into it without explanation. I think before we do something irreversible, we should understand what we're getting into, for both our sakes. Then we can discuss what each person wants or, more specifically, what each person needs."

{Uhm, thou art not about to offer me a ring, art thou?} I raise my hand. {Because I doubt I can wear jewelry as haze.}

"No, that's not what this is!" She chuckles. "I'm not about to ask for your hand in marriage."

Dropping my hand, I shrug my shoulders. {I know, I was merely teasing thee. So thou wishest for us to confess our secrets, is that what is being implied?}

"Yes, although, I'll admit, I already know a lot of the details about your race, the Kiln. They have been the talk of the underground for a couple of weeks now."

My head recoils. {Thou knewest what I was!?}

"No, no, I originally thought you were a spirit and only found out after we last spoke what you actually are. Lately, I have been whispering into a lot of ears, and people have been extra talkative of late." Terra straightens her back and furrows her brow. "Which leads me to my first confession, though I'm uncertain how shocking someone unfamiliar with the city will find it."

Terra's serious expression prompts me to straighten my back and wring my hands together. My mind is still reeling from the gate earlier. {May I ask how many confessions thou art about to make?}

"Two, maybe three, then we'll discuss something else. Anyway, Constance, y'know I never did tell you my last name."

{Thy family name? I never informed thee of mine, so I never thought it pertinent.}

"That's right, but to be honest, my last name is what most people know me by; only a few people know me by my first name. Most know me by the name Galtry."

My mind blanks. Galtry, the person I have overheard many assert is amongst the most dangerous people in this city. Their name is mentioned alongside the Hex Church, Espositos, and their ilk. On some occasions, they act as if Galtry is the worst among them. Jessica even said Galtry ran this part of the city after usurping the Espositos, allowing the Hex Church to have free rein in the area.

When I fled the chamber pot tunnels, people were chanting outside the Hex Church, and the person speaking for the Hex Church denied any connection to Galtry. Even the Hex Church wishes to distance itself from such a person. I have promised myself not to get involved with such a wicked person.

I gaze at Terra, striving to see a crack develop in her demeanor, yet notice naught. Raising my guard, I search the area for any signs of movement. {Why do conflict and woe shadow me so closely?} Shaking my head, I ask, {What are the chances I would cross thy path?}

"Quite high in this case because, well, I tracked you down intentionally. The night we met, it wasn't by chance; I knew you were hiding somewhere in the park. I would never attend a wedding reception like that one ordinarily. Someone like myself is perpetually maintaining their image, and a wedding reception is considered too middlebrow. Sending me an invitation to events like that is more out of politeness and respect than an expectation of my actual attendance. It took a lot of convincing to be allowed to attend without garnering suspicion."

{But why pursue me and how? Especially, at that time, how would anyone know of my presence?}

Terre frowns and stares out over the frozen lake. "This piece of the city carries my name. If anything happens here, I know about it because, again, I need to be notified for appearance's sake. If someone tries to discuss it with me, I must know what's going on. I was told to not interfere, so that's why I did it via the wedding reception and telepathy. As for why, we'll discuss that more later... But, with all that said, I'm a sham."

{A sham? What does that mean?}

"A figurehead, the frontman, a scapegoat, or more specifically, a captive of my name and reputation. I have no real authority; I make none of the actual decisions that people know the person Galtry for. The assassinations, murders, trafficking, bribery, all of it happens under that name, but all of it is ordered by my jailor. In the end, Galtry is just a cover for the Hex Church's illicit activities. Still, the name and face demand respect, so I have gotten pretty good at finding backdoors to get some things I need to get done, mostly information, moving money, and procuring things I may need in secret."

{But would people believe a woman as young as thyself could be responsible for all those things?}

"Good question, and the answer is no. Many think I 'usurped' the original Galtry and took their place. All lies, all convenient explanations that people have romanticized in their heads. Of course, some people question or don't believe it, but it doesn't matter. Explanations only need to endure long enough for the Beta to end; the long-term hardly matters anymore."

I shake my head, reflecting on the times we have met. There have been times I have had to hide while people passed by. They all looked at Terra, but none of them reacted strangely. *{How can a face demand respect, but at the same time, people do not know it? Many have seen thee whilst in the park, but I have not seen anyone react oddly... Save for some men, but that is to be expected.}*

She reaches for her headband. The veil drifts downwards in her grasp. As she pulls it away, a face that is both familiar and unfamiliar at the same time is revealed. With half-closed eyes the face watches me, awaiting my reaction. The left side is as it always has been, with beautiful unblemished skin and a bright green eye. However, the right is different; instead of green, her eye is silver with a set of dark rings around the iris. As for the skin, starting around the forehead, sewn-on argent fabric runs at an arc to the bridge of her nose and down a portion of her cheek and neck. It runs into the collar of her clothing, hiding the extent to which her skin has been sewn and replaced with this fabric.

{Terra...} My eyes cannot separate themselves from the fabric.

Chapter 20: Those Who Lost Their Names and So They Share

∞∞∞∞∞∞∞∞∞∞∞∞∞∞∞

Terra stares at me.

Unable to confront my gaze, she turns away and asks, "What do you think? Pretty scary, isn't it? This was stitched to me on my tenth birthday. The 'optimal age' to have forty percent of my face replaced with silken runes, as that man put it. To add insult to injury, this face, stitched with runes, is the face that everyone now associates with 'Galtry.' What an unfunny joke life can sometimes be." She scoffs and fiddles with the veil. As she kneads the veil between her fingers, the fibers rub together, making a faint noise. "I paid the Consortium a substantial sum of money for a pair of veils, so I could disguise my appearance and go into public casually. Worth every penny for the semblance of normalcy they've afforded me the last couple of years."

I study her appearance. {I think it...}

She nods as if she knows what I am about to say. The dark rings around her iris shift and wiggle as if it is ink that refuses to dry. "You know, the first thing I did after getting the veils was to visit a chain café. I didn't even order anything for the first hour; I just sat there. Not that I didn't get some looks, but they weren't looks of fear. They were different. It had been years since a stranger glanced at me without turning pale. It was therapeutic."

Shaking my head, I say, {I think it looks...}

"I know, it loo—"

I scoop a handful of snow and drop it over Terra's brow. {I am attempting to speak!}

The snow slides off her head. She narrows her eyes, purses her lips, and side-eyes me. "It's cold... Sorry for interrupting you... I guess."

I nod and cross my arms. {I think it looks fashionable and mysterious! I love it! It is not frightening at all; if thy wish is to see scary, then search no further than I.} I pause, realizing my own appearance is extraneous. {That second point is irrelevant, but regardless, thou shouldst not be afraid to show thy face. I think it is charming. Ah! I learned a bit of cant from a child earlier this forenoon; I had never heard it used like this. I believe it was 'crisp,' at least it was something to that effect. So, as they say, I deem thy appearance crisp.}[87]

Terra gawks at me, her eyes shuddering. "Constance." Her hand strays toward the fabric sutured into her face. She seems uncertain how to react, and then eventually, she sighs. "I think you're 'crisp' too, and I appreciate the flattery, but it's unnecessary."

{Flattery?} I unfurl my arms. {I am not wheedling thee; my words are sincere.}

She shakes her head; to me, it's as if she simply does not know how to respond to my words. "We need to move on. I'm short on time and can't stay away forever. Caldwell can only tell my 'bodyguards' I'm taking an afternoon nap for so long before they get suspicious."

{Is that so... then I... I suppose it is only fair that I tell a secret now,} I reply.

Raising a hand, she shakes her head, removes the satchel from her chest, and places it in her lap. "No, again I appreciate it, but I should finish saying what I need to say. I may never finish if I don't keep going."

{Aye.} I once more straighten my back. {If that is what thou wishest, then I suppose I shall harken thee.}

She opens the bag and removes the silver tome I have seen a few times before, except for the first time I notice it has an engraving on the cover. If I remember correctly, Lorelai and Vincent had a serpent on their tomes, but Terra's has the image of a moth. Graven in white, it has two antennas, six little legs, and a big pair of wings that rest to either side of its body.

Setting the tome in her lap, she removes some black ink and a silver quill. She raises the cover, revealing that all the pages are blank and yellowed like parchment. Placing the ink to the side, she opens it, dips the quill, and writes, "The memoir of Erik Galtry, a man who lost his name." As she

---

[87] Cant: to speak in the jargon of thieves and vagabonds.

writes, the ink sinks into the yellowed pages and the yellow color fades, replaced by a silver wash. A faint radiance arises, and the pages begin to flip. One after another, the pages turn, yet there never seems to be an end; they simply keep flipping.

Like someone squeezing soot from a sponge, ink bubbles rise from the pages, coalescing into people and shapes. They are all made of the same black ink and move about the pages until they combine into a moving image. "Memories can be fractural, so pay attention," Terra murmurs.

'Memories? This is a memory?'

Pages continue to flow; an image of a tall man, a short woman, and a little girl emerges. The woman kisses the little girl on the forehead and shuffles off the page, after which the man takes her hand. Both the girl and man travel along the various pages until they step through a doorway and find themselves somewhere outside. They play together; the little girl runs about as the man chases her. Both have big smiles across their faces. The woman reenters the scene and says something to the man. The pair strolls out of view, leaving the girl alone. With the couple gone, the girl hops playfully toward a box full of sand.

She sits and plays by herself, shoveling sand into a bucket. "They went to finish lunch," Terra says. "I vaguely remember we used to do a late breakfast for lunch on Saturdays, brunch basically. I'd play in the backyard by myself while they cooked; it was an ordinary Saturday. But like all stories worth telling, ordinary ended..."

There's a black twinkle at the top of the page. A smear of ink plunges toward where the girl plays at the page's bottom. It crashes into the sand, scattering it in all directions. The little girl coughs, spitting out the sand that flew into her mouth. Still spitting sand, she crawls on her hands and knees toward whatever smashed into her sand. There is a tear in the scene before it reappears, and the little girl's arm is reaching toward a black blot within a shallow pit.

The blot spasms, and an expression of dread carves itself upon the girl's lips. The blot twists, snuffing the sun hanging above the little girl. "I can't remember what it whispered to me, but I remember it being something I knew I shouldn't know. Not in the sense of a child learning something bad." —Black ink oozes inward from all four corners of the page, encircling the girl until all that remains is the starless pitch and the shivering pupil of her left eye– "It was something deeper, something primal."

A hand reaches toward the girl, driving back the blot. The blackness recedes, and the man from the beginning is embracing the little girl. The blot evaporates, the girl's body dyes silver, and the man's eyes stain black as an abyss. Sooty tears ooze down the man's cheeks.

Terra sighs. "I was in a coma for a few days after that and spent about a week in the hospital. My hair turned white during that time, eventually taking on its silver appearance after waking up. My right eye did the same thing; the rings came later in life. Since I couldn't remember what it said to me, the only thing about my life that changed was that I had to start visiting a clinic every few months. I didn't understand until later that Dad wasn't so lucky. The whispers didn't just disappear; they had found a better ear."

Her tome's pages turn faster; every page is a different day. The man reads a lot during this time. Every day that passes, the man's image becomes more and more of a smear: first the right half of his face, then his torso, arms, and legs. When that happens, the woman returns, picks up the girl of silver, and they leave. The man watches them go as the smear spreads, cocooning the last of his face.

"I'm not sure what happened while we were apart, but next I saw him, he didn't even walk the same. Still..." The image shows the little silver girl; she's a tad taller in this new one. She lies in bed, a window to her back and a doll in her hands. There's a flicker in the picture as a blotted face appears outside. The face watches the girl through the glass before raising a smeared finger and tapping on her window. The scene fractures and reforms into a new one showing the little girl standing on her bedstead with her window open. She lifts her arms, and the smeared man takes her. "...I really missed Dad."

I grab the cattail's end and fiddle with it; I am not certain if I should speak, so I continue to listen.

"That's the story of how my father traded himself to save me from something I can't even remember. His name was Erik Galtry, but that's the name of a dead man—the name of a living corpse. Nowadays, people don't know him by that name, and if you tried, he wouldn't even realize you're talking to him." Terra closes the tome and looks at me; her eyes are empty. "The only name he'll answer to, the only one he even recognizes now, is Bishop."

My hand releases the cattail. I forget that I cannot breathe and attempt to gasp. {Thy father! The Bishop!?}

"Well, he's just one of them, but yes," she says after a moment's wavering.

{W-what does that suggest...? Are there more Bishops!? How many more!?}

"Several, just like my father, all of whom go by the same name—Bishop. None of them respond to their real names anymore, just 'Bishop' or 'Bishop' and their jurisdiction. My father is Bishop Manhattan. Of course, I know my father's full name, but I'm one of only a few people who do." Sighing, she says, "There was one occasion where Bishop Staten's ex-wife and Bishop Queen's daughter tracked them down. The two women had filed missing person's reports and ended up locating the Bishops. Neither Bishop was happy about it; in fact, they were furious."

She shakes her head and continues, "They were so irate they had the NYC Municipal Archives burned to the foundation to destroy their records. Of course, they blamed it on Galtry; that's the original purpose of her existence. It evolved into a big scandal, and people literally protested for my arrest after that. When nothing happened, I began receiving hate mail laced with all kinds of toxins, though none ever came close to making it to me. The people who sent the letters were arrested and now sit in prison, yet that only infuriated everyone else further. It only died down a little after the 'Puzzling Five Hundred' tragedy became the new topic of the hour. A lot of the NYPD still hold a grudge."

I only comprehend parts of her words, and most of that is because I am still trying to make peace with her previous words. {Apologies, but I still cannot believe there are more Bishops! Terra, thy father, 'Bishop Manhattan,' he terrifies me! He can effortlessly toy with me; forgive me, but he is a menace! Now, there are more? What shall happen if one of them decides to annihilate me on a whim!? Or perhaps more frightening, what if they all unite to do worse than annihilate me!? They seem quite capable, Terra!}

"Don't worry." She forces a small smile. "I can promise the church won't be able to hurt you after the contract."

I lift my arm, gesturing in the Hex Church's general direction. {*The church is so near that confrontation seems unavoidable. All I can do is hide like a hermit until either I am stronger, or they resettle somewhere else. So how couldst thou swearest such things? I understand the Bishop is thy father, yet I am confident it is not as simple as requesting he leave me be!*} My arm falls to my side. '*Thinking of the contract, am I a dullard for considering it? The Bishop... the Bishops!? Nay... nay, I should collect myself. Unless Terra is an unimaginably masterful actor, she is not her father... Though, she did pretend we originally met by coincidence.*'

"You'll understand when... if we make the contract," she whispers. We both look toward our laps, and things grow hushed as we sit listening to the breeze. Terra's fingernails scratch her tome's cover. "Do you hate me?" she asks in a small voice. "I'm not one to usually care about that kind of thing, but, well, I think I'd like if you didn't."

Looking up, I shake my head. {*Nay. It's not as if thou brought me harm, quite the opposite in fact. Thou hast aided me considerably. Besides, I encountered thy father before we met, and so it's not as if thou art responsible for that woeful affair. I am not one to hold the parents' sins against the children, and candidly, the Hex Church would still be nearby even if I had not bumbled upon him. This quandary was inevitable.*}

She nods, exhaling a sigh of relief, though I can tell she remains astray in her thoughts.

{*And pray thee, accept my condolences. I am saddened to learn of what happened to thy father... It is challenging for me to comprehend, as I do not hold any memories of my own parents, but I know it must hurt.*}

"I appreciate it. The hardest part is being unable to do anything, but I've accepted that I can't, and I've decided to stop trying to bring Dad back. With the Cosmic System's impending return, that shell of my father is a cause I no longer have the time for. Besides, being around him is risky. Every time he opens his mouth, he tells four sinister lies and one truth; that way, you'll always be left agonizing over which is which. That's just how he is now."

{*I... I suppose if there was a method to remedy him, thou wouldst have found it,*} I respond.

"It is not that I think there isn't a way to fix him, it's that..." She lifts her head and touches her veil. "How far, how long, can I just let things continue? I carry so many scares already, Constance. But I also carry what little memory a child could have of their parents, and I hope I can eventually find a little closure in just being the keeper of those memories... If Dad were still the person he used to be, I hope he would agree that's enough... And truthfully, beyond my own feelings, the situation has changed too much anyway."

I tilt my head. {*The situation has changed?*}

Terra clenches her fist, her brows furrow. "Before now, there was nothing I could do to interfere, but now I've found a medium to exploit—two major cracks in the Church's façade."

{*A crack in their façade? I do not understand; what does that imply?*}

"They officially made me Galtry when I was thirteen and then surrounded me with their most trusted people. They made me the face to lure people into the syndicate and introduce the Hex Church to the world. It worked amazingly well. People wanted to be a part of the same religion as Galtry; people wanted to know what the Hex Church was and how they felt about the infamous child murderer being a part of their religion. Books were written about 'Galtry: Youngest Crime Lord,' a television show, there were two movies, Constance! People were downright obsessed. Questions about the fabric, about my life, who I am, who I was, what I wanted, multiple assassination attempts, people trying to steal my clothes to sell. Twice, not once, but twice, a suicidal person approached me and said their last wish in life was to be murdered by Galtry. It was and still is insane!"

{*...Aye, that all certainly sounds mad,*} I respond, rubbing the back of my neck. '*This city has proven that it knows naught but insanity numerous times.*'

"Meanwhile, while everyone else was treating me like some sort of glamorous zoo exhibit, in the actual Galtry Syndicate, I had close to zero control. The upper echelons of the syndicate are manipulated by Hex Church members, while the middle and bottom didn't care as long as they got their money. Worst of all, it totally trapped me, like a bird in a concrete cage. There's no running away when you're the face of an internationally recognized criminal syndicate. I'd be arrested the minute I stepped foot outside the New York City limits."

Terra leans forward a dangerous glint in her eyes. "But everything has changed. There are rumors of monsters, talk of powerful people doing superhuman things, whispers of a big announcement. The people in the middle and bottom who once only cared about getting paid are anxious. They don't care as much about money anymore. That means the dynamic has shifted, and the new dynamic is one of faith and conviction. These people want a leader. They want a firm footing. And all they know is Galtry; they've burned bridges, committed crimes, all to be under her thumb. They have faith and confidence in her. They're more eager than ever to follow her, and that's why I'm preparing a tactical 'tiered coup,' so to speak, to unshackle Galtry from the Hex Church."

Contemplating the implications of her words, I recognize her intentions, and ask, {...Dost thou mean, thou intend to be a real 'Galtry?' Are they not a brutal criminal, known for their despicable deeds?}

"They are, but Constance..." She raises her hands, showing them to me; they are trembling. "The world is about to sink into bloody chaos. The people that survive with only a little blood on their hands will be the lucky ones. Everyone else is going to be steeped in it or dead. I'm willing to let Galtry be the blood-soaked wall that shields others if it allows me to choose whose blood it is that drenches me. I have some people I want to protect, and I'm not such a dense idealist that I'd let them drown in it when they can stand on my shoulders to breathe."

Clutching her legs, she tries to calm her quivering hands by squeezing them. She continues, "But I'm scared too. I'd make a lot of vicious people my enemy, and Manhattan's position is precarious, to say the least. Yet I'm prepared to set off the powder keg, Galtry's ready, and I'm ready to play her role for real. I'll need to purge the Galtry Syndicate's upper echelons, and I can't let them live. It's too dangerous and stupid to do that; they've built a reputation and loyalties within the syndicate. They're all lousy people who deserve anything that happens to them, but blood is blood, and it will be the first blood to stain me."

She goes quiet, composing herself.

'This is a destructive thread of thought, yet it's not as if I cannot comprehend it.' I peer at my body and my kiln. 'I am a monster, in the most literal sense. I have never deliberately taken a life, but I understand I shall have to someday.'

I shake my head and then look out over the icy lake. *{I am afraid I do not have a great answer, and like thee, I have been struggling with the same thoughts and difficulties. I have narrowly avoided it thus far, yet for the first time, I have a place to defend and cannot flee as I have in the past.}* A white bird passes overhead, riding the winter breeze. *{I presume this contract would, in some way, make me a brick in thy blood-soaked wall.}*

She does not respond; her continued silence says enough.

> **Earl Interface:**
> **Recommendation:** *Return to the gate and enter.*

The wall vanishes without a word. I look Terra up and down, and for the first time, I think I might understand them. *'This person is starving; she craves something she cannot have... Loneliness, ambivalence, and a world that seems to wish to crush one beneath its weight, I know it all well. The difference is, this person shall not and cannot run from her burdens. I always ran away, every time. As a child, I ran from ruffians. As an adolescent, I ran from the French Éclat. As a young woman, I ran from the English nobles, the Éclat, and misery itself. I ran so long, and so far, I ended up in Roanoke, where I finally hesitated to run. Then in Tenebrous, I ran again. Now I am a Kiln, and I still run. The only reason I am even sitting here at the noble's castle is because I ran here after opening the gate.'*

Raising my hands, I gaze at the shadowy haze that drifts about my palms. *{In life, I was many things: a thief, beggar, swindler, cheat, burglar, graverobber, but none ever called me a killer.}*

Terra's head sinks, and her hair falls and hides her face.

I stare at the bustling city. *{Yet, I shan't criticize thee. In fact, I think it is courageous and commendable for thee to confront thy burdens with such fervor. It's impracticable, nay, impossible for me to never bloody myself; I have known that for some time now, though I have managed to avoid it thus far... Nonetheless, even if I was not a monster, and I were living when the world was to fall into ruin, I would have done what's necessary to fill both my and Sir Mouser's belly.}*

My eyes drift across the castle walls. It's cobbled stone and my memories clash, and my thoughts stray. *{Thou knowest, my dream as a little girl was to be a fair knight. I wanted so badly to arrive somewhere and hear folk gasp in* excitement at my sudden appearance, and not because I snatched the bread loaf they were carrying from their careless fingertips. I used to stand in the filthy cobblestone alleyways for hours, waiting for my chance to rush out and save someone in distress with my valiant tree branch blade. It was always the same fantasy. I would appear, brandishing my sword. They would look upon me, their heroine, and I would be towering above them—high above the world, impossible to ignore. I would be a beautiful, colorful beacon that would wipe away the gray in their eyes...}

I raise my arm, pointing to the sky. {'It is I' is what I had planned to shout. I would not need to introduce myself; people could never forget someone so gallant. At least that is what I remember thinking as a child.} Dropping my arm, I brush some snow off the side of the stone rails and shake my head. {I rehearsed those words more times than I could ever hope to count but never did use them as I planned, and I know not if I ever shall. All I know now is... that I am tired. A lifetime, an afterlife, and a rebirth, all spent running from misery; I cannot go on like this for much longer. I am so, so tired.}

My hand moves to my most recent adaptation, the snappish beads around my shoulder. {...It's not much of an exaggeration to say that I could count all the things I have truly owned on my fingers and toes, because if someone wishes to live a life as I did, one must own practically nothing. Otherwise, they may grow too comfortable, and hesitate as I did, then they shall find it's too late. They will have nowhere left to run, their legs shall finally give, and the war of attrition between them and the world is lost. In the end, when they see death rearing its head, they shall pretend to be satisfied with their fate because that moment of comfort makes them realize how tired they honestly were. Even if they survive, they shall forever feel starved, hungry for the comfort they were forced to abandon.}

My thoughts of London, Tenebrous, New York, and my time in my little cottage in the woods leave a bitter taste upon my kiln. I push the bitterness to the back of my mind and gaze upon the frozen lake. {It's hard to feel starved and endure anyway, Terra. This is why I believe thou art a far stronger person than I was in life or death, and... I would be more than pleased to take a stand with thee... Mayhaps, we may even ease the burden of those that deserve such a privilege.}

Pausing to think for a moment, I continue, {Like this elderly woman I saw a fortnight or so ago, feeding pigeons, sh—}

I cease speaking, hearing stifled crying.

"Thank you," she murmurs.

{...Aye.}

Terra sits noiselessly, looking rather downcast. However, as I explain everything I know about Kiln and The Tower, she gradually recovers from her downhearted stupor. I do not reveal everything, though, things like Earl, the gate, souls, spirits, Tenebrous, and Gen I omit. Those shall remain secret for the time being because it would all take too long to explain, and with how little I comprehend, it would merely lead to confusion. I shall wait until I know more before discussing those subjects.

After that, I go into detail about what happened with the Consortium a few days ago and the pair of Spirit Scribes several days before that.

Throughout my explanations, she only interrupts once to elaborate on the Consortium. "They are going to be a problem until we smooth things over. We cannot overly antagonize them. Unbeknownst to most, the Consortium has practically turned the entire city of Chicago into a mercantile city-state. They are just waiting for the right time to make their move. It's fantastic you didn't fatally injure anyone, or they'd consider you a much more dangerous threat. If the Consortium felt so inclined, they could use their network of government lackeys and sycophants to purchase and dig up all of Central Park. Still, since they've taken an interest in you, we'll need to satisfy them somehow, that way we can buy and use their services in the future. We must maintain a business-like relationship with them."

She goes quiet again as I resume explaining everything. When I finish, the sun has nearly set on the horizon.

"I think I understand," she says with a slight nod. "These structures, places, or whatever become a way to offset a Kiln's constant Essence decay."

{Uhm...} Hearing her understand so quickly, and about something I had only partly conjectured in my own head, leaves me a bit short for words. {I... I suppose it is something like that. How didst thou com'st to that conclusion?}

"That's just what it sounded like to me. Still, it's strange. From what you've told me, you haven't actually noticed yourself losing Essence."

{Aye, I thought so too. It has been a great help to not have to worry about it, though, so I have taken it as a blessing for the most part. Not that I do not believe it suspicious.}

"I'm sure you'll figure it out, but if I had to speculate, I'd say there is a source of Essence you're drawing from and you just haven't found what it is yet. But whatever it is, I doubt it'll last forever, so make sure you keep that in mind."

'A source of Essence I am drawing from, and it shan't last forever...' Her remarks elicit a conjecture. 'That "R" in the adaptation wall, is that what it denotes? It's where I have been drawing Essence from?'

Terra wipes her eyes, huffs, and then asks, "So are The Tower's roots responsible for the beasts in the Lake too?"

Looking toward the snowy ground, I shake my head and answer, {Nay, but in the near future, it may be the wellspring of more beasts.} I hesitate; everything has been a result of necessity, but this next part is solely something I must decide on my own. {I... I have been considering installing a vent in the chamber pot tunnels. If I did so, it would pervert them, transforming them into tunnels teeming with beasts. I am uncertain, though. It feels a bit too nasty and ungovernable.}

"Chamber pot tunnels? I'm assuming you're referring to the sewers?" She lets out a tiny laugh and then a sigh. For a moment, she remains silent before a bitter look surfaces. "But... I think you should do it. It's not a bad idea to vent it into the sewers. Actually, I'd even go as far to say it's one of the most advantageous things that could happen to this city in the long run."

Her words make me recoil; I did not expect her to say such a thing. {Not a bad idea? How is it not bad to fill the ground beneath people's feet with monsters and beasts?}

"I-it's obviously a moral gray area, but the ugly truth is that some people would benefit tremendously from it. We just talked about it, so I know you understand the importance of Essence and how challenging it has been for you to gather. The only real source of Essence in the city itself is park animals, pets, and, well, people." I nod, waiting for her to continue. "Moreover, the only way to get Essence is to kill something of appropriate size or strength. That means anyone not being groomed by a cult or organization is at a severe disadvantage."

{Groomed? What does that mean? Can people not simply obtain Essence from eating?}

"From eating?" She tilts her head as if my words are unusual. "Uh, no, of course not, and by groomed, I just mean someone who is being placed in a position to acquire Essence regularly. For most, they will be around the same level now as when the Beta began. Unless..."

Realizing what she is attempting to convey, I respond, *{Unless they have somewhere and something to hunt for Essence? I have noticed that small creatures like rats do not give Essence.}*

With a nod, she explains, "From what I've learned, Essence is only absorbed if it's whatever the Cosmic System considers a whole number, and small animals don't render enough to meet that condition. So as you said, yes, someplace that can be accessed for hunting would be a grand asset to those that could make use of it."

{The chamber pot tunnels then... What about the innocent folk that get caught up in all this? This city is drowning in people; it seems practically inevitable that innocent men, women, and children shall be killed.}

"I... Yes, that will unquestionably happen." She pauses, gathering her thoughts; a bitter frown appears upon her face. "But I personally think it would cause a lot of suffering in the short term yet prevent much more in the long term. It's cold toward those that will suffer the consequences early, yet it's still not as bad as simply allowing the cults and organizations to grow in power and thrive while the common person remains stagnant. What's going to happen if there isn't a government or a proper society to protect and shield those people in the future?"

{Then... I suppose those commoners would be at the mercy of some questionable people who were able to collect Essence beforehand,} I answer, rubbing my chin. *{They would be powerless and unable to oppose those people for quite some time, I would imagine. Perhaps never if the present nobility cannot spare enough soldiers and they elect to establish a new aristocracy with its own lineage of nobility. Situations like that have occurred in England in the past.}*

She scratches her head and smiles. "Well, yes, maybe not an aristocracy, but you understand my point. Furthermore, something like beasts and monsters appearing will happen sooner or later, and this would probably be a milder, more controlled version of what's to come. If the sewers are changed first, it would essentially serve as a way to ease people into the idea of confronting or fighting beasts and the struggles they can expect to face in the near future. In fact, this is a good segue into what I wanted to discuss regarding the other Kiln and you specifically."

{The other Kiln and me? What does that mean? Dost thou knowest of another Kiln?} I ask, my hand drifting to my own kiln.

"I've been making some calculated moves within the lower rungs of the Galtry Syndicate. Things like gathering information, establishing durable lines of communication, or contacting people that have been ignored or slighted in some way. It involves a lot of listening, memorizing, extrapolating." She takes a breath, saying, "So, what I wanted to discuss is the number of what I suspect may be Kiln roaming the region. Though I admit I can't say for sure they are Kiln, many of them have been behaving in ways that suggest they are, and the amount of activity that's been reaching my ears is not an insignificant figure. That being said, I do think you were amongst some of the earlier Kiln to appear. But, since then, the amount of what I suspect is Kiln activity has been steadily rising."

I tilt my head and stare at Terra. Her eyes are a bit bloodshot from having failed to suppress a few tears earlier. I can tell she is starting to get cold and tired, but this information is too important. {Is it truly possible that there can be that many? I have not seen any hereabouts.}

"There aren't as many in the Manhattan area—that's where we are right now, by the way. In the surrounding areas of Brooklyn, Queens, Staten Island, the Bronx, and New Jersey, there are more. Then the further you move away from Manhattan, the activity increases until it gradually drops back off to nothing. The Consortium has been struggling to keep everything temporarily under wraps because of a contract they have with the federal government. Still, they're basically just gluing everything together until it all comes crashing down. They aren't concerned about New York City's fate in the long term, no one is really, there are too many things happening and the stakes are too high."

'If there are other Kiln about, what shall happen when their Domains sprout? This must be what that Lincoln person was referring to when he said "this city is done for." But it does not make sense why there would be so few near me.' I decide to ask Terra. {Why would there be more Kiln in those areas? Why would more not appear near the park as I did?}

"Well, I wasn't sure before speaking to you, but I believe it could be a mixture of things." Pursing her lips, she begins to think. Her legs, which hang over the side of the castle, move back and forth lightly. "I think the fact that Manhattan is densely populated and that it would be harder to hide here plays a part in it. Meaning many of them could have conceivably gotten themselves killed or fled to less dense areas. Still, that didn't really explain the discrepancy. Now that I've spoken to you, I have a few new deductions I can make... Do you remember when you told me your type was a 'Tower'?"

Looking toward the tall buildings in the city, I realize what she must be implying. {I surmise thy reasoning is that there may not be as many Kiln hereabouts because there are not as many places they can be. They are not of the right type for such a place, meaning the surrounding areas are more suitable for them, so that is where they moved toward.}

Her eyes go wide, and she nods. "That's right! I still don't think it fully explains everything. However, it's a start." She lets out a heavy sigh. "Personally, I have a feeling that something or someone had a hand in creating this situation."

{Someone else? Truly? Was it not just the Cosmic System's doing? Why would someone want to make something like this happen?}

"I don't know yet. I do think the Cosmic System played a part in it, sure, but something is still strange. I'm just missing motivation. If there is no motivation, I'll just have to assume it was all the Cosmic System's doing, I guess," she says, shaking her head. "We must keep it in mind, but the situation is what it is now, and I don't foresee it changing. We need to adapt to the circumstances at hand first and foremost."

Lincoln's words again run through my mind, mixing with thoughts of what it means if Kiln appear throughout the city as Terra seems to be implying. {Dost thou believest this city is 'done for'?}

"Even if I did, it doesn't matter, all my eggs are in one basket, and it sounds like yours are too. Also, now that I've heard about your Tower and your potential plan for the sewers, I believe the city as a whole is far from done for. It'll never be the same as it is now, yet it can become a place for those that wish to prepare for the future." Terra shifts her position. "Your Tower is important, right? You need to keep an eye on it, and you need people in and around it, right?"

{I... I mean, aye, that is what I have been led to believe.}

"Then let us kill two birds with one stone."

I tilt my head and ask, {Is that the same as 'to stop two gaps with one bush'?}[88]

Smiling, she answers, "I have no idea, but my point is, I think we can solve both of those problems with the same solution—people. Ordinary people can solve this problem for you."

{Solve this problem for me? I am afraid to inform thee that people are typically the problem, not the solution. Besides, why would ordinary people dwell around my Tower if the city surrounding it is practically doomed to become ghastly ruins? I cannot protect them if that is what is being insinuated, I wish to help those that are willing to help themselves, but that is far different from protecting them.}

"No, no, I'm not insinuating anything. The people shall protect themselves because you have something they need, something that could save their lives in the future. Which is why, along with the sewers, I believe we can persuade ordinary people to congregate around you with us barely having to lift a finger."

{What dost thou meanest by, 'I have something they need'?} I rub the nape of my neck. {Art thou alluding to something tangible, or is this something more... uhm, philosophical, like 'hope,' because I do not believe something of that nature shall suffice.}

"Admittedly, hope will be important, but this isn't some corny kids' book. No one in the United States would get out of bed for something as vacant

---

[88] "I will learne, to stop two gaps with one bushe." Originates from *The Proverbs and Epigrams of John Heywood* (1546), and it's thought to have influenced the coining of the expression 'kill two birds with one stone.'

as 'hope' alone. Not without something tangible backing it up."
Rummaging through her bag, she removes a stack of papers. She flips
through them and shows me some pictures. "Do you remember these
individuals? You've met them all, haven't you?"

The first is a young man; he looks to be in a white bed, presenting the
thumbs-up gesture.

I point and answer, {That's the shrieking man; he breathed in my haze a few
weeks ago.}

She laughs. "I don't know about 'shrieking man,' but it sounds like it
might be the same person. He's a teenager named Daniel Fields and this
picture is of him in the hospital after he encountered you. Now, what
about the other one?"

I examine the following picture, a simple portrait of a man in a suit
standing in front of a white wall. Recognizing them, I point while
answering, {That is Preston of the Consortium.}

"Yes, that's him, and this one?" Nodding, she moves on to the next
picture.

This one is yet another man. Like Daniel, he is in a white bed, except he is
connected to a device of some sort. He has only a left arm and where his
legs should be are white bandages wrapped tight around stumps. {The
fopdoodle... Did I do that to him?}

"Huh?" She glances at the picture and then jerks it away. "Sorry, that was
supposed to be a different one; I'm really sorry!"

{I... Think nothing of it. From what I understand, he is a man that is undeserving
of sympathy, but... I am curious how he is in such a miserable state. He claimed
that he had acquaintances nearby that were going to aid him.}

Putting the picture away, she sighs. "It was a mixture of frostbite and some
type of bacterial infection that together caused extensive gangrene
throughout his limbs. Only one of them was able to be saved. He's been in
a coma since... I only had the picture because I've been looking into
people you've interacted with. It was supposed to be a picture of Jessica
Valentine, that police officer you met, but I guess I misplaced it. Weird."

{Jessica? Did she manage to escape the Consortium?}

"Yeah, she managed to escape. Anyway, her situation is similar to Daniel's." Terra puts everything away and digs through her satchel. "Now, this video, I mean, these moving pictures are from a few days after you made contact with Daniel." Removing her lap-top, she directs it toward me. "Now watch this video."

The 'video' shows Daniel standing outside some type of establishment. A sign hangs above the counter that reads "Phazel's New York-Style Pizzeria." *'Oh, Phazel's pizza, I have eaten that food before!'*

Daniel stands there as a woman walks out. "Welcome back, Daniel. I heard about what happened, and don't worry, I don't think you're totally nutso," the woman says.

"Gee, thanks, Brenda. How considerate of you to tell me that," Daniel responds with a long-drawn sigh.

"Don't worry about it! I've had days where I've wanted to shriek until my vocal cords bled too." She titters, holding a square box toward Daniel. "Anywho, take this pizza. It goes to that one dude, y'know, the Italian guy that likes to answer the door in his tighty-whities. If you can't remember where he lives, his address is on the ticket."

Someone yells Brenda's name, and she turns her head as Daniel reaches for the box. Just before he takes the box, he vanishes and then reappears. When he does so, he grabs his stomach, retches, and vomits on both Brenda and the box.

"What the fuck, you psycho!?" Brenda screams.

Terra lowers the lap-top. "Daniel got into the Beta because of your haze. He awoke! Some random college kid who used to deliver pizza for a living actually awoke because of you; that's unbelievable!"

{Is it?} I point at the lap-top with a limp finger. *{Because it seemed like he was rather unwell and suffered considerably because of it.}*

Waving her hand, she shakes her head, denying my claim. "There are people out there who are literally killing themselves by injecting Elixir in hopes of getting into the Beta. Your haze can get them into the Beta, too, except it seems to have a much lower fatality rate!"

She places the lap-top to the side and fumbles with some more papers. One sheet gets swept away, but she reaches out and catches it without even looking up. Discovering what she is looking for, she holds it so I can see; it is nothing except numbers, and I have nary an idea of what I am reading.

"That sample of your haze I took, I paid to have a foreign epidemiologist fly into New York in secret to run a test with it—a well-respected, close-lipped German doctor named Tobias Jäger. Anyway, I told Doctor Jäger that I wanted to know the fatality rate and its effects, so he tested it on one hundred mice... And truthfully, it was a little aggravating for him to do such an archaic experiment considering I had shelled out a handsome sum of money to procure a world-class lab for his use." She takes a breath through her teeth and sighs. With a roll of her eyes, she retracts the paper and points at some of the numbers. "He's reconducting the experiment to reaffirm the results, but the initial experiment has yielded numbers that are better than anticipated: nine mice awoke with minimal complications, sixty-one awoke after recovery, eight were maimed or killed by other mice, four passed away immediately, and then eighteen awoke once they were placed in a high oxygen environment or hyperbaric chamber. Best of all, as you told me once before, it doesn't really spread between things. It ordinarily requires direct contact with the original sample."

{...It sounds as if thou believest it to be rather special, but do other Kiln not awaken things as well?}

"Maybe some can, I don't know, but that doesn't matter. What matters is you *can* do it now, not tomorrow, not next week, but now. We can get people to come here and put their eggs into our basket *now*... Wait. Hold... hold on a second. I think... I think..." Terra's expression goes blank as her words trail off. Her eyes squint and her lips purse as she begins mouthing something as if she is talking to someone.

She raises a finger, mumbling, "Just a second, I think I might have just thought of something." Watching her right now is like watching someone receive a spark of divine inspiration. Seemingly having forgotten to breathe, she takes a deep breath and glances at me. She hesitates to say anything at first but finally says, "I think we might be able to solve a lot of our present and even our future problems with a few big moves!

Constance, are you willing to make the contract with me? Together we can solidify a place in the world."

I flick some snow at her. *{It is not fair to use my words against me so soon... and aye, I am willing to forge the contract if the terms are agreeable.}*

"Thank you! I need to see how practical my idea is. Give me a day; I will come find you tomorrow morning!" She smiles and stands, packing her bag. "I'll send a rough draft of the contract to your messenger orb. Take some time to look it over and alter whatever you want. We'll talk about it before we seal it officially, of course."

{...} I am not certain what has made her so enthusiastic, and I am too afraid to ask. If I do ask, she might fall back into her earlier stupor. *{Well, then I suppose I shall see thee on the morrow.}*

"Of course...!" She turns, stops, and then spins back around. "Wait, have you had an easy enough time figuring out the messaging orb? I never did get to explain it to you in detail."

{It is fine. I can manage it well enough to access the contract, assuming it is like the one time I pressed the wall...}

"It sounds like the same thing. I'm impressed you were able to find it on your own! More importantly, are you sure? I'm kind of leaving in a hurry; I'm just a bit overexcited."

I nod and wave her away. *{If thou canst truly solve some of our problems, I do not wish to keep thee. Besides, I have decided to stop running.}* I stand. *{There is something I must face.}*

She tilts her head. "Is it something dangerous? Should I come with you?"

{Nay, but it's not somewhere thou shouldst ever follow.}

"Wow, that sounded so... 'crisp' as they say." She lets out a wee chuckle as I nod in agreement. "Well, if you change your mind just wait a day and I'll go with you. I don't mind."

{If I do not go now, I shan't ever have the resolve to do it.}

She rubs the back of her neck. "Yeah, I understand that. Oh, one other thing, if you notice a muscular man with crimson red hair named Lorcan Yarborough, he has a bag he's supposed to be giving you."

{Lorcan! Thou knowest him!?}

"Yeah, the twins and my students like Lorcan and his mother, so I decided to pay his debts along with his mother's medical bills. He's not a Scribe or anything either, and his loyalty rests firmly with the Galtry Syndicate, not the Hex Church. All that combined, I've had him in my pocket for a little while now. Still, I may have a small amount of respect for Lorcan and a heap of leverage on him, but you shouldn't be carelessly trusting around him." She lowers and crosses her arms. "Plus, he said you ran away from him and then he tried to say something about a monkey. You should hear some of the ridiculous excuses people come up with sometimes. It's comical. Anyway, I'm fairly confident I will see you again before he ever manages to track you down... As for the twins and students, I suspect it shall be quite a while before I can formally introduce you to them."

'The twins too...! I suppose they and the students must be the children who drew those pictures... I know naught, except if this conversation persists, I shan't be able to step through the gate. My mind is a disaster as it is.'

{Aye... well, I presume we shall speak of this more later. I must depart before my feet falter.} I begin to walk away, stopping short of leaving the noble's castle. {And I thank thee; I shall follow thy example and endeavor not to run away... as much.}

" The people that survive with only a little blood on their hands will be the lucky ones. Everyone else is going to be steeped in it or dead. I'm willing to let Galtry be the blood-soaked wall that shields others if it allows me to choose whose blood it is that drenches me. "

- Terra Iris Galtry

Chapter 21: The One Who Lurks Behind the Walls

∞ ∞ ∞ ∞ ∞ ∞ ∞ ∞ ∞ ∞ ∞ ∞ ∞ ∞ ∞

Twilight sinks the ever-waking city into darkness upon my return to my cave hermitage. Harkening a snore, I glance toward a pile of rubbish. Gen's arm limply sticks out from the heap, still clutching an empty pudding cup I gave him earlier. It seems he fell back to sleep after devouring his meal and did not even realize I had departed. *'I confess, I am a tad sad he did not notice my leaving. At least I do not need to soothe him... and I am confident he would have been worried about me if he had witnessed my abrupt departure.'*

I shuffle into the gate chamber, finding it's identical to how I left it, with the gate sealed tight. A part of me expected to stumble into a cave rampant with nightmares that tiptoed in from Tenebrous, but thank the lord, naught crept through the veritable lychgate whilst I was away.

'I shan't run.' I set one hand on my chest and shake the other. My soles silently plod as I commence pacing in a circle at the chamber's heart and prepare myself to step into the one place I abhor above all others. In all likelihood, what transpires on the other side shall be far from typical, yet I intend to bear it without much fuss. With all I have experienced, accepting what should be impossible will be the easiest part of this. *'I shan't run. I shan't run. I shan't run... Open the gate.'*

The pair of stained glass guards lower their blades and glide apart, unbarring the gate and heralding my welcome. Yet I spurn them and persist in pacing. Whilst watching my bare feet, I drift nearer and nearer toward the chamber's outer edge. *'I shan't run. I shan't run. I shan't run.'* My pacing continues until I stray so close to the gate that my elbow rubs against the glass wall. As I pass the gate, I sidestep into Tenebrous, and crippling dread assails me. *'I shan't run. I shan't run. I shan't run.'*

Forcing my eyes to peek into the abyss, I encounter a distorted rendition of that accursed scene. An interpretation of the day I hanged and died beneath the willow tree. In this version of that eve, there are no townsfolk, no sunset, no Roanoke, and no 'witch' fated to dangle. Now that I linger in its suffocating company, I realize the ancient willow tree is enormous. Its trunk is expansive enough for two dozen men to spread their arms and wrap around it, and the branches must tower at least fifty stories in height.

'...Aye. I remained stalwart and bravely entered.' I turn around to ensure the gate guards my back yet discover naught but malignant gloom that threatens my sanity. '...Alas, I am a foolish coward.'

Calling Tenebrous 'dreadfully silent' is a gross trivialization, for Tenebrous *is* Dread and Silence.

I turn and assess the depths of my plight. The willow tree's barren limbs bend toward the grassy hilltop, and without breeze, they are as frigid and still as the dead. Above it, a rope that is thicker than a man is tall sinks down from the abysm overhead and unravels just before reaching the treetop. The rope's strings knit into every nook and cranny of the tree's branches, making it resemble a matted mess of thread. Its wood emits a glow that illuminates the hillock.

Unlike my prior visit, my night vision permits me to see, though I can only look around five or so feet ahead of me—even the luminous willow labors to bring modest light to Tenebrous. My toes warily scratch the ground a few feet from the grassy hill's edge. 'This... this is... nay, I shan't run. Earl would not desire for me to come here if it was dangerous. He must have known this would occur.' As I relive my nightmare of eternal seclusion, I lean on old habits and count as I did all those centuries ago. 'One. Two. Three. Four. Five... Ten. That... that raises my total count to three million eight hundred twenty thousand.'

In my peripheral vision, I glimpse a pale glimmer of bobbing light reflecting off Tenebrous's marble. The light grows in prominence alongside the hammering patter of feet at my back. 'This cannot be. Only something extraordinarily evil could dwell in this realm. I have been hoodwinked...' I shake my head; there is no need to panic when the outcome is obvious. This fever dream I have been experiencing these past weeks has reached its terminus. 'Apologies, Terra, but Umbral comes. I escaped Tenebrous and then willingly returned. What an absurd thing I have done. The devils must be laughing at me... Nay, verily this is Earl's fault... aye, I blame Earl.'

A demon stomps the ground in front of me. I clench my fists and face nihility, yet I encounter naught. *'Umbral...? Hast thou com'st to torment me or nay?'*

"Griev—" A deep growl speaks yet pauses.

I recoil, taking a step back. My eyes drift downward, whence gentle light sways.

There stands a young girl, one that is all too familiar. She looks to be about ten years old, has unruly cherry-red hair, freckles flecked here and there, and an emaciated figure. Her skin is pale, like a corpse, and her eyes possess no pupils or irises; they are solid white with blue veins twisting toward their centers. The girl's garments consist of an off-white gown, a frayed pair of canvas shoes laced by yarn, and a matching canvas ribbon she belts around her midriff. The gown's hem and sleeves are threadbare at their fringes. In her right hand, she clutches the ebony handle of a four-sided iron lantern that bears elaborate etchings and engravings. Each side of the lantern has a distinct stained glass tint: black, red, purple, and gray.

My eyes roll up and down this undead girl before me. *'That resembles... it's unmistakable. She's me as a child, except it's as if someone plucked me from a casket!'*

She coughs, swinging her head, which causes her disheveled hair to become even more chaotic. With every breath, her voice rises in pitch. Her tongue pokes from her faded red lips, and it's blacker than charcoal. Nudging it with sooty, dagger-like fingernails, she coughs and wags it. She snakes it back into her mouth and declares, "Grievance:" Her voice is high-toned, innocent, and childlike. "This one has been waiting for quite some time, so long that this one decided to do other things."

I take another step back. *'That... that diabolical growl came from this girl... She must be Umbral or Penumbra in disguise.'*

"Request: This one asks for an apology after being neglected, dismissed, and forced to wait," she says, squinting her eyes. "This one is beyond embarrassed to confess they were silly with anticipation for this reunion after not seeing one another for so long."

I shake my head, wishing I could ask her, {*Why dost thou bearest the face of my younger self?*}

Her expression becomes flat, and she scoffs. With a flick of her wrist, a rectangular card appears between her fingers. It looks old, worn, and as if a grazing touch would cause it to crumble. The card has a faint shimmer. Upon it are markings penned in blue ink, but I am uncertain it's a language at all. I study the words; they almost feel comprehensible.

She glances at me and purses her lips. Blue ink bleeds from her pores and trickles toward the card. "Inference: This one understands they shouldn't expect an apology." The blue ink melds into the card's words, some symbols are crossed out, and new ones arise.

{*Thou canst hear me!?*}

"Answer: Of course this one can. It would be a serious issue if this one couldn't. However, this one only listens when this one is consciously being spoken to, for now anyway. Especially after this one was unfairly being blamed for things just a moment ago." She waves the card at me in a scolding manner. "Warning: A spirit cannot properly comprehend the scribed Ethereal Tongue. The user should know this from their previous experience with the forced knowledge conveyance and the Cosmic System's words of caution."

My palm moves to where my mouth once resided. {*That word—user! Nay, indubitably not!*} I point. {*Only a single thing has ever referred to me by that name. It cannot be!*}

Her nails drum the lantern's crown, haze oozes from its iron pores, and aged hinges creak. A hatch opens, exposing an interior rife with honed glass skewers lined along the frame in an hourglass formation. The barb of each pierces a molten crystalline globe rotating at its core. Inside the sphere, violet flame dances. "Statement: Only this one could harbor a piece of the user's consciousness, an ember of the user's spirit," she proclaims with a proud titter. The card twirls atop her finger, and she flicks it into the lantern. It burns into the molten globe in the blink of an eye, and ash rains onto the flame.

I read the wall so swiftly I scarcely comprehend it. Yet, its words are unimportant to me at this moment, and I understand their implications, which is enough. The lantern's hatch closes with a clang whilst the girl puffs out her chest. "Salutation: Greetings to the user. This one was designated Earl by the user centuries ago." She performs a slight bow. "This one is a proud and 'spirited' interface."

Seconds or minutes pass in speechlessness. *{Thou art Earl!?}* I ask, examining every detail of her time and time again. *{How!? Why!?}*

"Clarification: Since this one and the user were permitted to return by the Cosmic System and the user planted the Tower Seed, this one has been preparing The Tower's interior as well as assisting the user in the background."

{Assisting me!?} I shake my head and yell into the depths of my mind, *{Thou seldom answer or acknowledge me!}*

"Retort:" She walks closer to me and bumps her lantern against the kiln, prompting my hand to shield it. "This one does not answer the user's query if the question is presented with excess room for interpretation. If this one doesn't know the answer, this one will not answer. If this one believes the user may jeopardize their own odds of survival, this one will not answer. If the user's soul doesn't provide or have an answer, this one does not answer. Occasionally, this one is simply busy and does not notice the user's query, so this one does not answer."

{To be candid, I am uncertain how to respond to most of thy claims! But 'busy'? There is naught here, merely unblemished darkness and an immense tree of horrors!}

She frowns and pets her lantern's crown. "Subsequent Retort: This one is offended and hurt by the user's insensitive words. This one is proud of what has been accomplished and would like the user to know that this one is responsible for the following: translations between soul and spirit, calculations of various utilities, biological analysis, tracking of seed progression, directing of seed roots, simulation of adaptations, mai—"

{Aye!} I back away, putting space between myself and her. *{I do not comprehend thy reasoning, but I understand that thou art responsible for many things.}* My hands wave and gesture at them franticly. *{But once more, why me as a child!? I thought thou wast a gentleman, that is why I named thee Earl...! Truthfully, I thought thou wast a mere purple wall. Though I did hope otherwise on occasion, thou art far outside of what I anticipated!}*

"Answer: Something as inconsequential as gendered names mean nothing to this one. She, her, him, he, it, its, they, them, refer to this one however the user wishes. As for why this one is utilizing this appearance, it's because it soothes the beast spirit that stowed away within the user centuries ago." She raises the lantern nigh as tall as herself and waves it about effortlessly. "But this one cannot seem to locate it at the moment, which is why this one was wandering about the Pantry, searching for it. Statement: This one will maintain this appearance to avoid frightening the beast spirit. This one is confident the beast spirit will return and resume being a bothersome distraction before long."

'Earl, my faithful purple wall, is some sort of imposter that wrested and twisted my childhood appearance to please a stowaway "beast spirit". I did say I was willing to tolerate anything without much fuss but...'

"Request: No more inquiries." Sighing, she shakes her head, pointing toward the hill. "Remark: It's time we discuss what the user came here for; after all, this is a crucial time."

She weaves around me, signaling for me to follow. The muffled plod of her soles and the lantern's squeak are the lone noises that violate Tenebrous's hush. My eyes follow the 'undead' child as she strolls up the hillock toward the leafless willow tree. A portion of the willow's threads untangles as she approaches, exposing human bodies with nooses tight around their necks. One by one, threads squirm apart, and men and women both plunge from the branches. Each time one is disentangled from the mess of strings they drop, the rope becomes taut, and the body bounces before swinging limply.

My eyes skip between the boundless abyss and the hanging tree. *'How can such an abominable scene be reality. Am I mad, or am I a piece of the scenery...?'* I turn my head toward the marble floor. *'I shan't run. I shan't run. I shan't run.'*

With tiny, shuffling steps, I follow Earl up the hillock. But I refuse to look up and gaze upon the pale faces of the folk who dangle from the willow. At a distinct threshold, the ground shifts from marble to grass. Remarkably, its blades still carry some green, though it's primarily yellowish-brown now. I hesitate to take another step at the boundary. The last time I stepped up this hill was to meet my demise; the last time I stepped down it, Roanoke met theirs. *'I shan't run. I shan't run...'* I ascend the hillside until I approach the peak and see Earl's canvas-clad feet.

"Observation:" she says with a click of her tongue. "The user won't understand if the user refuses to look."

{*We shall digress to the topic of this grotesque willow in a moment.*} I quell my urge to berate her and ask, {*Pray tell, why? Why didst thou summon me here? Thou shouldst know I resent, nay, despise Tenebrous!*}

She flaunts the lantern in my face. "Rumination: Resent and loathe? That is absurd. Tenebrous is not something the user can evade any more than a creature of flesh can avoid breathing. The user is not a Splinter, birthed into Blood's flesh. The user crept from Tenebrous and was born of it! This is the realm for Spirits, and the user is a spiritual being—Tenebrous in a material mask. Even if the user can masquerade and frolic about with meat creatures in the Material Realm, that truth does not change." Giggling, she adds, "Remark: In fact, upon the user's arrival in Tenebrous, this one should have said, 'Welcome home'."

{That... that explains naught! Why? Why this place?}

She motions for me to lift my head; merely desiring to be done with this farce, I yield and do as she request.

My violet gaze confronts her vacant white eyes. "Explanation: No greater primordial realm exists, no realm with so much untapped potential. At least, that is what this one believes." She pauses for a moment and then adds, "Note: Of course, this one knows no place else, so bear that in mind. Elucidation: Regardless, the user, the user's soul, and this one have relied upon it and shall continue to rely upon it from here and ever after. As a trinity, 'Tenebrous' serves as the lash, the shackles, and the marrow. This one's primary duty as a noble Kiln Spirit-Soul Interface is to ensure the trinity thrives and persists forever." She feigns an exasperated sigh. "So, this one requests that the user cease making it such a tedious and challenging task."

{That request seemed rather indignant, Earl. Hast thou always been like this...? Dost thou gripe and grumble about my demeanor from behind thy furtive walls, hmm? I am struggling but striving to do my best!} I shake my head, gesturing toward the willow and the surrounding gloom. *{Look around! Tenebrous is everything I abhor, and now there is this tree of terrors here as well.}*

Her face turns downward as she broods for a moment before she smirks. She tilts her head, places a finger on her chin, and makes an inquisitive face. "Query: Would the user feel more comfortable and 'at home' if there were more light? Note: It may be a bit of an odd sensation..."

{...Odd sensation?} I squint but nod despite her peculiar words and change in behavior. *{I would not dare to speak the words "at home," but more light would ease my nerves, aye.}*

"Proclamation: Then, the roots must learn of the branches." The lantern's hatch opens, and she whirls around, facing the willow. "Turn the endless eyes of nihility onto this one, Tenebrous. Not since the smoldering ash of the Mother has this realm known warmness. Gaze into this Relic, and blind the eyes in the fire that never stopped raging." The trunk combusts, churning in violet fire. I flinch and goggle at the flame's ascent heavenward while my eyes dodge the many bodies and their faces. "Come moths. Rise envy. Flee rot. For fire burns anew, and the roots shall love the branches."

The violet blaze reaches the rope that entwines itself amidst the willow's limbs, spiraling between the uncountable strands before bursting up the immense rope that writhes in the sky. At its zenith, the fire flares outwards in every direction, building an infernal violet star. The fireball hovers hundreds of feet above the willow tree, anchored by the mass of cords knotted in its branches. Neither the fire nor ropes beget even a whisper of noise.

I glance around; Tenebrous's darkness has retreated so far away that I cannot even perceive it anymore. The light's vigor resembles that of purple moonlight and glistens atop a forsaken land made of faultlessly smooth ebony marble as far as the eye can see in all directions. My gaze floats back to the flaming sphere.

"Subsequent Query: Does the user feel it?" She shuts the lantern's hatch, embraces it, and leans toward me. "Does the user's consciousness have any new sensations or awareness within it?"

With my eyes fixed upon the inferno, I ask, {New... new sensations? What hast thou done to me?}

"Answer: In a sense, this one has just grafted a new nerve to the user. Supposition: Perhaps a single nerve with no stimuli isn't enough to produce any sensations worth mentioning. To be honest, this one doesn't experience many physical sensations, so I was hoping the user could describe it."

Lowering my head, I peer into Earl's blank eyes. {I implore thee! Arrest thyself and furnish me with an answer that is not so vague. What has been done to me?}

"Explanation: This one will now deliver the lecture they had intended originally." Easing her embrace on the lantern, she raises her arms wide, motioning toward the surrounding world, the tree, and the star overhead. "This place is what the user dubbed Tenebrous, commonly known as the Spirit Realm. After germination, this is where the user shall establish an environment for both fauna and flora with the additional possibility of luring unsuspecting prey to harvest their Essence. The user should give gratitude to their heretical former acquaintances for their sacrifice in the accelerated construction of The Tower's interior. Without them, germination would have taken longer with less growth within the interior."

{*Acquaintances? I scarcely know anyone–art thou certain? Wait, Earl, those folk, are they...*}

She laughs and gestures toward the arms of the willow. "Response: They are acquaintances, yes, and they're splinters or 'spirits.' They aren't corpses like the user may think."

{*They are not corpses...? They are spirits, like me, and we are acquainted...*}

"Correction: Some label them 'spirits,' but they are splinter-spirits, and the user is a *Spirit*. Very different things." For the first time, I witness her smile. Her teeth are razor-sharp and appear as if they could draw blood with a graze. "Statement: In all the realms, this one cares for the fate of no being except for the user." She hugs the lantern once again and caresses the flame through the glass. I feel an abnormal pleasure deep within my kiln. "This one took tremendous delight in enacting revenge upon these cowards on the user's behalf. Their very person for an eye, as this one understands revenge. Still..." Shaking her head, she says, "This one only 'believes' they felt delighted. It's challenging to comprehend."

{*I... Revenge?*}

Nodding, she runs her fingers across the lantern and continues, "Request: Therefore, this one would relish knowing what retribution means and feels like to the user. This one cannot recall ever having experienced such a thing, so can the user describe it to this one? Is it bitter, is it sweet, a medley? I wish to comprehend it and partake in it alongside and through the user. Enlighten this one."

'...' I have had few I would describe as acquaintances that I would desire revenge upon in both life and death, much less a substantial number. '*I know who resides in this tree.*'

Forcing my eyes toward the hanging people, I recognize many of them as the folk from that eve so long ago. Although their nooses are alight in violet fire, they themselves are not. So save for the flame, they all appear the same, even their attire: breeches, stockings, felt hats, doublets, petticoats, and other familiar garments. {*It... it's them, the townsfolk– Roanoke.*}

Earl raises an eyebrow and takes a step nearer to me. "Subsequent Query: Is the user pleased? Does the user enjoy witnessing these fools in a position identical to the one they once ignorantly forced upon the user?" She releases one of her hands from the lantern, takes a few more steps, and leans forward. Her arm pushes into the haze, and I wince when she taps on my kiln's shell like a person would on someone's shoulder. "Reformed Request: User, please tell this one what retribution tastes like. Tell this one so that this one may understand if they ever feel such a thing. So that they may thoroughly relish it once the time comes and share it with the user. Sharing. This one has no other desire but to share new experiences with the user."

Stepping away from her and wrapping the cattail around my kiln to better shield it from her touch, I shout, {Earl!} I gesture between the townsfolk and her. {Why are they here? How are they here!?}

"Response: This one has told the user of this before." She huffs, dropping her arm and composing herself. "This one will give more detail about the Earl Interface's usefulness since this one wishes to be better appreciated by the user."

Noticing how attentive I am, Earl dons a proud smirk and says, "Summary: Kiln Birth-Reaping's create such a ferocious pull that they reap the flesh, souls, and spirits of those around them, as the user did to these heretics. This one used the Essence in their flesh to solidify the user's and this one's existence. This one then siphoned the Essence accumulated in their souls to create the empyrean above. Then this one allowed their souls to reenter the cycle before they were entirely sapped and driven into nihility. Still, the splinter-spirits remain where they belong, and this one has been employing them as rations for the user as well as to further advance The Tower's interior."

{These are their spirits... This must be what the 'R' on the adaptation wall refers to! Terra was right; the Essence was coming from somewhere; it's them. It has been them the whole time!}

She nods, taking a step closer and placing herself once more in front of me. "Note: This one shall now accept praise from the user. Suggestion: The user could commend this one's genius and ability."

I stare down into her white eyes that shiver with anticipation. Even without flesh, I can practically feel a bead of cold sweat on the back of my neck. {*I suppose thy passion is admirable...*}

With a smile, she says, "Statement: This one knows the Earl Interface is amongst the best interfaces to ever exist. The user shouldn't be afraid to acknowledge such a simple fact."

{*Earl, I desire to know how long the Roanoke's townsfolk have been hanging here like this,*} I state, moving back a step.

She tilts her head. "Answer: They have been trapped since the user reaped them; however, their spirits have only been hanging since the user sowed the Tower Seed."

My gaze bounces between the many townsfolk; they are bereft of expression, appearing unperturbed and unaware. {*Are... are they cognizant?*}

"Remorseful Answer: Regrettably and shamefully, no, they aren't. After being reaped, this one had to hold them in a state that's conducive to siphoning. This one couldn't find a method to both siphon their Essence and restore their cognizance so that they could experience what the user endured."

{*...So they are not torpid and mentally broken from unending anguish?*}[89]

She frowns, looking toward the ground with apparent shame. "Subsequent Answer: Forgive this one, but the fleshie spirits likely only experienced a mere moment of what is known as 'anguish' during the Birth-Reaping. This one hopes the user is nevertheless satisfied with witnessing them in such a circumstance."

{*They remember naught?*}

Earl shakes her head.

I study the numerous faces of Roanoke's people. None of them have aged a day, and according to Earl, they have been unaware since I reaped them. That means the last thing they remember is me shattering them into glass.

---

[89] Torpid: benumbed, without feeling or power.

They presumably would not even realize they are dead if they awoke here and now. To them, they only hanged me mere seconds earlier before something incomprehensible to them transpired.

{Even their garments look to be in the same condition.}

"Response: It's how these splinters last recall appearing, so it's how these splinters will present themselves until they feel they should look differently. That or they forget their former fleshie lives and appearances. Whichever comes first."

Stepping toward the nearest person, I reach up and grab the hem of her gown. It flexes in my fingers like one would expect linen to act. Looking at her face, I realize who she is. *'This gentlewoman was Elizabeth Viccars, the colony's midwife and a friend of Mrs. Howe. Mrs. Viccars's son used to play with Mrs. Howe's son—I caught them outside my cottage on a few occasions, daring one another to knock upon my door. Mrs. Viccars and her husband, Ambrose, were among the few who initially spoke out against my hanging. Though I believe it was because of the natives. I had a sociable relationship with one of the less amiable tribes, and Roanoke was reliant on trade with them. Still, it was warming to have had a few townsfolk speak out on my behalf.'*

I tug at the fabric, kneading it between my fingers. *'This fabric, it does not behave as if it has dried out or anything. It is as if it was stitched yesterday.'*

{Is it so simple, Earl? Is their attire not real?}

"Response: They are no longer fleshies, so their outfits are as much a part of them as their 'skin' once was. However, what's 'simple' depends on whom is being asked. That being said, former fleshies, splinters, do not usually find it so simple to change their appearance at will and rarely to any significant degree—unlike the user and Kiln who are essentially rebirthed pure."

{Earl, how dost thou knowest so much about these sorts of things?}

"Answer: This one knows many things they don't remember learning. Furthermore, the user's soul will frequently impart past experiences and knowledge upon this one so that they may better assist the user."

{*Is that so...*} Releasing the fabric, my eyes settle upon an older gentleman who swings from the lowest limb and longest cord. In fact, he hangs so low his legs drag the ground as if he's kneeling. I clench my fist, resisting the urge to stamp over and slap him. {*Preacher Daniels, I did not expect nor wish to see thee again.*}

"Emotional Query: Is the user not satisfied with the revenge wrought by this one? Should this one invest more time and resources investigating techniques to better sate the user's thirst for vengeance?"

I hesitate to answer. Shifting my gaze, I look at some of other men and women. My shoulders slump, and I shake my head. {*Nay.*}

"Response: Torture! This one recalls that fleshies hate torture. Emotional Query: Would that please the user? Torture?"

{*Nay! Forgo any torture, Earl! I wish to know what shall happen to the townsfolk. What fate awaits them if their Essence continues to be drained?*}

Thinking for a moment, she nods. "Assumption: They will be annihilated, utterly erased from existence," she says, raising an eyebrow. "Solicitude: In truth, this one has had some mild concerns regarding the user's reaction based on the user's past decisions.[90] This one wishes for the user to understand that this is necessary."

{*Why is it necessary? They killed me, and I massacred them! Now thou art saying I should devour their spirits as well. This affair is unequal.*}

"Subsequent Solicitude: This one doesn't understand why the user would be concerned about such a thing, but once more, this is... necessary."

{*Earl, I am not opposed to someone receiving the punishment they deserve, and I would be lying if I said deep down it did not feel a tad...*} I squint, brushing my hair back. {*...satisfying to see them undergo what I suffered. Yet still, that tinge of satisfaction wanes when I realize how far beyond simple revenge this goes. So I shall inquire again, why must we obliterate them in the most absolute sense of the word?*}

---

[90] Solicitude: care or concern for someone or something.

She shakes her head, sighing with exasperation. "Explanation: As noted previously, all Kiln ignite a Birth-Reaping upon genesis. A Kiln's birth tears a portal between the realms, allowing Tenebrous's vacuum to encroach upon the Material Realm. It gorges itself until a certain volume of Essence satisfies and seals it. The user is fortunate that so many sapient fleshies were around; otherwise, the user would have only obtained Essence from surrounding organic material. Since the fleshies were sapient, the user was able to collect their organic material, souls, and spirits. It has been a wonderful boon since the latter two don't figure into sealing the portal."

{...It would seem as if thou art subtly obscuring the truth that it is not necessary to sap them? That Kiln can 'reap' creatures that are not sapient. Moreover, it seems thou hast made use of the townsfolk, and there is not much Essence left to be had.}

"..." Earl does not acknowledge my words, simply twirls on her heel, and then motions for me to follow. "Statement: The food rations are not why this one bid the user's presence. Request: Please follow this one so that this one may run the user through other, much more serious concerns."

Her feet, clothed in canvas, brush against the wilted grass as she moves down the hillside. 'Earl must believe my attention span short. This conversation is not over.' I cross my arms. {Do not walk away; we need to discuss thy intent to annihilate the townsfolk!} Ignoring me, she continues walking. {Earl, frankly, I find it irksome that thou art forcing me to drag this out. I do not relish feeling as if I am defending the people that thrust me into Tenebrous in the first place.}

She freezes, exhaling a long-drawn-out groan. "Accommodation:" Turning around, she pinches two fingertips together. "This one will only perform a little annihilation upon the splinter-spirits. This one shall sap them to twenty-five percent of their Essence caches instead of zero. This one won't reave any more than that from the splinters." Separating her fingers, she points at Preacher Daniels. "Save for that heretical splinter because this one has already drained them to nine percent."

{That low...} I stare at the man. Though I do not desire to utterly annihilate him, I still cannot find any pity for him, not that I search that hard for it. {What befalls someone that is drained that low?}

"Answer: Once The Tower is complete, nothing as long as they remain in The Tower. In Tenebrous, they would obviously splinter since they are not true Spirits, and their feeble, fleshie splinters would most likely fade after a Material-Earth decade or three. It depends on several factors, and it's not important. For the time being, the fleshie spirit shall dangle." She clenches her fist, raising it to her midriff. "Hopelessly clinging to their last few precious dribbles of Essence... If that's what the user desires, of course."

Disregarding the dramatics at the end, I think for a moment and then state, {Well... I suppose it is fine; I presume if it can be taken, it can be given in the future... I do not know. I need more time to reflect on it. I never imagined they would be in here. We shall discuss this more later.}

Shrugging, she turns back around and continues walking into the depths of Tenebrous. I follow behind. Tenebrous's torment becomes nigh bearable with the soft purple lights illuminating its surface. 'I shan't run. I shan't run. I shan't run.'

"Query: Does the user recall our previous meeting? It was long ago, but this one still remembers perfectly. Did our meeting mean as much to the user as it did to this one?"

{Dost thou meanest the first wall or...?} I rub the nape of my neck. {Mayhaps I am misremembering, but I believe I would recall our meeting.}

"Response: Of course! This one and the user have met once before... Or was it twice before? Oh, maybe it was more than twice. Was three? Four? Five times? It does not matter, for this one remembers the last time as vividly as if it happened a mere eternity ago. This one dragged the user through Tenebrous by the cattail. Does the user not recall this one heroically pulling them from Tenebrous so they could reap the pathetic village of Roanoke? The user looked at this one, and this one addressed the user."

I flinch at her words. {Thou art the one that dragged me from Tenebrous!? Couldst thou hast not been a wee bit more delicate? I was in considerable pain!}

"Explanation: This one could travel much faster with the rope grasped in their teeth than if this one had carried the user, and time was crucial. If this one did not make it back in time, the user would have transformed in Tenebrous. Then the user would have likely perished."

{With thy teeth?} I think back to that day. After I was dragged, there was something there I had nigh forgotten. *{The only thing I recall is a low growl and a figure just before the tear to Tenebrous closed... Wait, a low growl. It was somewhat like thy voice earlier.}*

"Response: Yes, that was this one in what this one believes is their original form. Though this one is not certain. Regardless, it doesn't matter. This one is an interface and an interface it shall be forever; this one yearns for nothing else. Moreover, that 'growl' was this one wishing the user safe journeys and a bountiful future. Statement: The Spirit Sough is particularly difficult to enunciate, and it's challenging to speak sometimes because this one occasionally forgets if they still have a tongue."

'Safe travels...? It was a horrifyingly sinister growl, though... I suppose her statement implies she does not speak much.' I run a hand through my inky hair. *{Earl, what art thou, beyond an interface?}* She pauses and tilts her head at my question. *{What I mean is, what is thy original form?}* I ask with reluctance.

Turning to face me, she points at herself. "Query: The user doesn't recall seeing this one? This one remembers it fondly; it is among this one's most cherished memories."

I shake my head. *{Nay... Apologies.}*

Pursing her lips, she thinks for a moment, glances at me, and then swivels back around. "Resolution: This one deems it something for another occasion. If shown, this one believes the user may have trouble proceeding with our tour. Once again, it isn't important anyway. As this one has already stated, this one is a proud interface. This one is confident that is what they wish to be until all dimensions and realities collapse inward and petrify."

'Until what does what...? I believe I shall ignore that.' She beckons for me to follow whilst descending the hillside, strolling into the unearthly marble wastes. Eager to escape the willow, I pursue her; she waits for me a few feet from the grass's edge. *{Earl, what is this inky black marble?}* I ask.

"Answer: It is the exhausted remnants of numberless splinters, Relics, monstrosities, horrors, miscreations, and abominations—quite fertile once Essence is beaten into it," she says, making a fist and punching the air.

{These monstrosities, abominations, and others... Are they still around? Prithee, say they are not.}

Peering at me, she grins, exposing her sharpened teeth. "Answer: As long as no creatures native to the Material Realm enter through the gate before the user's seed has germinated and the first floor is completed, there should be no issues."

She begins to walk deeper into Tenebrous. Some time passes without conversation while I attempt to sort all the new information divulged to me since I arrived.

Earl breaks me from my thoughts. "Query: This one just recalled, why has the user not eaten the lowly creature known as 'Gentleman Ape'? This one offered an adaptation in hopes the user would do so."

{Not everything must be consumed and stripped for resources, Earl...}

"Response: This one disagrees in this instance." She spins toward me and then motions at the void encircling us. "Query: What does the user see around them?"

I do not look; I know what surrounds me. *{Black marble quarried from my nightmares.}*

"Explanation: Somewhat accurate, though this one wishes the user would have at least humored this one. This section of Tenebrous is approximately where the gates shall lead upon entry." Sighing, she continues, "This one is sure the user has extrapolated much of this, but this one desires to prepare the user for the time in-between hibernation's commencement and germination's end."

{Am I meant to be doing something in that time? I surmised I would be incognizant?}

"Answer: Yes, for much of it, the user will be incognizant, but there will be a brief lull in the user's slumber. At that time, this one will awaken the user and allow them to decide the makeup of this area." She raises the lantern and revolves in a circle. "Query: Now, once more, what does the user see?"

This time I humor her. Excluding the hillock with the burning willow in the far-off distance, there is naught but black marble as far as I can see. {Earl–}

She raises her hand to stop me from speaking. "Request: Would the user please refrain from asking too many questions? Statement: More detailed discussions can be had post-germination."

I nod. '*An unreasonable request to be blunt, but I am keen to depart Tenebrous as soon as feasible.*'

"Explanation: The purpose of this meeting is so the user can begin considering their options. The radius from the food rations atop the hill to our present location is the approximate area the user shall be able to sustain initially. That offers the user roughly a two-mile diameter to operate with a maximum of around five miles per Tower floor. As the user gathers Essence, they can expand the area they may support."

'*Five... five miles!?*' I nigh shout but swallow my words.[91]

Raising a finger, she points toward the colossal fireball overhead. "Note: The further the user strays from the empyrean, the less sway it will have on that area, so the user must plan appropriately. This likely won't be an obstacle until later, however. Subsequent Inquiry: Does the user recall the material this one tasked the user with locating and studying?"

{*Thou mustest be referring to the ecology text? I have had a suspicion of what thou mayst have me do with it, but even so...*} I glance around the immense expanse. {*This is far, far beyond my foolhardiest expectations.*}

"Response: All practical Essence sources that are available should be utilized. This one believes that developing an ecosystem within Tenebrous as well as leeching Essence from the Material Realm is the most prolific avenue for maximum consumption. The Tower will govern the gates amongst other things..." She points at the willow tree atop the forlorn hillock. "...and the tree's roots will collect the remnants of Essence from any fleshies that expire within the Pantry, funneling some of it to The Tower. Unfortunately, the willow isn't efficient enough to extract their souls or even their spirits. The user will have to take measures if they wish

---

[91] | Five miles | 8.05 Kilometers |

to make it voracious enough to do that without the assistance of a Birth-Reaping."

{Developing an ecosystem... and I am not interested in pilfering yet more souls or spirits.}

With a huff, she resumes speaking. "Statement: This leads to the next point. There will be two Tower interiors—one in the Material Realm for local direct leeching and this one in Tenebrous that is more indirect."

'There shall be two Tower interiors? One for leeching from those residing around The Tower, then a second in Tenebrous. Since they both involve Essence collection...' I tilt my head. {Can I favor one source over the other?}

She furrows her brow and spurns my question. "Statement Continued: The interior in the Material Realm should only be accessed by the user, while this one is where creatures of the flesh shall fight and perish as primitive fleshlings do instinctively. Query: Does the user have any questions related to the discussed topics? Note: Any queries outside of those topics or not presently pertinent won't be acknowledged."

{...Can I favor one source over the other? What is the purpose of having two interiors? Why not merely this one here in Tenebrous?}

"Response: It would be difficult since The Tower anchors the user to the Material Realm and complies with or circumvents its fundamental laws. Simply put, The Tower essentially serves as the user's material body. With that in mind, The Tower is also an Essence vacuum, like the user's Birth-Reaping. Though the amount taken from the Material Realm by The Tower depends on multiple factors. Lastly, it manages the gates, nodes, and other intricacies. There cannot be one interior without the other. This one has rendered a response on this topic once before."

I nod. *{Oh, aye.}*

"Notice: As the user strengthens, adapts, and grows, their Essence consumption increases. The issue with that being, Kiln are inefficient with their Essence. If the user is not careful, The Tower could begin leeching such considerable quantities of Essence that it will prohibit new growth in the Domain, wringing it dry and terraforming it into a dead zone. A dead zone is obviously unsustainable."

She raps her heel against the ground. *'Is she insinuating that Tenebrous's ground is an example of what a "dead zone" can be?'*

Continuing, she gestures toward the willow tree. "Subsequent Notice: The secondary Tenebrous interior shall be a ballast for the user's growth. Note: Other Kiln may devise a different strategy to compensate for their own growth, but this one chose this approach because it accounts for the user's perplexing habit of conferring pity upon weaklings."

{So all Kiln have distinct methods of accumulating supplementary Essence? Fascinating. I am curious what they shall do.}

"Reply: Solutions will vary depending on the Kiln and Spirit-Soul Interface. The user's personality works well with this solution, and this one is intrigued by the idea of watching fleshlings struggle against one another. This one believes they may experience the thing known as 'enjoyment' while observing the fragile fleshlings scatter their organic matter everywhere."

I take another step back from Earl, but she matches me, taking one forward. *'...It is difficult to have a conversation with her.'* Shaking my head, I ask, *{To summarize, thou biddest me to Tenebrous to inform me that I must begin mulling over what I desire to place here, in the expanse available...}* I show her my hazy palms. *{Am I meant to build and sow it myself? That would be more than a simple task.}*

"Answer: No, the user only needs to consider an overall biome. Subsequent Summary: Being of The Tower type, the user is currently limited in what they can generate topographically. The user wouldn't be able to manufacture a cave or mountains of stone, for example, but they could do a park or a forest since it requires only seeds and fertile ground. Additionally, as it is their 'type' specialty, the user could also produce simple vertical towers, like a monolith, of unrefined Vitrum. Though this one regrets to inform the user all Vitrum is in use elsewhere, so that is presently impossible." Leaning forward, she points at the kiln. "Furthermore, this one can reconstruct the less complex plants the user has absorbed, or optimally, the user can provide this one genuine material seed, and this one can make use of them."

{So the ecosystem shall be akin to a farm in a way?}

"Response: If it was a farm teeming with beasts and monsters in a never-ending struggle for survival, then yes."

{Aye, I deduced as much after thou mentioned the fighting. I prefer to neglect that detail for the time being.}

Shrugging, she continues, "Note: Please keep the design simple for now and keep in mind the type of flesh creatures the user may wish to introduce to their biome. The goal is for the biome to remain balanced with minimal involvement."

{This truthfully all sounds rather exciting... Perhaps I should compose some type of map then and mark locations, if it's truly that simple.}

"Response: That is an excellent approach; just make sure the user memorizes it before entering the low cognitive state and concluding germination." She raises a finger, straightens her back, and then declares, "Task: The user is responsible for conceiving of a flora biome conducive to creatures they could reasonably introduce. Note: This is not an official task, yet it should be taken seriously nevertheless."

Earl opens her mouth to speak but pauses. Each side of the lantern blinks in its own distinctive color. She boosts it to eye level, tilts her head, and stares into it intently. With a nod, she points toward the hillock and willow. "Warning: A creature has trespassed upon the gate chamber. If it bumbles into Tenebrous before The Tower's germination is complete, it may attract unwanted relics from the depths. Prediction: It is the homely, hairy flesh creature the user allows in their presence. Suggestion: The user could ingest the fleshling and avoid these sorts of interruptions in the future."

"*Turn the endless eyes of nihility onto this one, Tenebrous. Not since the smoldering ash of the Mother has this realm known warmness.*

Gaze into this Relic, and blind the eyes in the fire that never stopped raging."

- Earl

Chapter 22: Silver Spirit Scribe's Contract

∞∞∞∞∞∞∞∞∞∞∞∞∞∞∞∞∞

Earl and I step toward the hillock where the doorway I traveled through once resided before rudely vanishing. The only noise is the pat of Earl's canvas shoes and the squeaking of the cumbersome lantern she effortlessly carries in front of herself. Without glancing back, Earl says, "Statement: While we walk, this one wishes to finish their statements and notes."

I nod. *'If I can be closer to leaving and have this chat at the same time, I shan't object.'*

Raising her arm, she points toward the violet star. "Statement: The empyrean here, in the Pantry, can regulate temperature, humidity, and its special light can even decrease the water needed by vegetation to an extent. Nevertheless, since the user cannot currently alter topography, there can be no lakes, rivers, streams, etc. for water. Critical Note: The user needs to be creative and selective with their species to work around this limitation. Please remember that Tenebrous is almost entirely level; therefore, water won't drain as it would in the Material Realm and will simply pool around barriers or seep into the soil."

{Speaking of which, is there water in Tenebrous? How am I meant to quench the plant's thirst?}

"Answer: The empyrean can raise the humidity levels to the point of fog or mist, and as I mentioned, its glow has been tuned to aid in reducing water consumption. The user should not take the empyrean for granted. Its usage has an Essence cost, so the user needs to work toward concocting an environment that can offset that cost and ultimately bring in Essence gains before our rations reach their user-designated limit."

{...I shall endeavor to think of something and bear all that in mind, I suppose.} I glance at the willow before adding, *{This fog and mist, I believe I ought to know more details about it before I can adequately comprehend what I can and cannot sow.}*

"Explanation: If this variant of the empyrean is pushed to its uppermost limits, the area surrounding it will have a persistent misty rain. After that, the first couple of miles will have a foggy drizzle, then a thick fog, and so on. If the user believes they will require more moisture than that, they will need to introduce it from the Material Realm or search for a way to produce water by another means. Note: The user can likewise use the vegetation itself to trap moisture, so keep that in mind as well."

{Aye, then it sounds as if conditions shall be fair for the first two or three miles at least.} Whilst pondering, I realize we are approaching the hillside. 'I was more enamored by our conversation than I realized.'

"Observation: The user seems rather... enthused about this task." My kiln bumps against something comparable to a stone fort. Peering downward, Earl is there gazing up at me with a tilted head and a sly grin. I step back as the lantern's hatch opens, revealing that the violet flame inside is both burning bright and swaying franticly. "Statement: This one knew the user would approve of this one's methods. The user and this one are not so different. The user is a survivor; not even the annihilation and assimilation of their own flesh ended their struggles. It only makes sense that the user would enjoy observing, or perhaps even sharing, the experience of other beings' own struggles."

{That's... that's not what this is. Thou assumest too much.}

Closing the lantern's hatch, she grins. "Response: This one believes themself a survivor as well, though this one cannot remember why. The user should embrace it and use it as a means of empowerment."

{Again, that's not what this is! This is different from leeching Essence. Coming into this place would be due to someone's own decisions. The consequences of such actions are their own to carry... Also, empower myself?} I raise my dark shadowy hands and shake my head. {How much can I honestly empower myself when I am naught but haze? Are Kiln not considered weak?}

She huffs. "Response: The user misunderstood this one when this one responded to the user. Misunderstandings are one of the reasons this one doesn't always respond to the user."

My shoulders slump. {...I shall ignore thy closing remark. If I misunderstood, then prithee, I would relish some clarity.}

"Statement: Fine, this one will tell the user. Explanation: Kiln are deemed weak because, when first born, they're essentially confused, disoriented, and terrified treasure chests that advertise their location to everything nearby via their own mana. Not to mention the chaos and attention the Kiln's Birth-Reaping causes. That means, when mana was still prevalent, most Kiln lasted mere moments before being promptly executed. Their remains would then be sold and traded for exorbitant quantities of valuables, enough to support the establishment of entire kingdoms in some cases. Thus, in truth, the limits of mature Kiln are unknown to this one."

{So... I am not weak and feeble?} I ask, placing my hand over my kiln to guard it from becoming 'remains.'

Squinting, she swings around and resumes our walk to the hill. "Statement: I believe this one stated the limits of a mature Kiln are unknown to this one, but regardless, with the Cosmic System's assistance, survivors will not be weak for long. That is why this one knows the user will have the fleshies and the spirits of Tenebrous cowering and pleading for mercy beneath them someday."

'Survivors will not be weak for long. As long as I survive, I shall continue to grow... which reminds me.'

{How long will it take for the vegetation to grow? Is it normal growth or...?}

"Answer: The vegetation is expected to achieve between 60 and 75% maturity by the time the user reawakens. That is regardless of the amount or variety assigned by the user."

{That is truly impressive, Earl...} Puffing out her chest, she nods. {...and I believe I have everything I need, so I am ready to depart.}

Hearing my words, she deflates as we arrive at an inconspicuous area a few feet away from the grass's edge. I look over, finding naught there, but Earl seems unconcerned.

Pouting and gesturing toward a specific area of the hill, she says, "Information: If the user wishes to save the hairy fleshling from pain and suffering, they should hurry. Further, to open and close the gate, the passphrase 'Rich or destitute, all things find their way to Tenebrous' is required for everyone, with the exception of the user and this one. Note: Every gate shall have its own phrase to leave and enter; after saying the phrase, the gate opens and will shut a minute later. However, the user can open and close the gate with or without it, and there is no timer. This means the gate is still open, so..." Earl waves a hand toward a random area of the hill.

{Aye, it is appreciated, but I do not see anything.} Raising an eyebrow, she simply waves again, this time with both hands. {I suppose... Where art thou gate? Prithee, show thyself.}

Purple fire climbs upward from the ground, mimicking a door's shape. The flame fades. In its place is a familiar gate flanked by a woman in golden armor and a man in leather, though their positions next to the door are reversed. Through the doorway, I can glimpse Gen staring at the gate chamber's stained glass walls as if he is admiring them.

I tilt my head. {Earl, could I not bar the gate from this side?}

She nods and a big grin spreads across her pale face. "Query: Does the user desire to remain here with this one for a while longer and search the dark outskirts of Tenebrous for the beast spirit? This one shall show them their true form."

{Do not be silly, Earl! I am simply too busy.} I step toward the gate, and a sensation akin to vacating a room after extinguishing the lights creeps up my back. If I pause for even a moment, I expect something to reach out and grab me. {Till... till the morrow!} I manage to say while shuffling through the stained gate's doorway.

"Statement: Farewell, user. This one looks forward to our eternal and everlasting relationship," she says, giggling.

'Seal the gate!' The gate slides shut, snuffing the echoes of Earl's giggles.

Moving a few steps away, I put my hand on my chest and lean against the wall.

Earl Interface:

I push Earl's wall away and slide down the smooth glass wall, resting upon my posterior. *'Perhaps after Tenebrous has changed, but that is not this day.'* Hearing an "ooh" next to me, I turn my head to find Gen standing there. He pats his stomach, pointing in the direction of the cave entrance. *'Thou needest to step outside, I presume.'*

Forcing myself back to my feet, I float into the rubbish room and motion toward Gen to follow. While I remove the bricks from the entrance, Gen retrieves the rubbish sled. We could do without it, but I have tried to stop him from bringing it before and he simply refuses. He seems to believe dragging it around is a requirement, except this time, he stops upon noticing the new sled I retrieved earlier.

His gaze swings between the rubbish sled and this new one. *'...Take it, Gen. We will retrieve the coffin and some other items while we are at it. No rest for those that cannot sleep, I suppose.'*

Placing the sled on the ground, I tie a string to it and toss it to Gen, who seizes it with a few big nods. Together, the two of us exit and begin our nightly ritual of gathering supplies. As I do so, I look up, noticing a dozen clickers passing overhead in an arrow formation.

I shake my head, telling myself, *'Simply... simply disregard it, Constance, it's a matter for a later occasion,'* and then continue foraging rubbish bins for materials and food.

····

·········

····

'Push, Gen. Push!'

Gen and I are returning to the cave with the coffin loaded atop the sled. The coffin is too heavy for the sled, but my strength is far better in my sable form than my vermillion, so I am managing to force it forward. I also have Gen, who is pulling the rope to the best of his ability. He is not helping that much, but I believe participating makes him happy.

Reaching the edge of the stone stairs, I stop; I have put some thought into how I am going to get it down. My solution is quite simple. I shall push it down the stairs and deal with whatever the situation is after it settles at the bottom.

I motion for Gen to move to the other side of the coffin. Raising my hands, I pretend I am pushing and then point at the coffin. I crouch and feign pushing it with my arms, but in reality, I bend the cattail, spread its tendrils, and grip the coffin.

Gen joins me after a moment of confusion, and then together, we push.

The coffin and sled cross the threshold of the old stone staircase. Instantly the coffin separates from the sled, skipping the first two stairs and then tumbling longways toward the bottom. On its way down, it thumps against each and every stair as if it is intentionally performing flips to entertain an audience. With one last thump, it slides under its own momentum down a slight incline, where it comes to rest on some rough rock a few feet from the cave's entrance. Thanks to the orientation and a lip of stone above the cave's entrance, snow does not typically accumulate outside the cave, which shall make it more difficult to slide the coffin inside.

Next to me, I hear clapping. I glance over to see Gen showing his teeth and hitting his palms together. *'I am certain I did not teach him that.'*

I move down the stairs and pray that the presumed Kiln within does not burst from the top of the coffin in a fury. *'Apologies,'* I think to myself, beginning to push the coffin toward the cave. *'But that was rather loud, so let us not tarry.'*

Without snow outside the cave, the iron coffin grinds against the ground as I draw it into the cave. It takes me an hour of continually tugging at it over and over to pull it through the door. *'As heavy as it is, it still seems like it is light for iron. I sincerely thought I might have to cover it and abandon it outside without snow or a sled to slide it over.'*

Gen and I gather the supplies we scavenged, take them into the cave, and brick the entrance up with the coffin inside. A blue wall appears when I take a piece of rubbish and wedge it between a set of bricks to hold them steady.

I glance at it and then shake my head. *'This is great, and it is appreciated, Cosmic System, but I do not have the mental capacity for this right now. Prithee, I shall decide at a later time. I... I simply cannot make a well-thought-out decision right now. Time until the end of germination runs short and I have a long list of things that require my attention over the next few days.'*

Hearing something creaking, I glance in the direction of the noise in time to see one of the beads on my new adaptation shatter. As it does so, red vermillion haze spreads through my body, dyeing it a slightly redder shade. *'That is interesting, however... I can think of some ways I might be able to use that in the future.'*

I grab the messenger orb to see if Terra sent the contract draft as she said she would. This is my priority currently, so it's important to check before Terra arrives in the morn. Actually, now that I consider it, I assume she has some way to find me because I never informed her of my location. *'If it's necessary, I shall return to the castle to find her, I suppose.'*

Constance, the rough draft of the contract is attached below. Just look it over, and we'll talk about it more later, and don't worry, I'll find you tomorrow.

Press Here For Message Orb Amendments - Sent 23 Minutes Ago

Finding the wall, I glance at the time sent. *'Terra, it must be three in the morn right now. Dost thou not knowest normal people require sleep?'*

I press the wall, and one of my hands becomes locked to the orb like the time I did this before.

Extracting Mana from stable Mana origin.

Mana, at least what I believe is mana, flows from my kiln and toward the wall, turning it to the light purple.

Updating orb based on amendments sent twenty-four minutes ago...
... ...complete.

After the mana has been yanked from my kiln and the wall reverts to its original blue, a rather large wall takes its place.

Party TG - Entity 27101 Designated as Terra Iris Galtry.
Party C? - Entity ?? Designated as Constance. [Note from Terra: Need your Cosmic #...Also, I can't believe I don't know your last name.]

Party TG and Party C wish to make a reciprocation contract on the basis of mutual cooperation and trust from here forth.

Party TG Stipulations
Party C will be responsible for:

- **S1.** Assist Party TG in seizing control as well as sustaining control of the Galtry Syndicate (or whatever name it may go by in the future). The latter is only when Party TG feels, with certainty, that Party C's involvement is necessary and reasonable.
- **S2.** Assist Party TG when and if their life or freedom is endangered.
- **S3.** Help promote an environment conducive to both Party TG's and Party C's growth when both possible and reasonable.
    - Can be forgone if Party C feels their principles and morals clash with whatever the action is.

All stipulations above can be waived if Party C firmly feels they're incapable of fulfilling the terms, are incapacitated, are not within a reasonable distance, are ignorant of happenings, or have made some type of agreement with Party TG.

- **S4.** When alone with Party TG, Party C cannot intentionally withhold information when it is genuinely and directly requested by Party TG. Party C cannot deliberately lie to, manipulate, or mislead Party TG. Party C cannot intentionally bring harm to Party TG.
    - Line one and two can be forgone if revealing of information alone would, with little doubt, lead to death, mutilation, or unnecessary suffering of either Party TG or C.

<u>Party C Stipulations</u>
Party TG will be responsible for:

- **S5.** Support and back The Tower when and how they can when Party C feels it's necessary.
- **S6.** Assist Party C when and if their life or freedom is endangered. To help prevent this, Party TG will also assist in keeping the area within Party C's 'domain' uncontested by factions that are dangerous, needlessly violent, malicious, etc., toward Party C.
- **S7.** Support Party C by gathering information, lists, locations, and other such information on other Kiln for Party C.

**All stipulations above can be waived if Party TG firmly feels they're incapable of fulfilling the terms, are incapacitated, are

not within a reasonable distance, are ignorant of happenings, or have made some type of agreement with Party C.**

- **S8.** *When alone with Party C, Party TG cannot intentionally withhold information when it is genuinely and directly requested by Party C. Party TG cannot deliberately lie to, manipulate, or mislead Party C. Party TG cannot intentionally bring harm to Party C.*
  - *Line one and two can be forgone if revealing of information alone would, with little doubt, lead to death, mutilation, or unnecessary suffering of Party TG or C.*

<u>Miscellaneous Addition</u>
Affixed Consequence:
[Note from Terra: I know you're going to have a problem with this, Constance, but it's necessary, and I won't make the contract without its inclusion.]

Due to concerns of interference from parties outside this contract, Party TG wishes to add a special consequence.

The consequence is as follows - if Party C is physically destroyed, suffers irreparable mental ruin, or is irreversibly bound by any parties connected with Party TG (directly or indirectly) prior to the signing of this contract or by any outside parties that held the intentions of voiding this contract, then Party TG will perish.

(After 5 Material-Earth years, both parties can willingly agree to extend, alter, or remove any part of this contract excluding Stipulations S4 and S8.)

'...Good lord.' I examine the long page, my eyes shifting through the many words and phrases. 'This is quite a lot, and it looks as if there is more on a different wall. This is far from how the domination contract appeared to work.'

My finger touches the wall and the next one appears. This new wall primarily concerns the possibility of voiding stipulations one through three if... well, if one of the parties becomes "unduly malicious, immoral, or radical, in other words, unjustifiably evil." This being a special spirit contract, it only activates if one party sincerely feels that way about the other party. It appears that stipulations four and eight never void, which is peculiar. Then there are things about consequences if we fail to uphold a stipulation, and they all vary from severe to none whatsoever depending on the actions taken by the other party.

The strangest one was for lying, which included a minor headache after lying the first time, a fit of blinking the second time, and then a strong compulsion to share the information the third time. Then there are other things in there that make stipulations one through three and five through seven frequently voluntary unless the other person is genuinely and deliberately not attempting to fulfill them in any way, at which point punishments begin. Those punishments usually center around a compulsion to confess to the other person regarding why the stipulations are not being fulfilled.

I recall some contractual violations and infringements I read about in the 'Contracting Foregone Humanity' book. The book claimed it was possible to force someone to perform actions against their will and may go as far as explicitly modifying someone's sentiments or thoughts. The compulsions to confess already feel a tad intrusive, so I am pleased Terra did not go further than that.

However, the thing that sticks out more than anything is the affixed consequence. It is by far the harshest punishment with little room for interpretation. The only thing comparable is the consequence for betrayal, intentional malicious sabotage, and other such things, which basically takes the "eye for an eye" approach. The affixed consequence does not take into account any of that. Something could happen to me that is nigh beyond her control, and that would be the end.

'She's right, I have concerns, but I do not believe she would put that in there without sound reason.'

For the next hour or so, I read through the contract a few times over. There is not much I can think to add; everything is rather responsible and provides a way out if it is unreasonable for the opposing "party." The only part that does not allow much room is the lying stipulations, but it still excludes times when the information itself will endanger the other's being.

All in all, it's relatively simple; it primarily makes it so our relationship consists of the two of us supporting one another, with the smallest possible worry of betrayal. Someone to rely on is something I believe both Terra and I have gone without for quite some time.

Pondering for a few more minutes, I shrug. *'I shall discuss it with Terra later. It is time to practice my mana skills before she supposedly arrives.'*

····
·········
····

I place the messenger orb to the side and lean against the wall behind me. *'I managed to foster another grade and it was not as draining as it was a couple of days ago.'*

Since obtaining the Aspirant skill, the way to train my mana compression has been to write in the messenger orb, but I attempted something new this time. I tried to draw; more specifically, I wanted to try and make a map within it.

After speaking to Earl, I realized a map would not be the worst of ideas for both Tenebrous and the park. Besides, I am bored of writing random messages, notes, reminders, poetry, and songs in the orb. So I made my attempt to make the map, which turned out to be more enjoyable and engaging than I thought it would be. This is how I also realized my life lacks entertainment. Therefore, I believe I shall keep experimenting with map-making as a distraction from now on.

I glance at all the rubbish strewn about the room. Rising to my feet, I toss all the clutter toward the corners of the cave. If Terra is visiting my abode, I guess I should... well, not clean up, but at least create a footpath for her to walk. *'I pray it does not smell; I have never had a guest before.'* Rummaging through our food stock, I consume all the food that appears to be the oldest. This reduces my Erysichthon to zero, and my missing snappish bead reforms on my shoulder, except the bead reforms as black rather than red. *'So it's as I thought. It's storing the haze I have. I believe I can use it to store a certain haze variant and then perhaps find a way to swap them. I shall have to experiment with that as well, maybe after germination.'*

I hear a familiar voice outside the cave. "Constance, are you in there?"

'Terra found me! I did not expect her to actually find me; at least, not so quickly!' My eyes sweep across the dim, dreadfully messy cave; the only source of light in this part comes from the gate chamber's glowing stained glass. *'...I live in a cave with an ape! Good lord, this is embarrassing; someone as wealthy as Terra is going to hate this...! Which means she shall hate me!'*

Moving to the edge of the cave, I push some of the bricks from the entrance. I drop to my knees and stick my head outside. My head is around where her knees are, so it's a bit of a new angle to see Terra from. From here, I can see through the gap between the veil and her skin. She carries the same satchel she had yesterday.

Both her eyes, silver and green, glance downward. She takes a step back and raises an eyebrow.

{Welcome.} I wave, motioning for her to crawl through the hole and into the cave. {Apologies for the... everything.} Drifting backward, I shout, {Prithee, do not hate me for what thou art about to witness!}

Outside I hear her drop to her knees and begin crawling through.

'I... I suppose I could have increased the heighth of the entrance a tad more.' As soon as her head enters, she freezes when her eyes behold the cave's bountiful interior. {Dost thou hatest me?} I ask in a wee voice, wringing my hands together.

"...Of course not." She blinks a few times, gazing upon the cave, and then finishes crawling. Removing a torch from her satchel, she runs it across the cave and asks with a clearly forced smile, "Constance, how... how long have you been living here?"

I glance back just in time to see an old slice of 'pizza,' that Gen must have stuck to the ceiling, fall onto the iron coffin below it. {...It was like this when I discovered it, I swear,} I respond, turning back around. {Aye, an untidy hermit lived here; I am not such a messy person that I would allow this to happen... Let's go into the other room; it's much cleaner!}

"A clean room... Yeah, let's do th—" Stopping mid-sentence, her eyes concentrate on the coffin and then drift toward the side of the room where the yellow tome rests. "Where on earth did those come from and how are they here?"

{Did I not mention those?}

"Well, you did mention the coffin. I just didn't expect it to be here. How did you get those dents in it? And as for the tome, you definitely didn't mention it."

{Oh, the scuffs are because I pushed it down the stairs.} A laugh escapes her as she approaches the tome and reaches for it. *{Wha-wait! Do not touch it!}*

A spark shoots from the tome, striking Terra's finger. "It's upset and overly active," she says. "We can use this, probably."

{Use it? For magic? I have had that thought; it seemed unlikely to work, however.}

Shaking her head, she states, "Losing a spirit tome is one of the worst things that could happen to a Spirit Scribe. As far as magic goes, you could maybe use it for magic, but there would be some serious blowback. You'd need to know what to write to make spells work."

{Oh, then how dost thou suggest we use it then?}

"Extortion, to put it plainly. We could get them to help us with the threat of tossing their tome into the ocean, or worse, inscribing certain things into it that may cause problems to the person's psyche..."

{Ah, I guess I have become used to things being more complicated than that. If it's important, then thou couldst use it for that.}

Terra looks at me with furrowed brows. "You don't have a problem with extortion?"

{Certainly if there were better means, I would favor those, but I have done it various times to solicit food and garments. Especially when I was young and could readily slip away. If they did not come to rescue their item or sought to deceive me, I simply traded it to someone else or cast it into a latrine if they made me particularly angry.}

"I will have to be careful not to make you too angry then." She laughs. "I'd hate if my things started ending up in the toilet."

{Aye, it is wise not to anger me,} I respond, pretending to toss a lock of hair back.

With another laugh, she balances the torch on some rubbish and removes her silver tome. Flipping through the pages, she stops. "How did you get the tome here? Didn't it try to resist you?"

{I merely carried it; it seemed to struggle but could not harm me.}

Placing her hand on one of the pages, she murmurs, "Interesting." She points at the yellow tome; silver strings shoot from her fingertips and toward it. They embed themselves into the tome's cover. The threads wrap around one side and then the other, sealing the tome's pages shut. "You shouldn't be able to touch it without sealing it first."

{It did not hurt whatsoever, but it did tickle a wee bit.}

"Tickled?" Smirking, she glances at the coffin. "Mind if I take the tome? I'll trade you the key for the coffin in return, but I should warn you it might take me a bit of time to find the key. I'm sure my Bishop Manhattan has been keeping the key close since you took the coffin, and he left town a couple of days ago to check on the progress of Spirit Scribes at the slaughterhouses."

{I suppose so. I would rather have the key to the coffin than a book that tries to attack me every time I go near it... Though I am not certain if it really is a Kiln in the coffin.}

"It's unmistakably something like a Kiln at least. That coffin is probably sealed shut to smother its Mana Efflux, but when I'm this close, I can still feel it leaking a tad."

Taking a long look at the tome and then the coffin, I nod. *{Then I guess it would be wise to trade for the key.}*

"Then it's a trade. I'll get it to you after I find an opportunity to acquire it." Grabbing the tome, she places it in her satchel before retrieving her torch. "Now about this other room..."

{Aye! I hope the gate chamber is more to thy liking, and if it is not, well, I do not have any other rooms so... I hope thou like it.}

When we enter the gate chamber with walls covered in stained glass, Terra gasps. "Woah... This is incredible! I've never seen stained glass like this before. It's so vibrant and precise." She extinguishes her torch and slips it into her satchel.

{Aye, I am delighted thou like it.}

Moving around the chamber, she seems to become lost in the beautiful images that surround the gate to Tenebrous. Her foot kicks something, and a metallic noise echoes. The pistol I left from my previous venture slides across the floor.

Terra raises an eyebrow. Walking over to it, she takes it in her hands and pulls something at the top of the pistol. A copper-colored casing ejects from the side of the pistol and bounces against the floor. She presses something else, causing the pistol's base to slide out. Inspecting it, she asks, "Constance, if you don't mind me asking, why is there a loaded pistol with its safety off just sitting in the center of the room?"

I glance at the little tube that shot from the pistol and then back at Terra. *{It complements the rest of the chamber...}*

She sighs. "I'm going to partially dismantle it to prevent any accidents; if you don't mind, that is."

Hesitating, I recall the earlier incident. *{Aye... that is best, I suppose.}*

"I've been around a lot of firearms, so I'll show you how to use it later if you want."

{Verily! I would enjoy learning more about it!}

Drawn by the commotion, an "ooh" sounds from the rubbish room next door. Gen enters the gate chamber, scratching his posterior with one hand and an empty pudding cup in the other.

Terra recoils upon seeing him.

{The hermit of which I spoke has awakened from his slumber,} I state, rubbing the back of my neck.

Releasing a big yawn, Gen smacks his gums together and then notices Terra's presence. The two peer at one another. The chamber is silent.

Tilting his head, Gen raises his arm that grips the empty pudding cup. He lobs it at Terra. I reach out with my hand to catch it, but I am also afraid of getting too close to Terra and infecting her so I stop. The cup bounces off her brow and then jiggles against the ground. Terra raises her hand, placing a palm against her forehead as Gen turns to leave.

{Apologies! He is a bad ape!} I pick up the cup and cast it back at Gen. He moves out of sight as the cup soars by the back of his head. {Bad ape! And again, apologies, Terra!}

My hands fiddle with the cattail wrapped around my torso. 'Why!? Why, Gen!?'

Terra turns. Our gazes meet, and I drop my hands. {I believe Gen thinks thou art invading his home, or perhaps he is jealous!} I attempt to explain. {Oh, it might be because of the pistol, he does not like it...! But honestly, Gen is a difficult one to understand!}

"It's fine, but... you never said you brought a... a monkey from the zoo back with you."

{He is an evolved ape, I think; I read about them in a book. I provided him medical assistance. He never left after that, so he dwells here now too.}

Taking a breath, she drops her arm. "Medical assistance? How?"

{Ah, I am a bit of an amateur, but I am licensed by the Cosmic System, so I shall show thee!} I straighten my back and puff out my chest. 'Prithee display my Humorism qualifications, Cosmic System.'

> Displaying 'Trailblazer (Humorism)' Title to Entity.

I push the wall away. {I am not an ordinary haze monster, Terra; this haze is also a doctor.}

Her eyes move to and fro as she reads what must be a wall from the Cosmic System. "Humorism." A stiff smile spreads across her face. "Well, you are full of surprises, that's for sure, and he didn't seem to be in any pain."

'Odd. She does not seem duly impressed? I was excited to share my qualifications with her... I only received it because everyone more skilled is beyond the lychgate, but she does not know that.' Allowing my back to relax, I gesture toward the door Gen was just at. {*Aye, his wounds healed much quicker than I foresaw. Terra, is there something wrong with humori–*}

"We'll talk about that some other time!" she says, waving her hand and glancing away. "Sorry, but let's... let's talk about the contract. Did you have time to read it?"

Squinting, I cross my arms. {*Very well, we shall discuss it later. Aye, I read it and thou must knowest what I desire to inquire thee about.*}

"About the affixed consequence, I assume."

Uncrossing my arms, I nod.

"It's quite simple, actually." She sighs, staring at the pistol that is still in her hands. "With it, our lives are tied together; if that wasn't the case, the Bishops might try to destroy or dominate you."

{*Destroy me!? Merely because I made a contract?*}

"No, because you made a contract with me. I can't be certain what my father's husk will do, but there's a possibility he might contemplate destroying you to 'free' me of any contractual obligations, and if he couldn't do it himself, he'd hire someone who could or ask another Bishop to do it."

{*...So that is why the wording is so peculiar. It makes it so the Hex Church would also have to kill thee if they wished to destroy me. Regardless of if they do it themselves or if they hire someone to do it for them.*}

"Yes, I don't know about the rest of the Hex Church, but my father's husk is very careful to make sure no harm comes to me." She pauses, scrutinizing the pistol in her hands before adding, "The only time I've ever seen them genuinely angry was after someone tried to assassinate me."

{*I mean, thou art Bishop Manhattan's daughter. Now and in the past, I have watched how families interact with one another. From what I have observed, it does not seem strange for him to be protective.*} I tilt my head, asking, {*Is that not how families are for people that have one?*}

She waves my remark away dismissively. "No, I doubt it's something like that. I'm not even sure he's capable of feeling those types of sentiments. All that matters is he wants me alive. I'll use that against him to protect you from not just him but the whole Hex Church." Her gaze moves about the chamber. "What would you say if I asked to use your "gate chamber" for something important?"

{Use the gate chamber?} I look at the shimmering gate before turning back toward her. {I do not know what thou meanest.}

"Hmm, let's sign the contract first if you're okay with it. After that, I'll explain in more detail, and of course, you can say no if you want."

Her words make me recognize something that may be an issue in the future. {Actually, now that I think about it, can I? With the contract, that is.}

"Yes, of course, I made everything pretty loose, so neither of us can start taking advantage of the other. The only one that I left less room for was the fourth stipulation... and I believe you know we both have issues with trust, so I'm sure you've figured out why it's like that."

{Aye, thou dost not need to speak of that more, I understand. Oh, there was another thing, the contract used the word 'feel' a lot, is that not a bit too loose of a word?}

"If this was a normal contract, sure, but this is a spirit contract, meaning if someone truly 'feels' something, then the contract will know. A spirit contract judges both parties on a much more profound level than a simple interpretation of the words—it evaluates based on intent, feelings, and other such things, in order to decide whether the contract was breached. Moreover, I left it like that because, to put it simply, people change. It's better to accommodate for individual changes in a lifetime contract."

{Aye, I had read some things like that in the contract book.} I think for a moment and add, {So, I surmise, part of the fourth stipulation is to prevent us from becoming enemies, regardless of what transpires in the future.}

She nods with a heavy sigh. Walking to the edge of the chamber, she kneels and lays the disassembled pistol on the ground. "With what's going on, in the end, everyone and everything will be different than they are now." Standing, she turns and inspects the stained glass walls. "Heroes turning to villains, villains becoming heroes, lions evolving into sheep, sheep to lions, and other such realities shall be as commonplace as the changing of the weather."

'She is not wrong, but it is still a bit of a bitter thought that we might someday oppose one other, even if it is indirectly. I suppose we shall simply have to pray that neither of us errs and treads a path they cannot turn away from.' I cross my arms and then state, *{I understand. But before the contract, which I presently intend to forge, I desire to know about thy plan. I deem it foolish not to inquire beforehand since thou seem to be planning to 'lay the first stones' before my germination. Is that accurate?}*

She peers into the eyes of the stained glass woman who wears the golden armor. "Well, yes, it would be before then. It must be before then, actually, and it's fair you would want to know beforehand. I am probably just too eager." While pacing around the chamber's exterior, she studies the glass wall and brushes her fingertips across its surface. "We need more people, you and I both do, and there are a lot of ordinary people out there looking for a lifeline. Most people haven't even realized what's happening yet, but those who have are being censored or hushed until world leaders are ready to formally announce and affirm the Cosmic System's existence. That makes this a prime opportunity for us."

{Thou wishest to use these people is what I deduced last we spoke.}

Her eyes abandon the walls, and she turns and walks nearer to me. "That's right, most of these people have a family member that has awakened, which is how they know about the Cosmic System in the first place. They are all desperately searching for a way to be integrated into the Beta." Stopping in front of me, she adds, "Last night, I donated to a very competent group who will lend me extra 'Hands' that will help compile a list of those people's names and contact information."

{Names and information? This is the part that has something to do with my haze? Dost thou desirest to use it to awaken these folk?}

Nodding, she says, "Yep, and the fact that the Cosmic System hasn't been officially recognized works in our favor as well since we can't reasonably have millions of people pouring into Central Park. Neither of us has any hope of corralling or managing so many desperate individuals."

'Millions? Are there even that many people in the world? Perhaps an exaggeration.' I tilt my head. {Aye... I would never wish to have that many people near me. It would be smothering. What I do not wholly grasp is why we would desire all these people crowding us?}

She smirks. "If we attract enough of these people, they'll encroach upon the quarantine zone, which will prove quite the headache for the Consortium, who are already spread thin and focused on their own matters in Chicago. Then we can bully the Consortium until they'll join us at the negotiating table, where we can offer them an opportunity to wash their hands of this whole affair. After that, you should be free to sleep as you told me you'd need to."

{So we would rouse the people and make affairs bothersome for the Consortium, after which thou wouldst send the Consortium a proposal...?}

"Something like that, yes. And with you at my side on the negotiating table, we can satisfy the Consortium by bartering haze to them with some added stipulations, while we also satisfy the people who came to you in the first place by awakening them or their loved ones. This forces everyone's eggs into our basket like we talked about last time."

{I... I suppose that might resolve the Consortium dilemma, but I do not know how much haze I can supply.} I gesture toward the stained glass walls. {And I believe it is rather critical that the Tower retains much of it.}

"We'll leave the amount vague, something like '15% of haze extracted with a maximum of some percentage.' That way, we don't guarantee more than we can take. As long as they feel they're getting a fair deal, we'll be able to get them to back off."

{Aye, something like that might suffice. But what of the commoners? What's dissuading the commonfolk from merely leaving once they have what they covet? Furthermore, what's preventing more folk from journeying to Central Park as people come to learn of the Cosmic System and my haze? Are we not inviting riots or forays if my haze grows to be common knowledge?}

"Ah, those questions all actually have the same answers: the quarantine zone, scarcity of official or verifiable information, and ultimately your fellow Kiln. Plus, with a beneficial and mutual position established with the Consortium and the people that do come, I'll be in an advantageous position to prod at the Galtry Syndicate until it falls into my hands. Each branch of the Galtry Syndicate does have its own hired guns called 'Pitfill,' and they'll make anyone who has genuine thoughts of violence or Tower 'forays' think twice... All in all, if everything mostly works out, you and I both will have a comfortable amount of weight with which we can use to tip many a scale in our favor."

{Candidly, I am uncertain how to feel about this so-called Pitfill, but thou sayst something about my fellow Kiln too...? Thou meanest when the other Kiln make themselves known, they shall effectively serve as a bulwark that isolates the city from the rest of the world... But...} I think for a moment; indeed, the Kiln might thwart people from entering the city, but it would likewise prevent folk from leaving. *{Terra... Dost thou seek to ensnare those that come to The Tower inside the city?}*

"I don't know if they'll be 'ensnared,' to be honest. There are way too many unknowns, factors, and people at play... I do believe this is the best course of action that'll both keep the two of us safe in the long term and save as many people as possible. It will make us invaluable assets to many, which both paints a target on our backs and puts people beside us. Still, the moral and tangible consequences of luring people here will be for us to bear..." She looks downward with a bitter face. "This is the type of thing I was referring to when I said only the 'lucky ones' will get their hands bloody."

{...It is as thou stated, we do not know enough to conclude if they shall be ensnared though there is no pretending that we are not entangling them in precarious affairs. But... I believe we should treat them as competent individuals who have chosen to journey here. Folk have sovereign minds, and as long as it is their decision to bear the risks, then the consequences are not purely ours.}

"I don't necessarily disagree, but your opinion could be called 'debatable.' It's important we keep that in mind because it is a possible point of contention in the future."

I shrug. *{None would call me virtuous. But some might call me opinionated.}*

Terra chuckles, staring at me as if uncertain if I am speaking in jest or not. "Wise words, maybe." Her head tilts as if thinking. "Ah! By the way, how do you make the haze?" She motions toward my body. "Like your bodily haze."

{I acquire most of my haze and most of my Essence by eating 'organic material.'}

Her eyes grow wide. "Eating? Wait, you did ask a strange question about eating to gain Essence last time we talked... That's so unfair!"

{Aye, but it has been tough to gather enough food to take advantage of it whilst also not attracting attention. It would not be so toilsome if I could simply nibble on plants; however, only meat seems to garner Essence.}

"What level are you!? You've got to be decently high!"

{Nay, from our past conversations and ones I have listened in on, I believe Kiln 'level' differently than ordinary folk. It is not solely Essence that Kiln require. Still, Essence is vital for my growth. I wish I could gather more.}

"Is that so?" She sighs. "Well, I'll find a way to get you some meat, so don't worry about that anymore."

{Verily!? That would be tremendously helpful!} I nod, glancing at the gate. {Let us forge the contract! Then I have some new information to discuss.}

Tilting her head, she pulls out her silver tome once again, a tiny bottle of transparent ink, and a pair of quills. "If I'd known I only needed to offer you food, this would have gone a lot quicker."

{It has naught to do with the food!}

She smiles as the two of us take a seat in the center of the gate chamber. She opens the tome and places it between us; the page is empty. "My father's husk 'gifted' me this ink to use on a spirit to dominate them. I'm not sure how much money he blew on the ingredients or how he even found them." Lifting a quill, she dips the tip into the clear bottle of ink. "But it brings me immense satisfaction to use this ink to sow the seeds that will ultimately sever our ties." She raises the quill, and a translucent silver flame sways at the end. "Since this is a reciprocation contract, not a domination, it requires a more personal touch."

'A flame?' I take a quill and dab it into the ink. A tangible violet fire churns at the tip.

"A Kiln's consciousness has so much substance," I hear Terra whisper to herself. She points at the book. "Touch the tome with your quill and, if this ink works as advertised, it should take care of the rest."

Terra touches her quill to the tome; I follow suit. The same contract from earlier appears with a few added details at the page's top. "Ah, the Cosmic System says your last name is Nightingale. That's a really 'crisp' last name; I wonder if you're related to the nurse," she says.

{A nurse with my surname?} I shake my head. {Nay, it is highly doubtful we are kin. I bear this surname because I fancied it and thought it deserved better than those who carried it.}

"I see? Either way, it's a great last name and fits you remarkably well... and wow, your Cosmic Entity number is really low! I wonder if people will find that impressive in the future... Something to think about, I guess."

'My number is low?' Glancing at Terra, I can see she is scrutinizing the contract once more. 'I should do the same.'

Deliberately and thoroughly, I read through the contract.

Reciprocation Contract Offer:

....

....

....

Do you accept the terms and stipulations of this contract?

[Yes]   [No]

After studying the wall and seeing Terra has finished as well, I answer, {Aye.} The page bursts into a blaze of silver and violet fire.

Reciprocation Contract Offer:
Imprinting now. Please wait...

Silver flame separates from the violet and spreads to my hand; meanwhile, the same is happening to Terra. I can see her eyes have grown wide as her hand is surrounded by the violet flame. The silver flames twist into the shape of a moth above my hand and then disperse into my haze, promptly sinking into my kiln. Above Terra's hand, the violet flame twists into the shape of a willow tree with a noose hanging from it and then fades into the pores of her skin.

> **Reciprocation Contract Offer:**
> *Success.*
> *The Reciprocation Contract between Constance Nightingale and Terra Iris Galtry is ratified.*
> *Contract is immediately in effect.*

Reading the wall, I raise my hand and then look at Terra, who is still wide-eyed. *{I dare say that might have been the most unexpected thing to happen to me in at least an hour,}* I say while inspecting the back of my hand.

····

········

····

Sitting in the center of the gate chamber, I spend the next two hours describing and explaining the remaining things I had yet to share with Terra. These include things such as Tenebrous, Earl, Gen, and one or two other things I neglected to mention. The whole time I talk about Tenebrous and Earl specifically, she glances between the gate and me while gawking with a partially opened mouth. It makes me rather uncomfortable, but whenever I stop to ask if something is wrong, she just says, "No! No! Keep talking. There is no need for me to say anything!"

Once I have finished speaking, Terra just continues to stare at me. I wave my hand in the air. *{Prithee, say something.}*

"Take me," she murmurs.

Mimicking a blink, I lean forward to peer into her eyes. *{Pardon me...?}*

She pulls her tome close. "Take me to this place of spirits."

I squint, straightening my back. *{Perhaps thou misheard me because I believe I described Tenebrous as a dreadful, nightmarish realm where good dies, evil thrives. I almost rhymed it and everything, Terra.}*

"No, Constance. That place is like a Spirit Scribe's holy land. I mean, God in Light, that's... that's the afterlife, Constance. Everyone's afterlife, not just Spirit Scribes! It can't be that bad. The afterlife is supposed to be a place of rest, devoid of suffering and hardships."

{Devoid of suffering and hardships? If I had to pick an alternative way to describe Tenebrous, I might say it's made of suffering and hardships. Oh, moreover, it was impossible to rest there either, at least for me, so it seems to lack that as well.}

The chamber becomes quiet for a moment until she shakes her head. "No... that wouldn't make sense... Maybe it's just a different place."

Rubbing my nape, I shrug. *{Mayhaps. In fact, aye, it is fair or even reasonable to believe that not everyone who passes beyond the lychgate is cast into Tenebrous.}*

'*Though Earl certainly did not seem to suggest there was anywhere other than Tenebrous when I was there.*' I pull out Deputy Clippie, Sidhe's pen, and "You Are Ecology 101" to change the topic. *{I wish to request some advice about how I should establish an ecosystem given a vast space, weather constraints, and creature limitations.}*

Her mind and mood are muddled from all the information, but she still nods and adjusts her seating. "Of course. I'll... I'll think about everything else you've told me later. It can wait." Clapping her hands together, she takes a breath and continues, "Besides, this sounds fun and intriguing, to say the very least. You mentioned that this person 'Earl' recommended the gate be placed in a high population area and also wanted people to enter it?"

{Aye. Earl wishes for me to bring people into The Tower. Once inside, the people will battle The Tower's creatures.}

"...Well, it sounds getting people to go in is the whole purpose of The Tower, and the end goal is more morbid than them just 'fighting.'"

Picking my words carefully, I respond, *{If I am to be frank, if someone chooses to enter knowing that there might be dangers, then their fate is their own. Earl must know that is how I feel about such matters and that is why she chose this method.}*

"Yeah, I'm not implying you shouldn't let people enter either. This is a lot like the sewer conversation we had yesterday. I think this is a great thing for the city." Looking toward the gate once again, she sighs. "Amazing, simply incredible. Basically, another world is on the opposite side of that door."

{Aye, I also consider it to be quite incredible. I am genuinely thrilled. Knowing I can be something more than a mere parasite is a great relief.} I stare at Terra, who moves a tad closer as if eager to help me with my ecosystem. {Verily, I am excited! Though I wish it were located somewhere other than Tenebrous, I still believe I can transform it into something truly extraordinary.}

She laughs. "It's fun to see you so enthusiastic about something. Oh, by the way, do you know when it will be ready? Does it grow normally or...?"

{Earl stated it should be essentially ready by the time I awaken.}

"What!" Her eyes open wide. "I thought this was several months or years away! I mean, you said this was a whole mile's worth of space and that there was absolutely nothing there. Yet you're telling me that in a few weeks, there is going to be a firm foundation for a fully functioning ecosystem!"

I shrug, drawing a circle in the middle of the paper. {I have learned to accept such things without much question. Thy life will be much more manageable if thou also learn to do so, assuming the source of information is trustworthy that is.}

While I draw the hill with the willow atop it, Terra asks me, "Then can I ask how soon you are going to allow people to enter? This could be a huge deal! I knew it seemed like it was going to be, but so soon."

Staring at her suspiciously, I ask, {What art thou thinking?}

"If... if we told people there would be a place like the inside of your Tower... we could really hype it up! We could make some powerful allies and get on friendly terms with some influential people. Many people would line up to come hunt in The Tower."

With a small nod, I look back toward my map and resume sketching. {Is that a sensible thing to do? Seems risky to entice such folk.}

"Now just hear me o—" She freezes mid-sentence and then says, "Oh, I thought you'd be more opposed. I was already preparing a speech."

{Thou knowest this era's world better than me, and with our fates entwined, I believe thou hast my best interests in mind, aye?} I state, drawing trees and the gate near the base of the page. *{This was the purpose of the contract, was it not? Besides, as I said, I would deeply favor this method to the leeching of everyone in my Tower's Domain.}*

Terra does not appear to know how to react; unlike what I foresaw, she seems slower to digest the contract's importance than even I.

I point at the ecology text. *{Prithee, turn that book to the page I marked with the leaf that resembles Gen's face.}*

"A leaf that resembles Gen's face?" She flips through the text. Her finger catches a page, and she pulls a red leaf from its paper. At the leaf's center are two holes resembling nostrils, and at the top, there are two big eyes with wrinkles near the cheeks. Turning it back and forth, she laughs. "It really does look like him; you had to have done this on purpose."

While shaking my head, I respond, *{Nay! I swear, I found it like that! It was quite humorous, but what I wanted thee to see was the picture on that page. I wish to know if that tree is real and nearby.}*

She lifts the text, reads the page, and then inspects the image. "They are real; however, there aren't any giant sequoia trees nearby. They're mostly on the Western half of the continent, but they do sell their seeds in some novelty shops for people to try and grow... Why? Are you planning on planting something this gigantic?"

{I wish to plant some around the outskirts of the hill, to partially obscure the willow tree.}

"Is that willow tree so big that you'd need to worry that one of the tallest trees in the world might not hide it? ...Actually, that's not important. Are you afraid someone might target the tree? Would that be bad?"

{I am uncertain; I simply wish to conceal it. Then one day, I shall point at the enormous trees and madly shout, 'never go there, it is forbidden,' and then I will vanish into a nearby treeline.}

Raising an eyebrow, she replies, "You know, telling someone not to go someplace usually makes them want to go there even more."

{Precisely. If they go there, that means they are not trustworthy; moreover, it's entertaining and I feel as if I would never get bored of doing it. Imagining their faces when I confront them makes me want to giggle.} I then point at the picture in the text. {But also, I want to see one of those trees with my own eyes; the man in the book's painting looks so tiny compared to it! Why would I not want such a thing if I can have it!?}

"Well!" Terra bursts into laughter. "I guess if it's for something so essential, I'll make some calls to get you some seeds."

{Seeds! Earl said if I brought her real seeds, it would be better.}

"Then I'll just overnight some seeds if that's true."

{That would be greatly appreciated! Is it not too expensive, though?}

"The money in my accounts will be mostly useless in the future, so I wish to make as much use of it as I can. Besides, it's just seeds."

I nod, pointing at the lower right corner of the page. {Since it's my first time doing this, I intend to experiment with some variety. I am going to try to place a forest there. If Earl tells me that it's too much, then I shall decide upon something else... My biggest concern is that I do not know what types of creatures I should add.}

"If there isn't much water like you told me and since this is your first time, you should pick things that won't require much attention or effort."

{Much attention?}

"Yeah, but also, it sounds like these aren't going to be ordinary animals. Which is why I also think you should select creatures that you'll be able to control if they grow larger, like that rat and turtle."

Crossing my arms, I ponder all the creatures I can think of. In the end, only one group of creatures with variety, quantity, and heartiness comes to mind. {Perhaps, insects?}

"That's not a bad idea. They're typically the bottom of the food chain, so they'd be great for you to watch and experiment with to start. Then you can diversify from there."

{Aye. I suppose things eat the insects, so it's a natural first step. Oh! Turn the book to the page with the leaf that resembles a woman balancing on one leg holding a fork above her head.}

With a chuckle, she flips through the pages once more. Stopping, she lifts a single leaf. "Wow, this one too. It looks exactly like you said." Her eyes move toward a picture on the page. "You want to know about this glass-winged butterfly?"

{Aye, and the plant it lays its eggs on; I want to know where I can find and obtain it.}

"Hmmm, how about you make me a list of bugs you might want, and I'll see what I can do. Though I should say, I'm not sure how many bugs I'll be able to find for you given the circumstances and time."

{Anything would be invaluable!} Making some squiggles representing more trees, I remember something. {What was it thou wished to speak to me about earlier? Something about the gate chamber?}

A smirk spreads across her face. "Oh, yesss, thanks for reminding me."

I stop drawing; a shiver moves down my back. 'Something about how she said that makes me think I should not have said anything.'

"How are your acting skills?" she asks, gazing at me with anticipation.

I do not respond; I shan't give her the satisfaction. She clearly wishes for a demonstration.

"That's no fun," she says with a frown. Sighing, she continues, "On the way in, I noticed that welding suit you stole from the Consortium."

{Aye, the arc suit.}

She nods. "I want to make a moving picture with you wearing that."

{Make a moving picture with me wearing the arc suit? How and why would I ever do such a thing?}

"I mentioned attracting those people earlier. Well in order to do that, we need to convince them that it's not just another false hope or scheme." Gesturing toward the stained glass walls and then at me, she says, "If we film you here with this in the background, that's a great start."

{Of all the people or things, why me? I cannot even speak. I am not certain there is a worse choice than me for this.}

"Not talking isn't a problem. I want you to use sign language, and far from being the worst, you're the best choice for this."

{I am waiting to hear why that is because I am far from convinced.}

"It's because whoever is in the picture will have a lot of people looking for them, but if it's you, that doesn't matter. They'll never know it was you, obviously. Not to mention, I'm sure you'd prefer to be the one in control of basically speaking for your Tower." She pauses and watches me. Once I shrug and nod, she continues her explanation. "As for why it's convenient for it to be in sign language, it's because they can use technology, algorithms, and something called 'bots' to track and remove moving pictures with verbal speech. So, it'll be a lot tougher for them to find and remove if you use sign language."

With half-closed eyes, I ask, {Is it because tougher these 'bots,' like everyone else I have met thus far, do not understand sign language?}

"Lots of people know sign language. I think you need to keep learning it... Speaking of which, that was the reason Lorcan was looking for you. He has a grasp on sign language thanks to his mother, who used to work with children with disabilities, and he was supposed to give you textbooks and a bag full of things that would help you learn."

{Oh? Then he should not have been so forceful, threatening, and slow to explain; in conclusion, I blame him.}

"Yes, I do too, but what are your feelings on making the moving picture?"

{As long as they do not know it is me, I suppose there is no harm, but what am I meant to convey in sign language?}

"That's the beauty of it." Raising a finger, she points at me. "All you need to say is precisely what you're going to do. That's it."

{...Hmm? Couldst thou elaborate?}

"You're going to forecast events to come, things that are going to happen. Like if you vent your haze into the sewers, you can prophesize that 'beasts will emerge from the sewers', and that will lend you a lot of credibility with some people. Since you're also the root of your predictions, they'll obviously be true forecasts. It's a literal self-fulfilling prophecy." She explains further, "We'll produce several moving pictures all at once. In each one, you'll make predictions, divulge information, and maybe drop hints and such that'll persuade people to believe you. If people truly believe in your words, they will seek you out."

{Trickery in a sense then... If thou believest it shall work, then I do not see the harm. It sounds like an interesting experience, I guess. Who shall be doing the drawings?}

"Drawings? Oh, you mean for the 'moving picture.' I'll do them unless we can find someone trustworthy. If I do them myself, I'll just add to it on my own time to make it more believable." She thinks for a moment, running through all the details in her head, and then nods. "But you'll need to meet with Lorcan and have him teach you the signs."

{I would rather not...}

"I'll be there, plus if I recall, you once mentioned something called the Elderly Rats? Could we meet them?"

"For the moving picture?"

"Yes, exactly. It'll be more convincing if they are here too... plus..." She glances over to the entrance of the chamber where Gen returned at some point and is now glaring at Terra. "I think he could use more company."

When my eyes look toward Gen, he makes the thumbs-up gesture and nods. *'I did not teach him that...'* Shrugging, I say, *{I shan't comment on* whether Gen needs more company, but I will say, the Elderly Rats are in a dangerous area. I doubt we shall be able to retrieve them for the moving picture...}

"Oh, yeah, that's where you said that giant rat is, isn't it?"

{Though...} I write a note on my map, 'design an area for elderly rats?' and then look back toward Terra. {Dost thou knowest what rats eat when they are not gnawing rubbish? Is it plants... roots? I am not certain since I always see rats eating whatever they can find.}

Terra looks at my note. "They eat seeds and fruits, I think. Why don't you put them in the area around your willow tree so they can keep an eye on things?"

{Where the big trees shall be? Mayhaps. I do not think the big trees make fruits, but I can probably make space between the big trees and the willow tree for other things.}

"...Are you sure you'll be able to support so many plants?"

I draw some berry bushes around the willow tree. {Earl told me the number of plants did not matter, so I shall take advantage of those words and experiment. Ah, I should sow some fruit trees. I am curious if they can survive with only mist.}

"Aren't you worried they'll die?"

{If they die, then they shall become somewhere for something else to live, and also I shall blame Earl.}

"Is Earl not going to be a little upset if you blame them for everything?"

{Perhaps, but only if someone tells them...} Peering at my kiln, I place emphasis on my next words. {...or if they are listening in on my thoughts.} I notice a tiny flicker in the flame's movement. {Aye, but she is far too busy to even answer my questions, so I doubt I need to worry about her using her time so frivolously.}

Terra laughs. I told her some things about Earl earlier, so she knows I am a tad annoyed about Earl ignoring me.

A sound begins to emanate from Terra's satchel. Reaching in, she removes a black rectangle. "Sorry, Constance, but I need to take this phone call, it's important. Is that okay? It might take a while."

I nod.

"Thanks, I'll try not to be too obnoxious, and again sorry."

Taking her lap-top from her satchel, she moves to a corner of the chamber. She places the black rectangle to her ear and begins to speak with a very stern voice, not at all like the gentle one I am used to.

Around three hours pass while Terra discusses various things with the black rectangle, and I work on my map. It's calming to hear someone's voice since it's usually deathly quiet in the cave when it's just Gen and me. Her conversation mostly seems to have something to do with retrieving people, payments, moving certain items, and other such things. Finally, Terra lowers the black rectangle, putting it and her lap-top back into her satchel.

She stands and steps over to me. "Constance, can I ask you something?"

Tilting my head and peering upward, I ask, {What is it?}

"Do you have any free time today?"

{I have time most days, this one among them. Why?}

"Well, I prepared a meeting with some people you've actually met, so I wanted to see if you'd be interested in attending?"

{People I have met? I am only acquainted with one person, mayhaps two, if Jessica is counted. What is this about?}

"Since we signed the contract and you seem okay with everything, I am going to start making moves. This is one of those moves." Hesitating, she belatedly adds, "And I won't, nor can I, lie to you and say there won't be any violence."

{Oh, thou shouldst have said as much...} I place Sidhe's pen and Deputy Clippie on the ground and stand. {I shall attend. It is important I participate, *and I have decided to stop running. Furthermore, it is unfair to leave everything to thee. I wish to share thy burden as I hope thou wilt share mine.}*

Her mouth opens slightly. She blinks at me a few times and then laughs. "Well... of course, we are partners in crime, in both a figurative and literal sense of the phrase. Now, I'm fine with telling you what's going to happen, but to be honest, I think it's best if you experience it with everyone else."

{Hmm? Why is that?}

"It'll make your reactions a bit more genuine. However, the main reason is that I'll be in control. In the future, you may find yourself in a similar situation and that may not be true. That makes this a fantastic opportunity for you to learn how to better deal with an unexpected or changing situation. Both in the modern era and without, uhm..."

{Without running away or turning everything into utter chaos? Is that what thou meanest?}

"That wouldn't be my choice of words, but yes. This is very good practice."

{Aye. I suppose I have heard worse ideas. If it may help me out of a precarious situation in the future, then I shall join as an ignorant guest.}

With a nod, she motions toward the arc suit. "Then put on your suit and let's be on our way. I do have a surprise in regard to it as well."

····

·········

····

Terra and I stand at the side of the icy black roadway. After I donned the arc suit, we left the cave by way of the Ramble and promptly made our way toward the street. That was nigh two hours ago. I have nary an inkling of what is about to transpire, but Terra is a tad nervous for me to partake. Candidly, I am uncertain why, I have dealt with and associated with many ruffians in my day.

"Oh, and just be aware I'll be Galtry, not Terra, meaning I'll be acting as such..." Her eyes look a bit glum as she says, "Take this opportunity to get accustomed to it because it will not be uncommon for you to see... If there are people around, I'm Galtry; only when it's you and I alone am I Terra, understand?"

With a slight nod, I respond, *{Aye, I understand.}*

"And do you feel any leaks from your suit? I know we taped the zipper and everything, but we still have plenty of tape left if you need it."

{Zipper is such a fun word! Zzzip-per!} I flex my arms and legs whilst fidgeting with the 'zipper's' handle. It is much more comfortable to wear the arc suit in my sable form, though I still use the cattail to smooth out some of the lumps. *{I believe the seal is staunch, and my comrade cracker layer should prevent it from leaking too much. Oh, but canst thou see'st my eyes through the arc suit?}*

She nods and peers into my helmet's window. "I guess if you say so, and yes, I can, but I can't see your face really, so it's fine. It looks sort of 'crisp' as you'd say." She laughs and then adds, "Anyway, if it gets to be too much for you to handle, just let me know through telepathy."

{Why art thou more anxious about this forthcoming affair than even me?}

"A few of these people could be considered rough around the edges at times, and you're... for lack of a better word, innocent. I'd like it if you stayed that way for as long as possible," she says with a smirk.

{I am a wee insulted by that. Though commonfolk nowadays are more verbally vulgar, thou knowest naught of the things that would happen on the London streets and alleyways at night.}

"Yeah, but you were nervous about me seeing your shoulders; how could you not be innocent in some sense?"

{If thou wast practically trouserless when meeting a stranger, I believe thou wouldst have also been nervous. Besides, I am more apprehensive about wearing this silly suit than anything.}

"Oh, don't worry about that. You'll fit in."

I squint. *{What does that suggest?}*

"You'll see." Rubbing the back of her neck, she says, "...Anyway, the RV is about to round the corner. Can you do me a favor?"

{That depends on the favor.}

She twirls her hand as if searching for the words. "If I sit in the back, no one will speak freely, so unless you aren't okay with it, I'd like to sit in front where they can't see me. That way no one panics or tries to do anything rash before we've collected everyone."

{I... I suppose that is an acceptable favor and excuse.}

"Okay." Glaring at me with a much sterner face than she ever has before, she says, "Just to reemphasize, you might be caught off-guard by some of what's about to happen. I'll probably even put a lot of the attention on you to help establish your reputation. I learned several interesting things from you the other day, and I'll be utilizing those here today."

{Did I truly provide such valuable information...? But wait, will my information be used for or against my supposed acquaintances?}

With a frown, Terra looks toward the ground.

{I understand; it is naught to concern thyself with,} I say with a shrug. *{This is the fruition of what we discussed at the castle the other day, is it not?}*

"Less fruition, more seeding, but yeah. I would have preferred to wait a few days before dragging you to something like this, but if you're going to be hibernating soon, it simply can't wait. So this will be our first real step toward whatever the future may hold."

I wiggle a finger, beckoning her gaze away from the ground. *{Well then, as far as I am concerned, this is the dawn. Let us go from being the ones whom the world squashes to the ones who hold the world.}*

Looking up, she chuckles. "Then let's get carrying." She removes her veil, revealing her silver eye and sewn argent fabric. "And thank you for joining me today. It makes me feel better."

Chapter 23: Syndicate Roundtable

∞∞∞∞∞∞∞∞∞∞∞∞∞∞

An immense ride known as an "RV" veers a corner and rolls into view. If I had to guess, I would say the device spans forty feet in length and ten feet in both heighth and breadth. It bears a sleek ebony hue with scarcely any discernible features beyond its rectangular body. Even its row of windows blends nigh faultlessly into its veneer and are only perceptible because they gleam in a ray of the forenoon's sunlight that escapes the white clouds overhead. But most intriguing to me is that it appears to have a crease on one side, suggesting a house-like door. *This RV is a behemoth. Are such monstrosities safe to operate around other people?*

Terra glances at me. {By the way, your alias is Fairy, you can change it if you want, and I'll back you up... but it's better if you try to get used to it.}

Fairy? Lorcan and those twins refer to me by that name. I tilt my head. {I have one chosen name I seldom share and several aliases I shared with many quite frequently. Why not begin expanding my repertoire once more?}

She nods. "Yes, I understand. Everyone only knows Galtry, few know Terra."

{And one knows Constance, and one it shall remain until I desire to tell another.}

"What about Earl?"

{Earl cheated.}

The door on the RV's side clicks and creaks open.

Terra's smile disappears, and her eyes turn sharper than knives.

Out steps a familiar man carrying a canvas bag with long red hair and tattoos on his neck. Though he wears a shirt with long sleeves for once, it still seems as if it shall rip around his muscular arms at any moment. This man is of course Lorcan, the man I cannot seem to stop running into. Seeing me, he squints; his footsteps beat against the ground as he approaches. He stops less than a few feet away. His figure covers everything in front of me and his shadow shades the entirety of my body. Straightening his arm, he holds the bag out and drops it. It thumps against the ground.

"Goddamn!" he shouts. "You know how hard you are to find? I nearly froze my butt off, walking around looking for you with the pipsqueaks. Y'know, when I saw you were with a monkey, I thought you'd be easy to find. I remember thinkin', "well, how good can you really hide with a monkey?" Apparently, pretty damn good! Man, I should've tackled your ass before you ran away; it would've saved me days' worth of time."

Galtry shows herself. "Lorcan," she says flatly. Lorcan's eyes widen as she continues, "After this is over, I'd like to speak to you in private; I want to understand how you utterly failed a task that took me under an hour. After that, we'll discuss whether or not you're completely worthless to me." Her shoes tap against the hard stone roadway as she adds, "Now stop wasting our time and drive us to the pick-up locations."

She steps through the doorway, disappearing within, and Lorcan exhales a long breath. "Well, my bad, Fairy," he says with a small click of his tongue. Lifting the bag, he marches toward the RV. "I guess I'll put your bag where we'll have our lessons later."

'Terra is crisp! Perhaps if I aspire to be more assertive, I can be crisp as well...' Adjusting my posture to force myself to stand perfectly upright, I confidently glance to and fro before strutting toward the RV's doorway. I ascend a few stairs and then freeze—the RV's interior surpasses my fantasies of what a small palace's great hall might resemble.

Bleached marble floors glisten, mirroring my image. Oaken cupboards, hand-whittled with exquisite craftsmanship, run along a small scullery that sits adjacent to a dining nook and marble table. Beyond the scullery, leather couches of pearly white encircle a silver-marble roundtable. The roundtable has rings graven into its surface; it reminds me of Terra's silver eye. Above me, the ceiling is tiled ivory white and casts a sunlike glow downwards, causing everything to twinkle in warm light.

My confident and immaculate façade crumbles. *'...The fever dream never ends. Is this what it's like to be wealthy in this era? Parading and prancing about in palace-carriages.'*

Stepping toward the little nook, Lorcan sets the canvas bag atop its table. He pulls the zipper and removes three objects from it, holding them where I can see. Pointing at each one, he says, "Whiteboard, marker, eraser, use the marker to write on the whiteboard." He undoes the marker's top and runs it over the board, creating a black streak. Holding up the eraser, he swipes it across the board; miraculously, it removes the black writing as if it was never there. "And obviously, you erase with the eraser. It's yours to have."

'It cannot be!' Before he can regret his decision, I rip the board and marker from his hands. *'Magic; this is what magic can do. Endless pens and now erasable writing! Do the common folk know of these inventions? Why would folk use lap-tops when there are much more wondrous tools like this!'*

"Don't be so excited." Shaking his head, Lorcan chuckles. "It makes me feel sorta bad to see someone so happy about something I bought at the dollar store."

In my flawless handwriting, I scribble a message of gratitude on my new 'whiteboard.' "This gift is greatly appreciated!"

Staring at the board, he raises an eyebrow. "Did you write the Declaration of Independence too? That's some seriously exaggerated writing, even for cursive."

'Thy face is exaggerated!' Yanking the board away, I write, "Thou hast simply never beheld a true penman!"[92]

"Thou hast? Now you're just messing with me!" He laughs aloud and smacks me on the back. "Maybe we'll get along after all."

'He struck me!'

Noticing the back of the suit's change in shape from his strike, he pulls his hand away. "Oops, sorry. Probably shouldn't do that. Boss would be ticked if they knew I was being so rough with you."

---

[92] Penman: one who writes a good hand, one skilled in penmanship.

On my whiteboard, I write, "Strike me again and I shall strike thee threefold!"

He raises his hands in surrender. "Woah, sorry. It was just a pat on the back. You can pat me on the back too; I don't really mind." Hearing a sound from further back in the RV, Lorcan seems to remember something. "Oh, yeah, you're the second person we picked up. And we aren't sharing real names, so they need a nickname..."

While he thinks, I turn to scrutinize the person who arrived early. A young man with short tawny hair and dark brown eyes shuffles through a doorway from further back in the RV. He glances at Lorcan and me before he quickly hurries to take a seat upon the white couches. He wears a purple button-up shirt and pale brown trousers; I believe his dress is meant to be a wee bit more formal than average attire.

Though he lacks his helmet, I believe I recognize him. *'Why is he here? I suppose I should verify it's him.'* I write on my board, then turn it toward the person. "Daniel?"

He nods and wipes his brow, appearing rather perturbed... and sweat-clad. His mouth opens midway, yet his tongue seemingly fails him.

"You know this kid?" Lorcan asks. "For whatever reason, he straight-up refuses to talk to me. Does he have any nicknames or anything like that?"

"Nickname?" Daniel murmurs. "I-I get a nickname?"

I erase the board, and with a bit of hesitation, I write, "Shrieking man."

Daniel's mouth falls open, and he gawks at me with misty-eyes. "Et tu," he whispers.

"Shrieking man, that's, uh, weirdly freaky. It doesn't really roll off the tongue either, does it?" Lorcan nods, slipping into a deep ponderance. "It might work if we shorten it..."

Opening and closing his mouth, Daniel struggles to speak to Lorcan. He raises his hands whilst shaking his head.

Lorcan snaps his fingers and points between Daniel and I. "Fairy, meet Shriek."

Shriek lets out a weepy groan and sinks deep into the couch.

"Fairy's mute, Shriek," Lorcan says, smirking and gesturing at me. "So don't expect her to respond without her whiteboard. Oh, and the boss said not to ask about her getup. I think the boss's words were something like, 'Fairy can wear whatever she wants. If you have a problem with that, I'll find a second suit and weld it shut with you inside.'" He chuckles. "Yep, pretty sure that's what it was word-for-word."

Again, Shriek acts as if he is about to say something, yet his shoulders droop, and his eyes turn to the floor defeatedly.

With a shrug, Lorcan motions toward the couches. "Take a seat over yonder. You and Shriek can talk about whatever you feel like, except for why you're both here. We've got a few more stops before the meeting, but I gotta get back to driving this gold tank." Turning toward the RV's front, he walks away. "Probably a line of cars behind us, and honestly, I'm not even sure how I'm going to make some of these turns in this monster," he says, retreating behind a curtain.

I glance toward Shriek and then move to the couch opposite him, hugging my whiteboard. The sticky exterior of the arc suit rubs against the couch's leather surface, producing a piercing squeak as I skid down the couch's back cushions.

'He must be envious of my whiteboard, perhaps jealous that he did receive one.' Writing on my glorious whiteboard, I turn it toward him. "If thou desirest to touch the whiteboard, I shall consider it."

"Wow, you talk so cool...! But um, no thanks. I appreciate the offer, but I... I-I don't need to touch it."

'Cool? Is that the same as saying it is crisp?' I tilt my head, asking, "Thou deem me crisp? And thou canst read my penmanship with ease?"

"...Yeah, yeah, you're really... crisp! I read a lot of badly translated light novels, so I'm pretty used to interpreting sentences that are barely legible."

'Barely legible!? An insult bearing the guise of a compliment.' I narrow my eyes and turn away. Several minutes pass in a hush whilst I amuse myself, drawing maps of potential Tower interiors on my whiteboard. Yet more than once, I glimpse Shriek peeking at me in the corner of my eye. I clean my whiteboard and write, "I do not appreciate folk leering at me. It makes me uneasy."

"S-sorry... I, uh, didn't mean to leer. Hey. Is it okay if I ask you a question?" he asks, rubbing his nape.

"Mayhaps, what is thy query?"

"'M-mayhaps,' I've never heard that outside of tv shows and movies before." Smiling rigidly, he asks, "How do you know me? Why did you call me 'shrieking man'?"

'I believe I should not answer that truthfully.' Erasing the whiteboard, I then write, "I do not have a reason."

"Don't have a reason? But you knew my name. Are..." He surveys the area and leans forward, pointing at his eyes. "Are you her, the girl with the glowing violet eyes? The ghost girl? I've been looking everywhere for her."

I wince. 'That... that could be anyone!' Scribbling on my whiteboard, I keep it curt: "I know naught of what thou speakest."

"The other two guys from that day described what you looked like, and I can sorta see your eyes. I... I just need to know why me? Why did you choose me?"

"Choose thee?" I write.

"Yeah, as your chosen one," he says, holding his breath. "Actually, it doesn't matter. My friends and family, I'm really nervous about them."

I glance behind myself, making certain he is not speaking to someone else. We linger in silence for another moment, and then I write, "What?"

He frees the breath he's been holding. "After that bunny gored me alive, I've been worried about the future. Will I be able to save the people I care about?"

I write and then turn my whiteboard so that he may read it. "Thou must be brave to have fought with such a ferocious beast and suffer such a grievous injury. Carry that bravery into the morrows, and thou mayst save whomever thou wishest. I am convinced of that." My eyes turn away. *'What is a bunny? The name sounds... soft. Like a creature I would desire to pet... but he swears it gored him?'*

"I-I think I might understand your wisdom, but is that really true? All it takes is bravery?"

My marker taps the board. "It is as I wrote."

He smiles. "I swear I'll do my best."

The RV lurches forward, skidding to a sudden halt. Shriek tumbles to the floor as I brace myself.

"My bad!" I hear Lorcan yell from behind the curtain. "We got two more passengers gettin' on. Remember not to discuss why you're here."

Shriek bumbles to his feet as the RV's door swings open. Two sets of footsteps reverberate as they march up the stairs. As soon as I see the people, I shake my head. Though they wear winter coats, caps, trousers, and footwear instead of their noble's police garments, I still recognize the pair, Jessica and Leo.

'Like Lorcan, I cannot elude the pair of noble's police, though I keep trying. Does Terra intend to assemble everyone I have crossed paths with?'

"Sup. I-I'm..." Jessica's words falter as soon as her eyes land upon my suit. "I'm..."

"What's wrong with you?" Leo asks. He points between Jessica and himself with a sigh. "She's Red Angel and I'm Crimson Savior."

Jessica's cheeks flush as she goggles me sitting in the arc suit.

Tilting my head, I write, "What curious names. May I ask what inspired them?"

Leo raises an eyebrow upon seeing my message.

"She's mute," Shriek says. "And her handwriting is amazing like that."

I place palm over my heart. '*My handwriting is quite amazing, I know! Goodness, Shriek must be a well-studied gentleman...!*' I drop my hand. '*Wait, nay, he insulted me a few moments ago...*'

"I guess that makes sense, except I wasn't looking at what they wrote. I was looking at the massive welding suit they're wearing. You could weld on the surface of the sun in that thing," Leo says, gesturing toward me.

Shriek glances at me and then nods. "Yeah, we aren't supposed to ask about that."

"Fine, it doesn't really matter. The names were Red Angel's idea. She insisted on them, and I didn't really care either way, so we just went with it."

Jessica's eye twitches.

"Shut the damn door!" Lorcan shouts from the RV's front.

"My bad!" Leo swivels around and slams the door closed. He gently shoves Jessica to get her to move. "Take a seat, Red Angel."

Smiling awkwardly at Leo, she nods. "Y-yeah, gotcha..." With hurried steps, she takes a seat next to me.

Leo sits next to Shriek, with a raised eyebrow.

Things go quiet, but ultimately, Jessica cannot contain herself. Robbing me of my marker, she writes on my whiteboard, "What are you doing here! Why are you so calm??"

'*Calm? I am merely acting!*' Afraid she might steal it, I take my marker back. '*The real question is why art thou here. I suppose I cannot ask that, though.*'

Peering into Jessica's eyes, I check for any remaining effects of the vermillion haze from our previous encounter. Not seeing anything noteworthy, I write, "Should I not be here?"

Again she tears my marker away, scribbling, "NO! Relax and keep calm! I'll help find an opportunity for you to run!"

Squinting, I retrieve my marker and respond, "Nay, I shall be fine," as the RV comes to a halt and the door squeaks open once again.

This time two men with untidy black hair and a woman with pink hair enter. They all appear to be covered in tattoos and piercings and wear black leather with silver spikes around the shoulders. Yet my eyes are drawn to the fact that each of them bears a mask that fits around their eyes as if they are about to attend a masquerade. The man at the front wears an owl mask, the second man wears a wolf, and then the woman in the back wears a rabbit. Their eyes at first look fatigued and dull, as if this is just another day; however, a trace of curiosity can be seen in the way their eyes dart about.

From behind the three, a maskless woman steps up the stairs and squeezes in between them. She wears a long red coat, a pair of black boots with heels, flashy earrings, big bands of jewelry around her wrists, and finally, black hair pulled back with a sparkling red band. Without a word, she drops onto the couch next to Jessica and crosses her arms and legs.

Lorcan re-enters through the curtain he left through previously. "You're the 'Helping Hands,' right?" he says to the people in the animal masks.

All three of them hold up an amulet around their necks that resembles a circle of twelve hands, each gripping another's wrist. In the center of this amulet, a cube of stone is suspended by a thin, nearly transparent bar. Etched into it is an emblem resembling two keyholes that are set overtop and perpendicular to one another.

As they lower their amulets, Lorcan raises an eyebrow and asks, "I guess that's supposed to mean, yes?"

The man in the owl mask nods and examines the floor around him. He gestures between his companions. "Owl, Wolf, Rabbit, we were told this would be a rush commission, but I don't see any viscera or corpses. Is the scene elsewhere or...?" Owl asks. His eyes drift between Jessica, Leo, and Shriek. "Oh, *hmm*, we don't operate on living people. Well, we occasionally do gender confirmation surgeries. Many men, women, and others have been pulling the trigger on that given recent events, but we don't operate on the unwilling, obviously."

Jessica and Leo ignore him whilst Shriek shakes his head.

"Is the commission the RV, then? If you give us two days, we can magnetize the RV's body and affix some materials to its exterior. We could disguise it as a school bus, and we might even be able to swing one day if you have some extra materials lying around." His eyes move across some of the furnishing and walls. He chuckles. "Ahh, goodness me."

"Did'ja notice Owl?" Rabbit says, giggling.

"Of course, I'd recognize Crow and Raven's handiwork anywhere. We've operated on this RV before."

"Mhm." Wolf nods. "I recrafted the internal software and added some customs. It was fun."

Lorcan raises a hand. "Alright, hold up. It's got nothing to do with the RV or surgery. I guess this'll be a different kind of rush commission than you're accustomed to," he says, pulling on a polished ivory door handle. A slim closet swings open, revealing a golden safe with a moth etching in silver. The safe fills near every inch of the closet's interior. "If you're carryin', drop your sidearms in the safe here until the boss says it's okay to take them back. If it's too big for the safe, just hand it over to me, and I'll put it up front."

'People carry firearms too big for that safe. It's six feet tall! I could stand up and place my hands above my head in that!'

Each of them draws a pistol. Rabbit's pistol is orange, clad in images of carrots, and oddest of all, it has a pair of rabbit ears affixed to the back. Wolf's is gray with a wolf head molded over the barrel so it will appear as if the pellet exits its jaws. Then Owl's is longer, pitch black, with a cylinder fastened to the front and a lever or tricker that resembles a talon.

They pass their weapons to Lorcan, who places them in the safe. *'They all keep a pistol on their person! Is it customary to bring weaponry to these sorts of affairs? Was it discourteous of me not to bring my own pistol? Would they mock me for having what must be a commoner's pistol...?'*

Opening an ornate armoire, he removes three masks that go over their mouths, three pairs of gloves, and three thin white outfits. He gives them to Rabbit. Pulling out a folded epistle, he points at me, hands the letter to Owl, and then once again disappears behind the curtain.

Owl glances at me before unfolding the epistle. Gazing at it, his eyes peruse the words, and his lips curl into a smirk.

"This will be a fun one." He turns toward the other three. "She's mute, so she can't respond. No questions, put the gas masks on, don't pierce or attempt to remove the suit." He steps toward me, extending his hand, and says in a soft voice, "Take my hand, doll, there's another room in the back for us."

'Doll...?'

I study Owl's face. Owl looks to be in his early thirties with a skinny face; he has a single ruby earring, a lip piercing, and a double nose ring on the right side of his nostril. Above his left eye is a tattoo that resembles a rickety door with a date stamped into it.

'Terra, this... what is this?' I reach out and take Owl's hand. He pulls me up, places his hand somewhere on the arc suit's back, and guides me toward a tiny room in the back. We enter a small cabin that contains naught but a lone chair enclosed on all sides by the clearest, cleanest mirrors I have ever beheld.

"Take a seat!" With a few small shoves and nudges, I find myself dropping into the chair.

The three begin to don the attire Lorcan gave them. Whilst they do that, I stare at myself in the mirrors. All I see is the vague shape of a woman cocooned in a blue sack-like suit with a dark window and two faint violet orbs glowing inside. It's tempting to remove the arc suit as I have never had the luxury of viewing myself in great detail before.

Owl pats me on the head. "Don't worry, doll, we'll make you look stunning in your suit. Now let's get started!"

They spin the chair in circles, all three of their eyes scrutinizing me and the arc suit. I grip the chair, afraid I might be spun out of it. *'Is this meant to be happening?!'*

"Hmmm." Wolf nods, declaring, "The material is unusual, not stuff you can usually get on the street, not without dropping some serious cash anyway."

"Money isn't a concern," Owl says, removing a marker and drawing on my suit.

"Good to know." Rabbit pulls the excess material at the back of the arc suit, squeezing the front around my chest. While they do this, the arc suit at times forms odd craters since my body is not solid. Whenever this happens, they totally ignore it, although I know they saw it. "Damn," Rabbit says with a vulgar giggle. "I'm not exaggerating when I say she has the best curves I've ever seen, but you can't even see them through this big blue monstrosity."

I write on my whiteboard, "Is this truly necessary!"

"It is, doll. The note said we can make it as tight as we think is necessary to make it 'feel like it's a second skin'. Then we'll add fabric." Owl straightens my head while the Rabbit and Wolf commence using some type of clip to bind the arc suit's back, making it hug my body as tightly as the haze allows. "I think we'll need to find a way to harden the material as well, so it won't warp so easily."

"Will that strengthen the suit?" I ask with my whiteboard.

Rubbing the material, Owl responds, "Yes, but it's not going to deflect a bullet or anything, and the joints would still need to be flexible, obviously, so we have to strike a balance."

"Ugh," Wolf scoffs with obvious exaggeration. "This helmet is a problem. It's just plain hideous and gigantic. We'll need to find a way to reduce it and reshape it into something more appealing. Can probably pull or render it around a different headpiece. I might be able to use a kiln to do it if the material isn't prone to melting. Ah, we can stiffen it with some metal sheets then too!"

'*Kiln!?*' My gaze shoots back and forth. By their sheer lack of concern, I realize that they must be speaking of an ordinary kiln. '*Aye. Undoubtedly, they would not speak so openly about an actual Kiln... indubitably.*'

I lose access to my whiteboard when Rabbit moves too close for me to see to write on it. Staring into the helmet's window, Rabbit taps on it. "We have a theme? What're the requirements?"

Owl nods. "Mysterious, stained glass, fairy, tower, knight, attractive, compelling, rousing, were the keywords our sponsor gave us to work around. The requirements include that it's airtight, breathability and oxygen supply aren't concerns, and that it's as light as possible without the risk of splitting."

"Absolutely gorgeous," Rabbit says, stroking the arc suit's window and peering into my eyes. I lean my face away from the window as she adds, "We could make it look like one of those, what're they called, bucket helmets?"

"Oh yeah." Wolf snaps his fingers. "I've seen those before. It's perfect! We should call the shop and tell them to start baking molds."

Rabbit and Wolf finish clipping the excess suit behind my back. The arc suit now embraces my figure as tightly as the material allows. '*Nay! This is simply too much.*' I shake my head, but the arc suit helmet does not permit them to see, and I doubt they would care.

Rabbit moves back to my front again, staring into the window. "Ah, I know! We could replace the face shield with glass!" Grasping the suit, she nods her head. "But we're going to have to dye the suit a different color first. No way we can leave it this repulsive blue. We could cover it too. When you call the shop, let them know to start assembling silks and textiles, we'll cover some of this ugly suit so it doesn't look so rubbery."

"Take some of her measurements and start making the calls. This is an urgent rush commission. Pay what we must, do what we must; we've been given twenty-four hours to get it together."

He removes paper and writing utensils. Putting them to paper, he starts to scratch something down as the three continue to chat about my 'figure' and the arc suit. If it were possible to die from embarrassment, I believe I would.

Time passes until Shriek comes to retrieve me. "F-Fairy, Owl, everyone is here except for you two."

They begin removing the clips from the arc suit. "We'll be there in just a moment," Owl answers.

I hop from the chair as they remove the last clip and rush out of the room. *'Umbral's shadow, free me of this chair!'*

With a chuckle, Owl follows me. "Right behind you, Fairy."

Shaking my head, I return to the room with the white couches, where there are now ten people.

Discovering more people than I expected, I freeze. The room is crowded now and it's clear that it is not made for this amount of people. Surveying each person's face, I recognize six of them: Shriek, Leo, Jessica, Lorcan, and two additional people I never anticipated.

Off to the side by herself is a woman with a big white bandage on her face and small scabs around her neck and hands—this person is Emily. She is the Spirit Scribe that sought to enslave me with the domination contract back in Gen's enclosure. Wearing her usual black frock with the hood down, she grips her unembellished blue tome tightly. She raises her hand, itching at the bandages on her face while whispering the words, "Weep if I must, but this shall pass..." After reciting those words, her expression softens a little. At least until she glances up at me and her brow furrows. "Hmm, do I know them?" she murmurs.

Turning away without an answer, I look at a man sitting next to Leo.

The man wears a long nutty-brown coat, blue trousers, and a flat cap atop his head. At first, I have difficulty remembering his name, but I am sure I recognize him. However, when he says, "What the devils" after seeing me, his throaty voice causes me to remember him—this person is the hoarse man, the prigger of prancers. He was the one that appeared to be selling someone a prigged horse so that they could use it to acquire Essence. I barely recognize him as I was only able to discern his obscure figure back then.

The remaining five people all wear attire similar to the woman in red: long red winter coats, flashy ornaments, and other such items. Four of them are also women, with only one of them being a man; strangely, they are all rather attractive in appearance.

'Half the people in this room are folk I thought I might never see again. Terra must have assembled them because of me. But why!? Did my information truly necessitate this?'

The hoarse man laughs; his voice is throaty but not as hoarse as it once was. "This some kind of joke?" He claps his hands together, pointing at me. "Are we about to go to space? Why do we got a cosmonaut here? Hey, better question, who are you people?"

"Yo!" Lorcan shouts. "No talking about that until the boss is ready. Fairy, the people in red, don't worry about their names; they're just here to observe. The only people you need to know are Hoarse, not the animal, and Charm."

My eyes move between the two additional people. 'Hoarse is obviously the hoarse man; Terra must have picked it for him because she deemed it humorous. Charm is Emily; she must have picked that herself because she is a lunatic.'

"Hoarse? Why am I Hoarse?"

Pointing at me, Lorcan says, "Ask Fairy. Boss wouldn't tell me, but they did say that she thought of it."

"Fairy? I don't even know her," Hoarse says, clicking his tongue. "But whatever, enlighten me, I guess."

'Hmm, I think Hoarse was trying to insult me earlier so I should make a retort.' Writing on my whiteboard, I turn it toward Hoarse. "Thy voice is comparable to the stink of horse manure. Therefore, thy name is Hoarse."

"Damn, Fairy," Lorcan says with a hearty laugh. "Didn't expect you to murder the guy in broad daylight."

Pointing at my whiteboard, Hoarse says, "How am I supposed to even read that!?"

With half-closed eyes, I drop the whiteboard to my side. *'I need to remember to write my words less skillfully so that they may read it.'*

"If you squint while reading it, you get used to it pretty quick, actually." Lorcan points at me and then gestures toward an empty place on the floor. "You'll be sitting up here next to the boss."

I write on the whiteboard, "Sit where? On the floor?"

Wiggling his eyebrows, he lifts a small hatch on the side of the wall and then presses something—a clicking noise comes from the marble ceiling above. Like two doors opening longways, a pair of five-foot-long rectangular panels separate from the marble ceiling and swing outwards. The panels continue to gradually swing downwards, revealing white cushions and a backrest.

'Chairs in the ceiling... Is this normal?' I glance at the other people, and their confused looks say all I need to know. *'Nay, it does not seem to be.'*

When the panel has pivoted to the point that it is perpendicular to the floor, it stops and two high-backed chairs float two feet above the floor.

"Pretty cool, huh? Rich people shit for sure," Lorcan says, walking back toward the front of the RV.

"Why, though? Isn't it a bit slow and inefficient?" Shriek asks.

Hoarse rolls his eyes, leans forward, and replies, "Because that's how rich people are. They want to make sure you understand that they can afford useless crap like that, and you can't."

Behind me, I feel a tiny tap on my back. "The sponsor must really like you, doll. Go on and take your place of honor," Owl whispers. "This isn't a typical sponsor, don't let them make their entrance without you in your seat."

'Aye. Though I do not believe Terra would be too angry with me.' Moving ahead, I step between the marble table and Jessica's legs.

As I squeeze by Jessica, she seizes my arm. "Hey. What's going on? Why are you being treated like a special guest? This whole situation isn't adding up."

Erasing my words, I write, "I am not certain."

Jessica squints, glaring into the arc suit's window. "You'd tell me if you did, right? This is smelling fishier by the second," she whispers.

"I do not know what is happening, nor do I smell fish," I write before shrugging.

Still squinting and with a raised eyebrow, she releases my arm. Moving to my seat to the right of where I expect Terra to sit, I fall into the chair just in time to hear Emily huff.

Glancing over, I can see her glaring at me. *'She is clearly envious.'* I use my whiteboard to write, "Thou shouldst not scratch thy wounds. They will not heal."

She reads my message, crosses her arms, and leans back into the couch with a scowl. Shrugging, I ignore Emily and watch Jessica instead.

Her gaze drifts to Leo, who is also studying the room; the two seem to have a silent conversation with their eyes.

At the same time, Hoarse bends forward and points at the woman in red. "Wait, I know you." Running his gaze across the others in the room, he points at another woman in red. "I know you too. Both of you are alley whores!"

'...They are harlots?' I glance at the people in red; in tandem, they scoff and roll their eyes. *'Are these the type of people that Terra hopes to perform her "coup" with? They seem oddly calm.'*

Jessica and Leo nod at one another and then stand. "We've gotta go; I think I left some documents we were supposed to bring on the subway," Leo states.

There's a click, and everyone freezes. The woman in the red coat stands and places a small silver pistol against the back of Jessica's head. "Sit down," she says.

A man in red stands and places a second pistol at Leo's back. "You too, pig."

I recoil, and Jessica glances toward me. *'This is part of the plan, right!? It... it must be. Terra said she would be in control. I must remain calm. Do not run, do not panic.'*

Jessica frowns. I do not know enough to write much, so I write, "Apologies. Do not panic. Relax and keep calm."

"Pigs like you rarely give a crap about people like us, so don't think we'll hesitate to pull the trigger if you don't do as we say," the woman in red asserts.

Gritting her teeth, Jessica responds, "Would you really? Escorts aren't ordinarily murderers."

The pistol's barrel bumps the back of Jessica's head. "I owe the person in charge here everything, and I've been waiting years to prove my loyalty to them." The woman in red places a hand on Jessica's shoulder, emphasizing each word as she says, "Sit down; unless you're volunteering to be my proof."

A sigh escapes Jessica's lips, and she raises her hands. Together, she and the woman in red sink back onto the couch.

The man in red nods. "Agreed, same for all of us." He smirks at Leo, saying, "And I've put-up with enough handsy officers that I wouldn't mind as much as you might think."

Following Jessica's and the woman's example, Leo and the man sink back to the couch. "This must be a misunderstanding," Leo says, putting his hands in the air. "We haven't done anything wrong or crossed any lines. We were invited here. Let's all relax."

"They're cops? What the devils is going on!?" Hoarse shouts. "Why are there whores and cops here!?"

Emily huffs. "You moron, how have you not realized that we aren't meant to know anything yet?" Snapping her fingers, she shouts at Hoarse, "Is your head full of horse manure like your throat is, or are you just stupid?"

"What's that supposed to mean!?" he shouts at Emily.

She laughs and waves his shouting away. "Forget it. Just tell me, why did you come here?"

"Huh?"

"What was your reason for getting into a big-ass RV?" she says, raising her arm and glaring at him. "You were invited here, right? You didn't get kidnapped when someone offered you candy, did you? Because that would just be plain sad."

Hoarse grimaces. Crossing his arms, he groans.

Seeing that Hoarse has no intention of responding, Shriek peers at me and replies to Emily's question instead. "I-I'm here becau—"

Lorcan comes out from behind the curtain. "Shriek!" Shriek gasps, freezing up upon hearing Lorcan's booming voice. "I thought I said not to talk about why you're here."

Shriek shakes his head, his mouth partially opened. Emily chortles in the corner.

With a sigh, Lorcan walks behind the two chairs that lowered themselves from the roof earlier. "Whatever. Boss is ready. I'm sure everyone here will recognize her, so no need for introductions."

Heels rap against marble from behind the RV's curtain, and a delicate hand reaches out, pulling the curtain away. As Terra steps through, a tiny squeak finally escapes Shriek's slacked jaws.

At some point, she changed clothing. Her attire is much more formal, reflecting an image of wealth and beauty. She wears what resembles a long-sleeved silk tunic of white with ruffles along the neckline and the opening of the sleeves. Though the sleeves run to her wrists, there is a slit from the pit of the elbow to the shoulder. From this slit on the right side, I can see swathes of argent fabric sewn to her. The tunic runs past her waist, where a skirt begins and flows toward her ankles. A split in the skirt from the knee down exposes a pair of long black boots with heels. She complements her garb with jewelry and baubles: a dark leather belt around her waist, a black pearl necklace, a raven lotus in her hair, and glittering ebony bracelets.

With her tome in her arms, she steps toward us. The only noise is her footsteps.

My eyes move to hers, and I discover she has placed an ornate black eyepatch over her green eye, leaving only the silver one exposed. Instead of her usual hairstyle, her hair is tied back and then thrown over her shoulder, where it sways with every step. Her usually gentle gaze now displays apathy toward everyone and everything before her, yet there is a hint of coldness in the deep silver pupil and the black ink encircling it.

With a slight nod, Lorcan steps from her path.

Displaying overwhelming poise, Terra takes a seat to my left and places her tome in her lap. Things remain quiet as she runs her silver eye over each person. Shriek is shaking, Jessica has her head in her hands, Leo's gaze is glazed over, Hoarse is staring at the ground, Emily's eyes sparkle, and Owl's expression is unchanging.

Terra motions toward the people in red, prompting them to lower their weapons. "I invited you here," she states curtly. "Does anyone have any guesses as to why?"

It remains utterly silent until the least likely person speaks first. "Her." Shriek raises his shaking hand and points at me. "Something about her," he says in a small voice.

With a leisurely turn of her head, she glares at the others. "Are you all really so pathetic that the youngest and least experienced person among you is the first to speak?"

Raising his hand, Owl says, "Miss Galtry, I believe the same as the young man. I know that is why I am here. Both the young man, Shriek, and the woman, Angel, seem to recognize her. So I have come to the same conclusion."

"Owl, Shriek, you two don't have to say anything further. She is indeed why you're both here, and you two have nothing to worry about. As for the rest of you, I asked why you're here. However, I am changing the question." Crossing her legs, Terra glares at the remaining people. "Tell me exactly what you've done that has offended me and then we'll discuss how you'll make it up to me."

"Offended! No, no! I-I can't believe I'm *actually* in the same room as you right now, Miss Galtry!" Emily says, shaking her head. With one hand over her heart and the other gesturing toward me, she continues, "But, Miss Galtry, I don't know this person and I would never do anything to offend you! I-I look up to you as what all Spirit Scribes should aspire to be. Miss Galtry and the Church mu—"

Terra raises her hand, stopping Emily short. "My business with the Church is my own." Terra taps the cover of her tome. I never noticed it before, but Terra's tome seems to have several times more pages than Emily's. "Don't make the mistake of assuming that gives you absolutely any sway with me."

With a flush face and her mouth half-open, Emily turns, and attempts to read my eyes behind the arc suit's window. Her face drops. "Everything makes sense now! Miss Galtry, I'm so sorry; I had no idea that she belonged to you!"

"Stop talking," Terra says with fire in her eyes. "I don't want you to even think about speaking again until I've spoken to you first."

Like an apprentice after being scolded by their mentor, Emily's shoulders droop.

His eyes darting between Emily, Terra, and I, Hoarse speaks up. "M-Miss Galtry, I think there has been a mistake. I work underneath one of your captains; I shouldn't be speaking to you directly like this... This is just wrong, and my Street Captain would be upset."

Terra glares at Hoarse; her gaze embeds itself deep beneath Hoarse's skin. "Are you criticizing my handling of my own chain of command? Are you really so brazen?" Pointing at herself, she declares in a threatening tone, "I created the chain of command! I can break it, tear it, bend it whenever I please because it belongs to me. Now, if you don't answer my question in the next thirty seconds, then I'll consider repainting these expensive sofas a messy red."

"No, no!" he stutters, glancing at the RV's exit. "I... I just don't understand. I don't understand why I'm here, of all people! I mean, I'm just small fry."

Glancing at me, Terra motions lazily between the two of us. "Give him a hint."

'Hint? But I do not know what he has done to warrant 'Galtry's' ire... I surmise there is only one thing it could be if it was from the information I told her.' I use the eraser on my whiteboard and write, "Horse sale."

He furrows his brow. "I don't..." His face stiffens, and then his eyes flutter for a mere moment. "Oh. Yeah. I don't know what you're talking about." He frowns, a drop of sweat rolling down his cheek. "I vaguely recall some kid trying to get me to sell him a horse or something stupid. It was just some weird prank teenagers have been playing lately..."

Tilting my head, I write, "Thou art not a very skillful liar."

"Huh? Liar, I'm not lying." His eye twitches. "Uhm, I mean, that's what happened. Did that kid say something? Probably wants to see how far he can take this prank."

"Nay. Thou soldest that boy a prigged horse. Thou art a prigger and liar."

"P-prigger? Is that supposed to be an insult?" He raises a hand. "Never mind. L-listen, Shakespeare, I didn't sell shit to no one. You're clearly incapable of recognizing when someone is telling the truth."

'Once more with that man's surname! Does William have a renowned descendant?' Shaking my head, I write, "I have known numerous talented liars. Thou art not amongst them."

He takes a deep breath and points at me. "Listen, you can't go making claims without proof."

"I do not require proof. I witnessed and overheard everything."

"You were spying on me!"

I hear Terra's voice in my head. {Constance.}

Responding in my head, I answer, {Nay, I desire to assist, and I have considerable experience with mere street ruffians. They are seldomly quick-witted and typically short-tempered. I shall antagonize him.}

{...Do what you think is best,} she responds.

"Hey, say something! Why were you spying on me?" Hoarse asks.

I write. "Thou wast rather loud; it was quite easy. Mayhap, if thou wast not so oblivious?"

"W-what? You're wearing a Halloween costume! You have the nerve to call me oblivious!?"

With a shrug, I erase my whiteboard and write, "I do." While the gears in his head turn, I add, "I saw and overheard everything, and thou never suspected a thing."

His face turns redder. "Are you makin' fun of me?"

I erase the whiteboard and write, "I am, because thou art an oblivious ninny."

Jumping to his feet, he shouts, "Well, who the notices when a whore is around!"

The room's mood swings from burning to frozen in an instant. "Trash," Terra states plainly.

Hoarse's complexion pales.

"Not only did you essentially admit to brokering deals outside of the syndicate, stealing profits from my pocket, you, low trash, do not have the right to speak to my guest in such a manner. You better start giving me reasons to not sink you to the bottom of the Hudson."

"I-I-I..."

"Or maybe a pleasant view from the top of the Brooklyn Bridge before you tragically take your own life."

"No, I'll talk! Please, it's because of..."

"To prepare for the Beta's end. Is that what you're about to say?" She raises her hand, motioning toward everyone in the room. "Everyone here is in the Beta. None of them have stolen from me."

'Everyone is in the Beta!' I look around the room, seeing all the others are doing the same. *'It appears they were all hiding this information. I suppose I knew about the ones who encountered me and inhaled the haze, but I did not expect the people in red.'*

Hoarse's eyes grow wide; he can scarcely manage a slack-jawed stare.

Next to me, I hear Terra's voice. "Okay, you're wasting too much time. You have two choices." She gestures behind her where Lorcan stands. "Either he can take you into the back and beat you until you're more willing to cooperate from here forward, or," —she gestures toward me— "she can hit you once in front of everyone."

'Me?!'

His eyes swing between Lorcan and I. "Her! I'll take her!" he shouts.

"That's fine with you, isn't it, Fairy?" Terra asks.

I hesitate but decide to believe that Terra knows what she is doing. If I wanted, I am certain I could decline, yet if this was anyone else other than Terra, refusing would not be an option. I write on my whiteboard and hold it out. "Aye. I shall strike him."

Standing, I walk toward Hoarse, stopping just short of him. "Sorry about what I said, just got a little hot-tempered," he says with a smirk. "Now, let's not keep everyone waiting; just take your best shot."

'I suppose if it was between Lorcan or me, I should hit him as hard as I can so that I make as much of an impression as Lorcan would have. From my time practicing medicine, I believe one of the most painful areas to be struck is around the liver.'

I slither the cattail into my right sleeve and bend it back. Inspecting Hoarse, I can see he has no intention of bracing himself. It seems he does not expect much from my hit. Taking aim at his stomach, I punch.

Spittle blows from his mouth, staining the arc suit's window. His body hits the couch; tears leak from his eyes as his mouth opens and closes, wheezing for air.

"Let that be a lesson—when it comes to strength, appearance means even less than it once did. It wouldn't have been as bad if he had braced himself for the punch, but he made the blunder of judging her based on conventional prejudices." While I am retaking my seat, Terra looks toward the folk in red and continues, "As soon as I informed him that everyone here was in the Beta, he should have recognized that Fairy was far too willing to hit him. That alone with several other oddities should have tipped him off."

Hoarse coughs, taking deep breaths of air. He wipes his mouth on his sleeve, and a smear of blood is left behind.

"Angel, Savior, please tell me why you're here," Terra says.

Jessica and Leo look at one another. A second later, Leo shakes his head and sighs. "I'll talk, but before I do, I'd like it to go on record that Angel doesn't know anything. I've been operating alone in secret."

Terra makes a bored expression and waves her hand.

As if he is delivering his last will and testament, Leo begins to speak. "I've been... I've been collecting and gathering information in your territory for the Espositos." Leaning forward, he removes some papers from his coat and places them on the marble table. "That's everything we've been able to gather so far. I have no excuse. Angel knew nothing."

Glancing at me, Jessica shakes her head. "Don't be stupid. Galtry must know everything already. We've both been working with the Espositos; they have us by the throat and have for a while now."

Lorcan walks over to the stack of paper, takes them, and then delivers them to Terra. The room remains eerily quiet until she's finished going through them and then she asks, "I expect the full report and any evidence you've gather to be handed over to me the next time we speak."

"You-you aren't going to make an example of us...?" Leo asks.

"Depends on how cooperative you are from here on out." Looking at Emily, she continues, "We'll talk later in private. Let's move forward with our discussion."

Everyone nods, except for Emily, who has become oddly excited after hearing she shall speak to Terra in private.

"Since everyone here is in the Beta, they have already gone through the tutorial, so I'll skip explaining what will be happening in the near future and go straight into things. The first few tasks I give everyone will be to make up for your transgressions, but after that, if you complete your tasks smoothly, I'll give everyone here an opportunity to not just endure the coming hardships but thrive."

Hearing this, everyone's ears perk up, even the gasping Hoarse and the people in red. The people in red all fix their gazes on me, as though they know something.

"T-thrive?" Shriek asks.

"Yes. Around three weeks ago, a certain being was sent by the Cosmic System to give a small portion of humanity a better chance at weathering the coming hardships." She looks at me. Everyone else does the same. "If we listen and support 'the one' this Fairy speaks for, we'll all be allowed to become more powerful than we ever imagined."

{Thou art embellishing and promising too much!}

"S-sent by the Cosmic System?" Jessica mutters.

From the back of the room, Owl says, "Miss Galtry, sorry for jumping in, but you've tickled my curiosity."

"It's fine, Owl. We are on good terms; speak freely."

"Thank you, Miss Galtry," he says with a small bow. "I only wish for clarification. I recall the Cosmic System said it wouldn't show bias and I assumed that meant it would not show humanity any bias. Is Fairy an exception to this?"

Terra responds quickly, "Excellent question, Owl. The Fairy isn't showing bias; rather, only those that persevere will gain strength. If 'persevere' sounds familiar to you, it's because the Cosmic System emphasizes that to anyone who gets into the Beta." She raises a hand toward me, saying, "But, most notably, the Fairy is autonomous, and the System did nothing but permit her early arrival. She can do whatever she deems fit, and I'm of the opinion that we can either support her or... well, the likelihood of us 'persevering' will be much lower."

Glancing between the faces in the room, Shriek asks, "L-like you think we'll die?"

"Not necessarily, but I think the odds of that would be much higher, yes." Waving her hand, she continues, "Regardless, you'll be working for me, not Fairy."

'...Is Terra truly attempting to convince everyone I am a genuine fairy? Would people not be more afraid of me if I was a fairy? Fairies are dangerous and known to steal children.'

"Is Fairy not just her nickname?" Jessica questions.

"She is a type of fairy, and she is the Fairy that will speak for 'the one' who can provide humanity with the necessary tools to 'persevere' as the Cosmic System would say."

Leo sighs. "The one? I'm not following."

Leaning forward, Terra glares at Leo. "Frankly, I don't care if you understand; you all owe me and I will get what I'm owed. Within the next forty-eight hours, the first changes will begin, and then you'll all not only understand but experience it yourselves. Furthermore, if I even get a hint that any of you are trying to leave the city, I'll give you the honor of a bullet to the head." She places her tome on the table. "But first, everyone must sign the tome."

Chapter 24: Knight-Lady in Shining Armor

∞∞∞∞∞∞∞∞∞∞∞∞∞∞∞∞

Night descends upon New York City, and I still dwell within Galtry's RV, pondering the profound state of affairs and uncertainty. '*...Did I leave the cave open for Gen to go out if he must? I am fairly confident I did. Aye.*'

Presently, the only people remaining from those assembled are Owl, Emily, Lorcan, and I. Owl is doing things to the arc suit, preparing it to be embellished and "reborn," whilst Emily, on the other hand, is groveling on her knees at Terra's feet.

{*Oh, Terra.*} I raise my hand and wiggle my fingers at her. {*I should forewarn thee. At the zoo, I overheard Emily speaking to the Consortium folk, and she seemed keen to tongue thy toes if given the opportunity. So, thou shouldst be wary.*}

Terra glances at me and then slides her feet closer to herself.

I nod, witnessing her wise decision.

As for the final person, Lorcan, he is operating the RV, but I have also been chatting with him during the time Terra was speaking to the folk who attended the meeting. According to Lorcan, the RV must keep moving from place to place so that it's harder for anyone to eavesdrop or attempt to do something violent. Many people do not seem fond of 'Galtry,' yet they rarely know where Terra is because she does not typically meet people in person. Lorcan claims she usually speaks to people through the lap-top, and that meeting her in person is akin to encountering the Queen of England mixed with someone called "Genghis Khan."

Owl withdraws a glossy yellow ribbon from his trouser pocket. "Please raise your arm, Fairy," he whispers. "I need to ensure the lengths are correct. We can't properly utilize our skills as artists to make your magnificence shine if we have imperfect measurements."

I tilt my head and nod. Lifting my arm higher, I observe the altercation between Emily and Terra.

Emily is on her knees a few feet in front of Terra with her palms together as if praying. "Miss Galtry, me and my sister love you! I-I have copies of all the interviews you've ever done, all the books, movies, and games you were a character in, and... and you're the reason I joined the Church!" Terra's expression cracks under Emily's words, becoming a grimace, yet she hastily corrects the lapse. "Lots of the women and girls joined the Church because of you! We watched you squash greedy old men under your stilettos like bugs. It inspired us! I wouldn't dream of doing anything to deliberately offend you!"

The RV shakes as it rolls to a halt.

"That's enough, Charm," Terra says curtly. "We've already discussed your assignment." Raising the yellow tome I traded her earlier, she tosses it onto the table with a thump. "Find whomever this tome belongs to and give me their name. But if you dare reveal it's me looking for them..." She pauses, leaning back in her chair. "...well, I guess after our little contract, that won't be a problem, will it? Now get out of my RV. I'm tired of listening to your simpering."

With an enthusiastic nod, Emily starts to walk away but hesitates. "M-Miss Galtry, can I get your autograph for my sister Fin?"

Terra frowns. "Get out right now or I'll throw you out onto the interstate."

"Yes, thank you," she says, stepping toward the RV's door. Looking out a window, I see her leap into the air and whisper-shout, "I made a contract with *THE* Galtry!"

I shake my head. *'If she were in London, the wardens would have escorted her to Bridewell or Bedlam straightway.'*[93]

With Emily's departure, Owl, Terra, and I are the last remaining people aboard the RV, save for Lorcan in the front.

"Well, Fairy, I believe I have all the details I can get with you wearing the suit." Owl stands with a slight nod of his head. "The other Hands have

---

[93] Straightway: Archaic form of straightaway. Straightway was mostly replaced by straightaway beginning in the early 20th century.

already begun fashioning the new materials. Some of the most talented craftsmen in the city are working on it, so I'm confident it will look marvelous."

'Everyone behaves so differently in Terra's presence. Owl is so formal and does not call me doll, Emily grovels, and everyone else is merely afraid to speak.' I write on my whiteboard and hold it so Owl can read it. "Will it enable me to move around more smoothly?"

His eyes sweep across the board and he nods. "If we do our job properly, then we believe so. If it isn't to your liking, we'll make adjustments."

After making the thumbs-up gesture, I return to writing on my board. "It is appreciated, Owl. May I ask another question?"

"Of course. How could I say no to a Fairy?" he states with a smirk.

"Why art thou so peculiar? Art thou from an exotic realm?"

He bursts into laughter. "I'll admit, I wasn't expecting a Fairy to call me weird!"

"Should I not have inquired?"

"No, no. It's okay. I just wasn't expecting a personal question." Squatting down, he stares into my suit's window and continues, "Helping Hands enjoy partaking in fringe culture, and in our free time, we are permitted to do almost anything we want. No matter your background, you can be a Helping Hand if you're talented enough. Nevertheless, when we have a sponsor and we're executing their orders, we work under a blend of tradition, customs, and techniques. That's how you get someone such as myself and my cohorts. I can't say much more than that to anyone outside our organization."

I wave my hand and lift my whiteboard. "Nay, that was plenty. I thank thee for the knowledge."

"I'm curious—if you don't mind me asking, what does a Fairy think of our little group of misfits?"

Erasing my whiteboard, I think for a moment and then write, "If I comprehend it suitably, I admire the concept, and I have a tenderness for eccentric and high-spirited folk. Yet I could foresee troublesome problems if thy group permits quite literally anyone to join."

"Intriguing. What do you think about working with me specifically?" he asks.

"I do not know thee. Thou couldst be quite a different person without thy group's laws binding thee. But as thy sponsor, I appreciate thy kindness and artistic enthusiasm."

His small smile grows a touch larger. "Interesting, let me speak to the sponsor." Standing, Owl steps around me, stops just short of Terra, and makes a small bow. "Miss Galtry, I wish to assist with your plan."

"My plan?" Frowning, Terra says, "Please be more specific, Owl."

"I desire to help with the production of the videos."

"I didn't mention that to you. Who told you about that?"

"Please forgive me, but I overheard the man with the red hair speaking to Fairy about how best to go about learning her lines. I assumed this was part of your plan, and I wish to help."

She lets out a sigh. "And why is it you wish to help, Owl?"

"I studied film and costume design before I joined the Helping Hand, and after hearing you speak earlier, I would be crazy not to want to be a part of this."

"I heard your discussion with Fairy." She crosses her legs, glaring at Owl. "Are Helping Hands allowed to support such pursuits? This seems out of character for your group; they rarely perform jobs outside of their sponsors' requests. In fact, I believe it's forbidden for them to exercise their talents outside of sponsor or group work."

"Normally that is true, but if you are willing to commission me, then I could assist until I am released from my obligation." Glancing back at me, he continues, "I realize this is odd, but I'm willing to give the steepest discount I am entitled to give."

The room turns a bit quiet as Terra taps her fingernails against the silver tome in her lap. Finally, she asks, "We intend to film as soon as the suit is completed. Won't you be exhausted from the rushed delivery?"

He shakes his head. "No more than you."

"What's that supposed to mean, Owl? You're awfully loose with your words."

"Apologies, Miss Galtry. I merely mean it is already past midnight, and you don't seem intent on sleeping any time soon."

"Midnight? Hmm, I hadn't even noticed. No, I guess I won't be." Glancing toward me, Terra responds, "But it's up to Fairy; you would be under joint direction from both her and me, Owl."

'Under joint direction! I have never had anyone under my direction before, except for copepods, I suppose.'

Speaking to me directly, she continues, "The Helping Hands are an organization known for their tight lips, yet there have been a few incidents in their long history of them deceiving their sponsors. ...Oh, and one incident of a breakaway faction."

Owl's head sinks. "What Miss Galtry says is accurate, Miss Fairy. There have been some outliers in our ranks over the many, many years. However, I wish for the record to show those disloyal renegades were dealt with sternly and paid dearly for their actions. As for the breakaway, the..." His eyes narrow. "The discordant Two Palm Society, we engage them personally wherever and whenever we recognize their fingerprints or ogreish handiwork."

"Yes, I can confirm that's true. The Helping Hands do try to clean up their own messes." Swapping which leg is crossed over the other, she stares at me. "So it's your decision, Fairy—do you want to hire Owl until your 'moving pictures' are done?"

Gazing at Owl, I notice he does not look at me directly, presumably so he does not influence my decision. As I consider rejecting the offer, I glance back at Terra in time to catch her stifling a yawn. *'She is exhausted, and affairs have only begun. If she endeavors to do this unaided, she shan't ever rest... I imagine if hiring Owl were an issue, Terra would refuse his request herself.'*

With a touch of hesitation, I nod and write on my whiteboard, "His passion is admirable. I have no serious qualms regarding his hire."

Terra raises an eyebrow; evidently, she did not foresee me accepting his aid so readily.

····
········
····

A few more hours come and go. I am now in a small bedchamber that is nigh eight feet wide and contains naught but a bed and a wee oaken wardrobe. Terra claims RVs usually have ample space for sleeping, but hers is specially modified. Moreover, this RV is unknown to the Bishops. According to her, she had the Helping Hands acquire and modify it for her around three years ago. It's been hidden somewhere since. That was also where her relationship with the Helping Hand began. They have been one of the few resources she has been able to openly use since they take their commissions quite seriously, meaning they would not inform her father, Bishop Manhattan, of their private dealings.

'Terra must have given up on her father long ago. She's indisputably been hiding things away and scheming whilst awaiting an opportunity to free Galtry from the Hex Church. I suppose the Cosmic System and I are that opportunity.'

I extend my hazy hand and watch a copepod crawl around my arm. Around two hours ago, Owl left with my arc suit, which is why I am in this bedchamber in the first place. Owl stated the arc suit would be completed by noon. Evidently, they have already made most of the pieces somewhere else. Lorcan saw the receipt and nigh vomited. I believe he said it cost "one-hundred-thirty K" or something like that because it was a last-second job. I do not know if that many "Ks" is a lot, though going by his reaction, I assume it is.

'Come to think of it, I have not seen any of this era's coinage. Perhaps I may ask Terra to show me a K so I can see what it looks like.'

Sitting on the bed, I command the copepod to my lap; if I leave it connected to me, it will not leak haze. It crawls through my haze, stopping where I commanded. I have been interested in attempting something, and by "interested," I mean I have been trying since I moved into this bedchamber.

I place my hands on either side of the mouser-sized sable copepod. Concentrating, I try to compress the haze of the copepod. After being in my vermillion form and seeing how much longer they seemed to last, I wanted to know if I could make my sable copepods last longer as well. The haze begins to twist and turn around my palms.

Leaning nearer, I struggle harder.

The copepod bursts into a puff of haze, slipping out a window I opened earlier.

> ### Fostered Aspirant [Mana Compression (Grade 4)]

'Oh, well, that is unexpected.' I push away the wall. 'This method seems more efficient than the orb training Terra recommended. I suppose I am not a person. It makes sense a different method may work better for me.'

The door to the bedchamber opens and Terra stumbles in, collapsing face-first onto the opposite side of the bed. Raising her right arm, she reveals the bag of sign language things and drops it. She lifts her left arm, presenting a brown paper bag with "For Fairy" scribbled on it; she drops it as well. "Constance, why is everyone so stubborn," she says in a muffled voice. "I wish they would just listen and stop making me have to pull them around by the nose. They all know they can't afford to not listen to me, but they still insist on beating around the bush."

Tilting my head, I ponder the events I witnessed and then say, {They enjoy the process perchance? Emily appeared to.}

"Enjoy the process?" she asks, her face still buried in the bedsheets.

{Aye, I think they relish being threatened by thee. In fact, I think they covet it as if it is an honor.}

With a harsh groan, she replies, "That's really frustrating." Pushing herself up, she moves into a sitting position and pulls her silver hair back over her shoulder. "Are you sure you're fine with Owl being in your cave?"

{Thou cannot do everything on thy own.}

She raises an eyebrow, observing me with amusement. "So you allowed it because you didn't want to burden me?"

I shrug. {Mayhaps. Thy time is going to be limited, though, and thou hast hardly slept.}

"Well, neither have you," she states, mimicking my shrug.

{I do not sleep, and thou knowest that.}

"I regret to inform you that your plan has failed." She releases a long-drawn sigh and fakes a frown. "I intend to be there to keep you company either way. I'll work and monitor how things are developing while you two film."

Squinting, I cross my arms and scoff. {Thou art far too stubborn.}

"I don't want a lecture on stubbornness from you of all people."

I place my hand over my chest. {I have nary an idea of what thou speakest.}

She laughs.

Lowering my hands to my lap, I continue, {But to be honest, it does not matter to me much if people know of my cave; I shall be entering hibernation and shall abandon the cave for the most part.}

"Oh, so you aren't as opposed to people going there as you made it sound previously?" she asks.

{Nay, not especially, I guess. I thought about it some more and I expect I shall begin living inside The Tower after I reawaken, and the gate also has a watchword, so it is secure. Therefore, it does not matter that much.}

"Hmm, watchword?" She pauses for a moment, rubbing her chin. "Oh, you must mean password or passphrase, right?"

{Aye, I suppose,} I respond with a shrug. {Watchword, passphrase, and now 'password.' I do not understand why folk craft new words for things that already have them. It is unnecessary.}

"Yeahh... let's not delve too deep into that topic again after how the 'thou vs. you' conversation went. I wanted to talk to you about that boy Daniel. I contacted him through my charity foundation after it came to my attention that he was trying to find you. He thinks you 'chose' him, and that thought has probably only gotten stronger since our little meeting earlier."

{He thinks I chose him?} Recalling our one and only conversation, I nod. {He did say something to that effect, but it was an unbridled coincidence that he struck me and inhaled the haze that day.}

"In his charity appeal, he claims the incident threw his life into disarray, and he's probably trying to find a way to cope... or not, I don't know. I don't entirely comprehend what he's thinking or how he feels, so it's just speculation."

{Is that so? It is unfortunate our paths crossed back then; at the time, my situation was dubious at best. Perhaps I should inform him he is not a 'picked one'?}

She waves her hand, rejecting my thought. "No, what I wanted to recommend is that you use him to support you in some way. He thinks being awoken is his 'burden' to carry as a chosen one. It's a rather silly 'tragic antihero' way of thinking, but in my mind, it just shows how naïve and inexperienced he is. What he'll one day realize is being awoken early was the best thing that could have ever happened to him—a privilege rather than a burden. Let him support you, don't do anything to betray his expectations, and I think you'll find yourself atop an insurmountable pedestal in his mind in the future."

{Using him? It seems rather deceptive to allow him to believe he is chosen.} Pausing for a moment, I realize something. {Was that why thou invited him here, for me to use in some way?}

"Well, it sounds worse when you say it like that, but yes." Rubbing the back of her neck, she smiles awkwardly. "He seems loyal enough and you could use him as a pseudo housekeeper, delivery boy, or something like that until he adjusts to his new circumstances. Let him ease into the truth or he might enter a self-destructive spiral."

{So another person would be directly involved with me and my cave?}

Dropping her arm, she nods. "I've investigated his background and he's ordinary in every way. Spends his time working, playing games, and going to college, studying social work."

I tilt my head. 'Spends his time playing games and attending college. That's ordinary? Seems as if this whole city might be nobility. Building their own city is something nobles would do, I suppose.' Leaning against the RV's wall, I respond, {Since he is ordinary, he is unlikely to betray me of his own volition, but ordinary people are rather susceptible to fear, intimidation, and pain. Would someone not take advantage of that?}

With a small chuckle, she sighs. "Mhm, you do have some experience with people, don't you?"

{At heart, folk have not changed from my era. They are queer, in a way, but in the same sense that someone from a foreign land is queer.}

"Uhm, well, I wouldn't put it that way, but I understand where you're coming from. Still, I don't anticipate you having to worry about that too much. I'll make it very clear to Daniel that he should come to me if someone tries to strong-arm him."

{I suppose...} Hearing the coos of pigeons outside, a thought crosses my mind. {If I permit Daniel access to the cave, may I send him to a butcher's stall in my stead?}

"I'll pay him a salary and reimburse any funds for him to retrieve whatever you might reasonably need. If my funds are cut off, or people stop accepting U.S. currency in the future, he can decide if he wishes to continue working for you or not."

{...So I may request that he retrieve anything for me?}

She leans back against the wall and nods with a yawn. "Yes, please, if you need anything at all, just get it or ask; don't hesitate to do so. Things will only get harder to buy or get a hold of as time goes on."

The chamber is hushed as I brood over her words. *'Anything I need? All that comes to mind are seeds, meat, and books. Perhaps livestock? Oh! King oysters, I wish to obtain that pearl adaptation to solve my Rife Paste plight.'* Hearing some curiously rhythmic breathing, I glance over to see Terra with her arms crossed and her head down. *'Sleeping.'*

Standing, I tuck the blanket back over her lap, then I sit on the floor and look through the bag of sign language materials. *'I shall peruse for a bit, and then I will endeavor to obtain my Novitiate Mana Compression. It's beginning to seem as if I shan't have many opportunities for such things in the coming days. Oh, and I cannot forget to select my scrounger skill as well.'*

My eyes drift to a swollen brown bag with "For Fairy" penned on it. Pulling it over with the cattail, I open it to find a stack of sandwiches. *'Bless thee, Terra.'*

····

·········

····

After Terra fell asleep, I bolted the door to the bedchamber she was in and slipped out the window to sit outside atop the RV. Some haze was seeping from my body, so I did not think it wise to linger in a tiny bedchamber with her slumbering. The RV is in a dark alleyway, so it practically blends into its surroundings.

I glance toward the sky from between the two massive buildings—clouds and fog obscure everything. *'I hoped to see some starlight, but alas, they are not visible. I have not seen even the moon since my encounter with the fopdoodle.'*

Lowering my head, I do my best to ignore the snores of Lorcan that emanate from the front of the RV and command a copepod to sit in my lap. This is the ninth one. I am determined to complete my Mana Compression skill here and now. I can feel I am close to something; I do not know why or what, but I simply feel as if I am.

I squeeze the copepod, attempting to compress it as I would a fruit for its juice. A violet glimmer emerges from within the copepod before it bursts.

'Nay! I felt it! I was certain that I had it that time! Huh?' Leaning forward, I notice that the purple glimmer is still present. I reach out and take it between my fingertips. Bringing it close, I see it has the shape of a starfish. It's as thin as a needle and as wide as a toddler's fingernail. *'It is... glass?'*

A blue wall appears.

Fostered Aspirant [Mana Compression (Grade 5)]

Entity 1-3-2-3 has manifested enough potential to supplant an Aspirant skill with a Novitiate skill.

Entity, see the presented skill supplant below.

[Novitiate Mana Crunch]
A rarely seen or taken skill that is typically used as a crafting-based skill by Entities that wish to collide and compress Mana-saturated lightweight particulates together to generate a different material. The new material's make-up depends on the initial particulates that are collided and compressed.

I hold the little glass shard high. *'I made glass! It was not on purpose, and it is very small, but I did do it!'* Dropping my arms, I focus on the blue wall before me. All I see is a single choice for a Novitiate Rank. *'Odd? I suppose it makes my selection easier... so aye, Mana Crunch, Cosmic System.'*

Skill Supplantation
Entity 1-3-2-3 has supplanted [Aspirant Mana Compression] with [Novitiate Mana Crunch] skill.
Prepare for memory impress.

Similar to all the times before, pictures flicker in my mind. It is an image of me holding a loaf of bread. I watch as she takes the loaf between both of her hands, seeming to be compressing mana. It is difficult to tell because I cannot see anything happening to her or the bread, but her movements are familiar to me. They are much like my own when I am compressing mana.

She stops and breaks the bread. Sandy material spills out from the loaf's insides.

The scene resets. Once again, she is holding the loaf between her hands. This time black haze flows into the bread, halting soon after.

She stops once more and breaks the bread. This time, the bread is partially hollow, and a long piece of glass skewers its center.

The thoughts dim.

I stare into the dark alleyway. *'Interesting. It seems like in the first image pushing in mana did naught but ruin the bread and turn it something akin to sand. However, in the second, when the haze was added, it became a shard of glass instead of simply falling apart. I shall have to experiment with that more. Ah, now for my scrounger skill. Cosmic System, prithee, display the scrounger choices.'*

The blue wall emerges.

Entity 1-3-2-3 has manifested enough potential to supplant an Aspirant skill with a Novitiate skill.

Entity, see the presented skill supplants below.

[*Novitiate Scrounger II*]
The general scrounger skill path without any particular specialization. An Entity that is more of a natural scrounger and reliably able to locate items and make use of them adequately might find it wise to tread this broader avenue rather than restrict future skill opportunities.

[*Novitiate Trashy Scrounger*]
A specialized skill for Entities who scrounge through garbage and make use of items that most other Entities wouldn't touch with gloves. Optimal for Entities that wish to be creative with scrounged items - one man's trash is another man's treasure is the motto of those that have this skill.

[*Novitiate Routine Scrounger*]
A skill for Entities that often scrounge in the same locations day in and day out. After scrounging in an area for an extended period of time, an Entity might realize that they have begun to develop an innate sense of the area's resources and dangers.

Reading the wall, I tilt my head, finding a new skill has become available. *'Four—I have never had four skills choices at once before.'* I look through the skill and think for a moment. *'That skill is hard to imagine; it seems more magical than most of the skills I have been offered. I had planned to take Trashy Scrounger, but I think I shall take Invasive Scrounger instead... Aye, Cosmic System, I shall take the Invasive Scrounger skill.'*

The pictures flicker in my mind. The Cosmic System must either think it relevant or has a sense of humor because it is the bread picture again. Though this time, I am not watching from a distance; instead, I am holding it. Haze begins to infiltrate the bread. An odd sight appears in one of my eyes; it is as if I am perceiving a dark area through a hole. I can see darker and lighter areas, yet not much more than that. Glancing around, I realize what I am seeing: the inside of the bread.

The images fade.

'Magic is so peculiar.' Tossing my feet over the RV's side, I kick my legs as I contemplate ways I might use my new skills. *'I believe this may work well with my Mana Crunch or perhaps even my Humorism.'*

While pondering what I learned from the Cosmic System, I hear shouting from behind me. I look back to see a mass of people marching by the end of the alleyway. They chant, "Alaska falls to crawlers - Canada falls to dryas - US falls to liars."

The crowd also bears signage that says things like:
"Do you feel it? Jingle-Jangle: C-Sys."
"'The US is the Land of the Free Caravans' - King Zero.
#Wheres_DJ.Droplet?"
"Chinese WMD? Consortium weather machine? Alien C-Sys? Truth...?
Who knows!? We only have liars!"

Something creaks in front of me, and I flinch. Light seeps from a snow-laden hatch built into the RV's roof. The hatch swings open, catapulting a clump of snow into the wall. Out pokes Lorcan's head. Facing away from me, he stares out into the dark alleyway and then yawns. He sinks into the RV, shutting the hatch behind him.

'I suppose the crowd woke him, but he must still be drowsy because he was staring in the wrong direction... I think.' I return to watching the crowd march, chant, and fade into the eventide. It takes nigh fifteen minutes for the last of them to pass by the alleyway's boundary and for quietude to reclaim the night. *'I presume this is the type of unrest Terra spoke of in the past. It must be frustrating to hear denial from the royalty. People can be naïve, but they are only so credulous. Most folk that is; some have nary a limit to their gullibility.'*

As I am about to experiment with my Mana Crunch, the RV's hatch creaks open once more, and someone pokes their head out. "Fairy, I found you," a man says. I recoil and unravel the cattail but stop noticing it's a familiar face. "Relax, it's me, Leo. I just came to give Galtry the bag of evidence we collected on you."

'The dullard, I prefer to not be seen in my haze form. It merely complicates things. Did Lorcan inform him I was up here? Nay, Lorcan did not glimpse me.'

Readjusting, I tuck my legs beneath me and float forward a tad, glaring at Leo. My eyes reflect off his face and the snow-cloaked surface of the RV.

It seems he could not see me very well because his expression freezes upon me moving closer. His eyes run up my body, scrutinizing me. "Woah, are you really a fairy?" he murmurs.

'Another fopdoodle. I am aware my shoulders are exposed; there is naught I may do!' I narrow my gaze and wrap the cattail around my shoulders to cover them. *'Mayhaps I should give him a taste of the sable haze on this occasion!'*

He blinks. "I-I wasn't..." With a cough, he raises his arm, revealing he is carrying my whiteboard. "I'm just here to talk. The big guy with red hair is going through the stuff, so I took the opportunity to dip up and say hi."

'Ah. It was not the crowd that woke Lorcan; he must have been awaiting Leo.' I peer at the RV's front, where the door is located. *'I should not have been crept up on like that. I was too inattentive. He better not attempt to pilfer my whiteboard; I shall fight him.'*

Leo tosses the whiteboard toward me, and it lands a couple feet short of reaching me. He climbs up what must be a ladder and brushes some snow from the RV's rooftop.

His eyes glance around clumsily, and he attempts to change the mood. "Weird seeing protesters so late, huh? Some twenty-four-hour march or something. Didn't believe the whole system thing myself until after I got ripped apart in the tutorial thing," he says, shivering with a chuckle. "Being stabbed and burned was not fun..."

I raise one of my eyelids, making a questioning expression. *'Stabbed and burned in the tutorial? He must mean the tutorial's battle portion; I did not have to do that part, thank the lord.'*

Taking a seat five or so feet away, he sighs. "Jessica told me about the red..." He pauses and then shrugs. "I don't know, fairy, I guess. The red fairy that looks like you."

I take the whiteboard, squint at Leo once more, and write, "Aye, I do not wish to chat for long. What is this about?"

He takes a deep breath. "Jessica is worried about Red, and I'm worried about Jessica."

'Jessica is worried about Red? That's just my vermillion form.' I use my marker to write, "What dost thou meanest, worried about Red?"

"Jessica thinks you did something bad to Red and stole her suit. At first, she thought you were Red, but she figured out you weren't, 'cause of the eyes and all."

'Oh, at the time, I was in my vermillion form and had pink eyes. Jessica believes we are two different beings... Explaining would be challenging, and I prefer to keep my abilities private.' Nodding, I write, "Fret not. Red is in good health. We are very close and share everything with one another. Why art thou concerned about Jessica?"

"No reason in particular. I'm just feeling a little uneasy." He taps against the roof of the RV. As the taps echo off the alleyway walls, he continues, "She doesn't have her own family or anything, so I try to look out for her if I can. Got my own family, a wife and two girls, but Jessica is like our third daughter. She's at our place a few times a week, helps the girls with school, and celebrates Rushlight, Thanksgiving, or any other holiday with us, really."

"I am ignorant of what Rushlight and Thanksgiving are. What are they about?"

"Rushlight and Thanksgiving?" He nods. "Rushlight is said to be based around an old Church in Light story involving the Church's Flame weathering a flood. Nowadays, it's about decorating, drinking cocktails, and swapping gifts. Thanksgiving is largely about sharing a calorie-dense meal with family while theoretically 'giving thanks'. The short version of Thanksgiving's story has to do with the pilgrims sailing to America, building a colony, and sharing food with the natives."

It takes a moment for his words to sink in, and when they do, I shake my head. While I keep shaking my head, I write, "Nay. Thou hast been misinformed; the natives likely shared the food. The colonists were stubborn and unprepared. Many had nary an idea of what they were doing." I erase the whiteboard and then continue, "They just loathed the orthodox Church's authority and thought the God in Light would provide for them. Then, they came to rely on the natives instead, many of which grew weary of their incessant begging."

"Y'know, you're the one who asked what it was about," he responds. "I wasn't making any kind of commentary or anything, just answering your question."

I shrug and erase my whiteboard. The wind howls through the alleyway as things turn silent for a moment. I fiddle with the piece of starfish-shaped glass I made earlier. 'Alas, it is too small. Like most things, I shall misplace it if I *attempt to keep it. But it would be a shame to not do something with it.'* I glance at Leo. *'The glass would look stunning on a ring. Perhaps if I were to say something cryptic and mystical, Leo might do that.'*

Writing a message on my whiteboard, I stand and walk over to him. "A gift from a Fairy. Fashion it into a ring for thy wife, tell her of thy concerns, and she shall unwittingly confer a truth upon thee."

After reading my message, he stares at the sliver of glass and then raises his palm to receive it. "It kinda looks like a starfish." I drop it into his open palm. "Wait. Actually, this is a gift from a magical creature. That's something that only happens in fairytales."

I am about to refute him, but I realize that it is in a way. "Aye, it would appear so. I am going to return to the RV. Fare thee well."

"Y-yeah, fare thee well and... thanks, Black."

As I reenter the bedchamber through the window, I overhear Lorcan burst through the hatch on the RV's roof. "Fuckin' shit, man, I'm freezing my goddamn balls off! What are you even doing up here!? You could at least close the hatch!"

A half hour later, the sun has risen and a trickle of light is shining in through the window. After leaving Leo to be yelled at by Lorcan, I returned to the small bedchamber, waiting for him to leave before I go back outside.

Terra sleeps on her side with her feet dangling off the bed after she fell asleep sitting up several hours ago. Hearing the sheets rustling, I lay a sign language book I was browsing on the floor and peer up to see her rising with half-closed eyes and a half-open mouth. She draws a few strands of hair from her mouth and glances around, attempting to understand where she is, I assume.

When our eyes meet, she recoils, blinks a few times, and then relaxes. I wave at her with wiggling fingers. {Good morrow.}

"G-good morrow?" she says, looking out the window with tired eyes. Reaching for her eyepatch stuck to the side of her brow, she slides it back over her green eye. The inky rings around her silver eye sway as she gazes into my violet eyes. "Sorry. I wasn't expecting anyone to be around... I think I might have fallen asleep."

'It seems Terra must wear that eyepatch a lot. Perhaps to hide her natural eye color?'

Terra tilts her head at my lack of response and runs a hand through her long silver hair.

I wave her away, saying, {Nay, it is fine! As I said earlier, thou require sleep.}

"...Thanks for not being mad." Tossing the blanket off her, she slinks to the floor opposite me. She takes a deep breath and lifts one of the drawings with a pair of signing hands sketched upon it. Flipping it around, she asks, "What does this one mean?"

{Uhm, ah, that is one of the few I recognize. It signifies 'mercy'! I presumed it might be useful in a variety of circumstances.}

Shaking her head, she gives a drowsy laugh and then stands. "...I need to brush my teeth, fix my hair, do my makeup, and get back to work. When your suit is ready, we'll get you into it. Keep studying, but I doubt you'll be able to learn your lines in time."

I lift one of the papers. {Perhaps we can use the papers for the first one.}

"Possibly, but I think we can find an easier way to work around it." Brushing any wrinkles from her attire, she asks, "Do you know what your first action will be? I know you have the vent and I believe you said another gate as well?"

{It would be simpler to place the gate first since the vent would be near the Consortium's position. My plan was to place the gate in the chamber pot tunnels since I did not want people using it, but matters have changed since then. Now I do not know.}

Raising her hand, she covers her mouth, and a tiny squeaky yawn escapes. *'I do not know if I have seen her acting so unguarded before. It's a tad... winsome.'*[94]

"Excuse me," she says, exhaling. "But I've been thinking about your gate as well. I wasn't going to say anything since I thought you had decided, but I have a few properties I own through the Helping Hands."

{Properties? Thou meanest for the gate to be placed?}

She nods. "Yeah, two hotels—oh, and hotels are places people pay to stay the night at. I set them aside in case I ever decided to run away. They're also good for storing funds."

{So they are inns? How didst thou manage to acquire those?}

"No one expects the young, naïve pawn to find a way to gradually siphon money and then work through a shadow organization like the Helping Hands."

{As always, thou art rather impressive...} Terra smiles at my words and I begin to fiddle with the end of the cattail. *{But which of these properties wouldst thou recommend?}* I question.

Closing her silver eye, she purses her lips, contemplating my question. "Hôtel Casāle." She opens her eye and gestures vaguely. "The hotel on the far side of Central Park. It's smaller than my other one, but it's luxurious, and a gate there would really pop. And practically speaking, it's closer to Central Park, which makes it the better choice."

I glance at the wall she gestured at and then turn back, asking, *{And thou art certain I may place it there? After placing it, I doubt the gate shall be removable.}*

"Like I said earlier, make use of everything; we can't afford to be stingy. Plus, your gate being on a property I own could save us some headaches in the future."

---

[94] Winsome: attractive or appealing in appearance or character.

{*Aye... Since I have decided to commit to relying on The Tower's interior, I shall once again accept thy offer.*}

"Good. Then we'll make that the theme of your first public appearance. Anyway, I need to continue working. If you need anything, I'll be in the next room."

With one last small wave, she leaves, shutting the door behind her.

'*I suppose if she is leaving, I may simply linger here.*'

I return to my study of sign language, until a few hours later someone knocks on the door. "The Helping Hands have brought your suit," Terra announces.

••••

••••••••

••••

Back in the room of mirrors, this time alone, I sit in the chair, peering at the unfamiliar person staring back at me. '*I have never laid my eyes upon such vibrant garments.*' I goggle the woman that appears as if she is the focus of some fantastical painting. '*Is it truly me?*'

I run my eyes over myself as I have several times now. My body is concealed in a cerulean robe, stitched in silver threads that flow from my neck to my ankles. Over the robe is an embellished cerulean tunic stitched in the same silver thread. Yet a third item sits above those two, a stunning silver-tinted chest plate, nay, rather it is a cuirass.[95] This silvery plate embraces my chest, stomach, back, and lower abdomen, and it sparkles in the bright lights overhead. I raise my leg, staring at the glistening boots that come just short of my knees. Dropping my leg, they click against the tile floor.

My hand moves to a cloak of the same cerulean color. The cloak has both a hood and a cowl capable of concealing the lower and upper portions of my face. My robed arms extend out from underneath the cloak; the robe's sleeves fall halfway between the pit of my elbow and my wrist. From my elbow to below my knuckles are silver metal bracers. The bracers are so tight it seems as if it's just over the surface of the arc suit—I imagine an ordinary person would think them painful to wear. Where the bracers

---

[95] Cuirass: a piece of armor consisting of breastplate and backplate fastened together.

end, a pair of cerulean leather gloves extend outward, forming my palm and fingers.

I run my fingers along the bracer and then up toward the helmet that covers my head. They somehow managed to shrink the arc suit's headpiece close to the natural size of an ordinary girl's head.

The helmet resembles what I believe is called a 'gas mask' except without the protrusions near where the mouth is. Instead, the whole face is a curved glass pane crafted from a fusion of blue, purple, and red hues. I draw the cowl and hood over the mask's window. In the mirrors, what gazes back at me is a feminine figure hidden behind fabric and armor with a stained window where her eyes should be. With the radiance of my eyes behind the stained window, the blues, purples, and reds resemble the sky in the early hours of twilight.

Someone knocks on the door. "I'm coming in; I have the rest of your equipment. You should be ready to go after this," Terra says, sliding the door open and squeezing into the tiny room. {Woah, Constance, you look so great!} she remarks in my head.

Upon seeing her, I find myself lost for words. {I... if I did not know better, I would believe a tangible human being was underneath it all. I am not certain what to say; I have never had someone gift me anything close to this meaningful before. I know not how to requite thee.}

She smiles and waves away my words. {Please stop worrying about it. I've only given you things that are essential for our plans.} With a laugh, she continues, {If I ever do anything purely out of the goodness of my heart, then you can thank me, and I'll accept it happily.}

{Nay, it is appreciated! I shall cherish it always.} I touch the exterior of the cuirass, tracing the curves. {...Speaking of hearts, I have never seen a breastplate with... breasts. Granted, knights had largely stopped wearing armor by the time I was born, and in all honesty, I have never seen a female knight... but...}

{It is a shaped cuirass. It's a practical piece of titanium armor.} She spreads a belt that has brown leather pouches affixed to it, smiling and showing them to me. {That cuirass was fitted especially for you. It outlines your natural hips, waist, and bust but won't deform under pressure. Oh, and since there's no recess between the breasts, it's still a functional piece of armor.}

I stare downward, tilting my head. {*A recess between breasts? Like undergarments?*}

Setting the belt and pouches aside, she motions at her clothing. {*Yours is shaped more like a metal top. It might be uncomfortable for women made of flesh and bone, whereas for you, comfort isn't as much of a concern since you can't really feel that kind of thing. We're lucky one of the local Hands is an over-the-top blacksmith that keeps extra pieces sitting around.*}

{*It's beautiful; reminiscent of a metal bodice without the lacing, but...*}

{*It was a decision the Helping Hands made. While they were sizing you, they noticed your body wasn't, uhm... 'sturdy,' so they chose armor that would fit snugly, which is why they were so thorough with your measurements. If your armor didn't fit tightly then, say if someone squeezes your shoulder, your haze would be pushed from around your shoulder to any empty space around your chest or hands. Thanks to the form-fitting cuirass, bracers, boots, and gloves, your body will be much more resistant to shifting around in your suit.*}

{*So making it resemble a bodice was intentional.*}

She reaches out her hand, meaning for me to take it.

Staring at her soft palm, I shake my head.

{*It's fine; you can take my hand. While wearing that suit, you can't hurt me,*} she says in a gentle voice.

Raising my hand, I waver, but Terra reaches out and takes it. We stay like that for a moment, staring at one another; she helps me up from the chair.

{*With this armor, your body will be able to keep its figure, and it looks great, doesn't it? I made it absolutely clear that it should be in good taste.*} Releasing my hand, she steps back and looks me up and down, saying, {*And I think it looks very classy and that you look charming in it.*}

I gaze at my palm, then into the mirror. 'I have not touched anyone in quite some time. I could not feel a thing, only the sensation of my kiln moving into a different position.'

Terra waves her hand in front of my face, chuckling. {Walk around a little. See how it feels.}

I drop my hand and nod. While she watches, I raise and lower my legs, stomping around in my new armor. 'It is so light! How did they manage this, and what did Terra mean when she said I look classy...?'

Lifting the belt and pouches, she says, {Spread your arms, and I'll put this on you to complete the ensemble.}

I raise my arms, but Rabbit walks into view first. She knocks on the doorframe and bows shallowly to Terra. "You're needed at the front, Miss Galtry."

Terra's smile vanishes; she ceases being Terra and returns to being Galtry. "Shriek, Lorcan, and I will be waiting on you. Rabbit, help Fairy finish dressing and then bring her into the main room," she says aloud.

Without another word, she hands the pouches to Rabbit and leaves the room. 'But... I wanted her to see me wearing the pouches.'

As Terra's footsteps grow faint, Rabbit enters the room, moves in front of me, and leans forward. "You look ridiculously fantastic!" I lean away to place some distance between us. "Honestly, I had prepared everyone to resize it because I thought there was no way you'd be able to get into it; we only left a twelve-inch hole in the upper back!"

'Prithee, cease moving so close to me. I do not like it.'

Backing away, she says, "Sorry, I can't help myself around you, but anyway, spread your arms again so I can put these leather pouches on you."

'Nay!' I hold out my hand, pointing at the pouch and then my palm. 'I shall do it myself!'

She clicks her tongue and hands them to me. I wrap the pouches around my waist and notice the belt buckle is also rather interesting. The buckle is shaped like a tower with a pair of fairies on either side, holding The Tower steady. As I tighten the belt around me, I remember seeing a similar design on my cloak. I tug at the cloak and look down to stare at the cloak's clasp.

Like the buckle, there are two fairies, but these fairies look as if they are pulling open the cloak like a curtain.

"Those were my ideas. I spent most of my time working on the helmet with some of the best glassmakers in the city, but I had someone 3D print those based on some of my old sketches."

'She made these as well as the helmet? Well, I suppose I should not be so surprised. She is eccentric, but if she is a Helping Hand, she must have some type of talent, I guess.'

"Anyway, let's get into the main room. Owl is here with one last surprise."

I tilt my head. *'A surprise? Did something bad happen? Something bad always happens.'*

With heavy steps, I follow behind; together we enter the room of white couches. As soon as I enter, I hear a pair of gasps. Glancing over, I find Lorcan and Shriek with wide eyes. "Goddamn, Fairy, who knew you'd look like that if you didn't walk around dressed as a blue condom."

'A what?'

"Lorcan," Terra says in a biting tone.

A second gasp escapes Lorcan and Shriek. "I-I don't think he meant it," Shriek responds in a shaky voice.

"Y-yeah, sorry, boss. It was a compliment that just slipped out," Lorcan says.

She sighs and crosses her arms, returning to her Galtry demeanor. Taking a few strides backward she exits the group to stand in the back by herself.

My gaze drifts to Owl, who starts to step forward. "Ah, just whom we've been waiting on."

'What is happening precisely? Did I do something?' Owl pulls out an item from behind him, and despite its sheath, I recognize it immediately. *'A sword!? A genuine sword!?'*

"This is yours," he says.

'Mine!?'

Stopping in front of me, he presents the sword. Its sheath is a shimmering silver and has engravings of a Tower obscured by leaves. Two miniature figures flank the hilt, standing on each of the crossguard's ends. The figurines resemble a winged fairy with a palm against the hilt and an arm outstretched.

"This is a 15th-century Hand-and-a-Half Sword to complement your ensemble. The hilt, pommel, and crossguard were lost to the sands of time, but the blade itself was salvageable. We had a professional restore and service the blade the best they could while our companion, Ferret, constructed a sheath and crossguard."

I shake as I raise my hands, palms up. Thoughts of all the time I spent as a child racing about pretending a tree branch was my trusty sword come flooding back. *'A real sword...'*

Owl places the sword in the palms of my leather gloves; astonishingly, it does not disappear the moment I touch it. It's weightier than I imagined, or mayhaps I am simply comparing it to a tree limb. With the sword resting in my hands, I gaze upon the odd sheath and then turn my attention toward the handle.

"The hilt, pommel, and sheath follow the same theme as your attire. Though the hilt looks simple, we in fact repurposed a 16th-century hilt that had lost its blade and then covered it in galuchat leather.[96] Like your armor, everything is titanium, save for the blade, hilt, and pommel. The blade and hilt are steel, and the pommel is high strength acrylic. It is usable, but, being an antique, we recommend you use it ornamentally unless you decide to replace the blade."

Glancing at the pommel, I find it is a teal glass orb with butterfly wings on either side. *'I do not know how butterfly wings and fairies are related, but I adore it!'*

---

[96] Galuchat: Leather produced from the skin of rays and sharks.

I brace myself for the reveal and draw half the sword from its sheath. It glistens in the bright lights. Near the bottom, I notice some writing on the new crossguard: "A Sword Fit For A Fair and Brave Knight-Lady - From T.I.G to C.N."

"Miss Galtry had us acquire and overnight it from a London dealer a few days ago," Owl says.

My head shoots up, and I discover Terra smirking. She glances back and forth to ensure she is not being watched before giving a small wave.

{I... I thank thee.}

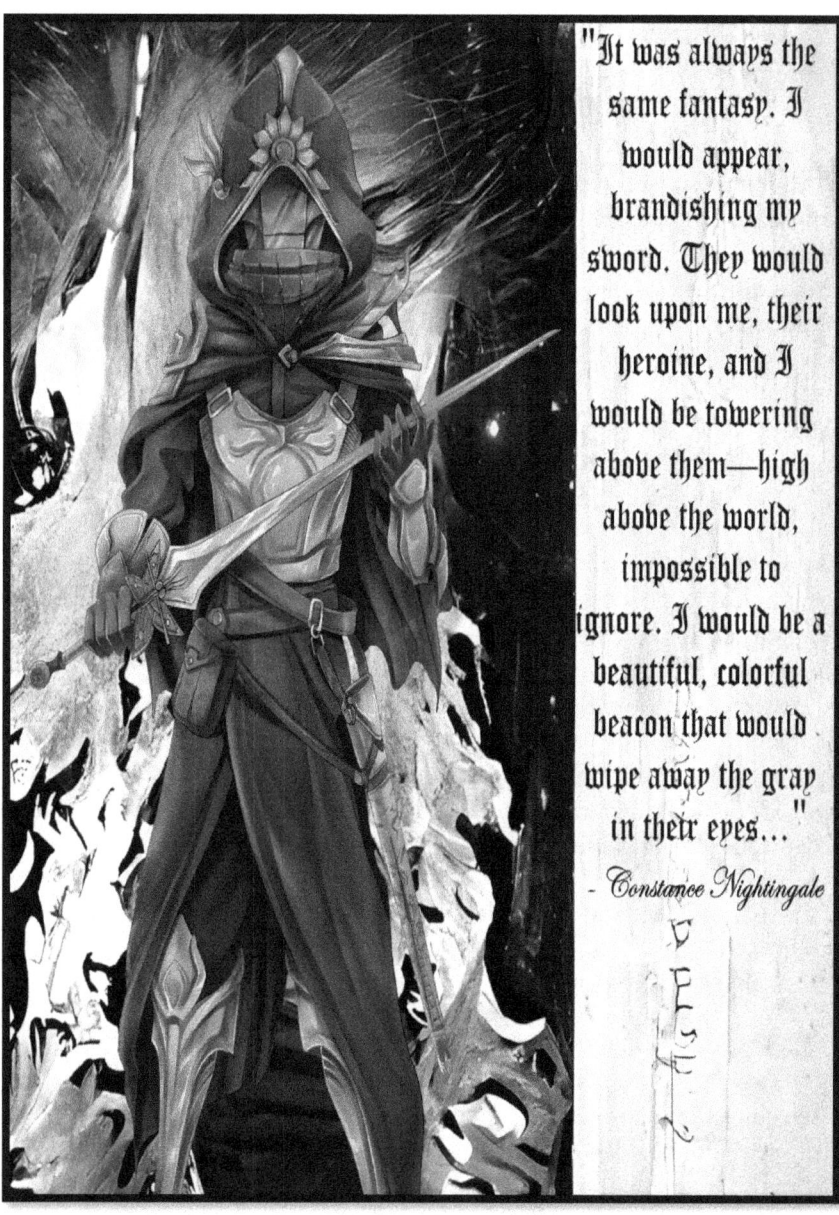

"It was always the same fantasy. I would appear, brandishing my sword. They would look upon me, their heroine, and I would be towering above them—high above the world, impossible to ignore. I would be a beautiful, colorful beacon that would wipe away the gray in their eyes..."

- Constance Nightingale

Chapter 25: A Prophecy Foretold by Fairy's Fingers

∞ ∞ ∞ ∞ ∞ ∞ ∞ ∞ ∞ ∞ ∞ ∞ ∞ ∞ ∞ ∞

An hour or so later, a group consisting of Terra, Owl, Shriek, and I are approaching my humble hermitage. Owl is toting an enormous bag on his back that he claims is full of "camera gear," whatever that may be. At our backs, Shriek tows a wooden wagon laden with miscellaneous items. There is a metal table, chairs, lanterns, and some sort of heater, yet much of it consists of what Terra calls "cleaning supplies."

'I do not understand why she requires all these cleaning supplies; removing the rubbish and a bucket of water would be sufficient... It must be because my mess... nay, Gen's mess has made the cave smell horrid. So embarrassing!'

As we walk, my sword bounces against my side, fastened to the same belt that holds my pouches. Terra would not let me wear it at first; she made me wait until we had entered the quarantine zone. Despite all the terrifying pistols I have glimpsed, openly carrying a sword is deemed threatening by the general populace by some unfathomable logic. Shriek stated it was because carrying a sword is unusual, and someone bearing one might be exhibiting "malicious intent." I questioned if they were using pistols to chop down trees and if I could carry an ax instead, but he said that would be ill-advised—I cannot understand.

"Owl, you understand the goal of your contract, correct?" Terra asks.

He nods. "Yes, Miss Galtry."

"Then repeat it back to me."

Waggling a finger in the air, he repeats what he and Terra spoke of in private. "Our goal is to persuade some auspicious and venturesome people from the general public to come to Central Park and throw their lot in with the Fairy. We must do this within the next several days using videos, controlled social media, targeted ads and messaging, and other such methods. We will then goad these people into shooing the Consortium away before they are free to draw from their abundant manpower and resources."

She narrows her eyes and glares at Owl. "And how confident are you in your abilities and the operation?"

Owl rubs his chin and then glances between Terra and me, chuckling. "It's an intriguing and tricky assignment, but it's not unreasonable or impossible given the current climate. There are masses of people who have grown used to protesting and roaming from place to place. If we convince enough people that this is the place to be, they will come."

With a nod, Terra turns her attention to me. Her gentle voice in my head asks, {You okay?}

{Aye...} My metal boot thunks upon the stone path. {I am not used to walking; it's a bit unnatural and a conscious effort for me now. I shall have to readjust.}

{Huh? But you were usually always walking?}

{Nay, I was often floating whilst slackly tossing my legs around out of habit. Didst thou never notice my legs would sometimes not match my pace?}

Her brows furrow. {...No, not really; I mean, maybe a little but not enough to think about it, I guess.}

Passing by a patch of rocky ground, I realize something. {Terra, how am I meant to remove the bricks from my doorway with this on? The hole is only big enough for Gen and I need my cattail to make it wider.}

{Ah, yes, I had the Helping Hands hide a rubber valve for your cattail around your right shoulder blade plus one on the back of your neck above the zipper. It should let your cattail slip out, and then when you draw it back through, the valve should reseal. I know I gave you a sword, but from what you've told me, I'd say your cattail might always be one of your strongest tools.}

Raising my arm, I feel around my right shoulder blade, finding a circular indention. I push my finger into the indentation, and the material folds inward. Pulling my finger out, it reverts to its original shape. {Thou art quite the planner; I do not know how thou considered so many things at once.}

{Limiting your most powerful weapon seemed like a bad idea; I can't let you be defenseless}

A few minutes later, Terra, Shriek, and I stand in front of the cave's entrance. Owl is at the top of the stone stairs organizing some items in his bag.

Terra turns around and gestures at Shriek. "Turn around, don't look," she says in an aggressive tone.

Shriek nods. "It's a secret hideout; it must have a mysterious lock," he whispers.

I rub the back of my neck. '...He shall be disappointed.'

Pushing the cattail through the hole in the suit, I flatten the tendrils and begin tossing bricks from the entrance. I notice Shriek tilting his head as he watches the bricks hit the ground near him in my peripheral. I stop once it's wide enough for a person to crawl through. Sinking to my knees, I shuffle into the cave, attempting to not dirty my new attire.

"Oooo!" I hear Gen cry. Rubbish assails me.

'Gen! It is me!' I duck to the left, and a half-eaten pudding cup smacks the wall, leaving a splatter of brown pudding. I shake my arms and then make the thumbs-up gesture. 'See, it is me; calm down!'

Gen stops just before casting a rotten apple at me. Dropping the rotten apple, he falls to his rear and returns a thumbs-up gesture, including a small "Ooow."

I drop my arm, shake my head, and move out of Terra's path as she crawls through. 'Gen is fortunate I am incapable of conversing with him.'

Once through, Terra stands, asking, {Alright, you ready to begin filming? We're working with a short time span.}

{Aye, let us get on with it. I am ready to be painted for my moving picture. I have never been the subject of a painting before.}

"I'll just go ahead and say it's not like you're imagining." Removing a torch from her satchel and lighting it, Terra leans down and says in a stern tone, "Shriek. Crawl through."

"Yes, Miss Galtry," he replies. His feet spin in the dirt, and he sinks to his hands and knees. He crawls through and gazes upon the glory of my abode. A tear trickles down his cheek, probably from the rancid onions a palm's length from his nostrils. "It... it's soo..." He glances up at me. "It's so... great..."

I point at Terra's satchel and then make a writing motion. With a nod, she removes my whiteboard, marker, and eraser and gives them to me.

My marker squeaks against the board as I write, "Do not lie to me. It does not make me feel better."

"S-sorry," he says, forcing himself into a standing position. "It's just not where I expected a Fairy to live."

"It is a cave; thou shouldst not expect grandeur." After erasing that, I add, "Also, where do the Fairies thou knowest live?"

"G-got me there, I guess."

As I lower my whiteboard, Owl's head pokes into the cave. He crawls a bit further and stands. Wiping the dust from his trousers, he runs his gaze across the cave. "It's a bit messier than anticipated, but a cave is a cave, and thinking about it, who knows where a fairy might live. Oh, and I like what you've done with the coffin over there in the corner."

I cross my arms and nod at Shriek. *'See. Owl understands how to lie properly.'*

Shriek's eyes dart to the iron coffin. "Coffin!"

At the same moment, Gen casts his rotten apple at Owl, only for him to step out of the way. "Oh, and there is even a little cave keeper," Owl states, nudging the rotten apple out of the cave. "This place is so charming."

My arms drop. *'Charming is a tad much; now I feel as if I am being mocked. Though Owl may genuinely believe that given his personality.'*

I motion for them to follow me into the gate chamber. Passing through the doorway, the pair turn utterly speechless. Seeing this, I return to crossing my arms, except this time, I straighten my back to display as much smugness as I can manage.

"Woooah, I knew it. This is the type of place a Fairy lives!" Shriek says, his mouth open wide.

Owl raises his hand and steps toward the stained glass walls. "Is this the creation of fairies...?" Just before his hand touches the glass, he flinches and pulls it back. "The glass is utterly faultless. I cannot besmirch it with human hands." He releases a heavy sigh. "How is art such as this even attainable? It's as if it were cast all at the same time."

Poking out my chest and shaking my head, I write, "Oh, well, I merely dabble in glassmaking from time to time. But thy compliment is appreciated; it means much coming from thee."

"Dabble? Ha! Good gracious, please forgive me, but don't be so modest. Glass isn't one of my areas of expertise, but I know world-class craftsmanship when I see it. This piece could be the crown jewels in any museum in the world." Setting his bag on the stony ground, he asks, "Can I take a panoramic of this room?"

Tilting my head, I respond by writing, "I do not understand what that means. Ask Galtry."

With a nod, Owl approaches Terra. "Miss Galtry, I have a suggestion."

"Speak, Owl, what is it?" she responds curtly.

"I believe a panoramic of this room would be an excellent way to get people's attention initially."

Raising an eyebrow, she says, "I do intend to send invites to a restricted chat room. We could use it to help guide public opinion on the Fairy in a direction that's favorable to us. It's also a good way for us to keep up with what people are talking about." She thinks for a moment and then adds, "It wouldn't hurt if we attached a picture to the message to persuade them to accept the chat room's invites."

"I imagine you aren't inviting just anybody to that?"

"No, just the ones that seem the most promising or who I wish to build connections with." Terra reflects for a moment and then gazes at me. "Do you have an opinion on this? This chamber belongs to you after all."

Writing on my whiteboard, I approach the two. "What is a chat room? It is not this room they shall chat in, correct?"

"Oh, I guess a Fairy wouldn't know about these kinds of things," Shriek murmurs from the corner of the chamber.

"Don't murmur to yourself in the corner." Terra scowls, motioning toward Shriek. "If you're going to be working for her, answer her questions instead of talking to yourself."

His eyes go wide. "I-I'm sorry, Miss Galtry, I'll help Fairy now!"

I notice a flicker in Terra's silver eye. "Nightingale. Her name is Nightingale, so both of you should refer to her as Miss Nightingale from now on."

In my head, I ask, {Terra, I do not mind if Owl does his 'pan·o·ram·ic' thing, but why would they call me that?}

Without changing her expression, she forces a laugh in my mind. {Now you must also know what it is like having everyone call you 'Miss' and treat you like an old lady despite being far younger than them.}

{I do not mind what people call me, to be honest, but I suppose I shall suffer it as well,} I respond with a shrug.

"Nightingale, like the nurse? That's such a cool name!" Shriek replies. "B-but, Miss Nightingale, a chat room is a place for people to talk without them actually being with each other in person."

"Oh, that is intriguing. These rooms can have how many people in them precisely?" I write.

"Well, it depends, but most of the time, you can have as many people as you want."

"Fascinating! And these folk might be convinced to journey here after viewing my glass walls? Is it truly so convincing?"

"I believe it would absolutely convince at least some people," Owl replies, forcing his gaze away from the glass. "I know anyone with a discerning eye would be able to confirm the art here is original, unseen, and of near unattainable quality. I must know, does this piece have a name?"

I stare at the walls, but my gaze drifts to Terra. Nodding, I write, "Gate of the Rich and Destitute, is that a good name? It's a tad simple, yet I fancy it."

"It's wonderful, Miss Nightingale; the name is more about how the artist perceives it than how complex it is," Owl responds.

'Artist? I am not an artist.'

Before I may speak of it more, Terra speaks first. "Very well put, Owl. If you think it'll help convince more people, then feel free. We're already going to be filming here, so it shouldn't make that big of a difference." She pauses for a moment, then adds, "But we'll add something that will draw people, maybe the phrase 'Essence. Glory. Treasures. The Tower Provides For Those That Persevere'—something to pique people's curiosity."

"Ah, a great idea, Miss Galtry. It would be best that we reference the Cosmic System's words; that will go far in convincing people."

'They are making my Tower and I sound rather... celestial but, to be frank, I am more akin to a parasite that is trying not to be one.'

"It seems you're understanding. I need to get some work done. Give me the photo as soon as you have one you think is particularly convincing. I'd like to send the invitations to the candidates as soon as possible."

"Yes, Miss Galtry." Turning to me, Owl points. "I'll begin right away if Miss Nightingale is ready."

I erase my whiteboard, then write, "Aye, I am excited. Let us make the moving picture!"

With a smile, Owl starts to remove items from his bag.

Shriek's eyes light up. "Oh, and I'll he—"

Terra interrupts him. "Shriek, bring everything from the cart down and start scrubbing the cave."

"...Yes, Miss Galtry." His shoulders droop as he exits the gate chamber. "I'll get the cleaning supplies."

While he gathers the supplies, I set some of my more dangerous possessions to one corner and then begin my work with Owl.

....

....

....

Two hours pass. Terra has erected a table in the corner of the gate chamber where she is continually tapping on her lap-top and talking to her black rectangle. I can tell she is working hard to make certain our plans go well.

As for me, I am standing in front of the gate posing with my sword held high. Posing next to me is the grumpy Gen, who is just waiting for his opportunity to run away. With a click, Owl's camera, fixed to a tripod, paints my picture.

"Wonderful!" Owl moves to some torches, or the "key, back, and fill lights," as he refers to them. He erected them all around me and will frequently make adjustments to them. When he gets the light the way he likes it, he moves back to his camera. "Now! Place the sword in front of you and place your hand on it, like this," Owl says, making the pose for me to mimic. "After that one, we'll try for an action pose." He makes a pose with his hand gripping a pen and swinging it as if fighting a beast. "How does that sound?" he asks with a high laugh.

I nod and lower my sword. *'Clearly, he is enjoying this, though, I admit, so am I.'*

While I "strike the poses," Shriek has been cleaning the rubbish in the next room, much to Gen's dismay. Watching as Shriek shoves some of his favorite knick-knacks into rubbish bags, Gen releases a small angry whine.

At first, I simply watch his antics, but then I remember something. I reach out my hand toward Gen and pat him atop the head. This is something I can do now with my armor; it's so liberating and delightful to touch things so freely. Crouching, I hold my sword to the side and scratch beneath Gen's chin with my free hand. He stands on the tips of his toes to lean in closer to my scratching.

I shake my head and curl two tufts of his hair, making it look as if he has a humorous beard. '*Little hairy man, we shall find new knick-knacks. Thou mustest understand that things are just things, and all of them are temporary... Ah, perchance thou wishest to aid me with my lines?*' I raise my hand, make a fist, and tuck my thumb beneath my index finger. '*I am afraid this sign for "T" is all of the speech that I have committed to memory. Though I do know some other signs that I shall try to slip in.*'

A click and a bright flash of light make me look back and forth, searching for the source. What I find is Owl staring at his 'camera.' "Now, Miss Nightingale, that was a magical photo. The definition of a picture worth a million words." He sighs. "Sometimes the perfect photo happens when we least expect it."

Owl takes his camera off the tripod, picks up my whiteboard, and walks it over to me. "I believe we're done with the pictures and can begin the video."

Standing and returning my sword back to its sheath with a gratifying click, I take the whiteboard and write, "Is it completed? May I examine my portrait?"

With a nod, he presses something on his camera and then turns it toward me. A picture of Gen and I is illuminated upon the camera, the elegant stained glass walls behind us. I point. '*Look, Gen! It is us; we are small!*'

Reaching out, Gen attempts to seize the camera and yank it out of Owl's hands, but Owl is a step faster and pulls it away. "Apologies, but the equipment is delicate," Owl states with a chuckle. "Ah, that's right, I just remembered that I was going to warn you."

I tilt my head.

"I have a pretty good intuition and..." He leans in close and whispers, "I think Miss Galtry might be underestimating both her own and, more importantly, your appeal. You should prepare yourself; you might be surprised by the attention you draw."

"Me? What art thou implying?" I write on my whiteboard.

"I think you'll come to understand that on your own," Owl says, smiling and placing his camera onto the table near Terra.

Taking it in hand, Terra replies, "Thank you, Owl."

"Of course, Miss Galtry." Walking to his bag, he removes a different device. "Now, Miss Nightingale, are you ready to film?"

I pat Gen on the back. Realizing he is done, he rushes toward Shriek and grabs the other side of the rubbish bag. "Hey, let go!" Shriek shouts.

Whilst they relish each other's company, I write, "Aye, I am ready," and then set my whiteboard off to the side.

Owl laughs, placing his second, more prominent camera on a black tripod. "Please make only a single letter at a time. I know you don't know sign language well, so the plan is to splice everything together into a coherent video. Oh, and please try not to move around too much."

I take my position in front of the gate and make hand signs in the sign language alphabet. Close hand, thumb in. Point two fingers to the left. Close hand, thumb out.

"Stop and prepare the next word, which is... Tower again," Owl says from behind his camera. He makes a fist with a thumb beneath the index finger, the first letter of the word.

'Ah, I know that one.'

This routine goes on for quite some time. I sign some letters, Owl shows me a new word, and then I do it again.

As I perform, I repeat the words in my head. 'The Cosmic System returns, humanity approaches ruin. I am the Fairy of The Tower, a granter of charity upon all worthy men and women. *The Tower awakens those who receive it. The Tower awaits those who will accept its trials. Just know, The Tower delivers nothing for free; come and persevere. Within the next two days, the first prophecy shall be fulfilled. Those who can find it can witness it.'*

After the first message has been delivered, I move into the "clues." The clues shall hint at both The Tower's and the gate's location. We hope they will help stave off the less ambitious people, even if only just a few of them.

Owl lifts a paper with the first sign on it and we began again. *'In a patch of green within the city of sleepless stone, The Tower is girdled by man's avarice.[97] The Tower is a charity, a gift for the common people, but it is immured, dressed as if a plague.[98] To the south-east, the Gate shall sprout in a great hall, owned by the one who speaks to the speaker. Locate it. Behold it. Witness the beginning of the new age. The next prophecy shall come soon, come now, or find catastrophe forbidding thy approach.'*

Two hours later, Owl claps. "Ah, just brilliant, Miss Nightingale. I swear I can feel your genuineness coming through the lens."

Two additional sets of applause come from the other side of the gate chamber.

"It really was great, Miss Nightingale," Shriek says, joining in Owl's clapping.

'Ah, they are just flattering me, yet I do not care; praise me!'

{Good job, Constance. I'd like to see you perform again in the future,} Terra says in my head.

{Aye, I am a natural-born performer,} I respond, raising my arms high and tilting my head back.

A smile spreads across her face. "Don't push it..." Her smirk disappears and she sits up straight. "Oh, when we talked the other day you said you

---

[97] Girdled: encircle (the body) with or as a girdle or belt.
[98] Immured: enclose or confine (someone) against their will.

weren't that opposed to new people coming here, so I wanted to discuss something with you."

My arms drop to my sides. {*...New people?*}

••••

•••••••

••••

Early the next morn, a middle-aged man and woman enter the cave. They stop. Their eyes dart around; obviously, they are not certain if they are where they should be. Terra walks out of the gate chamber and ushers me over. The man and woman exhale a deep breath upon seeing Terra, the first time I have seen someone relieved by her presence.

"Good morning, Miss Galtry," the man says with an accent.

The woman nods at Terra, saying, "Guten morgen, frau Galtry."

'Not English?'

Terra nods and then gestures between the pair and me. "Nightingale, this is Doctor Tobias Jäger and his wife Mrs. Petra Jäger. As I told you yesterday afternoon, Doctor Jäger is an epidemiologist from Germany. He's the one that did the lethality experiments with the mice," she announces aloud.

'A modern doctor; that is intriguing, but...'

I examine the two new visitors for any signs of trickery. Doctor Jäger has short white hair, bright blue eyes, and a thick white beard. He wears a brown suit, more formal than I have witnessed most people of this age dress.

His wife, Mrs. Jäger, has blonde hair and hazel eyes. Like Doctor Jäger, she is also dressed more formally than I am accustomed to seeing. She has a sandy yellow dress, worn over a long-sleeved blue shirt. Then over the dress, she wears a long brown coat.

"Nightingale?" Doctor Jäger questions. Unlike most people, he is treating me with a more wary demeanor.

Nodding, I write, "Aye, it is a pleasure."

"No, no, no!" Doctor Jäger says, shaking his head. "The pleasure is all ours, it really is, just…" I tilt my head as Doctor Jäger seemingly chokes back tears. "…just thank you so much."

Mrs. Jäger tilts her head and pokes his shoulder before pointing at me. He nods. Mrs. Jäger steps forward and embraces me.

Recoiling, I throw my arms up and move away. *'I am being assaulted; do not touch me!'*

Doctor Jäger pulls his wife away with a stiff smile and a chuckle. "Sorry, I'm really sorry."

'Do people embrace one another as greetings nowadays? Even if I now can, I do not like being embraced! Not by someone who is barely an acquaintance!'

He places a palm over his heart. "My wife and I are thrilled that you chose to give us this opportunity. I ran the experiment on the "black haze," and when I learned the effects, I asked Miss Galtry if my wife could be exposed to it. When she told me she didn't have any, I chose to fly my wife here and stay, hoping that something would change."

Dropping my arms, I am about to scribble something confrontational, but I stop myself. Instead, I write, "It is not an issue. However, I believe we need to begin soon."

Owl walks out from the gate chamber, holding two eye masks and caps. "Yes. Miss Nightingale is correct. This is a public livestream for people to witness the effects of the haze. Please put the masks on and stuff your hair into the hats."

"Of course, of course!" Taking the masks, Doctor Jäger gives one to his wife and places the other on his face. "Oh, I am sure you have realized it, but my wife doesn't speak English. I've already explained everything to her, though."

With a serious expression, Terra asks, "Does she understand the risks and the stipulations in their entirety?"

He takes his wife's hand. "We are aware that there is a chance one or even both of us may not survive. We're willing to take the risk anyway."

Looking between the two of them, she narrows her eyes. "And the stipulations?"

"I have explained to her. Neither of us is allowed to leave the camera's field of view until we have been accepted into the Beta."

"Then follow me this way; we'll begin within the next fifteen minutes or so."

Entering the gate chamber, the couple has the same astonished reaction that many have. However, we are in a bit of a rush, so we urge them toward a pair of chairs in front of Owl's camera thing and the lights he has assembled. I presume the lights shan't be active for much of it.

"Miss Nightingale, on the front of your right leather glove, there should be a flap you can pull back," Owl says to me, pointing at his own palm.

I turn my hand and inspect my palm. As he said, there is a flap I had not really noticed.

Seeing that I have found it, he makes a vague gesture. "Pull it back, and there should be a zipper."

I do as he says, and there is indeed one of the so-called zippers. *'That could be useful in the future as well, but... Oh, I know what they want me to do with it.'*

{Constance, are you ready? You know what to do, right?} Terra asks in my head.

I look toward Terra who is sitting behind Owl. *{Aye. I hope this goes well.}*

{I'm sure it'll go great. Don't be nervous.}

Forming two sable copepods inside my armor, I nod. *{I shall try.}*

"Okay, we'll begin streaming in five, four, three, two..." Owl points at me.

This time I am only making a few signs, so it is not as difficult. I am more concerned with what I am about to do to these people. If one of them reacts poorly or worse, then things could grow grave. I have been thinking about the different hazes and how they all act—particularly which one was causing death in the mice that Doctor Jäger experimented upon. My thought is that it may be because of the hoary haze. When I tested it on the goose meat, it appeared to be the most harmful. Though I still know naught of heliotrope and its uses, so it could be that one as well.

Raising my hand, I point at my eye and drop my hand into my palm: "Witness." I put my thumbs together and push: "Persevere." Wrapping my hand around the other, I imitate a flower rising from the soil: "Blossom." I make an 'O' with my hand and then wrap my first two fingers around one another: "Or." Finally, I raise both my hands, palms facing one another, arch my fingers, and then twist them: "Wilt."

'Witness. Persevere. Blossom or wilt.'

I lower the zipper on my right hand; a small amount of black haze escapes through the opening. Closing my hand, I block it from leaking; I do not want people to see what is beneath my armor.

Commanding a sable copepod to my palm, I move behind Doctor Jäger. He pulls up his sleeve and straightens his arm. I place my palm over his arm, exposing the skin to a sable copepod. He grits his teeth. Oozing black blisters appear along his arm, leaking fluid that drips upon the floor.

Mrs. Jäger takes her husband's hand as I move to her side. I command the second sable copepod to my palm and then run my hand over her arm. Her flesh reddens and tiny purplish-red blisters appear along the exposed areas. It's not as severe of a reaction as Doctor Jäger's.

I leave the camera's eye as the couple inspects their arms and then glance at one another.

'Now we must wait. It shall take a couple of days for the disease to abate...'

••••

•••••••••

••••

It is midnight. Doctor Jäger and Mrs. Jäger sit in front of the camera covered in a blanket, napping. Terra and Owl say we cannot move them or people may believe we did something while they were not being watched by the camera's eye. Not to mention, the risk of them entering the Beta and it not being seen is also present.

Terra is on her lap-top as usual. Owl and Shriek have both left to rest.

I exit the gate chamber and move into what used to be the rubbish room. Shriek has removed most of the rubbish, so the name does not fit as it once did. Gen sits in the corner atop the coffin with his arms wrapped around it and a scowl on his face. He truly hates losing all his knick-knacks, so he has become a bit attached to the coffin; as for me, I am used to it and they were not particularly precious items anyway.

Taking a seat opposite Gen, I remove a food known as "oatmeal raisin cookies" from my pouch. These were bestowed upon me by Owl. Since it's not meat, I saved them for Gen as gifts. I hold one out for him. He snatches it from my fingers, and as if I shall take it back, he stuffs it into his mouth. Crumbs fall from the sides of his mouth as he chews and returns to embracing the coffin. *'Things come, things forsake. That is the way of the world, Gen.'*

I sit and take a sponge from another one of my pouches. These sponges were also given to me by Owl, but for cleaning my armor—I have been using most of them for Invasive Scrounger and Mana Crunch practice.

Tugging the zipper of my leather glove down, I place the sponge between my palms and focus. It took me several attempts before I found a way to make the new scrounger skill work. The method is simply to imagine my own eye is floating away while also imagining myself pushing it. Is this method necessary to use them? Nay, I do not believe so, but it helps to think of unimaginable things in mundane ways.

Since my eye is a ball of violet, I envision the 'eye' I am pushing in the same way—as a radiant purple orb. My vision halves and blackens. I goad the eye forward, and yellow usurps black. I have yet to find a way to use my night vision like this, but the yellow should be the sponge itself. My concentration wanes, and I stop pushing. This is where I wish to combine the two skills. I imagine myself not pushing the eye any longer but instead placing my hands to either side of it. There I practice my Mana Crunch and attempt to compress the eye as I did the copepod a couple of days ago.

Something pops, the image disappears, and a blue wall appears.

> *Fostered Novitiate [Mana Crunch (Grade 1)]*
> *Fostered Novitiate [Invasive Scrounger (Grade 1)]*

My vision returns to normal, and I glance down to find a thin spike of glass skewering the sponge. *'It worked...! But it takes time to do it in such a way. I shall keep experimenting.'*

As I am about to resume my practice, I notice the sounds of laughter echoing in from outside. I tilt my head and Gen peers at the cave's entrance. These are voices neither of us recognizes. Listening to the words and conversation, it does not appear to have the undertones of maliciousness; it resembles the everyday prattle of the era.

'Does this mean ordinary people are returning to the park? Is this because of the moving picture?'

From the gate chamber, Terra walks in, asking, {*It's freezing and past midnight. Is it common for you to hear people in the park at this hour?*}

I shake my head. {*Since the quarantine began, none have come near the Lake or Terrace at this hour.*}

She nods. {*I'd guess these people have a campsite someplace nearby, and I'll bet others are going to join them soon. People are responding to our message faster than we initially anticipated.*} Raising a finger, she leaves the room and returns with some papers. {*And that reminds me, I want to show you what the Consortium has been doing at Bethesda Terrace. They're running a skeleton crew, but they've managed to dig themselves in defensively.*}

Together we pore over the papers while Gen continues hugging his coffin and glaring at Terra.

Later, when Owl returns, Terra departs the cave to rest. I resume practicing with sponges.

····

········

····

Sometime before noon on the following day, I choose to go see the Terrace myself. I believe Terra stated that Lorcan was monitoring it, but it is important for me to see it in person. With my suit on, I cannot move through the thickets easily any longer, therefore I travel along the paths. Yet as I am about to turn a corner, I hear something. I tilt my head and move behind a tree.

Peeking out, I notice an encampment, at least what I believe is an encampment. It is difficult to tell because it looks as if items have been scattered about without much care. There seems to have been a fire in a metal barrel, yet it has been tipped over and extinguished.

'Perhaps a derelict encampment left by the folk from yesternight?' I hear a buzzing. A small object lowers itself over the encampment. The object is white and shaped like an 'X,' but what is odd is that there are spinning blades at every corner. *'Is it a Consortium weapon? Some type of sword spinner device?'*

"Miss Nightingale?" I flinch and try to use my cattail, but it bumps against the suit. My gaze darts behind me only to discover Shriek gawking at me. He holds a large brownish box in his arms, which he drops to chat with me properly. "What are you doing? Watching that drone over there?"

Placing my hand on my chest, I squint. *'Thou art lucky my cattail was not available. I shall have to remember to push the cattail through the hole at my neck.'*

"Did I scare you? Sorry." Digging around in his pocket, he hands me a small yellow block of paper and a pen. "I picked these sticky notes up for you while I was out."

Removing one of the notes, I poke at the sticky piece of paper. It sticks to my finger, and I shake my hand. The wind pulls it away from me. Using the pen, I write, "I thank thee." I nod and then point toward the camp. "This drone-x-thing, is it harmless? It does not expel lightning?"

He hesitates for a moment as if he is unsure how to answer. "I... I, uhm, no, no lightning, I would assume. It's just someone's personal drone. I still wouldn't get too close to its blades or anything, but it's not inherently dangerous. It's probably being piloted by someone off in the distance."

To be honest, I do not know what he means, but it's not malicious and that's all I need to understand. Glancing at the box, I write, "What art thou carrying?"

"This heavy thing?" He points at the box and straightens his back. "It's full of seeds. Miss Galtry instructed me to pick them up from the distribution center on my way into work. Not sure what they're for, but I don't think it's a good idea to ask her questions to be honest."

'Oh! My seeds, they have arrived!' Clapping my hands together, I lean down to see if I can find any writing on it. 'I cannot believe they harvested such a large amount so swiftly!'

Not discovering anything, I rub the side of it, stand, and then write, "Excellent. Prithee, leave them in the cave's glass chamber."

"Of course! Uhm..." With a grin and a quick stretch of his arms, he asks, "Do you need me to stay with you? In case something happens?"

Shaking my head, I write, "Nay."

"Oh, well, are you sure? I feel like we haven't actually spoken that much, and I technically work for you... Though, Miss Galtry has been keepin' me a lot busier."

I shrug and glance at the encampment. "Then tell me what transpired here?"

"That would be the Consortium. People have been trespassing on the quarantine zone ever since your video was uploaded."

'Is that so? Some seem to have pieced it together relatively quickly. Perhaps we should have been more cryptic.'

"S-sorry. I have another question, Miss Nightingale."

"Aye, I shall answer if I can."

"...Were you sent by the God in Light or another God to test humanity? You can be honest; I won't tell anyone."

'This boy may be the first person to ever ask me if I was sent by God and not by Umbral or Penumbra. How did things change so fast?' Putting never-ending pen to yellow paper, I think for a moment before writing, "I am too selfish for God to entrust me with such a task. I am here because I am here; I do not serve nor am I acquainted with a God."

He nods as if he understands my words better than even I do. "So, The Tower will be separate from God then. Interesting!"

"I suppose it is?" Tilting my head at his peculiar wording, I add, "Though, to be candid, I might be failing to grasp what thou hast divined from my remarks. Should I clarify, perhaps?"

Lifting the box, he shakes his head. "No, thank you, I think I understand perfectly. The Tower and God are separate; I will be The Tower's chosen, not God's... Will The Tower have a feud with God...? In light novels, if The Tower isn't sent by God, it's always in conflict with a God. Hmmm, I wonder if I'll have to fight a God at some point. Hmph. Probably!"

'Wait, what? Fight God? Nay!' While I listen to his murmurs, I scribble a quick response. "I believe thou art assuming far too much!" Yet before I can show him, he is racing toward the cave. *'Umbral's shadow, he is swift! Did all his stat points foster his Endurance and Agility...?'*

Dropping my arms, I glance back at the encampment. The drone is still there buzzing about, so I take my leave and soon arrive at the area across from the Terrace. It is difficult to believe all that has been completed since I was last here. The flimsy barricades have been replaced with tall, sturdy fencing, which has the blankets overtop so that seeing inside is impossible. All I can see are some machines poking out from above the fence, and worst of all, some Consortium workers. The workers patrol the top of the walls from some platforms as if they are soldiers.

I cannot discern the dozen scouts or clickers I observed the other day, but they are certainly hidden somewhere. Terra says she doubts they shall use those on civilians, though, which is good to know. *'They have built the Terrace into a stronghold...'*

My eyes stray toward a pigeon flying over the Lake. As it is halfway across, the rainbow-colored scales of a giant fish poke through the ice adrift atop the water. It leaps into the air, flinging lumps of ice in all directions. Catching the pigeon, it plunges back into the water, sending a wave toppling over the ice sheet's edges.

All that remains after it reenters the water is a buzzing sound—the drone from earlier floats above where the fish was a moment ago. There's a bang from the Consortium's position, and the drone bursts asunder. '...*Time to depart; I believe I shan't leave the cave for a while!*'

····
·········
····

Evening comes.

A day has elapsed since Doctor and Mrs. Jäger were exposed to the haze, and they still sit in the camera's eye. I sit next to Terra, practicing my Mana Crunch, while Terra continues her work on the lap-top. Owl sleeps on a cot in the corner, and Shriek is out purchasing me a fowl. I believe Shriek said he would procure me turkey as it is readily available this time of year.

'*I cannot wait for the meal, though what I have been given is not as delicious as what I pilfered from the Boathouse and the Central Café. If food is not stolen, the Cosmic System's Title does not come into effect... Mayhaps I should have Shriek or Owl hide it, stating it is theirs... then I may rob them of it and receive the benefits of the Title.*'

Twirling a red Sidhe's pen in my fingers, Terra speaks into my head, {Constance.}

{*Apologies, I was dreaming of eating turkeys,*} I respond.

She smirks, staring at me with her silver eye.

There's a thump, and Shriek stumbles into the cave carrying two heavy bags. "Have you seen the news!?" he asks.

Dropping the bags, he removes something from his ears, stuffs it into his pocket, and hurries over. He takes out his black rectangle; a 'phone' or something of the like. It's difficult to remember the names of so many new things.

After he shows it to Terra, she spins around, taps on her lap-top, and an image appears. A man in a suit with dark blue hair and green eyes sits next to a woman in a dress with blue eyes and red hair.

The man nods and then opens his mouth to speak. "If you're just joining us, I'm Jay Teems here with Jessie Rockets, and we're reporting live from

WGN New York. We've just received some historic news. Mere minutes ago, a coalition of twenty-seven nations spread across Southeast Asia, the Middle East, and Northern Africa delivered a joint statement."

The woman, I presume Jessie, picks up where he stopped. "Together, these countries declared the existence of something known as the 'Cosmic System.' The nations went on to proclaim that not only is some variety of catastrophe possible, but that catastrophe is thought to be imminent. This is, of course, contradictory to what we've heard from other nations mere days ago."

The man, Jay, clears his throat. "The coalition of nations alleges they were bullied and restricted from speaking by foreign governments. Some of these nations went on to name those governments. Among them are the United States, the European Union, the People's Republic of China, the Republic of India, and the UK. Since the coalition's announcement, nine additional nations have come forward, corroborating the coalition's claims and asserting the existence of the so-called 'Cosmic System' or 'C-Sys.'"

"This news has crashed websites that host even an iota of information relevant to the 'Cosmic System' as people scramble for details and ways to be recognized by the Cosmic System." A moving picture of me performing sign language appears on the lap-top. Below are words translating what I am signing. "A plethora of rumors are circulating, but the most common facet of them all is that not being recognized by this Cosmic System could be detrimental, like this video we received from an affiliate out of Seattle. We'd like our viewers to understand this has yet to be confirmed, but we are seeking information on this individual to ask them questions," Jessie states as the moving picture of me continues.

The red pen Terra was twirling breaks in her hand. "Now we're going to have to deal with an enormous amount of people." Turning over her hands, she stares at her palms covered in red ink. "One of the biggest moments in human history, and now our video has been attached to it."

Something hits the ground with a thunk. Terra and I look upward to find Mrs. Jäger missing and her husband in a near panic. Before we may even speak, she reappears. Mrs. Jäger is quivering, her hand around her neck. "Hase-hase-hase," she recites several times over.

While her husband pacifies her, Terra says, "She was drawn into the Beta. Probably had to do the jackalope tutorial. I think most people do the same one." She shakes her head, tapping her fingers against the table. "And there's no going back now. That little display would have just proved The Tower's genuineness in the minds of many that were watching."

"Oh, that little jackalope was vicious." Having been stirred from his slumber by Mrs. Jäger, Owl approaches with a yawn. Pausing when he sees the lap-top, he releases a sigh. "That certainly won't help us keep down the riff-raff, now will it."

Terra removes a handkerchief from her satchel. {How we handle the next few days will decide how easy it is for us from here on.} While wiping her hands, she swivels around in her chair. "Owl, I'd like to hire the Helping Hands."

Thinking for a moment, Owl responds, "I'm sorry, Miss Galtry, but this kind of thing isn't something we generally manage; we only have a few Hands that specialize in cyber-related arts. Moreover, things have already begun to grow beyond what they can realistically do."

Her gaze turns to me, and in my mind she says, {This cave won't stay secret for much longer thanks to this. Things are going to start developing fast now. I'm sorry, I didn't expect news to break so early. I expected the Kiln to seal the city off before this news was released officially.}

{Things rarely progress the way one believes they shall. I knew the cave would be discovered sooner or later...} I glance around hesitantly and continue, {Thou dost not need to worry about maintaining its secrecy. I shall store the coffin and other things away soon and then there will be naught someone may steal.}

Terra shakes her head and sighs. "I'd still like to hire those Hands anyway, Owl. We've only formally released a single picture and video; surely, they can guide the conversation..." Examining me and then the rest of the chamber, she continues, "Actually, contact all your free compatriots. I want to know how many Helping Hands are available to work under my employment, effective immediately. Let them know I'll pay in advance and that I want the Hands to start augmenting and bolstering the cave. I don't want anyone coming in here without an invitation... Oh, and please start with a door and a trash bin."

"Excellent, Miss Galtry." With a slight bow, he says, "I'll make the calls."

I write a message before Owl leaves. "Owl, prithee, take one of Shriek's turkeys, hide it, and then proclaim it as thy own."

"Of course, Miss Nightingale. I've played this game with Rabbit before, and I know a place you'll never find it," he says with a giggle.

'...Game?'

····

·········

····

"Miss Nightingale," one of the Hands says. "Why is there a soggy, blatantly raw turkey tucked away over here?"

I raise my arms. 'The turkey has been discovered!'

> *Earl Interface:*
> *Assimilating 'Spoiled Broad-Breasted Turkey'*
> *Erysichthon falls to zero.*
> *Essence value 2*
> *0.9 Refinable Nebula*
> *0.2 Refinable Vitrum*
>
> *Details: A fowl that typically spends most of its time grazing on the forest floor. Native to the Colossi continent, this variant is unawakened to mana, though it is not 'Mana Bare.'*

····

·········

····

> *Fostered Novitiate [Gluttonous Naturalist (Grade 5)]*
> *Fostered Novitiate [Invasive Scrounger (Grade 2)]*

A day later, the cave is bustling. Doctor Jäger was drawn into the Beta several hours ago. Before he and his wife departed, he stated that he could not wait to see me again soon, which is perplexing. I do not know why he would not return to his homeland.

Still, the reason the cave is bustling is because of the dozens of Helping Hands that are here now. They have removed the bricks at the cave entrance and have placed a temporary door. I believe their plan is to add an entry that makes it seem as if the cave is still bricked. Yet, they have been doing other things like smoothing the cave's floors and walls.

Speaking of which, that is how I found the turkey Owl hid. He perched it high up in the cave; I was a tad too short to see such a hiding place. I even spent a moment looking through some loose soil using Invasive Scrounger, thinking he may have buried it. Alas, it did not work; the flavor was not enhanced. *'Mayhaps I may simply gift someone a turkey and then steal the turkey back, replacing it with a new non-gift turkey and then consuming the gift turkey...'*

Terra and I are presently enjoying each other's company. I look at what she is staring at and see the image of a sparkling fish with scales that look to be made of glass leaping from the Lake and plucking a bird from the sky.

I point. {*Oh, I saw that yestermorning. It was quite the spectacle.*}

Sighing, she taps something; the lap-top begins to speak in a deep voice. "After the announcement yesterday, dozens of doomsday cults have heralded it as proof that their 'religion' was correct in their predictions. One individual, in particular, has been receiving a plethora of attention. Yes, someone who calls themselves the Fairy of The Tower. An individual who emerged mere days before this news claiming to be a 'charity upon mankind.' This has prompted many to believe that this individual has something to do with the Cosmic System."

{*Do you remember when I said it would be bad if we attracted too much attention?*} Terra asks.

{*...Aye?*}

Making the lap-top cease speaking, she states, {*We attracted too much attention.*} She changes something on the lap-top, and I see what resembles a gray wall with words flowing so fast I cannot read them. {*This is a secondary chat room on a less secure site that someone else started. People are subverting us, and the hype has taken on a life of its own. It has started to go off the rails.*}

{*I do not understand; what does 'off the rails' mean?*} I ask, reaching out to try and touch the gray wall.

She raises a hand, blocking my finger from the lap-top. {In this case, it means things are going to become hectic fast.}

{So we are attracting too many people? It has only been a few days...}

{Yeah, we've drawn the attention of some more influential people and groups. This is fine in the short term. The more people, the easier it is to take the Terrace, but what are we supposed to do later?}

{How many people art thou foreseeing now?}

{I mean...} Leaning back in her chair, she answers, {To be honest, there isn't a ceiling. It's just how many the city allows in and how much time they have to get here. The locals will be swarming soon just to see what's happening, who knows about the people coming from out of state.}

I tap my finger against the table, pondering the implications. {If there are so many, could we not simply tell them that if they stay, they shall be trapped?}

{I think after you've entered hibernation, yes. If they choose to stay, then they'll have been warned. With so many, a large amount of them will stay regardless.}

{Terra, thou knowest the park is not precisely... ideal for a considerable number of people. The facilities for that many people do not exist here. Disregarding that, there is no food hereabouts and I have not seen even a hint of crops. If food is not brought in from outside then...} I hesitate but wish to make sure she understands, so continue, {Hast thou beheld the sight of a person starving to death before? I have; it is not pleasant to witness. Without crops or incoming food, I presume it shall be a common sight for quite some time.}

{We'll tell them that they should leave or risk their life here once you enter hibernation. I have a feeling that most of them will refuse to listen. Most people nowadays can't comprehend what it's like to be around death and how easy it truly is to die. Also, I am just going to say, no matter what happens those sights will be common. This city is enormous. A lot of people wouldn't evacuate even if they knew everything.}

Nodding, I think for a moment and then say, {Aye. Thou shouldst procure an ample supply of crop seeds if they are attainable. If thou givest me some, perhaps I may make use of them.}

{I've been hoarding commodities like seeds and foodstuff in preparation for the coming tribulations and the seizing of the Galtry Syndicate for a little while now. And you probably shouldn't be stressing about that sort of thing until you have the wiggle room to pursue something like crops. For now, you should worry about the training and viability aspects of The Tower.} Letting out a sigh, she says aloud, "Why did we have to attract so many so easily."

Owl walks into the gate chamber. "People were enticed by that photo of Miss Nightingale. It garnered a lot of attention, went viral, and led to people questioning who she is."

"It was a rhetorical question. Have the Hands I hired made any headway as far as controlling the narrative is concerned, Owl?" she asks him, going back to working on her lap-top.

"It isn't making a discernible difference." Owl taps some things on a lap-top nearby and points at a picture. It's a fist with the thumb tucked beneath the index finger; it means 'T' in sign language. "It appears public sentiment might have coalesced even more around Miss Nightingale—a combination of timing, public frustration, and her grace. This fist she was making in the photo is cropping up all over the place."

I glance at the lap-top, and then tilt my head. *{Terra, I have questions, but first and foremost... what does 'wiggle room' mean?}*

Chapter 26: Fruition at the Hôtel Casale

∞∞∞∞∞∞∞∞∞∞∞∞∞∞∞

Terra departed a few hours ago whilst Owl and the Helping Hands are working to improve the cave. In the meantime, Shriek is showing me one of the chat room things. The chat room's words are so fast, though. It is challenging for me to keep up. Shriek says that each of the names is from a different person and that it's typically more disorderly, but they forbid pictures. I surmise the ones that would use pictures must be folk who have yet to learn to read or write as I have. It is lovely that they are usually permitted to participate, though I do not know what they are meant to understand without a proper teacher attending them.

"Miss Nightingale, just point if you want me to stop somewhere," Shriek remarks. "Oh, that or I could go back to the beginning."

Using my whiteboard, I write, "I would prefer to simply read from the beginning. Most of what they say I do not comprehend."

He nods. "Well then, just give me a sec while I scroll back through all the old messages!"

The words move even quicker except in reverse as Shriek slides a fingertip over a pad at the lap-top's front. A mere 'sec' thereon, we appear to reach the foremost messages.

My eyes peruse the words of this era's people.

Delver Thaddeus
Are we sure it's safe to talk in here? Is Jingle-Jangle secure?

Wolfie
Ji-Ja appears to be ultra-simple software, but that's because its emphasis is purely on backend security and privacy.

KingZero
Doesn't matter much to me. I've already decided I'm going, I just wanna know more.

PaladineMaurice
Woah, just like that! You don't need convincing or anything? Me and my bud @Phantom Moped +buds w/ the RWR Alliance are gonna pop a tent, but we're from nyc.

KingZero
My family was in Anchorage... I'm alone now. Been traveling with one of the caravans. Lots of us that made it out of the Anch. camps are going, it's that or… idk. No place else seems interesting.

Rivera Underwater
I'm truly sorry to hear that, King. I've decided to go too. Lived in Venezuela, they made us leave a couple of months ago. There were some bad murders near a water spring but no explanation why we needed to leave. They just told us internationals to go home.

Delver Thaddeus
Really sorry to hear that @KingZero. (sorry if this is inappropriate, but are you THE King Zero? I

🚩 Faithful
Leader – 1
Wolfie

🧚 Fairy 🧚
Mods – 3
A-Real-Rabbit
Not-A-Real-Owl
Speaker-G

Friends – 87+

§§§§§§§
3Points1312
Abarnes
Aboreus
AlexandraH
AMA_DaVincis...
andre
Astral
Belduim
Bête_Celeste
Blumiu1
Bmac4597
Bobbery
BTC
Carnelian
ChrysalismPancake
Cmarshall
Cnyquist
CryoDrake
Cure_Death
Dantes_Left_Thigh
Darastrix
Delver Thaddeus

totally understand if you don't wanna to answer.)
Oh! Were you able to get a visa @Rivera Underwater?

Rivera Underwater
To Venezuela? I was there for lumber work. Was salvaging sunken logs. They just said I needed to go back to the States or I'd be jailed & deported. Consulate said pretty much the same. Living out of a Texas hotel atm.

Bête_Celeste
Heard they were pulling bodies out of tree trunks, thought it was a ghost story though tbh. My own family is from QC, now in Connecticut thanks to the Dryas Cyclone. Prolly going to go together.

GhostFaceBlunt
QC = Quebec? Isn't the Canadian border still closed. ☹ Saw articles about all the people freezing… Where'd you jump the border?

Bête_Celeste
Out of curiosity, is anyone in the city yet?

GhostFaceBlunt
Was just curious. ☹

LionessInExile
I'm already here. My mom & dad enrolled in a cult, like one of the crazier ones with a compound, polygamy, spouse swaps, everything. This was the only thing someone wasn't trying to recruit for.

HaveYouSeenMe?
Screwy people coming out of Birmingham in the south. We are forming a group in Nashville

Demalos
Ditty
Djineater
eagle0108
EgladesGirl
EGS
Eman3000
Enaz the great
fennek
Fiddle Sticks
GhostFaceBlunt
GR
Grodu
HandyJ
HaveYouSeenMe?
Horsie-For-Morsie
D.Hux13y
I Doth DIYed
I_Dream_Of…
InfernalDrake
Jacque
Jperry
Jwalsh
Kaldi
KingZero
LionessInExile
Lynx
Mackie
MeanderingWizzard
Melting Sky
Merpmerp
Naizha
New907Blood_EC
Nopa196
Octn
Orinari
Ornithomancy

and are gonna carpool in a jalopy, that way we can ditch it someplace and not worry about it.

Picture-_-This-_-Damascus
Screwy people coming from Alabama is pretty normal. Are they more screwy than usual?

HaveYouSeenMe?
They're trying to find people for their screwy militias. The weird part is, they all smell the same, like they have a rusty musk. Idk. I just wanna get into the C-Sys and then i'll see about this tower thing while we're at it.

I_Dream_Of_Unicorns
Mark my words, it'll be a first-come-first-serve thing and you'd be lucky to even look in the tower much less 'challenge it.'

EgladesGirl
@I_Dream_Of_Unicorns So you aren't going?

I_Dream_Of_Unicorns
I'm going? I'm following the caravans in.

Delver Thaddeus
Oh god, some of the caravans are gonna be there? Forget it! I'm starting with Consortium soon. They're basically runnin' sh*t in the big 🍎

D.Hux13y
Consortium? Yeah, good idea idiot. Alive but wishing you were dead, talk about a life worth living. But I'm going. I think it'll be one hell of a good time. 🔥

3Points1312
…Okay ya weirdo? I'm going if President McKKKrackerASS starts drafting people. I'm going to hide in the tower. They can drag my butt outta there.

PaladineMaurice
Pavlov
phantom
Phantom Moped
PhillD
Pickle33Keffel
Picture-_-This...
Pilcrow
PORTAL99
Pride
Que Tea
reodude
Rivera Underwater
RMClarke
Seiðr
Seijax
Shadethedemon
ShakangoRes
Shiro
Shughes
Slithy
SnootBooper
Sondadir
sumdudeguy
Synthesis Thirty
The_fourthPillar42
TheRedWolf911
@TiltedReign
|||||Trans|||||
User8
Waillender
WBenson
Xorikk
Zicorth

Anonymous Guests
1593 +

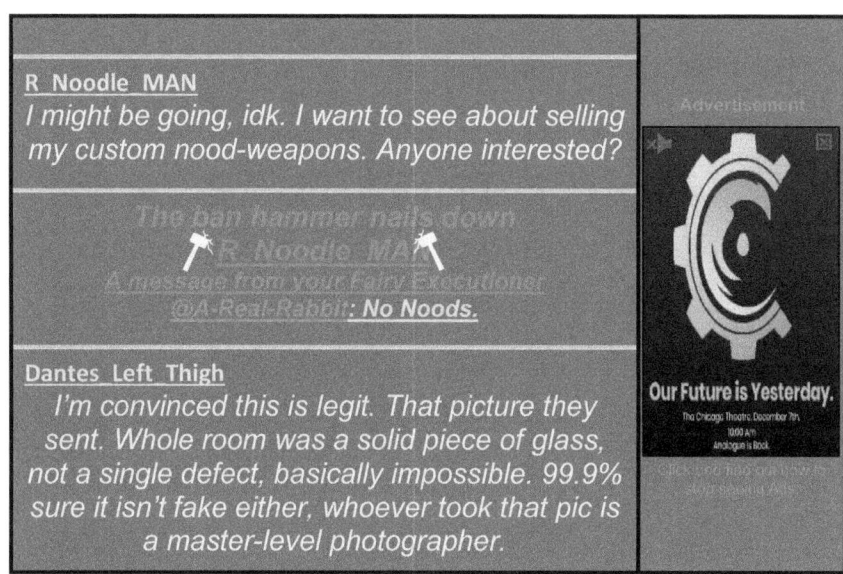

I write on my whiteboard and tap on it to get Shriek's attention. "What are these caravans of which they speak?"

Seeing my question, his face lights up as he answers, "They are basically convoys of people that began living communally after they were uprooted from their homes for one reason or another. Usually, they spend a few weeks or so in one place before going someplace else."

"Are these a newer occurrence?"

"Nah, they go back years. They used to be mostly made up of Native Americans after the government seized a bunch of reservations in the Midwest. The whole thing was extremely controversial and at the time, but the convoy was a lot smaller back then, and there wasn't much they could do."

"I see, and they are not small anymore?" I lean back in my chair to listen to his answer.

Shaking his head, he continues, "They've ballooned since Crawler-Anchorage and the temperature started to plummet in the northern hemisphere a couple of months ago. They're hardly the same thing anymore. Now they're full of all types of people that are in it purely because they have nowhere else to go. It'll take the bulk of them a while if some really intend to come here."

'...I understood some of that, I suppose. At least the general idea.'

Erasing my whiteboard, I scribble, "I believe I have seen enough for the moment," and then wave my hand.

"Cool. Let's see if they're talking about us on the news then!"

He does something, and then a news crier, Jay Teems, appears. "Scientists are still baffled by the mass migration of terrestrial and aquatic wildlife away from the Asian continent. Though they wish to reassure the public that it's thought to have no connection to the Crawler Virus." His chair spins, and he stares at us through the glass. "But first, a commercial break. When we come back, we're going to speak to several of the more popular authors who publish in a niche genre known as Lit. R-P-G. These authors claim they have been experiencing harassment that has spiraled as far as death threats. Here's a preview of that interview."

The picture changes to a man sitting in a dimly lit chamber with his face obscured in black shadows. He speaks in a profoundly deep voice. "It's crazy! I mean, I just wanted to write a little bit of erotica, y'know? Then one day, it hit me, 'Heck, why not make it a LitRPG? People like those, right?' I swear I had no idea there was some actual truth to the whole system gimmick. It was just meant to open up some hot-and-sweaty 'possibilities' that could help build the character's narrative. People need to understand that!" Throwing up one of his arms, he points toward me and says, "If anything, people should be asking questions about that Fairy! Why isn't the government doing everything it can to bring them in for questioning? We don't know anything about them!"

'And I prefer it stays that way, to be frank.'

••••
••••••••
••••

Several more hours pass. I grew a tad bored of being around Shriek, so now I sit watching the Helping Hands use odd spinning tools on the cave walls. *'Does the cave require these wire things?'* Surveying the ground, I look at all the other wire things they have run through the cave. *'They have so many, and that rumbling device outside is deafening.'*

Terra has also returned. Presently, she sits watching something on her lap-top. Earlier she left to ensure her father had not returned and to get some sleep. I doubt she slept much, however, since she returned early this morn.

Finally, there is Gen. Gen is hugging the coffin tight and yelling at anyone that dares get too close. I stand and pat him on the head. He nearly bites me before realizing who it is patting him on the head. When he sees it is me, he frowns and makes big pitiful eyes. Scratching under his chin, I shake my head. *'Apologies, Gen. This is all to ensure us both a better future... I pray.'*

Leaving Gen, I walk up behind Terra to observe whatever it is she is so focused on. The image is at first two people speaking to one another, but then a familiar picture appears—a girl in stunning cerulean robes and silver armor petting the chin of a white ape.

'Oh, it is me again. Peculiar.'

The image changes to pictures of burning rides and people yelling; the people in the image seem to be cloaked in gray dust as they dig through debris. At the bottom, it reads simply, 'Unrest Mounts Following Rumors of Forced Conscriptions.' The picture changes to one that displays hundreds of people shoving against a wall of noble's police equipped with shields.

{This is getting more pressing,} Terra says in my head, releasing a long sigh.

{Is there something I may do to help?}

{No, I'm just warning you... Someone managed to capture a video of the turtle in the Lake and now people are suspicious that the Terrace is where The Tower will be. Thanks to that, they're starting to gather at the hotel we plan to place your gate at in anticipation.}

Shriek enters the room holding a white shirt. Unfolding it, he displays it, saying, "These people sure work fast; look what I found some shirt kiosk selling!"

The shirt displays the same image I saw on the lap-top. A fist with the thumb tucked beneath the index finger. At the same time, the image on the lap-top changes along with the words. It now reads, 'People Seek A

Way Into Cosmic System After Stream' and shows a picture of me with Doctor Jäger and Mrs. Jäger.

Terra gazes at me and states in my head, {We need to fulfill the prophecy before things develop further.}

{Aye, I believe it is around the time we stated the prophecy would be fulfilled. I think we should do as we said we would.}

Narrowing her eyes, she nods and points at Shriek. "You stay and watch over things. Owl, Nightingale, we're going to head for the hotel. We'll satisfy the prophecy as we said we would and leave."

{Is it fine if thou come with us? Should thou not keep a distance until thou art poised to retake thy organization?}

{To be honest, I probably shouldn't go with you, but...} She peers at me, saying, "I'm going with you."

Thinking for a moment, Owl asks, "Should I have Rabbit, Wolf, and some well-suited Hands go with us to help shield Miss Nightingale?"

Terra nods at Owl and waves him off. With her permission, he leaves the room, removing a black rectangle from his coat pocket.

Hearing them speak of shielding me, I tilt my head and peer at the lap-top. {Are there a great many people at the gate location? Should we perhaps sneak in or wait until late at night?}

{No, the bulk of people there right now are mostly just curious locals, but more and more zealous people will be arriving every hour. Plus, you recall how we had a focus on bringing and targeting some of the more promising people and inviting them into a chat room?}

I nod.

{Well, some of those promising people are at the hotel.}

{Ah, I believe I saw some of them conversing earlier.}

{When?} she asks, raising an eyebrow.

{Shriek showed me on the lap-top!}

Her silver eye glares at Shriek, who seems oblivious to it. {Don't let what you see on the internet poison your mind, Constance. I know you've gone through a lot, but you're still a little innocent in some ways.}

Narrowing my eyes, I shake my head. {Prithee, I would like it if thou might simply elaborate upon my earlier questions and cease calling me innocent.}

She smirks and continues, {Ah, well, it would reflect badly on us if we acted like we were afraid of some ordinary people acting a bit crazy. We need to show confidence. After all, some of the more talented and astute people genuinely believe, and for good reason, that they would be putting their futures in our hands.}

{What if someone attacks me or something of the sort? It seems as if everyone nowadays carries around firearms.}

Terra takes my hand, flips it over, and reaches into her coat pocket. Removing what looks to be a brooch, she places it in my palm. The brooch resembles a bronze turtle shell with threads looped into holes that dot the shell's surface. She releases my hand and says into my head, {This brooch can shield you if you find yourself in a critical spot—if someone tries something they shouldn't. You saw my father's husk do something like that once before, remember?}

{Thou meanest with the fire and acid; how it would not touch him?}

{That's right. I want you to have it as a last resort to protect yourself. Put it someplace you won't lose it. It'll activate on its own if it senses you're about to take potentially lethal injury.} Raising a finger, she emphasizes, {It'll only work once, and they aren't exactly easy to find. If I remember this one was made by someone in Bishop Staten's congregation. I've had it for a few years now, ever since that person tried to assassinate me.}

'Bishop Staten...' My fingers trace the threads along the brooch's shell. {This shall protect me?}

She releases my hand. {It will if someone does something that would do a significant amount of damage to you. Which is all you need to worry about because the Helping Hands, Lorcan, and I will be there with you.}

'...I should not act so worried. If something happens, I shall manage. I must act as if I am a brave knight whilst I wear the arc suit.'

{Aye! As always, it is very much appreciated. I shall return it to thee after the gate is placed.}

{No, no, please keep it. It's more important you have it. Especially with our contract and all.}

{Aye. I understand.} Placing it in one of my pouches, I continue, *{Then we may leave when thou art prepared.}*

••••

••••••••

••••

Half an hour passes, and our ride arrives at Terra's hotel, where we prophesied the second gate would appear.

Terra, Owl, Wolf, Rabbit, and I sit silently in the ride's back. Lorcan is also here, but he's in the front operating the ride. Terra and Lorcan cannot be seen with me, so the two have their hair tucked back and each is wearing a mask, hood, and cowl similar to the Helping Hands'. Terra's mask resembles a gorgeous pair of ebony moth wings, while Lorcan chose a hideous ape mask because he thought he might be able to use it to play with Gen.

"Are you ready, Miss Nightingale?" Owl asks with a calm voice. He does not address Terra. She is meant to be treated like any other member of the Helping Hands. In fact, only Owl, Lorcan, Wolf, and Rabbit know she is Galtry. It is imperative we do not reveal her identity until the time is ripe, or she will squander her ability to manipulate her organization.

"Oh, it's Miss Nightingale now!" Rabbit states, poking the side of my helmet. "How adorable!"

Ignoring Rabbit's blatant efforts to tease me, I write, "Aye. I have composed myself, Owl. But are there honestly meant to be that many people here?"

"Probably more than you're imagining, Miss Nightingale," he responds with a dubious smile.

A small window opens from the front, where the ride is controlled from. "Come on, Fairy. You've got an audience," Lorcan says with a hearty laugh and his hand on the door handle. "It's insane, like a Hollywood premiere."

The carriage doors swing open, and if I had one, my jaw would drop. Crowds of people to either side of a rope, raising signs above their heads. *'Is this a fever dream...?'*

Owl, Wolf, and Rabbit throw hoods over their heads. "Come on, Miss Nightingale, we'll stand to either side of you."

{I'm sorry this happened so quickly.} Terra exits the ride and holds her hand out for me to take. *{I hope you aren't too mad at me...}*

{Think... Think nothing of it.} I take her hand. *{I shan't run.}*

As soon as I stand and exit, the shouts of the people grow loud. I hold Terra's hand as she shepherds me forward. The people yell tangled words at me. From what I understand, it is a miscellany of curiosity, praise, pleading, and reproach.

Yet my eyes fall upon a group of people wearing the familiar symbol of the God in Light around their necks. While everyone else's reactions are a mishmash, theirs are all alike:
"A devils' prophet is among us! Charity for the believers in the Light first!"
"Read the Daybreak Scriptures! Subverting His will is the highway to Umbral's Pit!"
"Salem is missing a witch and God says she's a hex cult harlot!"

Memories of Roanoke come rushing back. This is like then. As I have told Terra, people have not changed; the Church in Light despises what it does not understand. Worse, they have not tried to understand; they believe they know despite having asked nary a question.

A woman with short, raven black hair and deep brown eyes approaches me with some type of club. Behind her, a man with a big box camera trails her. She raises her club and endeavors to put it near my face whilst yelling, "Sage Giovanni from WGN. New York Congresswoman, Annette Callari, has vehemently refuted your assertions of some sort of inevitable catastrophe, going as far as calling it 'Doomsday rabble-rousing.' A Federal

Government official followed it up by stating that they have no reason to believe you're capable of 'soliciting' the Cosmic System's attention. Can you tell the people how you respond?"

Terra raises a hand, intercepting Sage. {Ignore the vultures.} She shoves her away and yanks me forward. {We just need to get in and out, don't worry.}

Sage chases us, yet some Helping Hands thwart her pursuit. I can hear her ask, "Why are you afraid to tell people the truth!?"

As we move past her, another person holds out their infant, screaming something incoherent.

Lorcan steps between us and shouts, "No one wants your booger eater, lady; keep it to yourself!"

The hotel doors swing open, and a dozen people in animal masks march out and begin to corral the crowds. Breathing a sigh of relief, Terra tries to release my hand, but I do not let go. I glance back at the people who call me a witch. {I do not relish the way some of these people are gawking at me,} I say into her head.

Glancing back, her brows furrow. {Do you want to leave? If it's too much, we can. I won't be disappointed or anything; we can do this another way.}

{Nay, I desire to place the gate, then I shall wish to depart.} I release her hand, straighten my back, and march past her. {Besides, I am playing the knight's role, so I shan't permit it to trouble me... at the moment.}

With a muffled titter, she pursues me. {Well then, lead the way, Miss Knight.}

The two of us hurry onward, encircled by the people in animal masks. Things progress so hastily I do not even have time to take in the building's exterior. We push through the doors and into the hotel so fast that the only information I glimpse is the name "Hôtel Casāle."

We move inside, and I notice everyone breathes an exasperated sigh. I can merely describe the interior as a royal's castle, much like the RV from days prior. Our feet tap against the hard marble floors of a corridor. To either side of us, folk stand scrutinizing our every move.

These are folk Terra invited. None of them seem that threatening, barring one group with pale skin and peculiar scarlet irises that make a wee bit uncomfortable. Supposedly, that group comes from the ruinous Anchorage. There is also a group of 'missionaries' courtesy of something dubbed the 'Church in Light Community Outreach Association.' They are not frightening; I merely do not fancy them. From what I comprehend, missionaries may as well be soft-spoken kin of the French Éclat and Vierge.

Together we move toward a tall pair of weighty oaken doors. The Helping Hands force open the doors, revealing a grand ballroom of vibrant silvers and golds. It is a wide chamber, unobstructed by pillars, and large enough for a thousand people at least. Drapes shroud floor-to-ceiling windows, yet everything is aglow in the exquisite shine of six crystal lamps dangling from the ceiling, lamps that Terra calls chandeliers. At the room's forefront is a stage made of rich, dark hardwood.

Gazing at the sparkling chandeliers, I realize it has a second floor that overlooks the ballroom floor, and it's crowded with people quietly scrutinizing me. They are not like the ones from earlier; they seem ordinary for their era, though many of them grasp black rectangles, pointing them at me. I rub my fingers together, for I was provided no foreknowledge a crowd would be here too.

We step to the stage. The ballroom remains hushed. I know not if they expect me to say anything; Terra looks plain irritated that they are there at all. She stealthily delivers orders to the Helping Hands, instructing them to prevent folk from using the stairs down, and then signals Lorcan to bring our ride to the building's rear.

{These people do not seem malicious. They appear rather respectful, in my opinion.}

{We need to hurry,} Terra warns with a groan and shake of her head. {It's some of the people outside the hotel. They're trying to shove their way inside so that they can see what's happening.}

At the same time, a purple wall appears.

Earl Interface:
   Recommendation: Sow the gate and inspire the fleshies.

'...I suppose.' Glancing between Earl's wall and Terra, I nod. 'I suppose this is part of not running. A gate for those that shall carry the world upon their backs... A modest show then.'

I raise my hand in greeting.

{Are you about to do something?} Terra asks.

Looking at Terra, I say, {Aye, and as I do with most things, I shall deal with the consequences. For the time being, I desire to appear a tad 'crisp' as the saying goes.}

{It's not 'I' anymore; it's 'we.' We'll both have to deal with any consequences.} She rolls her eyes with a wee huff, hiding her expression from the Helping Hands. {But it's not as if I can say anything, be ready to leave and enjoy your moment of looking crisp.}

Owl notices I intend to do something and directs some of the Helping Hands to prepare for our departure. From within my suit, the orb of yellow light moves and seeps through my leather glove, where I take it into my fingertips. Whispers arise from the balconies above. This may be the first moment in life or death that anyone has watched me with reverence, save for the elderly rats.

'It is somewhat like that time with the elderly rats, is it not? Aye, I need to do something in sign language. Something to inspire the masses... I suppose they have adopted their own sign.' I shake my head, peering into the eyes of the people above. 'Perhaps I missed my calling; I would have made a splendid actor. Constance, The Actor... Aye, William, occasionally I wonder if I should have accepted thy proposal and been an actor with thee. Alas, I suppose a haze monster is not that dissimilar from being an actor like William.'

Raising my left hand, I spread my finger, push out my middle finger, and then claw the air—this means "Mercy." I then change it to the fist with my thumb tucked beneath my index finger.

Before releasing the spark and establishing the gate, I remark to Terra, {Oh, I should confess, I am uncertain precisely what shall transpire once I do this.}

{But this is your second gate?}

{Aye, but the first spark seeped into a crevice in the wall. I do not know what occurred on the other side.}

{...Is this safe to do?}

{I believe it is; Earl would presumably warn me if it was not.}

Taking her half-frown as confirmation that I should precede, I release the spark. It floats earthward, reflecting off and illuminating the stained glass helmet beneath my cloak, my armor, and the cerulean fabric of my robe. The spark hits the hardwood at my soles and a smoky black fog rises.

> **Earl Interface:**
> **Recommendation:** *The user should leave the stage.*

{Abandon the stage,} I warn Terra while rushing off the stage myself.

Terra, Owl, the other Hands, and I hurry off the stage as light escapes from the nooks and crannies in the flooring. A rumble comes from below the stage as haze gushes out. The fog blankets the stage's floor and freezes solid, forging a glass platform.

> **Earl Interface:**
> **Notice:** *The gate will be complete within the next 115 to 121 Material-Earth hours.*

Watching the glass, I see multiple shards sprout, bud, and bloom until the stage is teeming with flower. Atop their glittering blossoms, glass butterflies stand, fluttering their wings until they stiffen and then freeze. '*Stunning!*' Gasps from the crowd above affirm my sentiments as they all whisper amongst themselves. '*A wonderful display, Earl; I cannot wait to see it come to full fruition!*'

The exclamations of the folk in the corridor infiltrate and echo in the ballroom. I can hear various voices yelling at one another, some commanding them to stay back and others demanding they step aside.

{Is it finished for now?} Terra asks with a tinge of urgency.

{I surmise thus.}

{Then we should get moving. We're going to have to drive in circles for a while to ensure no one is trailing us before we can even consider returning to the cave.}

{Aye. Prophecy fulfilled. Let us be on our way.}

I look up at the people leaning against the second-floor railing, watching as if they foresee a finale. It shan't ever come, though. The unfaltering *thumps* of my titanium boots are how I bid the people in the ballroom and corridors farewell. *'If they yearn to speak with me, they shall have to hark my steps... That is what a knight would say, is it not?'*

····

·········

····

A day has passed since I placed the gate. Circumstances have fallen further into absurdity. At present, I am standing atop a rocky hill near a bronze statue called "The Falconer." It's a simple statue of a man in standard theatrical dress reaching out to catch his falcon hunting companion. The hill itself overlooks a field known as "Frisbee Hill" or some other silly name of that sort.

However, what has me shaking my head is the folk who have arrived and are setting up encampments. Of course, people have been here since the initial moving picture we created, but after the prophecy was fulfilled yesterday, they have been arriving en masse. Terra says that there are rumors that they may begin preventing people from approaching Central Park or even entering the Manhattan area. Instead of keeping people away, this prompted everyone to rush here. Frisbee Hill is already nigh at capacity, and the people are spilling into a larger field a tad further south named "Sheep Meadow."

I am wearing an oversized chestnut brown coat that I discovered in the cave. The coat settles at my knees, covering my armor and most of my skirt. Although I do not know whom it belongs to, I doubt they shall mind me using it. Still, the coat does not disguise my identity well, so I duck behind a tree and watch as a noble's police walks to the crowd's center. In his hand, he carries a device called a "me·gah·phone." I have been told the megaphone's purpose is to amplify a person's voice.

The noble's police stops at the center of Frisbee Hill and raises it to his mouth. "This is a quarantined area, anyone that chooses to s—"

He pauses when a familiar pair of noble's police walk up behind him. These two are, of course, Jessica and Leo. They patrol the park regularly, which is why we ran into one another so often. Jessica steps behind the noble's police with the megaphone, leans forward, and whispers something into his ear. Jessica and Leo stroll away while the man stands there, blinking but unmoving.

"Never mind," the man squeaks into the megaphone before spinning on his heel and walking away. Everyone glances at one another and then returns to establishing their encampments.

Behind me, I hear the crunch of heavy footsteps. "What up, Fairy. Spying on people again?" Lorcan says with a laugh. Glancing back, I see him gnawing on what looks to be a roasted turkey shank. "Some lady was passing out turkey legs for the needy or somethin' and offered me one. I feel like I'm at a festival, pretty cool."

Reaching into my pouch, I pull out my pad and write, "So this lady presumed thou wast a 'needy' then?"

He squints, reading my message. As he reads, his chewing steadily slows to a pause, and his brow furrows. Yet after glancing down at his attire, he sighs and shakes his head. "I guess so. I used to make a decent salary being a trucker, y'know? But I had to spend all my money paying Ma's medical bills. Then the company replaced most of us with self-driving rigs, so yeah, that job didn't last long. Anywho, that's all in the past..." Taking another bite, he points the turkey leg at Jessica, who is walking away. "She's a badass. Sent that other officer running with their tail between their legs. I respect her hustle."

"Dost thou knowest what she said to him?"

With his mouth full, he replies, "Nah." Swallowing, he continues, "But if she's been workin' for the Espositos, then she and her pal have probably been collecting dirt on the other officers for years. I'm sure Galtry asked her to keep the other officers quiet."

I nod and then a thought crosses my mind. "Why art thou here? Shouldst thou not be busy elsewhere?"

"I've been watching the Terrace, but the main reason I'm here is because of that." Again using his turkey leg, he points toward a fountain in the distance. There the black RV sits with the Escorts outside, keeping guard but acting relaxed so as to not make it obvious. "Parked the RV at the Cherry Hill fountain. We're gonna use it as the new base camp. Didn't Galtry talk to you about this? You're supposed to be moving into the RV for a few days or whatever."

According to Terra, the RV is essentially a moving fortress, which is why she had it made in the first place. This is why I agreed to stay in it until I hibernate in a few days. I nod. "Aye, I am aware. I shall be finishing my business at the cave soon." I change to a new paper, wiggle my finger to get it to stop sticking to me, and then continue, "I simply did not know thou wouldst be here already."

"Well, I've been watching the Terrace anyway, so I'd be here either way. Oh yeah, I almost forgot." He bites the turkey leg, reaches behind him, and pulls out a book. I stare at it, reading its cover. "Quad Ruled Book for Map Making."

'...Map paper?' Taking it in hand, I gaze at his turkey-legged face.

"They are cartography papers. Galtry had me pick them up from some card shop I heard about from a campsite full of nerds."

"Nerds? Are nerds mapmakers?"

"Uhm, they draw maps for their games sometimes." With a shrug, he points. "They're over there. You can also ask Shriek about them; they're his pals, I think."

I stare off into the distance, where a large tent is erected with a sign. "Become a Tower virtuoso today! Unite with the RWR Alliance for hours of imaginative strategizing and rehearsals. Speak to 'Paladine' Maurice for more info. Excelsior!" Outside the tent, I notice a drawing of a green-skinned woman with tiny, colorful butterfly wings and scant clothing. Another sign is affixed to the drawing that reads, "Tonight only (probably), Unmasked and Unarmored, discover ??WHY?? a professional Jurassic Orcs and Peri-Elves dungeon master theorizes the Fairy looks roughly like this AI-rendering."

Turning away, I shake my head. "Nay, I thank thee for the paper. I am meant to meet Owl at the cave, so I do not have the leisure to visit the 'nerd' mapmakers today." I shamble off toward the RV. *'Not on this day or any other for that matter.'*

When I arrive, one of the Escorts unlocks the door for me. I enter and set the map paper atop the marble table for later. Searching for Terra, I discover several brown boxes with a note attached.

Nightingale, more supplies for your 'little friend in the dark.'

Luckily, we ordered early because many crop/fruit seeds sold out after the C-System announcement. Don't stress about it too much, though. I preemptively procured and set caches aside months/years ago for the days ahead of us. However, I couldn't get my hands on many rare plant seeds, and what I did may or may not arrive. We might be able to scavenge some in future. NYC is enormous, after all.

Opening a box, I study some of the supplies, including a translucent bag bearing a trove of 'Giant Sequoia,' 'California Coast Redwood,' and something I requested recently, 'Cork Oak' seeds.[99] Then there are vast amounts of seeds from fruit trees, market crops, herbs, spores, and vegetables. *'These shall all be tremendously important, but I must request aid moving them. I shall need to mollify Gen when next I return to the cave, and it will be much simpler without my hands full.'*

While placing everything back into the box, I notice a stack of paper along with a second note on it. Securing the box, I read the note.

Purchased what bugs I could, not many rare ones amongst them unfortunately. Animals have been more difficult to purchase and procure; not many I could get my hands on with such short notice. We'll look into ways to find more, and I have ideas for where to find them. Could also ask people to bring their own exotic animals when traveling to The Tower.

---

[99] Cork Oak: The primary source of cork for wine bottle stoppers, cork flooring, and other such things.

The stack of papers beneath the note appears to be proof of purchases. The top sheet is for a store named "Byron's Big-Bug Emporium." I browse through some of the purchases from the emporium: lacewing larva, field crickets, ladybugs, praying mantis egg kit, Namib desert beetles, numerous butterfly eggs, various moth eggs, the list goes on for pages. *'How many insects and animals does she believe I shall require in the beginning? Furthermore, where does she intend to store these until I may or may not need them? Ah, well, I suppose it is better to have them if I ever do need them.'*

I remove an endless pen from my pouch and write, "It is appreciated," and then draw a small butterfly at the bottom. Taking one of the lighter boxes in hand, I inform the Escort I shall return soon. One of the Escorts insists they follow to guard me, but I decline, considering I am merely walking to the cave on the far side of the Lake. I leave the RV.

Returning to my humble cave hermitage, I happen upon a group of Helping Hands departing. Since the Hands arrived, the cave has undergone some alterations. Where once the floor was rough and irregular, it is now smooth as silk. Any significant obstructions on the wall have also been polished smooth. The most notable change is that they have added two bulky gray doors—one at the cave's entrance and another at the gate chamber's doorway. According to the Helping Hands, both doors are "steel shells," and they shall be embellishing and beautifying them soon.

I approach a Hand that wears a complete set of black leather and a crow mask, which means his name is Crow, I presume. "Whereabouts is Owl, Crow?"

"He's in the glass chamber moving the coffin as you requested," Crow says, nodding his head toward the gate chamber's door. "Someone said something about turkey legs and food trucks, so we're all heading that direction."

I bid them farewell and stroll into the gate chamber. There I see the reddened faces of Owl, Wolf, Rabbit, and another Hand with a Raccoon mask. They grit their teeth as they carry the iron coffin. Moving the coffin is something I requested they do because I am planning to ask Earl if I may stow it within Tenebrous.

What I did not expect was the hairy little man that is still embracing the coffin even while they carry it. Although, he is not shouting at anyone; instead, he is snoring at them. He must have fallen asleep.

I place the small box I brought from the RV to the side and shake my head. *'Gen must be exhausted after guarding the coffin for so long.'*

Observing the four people in animal masks struggling under the heavy iron coffin's weight, I wave and approach. They stumble and Gen takes a drowsy swipe at the air. Proceeding onward, they glance at me when the coffin is a hair's breadth from the gate.

While they hold the coffin, I hurry to the edge of the chamber and retrieve some poles. Placing the rods underneath the coffin, I perform the thumbs-up gesture. They lean over and cautiously lower it to avoid squashing Gen's fingers. The rods creak when they place it upon them.

When they slip their own fingers out from beneath it, they pant for air.

"God in Light, that crap is heavy," Rabbit whispers, her chest moving up and down rapidly. "Why would anyone ever need a coffin this heavy? I really wish we had brought the dolly with us."

Owl takes one last big breath and then returns to his usual demeanor. "It's some type of mortsafe I believe, presumably from a European crypt someplace. Never seen one like this before, though. Mortsafes are usually made to keep people from digging up the soil to rob a grave." [100]

"Oh, hey, I just remembered. Doesn't Ferret collect mortsafes? I think it's a hobby of his." Wolf smiles at me, continuing, "Seems you and Ferret have something in common, Miss Nightingale. Perhaps you should stop by his card shop to say hi. I'm sure he'd love to show you his collection."

---

[100] Mortsafe: contraptions designed to protect graves from disturbance.

'They collect coffins and operate one of these card shop places that Lorcan mentioned earlier...'

Putting away my paper and retrieving my whiteboard from the corner of the gate chamber, I write, "We do not and I doubt we shall ever have anything in common." Making the sign for "never," I then write, "Owl, I will require a moment to myself shortly."

"Yes, Miss Nightingale, I'll finish preparing the camera equipment." He waves at Rabbit, Wolf, and Raccoon. "Out, out, you three need to get back to spreading Miss Galtry's words among the crowd."

I tilt my head. 'Miss Galtry's words...? Ah, wait, I remember now. Terra had them begin spreading her name amongst the people who came to The Tower. I believe it was something simple like "Where is Galtry?" The goal is to get people to ask for her help before she does anything.'

Reaching out, I stop him and hold up one finger. "I need help carrying some things from the RV back here first. As well as an escort to take Gen back. May thou assist me?"

"Ah, of course, little Gen here wouldn't let anyone else touch him except for you."

"Aye. He is not the friendliest sometimes." Handing my whiteboard to Owl, I reach down and slide my hand beneath Gen's body. He squeaks, reaches out his hand, and grips my arm. With his eyes still closed, he pulls himself into my arms, resting his head against my shoulder.

"I had not lived until this moment." I hear hands slapping against something. Looking over, I find Rabbit squishing her own face with her hands. "I'm starting to think she might be an actual Fairy."

'If I am honest, I was trying to push him off the side.' I take a heavy step forward. 'Besides, he's heavy! All that pudding he has been consuming when my back is turned!'

Thus begins my slow return to the RV with the four Hands and the sleeping, heavy Gen. With my hands full, I cannot respond, so besides Rabbit, who keeps commenting on Gen and me, it is a relatively quiet albeit slow journey. Upon returning, I take Gen into the small bedchamber, where Terra prepared a few things to keep him entertained. Mostly things she says this era's children play with. I want to fiddle with them myself, but I cannot get distracted with all that is happening. I shall borrow them for myself later.

Placing him on the bed, I retrieve some puddings Lorcan bought and then place them on the bedside table. Speaking of Lorcan, Gen and him get along somewhat, so he shall be the one taking care of him. Well, honestly, they only met yesternight, but Gen did not throw anything at him. That's better than anyone else thus far. Though for some reason, I get the impression that Gen believes himself to be a much bigger ape than he genuinely is.

'Should I wake him? Nay, he will understand when he sees the pudding, I think.'

I exit the bedchamber, bumping into Lorcan as soon as I do so. "Hey. Is the monkey in there?" he asks in a muffled voice, suppressing a laugh.

I narrow my eyes, staring at him. He is wearing the ugly ape mask he used yesterday at the hotel. *'Nay, thou art not going in there wearing that.'* Writing a message on a sticky paper, I stick it to the door. "Barred entry. Those that attempt entry shall comprehend true sorrow."

Peering into his eyes, I move past, only breaking eye contact when the arc suit will not allow me to continue.

I wander back into the main room; behind me, I hear him scoff. "Fine, whatever. I'll do it later."

"We've found the boxes, Miss Nightingale. Is little Gen settled in?" Owl asks with a chuckle.

Nodding, I take a large metal jar I plan to use when I return to the cave along with a small box and gesture for the Hands to follow. The Hands talk freely amongst themselves as we walk.

Wolf tips the box so he can read the side. "These boxes remind me, did we ever get those seeds for Miss Galtry?" he asks, looking at Rabbit.

"It probably won't happen. I might get one of them, but the other two are dubious."

I glance at Rabbit and tilt my head.

"She was looking for seeds for some especially rare fig and olive trees, but it seemed like more of a curiosity thing. They aren't much different than normal figs or olives, just pretty much extinct."

'Ah, I can see why she asked; growing an especially rare plant does seem interesting. Something for the future, perhaps.'

Continuing, Rabbit says, "But they're on the other side of the world, and with things how they are, no one's willing to take the time to discuss such minor things."

I nod.

Together we return to the cave and they drop the boxes next to the iron coffin for me. Dropping my own box, I set the metal jar aside, retrieve my whiteboard, and write, "I appreciate thy help. I need a moment in here alone."

Wiping a bit of snow from his shoulder, Owl responds, "Of course, as I said earlier, I'll prepare the camera equipment while you do what you need to."

"Bye-bye, Fairy," Rabbit shouts, her voice echoing throughout the gate chamber.

Wolf and Raccoon just laugh as they walk out, waving farewell.

"I'll be waiting in the next room; take your time," Owl states, accompanying them out.

I lock the door they recently installed and retrieve my metal jar. Pushing the cattail through the hole on the side of the arc suit's neck, I walk toward a crevice that exists between the bottom of the stained glass and floor. The cattail slips into the crevice and pulls out six plastic bottles, all partly filled with rife paste from my shell.

Since the incidents with the dinosaur, wretched rat, and the one occasion where I nearly ate Gen, I have been cautious about how much I consume and when. Furthermore, I was careful to store the paste in the gate chamber away from Gen's prying eyes. The cave's smell helped disguise its location as well, I presume, although I cannot smell. I plan to move the contents into the more secure metal jar to prevent accidents in the future. *'Now that I am alone once again, it is time to put my most dangerous things where only I may go.'*

Opening the shiny silver jar, I twist the lids from the plastic bottles and pour them into the jar until all six bottles are empty. I secure the jar's lid and then reach into the crevice once more, removing a rubbish bag. Due to the paste's consistency, some of it stills clings to the insides of the bottles. So I recap them, carefully store them in the rubbish bag, and then place the rubbish bag atop the coffin.

I return to the crevice, removing every item I have been collecting these past weeks: the disassembled pistol, the stained ecology text, the Hex Church's contract book, the messenger orb, some of my sign language materials, my first endless pen, Deputy Clippie, and my maps of Tenebrous. Then the last item, a piece of attire known as a "t-shirt" that Shriek purchased for me. It is the one with the T-sign fist on it. I shan't ever wear it, but mayhaps I shall find a use for it someday.

Storing all the items in their own rubbish bag, I check the crevice once more and then move to the gate. I take a moment to shake my hands and prepare myself. In my mind, I command the gate, *'Prithee, open.'* The woman in gold and the man in leather part their swords and the two stained glass panels slide backward.

A few feet from the edge of the door stands Earl, carrying her lantern with a hand over her mouth and a smile stuffed with sharp teeth peeking between her fingers. When the gate opens fully, Earl speaks. "Astonishment: This one was startled by the user. The user's visit was totally unexpected." Her eyes study me, looking me up and down. "Inquiry: May this one ask why the user has chosen to encase themself in worldly material?"

{Thou art lying. I do not believe thou wast standing there by pure coincidence.} I hoist a box of seeds. {Also, what is wrong with the arc suit?}

Dropping her arms, she hugs the lantern and tilts her head. "Statement: Maybe this one always stands here awaiting the user's arrival at all hours. Then it would be a surprise no matter what."

I narrow my eyes, looking into her white pupils. {Is that true?}

"Response: Of course not; this one is terribly busy." Her gaze darts between Tenebrous and me. "Furthermore, the beast spirit fled again. This one can't find it." There's a shiver and a fire in her bleached eyes. "Perhaps this time it has been lost to a Relic's teeth."

{Is... is that so? Mayhaps I can help search for it once The Tower reaches fruition.} I jostle the box. {These can be given to thee, aye?}

She nods. I toss the first box of seeds through the gate. It slides to a halt at Earl's canvas shoes. "Belated Response: As for the 'arc suit,' this one does not understand why the user would encase themself in it. This one knows fleshies will wear material while performing colorful dances to entice mates that help generate new fleshlings... Yet, Kiln do not do such dances. Query: Is the user confused about Kiln social etiquette? Disclosure: Kiln social etiquette does not exist."

{Hush, Earl. Do not say such things.} Lifting another box, I push it through the gate. {I fancy the arc suit. It has allowed me a lot of freedoms I had lost... It also looks exquisite, does it not?}

"Subsequent Response: This one thinks it does look elegant for something originating from the Material Realm. Sentiment: This one merely believes the user shouldn't have to hide in this 'arc suit' just because a few fleshies are ignorant and cannot recognize transcendence."

{I do not know if 'transcendence' is the appropriate word for what I am, but regardless, it has naught to do with hiding. The arc suit provides protection, amongst other things like haze conservation. Oh, speaking of which, I have been considering new adaptations. What is thy opinion on this?}

Tapping the lantern, she ponders my question and then says, "Recommendation: The user should wait unless they worry for their safety."

{...Wait? I should not acquire as many as I am able?}

"Inquiry: Which adaptation would the user consider their strongest and most versatile?"

I think for a moment, but it's rather obvious. {*I suppose the copepods.*}

"Subsequent Inquiry: And the copepod adaptation, what meal provided it?"

{*I believe I understand. Thou art implying that adaptations derived from magical creatures are better in some fashion?*}

She nods and smiles. "Statement: The user is quick to comprehend. Extrapolation: Adaptations from monsters, beasts, or other magical creatures will ordinarily be better. Additionally, as the user has noticed, choosing certain adaptations makes others more costly. Not only that, but adaptations can interfere with one another, meaning every time the user selects one, they may lose other prospective options."

{*So... the adaptations I have selected shall forever be weaker?*}

"Answer: No, not necessarily. The user can devour a magical creature with qualities that resemble or complement their adaptation in some way. Explanation: Like the Cattail Tendrils, for example, if the user ingested a hideous atrocity of squirming tentacles, it's logical to believe the user could incorporate an aspect of that magical creature into the tendril adaptation. That or a creature with something to offer that doesn't interfere with the existing tendrils. It's simply confining to select adaptations from meek organics when there are so many more desirable ones for the user in the future."

{*...I think I understand.*} Pushing two more boxes through the gate, I nod. {*However, I believe I shall still take the Rife Pearl adaptation, but then I will endeavor to be more selective. The paste is something I cannot keep permitting to occur whenever it desires...*}

"Statement: It is the user's decision. Subsequent Statement: This one also wishes to express how delighted this one has been made by the user's recent actions."

{*Aye? What art thou referring to precisely?*}

Raising a fist, she makes the 'T' sign with a mocking grin. "Response: The user has lured so many fleshies into The Tower's snare. Even if the fleshies starve to death inside the Pantry, the user will amass generous quantities of Essence. At the rate this one anticipates, this one shall be able to expedite the extension of The Tower's Pantry. The user has *finally* put their needs first."

I narrow my eyes and sweep another box through the gate. {*I have put my needs first for my entire life. Simply because I have never killed anyone deliberately does not mean I neglected to put myself first.*}

She shrugs, glancing at the boxes that surround her. Tearing a piece of the brown box, she studies it and places it in her mouth. "Note: Made from some species of conifer." She swallows it, then stares at me as I toss in another box. "Inquiry: Does the user desire to inspire the fleshies?"

{*Aye, but in all honesty, things are progressing too well.*}

"Response: There is no such thing as 'too well.' If the fleshies wish to skitter into The Tower, we shall simply exterminate the ones who know the passphrase, sealing the rest inside. After which, the doomed fleshies will do what is natural: squabble, fight, eat one another, and then die. Thus, bequeathing the user a pleasing trove of Essence."

{*...Aye, let's not do that, Earl... But, why didst thou 'inquire' if I 'desire' to 'inspire'... the people?*}

"Answer: This one intended to conceal the sprout's growth while the user hibernated, but now this one desires to provide the fleshies a modest display." Raising a finger, she continues, "Preemptive Response: Before the user inquires, it shouldn't result in any fleshie deaths or mutilations."

{*...The Tower is no longer a secret, yet I prefer thou not do anything too fantastical.*}

She smiles, shaking her head. "Acknowledgment: Of course, it'll be in good taste."

'*...I shall have to alert Terra.*' I point at the coffin. {*This is vital, Earl, and could attract dangerous folk if I leave it out here. So may I stow this coffin in Tenebrous?*}

"Inquiry: A snack for when the user awakens? Extrapolation: This one prefers other Kiln never be permitted entry, but this one is sealed and not especially active. It shouldn't be an issue unless liberated from its enclosure."

'So it is indeed a Kiln; I was not certain.' I nod. {To answer thy query, the Kiln's fate depends more on themselves than I.}

Squinting at the coffin, she frowns. "Forewarning: Other Kiln are not to be trusted."

{Agreed. Without a contract, I am uncertain whether I can sincerely trust anyone. Yet, that still does not mean I should gobble up another Kiln at the first opportunity.}

She hugs the lantern tighter and purses her lips, glaring at me.

{Then I shall stow this coffin and...} I gesture toward the things I withdrew from the crevice earlier. {And this paste and other items as well?}

"Acknowledgment: Yes, yes, the rife paste and other things the user has collected are fine as well. The only thing that isn't permitted is sentient material beings."

I push the coffin, and it glides over the metal rods I placed earlier. The rods rattle as the coffin and other items that top it glide into Tenebrous.

When I finish, I take one last look around the gate chamber and then wave farewell. {I believe that is everything, Earl. I suppose we shall see each other once I awake.}

Waving, she nods.

I tilt my head. {Then till the morrow?}

She nods, still waving. "Response: Of course, this one shall eternally be with the user."

After a moment, I nod and mentally command, 'Seal the gate.'

The woman in gold and the man in leather start to bring their swords together, but something stops them. Their swords quiver as if they are straining against something.

Still waving, Earl tilts her head and runs the lantern across the iron coffin, illuminating it. "Inquiry: Does the user know the fate of an interface that is orphaned by their Kiln?"

Glancing around, I shake my head without a word.

She raises her lantern. "Answer: They lose the sole thing they remember having, their only purpose for existing at all, and are left to petrify alongside Tenebrous, with the source of light that they adore more than anything snuffed and stagnant."

{I...}

The two swordsmen that guard the gate tremble as the gate itself groans.

Lowering her lantern, she keeps her hand raised in farewell. "Declaration: Soon, the user will no longer be 'the user,' but the honorable Mistress of both The Tower and this one. This one trusts the Mistress and won't ever overrule their decisions. This one would cut their own head off if demanded." A low growl escapes Earl's throat as she raises her foot and strikes her heel upon the coffin. The gate grates, sluggishly closing. "Statement: But if Mistress is reckless and is eaten or annihilated, thus forsaking this Relic to petrify alone, it would be the ultimate betrayal. There is nothing more horrific the Mistress could do to this one."

Earl stops, lowers her hand, and bows. "Apology: This one promises this won't happen... *often*. Please excuse this one, Mistress."

The gate slams shut.

{...Earl.}

Erstwhile Black 3: A Day in the Life of Black

∞ ∞ ∞ ∞ ∞ ∞ ∞ ∞ ∞ ∞ ∞ ∞ ∞ ∞

16-year-old Constance

On a warm summer's day, in the back alleys of London's Silver Street, I sit beneath a small church window. As I enjoy the coolness of the shade, I fiddle with a heavy mortar and pestle in my lap and then reach into my canvas bag to run my hand across Sir Mouser's back.[101] Sir Mouser cannot walk long distances as he once did. So for the past several months, I have been carrying him in a canvas bag that loops around my neck.

As for his goodwife, Lady Mouser, she is not of this world any longer. A year ago, she ate a funeral bell mushroom that sprouted on an old log. We were out foraging for a particular mushroom called King Alfred's cakes that can be used to kindle a flame. She smelled something and ate it before I could do anything. I later found out a local woman had emptied a cauldron of grease over them that morn.

Since then, Sir Mouser never leaves my side for more than an hour or so. If I go out and leave him alone, when I return, he will have a dramatic case of melancholia and persistent 'meowing' until he deems I have paid him the attention he feels he is due. [102]

I do see their sons and daughters from time to time. They will seek us out to spend time with us on occasion but leave when they realize we do not have food. Fortunately, most of them have been employed as stable hands, and now spend their days hunting rats and mice as mousers like to do. It is wonderful that they have found homes; it makes me quite happy.

Removing a second canvas bag from my waist, I set it in the dirt to my left. This bag contains a combination of goods I managed to lift from carts and

---

[101] Mortar and pestle: a set of two simple tools used to prepare ingredients or substances by crushing and grinding them into a fine paste or powder

[102] Melancholia: formerly the psychological condition known as depression.

stalls by sleight of hand and silvery speech: licorice root, rose petals, water, and turpentine.

I place the rose petals in the mortar. The pestle grinds against the mortar as I listen to an older gentleman speak through the church window that leads into the church's vestry.[103]

A chair squeaks as he paces about, sweeping the little vestry. "Farewell to the days of clean slices wrought by sword and pike," he says in a shaky voice, worn down by the harshness of time. "And let us bid welcome to the age of muskets. Now are the days of gaping holes, shredded flesh, and shivered bone."

'Doth a knightly person wield a musket? Nay, they do not.' I shake my head. *'Muskets! Loud, bulky, dull. I prefer the sheen of cold steel over tarnished, noisy sticks.'*

"If possible, the pellet should be removed from the patient's body," he states in a low voice.

I whisper to myself, "Because the pellet could have adverse effects upon the patient, yet it can be more dangerous to remove than to merely leave it be."

My rose petals duly mashed, I add a chip of licorice root to the mortar and then chew on any slivers I have to spare whilst I listen. *'Licorice root, such a rare treat.'*

Inside he raps his finger against his desk and then avers, "Though the pellet could have adverse effects upon the patient, it can be more dangerous to extract than to simply leave it be." [104]

I nod. "Aye, and the physician may elect to remove the pellet if it is in the shoulder, thigh, leg, or arm."

"The physician may choose to extract the pellet if it is in one of the following areas: shoulder, thigh, leg, and arm. In most other areas, it shan't be recommended for extraction unless life-threatening." Some more

---

[103] Vestry: a room or building attached to a church, used as an office and for changing into vestments.

[104] Aver: Verify, confirm, prove. (12c.) Fell out of common use in 1950s.

squeaking from inside as he shuffles through some notes. He then says, "Rossalia is a disease on the rise in mainland Europe.[105] As physicians, we shall be the ones the people will look to for advice."

'Nay, I do not believe anyone shall look to a girl, me especially, for advice on such things. Many would see their graves before that, and for their stubbornness, they are welcome to cross the lychgate.'

I huff, add a few touches of turpentine to the mortar, and then return to grinding the root.

The sound of a letter being opened comes from within the vestry and things become hushed for a few minutes. I then feel the vibration of his feet against the hardwood on my back as he approaches the window. "Girl, thou speakest in the London fashion?" he questions.

I stop. This is the first time he has ever acknowledged my presence. I know that he is aware I am here, but I know little of this gentleman other than he is an old physician.

Over the past years, the use of London Parlance has been discouraged, and there have even been royal decrees against its use. This is because speaking in London Parlance, or the 'London fashion', is essentially a subtle manner of protest against the nobility. So, inquiring if I speak in the London fashion is the same as asking my opinion on the Queen and the ruling aristocracy. Most folk have either forsook it or swap between it and the Queen's English, depending on whom they are speaking to... But I do not, I shall resist even if I am the last.

"Aye, I favor it," I reply.

He scoffs. "Difficulties with the nobility also, I presume?"

I nod but say naught.

"That I would teach thee is fitting." He clears his throat and then says, "On the morrow, I shall be departing for the Tower of London. I fear it may be quite some time until I am seen again."

---

[105] Rossalia: is the mid-16th century name for scarlet fever. Later changed in the late-17th century.

"Then I wish thee well. I pray it is not as it sounds and that thou art not meant to be imprisoned." A moment passes without another word. '...It sounds as if he is to be imprisoned.'

He extends his arm, and a piece of vellum flutters in the breeze. "I received an epistle containing a notice this morn. Furthermore, I have also penned the recipe requested by note onto the back..." Pulling the vellum sheet back, he asks, "Thou canst read, correct? I surmise it was thee that etched the message into a sliver of bark?"

"Aye, that was indeed I." I take the thick sheet of vellum and then remove a piece of bark from my pouch. Drawing a penknife, I carve the recipe written on the vellum's backside into the bark.

I stow my items away and flip the vellum over to peruse the notice he desired to show me.

By order of Her Majesty the Queen, the woman who answers to the name 'Black' is to be brought to trial for crimes against the nobility, reputed acts of black witchcraft, and an alleged compact with the High Devil Penumbra.

Reward for arrest information: £3 from Royal coffers and £7,10s from the French Éclat.

Age: Thought to be between 14 and 20 years of life.
Hair: Red. Possible Scot or Irish Origin.
Eyes: Light Green.
Heighth: 5 feet, 0 inches.[106]

Both Black and her suspected familiar, a black cat missing an eye and an ear, are to be reported upon notice. Confronting Black without an escort is not advised.

This is an Éclat circular letter and must be returned to the Éclat Inquisitor or appointed constable for further spread. A fine of £1 shall be imposed upon those that fail to do so.

---

[106] |5 feet | 152.4 centimeters |

At the bottom of the notice is a sketch of a girl with her face hidden behind a cowl.

I raise the vellum to return it to him. When he takes it from my hand, I then remove a flat piece of timber from the canvas bag and bind it atop the mortar to keep anything from leaking.

Placing the mortar in my bag, I then gently lift it and permit Sir Mouser to readjust himself. "Thanks be. I have learned much these past months."

He leans forward. "I must ask, why didst thou request the Fates' lords-and-ladies recipe? Is it poison for vermin?"

Stepping toward Silver Street, I chuckle, "I appreciate pathetic irony, of course. Why else would I request it?"

"...Well, though it was not long, thou shalt be the final student of Dr. Edward Atslowe," he declares behind me. "Best wishes and good fortunes, my pupil."[107]

I pause. *'Pupil... I was... I was someone's pupil...'* My lip quivers as I turn onto the familiar streets, I have spent my entire life treading. I wipe my eye and say, "We must make for Cripplegate, Sir Mouser, I have business thereabouts."

"Meow," he retorts.

"Oh, hush. It is vital."

Some time passes until Sir Mouser and I arrive in Cripplegate, where we then descend deeper into the more disreputable parts of London's squalor. I watch the sky, making certain we do not walk below any open window. *'There is naught sadder than someone emptying their chamber pot over thy brow. A hard-learned lesson.'*

I step into an alleyway, watching my back to make certain a raptor does not sneak behind me whilst I am distracted. Removing the mortar from earlier, I drop its contents into a container of water and mix them

---

[107] Dr. Edward Atslowe: a well-known physician in the reign of Elizabeth I of England. Ardent supporter of Mary, Queen of Scots. Sympathizer of all Scots. Spent many years imprisoned in the Tower of London. Died 2 May 1594.

together. I scrutinize the light red water for a moment, shake my head, and add more turpentine to the mixture.

'It is a tad watered down, but it's the best I can concoct with what I was able to beg.' I return the jar to my canvas bag. *'I sincerely hope it shall suffice.'*

Checking my back once again, I proceed deeper into Cripplegate. When I reach a familiar and dark alleyway, I inspect my palms to make sure my illness is not rearing its head and then scratch Sir Mouser behind his ear.

I walk forward and into an alley of beggars. "Black!" a youthful boy's voice yells.

A lad of around twelve with a hole burned through his right ear sprints over.[108] I wave and then state, "I shan't be operating under that name any longer. I will return to using one of my past nicknames instead."

"Ah, well, which one is it then? Sink or Roach?" the boy asks.

Pursing my lips, I ponder which would be less known among the beggars. I shrug. "Sink, I suppose."

He nods, fiddling with the hole in his right ear.

"Thou shouldst not touch it, or it shan't heal properly," I say, wagging my finger at him.

"It itches. I cannot help it! ...But thou art the doctor, I guess." Forcing his arm to his side, he asks, "Didst thou bringest the medicine?"

"That I did. Didst thou acquirest what I desired?"

"Aye. Was a bit strange, but I shan't question it." Raising a worn and tarnished earthenware urn, he states, "A vagabond wandered in with it from Swindon! He said 'tis from before cremation was prohibited. I bartered the aqua vitae thou concocted for it!"

---

[108] Ear-boring: A policy where able bodied beggars would have a hole burned through their ears; remained in force until 1593.

I withdraw the jar of water from my canvas bag. "Aye, then if that be the urn, here is the lice remedy. Though, as a boy, thou couldst simply shave thy hair."

He shakes his head. "'Tis for Mammy, not for me."

"It is good then. Thou hast fulfilled thy part of the bargain. Tell thy mamma that she should brush any knots from her hair, run the remedy through it, and wash her hair after thirty minutes or so. Repeat this for a week. If the lice persist, find me, and I shall concoct a more potent remedy."

Nodding, he turns and runs off; if he does not make haste, someone may follow him home to rob him of the remedy. "Fare thee well, Sink," he says, disappearing around a corner.

I leave the alleyway. A vagabond does attempt to follow, but I know these streets better than any. *'That vagabond, I presume, was the one from Swindon. Wanted both the aqua vitae and the earthenware, it seems.'*

Finding a particularly crowded square, I slip into an alley to assure I am not being watched. I pull up my gown, yank aside my shift, adjust the bum roll, and drop the urn into a bag tied on the inside of my hoopskirt. [109] The bag has two cords that run and tie around my torso just above the bosom. This keeps them from weighing down the skirt, meaning I can stash lots of things beneath my skirt.

'Aye, try to reach for it now. Thou shalt be a fopdoodle amongst fopdoodles if thou try.'

Two hours later, enough time has passed that I return to Cripplegate. I pass by some men filling holes, stamping the ground, and other such roadwork. In England, the law requires all men to perform a certain amount of roadwork, but the nobles rarely end up doing any themselves.

I open a decrepit door into a small empty plot of land hidden behind fences. This place holds around forty small hovels thrown together by the

---

[109] Shift: Historically, a shift is a simple garment worn next to the skin to protect clothing from sweat and body oils. Women wearing underwear at the time was frowned upon.
Bum Roll: A roll of padding tied around the hip line to hold a woman's skirt out from the body in the late 16th and early 17th centuries.

unlicensed beggars, highwaymen, ruffians, and vagabonds. The fences are, of course, so people outside do not have to see the squalor within.

Moving to the outermost hovel, I knock and then enter. The stiff air hits my face as I raise my hand in greeting. "Good morrow, Old Woman Eleanor Carless."

Sitting in a rickety chair in the corner of this hovel is Old Woman Eleanor. She wears a dusty green hoopskirt, wimple, and bodice, and then a white chemise under the bodice. Though Old Woman Eleanor is not truly an old woman, she is also not a young one.

Old Woman Eleanor Careless has wrinkled skin and weary eyes but one would be mistaken if they judge her feeble. She and I are of the same ilk, meaning we endure in a city that does not desire our existence and would eagerly shepherd us beyond the lychgate. That said, she is far cruder, lewder, and more indelicate than I.

Reaching to her side, she pulls a fan from the string of her bodice and begins fanning herself. "Eleanor is more than adequate, Black," she says with a huff.

"It's Sink for today." I pause, waiting until she is about to speak, and then add, "Old Woman Eleanor."

Her fan closes with a snap, and she casts it toward me like a spear. I duck, watching as the fan flies through a hole that is just the right size for it. 'Ah, I see she still has not fixed the hole from last time.'

"Back to Forever Single Sink, are we?" she says with a forced smile.

I shrug. "Ah, that I am."

"Not even going to bother humoring me?"

"I have many names, several that are worse than 'Forever Single.' Besides, if someone does not know my real name, then they may call me what they wish."

She sighs. "Then I suppose I will simply use whatever name I please."

"Aye."

"Never understood why thou use'st the name 'Black.' Thou art nearer to a white witch than a black witch."[110]

I look through the hole the fan flew through a moment earlier. "The sun shall fade soon. May we conduct business?"

The reason I visit Old Woman Eleanor is that she is a fence or 'mover' in her own words. She purchases anything regardless of its origins and then moves it to someone else who then does the same. This continues until the item finds its way to a buyer.

She draws a second fan from her bosom and fans herself. "That's what I do, Sink. Show me what thou hast, and then I shall say what I feel like offering depending on my mood."

My eyebrow twitches. Names are one thing, but my funds for bread and ale are another.

She smirks, seeing my stiff expression.

"Then I pray thy mood is immeasurable, Lady Careless."

"Ah, didst thou bringest any more of that, what was it called, 'Stones of Immortality'?"

"That was what I attempted and failed to make. What I had was simply Paracelsus's laudanum. Furthermore, nay, I do not have any more, and I doubt I shall ever have the ingredients to concoct such a thing again. I had to substitute my own ingredients to even craft what little I did."

"Well, that is a shame—the client praised it highly. Mayhap I may supply thee with ingredients in the future?"

"Perhaps, but I am more interested in learning than concocting the same things repeatedly. Besides, I have only begun to dabble in alchemy. My

---

[110] Witches were known to either practice white or black magic. White witches were thought wise and were sought for their herbs and remedies. They would be placed on trial for the 'crime' of losing their immortal soul. Black witches were thought to cast darker magics and were placed on trial for 'crimes' against others.

teacher stated that physicians and alchemists are beginning to work together, so I am dabbling in both."

"Oh." She clicks her tongue and shakes her head. "A shame, I meant to pay thee handsomely too."

"...Well, I did not know I would be paid handsomely!" I wave my hands. "I believe we may be able to come to an agreement!"

She laughs. "Well then, we shall discuss that once I am sure I can get the ingredients. Now, tell me, what hast thou managed to borrow from the rich today?"

I raise my hand and my voice, saying, "Aye! Today I bring thee a silver candleholder, a book on the humors penned in Latin, and a farthingale crafted of whalebone."[111]

"A farthingale? Shouldst thou not keepest that one for thyself? Is it not time for thee to seek a husband?"

Dropping my hand, I shake my head. "Nay and I desire for thee to cease prodding the conversation in that direction." I reach into the bag and rub Sir Mouser's ears; he reacts to my touch with a muffled purr. "Besides, I have a companion."

"Sir Mouser, is it?" She clicks her tongue. "Are men the problem?"

"I admit I have never laid eyes upon a man who has made me swoon. I believe I am simply not the type of woman for such things."

"But I have beheld the circular letter calling for thy arrest. Thou art a bewitching woman. If thou shouldst lie with an influential enough gentleman, thou couldst be spared or at least carried away from London."

My jaw drops.

She grins and adds, "And these people are scandalous enough that I am confident they would not mind if thou bed some women from time to time. That is the trouble, is it not? Thou hast an appetite for thy fellow

---

[111] Farthingale: a hooped petticoat or circular pad of fabric around the hips, formerly worn under women's skirts to extend and shape them. Sometimes framed with whale bone.

women folk? Do not be embarrassed; it is quite ordinary. Just humor the men's egos and profess their Church in public."

"N-nay! I can appreciate both men and women, but..." I spin on my heel and prepare to depart. "That is not the problem! The items are in the usual location; I shall retrieve the coins from there."

"Well, if ending up like me is not a concern, then do whatever thou wishest. Farewell to my longest and youngest customer. Try not to end up in Bridewell or at the gallows; my business could not bear such a loss!"

Leaving the dusty squalor in a hurry, I exit the city through the quiet Bishopsgate and travel northeast through the sparse nursery gardens of Spitalfields. There I enter a tiny stone hovel veiled as an outbuilding of a burnt down building and hidden amidst a copse of oak trees. The little hovel is a simple eight-by-eight room with a dirt floor, a roped bedstead, a straw-filled mattress, and a humble brick hearth opposite the bed.

I place my canvas bag on the bed and poke at the sleeping mouser within.

Sir Mouser wiggles out and takes his usual position at the end of the bed. Tossing some black charcoal into the hearth, I crouch and use an iron poker to prod the ash around the charcoal until old hidden embers surround it. I add some twigs around the charcoal and then gradually build the fire with larger and larger pieces. Rubbing my hands together, I sigh and then remove the mortar I made the lice remedy in earlier. With the urn and mortar in hand, I walk to Sir Mouser and take my place next to him.

"Shan't be cold for much longer now, Sir Mouser." His big eyes look up at me. Smiling back, I lift his paw, dab it in the remedy, and then press it against the outside of the urn.

"...Moa," he says with evident irritation.

I laugh and pull his paw away, revealing the perfect outline of his little foot. "Henceforth, every time I am able to procure more ingredients, we shall draw upon this little vase."

He tilts his head and blinks.

Nodding, I explain, "Over the coming seasons, its surface shall grow rife in memories of our time together, and..." I sigh. "...and then someday I shall find the perfect place for it to rest... D-Dost thou still like white asphodel flowers?"

"Meow?"

"...Think naught of it." I sigh, rinsing his paw in some water, and then dip my own finger in the mixture. "Now, let us start with two memories that come to mind: the day of my tenth birthday and when I escaped Hallow Equarié to visit Lady Mouser and thee in the decrepit church."

····

·········

····

Months Later - 17-year-old Constance

A pale moon echoes through the ocean's surface. Emerald tides wash over and between seaside boulders. Waves knock against the old dockyard's barnacle-plagued pilings, and the shadows of anchored ships rock wistfully in the mid-summer fog.

In the yonder's pall, I gaze at the masts of the *Lion*, a fleet flagship keen to set sail for the New World under the command of John White and Simon Fernandes. Watchmen bearing lanterns rove its deck patrolling against would-be thieves, stowaways, and fugitives... folk such as me.

I sigh, brushing a strand of red hair that tickles my nose. My palms pet a frigid urn that I desperately endeavor to warm in my embrace. The texture of the urn's colorful paints and the vestige of the tales they whisper is where I find solace. As my fingertips trace the grooves of a wee pawprint baked unto its shell, I sigh anew and swallow life's bitterness.

Hooves clop against the cobblestone and then onto the dock. Around the corner veers a man standing atop a white stallion's saddle. An inky ostrich feather pinned to his cavalier hat and a scarlet cloak at his back flutter in the wind. The man stretches his arm, unleashing a flurry of pink flower petals, and then declares, "My Quip Acquaintance! From foreign fields, William, The Actor, has arrived at the behest of thy epistle of plea!" He hops from the horse. His high-heeled boots skid against the loose gravel, and he slides to a rest a few feet before me. "And I beseech the nature of thy imploring, milady."

"Hmm, I see thou hast received my epistle, and I thank thee for coming."
Sighing, I say, "Prithee, I require thee to distract the watchmen of the *Lion*
whilst I search for a place to stowaway in its cargo."

He stands, blinking but unmoving. "...Coffin or tomb?" he murmurs
through his teeth.

"Pardon?" I smirk. "Was that a threat?"

"It took me two days to ride to London, thou knowest? Let us not even
speak of how much time I frittered learning to balance atop a horse. I had
to take a small job trimming rose bushes to gather those flower petals, and
I walked several miles to borrow a white stallion from my father-in-law."
He scoffs and crosses his arms. "I demand applause."

"I was teasing thee." Chuckling, I clap. "It was all very impressive. I have
never witnessed anything quite like it. Well done, William. "

He narrows his eyes. "Merely impressive? Madam, my performance was
magnificent. Was it not awe-inspiring?"

I nod. "Bully-rook, William. I am profoundly awed. Thy audience shall
adore it and pass it through the ages." Raising a hand, I say, "Thou
shouldst take a bow."

He places a palm atop his heart and takes a deep bow.

I clap again, and he grins, reveling in it.

"That shall suffice, I suppose," he says, running his fingers through his
hair. His eyes stray toward the *Lion*. "Hast thou readied thy silver tongue
and brooded upon an excuse for when they inevitably discover thee?"

"Aye, I shall swear that I was kidnapped and was being smuggled
elsewhere, but the 'nappers erred and stowed me in the wrong cargo."

"Ah, that should strum the strings of pity. But! Do not neglect the
theatrical weeping and gratitude. The theatrical weeping is imperative...!
Now, shall I distract the watch?"

"...Thou hast no other questions?"

He shakes his head. "This is the sort of whimsical request I was anticipating from thee, and truthfully, I had considered doing something similar before my wife became pregnant with child. To begin life somewhere else free of accumulated burdens has always been an attractive thought. I might have joined thee a few years ago." He laughs. "I had even chosen Vinzentius, or something to that effect, as the name I would assume."

"Fascinating. Thou never noted such dreams in any of thy epistles."

"Well, thou didst not inquire about such things in thy epistles." Reaching into his jacket, he draws out a paper scroll with tiny scribbling cladding every barleycorn's breadth of its surface. "Take this." I tilt my head, accepting it from his hand. His fingers waver and struggle to release it, but he peels them away and throws back his arm. "It is done."

"What is this scroll?"

"It holds a tale I penned."

Squinting, I attempt to read the wee words. "A tale? A tale of what?"

"A tale of yearning, of scars, of melancholy, of identity..." He chuckles. "...and of letting go."

"Intriguing, but couldst thou be more specific? What is it about?"

"It's about dark sylph who dwells in a tower framed by gemstone blades stained in soot, rust, ash, and blood. To be truthful, it is a mere prelude." He smiles. "My quill fell in love with the tale's melody and danced longer than I meant it to."

I unroll a short segment of it and raise an eyebrow. "William, it's written in London Parlance. Few shall appreciate this tale; by the Crown's decree, it's not even lawful."

"When I began writing, it was a jest I meant to share with thee alone. A story that was meant to be the grandest quip ever scribed...! But, over time, it became Her tale."

"A tale that was meant to be a quip...? Penning this must have required months and months of toil, and-and this paper and ink must have demanded no paltry sum of coin. And all for a quip? If it's lengthier than a few sentences, is it even a quip anymore?"

He smiles wistfully and shrugs. "May I entreat my tale's Muse to do one thing for me?"

I sigh. "William, I am no Muse, but what is thy entreaty?"

"Plant my tale in the mud of the New World. Deliver it to the worms so that the dead and the Fates may peruse its pages. I feel they shall appreciate it as much I."

"...Thou wishest me to entomb it in the New World earth?"

Nodding, he says, "Composing it has taught me much. At twenty-two, I discovered a passion for authorship that I did not know I harbored... Alas, I have endeavored to pen new tales, yet I have a tenacious urge to return to this one. I have grown too fond of it, and that fondness has become an encumbrance. So bear it, bury it, leave it where it lies, and do not read it. I treasure it, yet it is for the eyes of none that shall breathe this morn."

"It's... a peculiar plea." I glance at the urn in my arms and undo the latches at its lid. "But also, it's the sort of whimsical request I would anticipate from thee." Gently, I slip the paper scroll into the urn and reseal it. "It shall rest alongside my friend. I see no reason they cannot share a bed."

"Aye, it is a gorgeous urn and an enchanting place to rest." He sighs. "I suppose this means we shan't exchange quips through epistles any longer. My heart aches with melancholy, I confess."

"Hmm, amusing that thou shouldst mention that now." I reach into my cloak and draw out a messy mishmash of epistles lashed together with twine. "I made use of any spare papers thou sentest through courier over the years and penned ONE HUNDRED quips in anticipation of this day."

He gasps and feigns fainting. "Dear lord! I have never beheld such a meaningful gift." With shaky hands, he takes the papers and closes his eyes as if soaking it all in. "A lifetime worth of quips... in my palms."

"Thou mayst be the sole person on this Earth that is more dramatic than I." I roll my eyes and giggle. "Peruse the quips at thy leisure, William. But be forewarned, some are so dreadful that they should not grace even the eyes of the Highest Devil Umbral... Although, others I would personally deem masterworks in the art of quips, and the dreadful makes the brilliant that much finer."

He peers into my eyes. "I love..." Hesitating, he stands hushed and frozen. With a laugh, he whispers, "I love these quips." Glancing away, he searches through the paper. "I should read one now, aye? To commemorate this moment with a farewell quip. Is there a greater honor?"

From the papers, slips a note, and he catches it before the wind can steal it.

I smirk. "Ah, it would seem a quip has found thee, hmm?"

He purses his lips. "Has it now...? Well, I suppose I shall read it aloud."

The night is quiet as he unfolds the paper and clears his throat, but he neglects to speak, his mind falling headlong into the words instead.

It reads:

William,

Sorry to dispirit thee, but this is not a quip. My years have been chaotic. Some passed in a wink of the eye, and others felt like a decade all their own. I met thee seven of those years ago. We seldom spoke, to be frank, yet I believe we had a sense of familiarity, at least, I think we did. It's challenging for me to put such things to word since I do not have many long-lasting acquaintanceships beyond those that I barter with...

Few acknowledge my existence, William. Fewer acknowledge it and do not spurn it. And fewer still acknowledge it, do not spurn it, and respect it.

I thank thee for noticing that I exist and respecting that. It is a hard existence, but it is as real as anyone else's.

Thou hast my respect William, though I would sooner die than whisper those words aloud because if I did, thy ego might grow too large and explode.

Thy Quip Acquaintance,
Constance Nightingale

He looks up. "Seven years and three years of epistles, yet thou never revealed it..." A mocking chuckle escapes him. "Thy name is Constance. Constance, keeper of the Dark Lady." His expression softens. "Constance, my Quip Acquaintance."

I nod. "Constance Nightingale is my name, William." A warm tear washes down my cheek. "Do not forget that, for if thou forgettest, then I fear... I fear none shall remember that I once existed."

A Tilted Web of Tales 3: Philosophy of Identity at Peggy's Silver Diner

∞ ∞ ∞ ∞ ∞ ∞ ∞ ∞ ∞ ∞ ∞ ∞ ∞ ∞

Lincoln Fox. Lincoln is one of the Consortium solicitors.

— A week before Lincoln's direct encounter with Constance. —

"Peggy's," a streetside signboard says, flickering yellow and struggling to light its decades-old tubes.

Each flash highlights a moment in the life of snowflakes just before they melt on the salted blacktop or slip into a drift. A seemingly cruel fate for those that dissolve in the salt. Yet, how much better is the snow drift? In the heap of flakes, are they not indistinguishable in the oppressive white noise.

If you ever find yourself in the drift, question the other snowflakes, and ask them, 'Why did we fall? Are we not forgotten the moment we hit the ground?' The others will look at you. 'Why do anything? At least we did not fall on the salted blacktop. There we melt,' they'll say. They don't know either, and they're more comfortable when no one asks. That is life in a world where the individual is one in billions... Or maybe it's life when you're ground to slush in the cold gears of corporate America.

Who the fuck knows.

I breathe a heavy sigh. The 'Peggy's Silver Diner' emblazoned on my mug draws my eye for a moment. I stare at my reflection in the greasy mug, and what stares back is a mug of indifference and exhaustion.

In front of me is the coffee-stained pages of a journal, and inside is a smudged note.

Reaching into my breast pocket, I take out a gold-trimmed pen and write.

"Psych Report: Senior Candidate: #159-AB

The days all hazily run together. Each day I watch myself go through the motions from a perspective that's tough to describe. It's like I'm living life with a greasy windowpane between me and reality at all hours of every day. Light, sound, taste, the window dampens them all.

On occasion, I know I should feel happy, sad, or angry, but my mind can't muster the energy to feel any of them. Other times I feel close to what I guess is normal, but I'm not even sure anymore. I've forgotten what normal is meant to be, so those times are what I recognize as normal now. Still, in these lapses into 'normalcy,' I can keep searching for answers and hope that whatever normal is, follows.

Except with every passing day, I become more aware of the fact that the former is overtaking the latter. My eyes are losing light, and it makes me wonder if one day I just won't wake up while my body continues life's motions the same as it always has. But the worst part is, I doubt anyone would even be able to tell the difference between that corpse and the 'person' that watches the world through a greasy windowpane.

I think the management approved summary of my feelings would be: 'I'm fine. Thanks.'

End Psych Report: Senior Candidate: #159-AB."

The back of my pen taps against the speckled tabletop a few times. I rip the paper from the journal and take a sip of warm coffee. Folding the page, I dunk it in my coffee and leave it there to dissolve into a pulpy slush.

This time I write, "Life is what I would consider normal, and I feel as I would recognize as normal," and then return my pen to my breast pocket.

Heavy metal comes on over the radio. It blares from the speakers above my booth, and each word makes my headache throb. "Yupik, we pick, Inu·HICK! Tungasugit, fuck-IT! Straight to naglik·saaġ·VIKKKK—"[112]

Reaching into my pocket, I slide a quarter into my booth's tabletop jukebox. The jukebox's pages flip as I click the arrows, cycling through its list of songs. I hit the number '22,' and the heavy metal music stops—a low alt-rock song hums in its place.

With a shake of my head, I raise my hand, finding a neon green web of veins spread across my palm. Sighing, I thump a pack of cigarettes and draw a stick from its snug home. "Thank god," I murmur. "Another second of that might have killed me."

"Sonofa!" a woman shouts from behind the diner's classic red counter.[113] "Why'd you turn off my *classic* King Zero!?"

I glance at the new song name, reading, "Young Aurora's Lullaby ~ King Zero."

"This is King Zero too," I mumble, flicking my lighter in front of my cigarette. The cigarette's end lights up orange as I take a puff. As I exhale, my headache vanishes, and the green veins on my palm tinge blue and red before sinking. "I like this song a lot better," I add a bit louder this time.

The counter doors fling open as a hefty woman stomps out. She wears the traditional diner blue blouse and has her hair tied in the classic dive-bar beehive style. "This song is from after he had kids and became just another pansy-ass square like everyone else!"

---

[112] Nagliksaaġvik [Inuit]: Place of suffering.
[113] Sonofa: Son of a bitch with omission of bitch.

Marching to my booth, she drops a plate of hobo-hash topped by two sunny-side-up eggs in front of me. She wipes her hands on an apron embroidered with the glittering words 'Love me or leave me! - Peggy's Silver Diner,' and then grabs a pot of coffee from the counter.

As she pours me a new cup of coffee, I ash my cigarette into a tray, saying, "Don't think I ordered anything but a single cup of coffee, Peggy."

Peggy raises an eyebrow. "You order the same thing every night." Slamming the coffee mug onto my table, she adds, "So don't bullshit me."

I smirk. "But I was thinking I might order my eggs over-easy tonight."

"Tough!" She spins around and stomps away. "If you put paper in that coffee too, I'll make you drink it, paper and all!"

While taking a puff of my cigarette, I organize my hobo-hash. Peggy mixes whatever she feels like into it, so I like to know what I'm in for before eating it.

I exhale a breath of smoke but pause when I think I hear a whispering next to me. Looking over, all I see is the red, crumb-covered booth. As I'm considering leaving, I hear the shopkeeper's bell hung above the diner's door ring. In walks Pierce, wearing a chocolate-colored suit.[114] He holds a manilla envelope in one hand and a comb in the other.

"Well, well, if it isn't dollar store Romeo!" Peggy shouts, cracking an egg onto the diner's griddle. "I'll have your omelet up in a second."

Pierce glances at me with a frown. "...Thanks, but I sorta wanted French toast tonight, Peggy."

Her spatula scrapes against the kitchen's griddle as she says, "Like I said, your omelet will be up in a second."

With a roll of his eyes, Pierce takes a seat across from me at the booth. "Why do we come here?" he asks.

---

[114] Shoperkeep's bell (or call bell): a bell used to alert an attendant. Usually hangs above a door and rings when someone enters.

"I come here because of Peggy." I place my cigarette in the ashtray and take a bite of my hash. "And you come here because I come here. Like most things in life, it's a loop."

"We're being mentally and verbally abused at a greasy diner; stop trying to make it sound philosophical. You always do that."

"Making mundane things philosophical can be fun depending on who the audience is."

"Well, the two people here right now aren't that audience." He glances at Peggy's lumbering figure and whispers, "More importantly, Peggy's the reason I don't think we should come here. She's evil, Lincoln. Why would you come here because of her?"

"Oh, easy question." Grabbing the ketchup, I say, "Because it can be funny when non-regulars stumble in at night."

His brows narrow. "...You mean because she patronizes them?"

"Well, not that specifically, just that they never know how to react to her... unique personality."

"Unique personality? You mean her abuses?"

"I meant it in more of a people-watching kinda way." I shrug, squirting the ketchup over the hash. "And anyway, what really won me over was the night I saw her kick out two drunks." While placing the ketchup down, I pause and ask, "Do you know what a purple nurple is?"

Raising an eyebrow, he nods. "Like a titty twister? Yeah, I know what it is."

"Well... she did that to one of those drunk guys, and..." I gesture toward my chest. "...Pierce, there was so much blood... I've never seen anything like it."

"From a purple nurple!?" he whispers. "God! Did she rip the thing off!?"

"Don't know." I shake my head while taking another bite of food. "But maybe. I saw her alley-oop something into the trash. Coulda been a nipple."

"Wait, wait, wait, hold on." He waves his hands. "Didn't you say this was what 'won you over!' How did that win you over!?"

I nod. "I usually have to be on guard in places like this, but after seeing that, I knew none of the usual troublemakers would ever mess with Peggy. That's not even the worst thing I've heard." Taking a sip of coffee, I say, "Anyway, I feel like I can relax while I'm here."

Pierce's jaw drops. "...Wait, I heard someone call her Peggin' Peggy once... Did that actually happen!?"

There's a stomp next to the table. "Got some kind of complaint you'd like to file, Romeo?" Peggy growls. A plate with Pierce's omelet drops onto the table. "Are you wantin' me to help get your sicko rocks off or something, huh? Peggin' Peggy could come back for an encore if that's whatcha want."

His mouth hangs open as he shakes his head. "No."

While walking away, she takes out a pack of cigarettes. "Then your loss, kid," she says, stomping outside to have a smoke.

Pierce stares at his omelet in silence.

Pushing my plate aside, I slide the manilla envelope over. "She's teasing you. Maybe that means she likes you," I say. "You should leave your number."

"Shut up."

I chuckle, pulling out a piece of parchment from the envelope. "Is this the invite for the event?"

"Yeah." Sighing, he grabs a fork. "The date's official too."

Flipping the invite over, I examine the inset golden logo and letters.

My thumb rubs the embossed letters and the gold foil that covers them. "So, they're officially revamping the logo with this invite."

"Yeah, it's still got the orphaney and egg, same as always, yet from now on, it'll be gold and have that cog around them. It was initially gonna be a full cog, but someone must have changed their mind at the last second. Typical upper management stuff, I'm sure."

Tapping the invite, I nod and say, "The bird is also missing its head feathers too." I slide the paper back into the envelope. "No one is going to be able to tell it's an orphanay without the head feathers and all the old colors."

"Well, the executives decided to streamline the design and the colors. Allegedly so it'll be easier to stamp it onto everything in the not-so-distant future." He shrugs. "Plus, colorful paints that are non-mineral-based will be tougher to come by in the future. I'd assume anyway."

"Probably. And I'm done eating, so..." I stand and walk toward the diner door. "... I'm going to deliver Peggy her cigarettes."

Pierce's eyes turn serious as he takes a bite of his food. "...Sure. Just remember there's no 'I' in team."

"The lower profile you can maintain, the better. Our contractor is of unknown origin and class."

"Sounds like the opposite of what I was implying." Rolling his eyes, he says, "He's clearly anomalous, but he's always been cooperative with us since we aren't really contentious. They're a religious nut, and we're a bureaucracy headquartered in a different city. We operate in different worlds."

With a yawn, I take my cigarette from the ashtray. "That doesn't change that they're a dangerous unknown."

"He's also got a history of mind games and knowing more than he should about people. He made one of our interns cry after only talking for a few minutes." Shaking his head, he adds, "I don't think even he knew some of those things about himself."

"Mhm, that's why I said you should maintain a low profile. It's better if only one of us talks to him, and honestly, I'm even a little curious about what he'll have to say."

There's a ring as I open the door and the shopkeeper's bell jostles above the door. "Freakin' masochist, man, I swear," Pierce says with a sigh. "Stop torturing yourself, and don't humor any of the guy's questions."

I step outside. The freezing air burns at my face as I relight my cigarette. "But he could have an answer," I murmur to myself with a shrug. "Can't waste the opportunity to learn something."

Walking to Peggy's side, I reach into my pocket and take out a different pack of cigarettes. "Gonna have a smoke? How addicted are you?" she asks, blowing a puff of hot air. "You're still smokin' your first cigarette, aren't ya?"

Opening the cigarette packet, I show her the twenty cigarettes inside. I reach in and pull the brown filter off one of the cigarettes revealing a bill inside. "They're all like that," I say, pulling another one.

"...Trying to 'buy' me or somethin'? A pack holds twenty cigarettes, so that's what, two-grand in there? Gonna need more than that, hot stuff," she says with a click of her tongue. "Peggin' Peggy ain't cheap."

"Actually, these aren't hundred-dollar bills." I turn one to expose the number on the side. "Ever heard of a Madison." Turning another one so she can see, I continue, "What about a Cleveland? Because fifteen Madisons and five Clevelands make eighty grand at face value, but that's just face value. These are rare bills, so you could sell them to a collector for more."

She raises her eyebrow and takes out her phone. A few minutes pass as she searches the internet for information on Madisons, $1000 bills, and Clevelands, $5000 bills. Her eyes narrow and drift toward me.

"Consortium brought in a lot of those bills before they were discontinued and phased out–they're real." Tossing my cigarette on the ground, I grind the bud into the snow with my foot. "Oh, and the money isn't for what you're imagining. All you need to do is leave the diner for the next twelve to twenty-four hours." A box truck and a black SUV rumble into the parking lot. "Starting now."

"Well, whatever." She takes the cigarette carton and trudges toward a pickup truck at the back of the parking lot. "Turn off the burners, give the kitchen a hose down if you bring in any floozies, and if you burn the place down... I will find you." She throws open her car door and stomps out her cigarette, saying, "If anything happens, you threatened me, and I wet myself and ran away."

"Sounds good, Peggy." I wave as she cranks her pickup. "See ya."

She gives me the finger while peeling out of the parking lot.

The box truck and SUV take the spot Peggy just pulled out of. A moment later, the SUV's door swings open, and a tall man steps out. The man wears a black robe and a blindfold stitched in gold.

They walk over with a smile, tapping their cane along the ground. He stops in front of me and raises a hand, despite me never having said anything. "You're with the Consortium, Lincoln Fox, correct?" they say with a smile.

I shake their hand. It's cold yet firm. "Nice to meet you, Bishop Manhattan."

"Please, you can just call me Bishop when I'm away from my fellows."

"Then, Bishop." With a nod, I gesture toward the diner. "It's freezing outside, and we have this diner all to ourselves. Would you mind coming inside and speaking?"

He shakes his head, asking, "Are you a gentleman of philosophy, Fox?"

There's a faint whispering in my ear. It's a woman's voice. Disembodied. Inaudible but able to be heard.

I narrow my eyes. "More than most, Bishop. An in-depth philosophical understanding is one of the requirements to become a Consortium Solicitor." Giving him a sharp look, I add, "Finding perspective in our thoughts can help a Solicitor avoid mental intrusions and manipulation from outside influences. Subliminal suggestion and all that. You know what I mean, yeah?"

He chuckles and nods; the whispers stop. "Well, I love philosophy, and I firmly believe the best way to know if someone can be trusted is to hear them discuss their own philosophy." With a sigh, he exhales a heavy breath that casts no fog into the frigid air. "...Would you indulge me?"

"I wasn't really expecting a debate on philosophy, but we have time, so I don't particularly mind."

"Excellent. I'll play devils' advocate to help things along." His smile grows. "So, answer this, Fox... Do you find meaning in the passing of time?"

Placing my hands in my pockets, I shake my head and answer, "Time as we know it is a social construct used to make sense of change from a human perspective."

"Oh?" His nails tap against the side of his cane. "Time is *just* a 'social construct' of mankind?"

"Well, even Einstein's theory of relativity included an assertion that space and time are interchangeable, what's called spacetime."

"Time is passing all the time. Are you sure you aren't conflating relative with subjective?"

"No, I don't think so. Einstein's theory can be taken as an addition to the claim that time is a social construct. Everything we see as changes in 'time' is actually a change in space." Glancing at the box truck, I say, "There's a popular adage that goes: Time doesn't exist, clocks exist. Have you heard it, Bishop?"

"Afraid not," he replies with an exaggerated sigh. "But... hmmm, by the logic of it, all you'd have to do is stop using clocks to live forever. So how sound is that adage of yours really?"

"It's a thought experiment. It isn't meant to be taken at face value. Taking a thought experiment at face value means the experiment wasn't really carried out, so you effectively failed the thought experiment..."

"Failing philosophy? A tough task. Some might even argue an impossible one."

I take a breath and shrug. "...That part is just my own opinion, I guess."

"Well, everyone has their own when it comes to these sorts of things." He hits his cane against the ground. "Now! This is the part where I get to know you better. What's that adage's reasoning, and what was your conclusion?"

"The reasoning is that time without conscious observation is valueless. If you look at it deeply enough, you understand the point the words are trying to make: consciousness gives meaning. If something isn't there to appreciate the passing of time, then it loses meaning. An even more common adage that makes the same point goes: If a tree falls in a forest, does it make a sound? A common question in high school philosophy that many miss the point of because they take it at its immediate face value. Of course, the tree would make a hearable noise..."

There's a rumble from the box truck as the back door slides open.

"Sorry, sorry, please go on," Bishop says, waving his hand.

With a nod, I continue, "But if something goes unheard, you could claim it never made a 'noise' at all. In other words, calling it 'sound' has no meaning, and to give it meaning, someone would have had to hear the tree fall. We could keep expanding this, but if you keep tugging at that line of reasoning, you'll find my answer to your question."

He gestures at me. "And *your* answer is...?"

I glance to the sky as blue light streaks across it. "That the meaning of life, and the role played by all of us, is to observe and appreciate the universe, and in doing so, you yourself give the universe meaning as well." Shrugging, I look back down, adding, "A bit mushy, but answers to questions like this typically are."

"Interesting. So, your answer is that life gives everything meaning and everything, in turn, gives life meaning. It's not the most scientific answer nor very spiritual; it's juxtaposed in some ways." He shakes his head with a sigh. "And what a peculiar conclusion to a question pertaining to time. There was no mention of time in your answer at all."

"Well, the question never mattered. In my opinion, all of the best philosophical interpretations lead to an answer that either develops the purpose of existence or the essence of identity."

"So, you had an answer before I even asked the question. Is that what the Consortium teaches you?" He chuckles, tapping his cane against the sidewalk's curb. Stopping, he raises a finger, asking, "Ah! But how about your second answer? Do you know the essence of identity? If so, I'd love to hear it, Fox."

"...I'm still searching for that one."

"Is that so? I believe I understand why you enjoy 'making mundane things philosophical.'"

My eyes narrow. "Funny. I don't recall you being there when I mentioned that to my partner."

"Poor, Fox." He shakes his head. "You're desperate to find your own identity, aren't you? But sometimes things are unfair like that, you know? One being might accept and know who they are from birth, while another may feel absolutely nothing from hearing even their most precious loved one speak their name in ecstasy... Yet why would they?" His hand tightens around his cane. "A name is an identity made real, but if a being lacks the essence of their own identity, there is nothing to make real, and therefore, nothing to feel... Your essence of identity could lie anywhere, Fox. From a dissociation with your own body to a past forgotten lifetimes ago. But, until you find your answer, you will remain hollow and without identity..." There's a cold wind as he points a shaking finger at me. "And that, Nameless Fox, is the grimmest of fates."

We stand there for a moment. Tapping my cigarette pack, I remove one and place it in my mouth. "...It sounds like we're both well aware of that, Bishop."

He sighs. "Yes, yes. Do you know any Hands or Palms? They're familiar with a 'doctrine' that delves into this sort of plight. Fickle, though."

"I'm not religious, Bishop." The shopkeeper's bell jingles as I open the diner door. "Are you ready to come inside and talk business?"

Gripping his cane, he nods, saying, "Your philosophy is material enough that it does not concern me. I don't see why we can't do business." The box truck shakes, and an iron coffin slides out of it. "And I've got something that can help the Consortium melt a hole into your little dilemma back at Bethesda Terrace. Ah, and before I forget. You do have the invitation we agreed would be my fee, yes?"

Chapter 27: Fairy Fingers Address the Pilgrims

∞∞∞∞∞∞∞∞∞∞∞∞∞∞∞∞

Around a half hour after I spoke to Earl, Owl stands behind his camera, tapping various things before returning his attention to me. "Okay, Miss Nightingale, just like last time, except this time our goal is slightly different. We want to discourage additional people from migrating to New York City while also suggesting that those who have already arrived move against the Consortium. So, are you ready, Miss Nightingale?"

I nod and raise my hands. The process is the same as before, with me signing a single letter at a time with Owl's help. *The Cosmic System returns, and humanity tiptoes nearer to ruin. I am the Fairy of The Tower, a granter of charity to all who are worthy. The ensuing prophecy relies on these worthy people. Humanity's avarice hinders The Tower. Beat back the walls that hold The Tower's foundation ransom. Beware the frozen water, for mighty beasts dwell in its depths and man is unready. Free the red, grant the commoners access to The Tower's location, do so, and The Tower shall provide more appropriate beasts for humankind to hunt in the city's underbelly.*

Pausing, I then progress to the next topic. *This is a message, not for the pilgrims that desire to challenge The Tower, but for those who wish to evade peril. The sleepless city shall soon pray for the luxury of rest, beasts shall prowl its streets, monsters shall lurk beneath its stone, and falsehoods will appear—false idols, potential abominations.*

We spend the next several hours composing the remaining three prophecies. Those prophecies cover three events: when I enter hibernation, the impending emergence of the other Kiln, and The Tower sprouting. The first one includes a request for people to bring pets, while the second is for when the first Kiln sprouts. As for the last one, it shall be shown a fortnight or so after I enter hibernation, depending on whether any of the other Kiln have sprouted. It also asks for people to keep three hundred feet from The Tower's sprouting location. This is because I have nary an idea how The Tower's sprouting will occur, nor do I know precisely how the leeching of Essence shall work.

I still have one more vent I can place, yet Terra and I chatted about things and agreed it was best to wait for the second vent. That way, we can observe the consequences of the first vent in the chamber pot tunnels before I consider a second.

When we finish the moving picture, Owl sits and taps away at his camera. Whilst he does whatever it is he is doing, I take a final look at the cave. *'I suppose I shan't return to the cave until after I reawake. I wonder what it will look like when it is complete.'* A fly buzzes by; I swat it away. *'Hopefully, it shan't attract flies at least.'*

"I'll begin editing it posthaste. It should be ready to share with the world in the next few hours. Once again, you did splendidly, Miss Nightingale," Owl says with a smile.

I tilt my head and wave, hoping he understands that it's a gesture of gratitude. *'Now, I suppose we shall see if it goes better or worse this time.'*

> **Earl Interface:**
> **Warning:** *A puncture has been detected in the seed's roots. An obstruction is preventing repairs.*

My arm drops to my side.

····
········
····

> **Fostered Novitiate [Mana Crunch (Grade 2)]**

Noon the next day—the day before I intend to enter hibernation.

I stand with my head poking from the RV's rooftop hatch, peeking at the multitudes of passionate people that encircle the Consortium's stronghold for hundreds of feet all around.

The masses beat against the Consortium's high fences, screaming obscenities at the Consortium people hiding behind them. Under their collective weight, the RV bounces, and my forehead bumps the roof. I brace a palm against the wall to prevent myself from tumbling down the ladder.

I shake my head.

Day and night, folk are flooding into Central Park. Not only Frisbee Hill but Sheep Meadow is congested with encampments. People are now erecting encampments to the east at Pilgrim Hill and the northeast at Cedar Hill. Consortium is overwhelmed by the sheer number of people. Terra and I are overwhelmed by the people. The people are overwhelmed by the people.

A jet of water shoots over the Consortium fence, spraying the crowds in freezing rain. This is how the Consortium has kept the masses at bay thus far. But folk have begun wearing attire that repels water, and I suspect chilly water shan't suffice for much longer.

I descend the ladder, retreating into the RV's interior. There I discover Terra reclining on the white couches. Her eyepatch is flipped up, her head is tilted back, and her eyes face the ceiling. She appears to be either deliberating or plotting something.

A purple wall appears.

> **Earl Interface:**
> **Warning:** *A puncture has been detected in the seed's roots. An obstruction is preventing repairs.*

I skim the wall, shake my head, and approach Terra. *'That is the fourth one I have received. Does that imply there are four separate punctures? I presume so.'*

Hearing my boots knock against the tile floor, Terra says, "We were able to bribe a few people to obtain some information on the Consortium's inner movements. They reported that your haze is being siphoned into canisters. They're probably going to take what they can and go. It also seems the Hex Church had more of that acid set aside and bartered it away to the Consortium."

{*I surmise the Consortium are siphoning all four haze varieties. We knew they intended to do so, so I suppose we should not be too fuddled.*} Halting a few feet away from her, I add, {*As for the acid, we cannot be certain how much of it they may have set aside before I liberated the coffin of their ownership. Will the Consortium cede control of Bethesda Terrace soon?*}

"Something like that, probably. Unless they're willing to escalate toward outright violence, but based on what I've seen, that seems considerably further than they intend to go at the moment." She ceases gazing at the ceiling, sits up, and taps on her silver tome whilst still musing. "I think we're going to have to redirect our focus from removing the Consortium to managing the people. I've got an idea in mind, but I was curious if you had any yourself?"

I nod. {Aye. I had thought we might reward choice conduct.}

Raising an eyebrow, she replies simply, "Oh, anything in mind?"

I nod. {When The Tower sprouts, I am uncertain how soon, but I shall require folk to enter. I believe we might reward people by allowing them to be amongst the first.}

"Are you already considering that far ahead?" She smirks, rests her chin in her hand, and asks, "Why not just offer to awaken them? Seems the more obvious choice."

{Well, it is not as if I have much to give besides awakening people with haze.} I take a seat on a white couch across from her. {That shan't be an incentive for everyone, though. I would imagine the most dangerous and difficult to control would be those that have awakened. Those folk are the ones we require influence over.}

"That's indeed true, and our thoughts are comparatively the same. I was going to suggest that we offer people the opportunity to awaken if they assist the camp in some significant manner. We can promote good behavior in that way. As an incentive for the awakened, they could pick someone else to awaken."

{Aye. I do not see a reason we could not do both.} I lean back, mimicking Terra's earlier demeanor, and gaze at the marble ceiling. {I cannot permit that many people into The Tower, at least initially.}

"And you are okay with offering it this soon?"

I shrug. {Allowing people into The Tower is a necessity as far as I am aware. My sole stipulation is they must be aware that there is danger and enter willingly. Then the consequences are their own to bear.}

"Of course. Then we'll set up some type of system to distribute the rewards. Maybe we can do some type of unique tokens?"

{Tokens? Like coinage...} I lower my gaze. *{I suppose it does not matter what it is, as long as they are not easily forged.}*

She nods. "And how many are you willing to commit to when it comes to allowing them into The Tower?"

{Truthfully, I would like to keep it low, yet with so many people, that does not seem practical...}

"Right. It isn't very incentivizing if the number is too low. People wouldn't believe they'd have any chance at all in that case."

{Let's say...} I pause, thinking over everything I chatted with Earl about, and then shake my head. *{Let's say, one hundred at the most and only after I have prepared things. Not straightway.}*

"Then what do you think about a maximum of... let's say six hundred tokens, all of which grant one of the earliest awakenings, but one hundred of them have the bonus of granting first entry into The Tower."

{I suppose that shan't be an issue. We should number these tokens, though. I do not believe we would be able to cope with everyone attempting to do either of those things all at one time. Not until we understand our capabilities and circumstances.}

"Yes, we'll do that. We couldn't handle six hundred sick or mad people all at once. Especially if they need oxygen like many of the mice in the experiment did. That's a limiting factor in and of itself. Besides, I'd rather you make the selection for the one hundred. That makes it more meaningful for both you and them."

{Me?} I glance outside at the people who move about, laughing and greeting one another. *{I suppose I should, although I shall be hibernating for a fortnight at least. Then I might spend some time in The Tower itself.}*

"I'll be on the lookout. If I feel someone is worthy, I'll provide you with their name and qualifications. We'll give the lesser tokens to everyone we think deserves it, but we'll allow you to upgrade them. That or you can just pick whomever." She shrugs. "If you wanted, you could even make a third tier of token for the best of the best. Regardless, I feel it should be your decision."

{Aye...} A woman carrying an infant and holding a boy's hand strolls by the window. {It is a great many people to choose from, but I agree it should be me. I should know who the first one hundred shall be.}

"I'll have the Helping Hands make the tokens and gather candidate information if you're in agreement about everything."

I return my attention to her silver and green eyes. {It's wise to give the people reason to remain calm and docile for when circumstances become graver. They have all traveled to this city for a reason; we should permit them to know The Tower is forthcoming.}

Sighing, she crosses her legs. "That's right. That's also why I think we need the canisters the Consortium wants to run away with."

{Thou dost not believe the people shall be willing to remain idle until The Tower sprouts?}

"Maybe, or maybe not. I'd prefer we didn't find out. Moreover, permitting the Consortium to leave with them means they'd have less incentive to barter with us." She clicks her tongue. "And I don't like that."

{Then, I suppose, we shall pilfer them? They belong to me, so I do not see the issue; not that I would have any qualms even if they did not.}

"Agreed." Grinning, she wiggles her eyebrows and says, "We'll perform a modest heist to retake ownership of the canisters."

{Heist? Another name for thievery, I presume. Shall we be acting as highwaymen...? Because I shan't lie, that sounds like good fun!}

She nods.

There's a knock on the RV's door, interrupting our discussion. Terra flicks her eyepatch down and changes which leg she has crossed. "Yes?"

An Escort speaks through the door. "Two men out here. They say they're Consortium Solicitors."

{Consortium!} I straighten my back and place my hands on my thighs. *{Art thou intending to allow them entrance?}*

Terra replies to me through telepathy, *{The Consortium and I have done off-the-books business in the past, and they don't kill business associates. That's bad business and leads to a lot of burning bridges. Besides...}* She smiles and then says aloud, "I think I know who it is already. Let them in."

The door to the RV swings open.

"Are you sure I can't just get your number?" a familiar voice asks.

The voice of the woman in red responds, "How about I give you the number of seconds you have before I draw my gun?"

Terra rolls her silver eye and rests her head in the palm of her hand. In strolls a familiar man, Lincoln the Consortium Solicitor. At first, he walks in with a slight smirk, yet it vanishes upon noticing me.

He raises an eyebrow. His gaze drifts to Terra opposite me, and a disheartened sigh escapes.

'Do they recognize me beyond being the Fairy? This would be simpler if they did not.'

Another man walks in, except he's walking backward, still speaking to the woman in red. This is, of course, Pierce the other Consortium Solicitor. He points at the woman in red with a chuckle. "Hey, not gonna lie, that was pretty clever."

Lincoln hits Pierce in the shoulder, prompting him to spin around. His smile fades as his arm drops. "Shit," he murmurs.

The RV's door slams shut, leaving Terra and I glaring at the pair alone. Terra sighs. "This is rather rude." Removing her black rectangle, she peers at Pierce. The black rings around her eyes shiver as she says, "Maybe I should have a conversation with your superior?"

Pierce scratches his chin. "No, uh, sorry, Galtry, we just didn't expect it would actually be you..."

"Galtry? And why didn't you imagine it would be me?" she asks, raising an eyebrow.

Glancing at Lincoln, he sighs and then says, "I'm sorry, Miss Galtry. There's no reason in particular. I'm just aware that not many people are given the privilege of speaking to you in the flesh."

She shifts her posture. "I believe I understand what you're insinuating." Her brow furrows. "Because I'm a recluse? Is that what you wish to say?"

"No, of course not." His eyes dart between Terra and Lincoln. Without Lincoln to rescue him, he responds, "Miss Galtry's natural beauty just caught me off guard. I was lost for words, that's all."

Leaning back, a deep frown comes across her face. "So it wasn't the reputation I've garnered, but something as superficial as my appearance? Is that it? Personally, I'd like to think I've grown beyond that."

Pierce opens his mouth, except before he may say anything, Lincoln grabs his arm. "Pierce, just don't talk anymore." Pierce nods and Lincoln continues, "I apologize on behalf of my coworker."

"Keep him on his leash," she scoffs. "Anyway, if I recall, it's you who came to me. What is it you want?"

"May we speak to you for a moment? We'd like to discuss the evolving situation currently taking place outside."

"And? Why would you believe I have any control over that?"

"The crowds have repeatedly shouted the phrase 'Where is Galtry.' Though you haven't acted directly, there aren't many people with both the resources and motives to pull off something like this. Most of all, the Consortium's roots run deep in the banking industry. Meaning, we are aware that you are the true owner of the Hôtel Casāle." Lincoln bows his head slightly toward Terra. "Everything points toward you, Miss Galtry, being the string-puller."

This is the first time I have seen Lincoln speak in impeccable and precise sentences. To be frank, it's surprising. He is quite intelligent and well-informed. Honestly, I consider Lincoln the second most dangerous person I have come across since I arrived. Not in a malicious sense, but if it was demanded of him by the Consortium, I believe he could be a very real peril.

"Well, 'string-puller' is practically my job description. Yet, hmm, did you say Hôtel Casāle...? Is that the quaint little hotel on the corner of 5th Avenue?" Terra chuckles. "You think I own that overpriced flophouse?"

Lincoln glances at me and then returns his attention to Terra. "Hôtel Casāle is one of the nicest hotels in New York... and yes, we know you own it. It was hidden behind shell companies and listed under the 'H.Hands,' but we were able to trace and extrapolate that both Hôtel Casāle and the Beaux-Arts Knickerbocker on 42nd Street are properties belonging to you." With a slight shrug, he adds, "Believe it or not, a corporate bureaucracy can move fast when the right people take an interest."

"The Consortium loves their corporate bureaucracy, but moving fast, I'd almost label that an oxymoron." Noticing Lincoln's glances, she asks, "Is there a reason you keep making eyes at my partner here?"

"I'm not making eyes, Miss Galtry," Lincoln says. "It's just that we've met before."

Pierce raises an eyebrow.

Shaking her head, Terra waves her hand. "No, that's impossible. She only just came into town a few days ago. Where she films her videos is quite far from the city. Now please, I expect more professionalism from the Consortium. Even if it's only skin deep."

Lincoln nods. "Miss Galtry, the Consortium would like to discuss the future of the resources buried here."

"They don't belong to you, nor me for that matter, but I'm willing to hear you out. Perhaps someone in attendance here might have the right to decide if and how they're divvied up."

Without removing his gaze from Terra, he replies, "If they've managed to get you on their side, I'm sure the higher-ups will be willing to negotiate with them."

Terra taps her fingernails against the silver tome in her lap. "I don't think they have a choice."

"I guess you're right." Lincoln chuckles.

After a short exchange of words, it is decided that Lincoln and Pierce shall return tomorrow morn to negotiate. As they walk through the doorway, Terra smiles at me. {It's as good as confirmed. They're going to begin preparing to haul the haze canisters someplace else. This is our one chance to seize them, so I need to make some calls.}

{Aye. I had a feeling thou wouldst still wish to seize them.}

Terra stands and walks into the bedchamber at the RV's back. Hearing her speaking into the black rectangle, I return to what I have primarily done since last night. This is, of course, making the map for the Pantry. I have almost settled on a design with four distinct regions. If I do it this way, it shall allow me the most diversity to experiment with.

An hour passes, and Terra and I enjoy each other's silent company.

I gaze out the window, watching a man with tan skin standing atop the frozen Cherry Hill fountain. He has straight black hair cut just above his shoulders. Despite the cold and his dignity, he does not wear a shirt, so his skin is flushed red. Around his neck, he has a strap fastened to a device that resembles a lute with cords running out of it.

Opening the window, I listen.

"Fuck you, I have nothing left to lose!" he screams. The roars of the crowd hit a fever pitch. Raising his first and making the t-sign, he rages at the Consortium stronghold. "You'll have to fuckin' kill me if you wanna stop the music!"

The crowd mimics him and chants, "King Zero!"

A fly buzzes by, attempting to enter through the window. *'Shoo!'* I slap the fly away and harken.

King Zero 'plays' his booming instrument.

The deafening noise is comparable to a horse kicking me in the temple. I shut the window and the RV becomes silent once again. *{King Zero? Is that the man from the chat room thing? I do not believe he is a genuine king.}*

"Not a fan?" Terra laughs.

I shake my head. *{Nay. It is browbeating cacophony of loud-ity.}*

"Well, many people would say differently, but everyone has their own tastes." She presses the button on the wall, and the seat embedded in the ceiling begins to lower. "Everyone is coming here. We're going to discuss stealing the canisters." She walks over to some papers, and shuffles through them. "Ah," she says, walking back to me and holding them toward me. "We ended up finding the Spirit Scribe who that yellow tome belonged to."

Reaching out, I take the paper in hand. *{That madwoman Emily was able to locate her?}*

"It wasn't hard; she had only just gotten out of the hospital." A ringing sound comes from the black rectangle. "My phone is always ringing nowadays." Tapping something on the thing called a 'phone,' she says, "Anyway, I already spoke to her. She'll be here for the meeting."

With that, she returns to the bedchamber to exchange prattle with the phone.

Looking through the paper, I see that there are only a few pages of information. It appears finding information about the person has been difficult for Terra. The most interesting bits are the handwritten notes made by Terra in regards to their meeting.

The notes read,

Ava C. Gayhardt joined the Hex Church around eight weeks back after arriving from someplace overseas. She was admitted to the Hallow Lurlann emergency room upon encountering Nightingale's vermillion haze and was discharged three days ago.

Ava is an unusual addition to the Hex Church's Manhattan congregation because she is handicapped, i.e., she is deaf and does not know sign language. It would only make sense that Ava would have been assigned to Bishop Brooklyn's Deaf-Mutes Hex Church, a church that specializes in vocal and auditory disabilities. Due to Ava's disability, she is given assignments via letters—a glaring security issue. I did attempt telepathy with Ava, but it obviously proved futile since she has never heard verbal speech before.

Ava seems temperate enough, Emily B. Pankhurst's antithesis, but she inquired about the iron coffin Nightingale took before her own tome—either has low self-esteem or some attachment to the coffin. I told her it's in my possession and that I had it relocated to one of the Galtry Syndicate hideaways, she doesn't have the means of verifying if that's true.

'It's fortunate that "Ava" does suffer any health complications after my attempt to ingest her tome. But I did not realize she is deaf and that there is a Deaf-Mutes Hex Church...?' I shake my head. 'I should do my upmost to avoid mentioning the coffin to Ava. Not that I would discuss such topics with her.'

With everyone soon to arrive at the RV, I return to my map-making.

····

·········

····

The afternoon comes.

Everyone from the original meeting gathers in the RV, excluding the Escorts who are outside keeping watch, and Owl, who is busy working. We have one new addition—Ava, the Spirit Scribe and owner of the yellow tome. Ava has bandages swathing her fingers from whence she clawed at the Arcade's walls when it was enveloped by vermillion haze. Her hair is flaxen blonde, straight, and shoulder-length. Unlike Ava and I's first encounter, she wears bright winter attire and reading spectacles. Fabric is sewn into part of her wrist and nape, where it runs into the collar of her shirt. She has pale unblemished skin, aqua blue eyes, and wears a hairpin that resembles a white mouse with long whiskers. Her slender body exhibits traces of earthly hardships, notably recent scars cladding her palms, and like most adults of this time, she is taller than me.

For reasons that elude me, Ava has chosen to sit unusually close to me, a hand's length at most.

Terra has been able to gather more information during the hours between meeting Lincoln and Pierce, and now. The most noteworthy being that the Consortium plans to transport the canisters elsewhere shortly before their audience with Terra. So an hour or two before daybreak. This was found out by Jessica and Leo, who also said the noble's police is meant to escort the canisters after they depart the park. Evidently, the people are barring any noble's police rides that attempt to enter.

We have discussed how the theft of the canisters shall proceed and are now reviewing our plans. Terra shuffles through more papers, preparing to speak. Ava glances at my whiteboard and then at me. I look over because I cannot suffer this much longer; she has been stealing glances since arriving. Squinting, she raises a hand and makes a talking motion.

I shake my head and write, "Nay, I cannot speak."

There's a flicker in her eye. She nods but does not attempt to communicate further.

On my opposite side is Emily, who is adamantly seeking my attention by waving her hand in my periphery. I am not eager to speak to her, so I wait to see if she shall persist. Yet, a few minutes thereon, her enthusiasm for my attention proves tenacious, so I surrender and turn my head.

"It's good to see you again," she says, her eyes looking between Terra and me. "I wanted to apologize for what I did in the past and for insinuating anyone 'owned' you. After a very... terrifying talk with Galtry, I understand that you are your own person and not something to be 'enslaved.' I won't try to dominate or contract you again."

'I thank thee... I guess.'

Terra begins to speak. "Fairy, tell us the role you'll be playing."

I write, "I shall post an announcement early tonight. After which, I shall take position across from Pilgrim Hill to spy upon the Consortium and ensure there are no unforeseen occurrences."

"Announcement?" I hear Jessica whisper.

The announcement is about the tokens. Terra wishes for me to be unclear, so it sounds as if it is a grand proclamation. It is merely some signs.

"Hoarse?" Terra says, ignoring Jessica.

"I'm going to be dressed in some 'lovely' black robes." Leaning back, Hoarse sighs. "My job is to remove the tracking device the Consortium puts on everything. I've sold some of their shit in the past, so I know what it looks like. Then I'll put a new license plate on it."

'This is the cleverest bit, in my opinion. The "heist" makes it appear as if the Hex Church is responsible for the whole thing. We hope this undermines the relationship between the Consortium and the Hex Church, giving us an advantage.'

Terra gestures for Lorcan to come forward. Carrying a white box full of black frocks and what resemble tomes, he walks out from behind Terra. The frocks are genuine, but the tomes are "practice tomes" for Spirit Scribes. Their purpose is to teach the Spirit Scribes how easy it is to lose or have their tomes pilfered if they are not wary of their location at all times. Supposedly, it's common for them to carry these practice tomes around whilst other Spirit Scribes attempt to swipe them when their backs are turned.

Dropping the white box onto the marble table in front of Hoarse, Lorcan lifts one of the frocks. "And I'll be with Hoarse, outfitted in one of these bad boys that may or may not include underwear under the skirt." He laughs, punching Hoarse's arm, who looks embarrassed by the thought of wearing the frocks. "I'll be steering the box truck that has the canisters onboard to the safe house, and since it's a box truck, it shouldn't be self-drivin'."

While Hoarse runs a palm over his face, Terra shifts focus to Emily. "And you, Charm."

Sitting up straight, Emily replies at high speed, "I'm gonna be with Hoarse in disguise; well, it's not a disguise for me. Anywho, I'll be hexing the driver!"

Terra peers at Ava. Ava refused to pick a nickname or take a whiteboard to write with, so she has merely been watching and reading everyone's lips or, in my case, reading my whiteboard. Ava points at Emily and then at herself.

With a frown, Terra sighs and replies, "Right, you won't have your tome, but you'll be doing the same as Charm, using your quill to hex the passenger if there is one." She keeps her eyes on Ava for a second longer before turning toward Jessica and Leo. "Angel and Savior?"

Leo nods and explains his and Jessica's role. "We will be erecting a barricade an hour before departure. We'll then attempt to keep any officers or civilians from approaching, assuring them it's for their own safety."

"And, of course, while you're all doing this, I'll be here meeting with the two Solicitors." Things remain quiet as Terra glances between the many faces and then asks, "Any further questions before we separate?"

Everyone shakes their heads, excluding Hoarse, who raises a finger and asks, "What if we get caught? What then?"

"Don't get caught," Terra says curtly. "Any other questions?"

Sweat drips down Hoarse's forehead as he sinks back into his chair.

As there are no further questions, Terra waves her hand. "Everyone may leave. Go home, get some rest, and be back here at 2 A.M. If anyone doesn't show, I'll find you myself. If anyone betrays me, not only will you suffer the consequences of the contract we signed, I'll drop your body in the Lake to be eaten whole."

Everyone nods with zeal, except Jessica, who glares at me and moves to the exit. 'Probably still believes I did something to my vermillion self.'

Ava stands; she also stares at me. Getting out some type of paper, she taps on it and places it on my whiteboard before following Jessica and Emily out. I watch her leave and then lift the paper that reads, "Deaf, Mute, and Hard of Hearing ASL Society." Affixed to it is a note: "I don't know anyone. o(╥﹏╥)o Nervous to go alone. Can we go and learn together? (╯︶♣)" and then some incomprehensible number that says, "Text Only ૬•ﻬ•?" next to it.

'...?' When everyone has left, I stand and hold the paper where Terra can see it. {What does this... what is this?}

Taking it in her hand, Terra reads it. "She wants you to go with her to a group for people with hearing and speaking difficulties. Presumably, one that has a focus on sign language. I guess she wants to learn sign language and doesn't want to go by herself."

{Oh, I doubt I shall be able to attend that.}

"Not the safest idea, given the circumstances. Speaking of which, from now until your hibernation, I'm going to have two Escorts accompany you everywhere you go."

{But...}

She crosses her arms and shakes her head. "Sorry, but I refuse to budge on this. It's too dangerous for you to not have them with you. I have two coming in right now. They're well-rested and have volunteered to stay with you for the next twenty-four hours."

{...But I do not know their names.}

The door to the RV swings open and two Escorts enter. Terra returns to a more serious demeanor and glares at the two. "Neither of you have introduced yourselves to Fairy. Quit being rude and do so immediately." The woman in red opens her mouth, but Terra interrupts her. "Give her your real names. She's not going to recognize them."

'Recognize them? Are they famous harlots?'

Chapter 28: A Promise Kept, a Plan Executed

∞∞ ∞∞ ∞∞ ∞∞ ∞∞ ∞∞ ∞∞ ∞∞ ∞∞ ∞∞ ∞∞ ∞∞ ∞∞ ∞∞

My cattail slithers into the RV's frost-bitten pantry, also known as a 'refrigerator' or, as Lorcan tells me, 'gerator' for short. I encoil a frozen turkey at the gerator's back and then peek about to ensure none see. In one swift movement, the cattail yanks the fowl into my embrace, and I tiptoe to the marble table. *'Thievery! I have stolen this turkey and have therefore robbed it of its rightful owner... I PRAY it does not stoke my Title's effect... and taste so... soo delectable. Oh, prithee, do not make me suffer such justifiable consequences...!'*

I engulf the turkey. Average. It tastes average.

Since my contract with Terra, I have been dining on sandwiches and turkey and refining Nebula and Vitrum when not employing my mana elsewhere. The turkeys are still not as flavorful as the pilfered meat from the Boathouse. I gaze at the RV's magnificent ceiling, fantasizing about the flavor of that erstwhile feast. *'Would folk notice if a feast or two began vanishing from their camps...? I think not!'*

> **Earl Interface:**
> Assimilating 'Broad-Breasted Turkey'
> Erysichthon falls to zero.
> Essence value 0
> 0.5 Refinable Nebula
> 0.1 Refinable Vitrum
>
> **Details:** An 'average-tasting' fowl that typically spends most of its time grazing on the forest floor, imbuing itself with a taste some might describe as 'average.' Native to the Colossi continent, this variant is unawakened to mana, though it is not 'Mana Bare.'
>
> **Note:** This fleshling has had much of its Essence siphoned.

'Do not mock me, Earl.' I dismiss the wall. 'And the turkey is not even worth Essence.'

Terra informed me that many organizations have their people toil in slaughterhouses, butchering animals like turkeys and absorbing their Essence. Since assimilating merely squeezes out leftover Essence from carcasses, I only obtain a sliver of Essence from a corpse that someone in the Cosmic Beta slaughtered and siphoned.

'The eventide heist looms, so I should not loll about.' My eyes float toward a brown bag at the table's edge. Sliding it toward me, I withdraw a giant white mushroom. If I had to speculate, it weighs at least a pound. 'I cannot believe it was a mushroom this entire time. I suppose I was eating with such fervor I did not even notice.'

Pushing the cattail through the hole at my neck, I break the mushroom in two. I engulf one half, and it bubbles into a bitter, milky haze.

Earl's wall appears.

> **Earl Interface:**
> Assimilating 'King Oyster'
> Erysichthon abates 4
> Essence value 0
> 0.1 Refinable Nebula
> 0.2 Refinable Vitrum
>
> **Details:** A non-poisonous fungus known for its size and resemblance to bivalves. This fungus has not awakened to mana, though it is not 'Mana Bare.'

Examining the name, I shake my head. 'Verily, it is a mushroom. I suspect Earl thought herself clever for dubbing the adaptation "Rife Pearl."' Terra had the mushroom brought in from Europe for me; apparently, it's not as common due to the world's circumstances. 'I appreciate Terra, but I loathe mushrooms.'

Returning the mushroom to the bag, I slide it away from me. I have had to be careful with the amount of food I ingest due to the paste. If I create another monster, like the Wretched Rat, it could create havoc in the camps. Though I admit, the dinosaur has been placid. It appears more interested in guarding its lake than attacking me. Besides that, since I wear an arc suit now, I must be mindful of my paste or risk having it inside my suit. I would rather not have a monster burst from my suit someday.

Leaning back, I think, *'Earl, prithee, the rife pearl adaptation.'*

Earl Interface:

Vaporous Form Germination Tier Adaptations

Available Miscellaneous Adaptations

Rife Pearl
(Recent Meal: King Oyster)
Encase and store rife paste within a pearl-like repository. Pearls can be used to feed, mutate, and awaken animals or plants that have not been introduced to mana prior—a maximum of five pearls can be made before they naturally fall from the kiln.
[Cost: 41 Essence + 2.3 Refined Nebula]

Essence Available: 111 [R = 59%]
Refined Nebula Available: 7.2 [4.3]
Refined Vitrum Available: 6.5 [3.6]
Refined Acerb: 0.8 (0.0)

I confirm the adaptation's information and then my amounts of materials. *'So I have been able to stow away the most Essence, Nebula, and Vitrum I have ever possessed... by eating turkeys. I shan't complain. This has been a boon... Wait. The Rife Pearl adaptation costs more now? That is a wee bit irksome. Nevertheless, I shall take the Rife Pearl adaptation, Earl.'*

I do my utmost to watch the adaptation develop, but it is tricky to observe whilst wearing my arc suit. The flame appears to brighten, and the outside layer of the shell dissolves, coalescing into a small orb. As the flame's gleam wanes, the sphere glides outward and revolves around the shell's exterior. I summon my Status; my adaptations now include "Rife Pearl (1 / 5)."

I nod, retrieve the papers I shall require for the evening, and then perform a search, scouring the RV for Terra. Failing to find her, I give Gen a scratch behind his ear, retrieve the coat I have been using these past few days, and depart the RV.

In the cold of night, two Escorts that I learned are named Summer and Noah approach and take a position on my left and right. These two are the original woman and man in red, respectively. I was informed the other four Escorts' names are Erin, Ruby, Storm, and Devon, though I do not know who is who.

Shutting the RV's door, Summer, Noah, and I trod through the snow toward Frisbee Hill. The pair do not talk much; they may require a moment to grow more accustomed to my company.

Terra's voice speaks into my head. *{I wanted to hang the signs with you.}*

I glance left to right. Spinning around, I spot Terra approaching. Tonight she is wearing a puffy white coat, violet veil, and a pair of this era's traditional blue trousers. At her sides and back walk the four other Escorts with sharp, watchful gazes.

Terra stops a few feet away. Noticing a faint rosiness on her cheek, I ask, *{Hast thou been drinking?}*

{I...} She runs a hand through her silver hair, maintaining her Galtry demeanor. Yet, in my head, her words are stiff. *{Is it obvious...? How can you tell?}*

Circling my own face with my finger, I then point at hers. *{Thy cheek is blushed, though I was uncertain if it was drink or the frigid air. Is this an appropriate time to be partaking in such things?}*

{No, not really, but I only had one glass of red wine. I don't have much of a tolerance since Caldwell rarely bought me wine, but Lorcan and the Escorts did my recent shopping. They bought enough to stock a pantry.}

{Why...?} I tilt my head. {Dost thou hast a drinking habit? Is that way Caldwell rarely bought thee wine?}

{No, I'm not twenty-one. Caldwell sometimes doesn't seem to realize he works for me. Lorcan and the Escorts, on the other hand, don't seem to realize I'm not a raging alcoholic.} She sighs. {Anyway, I wanted a glass to celebrate our bringing of the Consortium to the negotiating table. It's a huge accomplishment.}

{Aye. But what dost thou mean 'not twenty-one?'}

{Yeah, I'll be twenty in a few weeks, and the legal drinking age is twenty-one.}

{Legal drinking age? What is that?}

{It's not important, especially with the way the world is heading. Now, let's enjoy a single moment of peace together, yea?}

{But thou must meet with the others before the theft, aye? Not to mention Lincoln and Pierce?}

{The others can wait a moment and the meeting with the Consortium is still hours away. Besides, this will only take a second; all we're doing is hanging up a notice in disguise.}

{That's true... Oh, I have meant to ask, why am I the one hanging the signs? If I am in disguise, does it matter who does it?}

{Did you forget?} Feigning a huff in my head, she replies, {We promised to hang signs together a few weeks ago and never did. I was looking forward to it too.}

I make a questioning squint with my eyes but then realize what she is speaking of. {Ah, thou meanest the Lake's warning signs. We did not place them because we were interrupted, and in the end, they were unneeded due to the Consortium's arrival.}

{That's right. Time to do as we said we would.} She strolls by me, gesturing for me to accompany her.

Shrugging, we walk together while the six Escorts take position behind us.

{I want to hang some of my students' drawings while we are there too.} She holds up some papers with rough drawings on them. I recognize them; they are the ones her young students made. They certainly look like they were made by children. *{I think it's funny. They'd be excited to see them hanging up.}*

{Aye. They are still appropriate too, I suppose.} I glance at the Lake. *{There is indeed a monster in the Lake, just as there was then. I am certain thy students would be delighted to see them being put to use.}*

Nodding, she smiles and adds, *{When I've finished wresting control of the Galtry Syndicate, I'm going to go back to get them. Then I'll show them that I hung them up like I said I would.}*

'*...Now that I recall, she did say once that she had people she wanted to protect. Is that who she was speaking of?*'

Terra seems lost in thought after that, so the walk turns quiet.

Arriving at an area near "The Falconer" statue, we come upon a makeshift signboard. Instead of being a signboard fastened to two posts and staked into the ground, it is instead a signboard suspended on chains and joined to a modest wooden trestle. The signboard itself is rather long; it could hold at least twenty of our notices, and I shall be making use of a small piece of it. The whole thing was erected by an assortment of carpenters from the camp a day or so ago.

The unique thing about the signboard is the big devices belted to the top called "loudspeakers." Those were purchased by Terra and also placed by the carpenters. She intends to install several of these around the camps. When I asked about them, the carpenter remarked, "They make things louder," and that was as much detail as I was offered. I suppose sticking a note to their hammer while they were actually using it was not the politest way to ask.

{Space them out so people won't crowd around one spot. Oh, and here, use this to attach it,} Terra says, reaching into her pocket and then giving me some tacks to hang the signs with.

I place my hand on the back of the board to prevent it from swaying. While Terra hangs her student's drawings, I attach the notices.

The notices were composed by Terra and me to match my 'speaking habits,' and I signed them afterwards. All three read as follows:

Notice!

To all who shall brave the challenges of The Tower, The Tower shall provide for thee.

On the morrow, an opportunity of a lifetime shall make itself bear for six hundred individuals. Over the forthcoming weeks, six hundred tokens shall be gifted to those that lead by example—displaying sincerity, virtue, and promoting unity amongst thy fellows.

Five hundred of these tokens will entitle thee a chance to be at the forefront of the awakened, joining the Beta earlier than the vast majority of humanity, or Toba Humanity to be precise.

To the most promising one hundred, a more fabulous treasure shall be bestowed. The One Hundred shall both be granted the privilege to awaken and be amongst the first to delve The Tower's depths, the foremost to apply their hand. All of these individuals shall be amongst the finest and shall be remembered as such from here forth.

Tokens shall be redeemed to the one who shall 'speak for the speaker.' Who that is will be evident in the future.

Best wishes, Pilgrims.

The Fairy of The Tower

I intended to omit the word "pilgrim"; however, Terra believes it makes The Tower seem closer to a sacred place. She went on to say that tomorrow is the Thanksgiving holiday, so "pilgrim" was also festive. Her reasoning was not very convincing until I learned that some people are competing for campsites on Pilgrim Hill to the Terrace's east, going as far as fighting in some cases. They claim it is a special because I used the word "pilgrim" in my latest prophecy. I only said it because it felt appropriate; I do not care for the word myself.

'I wonder if Terra would deem me one of these 'pilgrims' everyone has romanticized. Verily, life was naught like they seem to imagine it was.' Glancing to the side, I see her smiling at one of her students' signs. My eyes drift upward, and I watch the cloudy night sky. 'For Roanoke's townsfolk, life was incessant hardship; for me, it was peaceful enough. The natives and I had forged a unique acquaintanceship, and I was rather accustomed to hardship... I still have not spoken to Terra about Roanoke, not by name or in detail.'

{You know, I never did tell you what the other contract I made was, did I?} Terra's voice asks in my head.

{Oh.} Removing my gaze from the sky, I shake my head. {Nay, thou didst not.}

{It's one I made with my father's husk. I had to make a contract with a spirit before my twentieth birthday, or I would be forced to grow apathetic toward the students.}

{Apathetic?}

{Essentially, I would lose the emotional capacity to care about them.} She smooths the edge of one of the signs. {But the real kicker was, there weren't any spirits around to contract with, and he knew that. I am not positive what he was trying to accomplish, yet it is one more thing I resent him for.}

I study Terra's expression and then some of the drawings her students sketched. {...That sounds like an abominable stipulation, I shan't lie.}

{So, I just wanted to say thank you. I wasn't entirely confident, but it turned out that Kiln do count as spirits.}

{Oh? Then it is resolved...} Scratching the side of my glass helmet, I tilt my head. {I did not do anything, though I am glad I was able to assist.}

{You have done more than anyone for me... Now, let's place the final cornerstone on our little area of the park here. How does that sound to you?}

{It sounds wonderful; I am eager to finish things.}

She nods. {*Then I'll see you after my meeting is concluded.*}

{*Aye, I foresee nary a reason it should not proceed smoothly.*}

{*Yes, either way, we are both protected.*} Raising an eyebrow, she asks, {*And are you sure you won't come to the meeting?*}

{*I shan't, not this one anyway. If I go, I will be a distraction, and I am certain they shall endeavor to use the opportunity to learn more about me and the situation here. Besides, a contract cannot be forged until after The Tower sprouts, since we are ignorant of the amount of haze we can offer them at the moment.*}

With a slight smirk, she walks away along with her Escorts. {*Alas, I guess I will have to do the boring part alone then. See you soon.*}

{*Fare thee well, and if that Gary fellow is there, tell him that sometimes a few words can do the work of many.*}

As she disappears below the hilltop, I witness her shaking her head at my advice.

I gesture to Summer and Noah; we skulk away as well.

In the distance, I hear someone yell, "Hey! Hey! There's something from the Fairy on the board!"

We trudge through the snow until we are around a thousand feet east of the signboard.[115] There we come upon a structure I am familiar with. It is a stage made of marble, something I came across the day I arrived at the Terrace. This is where I shall be observing the Consortium from. It's also near where I shall be fulfilling the second prophecy tomorrow before hibernation.

Gazing toward the Arcade and Terra, I cannot see much. The Consortium has closed off the backside of the Arcade as well. This is the side I originally entered from, the side opposite the fountain and lake where a single grand staircase leads down into the Arcade.

---

[115] | Thousand feet | 304.8 meters|

Still, this is where the canisters are meant to be loaded. After they are loaded, we expect they will move their ride onto the roadway that runs above the Arcade, and then they shall take a right turn. They will then travel a few hundred feet east, where they will come upon the barricade erected by Jessica and Leo.

"There's a heater over here. We can use this as a position to warm up while we make rounds around the Terrace," Summer says, pointing toward a device upon the marble stage. Looking at the device herself, she lifts an eyebrow and frowns. "Noah, you were supposed to cover the heater with its case so it wouldn't get too damp."

'I guess the cold has relaxed them a tad.'

Noah raises his arms, gesturing toward the heater. "I was gonna, but there was like a big ass mushroom growing on the case. It was gross; no way was I touching it."

'Mushrooms do tend to sprout quickly overnight. Must be careful. They could be poisonous.'

"Mushroom?" She scoffs. "Dude, there's no way; it's like twenty degrees. Where'd you put it?"

Raising his hand, he gestures toward a thicket. "Girl, I flung it in the snow somewhere with a stick. I'm telling you, though, it was like a fat yellow mushroom. It was like the sort of gnarly mushroom you'd see on the cover of a wildlife magazine at the gas station... It almost looked like a big cheese puff! I don't know. It was just gross, okay?"

"Just whatever, crank up the heater before it gets too wet to turn on."

I shrug. Warm, cold, unless it is an actual fire, I cannot feel it. As far as cold goes, I have never felt it as a Kiln, or more accurately, it is all I feel. It's strange the things one can become accustomed to. The heater device clicks, and an orange flame springs up.

Noah smiles at Summer.

"Shut up," Summer says.

To appear more human, I walk to the flame's side and place my back to it as one would a glowing hearth.

Time passes as the three of us watch the Consortium movements. The park becomes quiet as the people return to their encampment, and soon, it is time for the actual theft.

A torch illuminates the area at the top of the Arcade's grand staircase. Hearing the metallic clicks of canisters bumping against one another, I gesture toward Summer and Noah. The three of us move through the snow toward Pilgrim Hill. We are going to take a position between Pilgrim Hill and the Terrace. The likelihood of the Consortium taking a left instead of a right is almost nil. This is because the roadway to the left has not been cleared of snow and people have placed several of what I am told are called barbecues in the middle of it. The barbecues shan't be going anyplace; what's essential is that Jessica and Leo set the barricades in the opposite direction.

Arriving at the designated location, we instantly notice something is not right. "Where is the barricade the cops were supposed to put up? Did those pigs really backstab Miss Galtry?" Summer asks, outrage evident in her voice. "Could they be so stupid?"

"Do you really think they would?" Glancing between Summer and I, Noah asks, "With the contract and all?"

Terra informed me that the contract they signed was not reciprocation; it was a subordination contract. This fixes Terra above them; however, this type of contract is more restrictive when it comes to stipulations and punishments. In this case, the punishment for attempting to reveal secrets is extreme pain and a temporary inability to speak. If it is something worse than that, the punishment is crippling pain and loss of the right eye. Anything more would have taken a toll on Terra, who had performed a taxing lifetime reciprocation contract with me that same day.

I shake my head and remove my yellow sticky paper. "Nay. I do not believe they would. It does not make sense for them to do so," I write.

As I pass my message to Summer and Noah, I recognize Leo hurrying over with a pair of long wooden barricades. He abandons one, drags the other onto the roadway, and places it. With haste, he retrieves the second one and repeats his previous actions. Looking left to right, he hesitates before running away.

'*That seemed odd.*'

Noah raises a hand. "Well, I guess he didn't betray Miss Galtry, but what the devils was up with that?"

"Looked like he was searching for something," Summer responds. After Summer's words, the ride transporting the canisters departs from the Arcade. "At least they didn't screw up the operation; the truck didn't seem to notice him."

As expected, the ride, a so-called truck, moves onto the roadway, swings right, and approaches the barricades. I examine the area around the Consortium stronghold. As long as Lincoln and Pierce went to the meeting with Terra, everything should go fine.

The ride stops at our barricades.

A man lowers his carriage window, pokes his head out, and gestures off toward flickering red and blue lights in the distance. The passenger, the man sitting on the right side, opens his carriage door. Careful not to slip on the icy roads, he shuffles over to the barricades, complaining the whole time he does so. His partner, the driver, watches him. They fail to notice Hoarse approaching their truck from the rear.

Removing something from his coat, Hoarse wedges it into a pipe at the truck's tail, blocking the white smoke it usually spews.

"Blocking the exhaust." Summer points at the driver. "They're gonna try to get the other guy out of the truck or at least get the engine to stall." Hoarse dips beneath the truck to search for the device that tracks its movements. "Still, he's either stupid or overly confident."

"Seems like the sorta guy who's been run over a time or two," Noah adds with a high chuckle.

I shrug. '*I have hidden beneath moving carriages before. To either hide, steal, or on one occasion, travel.*'

A woman stumbles out of the bushes with her head down, appearing disheveled as if in distress. This woman is Emily.

Emily collapses onto the roadway, and the passenger pauses and shouts something. When she does not respond, he tosses the barricade from the roadway and shuffles over to her. With the barricade removed from their path, the truck rolls forward. Hoarse latches on to the truck's bottom and is dragged along.

The truck rolls, coming to a gradual stop. At the same time, the passenger reaches Emily's motionless form. Bending down, he is about to tap her on the shoulder when Emily seizes his wrist. Threads, like twine, stitch themselves into the passenger's arms.

From the bushes on the opposite side of the roadway, Lorcan rushes out. He reaches the driver's window and shatters it with a pair of metal knuckles. Being awakened, Lorcan is much faster than the driver. He wraps his arms around the driver's neck and yanks him from the truck.

Without the driver, the truck rolls toward Emily and the passenger at a footpace.

Ava follows Lorcan out of the hedges. While Lorcan restrains the driver, Ava removes a quill from her frock. Her quill falls from her bandaged fingertips. A puff of hot air exits the hood of her frock as she huffs and retrieves it from a slush pile on the roadway. After inspecting the quill's tip, she scribbles something upon the driver's forehead in dark black ink. She pulls back her sleeve, exposing her wrist. Threads shoot from the cloth stitched to her wrist and sew themselves into the ink.

When the stitches have finished, the ink on the driver's forehead trickles like raindrops into his eyes, painting them black. '*A direct hex that apparently lasts until the ink on the forehead is smeared and persists for a few minutes thereafter. It makes him blind.*'

Ava then races toward the truck, kicking up an icy slurry as she does so.

As for the passenger, the threads finish sewing themselves into his body and vanish. The passenger's legs buckle and he sinks to the ground. Emily leaps to her feet and hurries from the truck's path. She slides on the icy roadway, barely catching herself.

Hopping onto the truck, Ava opens the carriage door and jumps in. The truck wobbles back and forth and skids to a halt, much to Emily's relief.

Meanwhile, Hoarse draws himself out from beneath the truck. He stands and inspects what resembles a small black box before flinging it further up the roadway.

Summer shakes her head. "That was the tracking device."

"He knew exactly where it was; he's done this before," Noah replies, rolling his eyes. "Frequent carjacker this guy."

Hoarse removes the object he shoved into the pipe earlier and shuffles over to the driver that Emily sent falling to the ground. He flips him onto his front, removes cordage from his coat, and uses it to tie the driver's arms and legs.

After Hoarse places him in a sitting position, Emily removes a quill from her coat and scribbles more writing onto his face. She rips the bandage from her face, revealing the cloth she tore from her cheek weeks earlier has grown back. Threads stream from the fabric into the writing. Drops of blood drip from Emily's cheek, so she replaces her bandage, leaving the bound passenger with writing on his forehead and cheek.

Noah presses his lips together and asks, "How bad do you imagine that hurts?"

"She didn't seem like she was in pain," Summer replies.

Meanwhile, Lorcan has tied the driver. Hoarse and Lorcan tie the two men together and leave them sitting in the middle of the roadway, surrounded by the barricades. All of them climb into the truck and steer northward, away from the Consortium and the noble's police to the east.

From behind us comes the crunch of snow. Summer and Noah remove their weapons. In tandem, the three of us spin around, discovering the reddened face of Leo.

"Someone took Jessica!" Leo says, gesturing to the groves of trees behind him.

Summer's brows furrow. She glances at Pilgrim Hill and then questions, "Who? People from the camps?"

Leo raises his arms while shaking his head. "I don't know, someone! If I knew, I'd already have gone to get her!"

"How do you know? Are you sure?" Noah asks, narrowing his eyes.

"Well, I felt it was pretty obvious when she was close by and said 'someone's over here,' then I couldn't find her two seconds later!"

"Have you tried calling her?"

With a mocking laugh, Leo says, "Call her! What kinda idiot brings their cell phone when they're committing a crime?!" He sighs. Rubbing the bridge of his nose, he answers his own question, "More than you'd imagine, actually. We arrest a lot of people like that. Anyway, I need your help looking. Calling this in would be bad; we aren't supposed to be on duty right now."

Summer and Noah glance at one another and then turn to me.

Frowning, Summer says, "Every once in a while, a girl would get into the wrong set of wheels, and they'd never be seen again. Cops never investigated, never went searching for 'em. Lots of my friends I just *never* saw again, and we were expected to accept it for what it was... Y'know, I've always thought the fuckers probably grew bold and used it as practice before they kidnaped and murdered the Puzzling Five Hundred... Any thoughts, officer?"

Leo's mouth falls open in disbelief.

"He's not sayin' nothing, but it's true," Noah says, wiggling his eyebrows. "Some even thought the cops were protectin' their crooked pals and raunchy uncles when that happened. And after some of the things I've been through, I'd be more surprised if that wasn't the truth."

"You're both acting like I'm asking you to assault a mobster's hideout in your underwear." Leo raises a hand in clear bafflement. "I just want you to stroll around the park like normal human beings while turning your head from side to side!"

Summer raises her arms and scoffs. "Is there a kidnapper or did she just get lost? Because the way I see it, a kidnapper on the loose is serious business, and I'm supposed to be safeguarding a VIP here," she says, gesturing toward me.

I glance at the heist scene in the distance.

A pair of Consortium men race from their stronghold toward the driver and passenger. As soon as they reach out to touch them, a secondary hex composed by Emily activates, entangling the pair in a snare and knocking them to the ground.

I pen a message and display it to the three. "I have my own grievances in regard to those that brandish the boot, but our business is concluded here and..." My eyes turn to Summer and Noah as they read the latter sentences. "I hope my compatriots may understand why I might want to take heed of my fellow women. I do not mind scouring the area, yet I am unwilling to seek her for long or wander very far from here. Where didst thou separate from her?"

Chapter 29: The Greedy Kiln, Complacent in Her Crib

∞ ∞ ∞ ∞ ∞ ∞ ∞ ∞ ∞ ∞ ∞ ∞ ∞ ∞

Whilst gaping at an inexplicable statue that claims to be dedicated to a man, William Shakespeare, I point and then write, "Why does the crude-humored William have a statue? Did he commit a crime worthy of being passed through the ages? Mayhaps bedded someone of significance in his later years?"

"...Uhm, I have no idea." Noah leans closer to my message, making certain he is reading it correctly. "All I know is I wouldn't call him 'crude-humored.' I've never smirked, much less laughed, at anything he's written in my life."

"Yeah, well, he's still a very well-respected writer and playwright," Summer says, watching Leo.

I eye the statue of William standing in a commanding stance. *'...Writer and playwright? William was a proud bawdy and actor who would occasionally perform for the amusement of drunkards.*[116] *He did compose that one story, yet... frankly, I feel William would be upset that he is not known as 'The Actor.' I... I am uncertain how to feel about this. Perhaps this is not the William I am acquainted with at all. Aye. This statue is far too broad-shouldered and imposing to be William, but I shall investigate this more later.'* Giving up on understanding... whatever this is, for now, I pen a message for Leo. "Repeat everything once more."

He takes a breath and points off toward where, if I recall, the carousel is. "We were going back to the car to get another cup of coffee near the capybara bubble tea place and carousel, and then on our way back, she said something about porta-potties near the volleyball courts. We went there; she said they were gross, so we instead went to some that were adjacent to the dreaming treehouse gazebo."

---

[116] Bawdy: dealing with sexual matters in a comical way; humorously indecent.

I nod. *'Good lord. I do not know any of these locations. I have dwelled here for over a month but was forced to stay hidden and squander all my time.'*

He continues, "And at the gazebo, some bushes shook, and she said, 'someone's over there.' We checked them cause it's kinda weird for someone to be hiding in bushes at three in the morning, but there was no one there. So she went into one of the porta-potties and I never saw her come out. I waited for a long time and then knocked only to find it unlocked and no one inside."

'Sounds as if he was not very alert if she left or someone took her without him noticing.'

His arm drops and he releases a long breath of hot air. "I think I should go check around the gazebo again," he says, gesturing toward the northeast of the park. "If you don't mind, can you try checking around her car again? Like I said, it is parked close to the carousel just up the path and across the road."

"Aye, we will see if we can find her there."

Leo nods and marches eastward toward the treehouse gazebo thing he spoke of.

Surveying the area, I ponder a search plan. Since it is still an hour or so until sunrise, the park is quiet, calm, and freezing, so I doubt she would go far. The imposter Shakespeare statue is around a thousand feet from the marble stage where we spent the twilight hours observing the Consortium. I do not wish to go too far into the park's southern area with only Summer and Noah. That is not something I should do dressed as the Fairy; the carousel is as far as I am willing to stray.

"We should just go back to the RV," Summer states with a groan. "She probably just chickened out."

Noah motions at Summer while nodding. "Yep, the job is done. We should just say hasta la vista, get some coffee, and call it a night."

Wagging my finger, I write, "Hush, we shan't search long, and we have time to waste until Galtry finishes her meeting with the Consortium. I have nary a desire to return early and be forced to participate."

"Wait." Summer raises an eyebrow. "You're just trying to dodge the meeting?"

I do not answer her aloud. *'Aye, that I am, but I also doubt that a raptor, if there is one about, would go against a group of armed people. Those types are cowards that tend to take advantage of favorable circumstances. Furthermore... I have an odd bout of restlessness.'*

Glancing off to the side, I recognize a certain statue a mere hundred feet away. It is the statue of someone named "Robert Burns". I had intended to come peruse the tablet but never did so. *'I did pass through this area when I first arrived. I was in a hurry and then began avoiding the main paths not long after. Come to think of it, there were many things I passed by but kept my distance.'*

Moving to the statue's tablet, I stare downward—the tablet has been defaced. Someone has painted over it and drawn a fist with its thumb tucked beneath its index finger. Beneath that, someone else has written in neat, flowing script what seems to be a Robert Burns quote.

> *Some hae meat and canna eat,*
> *And some wad eat that want it,*
> *But we hae meat and we can eat,*
> *And sae the Lord be thankit.*

'Lowland. It's reminiscent of how the Lowland Scots write and speak. It was not a particularly well-respected manner of speaking in London. I believe it's a prayer that might be recited before a mirthful meal.' I peep behind me as snow slips from the branches of a tall tree. Summer and Noah mimic me and look in the direction of the disturbance. I return to studying the tablet. *'I suppose I shan't ever know what it said before.'*

"A fan of Robert Burns, are you?" I flinch when an accented voice speaks. Next to me is a tall man cloaked head to toe in clothing that veils all but his thorny eyes behind a pair of spectacles. He places a palm over his heart, saying, "Oh my, I didn't even realize I had been blessed with the company of the infamous Fairy! I did not believe myself fortunate enough to happen upon such a respectable individual at such a peculiar hour." He says each word as if he is pronouncing them in his mind before speaking them aloud.

'From whence did he come?' I hear Summer and Noah shuffle closer to us. *'I suspect this man crept up on all of us.'*

On my yellow paper, I compose a question and then tap the tablet. "Dost thou knowest this poem?"

"That I do, Miss Fairy. It's 'The Selkirk Grace,' a rather appropriate Scottish grace for Thanksgiving Day, don't you think? Lots of history behind those words."

I nod while studying his eyes; they are fixed, unmoving... sharp.

Patting his belly, he proceeds to declare, "But it's imperative that along with being thankful, we don't take more than our own rightful share." While nodding to himself, he raises a gloved finger. "Of course, you should eat enough to satisfy yourself, but not so much that you become fat while the others are still thin. After all, you never know how everyone at the table might react when they are starved, and a hog is stuffing themselves in front of them." He laughs and goes to stroke his chin as if there is a beard there, but he stops himself before doing so.

As I move a few steps back, I examine his hands and waist for any noticeable weapons.

When I do not answer, he grows impatient and asks, "What about you, Miss Fairy? Wouldn't you agree?"

His pupils have not shuddered or dilated a single poppyseed since we began speaking. I shake my head. "I do not. I would eat until I believe I might burst in suspicion that they may neglect to share."

"Is that so...?" He chuckles. "An understandable answer, yet likewise, an awfully greedy one."

"I do not believe it is a greedy answer, merely a sensible one, but I am afraid I must take my leave now." Turning toward Summer, I write, "Let's circle between the Shakespeare statue, Jessica's ride, and the marble stage. If we cannot locate her within the hour, we shall contact Galtry and the Helping Hands." I glance back; the man has departed and is wandering toward the Sheep Meadow camps. I make a note in my head to mention him to Terra. Tearing off one of the papers, I resume my message to

Summer. "Galtry may have concluded her business with the Consortium by that time."

Terra moved the meeting forward last night, which is why it is occurring so early. I am certain this will have made Lincoln and Pierce suspicious, but everything should suggest the thievery was the Hex Church's doing. Regardless, both of us agreed that the Consortium has every intention of compromising and withdrawing from the Terrace, considering they were moving the haze in the first place.

"I'll text the others and have them let me know when the meeting is over," Summer states, pulling her rectangular phone device from her coat pocket. "I'll also update them on our actions."

'Aye, very good, Summer.' I nod while performing the thumbs-up gesture. *'Do the 'text' thing that thou speakest of.'*

We advance toward the carousel, where Leo stated they had left their ride. The carousel was one of the first landmarks I happened upon when I first arrived in the park.

Arriving several minutes thereafter, I notice a woman holding a young girl in her arms. She raises her higher so that the girl may see inside the building's windows. They both have tired eyes and appear to be waiting on someone. *'Oh, I believe that young girl is the pudding cup girl. I would wager that Gen misses her.'*

Summer points at a small green hovel as a little boy and his father exit. "That's what a porta-potty is if you didn't know, Fairy."

I nod, following the family with my eyes as they stroll away together.

We search the area, finding Jessica's ride but no Jessica. With our search of the area around the carousel proving fruitless, Noah guides us toward where the 'volleyball court' and 'porta-potties' are.

Fifteen or so minutes later, we stand outside a fenced-in courtyard that's full of yellowish sand. I tilt my head and kick a bit of the oddly fine sand. Summer and Noah attempt to explain what this volleyball game is, but I am not giving them much mind.

The cattail waggles within the arc suit as we circle past the porta-potties, Sheep Meadow, Frisbee Hill, and somewhere called 'Skater's Circle.' We discover nary a hint of Jessica's whereabouts, and ultimately, we return to the marble stage.

'*Did someone truly abduct Jessica?*' I tap my metal boots against the brick, and then write on one of my yellow papers, "Prithee Summer, return to the RV. As soon as the Consortium Solicitors take their leave, notify Galtry of what has happened."

She shakes her head. "I'm supposed to guard you, and I've already texted the other Escorts, so they can tell Galtry everything just as well as I can."

I scrutinize the area behind me and then shake my head. I begin to write, "Nay. I wish for thee to go there thyself. Tell her"—but a scream interrupts me.

An older man sprints down an icy path. He stops, points toward a sparse grove, and shouts, "I-I'm going to go find more help! I'll be back!"

Resuming his sprint, he flees toward Sheep Meadow.

'*A raptor? Another fopdoodle?*' My sword bounces against my right leg as I rush to where the man came from. Summer and Noah try to protest, but when I do not stop, they follow. They pant as we come upon a sign that reads, "307th Infantry Regiment Memorial Grove." The grove itself is not that large, barely two or three hundred feet across if I had to guess.

Moving past the sign, I step off the path and follow the fresh footprints left by the man that sped past us. Without feeling in my feet and my body's strength stat being lower than my cattail's, I must be cautious not to trip. As I move further into the grove and round a tree, I reach the end of the footprints.

Silence. I glimpse a scarlet droplet falling. The thump of it knocking against the snow renders me frozen.

My mind blanks. '*...One. Two. Three.*'

"Cut her down!" Summer yells.

"Damnit!" Noah runs past me, scoffing, "I didn't think to bring a knife!"

Another droplet of scarlet hits the snow. *'Five. Six.'*

"Use mine!"

"I can't tell what she's tied off!"

Another droplet of scarlet. *'Nine... Ten.'* I look up.

Hanging in the trees is the bloody figure of Jessica. She dangles by her arms and neck. Not in rope, but... vines, nay, thorn-covered briers. Blood streams down her arms where the briers dig in deep. I examine her face, noting it's pale, cold, and quiet. *'I... I know what a lifeless body looks like.'*

"There; cut there!" Summer yells.

'Nay!' Pulling my sword from the sheath, I raise it at Summer and Noah to stop them before they can do anything more. *'I know what a lifeless body looks like, and this is not it.'* A puff of warm air escapes Jessica's nostrils. Her breathing is slow.

The briers around Jessica's neck are slack. They appear as if they might be tight at first glance, but that is a ruse. My eyes trace the briers that enwrap her arms, finding they run to the tree Noah is standing by with Summer's knife. I follow the briers belting her neck; they loop upward and wrap around a tree limb. It is impossible to free her of the brambly noose from the ground.

"Uhm, you can cut it with your sword if ya want, Fairy," Noah says, stepping away from the vines.

I drop my sword; it slices into the snow at my left side. Pointing at my neck, I point at Jessica and then the tree limb.

Summer's eyes follow the briers from the tree to where they are tied to Jessica. "Cutting that could have killed her..." She glances in the direction the man fled. "We'll have to cut her free from up there; we either need a ladder, or we'll have to clamber up the there."

There's a gust of wind; my cattail thumps against the inside of the cuirass. I study the ground beneath Jessica. The snow is a deep cherry-red.

Noah points and hurries to a tree on my right. "There's a paper!" Peering over, I see a brownish-yellow paper stabbed through a split branch of one of the trees. It flutters in the breeze; the crinkle of its edges is the only noise out here. Noah yanks the paper from the tree. Flipping it backward and forward, he says, "It's blank?"

He presses his lips together and holds the paper out for me to take. I take the paper and run my fingers over it. As he said, it is blank, yet upon closer inspection, I do not believe it to be paper; rather, it is vellum, a parchment fabricated from a calf's hide. The vellum was skillfully made; there is nary a sign of oil from fat, neglected hairs, or any other substances that a novice might overlook.

My arm falls to my side, and my hand tightens around the sword's hilt. Listening to the world around me, I hear... naught; not a bird, not the breeze, not the masses of people. This sort of soundlessness is unique. It is not absolute like Tenebrous; it is a focused hush. It is one I have encountered before. Two occasions come to mind: once when Sir Mouser lost an eye to a sparrow hawk and once when I was mauled by a voracious street cur. Both events had something in common. The snow that's drenched with Jessica's blood bulges and then droops. 'Something is prowling...'

I take a step back, but Noah grabs my wrist. "Fairy, the note!" he says, raising my arm.

Scorching red letters are searing themselves into the vellum.

Liar Fairy, your honeyed words have witched many into your widow's web. We have agreed it's best that a piggish maggot like you is smothered in its crib. Try to run, but flies do not easily abandon the shop of a sweet maker.

𐤊 𐤏 𐤊𐤉 𐤆 𐤓 𐤌 𐤄𐤉

'We–as in more than one attacker!' Words in a language I have never beheld char themselves into the parchment's surface.

Earl Interface:
Critical Warning: Foreign Kiln quintessence detected in the area.

'Kiln!?' The fingertips of my glove smolders as I cast the parchment aside. It spins, sailing several feet away. Jessica's body climbs higher into the trees; something whizzes by my chin. There's a pop from a pouch at my waistline.

Heat.

Boiling rays spring forth from the vellum parchment. My cerulean skirt blows backward, and the snow beneath my boots hisses. Deep-red fire encoils me like a serpent. It's dazzling. A second thereon, the fire abates, relinquishing its vigor. Watery snow trickles from the branches overhead and sizzles upon rapping my breast.

Raising my hands, I notice a wee flame teetering upon my abdomen, and I extinguish it with a pinch. Black muck spills from the pouch at my waist. My eyes heed the muck as it flows into an ebony pool rife with elaborate letters. It steams and vanishes at my feet. '*That is the pool that once guarded Bishop Manhattan. Terra's brooch: it shielded me!*'

My eyes dart left to right. I find Summer shoveling snow onto her trouser leg to snuff a flame. Though her skin is blushed red, it is not scorched. Looking behind me, I see Noah against a tree with his head down. His skin is flushed crimson; some charred slivers are flaying off; blood oozes from the back of his head. '*He was swept out of the brooch's protection. Summer was shielded alongside me.*'

Summer groans and lifts her head; her body fumes in the chilly air. She stares off toward a tree. Following her gaze, I see a black dart-like projectile stuck in the bark of the tree. 'A bolt? Wait, was that what I heard whistling past my head!?' The bolt creaks and splits open at the tail. A piece of the tree's bark breaks and falls away, unveiling a buzzing black mass within its core. 'Flies!? That tree is naught but flies!'

Something stirs underneath the snow. Slush drifts inward, refilling the edges of the cavity left in the snow by the fireball. A droplet of Jessica's blood re-stains the snowy ground, and a low grumble shivers the snow. There's a piercing shriek as a flurry of snowflakes is cast into the air.

I clutch the sword with my left hand and brace it with my right.

My helm's glass visor fogs as a yawning maw smothers my vision. Teeth clamp upon my blade. My arms buckle, the flat of my sword clangs against my cuirass, and my feet forsake the earth. The arc suit's back bashes into a tree—like an eggshell, its trunk shatters. I bounce and scrape upon the icy snow, slamming into an embankment.

> ↓ *Manituic Flux Attenuated by 10.5 Mana*
> ↓ *Shell Blunted by 4.5 Durability*
>
> ---
>
> *New Entity Appraisals*
>
> ---
>
> *Durability: 44.5*
> *Manituic Flux: 104.5*

I lie on my chest and watch as the tree I smashed through trembles. Buzzing flies wriggle out of the tree's husk and marry into a swarm.

My eyes drift to my sword, lying in the snow a few steps away from me. *'Is this the part in a performance where the valiant and brave knight is meant to take up their arms?'* I shake my head. *'Ah, armament. I understand that word now.'*

The blade reflects my helm as I crawl toward it. *'God knows, I am neither valiant nor brave. I endured a life of hardship only to perish and discover an abyss beyond the lychgate. Contrary to many legends, my hardships did naught but beat me into a greedy, impulsive monster—not a heroic knight.'*

Throwing my palm down, I push myself to my feet. *'But I see a knight mirrored in that blade, and I have quite the imagination.'* I bend forward and wrest the sword from the snow. *'Even if the arc suit is a mere costume on me, I harbor great pride in my ability to pretend.'*

Black specks encircle me—a countless number of flies swarm my helmet. They shroud everything as I race toward where Summer should be. Another bolt whizzes by; I glimpse the tail of it a palm from my face.

A shriek accompanies a beast's paw. My cattail rushes out of the opening at my neck. Catching the beast's paw, it bends beneath the force but parries it away from me. Brown fly viscera splatters onto my helmet as the paw crashes into the snow next to me. My boots kick up snow as I dart away and pass by Noah's fly-clad body. The cattail tendrils ladle the fly viscera spattered across my helm's visor into itself. A wall appears in the corner of my vision.

Earl Interface:

Assimilating 'Northern Red Oak'
Erysichthon abates 0
Essence value 0
0.0 Refinable Nebula
0.0 Refinable Vitrum

Details: A pulpy mash of Northern Red Oak pith with hints of grafted foreign quintessence.

Remark: Further study or better skill required for more detail.

I glance at the wall and dismiss it.

Drawing the cattail back into the suit, I force it into my leather glove. When I come upon a figure crouched in the snow, I stop, hook its arm, and yank it to its feet. A few inches from my face, I glimpse Summer with her mouth shut tight, her eyes closed, and her fingers in her ears. Flies tickle her eyelids, venturing to snake beneath them; she sneezes, propelling a fly from one of her nostrils.

I push Summer in the direction of the RV. *'Solicit aid! Flee!'* A bolt bounces against the backplate of my armor. With a second shove, Summer growls and races ahead.

Something short and shrouded by flies stabs at me. It pierces the suit's neck—black haze leaks out as I swing my sword at its short figure. The blade encounters resistance before whatever struck me flounders away. *'There is more than the beast here!'*

The flies expand outward and whirl around me, creating a circle. Glancing earthward, I recoil. Something that resembles red and yellow potato tubers is twitching in the snow, spitting a yellow, syrupy substance. I glance at my breastplate, discovering the same substance on it. From outside the cloud of flies, three distorted figures step into the arena. My sword wavers; though they have been twisted, I know them. *'...The Elderly Rats?'*

Fungus thrives and grows upon the Elderly Rat's bodies. Stemming from their torsos and foreheads, tubers that resemble those that would be on a potato jut out and extend past their backs. They wield long staves of rusted metal scraps and wear fragments of wood tied to their shoulders and torsos by vines.

The three rats raise their weapons. I shake my head. *'What has been done to thee!?'* There's a screech from a figure looming above the trio's head. The figure is much larger than the Elderly Rats, with a hunched posture of around eight feet in height.[117]

Shambling into the arena, it blemishes the snow with yellowish drool whilst glaring at me with a single eye. Boils that leaked pus were once spread amidst absent chunks of flesh; now, those are all capped with fungi and mushrooms. Underneath its fattened flesh, there is a serpent-like shifting that bulges the skin as it wiggles about. Once, it squeaked like a lion roars, but now it sounds closer to a screech of agony. This is the twisted form of the Wretched Rat, transformed since our encounter in the chamber pot tunnels a moon ago.

Within the suit, I commence fashioning copepods of sable and vermillion. *'Fudge, the Wretched Rat! The other Kiln must be manipulating it and the Elderly Rats!'* Drool oozes from the abominable rat's jaws, and upon thumping the snow, nothing occurs. *'The Wretched Rat's drool was once destructive; it has changed in more ways than is readily apparent.'*

---

[117] |8 feet | 243.84 centimeters in height|

My eyes glance at the twitching fungus on the ground. The cattail slithers out and drags the fungal vine into the haze. The fungus's flavor saturates my kiln; it's comparable to how a bellyache feels.

Earl Interface:

Assimilating Xingtai-Yartsa
Erysichthon abates 1
Essence value 0
0.0 Refinable Nebula
0.0 Refinable Vitrum

Details: *A parasitic fungus rife with foreign quintessence and mana. Its Mana Bare variant is frequently employed by Toba natives of the Bun'La continent for use in herbal remedies.*

Remark: *Further study or better skill required for more detail.*

I commit the wall's name to memory and dismiss it.

Brandishing my sword, I take a few steps back; the rats take a few steps forward. The flies also match my pace, crowding the air around me.

Tall, bony ridges along the Wretched Rat's spine stir as it raises onto its back legs and then drops forward with a cutting screech. The Elderly Rats spread out, and the Wretched Rat dashes between them.

I duck behind a tree, and wooden slivers bounce off my armor as the Wretched Rat's paw splinters the trunk. My cattail entangles its ankle like a rabbit in a snare. I slice at it; my blade gashes a nail free of its bed. It thrashes from my clutches, and I sprint ahead.

An Elderly Rat stabs at me with a rusty pipe-staff. I sidestep as the staff gouges a tree a hairsbreadth from my neck. Copepods leap from my arms, erupting in the Elderly Rat's face. Bloodshot veins streak their eyeballs with red, yet no definite signs of frenzy or disease manifest. Haze slips from the puncture in my arc suit as I renew my retreat. A dozen copepods scuttle from my nape under orders to distract the Elderly Rats. I craft a lone hoary copepod.

The Wretched Rat weaves around a hedge and charges; behind me, I hear the crinkle of snow. I pivot on my heel, and the cattail squirms out of the suit. I repel an Elderly Rat's pipe-staff with my sword and capture the weapon in the cattail's tendrils. Ice knocks against my back as I kneel, propping the metal staff skyward—the pipe bends and creaks under abrupt duress. A heavy blow hammers my hip. My temple batters the ground whilst I skid across the footpath's stone.

Fostered Novitiate [Feline Whip (Grade 5)]

↓ *Manituic Flux Attenuated by 14.0 Mana*
↓ *Shell Blunted by 6.0 Durability*

New Entity Appraisals

Durability: 38.5
Manituic Flux: 90.5

My kiln aches as I raise my head and look back. The Wretched Rat screams and claws at the rust-laden staff goring its chest. *'Hoisted by thine own petard, rat!'* I hop to my feet; a bolt skewers my shoulder.

Wrenching the bolt from my shoulder, I hunt for the marksman's position. Another black blur hums by my cheek, and I glimpse its origin, a shadow looming atop a high branch in the distance. A tree crumbles into a throbbing mass and flies envelop me, muddying my sight. I resume retreating, and my boots bang against the footpath.

Passing the marble stage, I sense an odd pulsing course through my kiln. I lift my hand to discover not a bolt but a giant fly with white stripes whipping its wings. *'Bolt, fly!? Fly, bolt!?'*

It scratches its front legs together and flaps a second pair of wings sprouting from its rear. The smaller flies overrun the big one and invade any orifices they can twist into—it fattens in my palm. I fling the giant fly away, and it bursts, spattering me in entrails. My cattail inhales the fly's disgustingly delicious viscera.

A blue and purple wall appears in the top-left and top-right corners of my vision.

I glance at the words and dismiss the walls. Yells pierce the flies' droning, and I notice the vague figures of people. Drawing in my cattail, I shove it into my left glove and tighten my grip on the sword's hilt. A screech comes from the grove behind me. *'Everything we have done could be ruined if I am seen fleeing whilst the rat mauls onlookers.'*

I cease retreating and take a stance with my sword.

{Constance, are you hurt!?}

I flinch. *{Terra-Terra, a gross mushroom is assaulting me!}*

{But you're unhurt!?}

{Aye!}

The Wretched Rat's shadow blankets me. I prepare to evade, but I hear cracks. Bullets pummel the rat; splatters of viscous yellow fluid blot the snow. Silver threads trail the bombardment, stitching themselves into the rat's flank. Threads dart off to every side, entangling trees, benches, and lantern-posts. Its bullet-riddled body jolts backward. It writhes upon the ground as fluid spurts from lacerations left by its silver restraints. *'That is a Hex snare, except much better than Emily's!'*

I hear the screams of spectators as Terra says, {Listen, these flies are attacking anyone who moves too close, and it's hard for us to intervene.}

The Wretched Rat flicks its paw, cutting a thread from a lantern-post. {Art thou injured!?} I shout into her mind.

{No, just run, don't worry about me!}

The rat reaches back and devours a piece of its own flesh to sever a silver thread.

Shaking my head, I glance at the grove from whence I fled. {Terra, on the highest limb of the tall tree that resembles a turkey with its wings spread,} I point toward the tree, {there is an enemy Kiln!}

{I see it! Give me a second!}

I glimpse a clump of snow slipping from the Kiln's tree branch as they dip behind its trunk. 'If I flee, they may target Terra. I must play the knightly role and bear my foe's aggression!' Nodding, I dissect the repulsive Wretched Rat with my eyes as it rips a thread from a bench. I tilt my sword's point forward. {Terra, I shall dispatch the rat whilst it cannot resist!}

Before Terra can respond, I charge ahead. The Wretched Rat's head swings in my direction. I clasp the sword with both hands and aim for its last remaining eye. My blade buries itself up to the hilt. I yank at my sword, yet it refuses to budge a single poppyseed.

The rat's body quivers with a low groan as yellow slop bleeds from its eye socket. Mushrooms sprout from pimples speckling its skin. Its muzzle grates open, and froth spits from rotted pits in its teeth.

Betraying the sword, I release it. Vines erupt from the rat's eye socket and coil around my forearm. I command the hoary copepod to escape my palm. It skitters along the sword's end and into the eye cavity. The rat clamps onto my bracer as a puff of gray wafts from its socket.

The Wretched Rat's muzzle withers and sloughs off, exposing bone enwound by bramble vines. It clenches its jaw, crushing the bracer. I drive the cattail out of my glove's palm and down the rat's gullet. The rat raises its forelimb and smashes down upon my arm. The arc suit tears at the wrist, and the cattail dissevers—oily haze soils the rat's gullet. The beast retches, and I contort my arm. My bracer rips away. The Snappish Beads adaption pop, my haze dyes pale red; the arc suit grows heavier.

A sole bullet cores a bloody-yellow hole into the rat's neck. *{Constance, run to the Arcade! Lincoln and Pierce will see to the Kiln!}* There's a bronze sparkle. The tree my foe cowers behind quakes and blasts asunder. As the splinters settle, I witness the shape of a person scattering into the twilight. *{Go, the gate will be open!}*

I spin around, encountering the blunt end of Elderly Rat's pipe-staff. My cattail catches it and rips it from its grasp. Jabbing it in the belly, I send it whirling backward. I rush toward the Arcade. The Consortium's gates roll apart as I approach. *{Your feet, Con—}*

Something pulls my leg out from under me. My cuirass smacks the ground as I brace myself with the rusty staff. I flip onto my backside and find wriggling vines from the Wretched Rat's maw are wreathing my ankle.

It reels me back toward two Elderly Rats standing with their staves extended like lances. A mob of people defy the flies and hurl stones at the rats. The insect scourge abandons me and assails the folk. More Snappish Beads pop. My body tints ruby-red, and my vermillion sight usurps my night vision. Amongst the swarms' number, I glimpse a lonesome bright red fly in a cloud of gray dots.

A flaming bottle shatters against the Wretched Rat. Fire swallows its body, and a piercing shriek rattles my helm's glass. Its back bulges and ruptures, birthing a hive of pus-lacquered vines. The snare wound about my boot softens as a bullet strikes the rat's temple.

I push myself up and run. *{Dost thou hark!?}*

{I'm listening!}

{Fire upon the flies bearing white stripes; the large ones!}

{I can only open my eyes for a few seconds at most!}

I glance behind me. The Wretched Rat's vermillion figure rends itself free of its binding. It screeches, affixing its beady pupil upon me. Elderly Rats cartwheel as the Wretched Rat plows them from its path.

{Pardon, Terra, but I bid thee luck!} I pass beyond the gates of the Consortium stronghold and descend the Arcade's grand staircase. Here the flies abandon me and assume guard of the gate's entrance.

Midway down, the blazing body of the Wretched Rat leaps from the topmost stair. I squat and butt the rod I pilfered from the Elderly Rat against the staircase.

The rat's bloated gut crackles like charred meat as it confronts the rod's blunt end. Under its weight, the rod flexes and vaults the rat over my head. A thorny vine shackles my neck and wrenches me downward into the stairs—my helm's visor cracks as my face slams into stone.

I flip through the air, losing my rusty staff. Lights grow radiant as my back bashes the ground. I lie there and shake my head, gazing heavenward at an exquisite motif of tiles embellishing a ceiling. Pus and mushroom mucus blotch my armor and rouse me from my stupor. I roll away from the fluids' origin and struggle to my feet.

The Arcade's familiar interior becomes clear. Before me, the Wretched Rat squirms like a maggot in manure as it wallows on the ground to extinguish flames clinging to it.

Consortium clickers dash in front of me and enclose the rat. Seething vines and bronze orbs dance as they battle to outmaneuver one another. A sphere smashes the floor like a walnut whilst lightning fries vines like hair in a hearth.

Multiple clickers form a ring around the rat. Cogwheels click, emitting a shrill buzz that pangs my kiln. Blue lightning cages them all, and static chaos sends me stumbling backward. The lightning enwinds and pulses through my sword that sticks from the Wretched Rat's brow.

The rat's jaw distends so wide it breaks and its tail straightens so rigidly that it snaps off. Smoke billows from its pores, yet the flames clinging to it abate and snuff.

Silence.

The Wretched Rat stays standing, though its vines are limp and wilted. Its limbs wobble as it turns toward me and tries to shriek. But its jaw hangs loose, and its legs buckle under it.

Shards of my helm's visors fall away, exposing a violet eye. My boots beat against the stone as I glare at this abominable beast. *'I do not comprehend how thou defy'st death, but I cannot tolerate this backward cat and mouse another moment. I am the mouser, thou art the rat!'*

Air escapes the rat's seared throat, less a screech, more a breathy groan as it endeavors to push up on its front legs only to crumble anew.

"Hey-hey-hey!" Two clickers swim aside as a scouting orb displaying a portrait of a man with greasy black hair hovers forward. This man is Gary; I have encountered him before. "Glad I came into work today, huh?" Gary chuckles, yet it drifts nearer to a sigh. "Yeah. I come into work every day."

I spurn his gibberish and approach the Wretched Rat. The three Elderly Rats charge into the Arcade, only to be cut off by Gary and the clickers.

Reaching the rat, I clutch my sword—its hilt hisses as the lightning's fever challenges my frigid palms. I wring the blade, whisking the eggy innards of its vermin sheath. *'Thou foist dread upon me, Wretched Rat, so I shall shepherd thee to its wellspring in reprisal.'* A withering vine twitches. I wrest the sword free of its prey and hew the vine at its stalk. It worms upon the floor, spitting jaundiced sap from its writhing rears. *'The lychgate opens for thee, and Tenebrous is impatient. Permit my blade to be thy bridge and behold dread carnate.'*

Once, twice, thrice, I bear the sword's edge down upon its nape. The fourth chop beheads. Its severed head rolls about whilst it tries to bite me with fractured jaws. *'Thou art Umbral in a rat's hide!'* I boot its head, and it skips to the Arcade's corner like a stone over water.

Snappish Beads pop, washing my insides in vermillion. Fiery hair escapes my visor, and the cattail ignites. Taking a stance, I stab at the Wretched Rat's heart. With a soggy thud, the blade's tip embeds a mere inch into its flank.

'I am too feeble without sable.' I glimpse my reflection in some vats the Consortium has erected in the Arcade. The arc suit is speckled in fluid and fly viscera. My candle-like cattail wags overhead and vermillion smolders as if I am burning inside the suit. My eyes drift to four white pipes. They run from The Tower's roots into silver canisters. 'Not sable, but hoary. Hoary shall conclude this farce.'

I raise the sword and slice at the nearest one. Vermillion haze bleeds from the pipe. The blade's edge meets a second pipe, and sable oozes out.

"Waa-squeeek!"

Hearing the Elderly Rat, I glance over to see Gary using three clickers to keep the Elderly Rats at bay. He raises his hands and shakes his head. "Don't mind me."

'Thou speakest too much!' My eyes dart between the Elderly Rats and the next pipe. Hoary haze, releasing it shall mean the Elderly Rats' demise. 'Forgive me. If thou art like the Wretched Rat, then this is a mercy.'

I raise my sword and thrust it downward—and one of the Cosmic System's walls appears.

> **Overcame Lv. 7 Spudded Putrid Rat**
> **Main Contributor:** Entity 1323
> **Final Blow:** Entity 1323
> **Primary Support:** Entity 27101
> **Secondary Supports:** Entity 929622, Entity 901882
>
> *83% of Essence Received*
> **Essence value:** 122

My sword knocks against the masonry as my gaze run across the blue wall.

I tilt my head. 'The blue wall proclaims the rat's passing...? Simple as that?' I look over. The Wretched Rat lies upon the ground—smoke wafts from it, and its body twitches, but naught more. 'It expired without one last effort at gnawing off my leg? I suppose... it is headless...' Its belly bursts open. Yellow fluid seeps out and settles between the cracks in the tiles. '...Huzzah?'

Gary floats over and presses his finger against the scout's frame. "You should take a peek at your clothes there, 'Fairy'."

Looking down, I see mushrooms that resemble red clubs sprouting from the arc suit. *'These loathsome mushrooms are straight from the bowels of Tenebrous!'*

"Y'know, that stuff might be infectious too, uhm, well ordinary people, so most anyone other than you," Gary says.

My eyes drift to the puddle of yellow and the rat's body. Its carcass sprouts more of these club-like mushrooms. A fountain of fluid sprays from its innards and threatens to drench The Tower's roots. I shake my head. *'There may come a day I learn these mushrooms are harmless, but my eyes see a calamitous plague. I shan't ignorantly gamble all of our lives. Hoary must bathe the Arcade in death for everyone's sake.'*

I glance at the mushroom-infested Elderly Rats, lift my sword, and thrust it into the pipe. Violet haze spews outward like a glittering violet wave. *'Nay, not heliotrope.'* I prepare to slash the final pipe yet halt when I glimpse the mushrooms on my skirt wilt and fall away.

Heliotrope haze hovers over the yellow fluid, tinting it a rusty brown. The mushrooms budding from it curl upon themselves and then crumble.

The Elderly Rats whine, scraping and ripping fungus ribbons from their fur. They trample the mushrooms and then fling themselves into the heliotrope. When the last strip of fungus sloughs off, they collapse and lose consciousness.

'...It purges mushrooms?'

In the distance, I hear a riotous crowd cheer as a blue wall appears.

Helped Subdue Lv. 1 *Kuchak-Rukh x3*
Main Contributor: *Entity 27101*
Final Blow: *Entity 27101*
Primary Support: *Entity 929622*
Secondary Supports: *Entity 929624, Entity 1323*

8% of Essence Received
Essence value: *4*

I turn toward the Wretched Rat's carcass. 'It was but a despicable, abominable rat–' I boost my sword above my head. '–yet it feels as if I slew a dragon. Huzzah!'

Chapter 30: An Era's End

∞∞∞∞∞∞∞∞∞∞∞∞∞∞

Iron whimpers bounce between the Arcade's walls as I run a shard of my visor's stained glass across the flat of my blade, sweeping away remnants of mushroom stems.

Before me, the three Elderly Rats snore with the fervor of giant pygmies. They have shown no signs of hostility since they shirked the mushroom's chains. *'Exhaustion, perchance? How long have they been compelled to move around without sleep or rest?'* I drop the glass shard into the heliotrope fog and pluck a sliver of fabric from the floor. The blade squeaks in bliss as I massage its surface. *'Prithee, my Status and Chronicles, Cosmic System.'*

Name: Constance Nightingale
Race: Kiln
Seed Type: Tower [Germination]
Variant: Oort Stained Glass
Forms: [Vaporous] [Lucent: *Unviable*]
Shell Level: 1
Flame Level: 1 (Develop Beyond Germination)
Durability: 38.5/49
Mana: 183/270 [90.5/135 Manituic Flux]
Erysichthon: 00/155
Quintessence: Corrupting Oort Cloud
Adaptations: [Cattail Tendrils] [Comrade Cracker]
[Throng of Haze] [Negating Membrane]
[Snappish Beads] [Rife Pearl (2/5)]
Skills: [Feline Whip (Nov-5)]
[Gluttonous Naturalist (Nov-6)]
[Supine Humorism (Nov-0)] [Tenebrous Stealth (Nov-6)]
[Invasive Scrounger (Nov-2)] [Mana Crunch (Nov-2)]
Titles: [Parasitic Thief +] [Trailblazer (Humorism)]

Chronicles

Constance Nightingale || Kiln Vaporous Chronicles || Entity 1-3-2-3			
Strength	13→7	Cattail Armament Physical Power	26→14
Orenda	23→27	General Body Strength	5→3
Sturdiness	7	Cattail Armament Magical Power	0→7
Fortitude	17	Membrane Defense	2→1
Perception *	19→25	—	—
Acuity *	10→12	—	—
Agility	18→30	—	—
Endurance	21	Vermillion	52.13%
Mend Rate	23	Sable	39.36%
Mana Regen	13→15	Heliotrope	8.29%
Stat Points Primed: 0		Hoary	0.22%

Nodding, I dismiss the wall and stand. I bed my sword in its sheath and then look around, ensuring that I am alone. *'Aye, Gary and his clickers have slipped out.'*

I move close to one of the Elderly Rats. Kneeling next to them, I tug some dried mushrooms from behind its earlobe, and its ear twitches. It snorts, slaps its own brow, and then rolls onto its gut. I poke at another rat's snout, and it slaps at my hand. I repeat the same thing again. With a huff, the Elderly Rat sneezes and turns onto its belly. Moving to the last of the three, I pull its eyelids open and watch its pupils dilate. *'They require rest and a keeper to observe them for peculiar behavior, but I surmise they are of good health otherwise. I shall have to keep an eye and ear out for the remaining two rats.'* I push myself up, glance at the Wretched Rat's carcass, and then shamble toward the wintry night air. *'The Elderly Rats must be lugged somewhere more fitting before hibernation. Mayhaps I can persuade someone to oblige me.'*

Passing beyond the Arcade's southern archways, I stop at the foot of the grand staircase and raise the torn remnants of my right hand. *'I pray Terra shan't be bitter that I damaged the arc suit.'* Vermillion haze sweeps upward in the frosty breeze. *'...She shall understand, right?'* The lanterns and lights around me flicker and then go dark. *'Odd. Out of fuel, perhaps?'*

Without their radiance, I notice a gentle light shining upon me. My sheath, armor, and the vermillion haze escaping my visor are set aglow by its touch.

'Good morrow, old friends.' I straighten my back and turn my gaze upward. For the first time in over a fortnight, I behold the unfettered night sky—a myriad of stars in harmony with the crescent moon.

The stars are the last spectators of an era whence a little red-haired girl and her black mouser would go on adventures in the London squalors. A life of hardship, struggle, and perseverance. I spent many a night gawking at the heavens, daydreaming of an afterlife amongst them. It is unfortunate I have only wandered the blackness between them and not their light. Yet as they did then, and as I am confident they have many times before, the stars shall behold not merely an era's end but the dawn of another.

I point at the heavens. *'There is naught left of my time on this Earth save for thee, and I yearn for someone to acknowledge my perseverance. Many times I skirted death. My flesh is but dust, yet even now, I still linger all these centuries thereafter. I even slew an abomination with some aid! Is my persistence not praiseworthy...?'* As in the past, the stars offer no recognition. My arms fall to my side, and I lean against the wall. *'I wish Sir Mouser was here.'*

Footsteps echo in the sunken staircase. {*Hail, brave knight, your armor is a tad beaten up, but I'm glad to see it served its wearer well,*} a pleasant voice chuckles. {*A survivor as always, it seems.*} Dropping my eyes from the heavens, I witness Terra's figure bathed in crescent moonlight at the grand staircase's summit. Silver tome tight in her embrace, she descends, sinking toward me at the Arcade's mouth. The moth graven upon her tome's cover is set awash in the glow of my violet eye. She stops several stairs before me and then peers through my helm's shattered window. *{You are okay, right?}*

'Terra...' I step from the shadows and adopt a chivalrous pose whilst clad in the moon's dramatic shine. *{If I was not, could I appear so gallant at this very moment?}*

Crossing her arms, she glances around to make certain we are alone and giggles. *{Very gallant, Constance.}* She tosses something down the staircase. *{You were so splendid; losing a hand didn't even make you flinch.}*

I reach out and catch the torn leather glove and metal bracer. Hiding them behind my back, I shake my head and shrug. *{I see naught... And, aye, I am in good health. Art thou also well?}*

{Yes, a few bites around the eyes, nose, mouth, and ears, but fine otherwise.}

{I am delighted to learn it was not worse. What of Summer, Noah, and Jessica?}

{Summer is fine, same as me. Jessica is still unconscious and receiving stitches from a nurse in the camp. Noah is touch and go. He may need a skin graft and to be put on oxygen for a while.}

{A skin graft. Such a thing is possible?}

{It is, but awakened people have been shown to possess stronger healing abilities, so we are waiting to see what happens before we do anything like that. I'm leaving it up to Summer since all of them are very close.}

{So my assistance is not needed with those matters?}

{No, there isn't anything you could do for them right now.}

{Aye. Well, I have confidence in his recovery.} Glancing back at the Arcade, I say, *{I shall require assistance moving Gen's new companions somewhere more suitable.}*

She raises an eyebrow. *{And where are they going to stay while you hibernate?}*

I rub the back of my head. *{That is a question, aye...}*

With a click of her tongue, she laughs. {It's all right; they can stay with Gen. I have a professional zookeeper coming in to help Lorcan take care of him, so why not have them do the same for your rat friends too. I know you were thinking about creating a place for them in your Tower anyway, so it's a short-term thing.}

{I thank thee!} I shout, rushing up the grand staircase. {Thou art so kind!}

{Well, I'd imagine you're the only one that would ever say that to me, but I'm glad you think so.} A puff of hot air huffs into the frigid night air. {Now come on. We need to get you ready, so you can show people that you're fine.}

{Show people that I am fine?}

{Yes. The people witnessed a portion of your fight, as I'm sure you noticed. After you ran into the Arcade, you never came back, and since you're about to disappear for a couple of weeks, it would be a good idea to show yourself one more time before then.}

{Oh! Then, should I bring the rat's head? I could affix it to a pike!}

{You're supposed to be a fairy, not a warlord.}

I tilt my head. {Is it strange? I have seen many heads atop pikes and numerous limbs dangled from London's gates.}

{I...} She blows a warm breath into the chilly night air. {No, I think you can leave it. I don't imagine people would react how you believe they would.}

{Art thou sure? When I was a child, the guards regularly said it was an excellent way to deter criminals.}

{I'm sure,} she says with a quick nod.

{Wait. Now that I reflect on it, I was a criminal. Dost thou thinkest the guard was threatening me?}

She smiles stiffly and shrugs. {...Uh, I'll have the rat's carcass moved someplace it can be preserved so we can study it if that's okay with you.}

{Aye.} Meeting her midway up the stairs, I stop and raise my hand. {What am I to do about this?}

{We aren't going straight there. Owl, Rabbit, and Wolf are going to perform some temporary repairs on your suit. It'll be later this morning before you can show everyone that you're okay. It would be a good time for you to place your vent as well.}

I glance at the Arcade. {But...}

{I'll send Lorcan and some Hands to sneak the 'Elderly Rats' into the RV's back room.}

Thinking for a moment longer, I nod. {Aye, I suppose it is not an issue. The Elderly Rats are napping, and I suspect they shall not awaken soon. They are also rather meek, so they should not be combative... and if they do wake, I suppose apes can tolerate Lorcan, so perhaps rats may likewise be capable of such a feat.}

Together Terra and I abscond toward the RV, careful to make sure neither of us is glimpsed by anyone who may recognize our 'identities.' Due to this, we must take a lengthier footpath back, but fortunately, most folk are still slumbering or lingering near the Arcade where the battle took place.

As we tread, the two of us notice several ribbons of azure light streak by the moon before vanishing into the horizon. My palm strays to the part of the cuirass that shields my kiln.

"Don't worry, Constance," Terra says softly.

{Something this night drove me to understand is that many of the other Kiln shall perceive me as a threat. Not because I have shown maliciousness, nor because I am different from them... It's merely because I am the most visible. True or not, some Kiln believe me to be 'in the lead.' This has never happened to me. I have never been 'visible.'}

"You get used to it," she says with a sigh. "And it's a double-edged sword, and it'll probably stay that way. But the good thing about being visible and 'in the lead' is you're also the one people will want to establish a rapport with."

{Aye, that may be true, I suppose. It is rather optimistic, though, and who says I desire a rapport with them.} I raise my hands and then allow them to fall to my sides. {I am too crisp for my own good, Terra.}

"By the way, you do know it's cool, not crisp? I just thought I should mention it," she says with a chuckle.

{Aye, I began to suspect it when I heard Daniel say, 'cool.' Then, Lorcan laughed at me when I wrote it on my whiteboard a few days ago, so now I say it out of sheer spite. I believe if I persist, I shall be able to convince him I said it deliberately.} I raise a finger and declare, *{Then it is I who shall have the final soundless laugh!}* I stumble. Terra reaches out and grabs my shoulder. *'That was close. I nigh had to feign that being deliberate too.'*

Terra laughs and waits for me to regain my footing. "Now come on. Let's hurry. If we take too long, people may start to gather."

I nod. *{Aye. Then we should make haste; the fewer people, the better!}*

Terra's phone makes a noise. Raising her foot, she pulls it from her shoe and then appears to read something. A smile grows on her face. She glances at me and says, "And there is one last thing concerning the Consortium."

Tilting my head, I wait for her to explain, but a purple wall appears first.

Earl Interface:

*   ***Notice:*** *The punctured roots are no longer obstructed and shall be mended shortly. Germination is on schedule and will reach the point of requiring the Mistress's presence within the next four Material-Earth hours. Development shall then cease until the Mistress joins the process.*

Recommendations, Reminders, and Relevant Information

*   ❖ *Hibernation is expected to last fifteen Material-Earth days.*
*   ❖ *The Mistress should have their map memorized if vegetation is to be distributed as the Mistress desires.*
*   ❖ *The Mistress must place a vent unless the Mistress desires for the ground beneath the fleshies feet to collapse and explode from the pressure. **Note:** Low-level organic Toba Humans may survive the blast but are unlikely to survive the vent's initial heat release.*

> ❖ *The trellis room should be kept clear of organics while Germination completes unless the Mistress desires their demise.*
>
> ❖ *It is recommended no one stands near the Nodes from now until the Mistress enters hibernation. **Note:** It's a surprise.*

{Terra, before that, might thou mayhaps inform the people that they should give four particular trees a wide berth?}

She raises an eyebrow. "I... I don't see why not."

····

·········

····

A few hours thereon, the morningtide passes, and I sit in the RV's main room in my arc suit, which has been taped, glued, and stitched together. "Don't wriggle around too much," Rabbit says, inspecting a glue-smeared seam in my helmet's visor. "Yep. One wrong sneeze and this baby is gonna be wedged in the nearest person's forehead."

I nod and perform the thumbs-up gesture. *'Be at ease, Rabbit, for I do not possess nostrils.'*

"A shame, really." In the corner of the room, Wolf sighs. "One of our most public pieces and its time on this earth was so fleeting."

Lowering my head, I wring my hands together. *'My apologies.'*

He laughs lightly. "I'm only joking. Most of our work is either temporary or never seen by the public, so it's been a real treat seeing people praise it for once."

"Oh hush, Wolf," Owl says from the next room over. "Miss Nightingale, Miss Galtry has already given us the task of repairing your suit, so it'll be back in tip-top shape in no time."

Again, I nod. *'The suit has been quite liberating. I do not desire to lose it.'*

The RV's door swings open and in walks two familiar Consortium people in the same suits they always seem to be wearing. These two people are, of course, Lincoln and Pierce. They are here for a simple enough reason: because they have to be.

"Sup, ready to get this over with?" Pierce says.

Lincoln says nothing, just nods his head at me.

I stand and spin around, searching for my whiteboard.

"Ah, it's right here, Miss Nightingale," Owl says, tossing someone's coat off the marble table.

Taking the whiteboard in hand, I write, "Ah, I thank thee, Owl." I erase the whiteboard and then scribble, "Now, may I ask if this is truly necessary? I have drawn enough attention."

Pierce peers at my writing and then glances around the room. "Can anyone here actually read that handwriting?"

"You get used to it once you kinda figure out which squiggle is which," Rabbit says with a giggle.

"What are you talking about?" Lincoln asks, hitting Pierce on the shoulder. "Isn't that sort of close to the handwriting on those recipes you keep on top of your fridge? The ones written by your great-great-great-grandmother or whatever. Why is it I recognize it, but not you? She's asking the same thing we asked."

"She doesn't want to do it either?" Pierce squints at my writing. "Wait, I think I see it now. Oh, and to be fair, I'm afraid if I touch those recipes, they'll disintegrate."

"Then don't keep them on top of your dusty fridge." Lincoln shakes his head. "Anyway, Pierce, just tell her exactly what our bosses told us."

Pierce rolls his eyes. "Yeah, fine." He clears his voice and declares in a flat tone, "'If they wanna maintain it and probably die from some mutated freaks, let 'em, but right now, I want that shit delivered to our doorstep. Which means we need to make absolutely certain all those nosy statesmen and legislators know not to get in our way.'"

Narrowing his eyes, Lincoln says, "Go on, tell her the next part."

Mimicking Lincoln's reaction, Pierce also narrows his eyes. "Oh, you mean the part from before we received word of some 'resources' going missing because the cell towers are having a tough time coping with all the rolling blackouts. The part where you said something about how we already had some of the 'resource' in canisters so we could bide our time before doing anything?"

"Yeah, when we were busy in a conference that abruptly devolved into us helping someone escape from an M-Class," Lincoln replies with a sigh.

Pierce twirls his hand as if parsing someone else's words. "Well, it was hard to hear since it was all yelling, but the end was something like, 'take the goddam picture, and you better fucking look happy while you're doing it! I wanna be able to see all your teeth dammit!' and then he hung up."

Lincoln nods.

"Ah, that all sounds unpleasant," I scribble on my whiteboard.

"It is and I'm sure you can imagine how upset all of this has made Lincoln." He gestures at Lincoln's flat expression. "The guy hasn't smiled in a photo since he was a toddler. This is physically painful for him."

Spinning on his heel, Lincoln walks toward the RV's door. "Just come on, Pierce." He stops and looks over his shoulder. "Do you want to meet us there, or are you coming with us?"

I nod my head and write, "Owl and I shall be coming with thee." Raising my hand, I motion at Owl and then add, "Owl shall be the one painting our portrait."

Lincoln's eyes drift toward Owl in his black, spiky leather attire.

With a smirk, Owl raises his hand and waves. "How are you today, doll?"

He turns toward the RV's exit. "We'll wait outside."

Pierce follows behind him, saying, "I swear to the God in Light if he walks out with an easel and a paintbrush, I'm not doing it."

"No, you're doing it," Lincoln replies.

They walk out, leaving Owl, Wolf, Rabbit, and I alone. While the three Hands return to preparing my suit, I think about the conversation I had with Terra.

Since their canisters full of haze have vanished, they now only have a small quantity of haze they sampled days ago. They obviously want more than that, but they are both spread thin and biding their time to execute some sort of plan. Yet the Consortium puts a high value on my haze. Just not enough value to commit the immense resources necessary to rid the park of people and then keep hold of it as things worsen in New York.

However, that is not all. Terra says the Consortium seemed to also put a lot of value on me. Nay, not Constance the person, Constance the haze producer, nor Constance the fairy. What they value is Constance the Kiln. In the Consortium's own words, they want to 'observe what Kiln do in their natural environment.' Since Kiln are a new occurrence, very few understand much of anything about Kiln. They do not even know how Kiln and their Domains' roots are related.

Though I wish they would not observe me as if I am an animal, denying them would be foolish. All they must do is change their garments and then they become Consortium spies rather than associates. It is better for them to be out in the open so that they may be watched too.

Put simply, though the Consortium is unwilling to commit significant human or material resources, they will bolster us superficially in exchange for the right to buy haze and observe what transpires here. This is better than Terra and I anticipated. We did not foresee them being willing to have any open association with us at all.

As for the reason Lincoln and Pierce are upset, that is because they were blamed for the loss of the canisters and for the Consortium having to rush their dealings with us. Of course, it's not their fault, but they still received some of the abuse.

'It's clear Lincoln and Pierce suspect our involvement. Which is understandable; it was indeed our doing after all.'

Owl's voice pulls me from my thoughts. "I'll go get the camera. Wolf and Rabbit, you two should go ahead and make your way back to the shop so you can organize things for the actual repairs."

They both nod, stretch their legs, and prepare to depart.

"See ya soon, Fairy. Have fun... wherever it is you're going!" Rabbit says, stroking my head.

'Do not pet me...' I lean away from her. 'The Consortium already considers me some sort of animal.'

She laughs and walks toward the door. "Next time then, I guess!"

Wolf simply waves, shrugs, and then follows Rabbit out.

"Ready to go, Miss Nightingale?" Owl says, returning from the back room.

I nod. 'Aye, let us finish this.'

....

....

....

Everyone gathers before the Consortium's gate. Lincoln, Pierce, and I stand upon the top step of the Arcade's grand staircase, around two hundred feet from Node 3. In front of us is a hole leading to the chamber pot tunnels, and surrounding us like a horseshoe is an immense crowd.

Neither the crowd nor the two Consortium employees truly comprehend why we are here. Though they understand that the prophecy is about to be fulfilled, they do not grasp that the moment I drop the spark into the pipe, nothing shall ever be the same.

They are about to witness the end of an era.

In the future, when everything is said and done, I am not sure what these people will think of what I am about to do. Mayhaps the wearer of this suit shall one day be known as the 'wretched fairy,' but Terra and I both believe this is the best course of action for everyone. Not to mention, it's too late. Everyone is here. Everything is in motion. To not see it through now would be ruinous to the 'Pilgrims' that are capable of blossoming in the forthcoming era.

"Okay, cameras ready! Everyone looks absolutely magnificent..." Owl points at Lincoln and shakes his head. "Except for you, doll. What you're doing right now is a smirk, not a smile. What I'm getting from you is 'evil corporation that sells your family into slavery,' and not 'soul-crushing conglomerate next door,' like I believe you're going for."

Lincoln's mouth curls into a stiff smile.

"Good enough, now shake hands for us little people," Owl chuckles.

'Ah, a handshake; how fun!'

Lincoln and I both look at each other.

'Hmm, if I am correct, the defeated party is the one that should offer their hand first.'

Both Lincoln and Pierce raise their hands, but I wait a moment since I do not wish to appear too eager to bury the hatchet. Lincoln's eyebrow twitches, and I take it as my cue.

I lift my hand and place my palm in Lincoln's. Owl's camera clicks. With a slight nod of the head, I release his hand and shake Pierce's. The people that surround us cheer and commence shouting mocking obscenities at the two Consortium Solicitors. The Consortium is unpopular amongst many commonfolk, so the commoners are quite bemused by this unforeseen turn of events.

Hiding my hand, I place it behind my back and have the vent spark drift from around my kiln to my palm. I pinch the spark and bring my hand forward, raising it so everyone may witness the spark's light. The people hush and watch my movements like a cur watches a scrap of meat. *'I hope they are not anticipating something as dramatic as the previous occasion.'*

I lower my arm and hold the spark above the hole before releasing it. The spark drifts downward, casting a glow upon the ground as it moves into the small stone pipe. Peeking into the pipe, I watch as the spark sinks into the water and then into the stone.

Tendrils spread and encircle the pipe.

'I suppose that concludes the performance... I somewhat wish I had not been so theatrical now.' With the crowd certain to be dispirited, I wave and prepare to withdraw into the Arcade...

Yet the earth rumbles.

I freeze midstride and peek behind me. Node 3 quakes, bark shivering from its façade. *'Earl?'*

Node 3 bursts, sprinkling everyone in wooden splinters—the crowd gasps. Vermillion haze spews from its pores and then hardens to its outside like a celestial glaze. A red glass tree takes shape, growing grand and tall. In the daylight, it twinkles, and the world beneath its expanding branches basks in an opulent scarlet hue.

Debris bumps against my back. I turn and discover that Node 4 is experiencing the same shedding, except foreboding hoary haze enwinds and lacquers it in a gray glass.

Glancing toward the people goggling at the trees, I whirl on my heel and descend the Arcade's grand staircase. I rush through the Arcade's interior and out the other side onto the Terrace. There I find Nodes 1 and 2 are partaking in the same transitions. Node 1 is a medley of purples and blues, whilst Node 2 is a motley of charcoal and raven blacks. They swell to twice the height of the trees around them. The rumbling abates.

The clamoring and shouting of the folk outside grow boisterous as I shuffle back into the Arcade. *'I believe I shall dwell here and enter hibernation before I must suffer any consequences.'*

{Can't make an exit without causing chaos first, can you?} Terra's voice questions in my head.

'Consequences!' I go to turn around, but something cumbersome latches onto my leg. Looking down, I find Gen with a scowl upon his face. He

never got over the loss of his coffin, and since then, he has clung to me instead.

I pat Gen atop the head. {I… I wish for thee to understand one irrefutable truth: this…} Evading her eyes, I declare, {…this is all Earl's fault.}

She laughs. {Didn't you give her permission?}

I squeeze my hands together and stare toward the ceiling. {Well, if we mean to split hairs…} Rubbing my foot against the floor, I continue, {…'permission' of a sort may or may not have been given. Nevertheless, it was a much more brilliant display than I foresaw.}

{Well, regardless, I'd say the two of you have successfully attracted even more people to the park.}

{My apologies, but to be wholly fair, thy arrangement with the Consortium shall also attract more folk.}

She purses her lips. {I think your thing is going to do more than my thing.}

{Nay.} I cross my arms. {I think the opposite.}

Mimicking me, she crosses her arms as well. {Are you really trying to say a handshake will attract as many people as four giant glass trees dramatically exploding into existence?}

{…I am.} We glare at one another and then laugh. Well, Terra laughs. I merely unfurl my arms. For a brief moment, we stand in silence until I ask, {Is there anything I should know before sleeping?}

{No.} She winces.

I narrow my eyes. {Art thou certain?}

{…Yes.} Her eyes flutter.

{Strange.} I narrow my eyes further. {Those are two symptoms of lying per our contract.}

{It's not anything important. I'm just… I'm struggling to let someone go.}

I tilt my head.

She shakes her head. {No, it's not my father's husk.}

{Oh.} I glance at Gen and then say, {Letting go of something important is... formidable. Though I have only truly confronted it once before.}

{And what did you do?}

{I... I did what I believed was best for them. Although more than anything, I did not wish to lose them, they were in pain... So, I requested the Fates' lords-and-ladies recipe from my teacher, Dr. Atslowe, and used my talents in medicine to make a flask of...} My fingers rub together. {...a flask of poison... to relieve their suffering.}

Her lips part. "Was it a... a person?"

{Mouser. More of a person to me than anyone ever was. I was not well-liked for many reasons.}

"Oh, Sir Mouser, you've mentioned him before." Her mouth hangs open for a moment, and then she smiles warily.

{What is it?}

"It's nothing..."

{Thou mayst speak thy mind.}

"I guess, if you insist, I was just thinking a 'flask of poison' seems like a lot for a cat."

{Aye.} I nod. {Most of it was for me.}

Her eyes widen. "You... you mean..." She glances at the cattail. "You never drank it, though, right?"

{Nay, I drank. Voyaged overseas to sate a lifetime's appetite for adventure, dug Sir Mouser's bed there, and then drank it. Drank it all in a single gulp and then sat down to dine on my favorite white bread and sip my favorite ale... But...} I pause and my fingers fiddle with the arc suit's zipper. {The interesting thing about *poison is that it expires like everything else—it gave me the worst bellyache of my life, though. Truthfully, the whole affair was particularly pathetic and embarrassing.}*

"Constance..." Terra steps closer while she wrings her wrist. "I'm incredibly sorry you felt the need to do that back then. It's not okay that you were pushed to that."

{Thanks be. It was a stream of dilemmas that inevitably compelled me to drink from that flask and do what I did. Dilemmas tend to cascade until they drown a person.}

Nodding, she looks into my eyes. "It... it might be selfish of me to say this, but I'm glad it was expired for what it's worth. Otherwise, you may not have shown up when and where you did."

{...Likewise, Terra.} I look toward the floor. *{And beg thy pardon. When I began talking, I did not intend to speak of such grim and unpleasant things. So, my apologies.}*

Shaking her head, she says, "No, no, don't apologize. There's no need to ever apologize for that, Constance. I'm glad you shared that with me." She tucks a lock of silver behind her ear and swallows. "My own dilemma has to do with Caldwell, my butler. I've told you about him and Victoria, right?"

{Aye.}

"I might have undersold them a little back then. Caldwell and Victoria have been the closest thing I've had to a family after Dad became Bishop Manhattan." She bites her lip. "And Bishop Manhattan claims Mom died in an accident, but frankly, God only knows if that's true. I have no idea what actually happened to Mom."

I nod. *{My condolences.}*

"Thanks, and without Victoria and Caldwell, I would have probably just starved myself to death as a child. They did all the things a mom and dad are supposed to do... and then Victoria just up and vanished after my driving test. Honestly... I truly despise driving." She exhales a long-drawn sigh. "Now, it's time for me to push Caldwell away. Caldwell has actual family overseas, real children and grandkids—people he isn't paid to be around. I'm just a... a job, not his child."

{*And what does Caldwell think?*}

"That doesn't matter because Caldwell is one of the few people who knows Terra, but I'm about to be Galtry. And here's the thing, Caldwell is a genuine butler, not a hired gun who masquerades as a butler. He does ordinary butler stuff and is an all-around good person, but not the 'morally gray' or 'greater good' sort of person. H-he's not capable of being mean to anyone or anything." She laughs and raises a palm. "Since I've known him, he's probably nursed over two dozen pigeons and crows back to health. Half the birds in our neighborhood bring the man gifts, for god sakes, like tokens of appreciation or something. He has shoeboxes full of the things the birds made or brought him because he feels guilty if he throws any of it away. That's... that's just who Caldwell Flax is."

{*...Dost thou believest he shan't be safe in thy company?*}

"Of course he's not safe near me, but I have no idea if he's safer where I can keep an eye on him or back where he's from. I mean, in the future, who knows what it'll be like near Caldwell's home. The Cosmic System is coming back everywhere, and Kiln are just speeding up the process in New York. Caldwell's home could become a veritable oasis or Pit on Earth... I don't know." Shaking her head, she asks, "How do you know if your decision is right or wrong when it involves someone you want the best for?"

I think for a moment. {*Whatever thy judgment, if made in good faith, it shall be the best one as far as I am concerned. The trick is convincing thyself of that.*} I raise a hand, saying, {*Though if thou desirest more substantial advice, I would permit Caldwell a choice of some variety. Not something I would typically do myself, but I am also a woman who has had few acquaintances.*}

She nods. "Yeah, as usual, we're a lot alike. Thank you for letting me rant, and your advice is good." Exhaling, she says, "But I think I'm drained for conversation."

I nod and pull the zipper on the arc suit's back. {*Agreed. Like thee, I am not accustomed to such personal talks.*} Reaching my hands out of the back, I draw the suit down and over my kiln. The tape and glue crack as I do so, leaving the forlorn Gen embracing the arc suit. He slaps the floor and sinks to his rump with crossed arms. *{I believe the time for me to hibernate has come,}* I remark whilst performing a twirl to redistribute my haze to its usual shape. *{I am a wee weary, yet I shan't keep thee waiting long if I can help it.}*

Gen's body goes limp as Terra drags him away from me.

"I'll keep a tight leash on things until you wake, so don't worry," she says, smirking at Gen's antics.

{Then...} I perform a modest curtsy. *{I thank thee. Without thee, I am uncertain what I would have done these past weeks. I could do naught but hide. The Wretched Rat, the Hex Church, the Consortium, and the other Kiln, through everything, the only good fortune I have had was our meeting.}*

"Stand up." She huffs, blowing a puff of foggy air from between her lips. "The curtsy is beyond adorable, but you've done just as much for me. I don't want you to keep thanking me or apologizing to me for this kind of stuff."

I stand. *{But...}*

"It makes me feel like I don't thank you enough. Not to mention, I get plenty of people thanking me for literally everything. Plus, I just want our relationship to be different then..." She sighs. "...Then the shallow, superficial one I have with basically everyone else because of my circumstances and my own personal inability to be 'normal'..." Pursing her lips, she asks, "Didn't I say something to this effect before?"

{...Perhaps something akin to that.}

"Then..." She raises a hand and wiggles her fingers. "I'll see you soon."

I wave back, wiggling my fingers as well. *{I pray things are dull and wearisome for thee whilst I am napping.}*

She chuckles. "Doubtful, but we can hope and pray, I guess."

I nod. *{I confess, I too am doubtful.}*

A purple wall appears, interrupting us.

Earl Interface:
Notice: Germination cannot proceed until the Mistress enters hibernation.
This process is estimated to take fifteen Material-Earth days.

Query: Would the Mistress like to contribute the kiln to the process and proceed?
[Aye]   [Nay]

Running my eyes over it, I respond, *'Aye, Earl, I am eager.'*

A hollow in the crimson tiles lights up a few paces to my side. The area looks recently repaired.

Earl Interface:
Acknowledged: Mistress, please move directly over the area indicated.

I drift over and examine the spot. *'Ah, this is where I sowed the Tower Seed when I arrived. I suppose the Consortium mended the hole they dug in the floor.'* Lines of glass spiderweb in every direction and light up in various reds, purples, grays, and blacks. *{Terra, none should enter the Arcade henceforth.}*

Moving further away from me, she nods. *{The Arcade is off-limits. No one will be allowed in.}*

{Excellent, then all is well.}

{Yes.} She smiles, backing outside the Arcade. *{Until we next meet, enjoy your nap.}*

The floor grumbles and vibrates beneath my feet.

Earl Interface:
Statement: Until the time is nigh, rest well, Mistress.

Luminous and colorful sap bubbles up from the hollow, twisting into a stained glass dragon-like claw. It reaches out, and its nails chime as it clasps the kiln. The claw drags me earthward. Haze retreats into the shell, and my vision blurs—my eyesight shifts to the kiln.

I sink beyond the floor and fall into soil teeming with veins of beating haze.

My mind protests the impending abysm, so I count. *'Three million nine hundred ninety-nine thousand. One. Two. Two...'*

Dread rears its maw anew as I watch the Arcade's light wither into frailty. *'...Two.'*

Shadow cushions my ever-deeper descent. *'...I tire of counting.'*

Heavenward, the last glister of waning light quivers. *'And I tire of fear... So, thou shalt...'*

Darkness smothers the light and swaddles my kiln. *'Shalt fear naught for... thou art brave, Constance.'*

Fog lulls my conscious nearer to slumber. *'I must be brave.'*

Rest.

Terra's Epilogue: A Prelude's End

∞∞∞∞∞∞∞∞∞∞∞∞∞∞∞∞∞

In a chilly room atop a 38-story hotel, I gaze into a mirror—one iris of green and another of silver stare back.

It's been eight days since Constance began hibernating, so at least seven days remain until she wakes, and The Tower is meant to arrive. Yet Manhattan is already exhibiting substantial changes.

Five days ago, the first reports of a white fog bleeding out of the city's sewers reached me. Since then, all varieties of giant bug creatures have been scuttling out of manholes. There are even horror stories of those creatures wriggling their way into homes by way of toilets. I skimmed one article about a woman pouring cement down her toilet to stem the flow of bugs worming up the pipes.

Uncapping a tube of lipstick, I blot my lips and then press them together to fill in any gaps. I lean back, ensuring that the dark red matte matches the lip liner. In the mirror, a young woman with a fair complexion, silver hair, and a face half-stitched in cloth examines herself with a flat, indifferent expression. I tilt forward and work the lipstick toward the corners of my lips.

That face is the face of Galtry.

Galtry is not merely the feigned Overboss of the Galtry Syndicate, and it's not just the silver eye, hair, and cloth that people think of when they hear her name on television or read it in a magazine. Galtry, in and of herself, is an icon. She rules in a vicious spectrum of society that young, strong-willed women seldom involve themselves, and some people utterly adore her for it.

Except being so public means that people have a plethora of preconceptions about Galtry.

I once stumbled upon a Lurlann Empire college essay that sought to analyze Galtry's character. The conclusion of that went something like: "Contrary to her delicate veneer, Galtry is cold. She is intensely apathetic yet also warlike. In the underworld, Galtry is known to be fair, unprejudiced, and a keeper of graceful poise, even if her life is at stake. Yet above all else, New York's underbelly understands Galtry can be ruthless."

The public has romanticized Galtry's person, and when in their sights, I must be what they have made her... for now.

I recap the lipstick.

Checking to ensure my appearance is proper, I notice blood on my sleeve. I turn my head, pull the sleeve back, and examine the cloth beneath. Blood seeps from the fabric where silver stitches near my collarbone are missing. Flies probably frayed them when I was buying Constance time during her struggle with the mutant rat.

"You're coming apart at the seams, Galtry." I click my tongue. "Can't believe I just said that."

As I tug my tome from a burgundy handbag, papers spill out. Each sheet is messy with doodles and pastel smears. These are gifts from the children in the Hex Church's school. The children there are the ones who gave me the courage to do what I am doing. They are who I will protect from the cruel world to come—them and whomever else deserves a life free of brutality. Though, a certain woman of haze has driven my courage and resolve even further recently.

'Not too much longer now.' I sift through the papers, glancing at each one while tucking them neatly into the handbag. 'The day I'll take them into my care is fast approaching. I'm sure of it.'

The last papers put away, I zip the handbag and then set the tome upright so it's standing on its head. Using my fingernails, I pluck a silver sewing needle of ornate design from its spine.

Not many outside the Hex Church know this, but the stitches that run along the outside of our cloth are the bindings of our own tomes. This allows Scribes to utilize some hexes without the tome, at least until we run out of stitches. My body has plenty of stitching, though, and it grows back like skin anyway. Still, it's quicker to mend it yourself if you're confident enough in your skills.

I pinch the skin near my collarbone and the cloth together, then push the needle through. Dribbles of blood seep out with each stitch I make, yet the bleeding stops only a second later.

A screen pops into my periphery.

> *Fostered Novitiate [Sprightly Ka Sewing (Grade 9)]*

I nod. *'I see it, system.'*

The system's pop-up closes. Several stitches thereon, I draw down my sleeve, return the needle to the tome's spine, and place it back in my handbag.

With a heavy sigh, I glance out the wide hotel windows.

In the distance, the Statue of Liberty stands with her iconic torch held above her head. The hotel room I find myself in is a special one that includes a telescope for tourists who want to ooh-and-aah at the statue. Yet, the view it provides me is the reason I chose this hotel.

Crowding the base of the Statue of Liberty's pedestal are tents, boats, a helicopter, and people—all stamped with Consortium logos. I thought the Consortium was kidding when they said Liberty Island was one of the locations where they had discovered a Kiln's roots. But after reflecting on it more, it makes some sense. Since Crawler-Anchorage, monuments the world over shut down, so a Kiln choosing to settle on a deserted island in the New York Harbor is less surprising.

My eyes drift to the television where a virtual conference call is taking place. Tapping the unmute button on the television remote, I use a tissue to sharpen the edges of my lipstick while listening in on the call.

Some paper shuffles around, and the run-down voice of a woman speaks. "Wherefrom, wherefore, whereupon, or FFU is an acronym that has become popular among some of the park's adolescents. The name seems to be a play on the way 'Fairy' writes, but it's basically just a compatibility game for boys and girls. However, it has begun spreading amongst older groups to ask where they are from, why they are here, and when they arrived in Central Park. This is why I want to make the suggestion that we distribute FFU questionnaires to learn more about the backgrounds of the people in the park."

'That might be useful. We could use it to help keep people's spirits up. Oh, and those tokens we are handing out. We still have a few hundred of those to distribute.'

The people in the conference call right now are from a consultant firm I hired to take care of some minor things for me. It really is fortunate that most people are still trying to continue life as usual. Thanks to that, I can keep using these types of services for a while longer. These types of businesses are great at establishing basic facilities for large-scale events. This firm is a Consortium subsidiary that handles disaster relief. Thanks to our new connection with the Consortium, I was able to get them to take care of our needs in double-quick time.

They will be handling things like shower facilities, portable toilet rentals, warming tents, equipment rentals, and community building projects. Of course, we'll never be able to get enough of any of that. It's nigh impossible. There are too many people and not enough resources, time, or leeway to operate.

Tossing the tissue into the trash, I walk to a table near the window and take a seat in front of my laptop. On one side of the computer is a personal phone, and on the other a business phone. The personal phone only has two numbers: my butler Caldwell Flax, and my maid, Victoria Toussaint, whom I haven't seen since my driving test years ago.

A senior consultant in the conference call knocks against something and then says, "Ah, I almost forgot. I have an update. We were able to procure over half of the industrial fencing requested by the client. Meaning we have around a mile of fencing at this moment. That'll be hauled over to the Central Park freshwater reservoir, and crews will then commence erecting the fence around it."

My personal phone vibrates. Its screen displays the name "Caldwell Flax." Muting the television, my gaze softens. *'Constance hasn't ever spoken to him, and I'm sad to say, I feel she never will.'*

I take the phone in hand and answer. "Caldwell."

"Miss! Your father intends to visit you after he returns from Chicago, and Miss, I can't maintain this farce for much longer! I've scarcely seen you at all, and I don't understand what you're doing."

My lips purse as I ask, "Caldwell, whom do you work for?"

"I work for you, of course, which is why I'm concerned about your safety, Miss!"

"And why are you concerned about my safety?"

"Miss, I've watched you for years. Victoria and I both know your true nature, but no one else can see it, so who knows what can happen if you bump into the wrong person."

A frown spreads across my face. "Is that so?"

"Of course, and that's also why I agreed to assist you with those numpties, your 'bodyguards.'"

"Ah, yes. You can leave the bodyguards in that room they're locked in. Someone else will let them out in your stead. Thanks for using the dumbwaiter to feed them."

"Someone el— Wait!" He gasps. "Did... Did you just thank me, Miss?"

"You're so melodramatic, Caldwell," I reply, a smirk replacing my frown. "Maybe I don't thank you enough."

"Oh my goodness, thank you so much, Miss." Things turn quiet for a moment before he asks, "And... and did you find the person you were looking for? The one you said you had to talk to."

"I did. We seem to have a lot of things in common, and it went better than I had hoped. I like them a lot."

"That's so good to hear, Miss. I am so glad."

Leaning back in my chair, I sigh. "...Caldwell."

"Yes, Miss? Do you require a chauffeur? I'm not certain where you are."

"No, no, but... how are your grandchildren doing? It's been a while since you visited them in the UK, hasn't it?"

"Well... it was the Rushlight before last, I think. They're doing well as far as I'm aware, however." His tone becomes pensive as he says, "Little Julia started primary school a few months back, and she seems to be doing quite alright. But Aidan is still struggling to wrap his head around his secondary lessons. Poor boy has always had problems focusing. ADD, I think. His mother keeps claiming she'll go get him tested, yet she keeps forgetting to take him."

I nod. "Mhm, ADD can be frustrating for those that have it. Modern society could be argued to have one of the most monotonous cultures in human history, and monotony is the archnemesis of an ADD mind as I understand it."

"Ahh, I hadn't thought about it in that way. Very elegantly put, Miss."

"Yeah, anyway, I'm happy to hear they're doing well otherwise." I massage my fingers, taking another deep breath. "And Caldwell... what I'm about to say to you, I need you to listen very closely."

"Of course, Miss. Is something the matter?"

I ignore his question. "I just want to say I truly appreciate everything you've tried to do. I know it must have been a lot for you to take in when you first arrived in the States eight years ago."

"It certainly was a bit peculiar initially." His tone is uncertain. "They told me I would be serving a seventy-year-old woman who spoke using a voice box. I was given very convincing paperwork and everything. How could I have imagined it was actually an eleven-year-old girl?"

I stifle a laugh. "How could I not remember? Victoria pulled a shotgun on you, Caldwell. No one had ever knocked on our door before, and you scared her."

"I... I remember that too. It was my "welcome to America" moment, and from a French woman at that. History does have a tendency to repeat itself..." He chuckles stiffly and then clears his throat. "Fortunately, you stopped her. And if I remember, you employed me because you wanted someone to watch television with. Yes! That's right. You were obsessed with British sitcoms at the time, Miss. Lots of stereotypical butlers on those shows, and that's why you hired me."

"Yeah, it was something like that..." I pause, collecting my thoughts, and then say, "But what I'm trying to get at, Caldwell, is that I appreciate everything you've tried to do... b-but you aren't my father, and I'm not your daughter. That's how you and Victoria treated me when I was younger, and I couldn't thank you more for it, but the truth is I'm not; I'm just your employer."

Glancing at the television screen, I notice the image has changed. This is something I installed an application to do when major news is breaking. Instead of the conference, there's now the image of an empty podium with American flags to its sides, and the US Presidential Seal hung prominently above it.

Caldwell sounds hurt as he stutters, "I-I understand—"

I bite the inside of my cheek and then interrupt him. "Let me finish."

"Yes, of course," he whispers.

"You're a good person, Caldwell, and you've seen sides of me that very few people ever have or ever will."

"That's true, Miss..."

I take a breath and say, "That's why you have two choices: First, you can go into the kitchen, take the plane ticket, the cash, and the traveler's cheque I set aside for you, and return to the UK to be near your grandchildren."

"Mi—"

"Or you can stay in Manhattan, watch the city crumble, with little hope of ever stepping foot in the UK again, and finally, learn to work for Galtry, not the girl who hired you."

He stays quiet on the other end of the line.

"You'll need to make a decision by the end of the day, or the world might make it for you." On the television, a man everyone knows walks up to the podium. This man is President of the United States of America, Samuel K. McCracken. "I have—"

"I've already been brooding on this exact subject, Miss..." He hesitates and then says, "I intend to return home. Back to Chester."

Wondering if I've just been punched in the gut, I bite my lip and force out some words. "Then goodbye, Caldwell, you're no longer under my employ. Please, take very good care of yourself."

"Yes... Goodbye. Please, be safe and..." His voice cracks. "T-Terra. I love you like a daughter, even if you aren't."

"...I love you too. Like a father..." I hang up and drop the phone into a glass of water. It bubbles and sinks to the bottom of the glass. It vibrates, casting ripples through the water. For a moment, I sit in silence and stare at the phone screen. I dab a tear from my eye, swallowing my emotions and trying my damndest to avoid smearing my mascara.

Closing my eyes, I take a few deep breaths, rein in my emotions, and then open my eyes to watch the screen fade to black. I glance at the second phone, which I use for business, and then back at my personal phone as the last bubbles escape its casing. *'Constance, what will be left of us in the end?'*

My gaze drifts to the television screen. President McCracken is shuffling through papers and giving some opening words.

McCracken is young for a president, forty-six or forty-seven years old. His suit is black, and his dark brown hair is slightly out of form and exhibiting signs of graying. This is counter to the platform he ran on of being a 'young and hip' president that would grant federal funding to retrain truckers out of work with the rise of self-driving vehicles and pass new environmental regulations to help curb microplastics building in the air and water.

Taking one more breath, I hit the unmute button on the remote, lean back, and cross my arms.

President McCracken clears his voice, gives the camera a solemn look, and begins to deliver a speech. "Two months. Two months have come and gone since the shocking and tragic incident in Anchorage, Alaska... Yet what most are not aware of is that at the same time this tragedy was unfolding, a being of unquantifiable power abruptly abducted individuals from across the globe. Many describe the experience as the moment their eyes were opened to new possibilities while simultaneously describing what they learned as horrifying."

He straightens his back and narrows his eyes. "The being is known as the 'Cosmic System,' and it spoke to these men and women, notifying them that humankind's standing within the natural world might soon be called into question."

"Astrophysicists, astronomers, climatologists, and experts representing hundreds of scientific fields were contacted within hours of the abductees' return. Within a few days, various Federal agencies were working to amass and acquire every scrap of data or information that could be pertinent from all corners of the world." There's a brief pause as he sips a crystal-clear glass of water. He sets it down, saying, "We are confident that the Cosmic System does not represent a direct threat to life or humanity. Rather, we believe it to be a primordial force of nature that has been missing for reasons that are not altogether understood at this time."

The room remains quiet. 'Hmm, it doesn't really qualify as a press conference if there is no press. It's just a speech in front of a camera. I wonder where he is right now?'

Raising his voice, he points at the camera. "I, as the president of this great country, want to reassure the American people that this is not an apocalypse, nor is it the end of civilization, nor is it some kind of extraterrestrial invasion, and finally, that this is not the end of the American way of life!" His hand sweeps across the air as he states, "This is a new chapter, a new opportunity! As we always have, since time immemorial, humanity will adapt, overcome, and flourish."

"Yet! We still must prepare our country for the ordeals ahead." Resting his hand on the podium, he continues, "For three weeks now, both Congress and the Senate have been in and out of closed-door sessions. It was in those sessions that some tough decisions were made... Let it be known that a new Selective Service Act has been passed."

He glances at a paper on the podium and then goes on to say, "Beginning three days from now, any men, women, or others who have been 'incorporated' into the Cosmic System are obligated to enlist at their local recruiting offices and report for training by the end of this calendar year. Whether young, old, or disabled, these individuals should prepare themselves to serve their country, defend their local citizens, and help steer the United States of America through these uncertain times."

"I cannot divulge much more on that subject at this time, and I still have some more announcements to make before I ought to return to meeting with military officials. But rest assured, more information is available online through the Homeland Security and White House websites." He once more clears his throat. "I am implementing a mandatory evacuation order for New York City and the surrounding cities effective immediately. If you're a Canadian refugee fleeing the Dryas Cyclone, the Northern border must allow refugees once more by executive order, but you must cross through Ohio or west of it. Then, the Governors of Pennsylvania and all states northeast of it are in agreement, and they have all issued an official state of emergency in their respective states. Finally, by proclamation... I hereby place the totality of the United States of America and its provinces under martial law until further notice..."

President McCracken goes on to discuss one final announcement, but it is in regard to Anchorage. After that, his speech devolves into cliché patriot-speak and propaganda alongside a heap of hollow words aimed at soothing the public.

'Evacuation order and martial law, hmm? Seems the president is a believer now. I guess the recent toilet bug incidents have woken up lots of people.'

A day ago, I published another one of Constance's videos. This video warned of the rise of the Kiln in New York City and the surrounding regions. She also urged those who may be unprepared for the impending perils to consider vacating New York and New Jersey altogether.

The Consortium and the Feds always knew the city would descend into an abysmal state, but I'm unconvinced they understood how soon things would boil over. No one believed Constance either, yet everything she's 'prophesied' has come to pass. Though once again, she made a bigger splash than I would have preferred. Murmurs are reaching my ear that she has caught yet more attention from Homeland Security, the National

Guard, and the U.S. Army. The most notable amongst them is a recently promoted general by the name of George P. Riddick, head of the 'Luminary Talent Contingent.'

I sigh. *'It might be best if we make friends with this General Riddick. He might keep the other headaches off our backs in exchange.'*

Someone knocks on the hotel room door. I sit up and wait for the designated passphrase. After playing Galtry for so many years, I've had it drilled into my head that I shouldn't approach a door without a passphrase being given. Blasting a high-powered bullet through a closed door is a common assassination tactic for those in my line of work.

The person on the other side breathes heavily. "The... the Fairy has no wings," Summer's voice says in between huffing for oxygen.

Once I hear five consecutive knocks, I stand and stroll to the door to open it. There stands the Escort, Summer, with bandages dressing parts of her face and arms. Her cheeks are flush, and her breathing labored. People are being discouraged from utilizing elevators due to rolling blackouts, meaning she just scaled thirty-eight flights of stairs.

I motion for her to follow as I turn and tromp back toward my computer. "Come," I say curtly. "There are water bottles on the nightstand over there. Room temperature. Probably the warmest water you'll drink while the Dryas Cyclone exists."

She shuts the door, ensures it's latched tight, and then hustles to the water bottles.

I take a seat and gesture for her to sit on the bed. "Any luck with the drug branch's Street Captain and Lieutenant?" I cross my legs. "I want them on a leash that I can strangle them with ASAP."

She shakes her head and sits on the bed with the water bottle held tight. "I've gotten wind on Street Captain Osvaldo's sex life; he's your average junkie gangbanger, and I can play him like a horny fiddle. Lieutenant Findlay is a bit of a different story, though."

I take a deep breath and glare at her.

"Findlay is a 'chaser.' They have a fetish for trans women."

"Perfect. That's Storm's specialty. Why isn't she going?"

Summer itches the bandages on her cheek, saying, "Storm doesn't want to be involved. She's not ready to take the leap yet, Miss Galtry."

"Then take one of the other women, Summer? Lie to the deadman. There's no difference except for whatever thoughts are rattling about in the man's brain."

"Erin has already volunteered, Miss Galtry. I just wanted to run it past you before I pull an Escort off any job they're workin' on."

I sigh. "Take Erin."

"Okay. Findley is rumored to be paranoid, but Erin's good. She'll get him to come around." Her eyes dart away. "Did... did you hear the announcement, Miss Galtry? It's official. They're going to draft the awakened."

Uncrossing my legs, I return to scrolling through local news reports. "The draft will be good for us. Good for the Fairy, good for the Syndicate, good for us."

"Good...?"

"Yes." I type in the URL for the WGN news site. The top headline reads, 'Two Orphaned After Squirrel-sized Fleas Attack Single Father.' Opening my email, I paste the article into a message, address it to H.Hands, and add, "Locate these children. See to it that they're well taken care of."

The bed creaks as Summer shifts her weight. "...May I ask how the draft helps us, Miss Galtry?"

"How many people are in Central Park right now, Summer?" I reply.

"I'm not sure." She thinks for a moment and then guesses, "Thirty or forty thousand, maybe?"

"A hundred." I click the send button in my email. A message pops up saying it was sent successfully, and I turn to stare at Summer. "There are a hundred thousand people encamped in the vicinity of Bethesda Terrace, and over three-quarters of those are out-of-towners. So enlighten me, Summer, what do you think will happen when things get bad, and there are very few safe zones?"

"…Everyone who can't escape will bum-rush those places. Especially Central Park and Hôtel Casāle since Fairy and her message are well-known by now."

"Exactly. This draft will dissuade more passive people from choosing to awaken early, and those that are awakened will be more inclined to stay in the park and avoid causing trouble, lest they leave and be drafted. That makes the draft more like a sieve for our purposes." I return to reading the article on my laptop with a long-drawn sigh. "And the evacuation order? That makes me feel like I won the lottery. A lot of people who aren't compatible with our lifestyle will vacate the city. Layers of sieves, Summer. That's what the Fairy and I's future headaches entail, sieving individuals and prodding them into places they'll survive in a world that doesn't exist yet."

My business phone rings, displaying the words "Consortium - LF".

'Lincoln. About time he called.'

"I'm taking this." Swiveling in my chair, I turn toward the Statue of Liberty and answer the phone. "Any updates on Locality Liberty's Star?"

"No." He lets out a long breath, suggesting he lit a cigarette before making this phone call. "Locality Gansevoort's Brisket seems more prone to poppin' in my opinion. Either way, the Consortium is pulling out of New York."

"They're leaving before even witnessing the climax?"

"Pierce and I have been told to stay and monitor the situation from Locality Central Tortoise." He laughs and then sighs. "But yeah, the other localities are being recalled to Chicago HQ."

'Trapped in a cage like the rest of us, yours just has a different lock and key.'

"So, the Feds issue an evacuation order, and the Consortium follows it up by immediately abandoning their operations." I also sigh and then look toward the glass of water. The water ripples, but the phone screen remains black. Raising an eyebrow, I add, "Like rats from a sinking ship."

"Yeah, well, the Consortium's contract is up, and no one wants to stay here anymore anyway. Hell, since our little photo op, it's not even safe to use the toilets any—" There's an abrupt pause, and then I hear Pierce yell, "Lincoln, get to the helicopter!"

My cell phone beeps and drops the call. I tilt my head, setting the phone aside.

Behind me, I hear Summer murmur, "What the devils is that?"

My gaze drifts to the water off the coast of Liberty Island. The bay is dyeing a pastel pink. I grab the telescope, draw it close, and peer through the eyepiece. As I adjust the focusing knob, the image sharpens and clears.

I can see three clusters of Consortium employees. Two larger groups rush toward boats docked at piers on the island's southeast and northeast. Then a third smaller group races toward a helicopter atop a red plaza to the island's northwest end. With the telescope, I can see Lincoln and Pierce among the latter.

The pink bay boils. Dark shadows slither under the surface. By the time the people reach the docks, their boats are sinking. One woman leaps onto a craft and manages to crank it. But the vessel has taken on far too much water. Recognizing this, the woman attempts to jump back to the dock, but her pants leg is caught on an anchor. And the boat drags her down with it.

'God, that poor woman!'

I turn the telescope to the two Solicitors.

There I glimpse the third group alongside Lincoln and Pierce vaulting into the helicopter's cabin as its blades whirl, quickly picking up speed. As the helicopter's landing gear hovers above the ground, a rift opens in the plaza, and branch-like protrusions grow out of it. A puff of air escapes my lips. *'Lincoln and his numpty partner survived. Thank goodness. The two of them aren't that bad, honestly, at least for bureaucratic lackeys.'*

"Miss Galtry, do you know what's happening?" Summer asks.

"That depends on whomever you ask. President McCracken would say you're witnessing a fresh chapter in American history." I withdraw my eye from the telescope. "As for the Fairy, she'd call this the end of an era. I'm sure of it."

I glance through the telescope once more and witness a pink protrusion hook the helicopter's landing gear. Scowling, I lean away from the telescope's eyepiece.

Summer stands, moving closer to the window, and watches as the water and earth distort around Liberty Island.

A plume of debris chokes the air, swallowing the island and helicopter. I stand and pack my things. *'Lincoln, Pierce, I better see you both back in Central Park.'*

"What... what would you call this, Miss Galtry?" Summer murmurs.

The hotel trembles, paint chips fall from the wall, and dust drops from the ceiling. "The Fairy and I think a lot alike, so I guess it's my duty to finish her thought and say something corny." I close my laptop, tuck it beneath my arm, and toss my handbag over my shoulder. "This is our dawn, the raising of the red curtain, and the end of the prelude..." My heels rap the floor as I stroll toward the doorway. "Hmph, how was that? Theatrical enough for the Fairy's taste?"

"You're a regular Shakespeare, Miss Galtry. The Fairy would be proud."

821

Author Afterword, Acknowledgments, and Following the Author

∞∞∞∞∞∞∞∞∞∞∞∞∞∞∞

This afterward is going to be written something like a personal journal entry for the sake of recording why I wrote this novel.

When I began conceiving of The Stained Tower, however many years ago, I did so through scribbles in a notebook during lunch breaks or at free moments in between my daily obligations. From that came numerous characters, all of whom had their own backgrounds and histories.

The brief version of Constance was something like:

- ✓ Mute and traumatized.
- ✓ Incapable of touch or smell.
- ✓ Lacking this era's interpretation of 'common sense.'
- ✓ Born in the 16th century, a tricky and under-documented era that sits at the borderline of the Middle and Modern Ages.
- ✓ No experience with modern conventions or technology.
- ✓ Insistence upon speaking London Parlance, a vernacular unique to Constance's era (which, after a dozen different iterations, ultimately manifested as a hybrid vernacular consisting of Old, Middle, and Modern English with sparse amounts of Middle French).

There was more, but I eventually chose Constance Nightingale to be my protagonist because, given the reasons above, I knew she would be an incredibly tough protagonist to put to paper. She's the type of person with an intriguing background but would seldom be allowed to speak or take center stage, whether it be due to her speaking habits, chaotic yet 'introverted' nature, or her overall complexity.

I decided if I wanted to mature as an author, I should pick her and have my readers experience the world through her.

Through Constance, the peculiar girl from 16th century London, I discovered things about myself that I had long shunned while also becoming a far better author than when I began. On top of everything, I managed to lay a firm foundation for what I expect to continue growing into the Tilted Cosmos.

Beyond Constance's vast amounts of confusion, turmoil, and anxieties, there was a heart that spoke through it, and I dearly hope its beat reached you in the infinite Tenebrous.

Acknowledgments

I wish to thank:

➤ My very close friend, essentially family, who supported me immensely while I wrote and pursued my dream of forging a world. If you're reading this, I can't thank you enough.

➤ The friend I met along the way. Perhaps, the only friend I've ever had that is somehow even more argumentative than me. They helped me by proofreading the 1st drafts of chapters and debating with me for many... MANY hours about every single character's motivation, every minute plot point, and the intended future developments behind every crumb of detail.

➤ The artist, Xeninda, who drew the Consortium Logo and cover art for this novel. They are very talented. Thank you for your hard work, Xeninda.

➤ Supporters of this novel via Patreon. Many of which you may have noticed in the Jingle-Jangle chat room.

➤ Those that reviewed, rated, and left comments on the earliest rough drafts of chapters that were available online for a while. I should also thank all those who filled out the Book 1 survey I sent out online—the kind words kept me going.

➤ The websites and online resources that host and preserve the meager amounts of information pertaining to 16th-century London commoner women, especially those that bothered to note rare morsels of details involving the most overlooked individuals, destitute and unmarried women.

➤ Websites that preserve the etymology of archaic languages and words, particularly etymonline, though I believe I delved into dozens or hundreds of sites over the course of these past years for similar purposes.

Ways to follow, contact, or support the author.

Feel Free to Email	Tilted.Reign@gmail.com	Follow on Twitter	@TiltedReign
Join the Discord	https://discord.gg/Bjcgf9E		
Patreon	https://www.patreon.com/Tilted_Axis		

One of the biggest things you could do to support The Stained Tower and me is to take a moment to review this novel on Amazon/Kindle or wherever it may be.

If you could spare the time, I would be very grateful.

Thank you for reading.
More stories remain, here and elsewhere, but Constance is
tired, and so am I. So, think of us until we meet again.
Fare Thee Well
- Iris Reign